GIOVANNI BOCCACCIO (1313-1375)
*is one of the great figures in world literature. The varied and high-spirited tales of* THE DECAMERON *reflect his own love of life and his very human insight into the foibles of man. The ribaldry, the humor and the earthy sincerity of the hundred stories have stood the test of time:* THE DECAMERON *long ago secured its place as one of the towering achievements in literary annals.*

ABOUT THE TRANSLATOR: *Richard Aldington is himself a novelist and poet. Among his books are:* COLLECTED POEMS; DEATH OF A HERO; ALL MEN ARE ENEMIES; REJECTED GUEST; LAWRENCE OF ARABIA. *He is the editor of the* VIKING BOOK OF POETRY OF THE ENGLISH SPEAKING WORLD.

# THE DECAMERON

## OF GIOVANNI BOCCACCIO

*Translated by Richard Aldington*

A LAUREL EDITION

Published by
DELL PUBLISHING CO., INC.
1 Dag Hammarskjold Plaza, New York, N.Y. 10017

Translation Copyright © 1930 by Doubleday &
Company, Inc.

Laurel ® TM 674623, Dell Publishing Co., Inc.

ISBN: 0-440-31866-1

Reprinted by permission of Doubleday
& Company, Inc., New York


First Dell printing—June, 1962
Second Dell printing—February, 1965
Third Dell printing—May, 1966
Fourth Dell printing—June, 1967
Fifth Dell printing—September, 1968
Sixth Dell printing—October, 1969
Seventh Dell printing—August, 1970
Eighth Dell printing—August, 1971
Ninth Dell printing—October, 1972
Tenth Dell printing—September, 1973
Eleventh Dell printing—September, 1974
Twelfth Dell printing—August, 1975
Thirteenth Dell printing—October, 1976
Fourteenth Dell printing—March, 1978


Printed in the U.S.A.

# Contents

OTHER TO GET OUT WHAT HE THINKS TO BE A DEAD BODY;
AS THEY FAIL IN THE TEST, SHE GETS RID OF THEM BOTH

## THE TENTH DAY 564

# THE DECAMERON

# FOREWORD

*Here begins the book called* Decameron, *also entitled* Prince Galeotto, *containing one hundred tales, told in ten days by seven ladies and three young men*

Tis human to have compassion upon the unhappy. Much is required of those who are happy, especially if they have needed comforting in the past, and have received it. Now if any man ever needed compassion, or found it dear to him, or ever received comfort, that man am I. From my earliest youth until this time present I was taken with a lofty and noble love, one that was perhaps too high for my lowly birth. Although I was praised and more highly esteemed by discreet persons who heard of this love, yet it caused me great pain and suffering, not indeed through the cruelty of my beloved lady, but through the excessive fire kindled in my soul by ill-regulated appetite. And since this brought me to no satisfactory end, I often suffered more distress than was needful.

While suffering this unhappiness I was comforted by the pleasant talk and consolation of a friend, but for whom I am firmly persuaded I should now be dead. But He that is Infinite has been pleased to decree immutably that all things shall have an end. Thus my love, which was more fervent than any other love, my love which no resolve, no advice, no evident shame, no risk of danger could ever break or bend, at length by the passage of time diminished of it-self, and now has left within my soul that delight which love is wont to grant those who do not adventure too far upon its dark seas. And whereas this love was once burden-some, now all torment is removed, and only delight re-mains.

But, though the pain has gone, I have not lost the mem-ory of kindness received from those who were moved by sorrow on account of their affection for me; nor do I think I shall ever forget these things, save through death alone. Now I think that gratitude is highly to be praised among the other virtues, while the opposite is blameworthy. And since I do not want to appear ungrateful, now that I may say I am free, I have determined to do what little I can in exchange for what I received, to provide amusement for those who helped me. If their wisdom or their good fortune makes this unnecessary, then it may be for others who need it. And however slender my support or comfort may be to them, still I think it should be offered to those who most need it, since it will there be more useful and be more valuable to them. And who will deny that it is far more fitting to give this to beautiful women than to men?

In fear and shamefacedness they conceal within their delicate breasts the hidden flames of love, whose strength is far greater than those of evident love, as is well known to those who have suffered them. Moreover, women are restricted by the authority of fathers, mothers, brothers and husbands. They spend most of their time shut up in the narrow circuit of their rooms, sitting in almost complete idleness, wanting and not wanting a thing in the same hour, turning over different thoughts which cannot always be gay ones.

Now if the melancholy born of fierce desire should enter their minds, they must be forced to remain in sadness unless it is driven away by new discourse; moreover, they have much less endurance than men. This does not happen with men in love, as may be evidently seen. If men are afflicted with melancholy or heavy thoughts, they have many ways of lightening them or avoiding them; whenever they wish, they can go out and hear and look at things, they can go hawking, hunting, fishing, riding; they can gamble or trade. By these means every man can divert his mind from himself wholly or partly, and free it from uneasy thought, at least for a time; and thus in one way and another consolation comes to him or the anguish grows less.

Therefore I mean to atone for the wrong done by Fortune, who is ever most miserly of comfort where there is least strength, as we may see in the case of delicate women. As an aid and comfort to women in love (for the needle, the distaff and the winder should suffice the others) I intend to relate one hundred tales or fables or parables or stories—whichever you choose to call them—as they were told in ten days by a band of seven ladies and three young men during the time of the recent plague, and also certain songs sung for their delight by the said ladies.

In these tales will be seen the gay and sad adventures of lovers and other happenings both of ancient and modern times. The ladies who read them may find delight in the pleasant things therein displayed; and they may also obtain useful advice, since they may learn what things to avoid and what to seek. Nor can all this happen without some soothing of their melancholy.

If this happens (and God grant it may!) let them render thanks to Love who, by freeing me from its bonds, granted me the power to serve their pleasure.

# THE FIRST DAY

# THE FIRST DAY

*Here begins the first day of the* Decameron, *wherein, after the author has showed the reasons why certain persons gathered to tell tales, they treat of any subject pleasing to them, under the rule of Pampinea*

Most gracious ladies, knowing that you are all by nature pitiful, I know that in your judgment this work will seem to have a painful and sad origin. For it brings to mind the unhappy recollection of that late dreadful plague, so pernicious to all who saw or heard of it. But I would not have this frighten you from reading further, as though you were to pass through nothing but sighs and tears in your reading. This dreary opening will be like climbing a steep mountain side to a most beautiful and delightful valley, which appears the more pleasant in proportion to the difficulty of the ascent. The end of happiness is pain, and in like manner misery ends in unexpected happiness.

This brief fatigue (I say brief, because it occupies only a few words) is quickly followed by pleasantness and delight, as I promised you above; which, if I had not promised, you would not expect perhaps from this opening. Indeed, if I could have taken you by any other way than this, which I know to be rough, I would gladly have done so; but since I cannot otherwise tell you how the tales you are about to read came to be told, I am forced by necessity to write in this manner.

In the year 1348 after the fruitful incarnation of the Son of God, that most beautiful of Italian cities, noble Florence, was attacked by deadly plague. It started in the East either through the influence of the heavenly bodies or because God's just anger with our wicked deeds sent it as a punishment to mortal men; and in a few years killed an innumerable quantity of people. Ceaselessly passing from place to place, it extended its miserable length over the West. Against this plague all human wisdom and foresight were vain. Orders had been given to cleanse the city of filth, the entry of any sick person was forbidden, much advice was given for keeping healthy; at the same time humble supplications were

made to God by pious persons in processions and otherwise. And yet, in the beginning of the spring of the year
mentioned, its horrible results began to appear, and in a
miraculous manner. The symptoms were not the same as in
the East, where a gush of blood from the nose was the plain
sign of inevitable death; but it began both in men and
women with certain swellings in the groin or under the
armpit. They grew to the size of a small apple or an egg,
more or less, and were vulgarly called tumours. In a short
space of time these tumours spread from the two parts
named all over the body. Soon after this the symptoms
changed and black or purple spots appeared on the arms or
thighs or any other part of the body, sometimes a few
large ones, sometimes many little ones. These spots were a
certain sign of death, just as the original tumour had been
and still remained.

No doctor's advice, no medicine could overcome or alle-
viate this disease. An enormous number of ignorant men
and women set up as doctors in addition to those who were
trained. Either the disease was such that no treatment was
possible or the doctors were so ignorant that they did not
know what caused it, and consequently could not administer the proper remedy. In any case very few recovered;
most people died within about three days of the appearance of the tumours described above, most of them without
any fever or other symptoms.

The violence of this disease was such that the sick communicated it to the healthy who came near them, just as a
fire catches anything dry or oily near it. And it even went
further. To speak to or go near the sick brought infec-
tion and a common death to the living; and moreover, to
touch the clothes or anything else the sick had touched or
worn gave the disease to the person touching.

What I am about to tell now is a marvellous thing to
hear; and if I and others had not seen it with our own eyes I
would not dare to write it, however much I was willing to
believe and whatever the good faith of the person from
whom I heard it. So violent was the malignancy of this
plague that it was communicated, not only from one man to
another, but from the garments of a sick or dead man
to animals of another species, which caught the
disease in that way and very quickly died of it. One day
among other occasions I saw with my own eyes (as I said
just now) the rags left lying in the street of a poor man
who had died of the plague; two pigs came along and, as
their habit is, turned the clothes over with their snouts and

then munched at them, with the result that they both fell dead almost at once on the rags, as if they had been poisoned.

From these and similar or greater occurrences, such fear and fanciful notions took possession of the living that almost all of them adopted the same cruel policy, which was entirely to avoid the sick and everything belonging to them. By so doing, each one thought he would secure his own safety.

Some thought that moderate living and the avoidance of all superfluity would preserve them from the epidemic. They formed small communities, living entirely separate from everybody else. They shut themselves up in houses where there were no sick, eating the finest food and drinking the best wine very temperately, avoiding all excess, allowing no news or discussion of death and sickness, and passing the time in music and suchlike pleasures. Others thought just the opposite. They thought the sure cure for the plague was to drink and be merry, to go about singing and amusing themselves, satisfying every appetite they could, laughing and jesting at what happened. They put their words into practice, spent day and night going from tavern to tavern, drinking immoderately, or went into other people's houses, doing only those things which pleased them. This they could easily do because everyone felt doomed and had abandoned his property, so that most houses became common property and any stranger who went in made use of them as if he had owned them. And with all this bestial behaviour, they avoided the sick as much as possible.

In this suffering and misery of our city, the authority of human and divine laws almost disappeared, for, like other men, the ministers and the executors of the laws were ll dead or sick or shut up with their families, so that no duties were carried out. Every man was therefore able to do as he pleased.

Many others adopted a course of life midway between the two just described. They did not restrict their victuals so much as the former, nor allow themselves to be drunken and dissolute like the latter, but satisfied their appetites moderately. They did not shut themselves up, but went about, carrying flowers or scented herbs or perfumes in their hands, in the belief that it was an excellent thing to comfort the brain with such odours; for the whole air was infected with the smell of dead bodies, of sick persons and medicines.

Others again held a still more cruel opinion, which they

thought would keep them safe. They said that the only medicine against the plaguestricken was to go right away from them. Men and women, convinced of this and caring about nothing but themselves, abandoned their own city, their own houses, their dwellings, their relatives, their property, and went abroad or at least to the country round Florence, as if God's wrath in punishing men's wickedness with this plague would not follow them but strike only those who remained within the walls of the city, or as if they thought nobody in the city would remain alive and that its last hour had come.

Not everyone who adopted any of these various opinions died, nor did all escape. Some when they were still healthy had set the example of avoiding the sick, and, falling ill themselves, died untended.

One citizen avoided another, hardly any neighbour troubled about others, relatives never or hardly ever visited each other. Moreover, such terror was struck into the hearts of men and women by this calamity, that brother abandoned brother, and the uncle his nephew, and the sister her brother, and very often the wife her husband. What is even worse and nearly incredible is that fathers and mothers refused to see and tend their children, as if they had not been theirs.

Thus, a multitude of sick men and women were left without any care except from the charity of friends (but these were few), or the greed of servants, though not many of these could be had even for high wages. Moreover, most of them were coarse-minded men and women, who did little more than bring the sick what they asked for or watch over them when they were dying. And very often these servants lost their lives and their earnings. Since the sick were thus abandoned by neighbours, relatives and friends, while servants were scarce, a habit sprang up which had never been heard of before. Beautiful and noble women, when they fell sick, did not scruple to take a young or old manservant, whoever he might be, and with no sort of shame, expose every part of their bodies to these men as if they had been women, for they were compelled by the necessity of their sickness to do so. This, perhaps, was a cause of looser morals in those women who survived.

In this way many people died who might have been saved if they had been looked after. Owing to the lack of attendants for the sick and the violence of the plague, such a multitude of people in the city died day and night that it was stupefying to hear of, let alone to see. From sheer necessity, then, several ancient customs were quite altered among the survivors.

The custom had been (as we still see it today), that women relatives and neighbours should gather at the house of the deceased, and there lament with the family. At the same time the men would gather at the door with the male neighbours and other citizens. Then came the clergy, few or many according to the dead person's rank; the coffin was placed on the shoulders of his friends and carried with funeral pomp of lighted candles and dirges to the church which the deceased had chosen before dying. But as the fury of the plague increased, this custom wholly or nearly disappeared, and new customs arose. Thus, people died, not only without having a number of women near them, but without a single witness. Very few indeed were honoured with the piteous laments and bitter tears of their relatives, who, on the contrary, spent their time in mirth, feasting and jesting. Even the women abandoned womanly pity and adopted this custom for their own safety. Few were they whose bodies were accompanied to church by more than ten or a dozen neighbours. Nor were these grave and honourable citizens but grave-diggers from the lowest of the people who got themselves called sextons, and performed the task for money. They took up the bier and hurried it off, not to the church chosen by the deceased but to the church nearest, preceded by four or six of the clergy with few candles and often none at all. With the aid of the grave-diggers, the clergy huddled the bodies away in any grave they could find, without giving themselves the trouble of a long or solemn burial service.

The plight of the lower and most of the middle classes was even more pitiful to behold. Most of them remained in their houses, either through poverty or in hopes of safety, and fell sick by thousands. Since they received no care and attention, almost all of them died. Many ended their lives in the streets both at night and during the day; and many others who died in their houses were only known to be dead because the neighbours smelled their decaying bodies. Dead bodies filled every corner. Most of them were treated in the same manner by the survivors, who were more concerned to get rid of their rotting bodies than moved by charity towards the dead. With the aid of porters, if they could get them, they carried the bodies out of the houses and laid them at the doors, where every morning quantities of the dead might be seen. They then were laid on biers, or, as these were often lacking, on tables.

Often a single bier carried two or three bodies, and it happened frequently that a husband and wife, two or three brothers, or father and son were taken off on the same bier. It frequently happened that two priests, each carrying a cross, would go out followed by three or four biers carried by porters; and where the priests thought there was one person to bury, there would be six or eight, and often, even more. Nor were these dead honoured by tears and lighted candles and mourners, for things had reached such a pass that people cared no more for dead men than we care for dead goats. Thus it plainly appeared that what the wise had not learned to endure with patience through the few calamities of ordinary life, became a matter of indifference even to the most ignorant people through the greatness of this misfortune.

Such was the multitude of corpses brought to the churches every day and almost every hour that there was not enough consecrated ground to give them burial, especially since they wanted to bury each person in the family grave, according to the old custom. Although the cemeteries were full they were forced to dig huge trenches, where they buried the bodies by hundreds. Here they stowed them away like bales in the hold of a ship and covered them with a little earth, until the whole trench was full.

Not to pry any further into all the details of the miseries which afflicted our city, I shall add that the surrounding country was spared nothing of what befell Florence. The villages on a smaller scale, were like the city; in the fields and isolated farms the poor wretched peasants and their families were without doctors and any assistance, and perished in the highways, in their fields and houses, night and day, more like beasts than men. Just as the townsmen became dissolute and indifferent to their work and property, so the peasants, when they saw that death was upon them, entirely neglected the future fruits of their past labours both from the earth and from cattle, and thought only of enjoying what they had. Thus it happened that crows, asses, sheep, goats, pigs, fowls and even dogs, those faithful companions of man, left the farms and wandered at their will through the fields, where the wheat crops stood abandoned, unreaped and ungarnered. Many of these animals seemed endowed with reason, for, after they had pastured all day, they returned to the farms for the night of their own free will, without being driven

Returning from the country to the city, it may be said that such was the cruelty of Heaven, and perhaps in part of men, that between March and July more than one hundred thousand persons died within the walls of Florence, what between the violence of the plague and the abandonment in which the sick were left by the cowardice of the healthy. And before the plague it was not thought that the whole city held so many people.

Oh, what great palaces, how many fair houses and noble dwellings, once filled with attendants and nobles and ladies, were emptied to the meanest servant! How many famous names and vast possessions and renowned estates were left without an heir! How many gallant men and fair ladies and handsome youths, whom Galen, Hippocrates and Æsculapius themselves would have said were in perfect health, at noon dined with their relatives and friends, and at night supped with their ancestors in the next world!

But it fills me with sorrow to go over so many miseries. Therefore, since I want to pass over all I can leave out, I shall go on to say that when our city was in this condition and almost emptied of inhabitants, one Tuesday morning the venerable church of Santa Maria Novella had scarcely any congregation for divine service except (as I have heard from a person worthy of belief) seven young women in the mourning garments suitable to the times, who were all related by ties of blood, friendship or neighbourship. None of them was older than twenty-eight or younger than eighteen; all were educated and of noble blood, fair to look upon, well-mannered and of graceful modesty.

I should tell you their real names if I had not a good reason for not doing so, which is that I would not have any of them blush in the future for the things they say and hearken to in the following pages. The laws are now strict again, whereas then, for the reasons already shown, they were very lax, not only for persons of their age but for those much older. Nor would I give an opportunity to the envious (always ready to sneer at every praiseworthy life) to attack the virtue of these modest ladies with vulgar speech. But so that you may understand without confusion what each one says, I intend to give them names wholly or partly suitable to the qualities of each.

The first and eldest I shall call Pampinea, the second Fiammetta, the third Filomena, the fourth Emilia, the fifth Lauretta, the sixth Neifile, and the last Elisa (or "the virgin") for a very good reason. They met, not by arrangement, but by chance, in the same part of the church, and sat down in a circle. After many sighs they ceased to pray and began to talk about the state of affairs and other things. After a short space of silence, Pampinea said:

"Dear ladies, you must often have heard, as I have, that to make a sensible use of one's reason harms nobody. It is natural for everybody to aid, preserve and defend his life as far as possible. And this is so far admitted that to save their own lives men often kill others who have done no harm. If this is permitted by the laws which are concerned with the general good, it must certainly be lawful for us to take any reasonable means for the preservation of our lives. When I think of what we have been doing this morning and still more on former days, when I remember what we have been saying, I perceive and you must perceive that each of us goes in fear of her life. I do not wonder at this, but, since each of us has a woman's judgment, I do wonder that we do not seek some remedy against what we dread.

"In my opinion we remain here for no other purpose than to witness how many bodies are buried, or listen whether the friars here (themselves reduced almost to nothing) sing their offices at the canonical hours, or to display by our clothes the quantity and quality of our miseries to anyone who comes here. If we leave this church we see the bodies of the dead and the sick being carried about. Or we see those who had been exiled from the city by the authority of the laws for their crimes, deriding this authority because they know the guardians of the law are sick or dead, and running loose about the place. Or we see the dregs of the city battening on our blood and calling themselves sextons, riding about on horseback in every direction and insulting our calamities with vile songs. On every side we hear nothing but "So-and-so is dead" or "So-and-so is dying." And if there were anyone left to weep we should hear nothing but piteous lamentations. I do not know if it is the same in your homes as in mine. But if I go home there is nobody left there but one of my maids, which fills me with such horror that the hair stands upon my head. Wherever I go or sit at home I seem to see the ghosts of the departed, not with the faces as I knew them but with dreadful looks which terrify me.

"I am ill at ease here and outside of here and at home; the more so since nobody who has the strength and ability to go away (as we have) now remains here, except ourselves. The few that remain (if there are any), according to what I see and hear, do anything which gives them pleasure or pleases their appetites, both by day and night, whether they are alone or in company, making no distinction between right and wrong. Not only laymen, but those cloistered in convents have broken their oaths and given themselves up to the delights of the flesh, and thus in trying to escape the plague by doing what they please, they have become lascivious and dissolute.

"If this is so (and we may plainly see it is) what are we doing here? What are we waiting for? What are we dreaming about? Are we less eager and active than other citizens in saving our lives? Are they less dear to us than to others? Or do we think that our lives are bound to our bodies with stronger chains than other people's, and so believe that we need fear nothing which might harm us? We were and are deceived. How stupid we should be to believe such a thing! We may see the plainest proofs from the number of young men and women who have died of this cruel plague.

"I do not know if you think as I do, but in my opinion if we, through carelessness, do not want to fall into this calamity when we can escape it, I think we should do well to leave this town, just as many others have done and are doing. Let us avoid the wicked examples of others like death itself, and go and live virtuously in our country houses, of which each of us possesses several. There let us take what happiness and pleasure we can, without ever breaking the rules of reason in any manner.

"There we shall hear the birds sing, we shall see the green hills and valleys, the wheat-fields rolling like a sea, and all kinds of trees. We shall see the open Heavens which, although now angered against man, do not withhold from us their eternal beauties that are so much fairer to look upon than the empty walls of our city. The air will be fresher there, we shall find a greater plenty of those things necessary to life at this time, and fewer troubles. Although the peasants are dying like the townsmen, still, since the houses and inhabitants are fewer, we shall see less of them and feel less misery. On the other hand I believe we are not abandoning anybody here. Indeed we can truthfully say that we are abandoned, since our relatives have either died or fled from death and have left us alone in this calamity as if we were nothing to them.

"If we do what I suggest, no blame can fall upon us; if we fail to do it, the result may be pain, trouble and perhaps death. Therefore I think that we should do well to take our servants and all things necessary, and go from one house to another, enjoying whatever merriment and pleasure these times allow. Let us live in this way (unless death comes upon us) until we see what end Heaven decrees to this plague. And remember that going away virtuously will not harm us so much as staying here in wickedness will harm others."

The other ladies listened to what Pampinea said, praised her advice, and in their eagerness to follow it began to discuss details, as if they were going to leave at once. But Filomena, who was a most prudent young woman, said:

"Ladies, although what Pampinea says is excellent advice, we must not rush off at once, as you seem to wish. Remember we are all women; and any girl can tell you how women behave together and conduct themselves without the direction of some man. We are fickle, wayward, suspicious, faint-hearted and cowardly. So if we have no guide but ourselves I greatly suspect that this company will very soon break up, without much honour to ourselves. Let us settle this matter before we start."

Elisa then broke in:

"Indeed men are a woman's head and we can rarely succeed in anything without their help; but how can we find any men? Each of us knows that most of her menfolk are dead, while the others are away, we know not where, flying with their companions from the end we wish to escape. To ask strangers would be unbecoming; for, if we mean to go away to save our lives we must take care that scandal and annoyance do not follow us where we are seeking rest and amusement."

While the ladies were thus arguing, three young men came into the church, the youngest of whom was not less than twenty-five. They were lovers whose love could not be quenched or even cooled by the horror of the times, the loss of relatives and friends, or even fear for themselves. The first was named Pamfilo, the second Filostrato, the third Dioneo. They were pleasant, well-mannered men, and in this public calamity they sought the consolation of looking upon the ladies they loved. These ladies happened to be among our seven, while some of the others were related to one or other of the three men. They no sooner came into sight than the ladies saw them; whereupon Pampinea said with a smile:

"See how Fortune favours our plan at once by sending us these valiant and discreet young men, who will gladly act as our guides and servants if we do not refuse to accept them for such duties."

Neifile then became crimson, for she was one of the ladies beloved by one of the young men, and said:

"For God's sake, Pampinea, be careful what you are saying. I know quite well that nothing but good can be said of any of them and I am sure they could achieve greater things than this. I also think that their company would be fitting and pleasant, not only to us, but to ladies far more beautiful and charming than we are. But it is known to everyone that they are in love with some of us women here; and so, if we take them with us, I am afraid that blame and infamy will fall upon us, through no fault of ours or theirs."

Then said Filomena:

"What does that matter? If I live virtuously, my conscience never pricks me, whatever people may say. God and the truth will fight for me. If these men would come with us, then indeed, as Pampinea said, fortune would be favourable to our plan of going away."

The others not only refrained from censuring what she said, but agreed by common consent that the men should be spoken to, told their plan, and asked if they would accompany the ladies on their expedition. Without more ado, Pampinea, who was related to one of them, arose and went towards them where they stood looking at the ladies, saluted them cheerfully, told them the plan, and begged them in the name of all the ladies to accompany them out of pure and fraternal affection.

At first the young men thought this was a jest. But when they saw the lady was speaking seriously, they said they were willing to go. And in order to start without delay they at once gave the orders necessary for departure. Everything necessary was made ready, and word was sent on ahead to the place they were going. At dawn next morning, which was Wednesday, the ladies with some of their servants, and the young men with a man servant each, left the city and set out. They had not gone more than two miles when they came to the first place where they were to stay.

This estate was on slightly raised ground, at some distance from any main road, with many trees and plants, fair to look upon. At the top of the rise was a country mansion with a large inner courtyard. It had open colonnades, galleries and rooms, all beautiful in themselves and ornamented with gay paintings. Roundabout were lawns and marvellous gardens and wells of cool water. There were cellars of fine wines, more suitable to wine connoisseurs than to sober and virtuous ladies. The whole house had been cleaned, the beds were prepared in the rooms, and every corner was strewn with the flowers of the season and fresh rushes. All of which the company beheld with no little pleasure.

They all sat down to discuss plans, and Dioneo, who was a most amusing young man and full of witticisms, remarked:

"Ladies, your good sense, rather than our foresight, has brought us here. I do not know what you are thinking of doing with your troubles here, but I dropped mine inside the gates of the city when I left it with you a little time ago. Therefore, either you must make up your minds to laugh and sing and amuse yourselves with me (that is, to the extent your dignity allows), or you must let me go back to my troubles and stay in the afflicted city."

Pampinea, who had driven away her woes in the same way, cheerfully replied:

"Dioneo, you speak well, let us amuse ourselves, for that was the reason why we fled from our sorrows. But when things are not organised they cannot long continue. And, since I began the discussion which brought this fair company together and since I wish our happiness to continue, I think it necessary that one of us should be made chief, whom the others will honour and obey, and whose duty shall be to regulate our pleasures. Now, so that everyone —both man and woman—may experience the cares as well as the pleasures of ruling and no one feel any envy at not sharing them, I think the weight and honour should be given to each of us in turn for one day. The first shall be elected by all of us. At vespers he or she shall choose the ruler for the next day, and so on. While their reigns last these rulers shall arrange where and how we are to spend our time."

These words pleased them all and they unanimously elected her for the first day. Filomena ran to a laurel bush, whose leaves she had always heard were most honourable in themselves and did great honour to anyone crowned with them, plucked off a few small branches and wove them into a fair garland of honour. When this was placed on the head of any one of them, it was a symbol of rule and authority over the rest so long as the party remained together.

Pampinea, thus elected queen, ordered silence. She then sent for the three servants of the young men and the four women servants the ladies had brought, and said:

"To set a first example to you all which may be bettered and thus allow our gathering to live pleasantly and orderly and without shame and to last as long as we desire, I appoint Dioneo's servant Parmeno as my steward, and hand over to him the care of the whole family and of everything connected with the dining hall. Pamfilo's servant Sirisco shall be our treasurer and buyer, and carry out Parmeno's instructions. Tindaro shall wait on Filostrato and Dioneo and Pamfilo in their rooms, when the other two servants are occupied with their new duties. Filomena's servant Licisca and my own servant Misia shall remain permanently in the kitchen and carefully prepare the food which Parmeno sends them. Lauretta's Chimera and Fiammetta's Stratilia shall take care of the ladies' rooms and see that the whole house is clean. Moreover we will and command that everyone who values our good grace shall bring back only cheerful news, wherever he may go or return from, and whatever he may hear or see."

Having given these orders, which were approved by everyone, she jumped gaily to her feet and said:

"Here are gardens and lawns and other delicious places, where each of us can wander and enjoy them at will. But let everyone be here at the hour of Tierce so that we can eat together while it is still cool."

The company of gay young men and women, thus given the queen's permission, went off together slowly through the gardens, talking of pleasant matters, weaving garlands of different leaves, and singing love songs. After the time allotted by the queen had elapsed they returned to the house and found that Parmeno had carefully carried out the duties of his office. Entering a ground floor room decorated everywhere with broom blossoms, they found tables covered with white cloths and set with glasses which shone like silver. They washed their hands and, at the queen's command, all sat down in the places allotted them by Parmeno. Delicately cooked food was brought, exquisite wines were at hand, and the three men servants waited at table. Everyone was delighted to see things so handsome and well arranged, and they ate merrily with much happy talk.

All the ladies and young men could dance and many of them could play and sing; so, when the tables were cleared, the queen called for musical instruments. At her command Dioneo took a lute and Fiammetta a viol, and began to play a dance tune. The queen sent the servants to their meal, and then with slow steps danced with the two young men and the other ladies. After that, they began to sing gay and charming songs.

In this way they amused themselves until the queen thought it was time for the siesta. So, at the queen's bidding, the three young men went off to their rooms (which were separated from the ladies') and found them filled with flowers as the dining hall had been. And similarly with the women. So they all undressed and went to sleep.

Not long after the hour of Nones the queen arose and made the other women and the young men also get up, saying that it was harmful to sleep too long during the daytime. Then they went out to a lawn of thick green grass entirely shaded from the sun. A soft breeze came to them there. The queen made them sit down in a circle on the grass, and said:

"As you see, the sun is high and the heat great, and nothing can be heard but the cicadas in the olive trees. To walk about at this hour would be foolish. Here it is cool and lovely, and, as you see, there are games of chess and draughts which everyone can amuse himself with, as he chooses. But, if my opinion is followed, we shall not play games, because in games the mind of one of the players must necessarily be distressed without any great pleasure to the other player or the onlookers. Let us rather spend this hot part of the day in telling tales, for thus one person can give pleasure to the whole company. When each of us has told a story, the sun will be going down and the heat less, and we can then go walking anywhere we choose for our amusement. If this pleases you (for here I am ready to follow your pleasure) let us do it. If it does not please you, let everyone do as he likes until evening."

The women and men all favoured the telling of stories.

"Then if it pleases you," said the queen, "on this first day I order that everyone shall tell his tale about any subject he likes."

She then turned to Pamfilo, who was seated on her right, and ordered him to begin with a tale. Hearing this command, Pamfilo at once began as follows, while all listened.

## FIRST TALE

*Ser Ciappelletto deceives a holy friar with a false confession and dies; and though he had been a most wicked man in his lifetime, in death he is deemed a saint, and called Saint Ciappelletto*

It is befitting, most dear ladies, that in everything a man does, he should begin with the excellent and Holy name of Him that was maker of all things. Wherefore, since I am the first to begin this telling of tales, I intend to start with one of His marvellous deeds, to the end that when you have heard it our faith in Him may rest unshakeable and His name be ever praised among us.

Since all things in this world are mortal and transitory, even so it is plain that within and without they are full of bitterness and woe and weariness and subject to infinite perils, so that we who live mingled with them and are a part of them could verily neither endure nor remedy them, if God's especial grace did not lend us strength and foresight. Nor should we believe that this grace descends upon us through any merit of our own, but from the motion of His own benignity and the prayers of those His Saints, who once were mortals as we are; and while they were alive they were obedient to His will, and now have become eternal and blessed with Him. And we ourselves address our prayers concerning those things we consider desirable for ourselves to the Saints, as unto advocates who by experience are aware of our fragility, when perhaps we dare not utter our prayers in the presence of so great a Judge.

Towards us He abounds in merciful bounty; and we may perceive that, since the gaze of mortal eye can in no wise pierce the secret of the divine mind, we, deceived by false opinion, may choose as advocate before His majesty one that is exiled from before Him forever. Nevertheless He, from Whom nothing is hidden, considering more His petitioner's purity of heart than ignorance or the eternal exile of the advocate, hearkens to those who pray to this advocate as if he stood before His sacred presence.

Manifestly will this appear in the tale I am about to tell; I say "manifestly" in accordance, not with God's judgment, but with that of men.

Now there was a great and very rich merchant, named Musciatto Franzesi, who became a knight. He was compelled to journey into Tuscany with Messer Carlo Senzaterra, brother to the King of France, at the request of Pope Boniface. Musciatto discovered that his affairs, like those of most merchants, were so involved in all directions that he could not lightly and abruptly cut free from them. He therefore determined to entrust them to different persons, and found means to dispose of everything. Only one difficulty remained—to find a trustworthy person to receive on his behalf the repayment of money he had lent to many Burgundians. The reason for his hesitation was that he knew the Burgundians to be quarrelsome, perfidious, ill-conditioned men; and he could not think of any man he could trust who would be sufficiently artful to hold his own against their artfulness.

After much cogitation, he remembered one Ser Ciapperetto da Prato who had often visited his house in Paris. This man was very short and always dapperly dressed. The French did not know what Ceparello means, and thinking it was a chaplet (that is, in their tongue, a garland) they did not call him Capello but Ciapelletto, because he was such a little fellow. So he was known to everyone as Ciappelletto, and very few knew him as Ser Ciapperetto.

The life of this Ciappelletto was in this wise. He was a notary, and was mightily ashamed when any document he had drawn (and he drew up many) was discovered to be anything but fraudulent. He had drawn as many of these as he had been asked to do, and he did such things more willingly for nothing than another man would do for a large reward. He bore false witness with the greatest delight, whether he was asked to do so, or not. In those days the French had the greatest trust in oaths and cared not to utter false ones, and so he wickedly gained every lawsuit where he was called upon to swear to tell the truth upon his faith and his life.

He had other pleasing ways, and took great pains to cause mischief, scandals and enmities between friends and relatives and anybody else; and the more evil resulted from all this, the more he was delighted. If he was bidden to a murder or some other questionable affair, he went most willingly and never refused. And often he gladly wounded or slew men with his own hands. He was a mighty blasphemer of God and the Saints, and on the smallest occasions, like a man who is more irascible than others.

He never went to church. He scoffed at all the sacraments with abominable words as if they were vile things. On the other hand, he cheerfully frequented taverns and other ungodly haunts. He was as attractive to women as sticks are to dogs; but he delighted in them more than any other vile man. He would rob and purloin with the clear conscience of a holy man making an offering. He was most gluttonous and a great drunkard, so that sometimes he foully injured himself. He was a gambler, and made use habitually of loaded dice.

Why do I expatiate at such length? He was perhaps the

wickedest man ever born. For a long time his cunning was of service to the power and position of Messer Musciatto, by whom he was often saved from private persons whom he frequently injured, and from the Court which he also had offended.

When Ser Ciappelletto came into the mind of Messer Musciatto—who was perfectly aware of his whole life—he concluded that Ser Ciappelletto was the one man required to meet the artfulness of the Burgundians. So, having sent for him, he spoke to him as follows:

"Ser Ciappelletto, as you know, I am retiring from everything here. Among others, I have to deal with those artful Burgundians, and I do not know of any person more suitable than yourself for me to leave to receive my money from them. And since this is something you have never done before, I purpose to obtain you the favour of the Court and to give you a reasonable share of the money you get in."

Ser Ciappelletto, who was a spendthrift and ill-provided with this world's goods, having to face the departure of the man who had long been his refuge and support, made up his mind without delay, being practically compelled by necessity, and replied that he would gladly agree.

So, having made their agreement, Messer Musciatto departed, and Ser Ciappelletto, having received his power of attorney and letters of protection from the King, went off to Burgundy, where scarcely anyone knew him. And there, contrary to his nature, he began mildly and gently to collect the money due, and to do what he had been sent to do, as if he were reserving his wickedness until the end.

While doing all this he lodged in the house of two Florentines, brothers, who there lent out money at usury, and who honoured him much, out of their respect for Messer Musciatto. In their house he fell ill. The brothers at once sent for doctors and servants to look after him, and for everything needed to restore him to health.

But all aid was useless since (according to what the doctors said) the good man was old and had lived a disorderly life, and so was daily going from bad to worse, like a man stricken with death; for which the two brothers felt great regret.

And one day they began to discuss the matter quite close to the room where Ser Ciappelletto lay ill:

"What shall we do about this man?" said they to each other. "On his account we have a bad business on our hands. To send him sick out of our house would be a great reproach to us and an obvious sign of lack of sense, for people would see that we had at first received him, and then most solicitously procured him doctors and servants, and afterwards when he could not have done anything to displease us, they would see him, at the point of death, suddenly cast out of our house. On the other hand, he has been such a wicked man that he will not confess himself or take any sacrament of the Church. So if he dies without confession, no church will receive his body and it will be cast into the ditch like a dog's. And suppose he did confess, his sins are so numerous and so horrible that the same thing will happen, for there is neither priest nor friar who can or will absolve him; and if he dies without absolution, he will also be cast into a ditch. And if that happens, the people of this country, partly on account of our occupation which they abuse every day as an iniquitous one, and partly on account of their eagerness to rob others, will rise up in tumult, yelling:

" 'These dogs of Lombards, no church will receive them, we won't endure them any longer.'

"And they will run to our house, and perhaps they will not only steal the goods in it but, in addition, burn the inhabitants. So, in any event we are in an unpleasant situation if he dies."

Ser Ciappelletto, as I said, was lying near where they were talking, and, as we often see with sick men, his hearing had become more acute, so that he heard what they said about him. Therefore he sent for them and said:

"I do not wish you to feel any doubts about me or to dread receiving any injury through me. I heard what you said about me, and I am certain it would turn out as you say, if the matter went as you think it will; but it will turn out quite differently. In my lifetime I have committed so many sins against God that if I commit another on my death-bed it can make no difference. Therefore, procure me a wise and holy friar, as wise and holy as possible, if one of the kind exists, and leave the rest to me. I shall arrange your affairs and mine in such a manner that all will be well, and you will be satisfied."

Although the two brothers did not feel very hopeful about this, still they went off to a friary, and asked for a holy and learned man to hear the confession of a Lombard lying sick in their house. They were given an old friar, of a good and holy life, a great master of the Scriptures, a most venerable man, for whom all the citizens felt a very great and special devotion; and they took him with them.

Now when the friar reached Ser Ciappelletto's room, he sat down beside him and began gently to comfort him. Then the friar asked how long it was since he had been to confession. Ser Ciappelletto, who had never been to confession in his life, replied:

"Father, it has been my custom to go to confession at least once a week, although there were many weeks when I confessed oftener. It is true that during the eight days which have passed since I fell sick, I have not confessed myself, so much have I been distressed by my sickness."

Then said the friar:

"My son, you have done well, and thus one should do as an example. Since you have confessed so often, I see I shall have little labour in asking and hearkening."

Said Ser Ciappelletto:

"Messer friar, say not so; I have not confessed so many times nor so often but that I ever desire to confess altogether all the sins I remember from the day I was born until the time when I am confessing. And therefore, good father, I beg that you will question me about everything as closely as if I had never been to confession. And do not spare me because I am sick, for I would much rather mortify my flesh than, by doing its will, do anything which might cause the perdition of my soul which my Saviour redeemed with His precious blood."

These words greatly pleased the holy man and seemed to him proofs of a well-disposed mind. After he had highly commended Ser Ciappelletto for this behaviour, he began by asking him if he had never sinned in lechery with any woman. To which Ser Ciappelletto replied with a sigh:

"Father, I am ashamed to tell you the truth concerning this matter, for fear of the sin of vainglory."

Whereupon the holy friar said:

"Speak out boldly, for never is there any sin in speaking the truth either in confession or anywhere else."

Then said Ser Ciappelletto:

"Since you assure me of this, I will tell you: I am as virgin as when I came out from my mother's body."

"Oh, blessed are you of God!" exclaimed the friar. "Well indeed have you done! And by so doing you have acquired the more merit, since you had more liberty to do the opposite than have we and others that are subject to a rule of discipline."

After this, he asked whether he had not displeased God by the sin of gluttony. Whereunto Ser Ciappelletto, sighing deeply, replied that he had many times done so, because, as well as the Lenten fasts which devout persons keep during the year, he had been wont to eat only bread and water for at least three days of each week, but he had drunk the water with the same appetite and delight—especially when he had endured any fatigue either in prayer or going on pilgrimage—as great drinkers find in their wine. And he had often longed for those gross salads of coarse herbs, such as the women make when they go to town. And sometimes eating had seemed to him better than he thought it ought to seem to someone fasting from devotion, as he had fasted.

To which the friar said:

"My son, these are natural sins and quite venial; and therefore I do not wish you to burden your conscience with them more than is needful. It happens to every man, howsoever holy he may be, that eating seems good to him after a long fast, and drinking after labour."

"O father," said Ser Ciappelletto, "do not say this only to comfort me. Well do you know that I know that everything which is done by a servant of God should be done frankly and with no grudging of spirit; and he that does otherwise, sins."

The friar in great delight replied:

"And I am glad that you think thus in your soul, and I am greatly pleased by your pure and good conscience in this matter. But, tell me, have you not sinned in avarice, either by desiring more than was befitting or by withholding that which you ought not to withhold?"

Unto which Ser Ciappelletto said:

"Father, I would not have you misjudge me because I am in the house of these usurers. I have nothing to do with them. I came hither only to admonish and chastise them, and to save them from this abominable lucre; and I believe I should have done so, if God had not thus visited me. But you must know that my father left me a rich man, and when he died I gave the greater portion of his goods to God's works. And then, to sustain my own life and to aid Christ's poor, I have carried on my little traffickings, and therein I have desired gain, but I have ever shared what I earned with God's poor, keeping one half for my own needs, and giving the other half to them. And herein so well has my Creator aided me that my affairs have ever prospered more and more."

"Well have you done," said the friar, "but have you not often been angry?"

"Oh," said Ser Ciappelletto, "there I must say I have often erred. For who can contain his anger, when every day he sees men doing foul deeds, neglecting God's commandments and going in no fear of His judgments? Many a time have there been days when I would rather have been dead than alive, when I saw the young men plunging into vanities, and beheld them swearing and perjuring themselves, going to taverns, never entering churches, and following rather the ways of this world than the way of God."

Then said the friar:

"My son, this is a worthy anger, and I can lay no penitence upon you because of it. But was there never any time when anger led you to commit homicide or to insult someone or to commit any other sin?"

To which Ser Ciappelletto replied:

"Alas, Messer! Oh, you seem to me a man of God, but how can you utter such words? If I had ever had the least thought of committing one or other of the things you speak of, do you think I should believe that God would have aided me so much? These are things committed by brigands and men of Belial, unto whom, whenever I have seen one of them, I have said: 'Go, and may God convert you.' "

"May the blessing of God be on you," said the friar, "but tell me, have you never borne false witness against another, have you never spoken ill of others, have you never deprived others of their goods against their will?"

"Indeed, Messer, aye, indeed," answered Ser Ciappelletto, "have I spoken ill of others. For once there was a neighbour of mine that for no reason in the world did nothing but beat his wife, and once I spoke ill of him to the wife's relatives, so much did I pity the poor wretched little woman, whom he tanned, as God be witness, whenever he had drunk too much."

Then said the friar:

"Now, you told me you have been a merchant. Did you never trick anyone, as merchants are wont to do?"

"Aye indeed, Messer," said Ser Ciappelletto, "but I do not know who they were, save for one man, and he brought me the money to pay for some cloth I had sold him, and I put the money in a chest without counting it, and a month later I found it was four farthings more than it should have been. But, not seeing the man again, after keeping the money a whole year to return to him, I gave it away for the love of God."

Said the friar:

"That was a small thing; and you did well to do what you did do."

And after this the holy friar questioned him about many other matters, to all of which he made answer in the same manner. But, when he was about to proceed to give absolution, Ser Ciappelletto said:

"Messer. I have yet another sin I have not confessed to you."

The friar asked what it was, and he replied:

"I remember that one Saturday after Nones I made the servant sweep out the house, and I have not held the Holy Sabbath in all the reverence I should have done."

"Oh," said the friar, "that is a small thing, my son."

"Nay," said Ser Ciappelletto, "say not that it is a small thing, for the Sabbath is to be greatly honoured, since on that day our Saviour rose from the dead to life."

Then said the friar:

"Well, have you any other sins?"

"Aye, Messer," answered Ser Ciappelletto, "for once, without realising what I was doing, I spat in a church of God."

The friar began to smile and said:

"That is nothing to trouble about, my son; for we monks spit in church all day long."

Then said Ser Ciappelletto:

"Then you do great ill, for nothing should be kept cleaner than the holy temple where we offer sacrifice to God."

And, in brief, he told him many such things, and finally began to sigh and then to weep, being one who knew full well how to do so when he wanted.

Said the holy friar:

"What is it, my son?"

"Alas, Messer, a sin remains with me which I have never confessed, so greatly am I ashamed to tell it. And every time I remember it, I weep as you see, and it seems to me most certain that God will never pardon me this sin."

Then the holy friar said:

"Come, come, my son, what are you saying? If all the sins that all men have ever committed, or all those which will be committed by men until the end of the world, were all in one man, yet if he were penitent and contrite as I see you are, God's mercy and loving kindness are so great that if that man confessed them, He would freely pardon them to him. Therefore speak out with good assurance."

Ser Ciappelletto, still weeping bitterly, said:

"Alas, father, my sin is too great. And unless your prayers are devoted to it, I can scarcely believe that God will ever forgive me."

To which the friar answered:

"Speak out boldly, and I promise you I will pray to God for you."

Ser Ciappelletto went on weeping and said nothing. And the friar exhorted him to speak out. Ser Ciappelletto went on weeping and for a long time kept the friar in suspense; then he heaved a deep sigh, and said:

"Father, since you have promised to pray to God for me, I will tell it you. You must know that once when I was a little child I cursed my mother."

And, having said this, he began to weep bitterly again. Said the friar:

"Oh, does that seem so great a sin to you, my son? Oh, men grievously curse God all day long and He gladly pardons those who repent of having cursed Him; and do you think He will not forgive you this? Weep not, be comforted, for with the contrition I perceive in you He would certainly pardon you, even if you had been one of those who laid Him on the Cross."

Said Ser Ciappelletto:

"Alas, father, what is this you are saying? It was too great a sin, too great evil did I commit by cursing my sweet mother, who night and day carried me in her body for nine months, and bore me on her breast more than a hundred times! And if you do not pray God for me, I shall never be pardoned."

When the friar saw that Ser Ciappelletto had nothing more to confess, he absolved him and gave him his blessing, looking upon him as a most holy man, for he fully believed everything that Ser Ciappelletto had said was true. And who would not have thought so, when he beheld a man on his deathbed speak in this way? And after all this, the friar said:

"Ser Ciappelletto, with God's aid you will soon be well again. But if it should happen that God should call to Himself your blessed and well-disposed soul, are you willing that your body should be buried in our convent?"

To which Ser Ciappelletto replied:

"Aye indeed, Messer. Nor do I wish to be anywhere else, since you have promised to pray God for me; and moreover I have always felt a special devotion to your Order. Wherefore I beseech you, when you return to your convent, to send me that most true Body of Christ which you consecrate upon the altar in the morning. For, although I am not worthy, I intend, with your permission, to partake of it, and afterwards to receive the holy Extreme Unction, so that though I have lived a sinner, I may at least die like a Christian."

The holy man said that he was well pleased with this, and that Ser Ciappelletto spoke well, and that they should be brought to him immediately. And so it was.

The two brothers, who greatly suspected that Ser Ciappelletto would deceive them, had hidden behind a partition which divided another room from that in which Ser Ciappelletto was lying. They listened, and easily heard and understood what Ser Ciappelletto said to the friar. And when they heard the things which he confessed he had done they sometimes had so great a desire to laugh that they almost burst out loudly, and said to themselves:

"What a man is this, whom neither old age nor sickness nor the fear of death (to which he sees himself close) nor even the fear of God (before Whose judgment he must expect to come within a few hours) can remove from his wickedness or make him wish to die otherwise than he has lived!"

But seeing that it had been said that he should be received for burial in the church, they cared nothing about the rest.

A little after this Ser Ciappelletto received the communion and, growing ever worse, Extreme Unction. And a little after vespers on the same day that he had made this good confession, he died. Wherefore the two brothers took measures (with the man's own money) for him to be honourably buried, and sent the news to the friars' convent for them to watch over the body that night, as is customary, and to come for it in the morning with all things befitting.

When the holy friar who had confessed him, heard that he was dead, he went to the prior of the convent and called the chapter together by sound of bell. And when the friars were gathered together he told them what a holy man Ser Ciappelletto had been, according to the opinion which the friar had formed from hearing his confession. And, with the hope that God through him would perform many miracles, the friar persuaded them that they ought to receive his body with the greatest reverence and devotion. To this the prior and the other credulous friars agreed. That evening they all went to the place where Ser Ciappelletto's body lay, and kept great and solemn vigils over it. Next morning, dressed in their albs and copes, with books in their hands and crosses borne before them, they set out chanting

to fetch the body and brought it to their church with great
pomp and solemnity, followed by nearly all the people, both
men and women, of the town. When they had set him down
in the church, the holy friar who had heard his confession,
went up into the pulpit and began to preach marvellous
things about him, his life, his fasts, his virginity, his simplicity and innocence and sanctity. And among other things
he related that which Ser Ciappelletto had confessed to him,
weeping, as his greatest sin, and how the friar could scarcely
bring him to believe that God would pardon him. From
this he turned aside to reprove the people listening to him,
and said:

"But you, accursed of God, at every wisp of straw that
catches your feet you curse God and His Mother and the
whole Court of Paradise."

Besides this, he said a lot more about his probity and
purity. In short, with his words—in which the country
folk had complete faith—the friar so beat him into their
heads and devotion that, as soon as the service was over,
all those present went crowding up to kiss his hands and
feet, and the clothes were torn off his back; and happy
was he who could get a fragment of them. And it was
agreed that he should remain there all day, so that all could
visit and behold him. Then, when night came, he was
honourably buried in a marble tomb within a side chapel.
And little by little on the following day the people began
to go and light candles to him and to adore him, and afterwards to make vows to him, and to hang up waxen images,
when leave was granted.

The fame of his sanctity and of the devotion to him increased so much that almost everyone who fell into ad-
versity made vows to him rather than to any other Saint.
They called him and still call him Saint Ciappelletto; and
they declare that through him God has performed and
every day still performs many miracles on behalf of those
who devoutly beseech his aid.

Thus lived and died Ser Ciappelletto da Prato, and thus
became a Saint, as you have heard. I am unwilling to deny
that it is possible he may be among the Blessed in God's
presence; for though his life was evil and wicked, he may
have repented at his last hour and God may have been merciful to him and have received him into His Kingdom. But
since this is hidden from us, I conclude from what appears
that he must rather be in the hands of the Devil in Hell,
than in Paradise. If this is so, we may recognise the greatness of God's mercy towards us, Who looks not at our errors

but at the purity of our faith; and when we, believing him to be God's friend, make His enemy our mediator, He grants our requests as though we had appealed to a true Saint as a mediator for His mercy. And therefore, since in this present calamity through His grace we are kept safe and sound and in such pleasant company, praising His Name (wherein we have begun this) and keeping Him in all reverence, let us in all our needs devoutly beseech Him in the certainty that we shall be heard.

Whereupon he was silent.

## SECOND TALE

*A Jew called Abraham, urged by Giannotto di Civigni, goes to Rome and, beholding the wickedness of the clergy there, returns to Paris and becomes a Christian*

The ladies commended the whole of Pamfilo's tale and laughed at parts of it. After this tale had been listened to eagerly and had come to an end, the queen commanded Neifile (who sat next to Pamfilo) to tell a story to follow the order of the entertainment thus begun. She, even as one that is no less ornamented with all courteous manners than with beauty, cheerfully replied that she would gladly do so, and began thus:

In his tale Pamfilo has showed us that God's mercy regards not our errors when they proceed from matters which are beyond our knowledge. Now, I mean to show how this same mercy patiently endures the faults of those who by their words and deeds should bear true witness to His mercy and yet do the exact contrary; nay, more, makes these things an argument of His infallible truth, in order that with more constancy of mind we may follow those things we believe.

Gracious ladies, I have heard it told that in Paris there dwelt a great merchant and good man named Giannotto di Civigni, a man of the utmost honesty and probity, with a large business in silk goods. He was the intimate friend of a rich Jew called Abraham, who was also a merchant and a very upright, honest man. Now, when Giannotto saw the man's honesty and goodness he began to feel great regret that through lack of faith the soul of such a wise, learned and good man should go to Hell. Wherefore, Giannotto began in a friendly way to beg him to abandon the errors of the Jewish faith and to return to Christian truth. For, as he said, the Jew might see that Christianity is so holy and so good that it continually prospers and increases, whereas, on the other hand, he could perceive that Judaism is diminishing and will soon vanish.

The Jew replied that he thought Judaism was the only holy and good faith, that he had been born in it, and intended to live and die in it. Nor could anything ever shift him from it. This did not prevent Giannotto from bringing up the subject again a few days later, and from pointing out to him, in the clumsy way most merchants would do, the reasons why our faith is better than Judaism. Although he was a great master of the Jewish law, yet, either because he was moved by his friendship for Giannotto or because the words which the Holy Spirit puts in the mouth of an ignorant man acted upon him, the Jew began to take a pleasure in Giannotto's explanations. However, he remained obstinate in his belief and did not allow himself to change. But the more stubborn he remained the more Giannotto continued to urge him, until at last the Jew was overcome by so much insistence and said:

"Look here, Giannotto, you want me to become a Christian, and I am quite prepared to do so. So much so, that I want first to go to Rome and see him whom you call God's Vicar on earth, to observe the ways and customs of him and his brother Cardinals. And if they seem to me such that, what between your words and them, I can come to see that your faith is better than mine, as you have laboured to prove to me, then I will do what I have said. But if not, I shall remain a Jew as I am."

When Giannotto heard this he was deeply pained and said to himself:

"I have wasted my labour, which I thought I had employed so well, in the belief that I had converted him. Now, if he goes to the Court of Rome and sees the filthy and rascally life of the clergy, not only will he not turn from a Jew to a Christian, but if he had turned Christian he would inevitably become a Jew again."

So he turned to Abraham and said:

"My dear friend, why undertake all the trouble and expense of going to Rome? Especially since the journey by sea and land is full of dangers for a rich man like you. Do you think you can find nobody here to baptise you? If you have any doubts concerning the faith I have expounded to you, where will you find greater masters and men more learned in these matters than those here, who will enlighten you concerning anything you wish or enquire about? In my opinion this journey is superfluous. The prelates there are like those you can see here, if not better, because they are nearer to the chief Shepherd. In my opinion, this troublesome journey will be of more avail to you later on as a pilgrimage to obtain remission of sins, and perhaps I will then accompany you."

To this the Jew replied:

"Giannotto, I believe that things are as you say. But, to condense many words in a few—if you want me to do what you have so often asked of me, I am determined to go to Rome; otherwise I shall do nothing."

Seeing he was obstinate, Giannotto said:

"Go then, and good luck to you."

But he thought to himself that the Jew would never become a Christian when he had seen the Court of Rome. However, having nothing to lose by it, he said nothing.

The Jew got to horse as soon as possible and went off to the Court of Rome, where he was honourably received by his Jewish friends. He told nobody why he had come there, but began cautiously to examine the behaviour of the Pope, the Cardinals, the other prelates and all the courtiers. From his own observation—for he was a very acute man—and from what he heard through others, he discovered that from the highest to the lowest they all generally and most unworthily indulged in the sin of lechery, not only in the natural way but sodomitically, without the slightest remorse or shame. And this to such an extent that the power of courtezans and boys was of considerable importance in obtaining any favour. Moreover, he observed that they were openly gluttons, wine-bibbers and drunkards, and after lechery were, like brute beasts, more servants of their bellies than of anything else.

Looking more closely, he saw that they were all avaricious and grasping after money, and that for money they bought and sold human, and even Christian, blood, and also every sort of divine thing whether appertaining to the sacraments or to benefices. They did more trade and had more brokers than there were for all the silks and other goods of Paris, and gave the name of "Procurator" to the most flagrant simony and that of "Maintenance" to gluttony; as if God, like us, suffered the meaning of words to impose on Him, and did not know the motives of evil souls, and, like men, let Himself be deceived by the names of things. These, and many other matters which must be kept in silence, grievously displeased the Jew, who was a sober and modest man; and when he thought he had seen enough, he determined to go back to Paris, which he did.

When Giannotto heard that the Jew had returned, he did not feel the slightest hope that he had become a Christian; but he went to see him, and they rejoiced together. And when the Jew had rested for a few days, Giannotto asked him what he thought of the Holy Father and the Cardinals and the other courtiers.

To this the Jew immediately replied:

"It seemed to me that God is very kind to them all. For, if my observation is of any value, I saw there no sanctity, no devotion, no good works or examples of life or otherwise among any of the clergy. But it seemed to me that lechery, avarice, gluttony and such like things, aye and worse (if there can be any worse) were so much in grace with them all that I consider Rome a forge of devilish rather than divine labours. In my opinion your Shepherd (and consequently all the others) endeavours with all haste and talent and art to reduce the Christian religion to nothing and to thrust it out of the world, in the very place where they ought to be its support and foundation.

"Now, since I perceive that what they endeavour to achieve does not occur, but that your religion continually increases and becomes brighter and more illustrious, I justly am of opinion that the Holy Spirit is its support and foundation, inasmuch as it is truer and more holy than any other. So, whereas I remained formerly unmoved by your exhortations and would not become a Christian, I now tell you openly that nothing shall prevent me from becoming a Christian. Let us go to a church, and there I will be baptised in accordance with the usual rites of your Holy Faith."

Giannotto had expected a completely contrary conclusion, and when he heard the Jew say this he was as happy as a man could be. So they went together to Notre Dame of Paris, and asked the clergy there to baptise Abraham. And when they heard what was requested, they did so immediately. Giannotto held the Jew at the font and gave him the name of Giovanni. Immediately afterwards Giannotto caused him to be perfectly instructed in our faith by the most eminent doctors. This he learned speedily and became a good and worthy man, of holy life.

# THIRD TALE

*By means of a tale about three rings, a Jew named Melchisedech escapes a trap laid for him by Saladin*

When Neifile was silent, her tale was praised by them all; and then, at the queen's command, Filomena began to speak as follows:

Neifile's tale brings back to my mind a dangerous adventure which once happened to a Jew. Now since God and the truth of our faith have already been well dealt with among us, we should not be forbidden to come down to the adventures and actions of men. I shall tell you this tale, and when you have heard it perhaps you will become more cautious in answering the questions which are put to you. You must be aware, my loving friends, that stupidity often drags people out of happiness into the greatest misery, while good sense saves the wise man from the greatest dangers and puts him in complete security. That stupidity brings people from happiness to misery may be seen from many examples, which I do not intend to relate now, seeing that a thousand instances of it occur every day. But, as I have promised, I will briefly show you by a little tale how wisdom may be the cause of joy.

Such was the valour of Saladin that not only did he rise from the people to be Sultan of Babylon but he won many victories over Saracen and Christian Kings. He found one day that he had spent the whole of his treasure in divers wars and magnificent displays, while something had occurred which made him need a large sum of money. He did not know where to get it as speedily as he needed, when he remembered a rich Jew named Melchisedech who lent money at usury in Alexandria; and Saladin thought that this Jew could be of use to him if he wanted. But the Jew was so miserly that he would never do it of his own free will, while Saladin did not wish to use force. Since necessity pressed him, Saladin tried to think of some means whereby the Jew would come to his aid, and finally decided that he would devise some colourable pretext for compelling Melchisedech. So he sent for the Jew, received him in a friendly way, made him sit down, and then said:

"Worthy man, I have heard from many people that you are very wise, and that you have a deep understanding of God's ways. So I should very much like to know from you which of the three Laws you think the true one—Judaism, Mohammedanism or Christianity?"

The Jew, who really was a wise man, saw at once that Saladin intended to catch him by his words in order to draw him into a dispute. So he thought he must not praise one of the three above another, otherwise Saladin would attain his object. So he sharpened his wits, like a man who needs to make an answer which will not entrap him, realised excellently beforehand what he ought to say, and said:

"My Lord, you have asked me a very good question, but if I am to tell you what I think about it I shall have to relate a little story, which you will now hear.

"If I err not, I remember that I have often heard that once upon a time there was a great and rich man who possessed a most beautiful and valuable ring among the other precious jewels in his treasure. Being desirous to do honour to it on account of its value and beauty and to make it a perpetual heirloom among his descendants, he commanded that whichever of his sons should be found in possession of the ring, which he would leave to him, should be looked upon as his heir, and that all his other children should reverence and honour this son as the greatest among them.

"The son to whom the ring was left gave similar orders to his descendants, and acted as his predecessor had done. In short, this ring passed from hand to hand through many succeeding generations, and finally came into the hands of a man who had three fine and virtuous sons who were all very obedient to their father. For which reason he loved all three of them equally. The young men knew the custom attached to the ring and each was desirous to be the most honoured, and therefore each of them to the best of his ability besought the father—now grown old—to leave him the ring when he died.

"The worthy man, who loved them all three equally, did not himself know which of the three he would choose to leave the ring, and, as he had promised it to each of them, he thought he would satisfy all three. So he caused a good artist secretly to make two other rings, which were so much like the first that even the man who had made them could scarcely tell which was the real one. When the old man was dying, he secretly gave one of the rings to each of his sons. And after their father's death, each of them claimed the honour and the inheritance, and each denied it to the others; and to prove that they were acting rightly, each one brought forth his own ring. And the rings were found to be so much alike that no one could tell which was the true one, so the question as to which was the father's real heir remained unsettled and is not settled yet.

"My Lord, I say it is the same with the three Laws given by God our Father to three peoples, concerning which you have questioned me. Each of them thinks it has the inheritance, the true Law, and carries out His Commandments; but which does have it is a question as far from being settled as that of the rings."

Saladin perceived that the Jew had most skilfully avoided the snare which he had woven to catch his feet. And therefore he decided to tell the man of his necessity and to find out whether he would aid him. And this Saladin did, telling the Jew what he had thought of doing if the Jew had not replied so discreetly.

The Jew freely put at Saladin's disposal all the money he needed, and Saladin afterwards repaid him in full. Moreover, Saladin gave him very great gifts and always looked upon him as a friend and kept the Jew near his person in great and honourable state.

## FOURTH TALE

*A monk falls into a sin deserving the most serious punishment, skilfully proves his abbot guilty of the same fault, and escapes the penalty*

Filomena ended her tale, and was silent. Dioneo, who sat next her, saw that he was next in order, and, without waiting for the queen's command, began as follows:

If I have understood your intention rightly, amorous ladies, we are here to amuse ourselves by telling stories. So long as we achieve that, I think each of us should be allowed to tell the story he thinks most likely to be amusing; and just now the queen said that we could do this. Well, we have heard how Abraham saved his soul through Giannotto di Civigni's good advice, and how Melchisedech defended his money from Saladin's wiles by his wisdom. So, without any fear of censure from you, I am going to tell you briefly how a monk's prudence saved his hide from serious punishment.

In Lunigiana, a district not far from here, there was a monastery which in the past abounded more in monks and sanctity than it does today. Among them was a young monk, whose virility and youth were unsubdued by fasts and vigils. One day he chanced to go out about noon when the other monks were asleep. He was walking round the church by himself—it was in a rather isolated spot—when he saw a very pretty girl, probably the daughter of one of the peasants, who was picking flowers in the meadows. As soon as he saw her, he was violently attacked by carnal desire.

He went up and began talking to her; he got on so well that they came to an understanding, and he took her up to his cell without anyone seeing them. Carried away by over-much good will, he was enjoying her too vigorously when the Abbot arose from sleep and, as he passed softly by the cell, heard the noise they were making together. To make certain of the voices, the Abbot stopped outside the cell to listen, and realised that a woman was there. At first, he was tempted to make them open the door; then he changed his mind and decided to act differently. So he went back to his own cell to wait until the monk came out.

Now, although the monk was extremely preoccupied with his pleasure and delight in the girl, he thought he heard a shuffling of feet in the dormitory. He looked through a crack and plainly saw the Abbot there listening, which meant that the Abbot knew he had a girl in his cell. This troubled him greatly, for he knew quite well he would be severely punished. However, he did not let the girl see his anxiety, but at once tried to think how he could escape. He hit upon a new scheme, which exactly achieved the end he wanted.

He pretended that he thought he had been long enough with the girl, and said:

"I must go and find some means for you to get away without being seen, so stay here quietly till I get back."

He went out, locking the cell behind him, and went straight to the Abbot's room, as every monk does when he wants to go out. He presented himself to the Abbot, and, putting a good face on things, said:

"Messer, this morning I couldn't get in all the logs needed, so with your permission I am going to the wood to fetch them."

The Abbot thought the monk did not know he had been

seen and, glad of the opportunity to enquire more closely
into the monk's offence, gave him the key and permission
to go out. When the monk had gone, the Abbot began to
wonder what he should do next. Should he open the cell in
the presence of all the monks for them to see the crime
and thereby prevent them from grumbling about him when
he punished the monk? Or should he first go and ask the
girl how it had happened? It then occurred to him that she
might be the wife or daughter of some respectable man,
whom he would prefer not to hold up to shame before all
the monks; so he thought he would see her first, and then
decide what to do. He went stealthily to the cell, opened
it, went in, and shut the door.

The girl was frightened when she saw the Abbot, felt she
would be shamed, and began to cry. Messer Abbot cast his
eye upon her, and saw that she was fresh and pretty. Although he was an old man, he suddenly felt the warm stings
of the flesh, just as the young monk had, and said to himself:

"Ah now, why shouldn't I take a little pleasure when I
can get it? I have enough worry and trouble every day,
without adding this. She's a pretty girl, and no one knows
she's here. If I can persuade her to pleasure me, I don't
know why I shouldn't do so. Who's to know? Nobody
will ever know it—and sin hidden is half forgiven. This
chance may never happen again. I think him a wise man
who can pick his own pleasure from what God sends to
others."

Having entirely changed his mind in this way, he went
nearer to the girl, gently comforted her and begged her not
to cry. So, going from one thing to another, he finally expressed his desires.

The girl was not made of iron or adamant, and willingly
yielded to the Abbot's pleasure. When he had fondled and
kissed her, he lay down on the monk's bed. It may be
that he thought of the weight of his own dignity, and the
girl's tender age, and was afraid to lay too much weight
on her; in any case, he did not lie on her breast but made
her lie on his, and for a long time enjoyed himself with her.

Meanwhile the monk, after pretending to go to the wood,
had hidden himself in the dormitory, and saw the Abbot
enter the cell alone. Completely reassured, he felt that his
little plan would succeed; and when he heard the Abbot
lock the door, he was quite sure of it. He left his hiding-
place, and through a crack heard and saw all the Abbot
said and did.

When the Abbot thought he had had enough of the girl, he locked her in the cell and went back to his own room. A little later he saw the monk and thought he had come back from the wood. The Abbot's plan was to reprimand him severely, and imprison him, to enjoy the well-earned prize all to himself. Therefore he called the monk up, frowned on him, severely reprimanded him, and ordered him to be imprisoned. But the monk promptly replied:

"Messer, I have not been long enough in the Order of Saint Benedict to know every particular connected with it; you did not tell me that monks should humble themselves beneath women, as with fasts and vigils. But now you have showed me, I promise you, if I am forgiven this time, that I will not go wrong again here, but will always do exactly as I saw you do."

The Abbot was a sharp fellow and saw at once that the monk was smarter than he was, and moreover had seen what he did. Remorseful at his own slip, he was ashamed to give the monk a punishment he deserved himself. So he pardoned him and told him to say nothing about what he had seen. He had the girl secretly sent out of the monastery, and it may be well supposed that he often had her brought back.

# FIFTH TALE

*With a dinner of fowls and a few witty words the Marchioness of Monferrato represses the King of France's indecent passion for her*

The tale told by Dioneo at first pricked the hearts of the listening ladies with a little modest shame, which appeared by their chaste blushes. But, as they glanced at each other, they could scarcely keep from laughing. However, they smiled to themselves as they listened. When the tale was finished, the queen reproved him with a few gentle words, just to show him that such tales should not be told before ladies, and then, turning to Fiammetta who sat next him on the grass, commanded her to follow on in her turn. So with a cheerful look she gracefully began:

I am glad that in our tales we have begun to show the power of quick and witty retorts. Now, in men it is always wise to love women of better families than themselves; and in women it is prudent to know how to preserve themselves from the love of men of higher station than they are. So it has occurred to me, fair ladies, to show you in the tale I have to tell how a gentlewoman saved herself by her action and words from such a man, and sent him off.

The Marquess of Monferrato, Standard-bearer to the Church, was a man of great valour, and went overseas with the army of the Crusaders. There was talk of his bravery at the Court of Philip the One-eyed, who was preparing to leave France on the same Crusade. One of the knights said there was not another couple under the stars like the Marquess and his wife; for, just as the Marquess excelled all knights in courage, so did his wife exceed all other ladies in beauty and virtue.

These words entered the King of France's mind so deeply that, although he had never seen her, he fell violently in love with her, and made up his mind that he would sail from nowhere but Genoa. If he went to that port by land he would have a reasonable pretext for going to see the Marchioness; and, as the husband was away, he thought he would be able to get what he wanted from her.

He proceeded to carry out his plan. He sent his army on ahead, and started out himself with only a few gentlemen. When he was one day's march from the Marquess's lands, he sent to tell the lady that he meant to dine with her next day. The lady, who was prudent and wise, cheerfully answered that she considered it a very great honour, and that he would be welcome. Then she began to wonder why a King should come to visit her when her husband was away. Nor was she wrong when she concluded that he was attracted by the fame of her beauty.

However, as she was a great lady, she determined to show him all honour, and called together all the eminent men remaining with her to make all suitable arrangements with their advice. But she reserved to herself the banquet and the food. Without delay she got together all the fowls in the countryside, and ordered her cooks to use them only for the different courses at the royal banquet.

The King arrived at the time appointed, and the lady received him with all honour and rejoicing. When he observed her, he found that she was far more beautiful and virtuous and polite than the knight had said. He marvelled at her, and praised her highly; and, finding that the lady was so much more excellent than he had imagined, his desires increased proportionately. He then went to take his repose in apartments richly furnished with everything necessary for a King's reception. When dinner time came, the King and the Marchioness sat down together at one table, and the rest, according to their rank, were served at other tables.

Here the King was highly delighted, for he was served successively with many courses and the finest wines, while in addition he kept gazing at the beautiful Marchioness with the greatest pleasure. However, as one course succeeded another, the King began to wonder, for however differently they were served up, they were all made of chicken. He knew that the country round about must be filled with game, and, since he had warned the lady that he was coming, there had been plenty of time to hunt and shoot. He marvelled so much at this, that he wanted to make her talk about nothing but fowls, and so turned to her gaily, saying:

"Why, Madam, are there only hens and no cocks born in this part of the country?"

The Marchioness perfectly understood what he meant, and felt that, just as she had wished, God had given her an opportunity to show the King her intentions. So, at the King's question, she turned bravely upon him and said:

"No, Sire, but the women are the same here as elsewhere, although they may differ in clothes and rank."

When the King heard her words, he understood the reason for the banquet of fowls and the virtue hidden in her words. He realised that words would be useless with such a woman, and he could not use force. And since he had so incautiously flamed up for her, the wisest thing to do for his own honour would be to extinguish this unlucky fire of passion. So he continued his dinner with no hope of success, and did not attempt to jest further with her, for he was afraid of her retorts. To cover up the cause of his unseemly visit by a swift departure, he thanked her immediately after dinner for the honour she had done him, commended her to God, and departed at once for Genoa.

## SIXTH TALE

*A worthy man censures the vile hypocrisy of the clergy
with a jest worthy of praise and laughter*

They all praised the Marchioness's virtue and her pretty
slap at the King of France. Emilia, who sat next to Fiammetta, at the queen's pleasure, began cheerfully to speak.

I mean to tell you how an honest layman scored off a
grasping monk with a jest worth your praise and laughter.

Not long ago, my dear friends, there lived in our city
a Minor Friar, attached to the Inquisition. Although he
pretended to be a holy man and a tender lover of the
Christian faith—as they all do—he was a no less expert
Inquisitor of those with fat purses than of those that were
lukewarm in the faith. He happened to come upon a good
man, with more money than sense, who, out of no dis-
respect to the faith, but possibly a little warm with wine or
overmuch merriment, thoughtlessly remarked in company
that he had a better wine than Christ himself ever had
drunk. This came to the ears of the Inquisitor, who knew
the man's farms were large and his purse fat. So he descended upon the poor man with sword and staves and
brought a serious charge against him, not so much with
the idea of strengthening his faith by the Holy Inquisition
as of filling his own hand with the man's money; which
he succeeded in doing.

He called the man before him and asked him if the
charge made against him were true. The poor man said
"Yes," and explained how it happened. And the Inquisitor,
a most holy man, greatly devoted to Saint George Goldbeard, answered:

"So you made Christ a drinker and a judge of good
wines, as if he were a swashbuckler or one of your drunken
sots and tavern-mates? And now you speak humbly and
try to prove that it was of no importance. It's far worse
than you think. If I treated you as you deserve, you would
be burned at the stake."

With a fierce countenance he spoke these and other
words to the poor man, as if the fellow had been Epicurus
denying the immortality of the soul. In short, he so terrified

the man that, by the aid of certain mediators he anointed
the monk's palms with a large quantity of Saint George
Goldbeard's grease (which vastly calms that malady of
pestilent avarice which afflicts the clergy, and particularly
the Minor Friars who are forbidden to touch money)
and thereby persuaded the Inquisitor to deal mercifully with
him. Although this ointment is nowhere mentioned by
Galen in his treatise on medicine, yet it is so potent that the
threatened stake was graciously changed into a cross. This
was made of yellow on black, as if they were giving him a
banner to go on a Crusade. In addition, after the money
was paid, the Inquisitor kept the man by him for a few
days; then, as penitence, made him go every morning to
hear Mass in Santa Croce and appear before the Inquisitor
at meal time. After which, he was free to do as he pleased
for the remainder of the day.

All this he diligently performed, and one morning at
Mass he heard the Gospel sung, containing the words:
"You shall receive a hundred for one, and possess eternal
life." These words stuck in his mind. Later on, according
to his orders, he went to the Inquisitor at meal time, and
found him dining. The Inquisitor asked if he had heard
Mass that morning.

"Messer, yes," he replied promptly.

Then said the Inquisitor:

"Did you hear anything which raised any doubts in you,
anything you would like to enquire about?"

"Indeed," replied the good man, "I doubted nothing
that I heard, and I believe firmly that it is all true. But I
heard one thing which filled me with the greatest pity for
you and all other friars, on account of the sad plight you
will be in when you get into the next world."

Said the Inquisitor:

"What was it you heard that made you pity us?"

"Messer," replied the good man, "it was the sentence
from the Gospel, which says: 'You shall receive a hundred
for one.' "

"That's true," said the Inquisitor. "But why did it trouble you?"

"Messer," replied the good man, "I will tell you. Since I
have been coming here, every day I see the poor people
outside are given one or two large cauldrons of soup,
which are simply the leavings of the other friars and yourself. So, if you are to receive a hundred for every one of
these, you will get so much soup that you will all be
drowned."

All those at the Inquisitor's table laughed at this, but the Inquisitor was enraged, for he felt it was a stab at their thick-soup hypocrisy. And the Inquisitor would have started another suit against him, if he had not already been blamed for bringing the first one—simply because the man had amusingly scored off him and other lazy rogues. And so in a rage he told the man to go about his business and not show his face there again.

## SEVENTH TALE

*With a tale about Primasso and the Abbot of Cluny, Bergamino wittily satirises the avarice which had begun to appear in Messer Cane della Scala*

Emilia's manner and the tale she told made the queen and the others laugh, and praise the jest of the man dressed out with a cross. But when the laughter was ended and everyone was silent, Filostrato, whose turn to speak came next, began thus:

To hit a fixed mark, virtuous ladies, is good, but when something unexpected suddenly appears and is brought down by an archer, then the shot is almost marvellous. The foul and scandalous life of the clergy, a sure sign of rottenness in many things, gives an easy opportunity for talk, satire and reproof to anyone who likes to take the trouble. I approve the good man who hit at the Inquisitor by way of the hypocritical charity of the friars, who give the poor what ought to be thrown away or fed to the pigs. But I think more praise is due to the man I am going to tell you about, of whom I was reminded by the last tale. By means of an amusing tale which put what he wanted to say into other persons' mouths, he satirised Messer Cane della Scala, a magnificent lord who had suddenly and unwontedly become miserly. And this was how he did it.

As almost everyone in the world knows Messer Cane della Scala was favoured by Fortune in many things, and was one of the greatest and most magnificent lords known in Italy since the Emperor Frederick II. Now, he had arranged to give a wonderful feast in Verona, and many people, especially all sorts of courtiers, came from all parts to it. Suddenly, for some reason, he changed his mind, and sent all these people away after he had compensated them. There was a man named Bergamino, whose wit and ready tongue will hardly be believed by those who did not know him. He alone remained without receiving any compensation or permission to leave, but in hopes that this would be of some future use to him. But Messer Cane had taken it into his head that anything given to Bergamino was as much wasted as if it had been thrown into the fire; and therefore said nothing to him directly or indirectly.

Some days passed and Bergamino saw he was not sent for or required for any service, while his horses and servants and himself were spending all his money at his inn. This made him very melancholy, but he continued to stay on, thinking it better not to leave. He had brought with him three handsome suits of clothes, given him by other lords so that he could cut a figure at their feasts. When the landlord of the inn insisted on payment, Bergamino gave him one of these suits. He stayed on, and had to give another suit to the landlord to pay his expenses. Finally, he was living on the third suit, and made up his mind that he would stay as long as it lasted, to see what might happen, and then depart.

While he was living on his third suit, and looking very gloomy, he happened one day to be in the presence of Messer Cane, who was at dinner. Messer Cane saw him, and with the idea of sneering at him rather than getting any amusement out of what he might say, remarked:

"What's the matter, Bergamino? You look very gloomy. Tell us what's the matter."

Quite spontaneously, but as skilfully as if he had long thought it out, Bergamino promptly told the following tale relevant to his affairs:

"My Lord, you must know that Primasso was a man very learned in Latin and wrote verses better and more easily than anyone else. These gifts made him so famous that, although very few people knew him by sight, almost everyone knew the name and fame of Primasso.

"On one occasion he was in Paris. He was poor, as he remained most of his life, for the rich take small interest in learning. He heard much talk of the Abbot of Cluny, who was supposed to be the richest prelate in revenues in the Church, except for the Pope. He heard wonderful and magnificent things about him, how he always kept his court, and how nobody was ever refused food and drink if he went and asked for it when the Abbot was at table. Pri-

masso was a man who liked to see worthy men and lords,
and when he heard this he decided to go and see the Abbot's magnificence. He asked how far the Abbot lived from
Paris, and was told that it might be about six miles to his
house. Primasso thought that if he started out early enough
he could get there in time for dinner.

"He enquired the road, but did not find anyone going
that way. He was afraid he might lose himself and arrive
somewhere else, where a dinner would be harder to find.
Therefore he took three bread rolls with him to have something to eat in case this happened, reflecting that you can
find water everywhere, although that was a drink that gave
him small pleasure. He put the rolls in his gown, started
out, and made such good progress that he arrived before
dinner.

"He entered and looked about him, and saw a multitude
of tables set out and great preparations in the kitchen and
other things preparing for dinner. And he said to himself:
'This is really as magnificent as people said.' While he was
gazing about him, dinner time arrived, and the Abbot's
steward ordered in the water for everyone to wash his
hands; after which, they all sat down at table. It happened
that Primasso found a seat just by the door which the Abbot had to come through to the dining hall.

"Now in that Court the custom was to serve no bread
and wine or any other food or drink until the Abbot was
seated. So when the steward had arranged the tables, he
sent word to the Abbot that dinner awaited his pleasure.
The Abbot had the door opened for him to enter the hall,
but, as he glanced in, the first man he saw was Primasso,
who was ill-dressed and unknown to the Abbot by sight.
When the Abbot saw him, an ungenerous thought which
had never struck him before, came into his mind; and he
said to himself: 'Is that the sort of man who eats my food?'
So he turned back and commanded the door to be locked,
and asked those about him if they knew who the ruffian
was sitting at the table just by the door. And everyone said
'No.'

"Primasso had the appetite of a man who has travelled
some distance and is not used to fasting. After waiting a
little time for the Abbot, he pulled out one of his three
rolls and began to eat. When the Abbot had delayed a
while, he told one of his attendants to go and see whether
Primasso had left. The attendant replied:

" 'No, Messer, he is eating bread which he must have
brought with him.'

"Then said the Abbot:

" 'Well, he can eat his own, if he has any, but he shan't eat mine today.'

"The Abbot hoped that Primasso would go away on his own, for he did not like to send him away. But when Primasso had eaten one roll, and still the Abbot did not arrive, he began to eat another; and this was told the Abbot, who had sent someone again to see if Primasso had gone.

"Finally, as the Abbot still did not arrive, Primasso having finished the second roll, began on the third. This also was told the Abbot, who began to think to himself:

" 'What new idea is this which has come into my mind? Why this avarice and scorn? And for whom? For many years now I have given food to anyone who asked for it, without enquiring whether he was a gentleman or a peasant, rich or poor, a merchant or a swindler. With my own eyes I have seen my food devoured by all sorts of ruffians, yet the thought which came to me about this man never occurred to me. Such avarice would not have attacked me for a nobody; this man I thought a scoundrel must be someone important, since I refused to do him honour.'

"Whereupon he made enquiries and found the man was Primasso, who, having long heard that the Abbot was a great man, had come there on purpose to see the magnificence of which he had heard so much. This made the Abbot feel ashamed, and, desirous to make amends, he strove to honour Primasso in every way. After a dinner befitting Primasso's honourable condition, the Abbot clothed him nobly, gave him money and a horse, and left him free to stay or depart. Primasso was highly pleased, gave the Abbot the greatest thanks possible, and returned on horseback to Paris whence he had come on foot."

Messer Cane, who was an intelligent lord, needed no further explanation to understand exactly what Bergamino meant. He smiled and said:

"Bergamino, you have skilfully exposed your wrongs, your worth, my avarice, and what you desire of me. I never was attacked by avarice before, but only in your case. But I shall drive it away with the stick you have invented."

Messer Cane paid Bergamino's landlord, most nobly clothed him in one of his own suits, gave him money and a horse, and this time allowed him to stay or leave as he chose.

# EIGHTH TALE

*With a witty saying Guglielmo Borsiere, a courtier,*
*overcomes the avarice of Messer Ermino de' Grimaldi*

Next to Filostrato sat Lauretta who, after listening to the
praise of Bergamino's adroitness, realised that it was her
turn to speak; so without waiting the order, she began
pleasantly to say as follows:

This tale, dearest friends, makes me wish to tell how
an excellent courtier similarly, and not without results, attacked the covetousness of a very rich merchant. Although
its purpose is like that of the preceding tale, it ought none
the less to please you, since good came of it in the end.

Some time ago there lived in Genoa a gentleman named
Messer Ermino de' Grimaldi. According to everyone's belief, in wealth and great possessions he vastly surpassed any
other rich citizen then known in Italy. Now, just as he
excelled every Italian in wealth, so he was more avaricious
and miserly than any other miser on earth. He not only
kept his purse shut against other people, but, contrary to
the usual custom of the Genoese who like to dress handsomely, he deprived himself of what was needed for his
own person, simply to save money. And he did the same
with food and drink. So he deservedly lost the surname of
Grimaldi, and everybody called him Messer Ermino Miser.

While by spending nothing he was increasing his wealth,
there arrived in Genoa one Guglielmo Borsiere, a valiant,
well-bred and witty courtier. He was quite unlike the courtiers of today who, rather than be called courtiers, to their
shame, wish to be considered gentlemen and lords in spite
of their corrupt and vile habits, when they should rather
be called asses, bred in the filth of all the wickedness of
the vilest men. Of old, gentlemen were wont to consider it
a duty to labour to keep the peace when wars or quarrels
occurred between other gentlemen; or they arranged marriages, alliances and friendships, enlivening unhappy persons and amusing the Court with fine and witty remarks; or,
like fathers, they earned little that way. But today they
speak ill of one another, they sow discord, they say wicked
and malevolent things, and, which is worse, perform them

in men's sight; they accuse each other of true and false wrongs, shameful things and wickedness. With false allurements they drag gentlemen down to base and wicked things, and devote all their ingenuity to wasting their time. The man who says and does the most abominable things is most beloved and honoured and richly rewarded by these lewd worthless lords. This indeed is a shame and reproach to the modern world and an evident proof that the virtues have departed from us and have left the wretched living to the dregs of vice.

But to return to what I was saying—for my just scorn has led me a little further out of my way than I thought—this Guglielmo was honoured and eagerly entertained by all the gentlemen of Genoa. After he had remained a few days in the city, he heard so much about Messer Ermino's avarice and miserliness, that he wished to see him.

Messer Ermino had heard the report of Guglielmo's worth; and since, despite his avarice, he still retained some small spark of honour, he received the gentleman with a cheerful visage and friendly words. They entered upon various discourse and, as they conversed, Messer Ermino took him and other Genoese there present, to a new house of his which he had had very handsomely built. After he had showed them all over it, he said:

"Messer Guglielmo, you have heard and seen much of the world; now, can you tell me of something which has never been seen which I can have painted in the hall of my house?"

To this inept speech, Guglielmo replied:

"Messer, I do not think I can suggest any subject never seen before, unless it were people sneezing or something like that. But, if you wish, I will tell you of something which I believe you have never seen."

Messer Ermino, not expecting the retort he was bringing down on himself, said:

"Oh, please tell me what it is, I beg you."

To which Guglielmo promptly replied: "Paint 'Liberality' on the wall."

When Messer Ermino heard that, he was so much ashamed of himself that the emotion changed his nature from what it had been almost to the contrary, and he said:

"Messer Guglielmo, I will have 'Liberality' painted in such a manner that neither you nor anyone else will be able to say again that I have not seen and known it."

Such virtue was in Guglielmo's remark that henceforth

he became a most liberal and gracious gentleman, entertaining strangers and his own countrymen beyond any man in Genoa.

## NINTH TALE

*The King of Cyprus, taunted by a lady of Gascony, changes from a bad to an energetic monarch*

Elisa was the only one left to receive the queen's command, and, without waiting for it, she began cheerfully.

Fair ladies, it often happens that a remark made accidentally and without design may succeed where various reproofs and much pains have been wasted. This appears plainly from the tale told by Lauretta, and I mean briefly to show you this with another tale. Whoever the speaker may be, these things always rejoice the virtuous and should be heedfully gathered together.

In the reign of the first King of Cyprus, after the conquest of the Holy Land by Godfrey of Boulogne, a gentlewoman of Gascony went on a pilgrimage to the Sepulchre. As she was returning, she was basely raped by certain villains in Cyprus. Having complained without receiving any redress, she thought she would go and complain to the King. But someone told her that she would be wasting her pains, for the King lived a very base and mean life, not only failing to avenge with justice the wrongs done to others, but enduring with shameful cowardice an infinity of insults to himself. So that if anyone was angry, he vented it without causing the King any shame or irritation.

When the lady heard this, she despaired of vengeance, but as some consolation to her woes she thought she would go and taunt the King with his baseness. So she came weeping before him, and said:

"Sire, I have not come to you for vengeance of the wrongs done me, but as some amends for them I beg that you will tell me how you endure those which I hear are done you. In this way I may learn from you patiently to bear my wrong, and, God knows, I would gladly give it to you if I could, since you bear them so well."

The King, who hitherto had been dull and lazy, seemed to awake from a dream. He began by sharply avenging the injury done this lady, and from that time forward became very severe in punishing those who did anything contrary to the honour of his crown.

## TENTH TALE

*Master Alberto da Bologna modestly shames a lady who had tried to do the same to him when she saw he was in love with her*

When Elisa was silent, it fell to the queen to tell the last tale; and she, in a womanly fashion, began to speak as follows:

Young and virtuous ladies, even as the stars in the bright cloudless sky are the ornaments of heaven, even as the spring flowers to the green meadows, so are graceful jests to good manners and pleasing conversation. And since they are brief, they are more befitting women than men. Much and long speech (especially when it might be avoided) is far more unseemly in women than in men. Nowadays few or no women understand a witty thing, or if they do understand it, do not know how to reply. This is a disgrace to us and all living women. That which the women of the past possessed in their minds, is placed by modern women in the ornaments of the body. She whose clothes are most variegated and striped, with most ornaments, feels she ought to be much more esteemed and honoured than other women, forgetting that if such things were put on an ass it could carry far more than any of them, and yet be esteemed no more than an ass.

I am ashamed to say this, for I cannot speak against other women without speaking against myself. These dressed-up, painted, gaudy things either stand mute and senseless as marble statues, or, if questioned, make such answers that they would do much better to remain silent. And they pretend that this ignorance of how to talk with ladies and men of worth is the result of purity of soul. Their stupidity they call modesty, as if the only modest women were those who talk with their maid or their washerwoman or the baker's wife. If Nature had meant this, as they pretend, she would have nipped short their chattering altogether.

True it is that here, as in other matters, we must consider time and place and the person with whom we talk. For it often happens that a woman or a man tries to make someone blush by a witty jest; but, having misjudged the other person's powers, she finds the blush she tried to put on another is put on her. So, that you may learn to take heed and, moreover, not verify the common proverb which says that women always choose the worst in everything, I mean to instruct you by means of today's last tale, which it is my turn to tell. And I shall show you how we may excel other women in nobility of soul as well as in good manners.

Not many years ago there lived in Bologna—and perhaps still lives—a great and famous doctor named Master Alberto. He was nearly seventy years old, but such was the nobility of his spirit that, although nearly all the natural heat had left his body, he did not reject the flames of love. One day at a feast he saw a beautiful widow whose name, according to some, was Madonna Malgherida de' Ghisolieri She was most pleasing to him, and he received these love-flames in his elderly bosom as if he had been a young man; so much so that he could not sleep well at night unless during the day he had seen the lovely and delicate face of his beautiful lady.

To this end he was continually passing in front of the lady's house, afoot or on horseback, whenever the opportunity arose; and she and other ladies naturally perceived the reason of his going to and fro. They often laughed together to see a man so old in years and wisdom fallen in love, as if they thought the delicious passion of love should only dwell in the foolish minds of young men, and nowhere else.

Master Alberto continued to pass in front of the house, and one feast day when the widow and other ladies were seated at her door, they saw Master Alberto in the distance coming towards them. So they proposed that they should receive and entertain him, and afterwards jest at him for being in love. They all stood up and invited him in. He was taken to a cool courtyard and served with sweetmeats and the finest wines. Finally they asked him as gently and politely as possible how he could be in love with such a beautiful lady when he knew she was beloved by numerous handsome, courteous and witty young men.

The Doctor at once saw they were quietly making fun of him, and with a cheerful countenance replied:

"Madonna, no wise person should be surprised that I

am in love, especially with you who are so deserving of love. And although old men are naturally lacking in the powers required for amorous exercises, they are not lacking in good will or in judgment as to whom they should love; for since they are more experienced, they have more knowledge than young men. I am an old man in love with a woman who is beloved by many young men; and this is why I feel hopeful about it. I have often seen women at lunch, eating lentils and leeks; and although leeks are not very good, still the bulb portion is the least unpleasant and the most agreeable to the taste. Now, you women have such perverse appetites that you hold the bulb in your hands and eat the leaves, which are not only worthless but taste unpleasant. Well, Madonna, how do I know that you will not do exactly the same in choosing a lover? If you did so, I should be the chosen lover, and the others would be sent about their business."

The lady, as well as all the others present, felt greatly ashamed, and said:

"Doctor, you have well and courteously punished our presumptuous attempt. Yet your love is dear to me, for it is the love of a wise and good man. Therefore, save for my honour, you may command me in all things."

The Doctor arose with the company, thanked the lady, cheerfully took leave of her, and departed.

In this way, by not being careful to estimate the man she was jesting at, the lady, in trying to bring him down, was herself brought down. And if you are wise, you will yourselves take care to avoid doing this.

When the ladies and the three young men had finished their tales, the sun was declining towards evening and the heat much less. So the queen said gaily:

"And now, dear companions, there is nothing left for me to do during today's reign save to provide you with a new queen, who will arrange our lives and hers tomorrow in all such virtuous amusements as she thinks fit. My reign should last until night, but those who have no time beforehand cannot well prepare what is to come; so, I think the future days should begin at this hour, to give the new queen time to prepare what she thinks fitting for the morrow. Therefore that most discreet young lady, Filomena, shall be queen of our kingdom tomorrow and guide us for our own amusement and in reverence to Him through Whom all things live."

So saying, she arose, put off her garland and reverently

placed it on Filomena, saluting her first as queen, followed by the other ladies and young men, who cheerfully submitted themselves to her rule.

Filomena modestly blushed a little when she found herself crowned, but remembering the words just uttered by Pampinea, she plucked up courage and, in order not to be remiss, first confirmed all the orders given by Pampinea, then arranged for the following morning and the supper that was to come. After which she said:

"Most dear companions, although Pampinea has made me your queen—more from her courtesy than my worth—I do not intend to follow my own judgment alone, but yours also, in arranging our life together. I shall tell you in a few words what I intend to do, and you can make any alterations you choose. If I have rightly observed Pampinea's arrangements for today, they are both praiseworthy and pleasant. So, unless they become tedious by repetition or for some other reason, I do not think they should be altered.

"Let us continue in the way we have begun. We will first get up from here and amuse ourselves. When the sun is setting we will dine in the open air and then, after a few songs and other pleasures, we shall do well to go to bed. Tomorrow, we will get up early, and walk somewhere for our pleasure, everyone to his choice. Then, at the proper time, we will come back for lunch, and afterwards dance. After the siesta, we will do as we did today, and tell stories, which seems to me equally useful and pleasant.

"Pampinea was elected queen so late that she could not limit our tales to a given subject, as I intend to do. This will give time for each of you to think of a good tale about the subject agreed on. Now, since the beginning of the world people have been led by Fortune into various adventures, and will be until the world ends. So each is to tell a tale about someone who after passing through various adventures reaches a happy end he had not hoped for."

The ladies and the men all praised this command and agreed to follow it. But when the others were silent, Dioneo said:

"Madonna, I agree with what the others have said, that the order you have just given is commendable and pleasant. But as a special grace I ask one privilege, which I want to enjoy as long as we are together. I ask that I shall not be compelled by this law to tell a tale on the given subject, if I do not want to, but to take any subject I like. And so that no one may suppose I ask this grace because I am short of tales, I am quite willing that henceforth I shall always be the last to speak."

The queen knew he was a gay and amusing man, and also knew that he only asked this with a view to livening up the party with a merry tale if they grew tired of the same subject; and so, with the others' consent, gladly gave him this permission.

They then arose from their seats and walked slowly towards a stream of the clearest water, which flowed down a slope into a valley shaded with many trees, among natural rocks and green plants. Bare-footed and with naked arms, they amused themselves in the water. And when supper time drew near, they returned to the house, and supped gaily.

After supper, musical instruments were brought and the queen ordered Lauretta to dance and Emilia to sing a song, accompanied by Dioneo on the lute. In obedience to which Lauretta immediately began to dance and Emilia tenderly sang the following song:

> *So much my beauty doth delight me, I shall never heed another love, nor seek delight therein.*
>
> *Whenever I gaze upon that mirrored beauty I behold the sovereign good which charms the mind; and no new hap or ancient thought can cheat me of this dear delight. What other lovely thing could I behold to waken new delight within my heart?*
>
> *This good flies not whenever I desire once more to gaze upon my solace; and to my pleasure this beauty is so delicate no words may speak it, and no mortal ever comprehend, save those who burn with like delight.*
>
> *Each hour, the more I fix my sight upon this loveliness, the more I burn; I give it all myself, yield myself wholly, enjoying now all it has promised me, and greater joy I trust shall soon be mine, that never such delight was felt by any.*

All gaily responded to this song, though some pondered greatly over its words. After they had spent part of the night with other songs, the queen was pleased to put an end to the First Day. Torches were lighted, and she ordered everyone to rest until the next day. And so all went to their bedrooms.

**END OF THE FIRST DAY**

# THE SECOND DAY

# THE SECOND DAY

*Here begins the second day of the* Decameron, *wherein under the rule of Filomena, stories are told of those who after passing through various adventures reach a happy end they had not hoped for*

The sun had already brought in a new day with his light, and the birds singing their pleasant verses among the green boughs bore witness thereof to men's ears, when the ladies and the three young men arose and went into the garden. There, with slow steps treading the dewy grass, they wove fair garlands, and for a long time walked for their delight. And as they had spent the previous day, so did they spend this. For having eaten in the open air, they danced, and then went to their siesta; and waking about the hour of Nones, as the queen had ordered, they went out to the greensward and sat down round about her.

Crowned with her garland the queen was beautiful and pleasant to look upon. And as they all gazed at her where she sat, she ordered Neifile to begin the first tale. And she, without making any excuse, gaily began to speak.

## FIRST TALE

*Martellino pretends to be a cripple and feigns that he is cured by the body of Saint Arrigo. His deceit is discovered and he is beaten; he is arrested and in danger of being hanged by the neck, but finally escapes*

Most dear ladies, it often happens that he who tries to mock others—especially in those matters which should be reverenced—often finds that he is mocked himself to his own hurt. To obey the queen and to start on the subject proposed with my tale, I mean to tell about one of our own citizens, and how things first fell out most unpleasantly for him but afterwards, contrary to his hopes, very luckily.

Not long ago there lived in Treviso a German named Arrigo. He was very poor, and hired himself out as a porter. But he was a man of most holy life and everyone thought him a good man. Whether this was so or not, the people of Treviso say that when he was dying the bells in the largest church of Treviso began to ring miraculously, untouched by human hand.

Considering this a miracle, they all said Arrigo was a saint. And all the people of the town went in a crowd to the house where his body lay, and bore it to their principal church as if it were a saint's body. Then they brought the lame and the blind and the crippled and everyone else diseased or deformed, almost all of whom became well when they touched Arrigo's body.

During this tumult and concourse of the people, three of our fellow countrymen happened to be in Treviso, whose names were Stecchi, Martellino and Marchese. These men were mummers, and went about to the courts of great lords, amusing people by acting and mimicking others. This was their first visit to Treviso, and they were greatly surprised to see everybody running about. When they heard the reason they wanted to go and see what was happening. So they left their baggage at an inn, and Marchese said:

"We want to see this Saint, but I don't see how we can get to see him. I am told the square is full of Swiss and other troops, placed there by the Lord of this city to prevent riots. Moreover, according to what they say, the church itself is so full of people that hardly anyone else can enter."

Martellino, who loved to look at things, then said:

"Don't let that worry you. I'll find some way to reach the Saint's body."

Said Marchese:

"How?"

And Martellino replied:

"I'll tell you. I will pretend to be a cripple. You and Stecchi will support me on either side as if I couldn't walk, and you will pretend to be taking me for the Saint to cure. Everyone who sees us will make way and let us pass."

This idea greatly pleased Marchese and Stecchi. Without delay they left the inn all three, and found a lonely place; there Martellino contorted his hands, fingers, arms and legs, and his eyes, mouth and whole face as well, until he was a fearful sight. Anyone who saw him would have said that he was really crippled in his whole person. Marchese and Stecchi took him up and went towards the church, with visages full of piety, asking everyone humbly and for the love of God to make way for them; which they easily obtained.

Everyone stared at them and almost everyone kept shouting, "Make way, make way!"; and so they came to Saint Arrigo's body. Martellino was lifted up and laid on the Saint's body for him to receive the gift of health.

Everyone gazed at Martellino to see what would happen. Martellino, who knew exactly what he was about, began to straighten out first a finger, then a hand, then one of his arms, and finally his whole body. When the people saw this they made such a clamour in honour of Saint Arrigo that you could not have heard a roll of thunder.

Now there happened to be present a Florentine who knew Martellino quite well, but had not recognised him when he was brought in so deformed. But when Martellino straightened himself out, the man recognised him and began to laugh, saying:

"God damn the man! Seeing him come in like that, who would not have believed that he was really crippled?"

Some of the people of Treviso heard what he said, and immediately asked:

"Why! Wasn't he a cripple?"

To which the Florentine replied:

"No, by God's grace! He has always been as well as any one of us. But, as you have just seen, he is more skilful than anyone in playing monkey-tricks and contorting himself into any shape he chooses."

When they heard this, it was quite enough. They forced a way forward, shouting:

"He's a traitor, a mocker of God and the Saints! He wasn't a cripple! He pretended to be a cripple to scorn us and our Saint!"

So saying, they seized him and dragged him away, pulled him by the hair, tore the clothes off his back, and began to punch and kick him. And everyone present who thought himself a man took his whack at him. Martellino shrieked for mercy in the name of God and defended himself as best he could. Useless—the crowd only grew thicker.

When Stecchi and Marchese saw this they began to think that things were going wrong, and fearing for their own skins, were in no hurry to help him. So they shouted, "Kill him!" with the rest of the people, but tried to think how they could get him out of the hands of the mob. They would certainly have killed him, if Marchese had not invented a plan. The whole of the police-forces were there outside, and Marchese made his way as quickly as he could to the Podestà, and said:

"Help, for God's sake. A thief has cut off my purse with a hundred gold florins in it. Come and seize him, and get me my money back."

As soon as they heard this, about a dozen sergeants rushed off to where the luckless Martellino was being carded without combs, beat off the mob with the greatest difficulty, snatched him all broken and bruised from their hands, and took him to the palace. Thither he was followed by many who considered he had mocked them; but, hearing he had been arrested as a cut-purse, they thought this a good way of harming him, so they all began to say he had stolen their purses.

The police magistrate was a rough fellow, and when he heard this, he had Martellino brought in at once and began to question him. Martellino answered him with jests, as if he had been arrested for nothing. This angered the judge so much that he ordered him to be bound on the rack and given several good turns to make him confess to what they said in order to hang him up by the neck. When he was laid on the ground, the judge asked him if what he was charged with was true. And since it was useless to say no, he said:

"My lord, I am ready to confess the truth; but if you will order each person who accuses me to say when and where I took his purse, I will tell you which I took and which I did not take."

Said the judge:

"I am content."

He called some of them up, and one said that Martellino had cut his purse a week before, another six days, another four days, and some said that very day.

Hearing this, Martellino said:

"My lord, they all lie in their throats. And I can give you a proof that what I say is true, for I was never in this country before, and only arrived here a very short time ago. As soon as I arrived, as ill luck would have it, I went to see the Saint's body, where I was beaten and scratched as you may see. That I speak truth may be verified by the official who interviews foreigners, and by his book, and by the inn landlord. Now if I speak truth you will surely not have me tortured and killed at the instigation of these base fellows."

While things were in this state, Marchese and Stecchi

perceived that the judge was dealing harshly with Martellino and putting him on the rack. They were alarmed and said to themselves: "We've done this badly; we've pulled him out of the frying-pan into the fire." While their attention was wholly given up to this, they came upon their landlord, and told him what had happened. He laughed heartily at it, and took them to one Sandro Agolanti, a man living in Treviso who had great influence with the Governor, to whom he told the whole story, begging him with the others to interest himself in Martellino's affair.

After much laughter, Sandro went off to the Governor, and asked that Martellino should be sent for; which was done. Those who went for him found him still in his shirt before the judge, bewildered and terrified because the judge would not listen to any excuse. Perhaps he hated the Florentines, for he had made up his mind to hang Martellino, and refused to give him up to the Governor, until he was compelled to yield against his will. When Martellino came before the Governor, he related exactly all that had happened, and begged as a supreme favour that he should be allowed to go away, "For," said he, "until I get back to Florence I shall always feel that halter round my neck." The Governor laughed extremely at all that had occurred, and gave them each a suit of clothes. Thus, beyond all their hopes, all three escaped this great danger and returned home safe and sound.

## SECOND TALE

*Rinaldo d'Asti is robbed, comes to Castel Guglielmo, is sheltered by a widow, recovers what he had lost, and goes home safe and sound*

The ladies laughed greatly at Neifile's account of Martellino's misfortunes, and among the young men Filostrato was most amused. As he sat next to Neifile, the queen commanded him to tell the next tale. And he began without any delay.

Fair ladies, the tale I am about to tell you concerns the duties of a Catholic; it is composed partly of misfortunes and partly of love; and to hear it may be useful to you,

especially to those who travel love's debatable lands,
wherein, if they have not said their prayer to Saint Giuliano
they may find a good bed but a bad lodging.

In the days of the Marquess Azzo da Ferrara, a merchant
named Rinaldo d'Asti came to Bologna on business. He was
returning home after completing his business when, on the
road from Ferrara to Verona he fell in with some pretended
merchants, who in fact were highwaymen and men of base
life and condition, whom he incautiously talked to and allowed to accompany him.

They saw he was a merchant and supposed he must have
money upon him; and so they determined to rob him at the
first opportunity. To prevent any suspicion in him, they pretended to be modest, well-conditioned men, went along
talking about honesty and fair dealing, and as far as they
knew how, acted courteously and modestly towards him.
And he believed that he was very fortunate to have met
them, since he was alone with only one servant on horseback. As they went along talking of one thing and another, the conversation fell upon the subject of what prayers
men make to God; and one of the three highwaymen said
to Rinaldo:

"And what prayer do you make, Sir, when you are on a
journey?"

To which Rinaldo replied:

"Indeed, I am a rough and awkward man in such matters
and I know very few prayers; I live in the old-fashioned
way. But still when I am travelling, every morning when I
leave my inn I say an Our Father and a Hail Mary for the
souls of Saint Giuliano's father and mother; and then I
pray God and Saint Giuliano to give me a good lodging that
night. And it has often happened to me when travelling that
I have been in great danger, and yet have escaped and
reached a good lodging for the night. And I firmly believe
that Saint Giuliano, in whose honour I tell this, has begged
this grace for me from God; and if I did not pray to him in
the morning I do not think I should travel well by day nor
lodge well at night."

And the highwayman said:

"Did you say your prayer today?"

And Rinaldo replied:

"I did indeed."

Then he, who knew how things would turn out, said to
himself: "You'll need it; for if I'm not mistaken, you'll
spend the night in rather a bad inn." But aloud he said:

"I have travelled a lot myself, but I never say that prayer

though I have often heard it recommended; however, I have always come to a good lodging. And perhaps this very evening you will see which of us two has the better lodging —you who say the prayer or I who do not. But it's true that instead of your prayer I say the 'Dirupisti' or the 'Intemerata' or the 'De profundis' which, as my grandmother used to tell me, are very useful prayers."

Thus talking they went on their way, awaiting time and place to carry out their base plot. When they came to a ford near Castel Guglielmo they saw the place was deserted and the hour late; so they fell upon him, robbed him, and left him afoot in nothing but his shirt. And as they departed, they said:

"Go, and if your Saint Giuliano gives you a good lodging tonight, remember ours will give us a good one too."

And they crossed the ford, and rode away. When Rinaldo's servant saw his master attacked, like a base fellow he did nothing to help him, but turned his horse round and rode hard till he came to Castel Guglielmo. He entered the town and without further ado, went to an inn. The weather was very cold and it began to snow. Rinaldo was barefoot and in nothing but his shirt, and did not know what to do. Night was coming on, he was shivering, his teeth were chattering, so he began to look about for some shelter where he could pass the night without perishing of cold. He saw none, for war had passed over that country not long before and everything had been burned. Urged by the cold, he set off at a jog-trot in the direction of Castel Guglielmo, not knowing whether his servant had fled there or elsewhere, but hoping that if he could enter the town God would send him some help.

The darkness of night fell on him when he was still about a mile from the town, and when he arrived there it was so late that the drawbridges were raised and the gates shut, and he could not enter. Weeping and in despair he looked about for some shelter from the snow at least, and saw a house built on the town wall and jutting out a little. He determined to shelter under this pent-house until dawn. Under the pent-house he found a locked door, and, gathering some straw, he lay down on it, complaining frequently to Saint Giuliano that all this was a poor return for his faith in the Saint. But Saint Giuliano had an eye on him, and soon found him a better lodging.

In this town there lived a widow of great beauty whom the Marquess Azzo loved more than life itself and kept there for his pleasure. And this lady lived in the house under whose pent Rinaldo had taken shelter. The Marquess had come there that day to lie with the lady, and she had secretly provided a bath and a good dinner for him. Everything was ready, and she was awaiting the Marquess, when a messenger arrived at the gate bringing news which compelled him to go to horse at once. He sent a message to the lady, and immediately rode away. The lady was somewhat displeased, and not knowing what to do, decided to take a bath herself, have dinner and go to bed. And so she got into the bath.

The bath was near the doorway where the unhappy Rinaldo was lying outside on the ground, and, while the lady was bathing, she heard Rinaldo complaining, and his teeth chattering with a noise like a stork's bill. Calling her maid-servant, she said:

"Go and look at the man in the doorway outside the wall, see who he is and what he is doing."

The maid went and saw in the dim light a shivering man sitting there bare-footed and in his shirt. She asked him who he was. Rinaldo was shivering so much that he could scarcely utter the words, but in a few words he managed to tell who he was and how and why he happened to be there. And then he piteously besought her not to leave him there all night to die of cold.

The maid felt sorry for him, went back to her mistress and told her everything. The widow also pitied him, and, remembering there was a key to the door which the Marquess sometimes used to enter secretly, she said:

"Go and open the door for him. Here is a dinner and nobody to eat it, and we can easily find room for him."

The maid highly commended her mistress's charity, went down and opened the door and brought him in. The lady saw he was nearly frozen, and said to him:

"Quick, good man, get into that bath—it's still warm."

Without waiting any further invitation he gladly did so, and, as he felt the warmth reviving him, it was as if he were coming back from death to life. The lady lent him some clothes of her husband, who had recently died, and when Rinaldo put them on, they fitted him as if they had been made for him. While waiting the lady's next orders, he thanked God and Saint Giuliano for saving him from the bad night he had been dreading and for bringing him to what seemed like a good lodging.

The lady rested a little and ordered a large fire to be lighted in her main room. When she came down to it, she asked what kind of a man he was. And the maid said:

"Madonna, he has dressed himself, and he's a good-looking man, and seems well-mannered and a gentleman."

"Go then," said the lady, "and call him, and tell him to come up by the fire here and dine, for I know he has had no dinner."

Rinaldo entered the room, and seeing the lady (apparently of quality), respectfully greeted her and gave her his warmest thanks for the favour she did him. The lady observed him and thought the maid was right about him; so she received him gaily, sat down by the fireside with him, and questioned him about his misfortune. And Rinaldo told her everything that had happened.

The lady believed what he said, for she had heard something about it, through Rinaldo's servant having come to the town. She told him what she knew about his servant, and that he could easily find the man next day. And when the table was ready Rinaldo and the lady washed their hands and, at her invitation, sat down to dinner.

Rinaldo was a tall man, handsome, with a pleasant face and good manners, in the prime of life. The lady kept throwing appreciative glances at him, and as her carnal desire had already been made lively by the prospect of the Marquess's lying with her, she let it occupy her mind.

When they left the table after dinner, she asked the maid whether, since the Marquess had abandoned her, she might not enjoy the gift which Fortune had sent her. The maid perceived the lady's desire, and urged her to gratify it; so the lady returned to the fireside where she had left Rinaldo seated alone, and, gazing amorously at him, said:

"Come, Rinaldo, why do you sit there so pensive? Are you so much worried by the loss of a horse and a few clothes? Console yourself and cheer up, you are in your own house here. I meant to tell you before, that when I see you here in my husband's clothes, you seem like him, and a hundred times tonight I have wanted to embrace and kiss you; which I should certainly have done, if I had not been afraid of displeasing you."

Hearing these words and seeing the gleam in the lady's eyes, Rinaldo, who was no fool in such affairs, went towards her with open arms, and said:

"Madonna, henceforth I may say I owe my life to you, considering what you saved me from, and it would be base in me not to do anything I can to please you. Therefore embrace and kiss me as much as you like, for I shall be more than willing to embrace and kiss you."

After this, no more words were needed. The lady, all

on fire with amorous desire, threw herself into his arms.
Holding him amorously, she kissed him a thousand times,
and was kissed by him. Then they arose and went to her
bedroom, and with no delay got to bed. And there they
fully satisfied their desires many times, until daybreak.

When the dawn came, he arose, as the lady wished him
to do. So that nobody should know what had happened, she
gave him some old clothes and filled his purse with money,
begging him to keep the secret; then she told him how he
could find his servant, and let him out by the door through
which he had entered.

When it was full day, he pretended to be coming from a
distance, entered the city after the gates were opened, and
found his servant. He put on some of his own clothes and
was about to mount his servant's horse, when as if by a divine miracle the three highwaymen who had robbed him
were brought into the town, having been arrested for another crime they had committed. They confessed the robbery, and Rinaldo regained his horse, his clothes and his
money; and the only thing he lost was a pair of garters,
which the highwaymen had mislaid.

Wherefore Rinaldo gave thanks to God and Saint
Giuliano, mounted his horse, and rode off homeward, safe
and sound. As for the thieves, the next day they were dangling their heels in the air.

## THIRD TALE

*Three young men waste their money foolishly and fall
into poverty. As he is returning home in despair, their
nephew meets a young abbot, who turns out to be the
daughter of the King of England; she marries him, and
he restores his uncles' fortunes*

The ladies listened in wonderment to the adventures of
Rinaldo d'Asti, giving thanks to God and Saint Giuliano
who had helped him in his great need, and praising his devotion. Nor—though they only half admitted it—did they
blame the lady for having enjoyed the good thing God sent
to her house. While they were talking and laughing about
Rinaldo's pleasant night, Pampinea, who sat next to Filo-

strato, saw that her turn was next, and thought over what she should say. When the queen ordered her, she began to speak no less confidently than gaily.

Virtuous ladies, when we look at things closely we see that the more we say about Fortune's deeds, the more remains to be said. No one should be surprised at this if he remembers that everything we foolishly call ours is in the hands of Fortune. Consequently, in her blind judgment she passes them successively from one person to another, without any method visible to us. Now, although this is plainly showed everywhere every day and has again been demonstrated in the former tales, yet, since the queen wishes us to take this subject, I propose to add my tale which I think should please and perhaps be useful.

Once there lived in our city a knight whose name was Messer Tedaldo. Some say he was of the dē̄ Lamberti family; others, perhaps influenced by his sons' trade, say he belonged to the Agolanti, since they always did and still do follow the same trade. But, whichever family he came from, he was a very rich knight in his day, and had three sons, the eldest of whom was named Lamberto, the second Tedaldo, and the youngest Agolante. They were already handsome and fashionable young men, although the eldest was not eighteen, when this rich Messer Tedaldo died, leaving all his goods and chattels to them as his lawful heirs.

When they found themselves very rich and with such great possessions, they began to spend money with no purpose but their own pleasure, and with no sort of control or restraint. They kept numerous servants, many good horses, dogs and hawks; they kept open house, gave tournaments, and not only did everything gentlemen should do but anything else which appealed to their youthful appetites. They had not lived this life long, when the money left by their father began to disappear. Since their income would not meet their expenses, they began to mortgage and sell their lands. Selling one thing one day and another the next, they were soon reduced to almost nothing; and their eyes, which had been closed by wealth, were opened by poverty.

Therefore Lamberto one day called his two brothers together, pointed out to them the splendour in which their father had lived, and they also, and how through their extravagance they were reduced to poverty. Consoling them to the best of his ability, he advised that they should sell the little they had left before they fell into misery, and go away. Without taking leave and with no display, they left Florence and went to London, where they took a small house. Spending as little as possible they began to lend out money on harsh terms of interest, and Fortune was so favourable to them that in a few years they made a great deal of money.

They returned one by one to Florence and with this money bought back a great portion of their estates and others as well, and married. Since they were still lending out money in England, they sent a young nephew named Alessandro to look after their affairs. All three remained in Florence, and though they now had families, they quite forgot the plight into which their former extravagance had brought them, and began to spend more excessively than ever, having credit up to almost any sum with every merchant. For some years these expenses were met by the sums Alessandro sent them, for he had lent money to the English barons on their castles and other revenues, which brought him in a large profit.

Meanwhile the three brothers went on spending freely, and being short of money, began to borrow, always relying on England. Now, contrary to everyone's expectation, a war broke out in England between the King and one of his sons, which split the whole island in two, some holding for one side and some for the other. Thereby all the barons' castles were taken from Alessandro, and he received no income at all. Alessandro did not leave the island, for every day he hoped that peace would be made between father and son, and that he would regain both his interest and his capital. And the three brothers in Florence went on spending at the same rate, and getting deeper into debt every day.

Several years passed, and their hopes were still disappointed. The three brothers not only lost their credit but were arrested by their creditors, and, since their estates were insufficient to meet their debts, they had to remain in prison. Their wives and little children were dispersed in various country places in a very poor state, with no prospects but that of a life of continual poverty.

Alessandro had waited several years in England hoping for peace, but seeing it did not come and that by lingering on he only endangered his own life, he decided to return to Italy. He set out by himself, and, as he left Bruges, he saw a young Abbot in white leaving the city with a long train of monks and numerous servants and a long baggage train. Behind him rode two elderly knights, relatives of the King; and since Alessandro knew them, he spoke to them, and was allowed to ride with them.

As Alessandro rode along with them, he politely asked

who were the monks riding on ahead with so many servants, and where they were going. One of the knights replied:

"The young man riding on ahead is a relative of ours, recently elected Abbot of one of the largest abbeys in England. Now, since he is too young to be legally inducted into such a See, we are going to Rome with him to request the Holy Father to grant him a dispensation, and to confirm the election in spite of his youth. But no one must know this."

The new Abbot rode sometimes ahead and sometimes with his attendants, as we see lords do every day; and on the road he saw Alessandro near him. Now Alessandro was still young, handsome in face and person, and as well-mannered and polite and pleasant as a man can be. At first glance he pleased the Abbot more than anything else had ever pleased him; so he called Alessandro over and began to talk pleasantly to him, asking him who he was, where he came from, and where he was going. In reply Alessandro explained his whole situation, and offered his services to the Abbot in any capacity, however slight.

The Abbot hearkened to his well-ordered talk and noticed his polite behaviour, and, considering that he must be a gentleman in spite of his servile occupation, was better pleased with him than ever. Already full of pity for him, the Abbot tried to console him for his misfortunes, telling him that since he was a man of worth, God would restore him to the position from which he had fallen, and perhaps even higher. And since they were both travelling in the direction of Tuscany, the Abbot asked him to stay in their company. Alessandro thanked him for his consolation, and said he was ready to obey his commands.

As the Abbot rode along, the sight of Alessandro seemed to have put new ideas into his head. A few days later they came to a town none too well furnished with inns. Here the Abbot insisted on stopping, and Alessandro made him stay at an inn whose landlord had once been his servant, and gave him the least uncomfortable room in the house. In this way he became the Abbot's steward, and, as the most practical member of the party, billeted out the remainder as well as he could. The Abbot had dined, it was late, and everyone else had already gone to bed when Alessandro asked the landlord where he should sleep. And the landlord replied:

"Truly, I don't know. You see everywhere is full, and my family and I are sleeping on benches. But there are some grain chests in the Abbot's room, where I can make you up a bed, and you can manage to spend the night there."

To this Alessandro said:

"How can I share the Abbot's room? You know it's small, and so narrow that none of his monks could lodge there. If I had known this at bed time, I should have put the monks on the grain chests, and have taken the place where they are sleeping."

Said the host:

"Well, that's how it is; if you like, you can be quite comfortable there. The Abbot is asleep and his curtains drawn. I can put you a mattress quietly there, and you can go to sleep."

Seeing that this could be done without any annoyance to the Abbot, Alessandro agreed, and lay down as quietly as he could. But the Abbot was not asleep. He had been thinking of the new desires which had come to him, and had heard Alessandro talking to the landlord and where Alessandro had lain down. In great delight, he said to himself:

"God has provided me with the opportunity I desired. If I do not take it, the like may not occur again for a long time."

Determined therefore to take the opportunity, the Abbot waited till all was quiet in the inn, and then called to Alessandro in a low voice, telling him to come and share the bed. After many polite refusals, Alessandro finally consented.

As soon as he was in bed, the Abbot laid a hand on his chest and began to touch him as girls touch their lovers. This greatly astounded Alessandro, and he began to think the Abbot was a person of unnatural tastes. Either from intuition or from Alessandro's movements, the Abbot guessed what he was thinking, and smiled. Then he quickly opened his shirt, laid Alessandro's hand on his breast, and said:

"Alessandro, get rid of that silly idea; seek, and find out what I am hiding."

Alessandro laid his hand on the Abbot's chest, and found two round, firm, delicate woman's breasts, as if carved out of ivory. When he touched them and realised the Abbot was a woman, he stayed for no further invitation, but quickly embraced and tried to kiss her. But she said:

"Before you come any nearer, wait and hear what I have to say. As you see, I am a girl and not a man. I left home a virgin and I am going to the Pope to be married. Your good luck or my misfortune, as time will show, made me fall in love with you deeper than ever woman loved a man.

I want you more than any other man as my husband; if you do not want me as your wife, get out of bed at once and return to where you were."

Now though Alessandro knew nothing about her, he judged from her companions that she must be noble and rich, and he could see that she was most beautiful. So, without hesitation, he replied that if such were her pleasure, it was his also.

She then sat up in bed opposite a little table bearing an image of Our Lord, and, giving Alessandro a ring, made him take her as his wife. After which they kissed each other, and spent the remainder of the night with great pleasure to both parties. And, having made certain arrangements, Alessandro got up at dawn, and left the room as silently as he had entered, without anyone knowing where he had spent the night. In great happiness he rode along with the Abbot and his companions, and after many days' travel they reached Rome.

A few days later the Abbot took the two knights and Alessandro to visit the Pope, and, after the customary reverence, she said:

"Holy Father, you should know better than anyone else that those who desire to live virtuously and well should avoid everything which might lead them to the opposite. To this end, I am sent to you in the dress of an abbot by my father, the King of England, with the greater part of his treasure, for your Holiness to marry me to the old King of Scotland whom my father wishes me to marry, young as I am. I am not so much repelled by the King of Scotland's age as by the fear that, if I marry him, the fragility of my youth may cause me to do something contrary to the laws of God and my father's royal blood.

"God knoweth what is best fitting for us all; and, as I came hither, He in His mercy (as I believe) brought to sight the man I should like to marry. It is this young man." (And she pointed to Alessandro.) "His virtue and his manners are worthy of any great lady, although perhaps his blood is not so noble as the blood royal. Him have I taken and him do I desire; nor will I ever take another man, whatever my father and other men may think. Thus the chief cause for my journey is already settled; but I choose to continue my journey, to visit the sacred places with which this town is filled, to see your Holiness, and to arrange that the contract of marriage made between Alessandro and me in the presence of God alone should be made also in your presence and in the presence of others. Humbly then do I beg you to accept him who is pleasing to God and to me, and to give us your blessing, so that we may live and at the last die together, honouring God and your Holiness, with more certainty of pleasing Him whose Vicar upon earth you are."

Greatly did Alessandro marvel to hear that his wife was the King of England's daughter, and he was filled with a wonderful secret joy. But the two knights were even more astounded, and, if they had not been in the Pope's presence, they would have slain Alessandro and perhaps the lady as well.

The Pope also was amazed both by the lady's clothes and her choice of a husband. But, since he saw there was nothing else to be done, he determined to grant the lady's request. First of all he soothed down the knights who, he could see, were very angry; and having made their peace with Alessandro and the lady, he gave the necessary orders.

On the day appointed, the Pope made a great feast to which he invited all the Cardinals and many other great nobles. Thither also came the lady royally dressed, so beautiful and of such pleasant aspect that she was deservedly appraised by all; Alessandro came too, so splendidly apparelled that he seemed rather of royal blood than an ordinary young man who had lent out money at usury, and he was much honoured by the two knights. Then the Pope solemnly celebrated the marriage, and, after the magnificent service, sent them away with his blessing.

Alessandro and the lady chose to leave Rome and to go to Florence, where the news of their marriage had already arrived, and where the citizens received them with the highest honours. The lady paid the creditors of the three brothers, freed them from prison, and restored them and their wives to their estates; for which they thanked her heartily. Alessandro and his wife then left Florence, taking Agolante with them, and came to Paris, where they were honourably received by the King.

Meanwhile the two knights went over to England and so worked upon the King that he forgave his daughter, and received her and his son-in-law with great festivity.

A little later the King knighted Alessandro with great pomp, and made him Earl of Cornwall. Alessandro acted so skilfully that he reconciled the King and his son, which was of great benefit to the island and obtained him the love and esteem of all the inhabitants. Agolante recovered every-

thing that was owing to him, and, after he had been
knighted by Lord Alessandro, returned to Florence with
very great wealth. The Earl lived gloriously with his Lady;
and some say that by his wisdom and valour, and with the
aid of his father-in-law, he conquered Scotland and was
crowned King.

### FOURTH TALE

*Landolfo Ruffolo becomes poor, turns pirate, is cap-
tured by the Genoese, and shipwrecked, but escapes on
a wooden chest full of jewels; in Corfu he is saved by a
woman and returns home a rich man*

Lauretta sat next to Pampinea, and, seeing her come to the
glorious end of her tale, began to speak without further
delay.

Most gracious ladies, in my judgment no greater act of
Fortune may be seen than to watch a man rise from miserable poverty to a royal estate, as Pampinea's tale has showed
us in the case of Alessandro. Now since each of us is to tell
a story on the same subject and must necessarily keep within
these limits, I feel no shame in telling you a tale which has
no such splendid ending, although it contains greater misfortunes. For this reason I feel sure my tale will be listened
to less eagerly; but as I can do no better, you will forgive
me.

I think that the coast from Reggio to Gaeta is about the
most beautiful part of Italy. Near Salerno there is a part
which the inhabitants call the Amalfi Coast. It is filled with
small towns, gardens and fountains, and rich men who gain
more by trading than the people in any other country.
Among these towns is one called Ravello, which has rich
men today and, in the past, had a very rich man called
Landolfo Ruffolo, who, not content with the wealth he had,
tried to double it, and came near to losing it all and himself
as well.

Having made his calculations, as a merchant does, he
bought a very large ship, spent all the rest of his money
in purchasing cargo, and set sail for Cyprus. There he found
several other ships which had brought the same sort of

cargo as he had. Consequently, he not only had to lower his prices but almost to give away his merchandise to get rid of it; which brought him to the verge of ruin.

He was exceedingly perturbed by this and did not know what to do. From a very rich man, within a short time he had become a poor man, and he decided that he must either kill himself or make up his losses by robbery, to avoid returning home poor after leaving rich. He found a purchaser for his large ship, and with this money and the money he had received for his cargo he bought a small, very swift ship, suitable for a pirate. He armed and fitted it out in every way necessary for this purpose, with the intention of stealing other men's goods, especially the Turks. And Fortune was far more favourable to him as a pirate than as a merchant.

Within a year he robbed so many Turkish ships that he regained all he had lost as a merchant and more than double that. Warned by his first loss he determined not to risk a second, and decided that what he had was sufficient. So he made up his mind to return home and, as he was still afraid of merchandise, he did not trouble to lay out his money, but set out homewards in the little boat whereby he had captured it. When he came to the Archipelago, a sirocco wind began to blow one evening, dead in their faces, making the sea very rough. His small ship could not ride out such a storm at sea, so he ran in under the lee of an island to a bay, intending to wait there for better weather. Soon afterwards two large Genoese merchantmen, coming from Constantinople, with difficulty got into the same bay to avoid the storm.

These two ships blocked up the entrance to the bay and the people on board, seeing the small ship and hearing it was Landolfo's (whom they knew to be very rich), determined to seize it, like the rapacious, money-loving men they were. They sent a landing party ashore with cross-bows, and posted them in such a position that no one could leave the ship without being shot down. The remainder got out their boats and, with the aid of the tide, soon came alongside Landolfo's ship, and in a very short time without much trouble they seized it and the whole crew, without the loss of a single man. They sent Landolfo on board one of the merchantmen dressed in an old jacket. And after taking everything out of the ship, they sank her.

Next day the wind changed, the carracks set sail on a westerly course, and everything that day went well. But towards evening a gale began to blow, with a very rough sea, and the two carracks were separated. The force of the wind was so great that the carrack with poor wretched Landolfo on board struck with a terrific shock on a sandbank off the island of Cephalonia, and broke up like a glass dashed against a wall. The sea was full of merchandise, of chests and tables, as usually happens at such moments. Although it was very dark and the sea raging, such of the poor wretches on board as could take notice of anything began to clutch at whatever was near them.

Among them was the unhappy Landolfo. Many times that day he had called upon death and had determined to kill himself rather than return home in such poverty; but when he saw death face to face, he was afraid. He did as the others did, and when a table came to his hands he clutched it, as though God, by delaying his being drowned, had sent him a means of safety. He lay straddled on it as best he could, and, tossed hither and thither by wind and waves, kept himself afloat until daylight. As he gazed around he could see nothing but clouds and sea and a chest he noticed floating on the water near him. With terror he found this chest coming nearer to him, for he was afraid that if the chest hit him he should be drowned. And each time it came very close he thrust it away with his hand as far as his weakness allowed.

Suddenly a blast of wind and a huge wave threw the chest on to Landolfo's table, which upset and plunged him under the waves. He came up again, more through terror than strength, and saw the table already drifting away in the distance. Fearing he could not reach it, he swam to the chest which was close at hand, resting his body on top of it and keeping it upright with his arms, as best he could. All that day and all the next night he was tossed about on the sea in this manner, with nothing to eat and a great deal too much to drink, not knowing where he was, and seeing nothing but the waves.

Next day, when he was nearly as waterlogged as a sponge, clinging on to the handles of the chest with both hands (as we see drowning men always clutch at anything near them), he was driven towards the coast of Corfu, either by the will of God or the force of the wind. A poor woman happened to be on the shore, scouring her pots with sand and sea water; and when she saw this shapeless object coming near, she screamed in terror and made off.

Landolfo could not speak and could hardly see, and therefore said nothing. But, as the waves brought him nearer to shore, the woman made out the form of the chest;

then, looking more intently, she first saw his arms on the chest and then his face, and guessed what he was. Moved by pity, she waded into the sea which was already calm, clutched him by the hair, and dragged him and the chest to land. With great difficulty she loosened his fingers from the chest, which she placed on the head of her daughter for her to carry. She herself bore Landolfo as if he were a little boy, put him in a bath of warm water, and washed and rubbed him until a little warmth came back and he recovered some of his strength. She took him out of the water when she thought it was time, and fed him with good wine and sweet macaroni, tending him for several days until his strength came back and he knew where he was. The good woman thought she ought to give him the chest which she had saved with him, and then told him to go and seek his fortune.

Landolfo had forgotten all about the chest, but took it when the woman offered it, thinking it could not be so valueless but that he could live for a few days from it. But when he found it very light, his hopes began to sink. However, when the woman was out of the house, he forced it open to see what was inside, and found it full of precious stones, some set and some unset. He had a knowledge of such things, and when he looked at them, he saw they were of value; wherefore he praised God who had not abandoned him, and felt entirely consoled. But since in a short time he had twice been badly buffeted by Fortune, he felt that great caution would be needed in getting these stones home, if he were to avoid a third misfortune. So he wrapped up the jewels in some rags and told the woman he did not need the chest, but that she could have it, if she would give him a sack.

This she willingly gave him, and, after he had thanked her heartily for what she had done for him, he threw his sack on his shoulder and departed. He found a ship to take him to Brindisi and thence coasted along to Trani, where he came upon some drapers, fellow countrymen of his. He told them all his adventures, except for the matter of the chest; and they, for the love of God, gave him clothes and lent him a horse and found him company to return to Ravello, where he said he wanted to go.

When he found himself safe home, he gave thanks to God who had guided him. Then he opened the sack and carefully examined everything in it. He found he had so many valuable stones that by selling them at a reasonable price or even less he would be twice as rich as when he set forth. When he had managed to sell the jewels, he sent a large sum of money to the poor woman of Corfu who had saved him from the sea, and he also sent money to the men who had given him clothes at Trani. He kept the rest without ever wishing to go adventuring again, and lived handsomely until his death.

### FIFTH TALE

*Andreuccio da Perugia goes to Naples to buy horses, falls into three unpleasant adventures in one night, escapes from them all, and returns home with a ruby*

The jewels found by Landolfo (said Fiammetta, whose turn it was to tell the next tale) remind me of a tale containing as many dangers as the one Lauretta has told; but with the difference that whereas in hers the adventures are spread over years, those I am about to relate occurred in one night.

According to what I have been told, there was a young horse-dealer in Perugia named Andreuccio di Pietro. He heard that Naples was a very good horse-market and, though he had never been away from home before, he put five hundred gold florins in his purse, and set out for Naples with several other tradesmen. He arrived one Sunday evening, and, on his landlord's advice, went next morning to the market where he saw a great many horses he liked, though after much chaffering he was not able to strike a bargain. To show that he was a genuine buyer he kept pulling out his purse of florins to show everybody coming and going, like the foolish rustic he was. As he was there displaying his purse, a very beautiful Sicilian girl (one of those who will pleasure any man for a small sum) happened to pass by without his noticing her, and saw the purse. Said she to herself: "If that money were mine who would be better off than me?"

With this girl was an old woman, likewise a Sicilian, who when she saw Andreuccio left the girl and ran up to embrace him. When the girl saw this, she said nothing but waited for the old woman. Andreuccio turned round, recognised the old woman, greeted her warmly, and arranged for her to come and see him at his inn. They then parted without further words. Andreuccio returned to his market, but bought nothing that morning.

The girl who had first noticed the purse and then the old woman's friendship with Andreuccio, meant to try to get hold of some or all his money, and therefore began cautiously to ask her who he was, where he came from, what he was doing in Naples, and how she knew him. The old woman told her all about Andreuccio as well as he could have done himself, how she had lived with his father for a long time in Sicily and then in Perugia. She also explained where he lived and what he had come for.

Having obtained full information about his relatives and their names, the girl determined to use what she had learned, to cheat him of his money by a cunning trick. On returning home she found work to keep the old woman occupied all day long, so that she could not return to Andreuccio. Towards evening she sent another girl, whom she had trained in such affairs, to Andreuccio's inn. By chance she arrived there when he was standing alone by the door, and asked for him of himself. When he said he was Andreuccio, she drew him aside and said:

"Messer, a lady of this town would like to speak with you at your leisure."

Hearing this and seeing the maid was a comely creature, he immediately concluded the lady must be in love with him, for he thought Naples did not contain another young man as handsome as he. He replied that he was ready, and asked her where and when the lady wished to speak to him. To which the maid replied:

"Whenever you like to come, Messer; she is waiting for you in her house."

Whereupon, without saying anything to the inn-keeper, Andreuccio said:

"Lead on then, and I'll follow."

The maid took him to the girl's house, which was in the Malpertugio quarter, whose ill-fame may be seen from its very name. But he knew and suspected nothing, and thought himself going to a lovely lady in a respectable quarter, and so, calmly, followed the maid into the house. As he went up the stairs, the maid called to her mistress: "Here's Andreuccio," and he saw her waiting on the landing.

She was still young, tall and very pretty, quite well dressed and adorned. As Andreuccio came up, she descended three stairs towards him with open arms, clasped them round his neck without saying a word, as if overwhelmed by emotion. Then she wept, kissed his forehead and said in a broken voice:

"O my Andreuccio, welcome, welcome!"

He was quite amazed by these tender caresses, and replied in astonishment:

"Glad to meet you, Madonna."

She then took him by the hand and, without saying another word, led him into her sitting room and from there straight to her bedroom, which was all scented with roses and orange blossom. He saw there was a handsome curtained bed and many dresses on pegs and other rich and beautiful things. As they were all new to him, he was firmly convinced that the girl must be some great lady. She made him sit down beside her on a chest at the foot of the bed, and said:

"Andreuccio, I am quite certain you must be surprised by my tears and caresses, since you do not know me, and perhaps do not remember to have heard of me. But you will soon hear something which will greatly surprise you— I am your sister! Since God has granted me the grace to see one of my brothers before I die (how much I should like to see them all!), if I died at this moment, I should die content. If you have never heard about this, I will tell you. Pietro, your father and mine, as I think you know, lived for a long time in Palermo. His kindness and pleasantness made and still make him beloved by all who know him. But among all who loved him, my mother, who was a lady and at that time a widow, loved him most. Setting aside her fear of her father and brothers, and her own honour, she became so familiar with him that I was born, and am as you see me.

"When Pietro went from Palermo to Perugia, he left me as a little girl with my mother, and for all I know never thought of me and her again. Were he not my father I should blame him severely for his ingratitude to my mother (quite apart from the fact that he owed me his love as his daughter by no servant or vile woman), since she had placed herself and everything she had freely in his hands, out of her great love for him, without knowing who he was.

"But there it is. Things ill done and long passed by are more easily blamed than amended. But so it was. He left me as a little girl in Palermo where I grew up to be much as I am now. My mother, who was rich, gave me as wife to a wealthy gentleman of Girgenti, who for love of me and my mother came to live at Palermo. He was a strong Guelf and began to intrigue with our King Charles, but was discovered before the plot took effect. So he had to fly from Sicily, when I was expecting to be the greatest lady ever known in the island. Taking the few things we could (I say 'few' in comparison with what we had), we left estates and palaces and took refuge here, where King Charles has been very generous to us, restoring to us part of what we lost in his cause and has given us possessions and houses. He makes ample provision for my husband and your brother-in-law, as you may see. This is how I come to be here, my sweet brother, where thanks to God rather than to you, I have at last met you."

So saying, she embraced him once more, and softly weeping kissed him once more on the forehead. Andreuccio, hearing this well-composed fable uttered so cleverly with no hesitation over a single word, remembered it was true that his father had lived in Palermo. From his own experience he knew how apt young men are to fall in love, while her tears, her embracings and modest kisses all combined to make him believe what she said. Therefore he replied:

"Madonna, you must not wonder that I am surprised. Indeed, either my father never spoke of you and your mother, or, if he did, I never heard of it, for I knew no more of you than if you did not exist. It gives me the more happiness to have found a sister because I am quite alone here, and did not hope for any such thing. I think you should be dear to any man however important, let alone a little tradesman like me. But tell me one thing—how did you know I was here?"

To this she answered:

"I learned it this morning from a poor woman whom I often see. According to what she says, she lived for a long time with our father in Palermo and Perugia. And if I had not thought it more fitting that you should come to my house than that I should go to you in a stranger's house, I should almost certainly have come to you."

After this, she enquired after his relatives by name, to all of which Andreuccio replied; and her questions made him believe the more firmly in what he should not have believed at all. They had talked for a long time and it was very hot, so she served him with sweetmeats and Greek wine. After which, Andreuccio got up to go, since it was time for supper. This she would not allow, and, pretending to be greatly offended, she embraced him and said:

"Alas! Now I see how little you care about me! Here you are with a sister you never saw before, in her own house, where you ought to be staying, and you want to sup at an inn! Indeed you shall sup with me. I am very sorry that my husband is not here, but I shall honour you as much as a woman can."

Not knowing what else to say, Andreuccio replied:

"You are as dear to me as a sister can be, but if I don't go, they'll wait all evening for me to come to supper, which will be very bad manners on my part."

Then she said:

"Let me send someone to tell them not to wait for you. But you would do better and show more courtesy to me if you would invite all your companions to sup here, and then if you must leave you can all leave together."

Andreuccio replied that he did not want his companions that evening, but that he would stay as she wished. She pretended to send a messenger to the inn to tell them not to wait supper for him. Then, after a lot more talk, she gave him a supper of several courses, which she skilfully prolonged until night had fallen. When Andreuccio got up to leave she told him she would not allow it, because Naples was not a town for anyone, especially a stranger, to walk about in at night. Moreover, she said that when she had sent the message about his staying for supper, she had also said he would stay the night.

He believed it all, and, delighted by his false belief and at being with her, remained. They went on talking for a long time, as she intended they should. Late at night she left Andreuccio to sleep in her room, with a little boy servant to show him anything he needed, while she went to another room with her women.

The night was very hot. When Andreuccio was alone, he stripped to his doublet and laid his breeches at the head of the bed. He then felt a natural necessity to relieve himself, and asked the boy where he should go. The boy pointed to a door in one corner of the room, and said:

"Go in there."

Andreuccio unsuspiciously entered, but at once trod on a board which was not secured to the rafter, and fell through the floor with it. By God's providence he did himself no harm, although the fall was a long one, but he was all daubed with the filth in the place. For you to understand what happened and what is to follow, I shall describe this place. It was in a narrow space, such as we see between two houses, on two beams laid from one house to the other, with the place to sit down and a few planks, one of which had fallen down with him. Finding himself at the bottom of this place in great discomfort, Andreuccio called to the boy. But the boy had run to tell his mistress as soon as he heard him fall. She ran to the room and immediately looked to see whether his breeches were there. She found the clothes and the money, which he had always carried about with him, in his mistrust of others. Once this Palermo lady who had pretended to be sister to a man of Perugia had got hold of the money for which she had laid this snare, she cared no more about him, but at once went and locked the door he had gone through when he fell.

When the boy did not answer, Andreuccio called louder, but with no result. He then began to feel suspicious and to realise that he had been tricked. He climbed over the wall which separated the place he was in from the street, and ran to the door of the house which he recognised easily. He shouted and knocked for a long time, but in vain. He then saw his misfortune clearly and began to weep, saying:

"Alas! In how short a time have I lost five hundred florins and a sister!"

After many more such exclamations, he began to beat his head against the door and to scream. He made such a din that many of the neighbours could not endure it, and got out of bed. One of the lady's servants came to a window, pretending to be very sleepy, and said angrily:

"Who's knocking down there?"

"Oh!" said Andreuccio. "Oh! Don't you know me? I am Andreuccio, brother to Madonna Fiordaliso."

To this she replied:

"Good man, if you have drunk too much, go home and sleep, and come back tomorrow. I know nothing about Andreuccio and the other nonsense you're talking. Get along with you, and let us sleep, if you please."

"What!" said Andreuccio, "you don't know what I'm talking about? Well, if these are your relatives from Sicily who forget a man so soon, give me back the clothes I left there, and I'll gladly go, in God's name."

But she replied, half laughing:

"You must be dreaming, my good man."

So saying, she went in and shut the window in a flash. Andreuccio, now certain of his misfortune, was so grieved that his anger became rage, and he attempted to get back by force what he could not recover with words. He picked up a large stone and began to batter at the door with it, much more violently than before. Many of the neighbors whom he had already awakened thought he was some disturber of the peace, who had invented all this to annoy the woman. Angry at the noise he made in knocking, they went to the windows and began to shout at him, as all the dogs of a countryside bark at a strange dog:

"It's a foul thing to come and talk nonsense like this outside a good woman's house at this hour of night. Go away, good man, in God's name. Let us sleep, if you please. If you have any business with her, come back tomorrow, but don't make all this uproar tonight."

The good woman's bully, whom Andreuccio had neither seen nor heard about, was in the house. Emboldened perhaps by his neighbours' voices, this bully came to the window and exclaimed in a deep, rough, threatening tone:

"Who's there?"

Hearing this voice Andreuccio gazed up and saw what seemed to be a foul ruffian with a great black beard, looking as if he had just got out of bed, yawning and rubbing his eyes. Somewhat fearfully, Andreuccio replied:

"I am a brother of the lady of the house . . ."

But the man did not wait for him to finish, and interrupted him even more rudely than before:

"I'll come down to you and give you such a beating that you'll soon move along, you drunken tedious ass, keeping people awake!"

And going in, he slammed the window. Some of the neighbours, who knew the man well, said to Andreuccio in low tones:

"For God's sake, good man, don't stay here to be killed; be off, for your own good."

Terrified by the man's voice and urged by the entreaties of the neighbours who seemed moved by charity towards him, Andreuccio, in despair at the loss of his money, went down the street along which the maid had led him the day before, trying to find his inn. He was revolting to himself from the stink of the filth on him, and thought he would go down to the sea and wash. So he turned to the left down a street called Ruga Catalana. As he went towards that end of the city he saw two men with a lantern coming towards him. Thinking they might be the watch or other men likely to harm him, he crept into a hut nearby to avoid them. But they came straight to the same place and went into that very hut. Putting down some iron instruments they were carrying, they began to look at them and to discuss them. While they were talking, one said to the other:

"What's the meaning of this? I can smell the worst stink I ever smelled in my life."

So saying, he turned up the lantern and saw the unfortunate Andreuccio, to whom he said in amazement:

"Who are you?"

Andreuccio said nothing, but they came up to him with the lantern and asked what he was doing there in such a state. Andreuccio then told them what had happened to him. They guessed where this must have taken place, and said to each other: "It must have been in Scarabone Buttafuoco's house." Then one of them turned to Andreuccio and said:

"Good man, although you lost your money, you ought to thank God that you fell down and could not get back into the house. For, if you had not fallen down you may be quite sure that you would have been murdered as soon as you went to sleep, and would have lost your life as well as your money. But what is the use of lamenting? You can no more recover a farthing of it than you can take the stars out of the sky. You even run a risk of being killed if the girl's lover knows that you've said a word about what happened."

After consulting with his companion, he went on:

"Look here, we're sorry for you. If you will come along and share in what we are going to do, it is quite certain that your part of the spoils will be worth much more than you have lost."

Since Andreuccio was in despair, he said he was ready.

That day Messer Filippo Minutolo, Archbishop of Naples, had been buried in very rich vestments and with a ruby ring on his finger worth more than five hundred florins. These things they meant to steal, and told Andreuccio their plan. With more greed than sense Andreuccio started out with them. As they went along towards the church Andreuccio stank so much that one of them said:

"Can't we find some means for this fellow to wash himself, so that he won't stink so abominably?"

Said the other:

"Near here is a well with a pulley and a large bucket. We'll go there and soon wash him."

When they got to the well they found the rope, but the bucket had been taken away. So they decided to tie the rope round him, lower him into the well to wash, and then when he had washed he was to shake the rope, and they would pull him up. While Andreuccio was down the well, certain of the watch came there for a drink, being thirsty with the heat and running after someone. When the two men saw them, they fled at once, before the watch noticed them.

Andreuccio down in the well had now washed himself,

and shook the rope. The watch had laid down their arms
and halberds, and began to haul up the rope, thinking they
were bringing up a large bucket of water. When Andreuccio came level with the well-head, he let go the rope and
grasped the brickwork. The watch saw him and, seized
with sudden terror, dropped the rope without a word, and
made off as fast as they could. Andreuccio was greatly surprised by this, and would have fallen back into the well if
he had not clung on tightly, and might have hurt or killed
himself. However, he managed to get out, and then came
upon the weapons. Since he knew they did not belong to
his companions, he was still more perplexed. Not knowing
what to think and grieving for his fate, he decided to leave
without touching anything, and went off not knowing where
he was going.

As he went along, he fell in with his two companions,
who were coming back to draw him out of the well. When
they saw him they were amazed, and asked him who had
pulled him out of the well. Andreuccio replied that he did
not know, told them what had happened and what he had
found lying near the well. They then saw what had happened, and, laughing heartily, they told him why they had
run away and who the men were who had pulled him up.
As it was now midnight they went to the cathedral without
further talk, and easily got into it. They went to the tomb,
which was a large one built of marble, and by the aid of
their crowbars they managed to lift the heavy top slab high
enough for a man to get in, and propped it up. Having done
this, one of them said:

"Who'll get in?"

Said the other:

"Not I."

"Nor I," said the first. "You get in, Andreuccio."

"That I won't do," said Andreuccio. Whereupon they
both turned on him, saying:

"You won't go in, won't you? Well, if you don't, by
God's faith, we'll give you such a knock on the head with
one of these crowbars that you'll fall dead."

Andreuccio in terror got into the tomb, but as he entered he thought to himself: "These two make me get in
to cheat me. After I've handed everything out to them
and am struggling to get out myself, they will run off with
the spoil and leave me with nothing."

So he thought he would make certain of his share at
once. He remembered the valuable ring they had talked

about, and, as soon as he got into the tomb, he took it from the Archbishop's finger and hid it in his clothes. Then he handed out the crozier, the mitre, the gloves, and everything down to the shirt, when he said that nothing else remained. The other two swore the ring must be there, and told him to look everywhere for it. He said he could not find it, and kept them waiting while he pretended to look for it. But they were more artful than he was, for, while they told him to look carefully, they suddenly pulled away the prop which held up the top of the tomb and ran away, leaving him shut up inside.

When Andreuccio heard this, you may imagine his state. He tried several times to lift the slab with his head and shoulders, but his labour was in vain. Overcome with despair, he fell down senseless on the Archbishop's dead body. And anyone who had looked in would have found it hard to tell whether he or the Archbishop was the dead man. When he regained consciousness, he began to weep floods of tears, seeing only two possible fates awaiting him: if nobody came to open the tomb he would die of hunger and the smell of the dead body; and if the tomb were opened, he would be arrested as a thief.

Filled with these gloomy thoughts and his agony, he heard some men come into the church and several persons talking. From this he gathered that they were about to attempt what he and his companions had done, which increased his terror. But when they had opened the tomb and propped up the slab, the question arose who should get in—which nobody wanted to do. After a long discussion, one of them, a priest, said:

"Why are you afraid? Do you think he'll eat you? Dead men don't eat people—I'll get in."

Seeing this, Andreuccio stood up, seized the priest by one of his legs and pretended to pull him in. Whereupon the priest uttered a piercing yell and scrambled rapidly out of the tomb. The rest were so much terrified that, leaving the tomb open, they ran off as if a hundred thousand devils were after them. Seeing this Andreuccio was delighted far beyond his wildest hopes, and at once climbed out, leaving the church by the way he had come in.

It was now nearly dawn and, as he wandered about with the ring on his finger, he came to the seashore, and from there made his way to the inn, where he found his companions and the inn-keeper who had been awake all night in their anxiety about him. When he had told them his adventures, the landlord advised that he should leave Naples at once. This he did without delay, and returned to Perugia, having invested his money in a ring when he had set out to buy horses.

### SIXTH TALE

*Madonna Beritola, having lost her two sons, is found on an island with two goats, and goes to Lunigiana. One of her sons enters the service of the lord of that place, lies with the lord's daughter, and is imprisoned. Sicily rebels against King Charles, the son is recognised by the mother, finds his brother and they all return to great wealth*

The ladies and the young men all laughed at Fiammetta's account of Andreuccio's adventures, and then, at the queen's command, Emilia began as follows:

Sad and painful are the various revolutions of Fortune, and whenever we hear them spoken of, it awakens our minds which are inclined to sleep under her flatteries. I think that to hear of them should please both the fortunate and the unhappy; since this is a warning to the former, a consolation to the latter. Although much has already been said about them, I mean to tell you a tale both piteous and true, wherein, although the end was happy, the bitterness was so great and lasted so long that I can scarcely believe it was sweetened by the happiness which came at length.

Most dear ladies, you must know that after the death of the Emperor Frederick II, Manfred was crowned King of Sicily. One of the most powerful of his barons was a gentleman of Naples named Arrighetto Capece, whose wife was also a Neapolitan, by name Beritola Caracciola. This Arrighetto was governor of the island, when he heard that King Charles I had conquered and slain Manfred at Benivento, and that the whole kingdom had gone over to him. Having very little belief in the fidelity of the Sicilians, and being unwilling to become a subject of his Lord's enemy, Arrighetto prepared to fly.

But when the Sicilians heard of this, they immediately

sent him and many other friends and servants of King Manfred as prisoners to King Charles, who took possession of the whole island.

In this sudden change of affairs Madonna Beritola lost sight of Arrighetto. Frightened by what had happened and dreading disgrace, she left everything she possessed, although pregnant and without money, and taking with her an eight-year-old son named Giusfredi, she fled to Lipari on a small boat. There she brought forth another son, whom she named Scacciato. She hired a nurse, and then they all took ship to return to her relatives in Naples. But events turned out contrary to their hopes. Instead of reaching Naples, the boat was driven by a gale into a bay in the island of Ponza, where they waited for calm weather to continue the voyage. Like the others, Madonna Beritola went on shore, and, finding there a remote and solitary place, began to lament by herself over the fate of Arrighetto.

This she did every day. And then one day when she was thus plunged in her grief, unaccompanied by any of the sailors or passengers, a pirate ship swooped down, captured everybody else without striking a blow, and immediately departed.

Having finished her daily lament, Madonna Beritola returned to the shore to see her children, as her custom was, but found nobody there. At first she was amazed but then, suspecting what had happened, she gazed out to sea and saw the pirate galley still not very distant, towing the other ship behind. Thus she perceived that she had lost her children as well as her husband. There she was, poor, alone and abandoned, not knowing whether anyone would ever come to the island and find her; and, uttering the names of her husband and children, she fell fainting on the shore.

Nobody was there to bring her round with cold water and other aids, so that her spirit could go wandering at will. But when her senses at last returned, along with tears and lamentation, she kept calling for her children and for a long time sought them in every cave on the island. But when she saw her labour was vain and that night was coming on, she began to think of herself, and, hoping she knew not what, she returned to the cave where she had been wont to lament and weep.

When at last the night with all its fears and infinite grief had passed and a new day dawned, she began to feel hungry, since she had eaten nothing the day before, and was forced to feed upon herbs. As she ate them weeping, her

mind was filled with conflicting thoughts about her future
life. While she was lost in thought she saw a goat enter a
cave near at hand and then come out again and disappear in
the wood. She got up and entered this cave, where she
found two kids, perhaps born that same day, who seemed
to her the most graceful and charming creatures imaginable. Her breasts had not yet lost the milk of her last baby,
and she tenderly picked up the two little creatures and
held them to her breasts. They did not refuse the offer, and
began to milk her as they would have suckled their own
mother. And thereafter they made no distinction between
their mother and her. In this way the lady felt that she had
found some company on this desert island. She had only
herbs to eat and water to drink, and she wept whenever she
thought of her husband and her children and her past life.
She made up her mind to live and die there, and became
as fond of the goats as if they had been her children. The
lady lived this wild life for several months until another
gale brought to the island a ship from Pisa, which remained there several days.

On this ship was a gentleman named Currado de Malespini with his saintly and virtuous wife. They had been on
a pilgrimage to all the holy places in Puglia, and were returning home. To ward off melancholy, this gentleman and
his wife and some of their friends set out to explore the
island with their dogs. At a short distance from where
Madonna Beritola was, the dogs began to chase the two
goats, which were already large enough to feed outside.
Pursued by the dogs, they rushed back to the cave where
Madonna Beritola was sitting. When she saw the dogs, she
jumped up, got a stick and drove them out. Currado and
his wife, following up their dogs, arrived and were amazed
to see this sunburned, thin, shaggy woman, who was still
more amazed to see them. When Currado at her request had
called off the dogs, he began to ask who she was and
what she was doing there, and she plainly told him all about
herself and her misfortunes and the bitter determination she
had formed. Hearing this, Currado, who had known Arrighetto Capece very well, wept with pity and attempted to
dissuade her from her intention, offering to take her to
his own house and treat her as his sister until God sent her
better fortune. When the lady refused these offers, Currado
left his wife with her and said he would send food up to
her; at the same time he asked his wife to give her some
of her own clothes (since Beritola was in rags) and to do
all she could to persuade her to come with them. Left be-

hind with Madonna Beritola, the gentlewoman first wept
over her misfortunes with her, then brought clothes and
food, and with extreme difficulty at last persuaded her to
dress and eat. After she had repeated many times that she
would never go anywhere where she was known, they finally
persuaded her to come with them to Lunigiana, together
with the two kids and the mother goat which meanwhile
had returned and greeted Beritola most affectionately, to
the great amazement of Currado's wife.

When the weather became fine, Madonna Beritola, Currado and his wife went on board ship, taking with them the
she-goat and the two kids. Many of those on board did
not know Beritola's name and they called her "the Goatherd." They sailed with a good wind and at last came to
the mouth of the Magra, where they landed and went to
their castle. There Madonna Beritola lived with Currado's
wife like a waiting-woman, modest, humble and obedient,
dressed in widow's weeds, and affectionately looking after
her goats.

The pirates who captured Madonna Beritola's ship and
unwittingly left her on the island, went to Genoa with
everyone on board. The spoils were there divided among
the owners of the galleys, and Madonna Beritola's nurse
and two children fell, along with other things, to the share
of one, Messer Guasparrino d'Oria, who sent them to his
house to make use of them as servants. The nurse wept
for a long time at the loss of her mistress and the unhappy
fate of herself and the two children. Although a poor
woman she was shrewd and prudent, and when she saw
that tears were useless and that she and the children were
all servants together, she did her best to cheer up. Pondering over their present condition, she felt that if the children's real names were known it might harm them. She
thought too that Fortune might change and that if they
lived they might regain their former station in life. She
therefore decided not to reveal their names to anyone
until the right moment, and told everyone who questioned
her that they were her own children. She changed the elder
boy's name from Giusfredi to Giannotto di Procida, but
did not think it necessary to change the baby's name. She
was most careful to impress on Giusfredi the reasons
why she changed his name and how dangerous it might be
for him if he were recognised. She repeated these, not once,
but many times; and, since the boy was intelligent, he carried out her instructions perfectly.

Ill-dressed and worse shod, the two boys spent several

years with the nurse in Messer Guasparrino's household, condemned to the most servile tasks. At the age of sixteen, Giannotto, who had more spirit than a servant and scorned the baseness of a servile state, left the service of Messer Guasparrino and went on board the galleys which made the voyage to Alexandria. He travelled about in various lands but failed to advance himself.

Within three or four years of leaving Messer Guasparrino, Giannotto became a tall and handsome young man. As he wandered about, despairing of his fortune, he heard that his father was not dead, as he had thought, but kept alive in prison by King Charles; and, coming to Lunigiana, he fell in with Currado de Malespini, and was thankful enough to take service with him. He rarely saw his mother, who was always with Currado's wife, and when he did, neither recognised the other, so much had time changed them from what they had been when they last saw each other.

While Giannotto was in Currado's service, the latter's daughter (named Spina) was left a widow by Niccolà da Grignano, and returned to her father's house. She was a handsome, pleasant girl, not yet sixteen, and, after she and Giannotto had looked upon each other, they both fell passionately in love. This love soon led to the usual result, and lasted thus several months without anyone noticing it. But they became too confident and behaved in a less cautious manner than is required in these affairs. One day when they were out, Giannotto and the girl left their companions and went into a thick wood. Thinking the others had gone on far ahead, they lay down in a place covered with grass and flowers and screened by trees, and began to take lovers' pleasure. They remained there a very long time (which their great delight made them think very short) and were surprised first by the girl's mother and then by Currado. Outraged by the sight, Currado without a word of explanation had them seized and bound by three of his servants and sent to one of his castles, intending in his rage to put them to a shameful death.

The girl's mother was also greatly angered and thought the daughter should be made to suffer cruelly for her slip; but when from certain words of Currado's she perceived his intentions towards the two sinners, she could not endure the thought. She went to her angry husband and besought him not to rush madly upon the murder of his own daughter in his old age nor to stain his hand with the blood of one of his servants. She said he could wreak his anger on them in other ways, by shutting them up in prison and making them labour and weep for their sin. These and many other things this holy lady said to her husband, and thus diverted him from murdering them. He ordered that each should be imprisoned in a separate cell, closely guarded, served with little food and much discomfort, and so kept until he had decided what further to do. Everyone may imagine for himself what their lives were, thus imprisoned, with many tears and much more fasting than they had been accustomed to.

Giannotto and Spina had spent a year in this painful life and Currado had taken no further notice of them, when King Pedro of Aragon (through the treachery of Messer Gian di Procida) stirred up a rebellion in Sicily and captured the island from King Charles; an event which greatly pleased Currado, who was a Ghibelline. Giannotto heard this news from some of his wardens, and, heaving a deep sigh, said:

"Alas! For fourteen years I have been wandering the world waiting only for this to happen. Now it has occurred; but, to keep me always void of hope, it happens when I am in a prison which I cannot hope to leave until I am dead."

"What!" said the gaoler. "How can it matter to you what great Kings do? What have you to do with Sicily?"

To which Giannotto replied:

"My heart feels as if it would break when I remember what my father once was there. I was only a child when I fled from Sicily, but I remember that I saw him Governor of Sicily when King Manfred was alive."

Said the gaoler:

"Who was your father?"

"I can now tell you who my father was," said Giannotto, "since I am in the danger I feared if I told it. His name was and still is, if he is alive, Arrighetto Capece, and my name is not Giannotto but Giusfredi. If I were free and could return to Sicily I have no doubt I could get some important post."

Without enquiring further, the worthy man related all this to Currado on the first opportunity. When Currado heard this he pretended to the warden that it was of no importance, but he went straight to Madonna Beritola and asked her if Arrighetto had a son named Giusfredi. The lady wept and said that if her elder son were alive that would be his name and his age about twenty-two. On hearing this Currado felt Giannotto must be the same person. It also occurred to him that he might at one and the same time perform a great act of mercy and wipe out his own and his daughter's shame by marrying her to Madonna Beritola's son. He therefore sent for Giannotto and questioned him closely about his past life. Finding from many plain indications that Giannotto was Giusfredi, son of Arrighetto Capece, Currado said to him:

"Giannotto, you know what wrong you have done me through the person of my daughter, whereas, since I always treated you well, you ought always to have defended my honour and my property, as becomes a servant. If you had done the like to many other men they would have slain you in some shameful way; but this my pity would not allow. Now, since things are as you say and you are the son of a gentleman and a gentlewoman, I shall be glad to put an end to your sufferings whenever you yourself wish, to bring you out of misery and captivity and at once restore your honour and mine. Spina, for whom you felt such amorous friendship (though unseemly in you both) is a widow, and her dowry a large one. What she is, and what her father and mother, you know. Of your present condition I say nothing. Therefore if you are willing, I too am willing to make her your chaste spouse instead of your unchaste mistress, and to have you live here as my son with her and me as long as you wish."

Prison had wasted away Giannotto's flesh but had not diminished the noble spirit he had inherited nor the love he bore his lady. Although he eagerly desired what Currado offered and knew he was in the man's power, yet he abated nothing of what his greatness of soul bade him say, and replied:

"Currado, neither desire of lordship nor eagerness for money nor any other cause has ever made me traitor to you or your possessions. I loved your daughter, I love her and always shall, because I think her worthy of my love. If I committed with her what the ignorant consider a sin, it is a sin which always goes with youth; and if you want to abolish it you will have to abolish youth as well. If old men would remember that they were once young and would measure their own faults and compare them with those of youth, they would see that this sin is not so serious as you and many others make it out to be. Moreover, I committed it as a friend, not as an enemy. I have always desired to do what you offer me, and if I had thought you would grant it I should long ago have asked for it. Now it is the more precious to me since I had so little hope of it. But if you do not really mean what you say, do not feed me on vain hopes. Send me back to prison and treat me as harshly as you please, for just as I love Spina, so out of love for her shall I always love and reverence you, whatever you may do to me."

Currado was amazed to hear this and thought him a man of great spirit and a true lover, and esteemed him greatly for it. Therefore he stood up and embraced and kissed Giannotto, and without any further delay ordered that Spina should be brought before him.

Imprisonment had made her thin, pale and weak, quite another woman from what she had been, just as Giannotto was another man. And they two, in the presence of Currado, by mutual consent took each other as man and wife, in accordance with our customs.

Currado furnished them with everything they needed and asked for, but told nobody what had happened. But after a few days he thought it time to make the two mothers happy, and therefore sent for his wife and "the Goatherd," and said:

"What would you say, Madonna, if I brought back to you your elder son married to one of my daughters?"

To which "the Goatherd" replied:

"I could only say that you would be dearer to me than ever, if that is possible, because you would have given me back someone who is more precious to me than myself. And if you bring him back in the way you say, to some extent you will give me back my lost hopes."

And then tears made her silent.

Then said Currado to his wife:

"And what would you say, wife, if I brought you such a son-in-law?"

To which the lady replied:

"Not only should I be pleased with one of that family, who are gentlemen, but with a peasant, if such were your pleasure."

Then said Currado:

"In a few days I hope to make you happy women."

When the two young people had recovered their health and were honourably dressed, he said to Giusfredi:

"Would it add to your present happiness if you saw your mother here?"

And Giusfredi replied:

"I cannot believe that she is still alive after all this unhappiness and misfortune. But if she is alive, she would be most dear to me, since by her advice I believe I could recover a large portion of my estate in Sicily."

Currado then sent for the two ladies. They both greeted

the newly-married pair with great joy, although they wondered what could have inspired such benevolence in Currado to make him marry his daughter to Giannotto. But, remembering Currado's former words, Madonna Beritola gazed at Giannotto. Some hidden virtue within her brought back some recollection of her son's childish features, and, waiting for no further proof, she threw her arms round his neck. The excess of her emotion and maternal love prevented her from uttering a word; indeed her senses left her and she fell as if dead in her son's arms. He was greatly surprised, for he remembered how he had often seen her before in that same castle and had never recognised her; yet now he immediately knew his mother's smell and blamed himself for his former neglect, and taking her in his arms kissed her tenderly and with tears. Currado's wife and Spina at once went to her aid with cold water and other assistance, and, when Madonna Beritola had recovered her senses, she embraced her son again with many tears and many gentle words. Filled with maternal feeling she kissed him again and again, and he gazed at her and responded most tenderly.

These glad and virtuous greetings were repeated three or four times to the great delight of the onlookers, and then each related his adventures to the other. Currado then announced the new marriage to his friends, and ordered a magnificent feast. Whereupon Giusfredi said:

"Currado, you have made me happy in many ways, and for a long time you have honoured my mother. Now, so that nothing which is in your power to do remains undone, I beg that you will make me and my mother and my wedding feast happy with the presence of my brother, who is kept a servant in the house of Messer Guasparrino d'Oria. As I have already told you, it was he who captured us both on the high seas. Also I beg you will send someone to Sicily, to enquire into the state and condition of the country, and to find out whether my father Arrighetto is alive or dead; and, if he is alive in what state he lives. And so bring us back full information."

Giusfredi's request pleased Currado, who at once sent very prudent persons to Genoa and Sicily. The man who went to Genoa found Messer Guasparrino and, in Currado's name, requested him to send back Scacciato and his nurse, telling him fully what Currado had done for Giusfredi and his mother. Messer Guasparrino was greatly surprised to hear this, and said:

"It is true I would do anything I could to please Currado. And for fourteen years I have had the boy you ask for and his mother in my house, and I will gladly send them to him. But tell him from me to beware how he trusts in the tales of Giannotto, who now calls himself Giusfredi, because he is far more of a rogue than Currado thinks."

Having said this, he did all honour to Currado's messenger. He then had the nurse brought secretly before him and began cautiously to question her. Now, she had heard of the rebellion in Sicily and believed Arrighetto to be alive; so she dismissed her former fears and told him everything as it had happened and why she had kept it all secret. When Messer Guasparrino found that the nurse's account was perfectly in harmony with that of Currado's messenger, he began to believe there was something in it. He enquired into it all very astutely and kept finding additional proofs of the facts, so that he grew ashamed of his vile treatment of the boy. To atone for this, and knowing what Arrighetto was and had been, he gave Scacciato his own daughter (who was aged eleven) as his wife, with a large dowry. After a great wedding feast, he went on board a well armed galley with the boy and his daughter and Currado's messenger and the nurse, and sailed to Lerici. Then he was received by Currado and the whole company rode to one of Currado's castles, which was not far away, where a great feast had been prepared.

No words can express, and I leave it to you, ladies, to imagine, the mother's joy at seeing her other son again, and the joy of the two brothers, and the greeting of all three to the faithful nurse, and the greeting of them all to Messer Guasparrino and his daughter, and his joy at them all, and the happiness of them all with Currado and his wife and the sons and the friends!

To fill up full their cup of joy, God (who is a most generous giver once He has begun) allowed news to arrive that Arrighetto Capece was alive and well. For, as the feast ran high and men and women were still at the first courses, there returned the messenger sent into Sicily. Among other things he related that Arrighetto was in prison when the revolt against King Charles started; the people slew the gaolers, took him out of prison, made him their leader (since he was an enemy of King Charles) and with his aid slew and drove out the French. This had set him high in the good graces of King Pedro, who had restored him to all his honours and estates. The messenger added that Arrighetto had received him with the greatest respect and had shown extreme happiness when he heard about his wife and son, of whom he had received no news since his imprisonment. Arrighetto had therefore sent a swift ship and some of his gentlemen to take them to Sicily. The messenger was greeted and listened to with great delight and rejoicing. Currado immediately went out with his friends to meet the gentlemen who had come for Madonna Beritola and Giusfredi, received them courteously, and brought them into the banquet, which was not yet half over.

The gentlemen were greeted by Giusfredi and his mother and all the others with such joy that the like has never been heard. Before they sat down to meat, the gentlemen, on Arrighetto's behalf, returned thanks to Currado and his wife for the honour they had done his wife and son; placing Arrighetto and all he had at their disposal. Then they turned to Messer Guasparrino (whose kindness was something unexpected) and told him that they were certain that when Arrighetto knew what he had done for Scacciato, he would receive similar or even greater thanks.

After this they feasted most merrily with the new brides and bridegrooms. And not that day alone did Currado feast his son-in-law and his relatives and friends, but many others as well.

At last Madonna Beritola and Giusfredi and the others felt they ought to depart. And, taking Spina with them, they went on board ship and sailed away, with many tears on the part of Currado and his wife and Messer Guasparrino. A favourable wind soon brought them to Sicily, where Arrighetto received his wife and children at Palermo with such rejoicing that words cannot describe it. There they lived happily for a long time, grateful to Almighty God for the benefits received from Him.

## SEVENTH TALE

*The Sultan of Babylon sends his daughter to marry the King of Garbo. In the space of four years she passes through many adventures in different lands and lies with nine men. She is finally restored to her father who is made to believe she is still a virgin, and marries the King of Garbo*

The pity felt by the ladies for Madonna Beritola's misfortunes would have made them shed tears perhaps if Emilia's tale had lasted much longer. But when it was ended the queen ordered Pamfilo to follow, which he obediently did.

Fair ladies, it is difficult for us to know what is truly useful to us. Thus, as we often see, there are many men who think they would live secure and carefree if only they were rich. To this end, they not only send up urgent prayers to God but eagerly brave every danger and fatigue to acquire wealth. And then when they are rich, it sometimes happens that they are slain by those who in poverty were their friends, but who are tempted by the hope of acquiring their riches. Again, men of humble birth have risen to the dignity of Kings through a thousand battles and the blood of their brothers and friends, thinking that all happiness lies in ruling. But they have found their thrones surrounded with cares and fears, and have learned at the cost of their lives that at royal tables poison may be drunk in gold cups. Others have ardently desired such gifts as bodily strength and beauty; and yet these very things have caused them misfortune or even death.

But I do not wish to name every human desire one by one; so I shall only add that we can choose no desire which will certainly bring us happiness. Wherefore, if we desire to labour rightly, we should resign ourselves to accept what is given us by Him Who alone knows what is necessary to us, and is able to give it. Men indeed sin by desiring many things; but you, most gracious ladies, are especially given to one sin, which is the desire to be beautiful. So much so that the beauties Nature gives do not suffice you, and you seek to increase them by wonderful arts. I shall therefore tell you a tale of the misfortunes of a beautiful Saracen girl, whose beauty caused her to lie with no less than nine men in the space of four years.

Long ago there was a Sultan of Babylon named Beminedab, fortunate in all his enterprises. Among his many male and female children he had a daughter called Alatiel, the most beautiful woman to be seen in the world in that age, if we may believe those who saw her. Now, the King of Garbo had given valuable aid to the Sultan in a fierce war he had waged with a vast horde of invading Arabs; and, at his request, the Sultan as a special favour granted him Alatiel as his wife. So the Sultan sent her on board a well-equipped and well-armed ship with an honourable escort of men and women and many rich and noble presents.

and, having commended her to God's care, despatched her to the King.

The weather was fine, the sailors set every sail as they came out of the port of Alexandria, and for many days their voyage was prosperous. They had passed Sardinia and saw the end of their journey in sight when suddenly one day furious and contrary winds arose and beat so heavily on the ship that more than once they gave themselves up for lost. But, like brave men, they made use of all their strength and every device, and for two days endured the infinite onslaught of the waves. The third night of the storm only increased its violence. The sailors did not know their position; all observation was impossible, for the sky was blotted out with clouds and mist; but they had drifted somewhere near Majorca when they found the ship had sprung a leak.

Seeing no other way of escape and everyone thinking of himself, the officers launched the long-boat and got into it, thinking they had better trust to it than a leaky ship. But although those first in the long-boat tried to fight the others off with knives, every man on the ship tried to jump into it; and, in trying to avoid death, fell into it. In such weather the long-boat could not hold so many; it capsized and everyone in it perished. Nobody was left on the ship but the lady and her women, who lay half dead with fear and the violence of the storm. Although the ship was leaking badly and was nearly full of water, it was driven rapidly by the force of the wind and struck on the coast of Majorca. So great was the shock that it stuck firmly in the sand about a stone's throw from the shore, and there remained all night beaten but not moved by the force of wind and sea.

At daybreak the storm calmed down somewhat. The lady, although almost half dead, weakly lifted her head and called one after another of her attendants by name; but she called in vain, for they were far away. Getting no reply and seeing no one, she was greatly amazed and began to feel terrified. She stood up as well as she was able, and saw the ladies in attendance on her and the other women lying about. She called first one and then another, but found that seasickness and fear had so exhausted them that most of them seemed dead, which greatly increased her terror. However, seeing that she was quite alone and did not know where she was, she took council of necessity and so shook those who were alive that she made them get up. Finding they did not know where the men were and seeing that the ship had struck and was full of water, she began to weep most piteously with them.

It was past the hour of Nones before they saw anyone on the shore or elsewhere from whom they could hope for assistance. About that hour a gentleman named Pericone da Visalgo was returning home that way on horseback with his attendants. He saw the ship, realised what had happened, and ordered one of his servants to get on board without delay and to report what he found there. With great difficulty the servant climbed on to the ship and found the lady with her few attendants hiding timorously under the bowsprit. When they saw the man they besought his pity with many tears; but finding he did not understand their language nor they his, they tried to communicate their plight by signs.

The servant went back and told Pericone what he had seen, and Pericone immediately had the ladies and the most valuable things in the ship brought on shore and carried to his castle. He saw that the women were given food and rest, and judged from Alatiel's rich clothes and the respect showed her by the other women that she was a lady of high birth. Although she was pale and dishevelled from the sea, yet her features seemed most beautiful to Pericone. So he immediately determined to make her his wife if she was not married, or, if he could not marry her, to have her as his mistress.

Pericone was a strong, haughty-looking man. For several days the lady was most carefully tended, and thus perfectly recovered. He saw that she was indeed extremely beautiful, and grieved that he could not understand her language, nor she his. But as her beauty moved him immensely he attempted by amorous and pleasant signs to induce her to yield to his pleasures without resistance. But to no avail. She flatly refused to lie with him, which merely inflamed Pericone's ardour. This the lady perceived. She had now been there for some days and guessed from the clothes of those about her that she was among Christians, and also approximately where she was. She saw that it was of no avail therefore to make known who she was, and she also saw that in the long run she would have to submit willingly or unwillingly to Pericone's desires; she therefore proudly resolved to spurn the misery of her fate. She ordered her women (only three of whom remained alive) never to reveal who she was, unless they found themselves in a position where they might reasonably expect some help towards getting free. In addition she urged them to preserve their chastity, asserting that she herself had made up her mind that no man should enjoy her save only her husband. Her women praised her, and said they would obey her faithfully.

Pericone, having the woman he desired ever before his eyes but yet denied him, became daily more ardent. He saw his allurements were useless, so had recourse to cunning and art, leaving force as a final resource. He had several times noted that the lady liked wine, as happens with those who are unaccustomed to it because their laws forbid it; and he thought he would use wine as an aid to Venus. Pretending not to care that she rejected him, he gave a fine supper one evening, to which the lady came. Everyone was very gay, and Pericone ordered the servant who waited upon her to give her various mixed wines to drink; which he did very skilfully. Attracted by the pleasure of drinking and not knowing what she was about, she took more than befitted her chastity. She forgot all about her misfortunes and became very merry; and when she saw some of the women dancing in the fashion of Majorca, she danced for them in the Alexandrian style.

When Pericone observed this, he felt he was drawing near the desired end. He therefore prolonged the supper far into the night, with abundance of food and drink. Finally, when the guests had all gone, he went alone with her to her bedroom. She, being hotter with wine than cool with chastity, unreservedly undressed herself before Pericone as if he had been one of her women, and got into bed. Pericone was not long in following her. He put out every light, nimbly got into bed with her, took her in his arms, and, without any resistance on her part, began to enjoy her amorously. She had never known before the horn with which men butt, but when she felt it she regretted that she had formerly refused Pericone's advances; and, thereafter she did not wait to be invited to such sweet nights, but herself often invited him, not with words (which he could not understand) but by actions. While she and Pericone thus enjoyed life, Fortune, not content with making a King's wife into a gentleman's mistress, was preparing a yet worse bed-mate for her.

Pericone had a brother named Marato, aged twenty-five, as handsome and fresh as a rose. He saw Alatiel and she pleased him mightily, while, from what he could gather by her signs, he was well in her good graces. In his opinion nothing kept them apart but Pericone's very strict watch over her, and so he devised a cruel plan to which he wickedly gave effect.

At that moment there happened to be in the harbour, a ship laden with merchandise, owned by two young Genoese, just about to sail for Chiarenza in the Greek Empire. Marato arranged with them to take him and the lady with them. That night he went to the castle of the unsuspecting Pericone together with several companions, to whom he had revealed his project, and hid them in the house as he had planned. In the middle of the night he called his companions and went with them to the room where Pericone was sleeping with the lady. They murdered Pericone in his sleep, and threatened the weeping lady with instant death if she made any noise. Unobserved they stole Pericone's most valuable goods, and fled to the shore, where Marato and the lady went on board, and the rest went to their homes. The sailors at once started out before a fresh breeze.

The lady grieved bitterly over this her second misfortune, as well as the first. But Marato, producing that holy crescent which God had given him, soon consoled her in such a manner that she forgot all about Pericone and settled down comfortably with him. But just as she began to feel happy again, Fortune, not content with her former woes, prepared her a new experience. As I have already said more than once, Alatiel was most beautiful and her manners graceful; consequently the two young Genoese fell in love with her, and thought of nothing but trying to please and serve her, though they took care that Marato should not notice anything.

Each perceived the other's love, and, after a secret discussion, they agreed to share her between them, as if love could be shared like money or merchandise. But they found that Marato watched her so carefully that they could not carry out their intentions. So one day when the ship was sailing very fast and Marato was standing at the poop looking out to sea and not noticing them, they crept up behind him and together threw him into the water. The ship had already gone over a mile before anyone noticed that Marato had fallen overboard. When the lady heard of this and saw there was no way to save him, she began to lament once more on the ship. The two lovers at once went to her and tried to comfort her with soft words and big promises; she understood little of what they said, and, as a matter of fact, was grieving far more over her own misfortunes than the loss of her lover. After they had talked to her for a long time and felt they had consoled her, they began to argue as to which of them should lie with her first.

Each wished to be first, and neither could agree with the other. So from high words they fell into a rage, drew their knives and attacked each other. Before the other men on board could separate them, they both fell, one dead and the other seriously wounded. This greatly grieved the lady, for she saw herself left without any help and advice, while she dreaded lest the anger of the two Genoeses' relatives and friends should fall on her. But the wounded man's entreaties and their speedy arrival at Chiarenza saved her from the danger of death. She landed with the wounded man and went to an inn with him. The fame of her beauty immediately ran through the town and reached the ears of the Prince of the Morea, who was in Chiarenza at that time. He therefore desired to see her; and, when he saw her, she seemed to him far more beautiful than common report had said, and he fell so deeply in love with her that he could think of nothing else.

The Prince discovered how she had come to Chiarenza, and began to wonder how he could get hold of her. While he was examining ways and means, the wounded man's relatives heard of it, and immediately sent her to him without any delay. This delighted the Prince and the lady too, for she felt she had escaped a great danger. The Prince saw that she possessed royal manners as well as great beauty; he felt she must be a noblewoman (although he could not find out who she was), and this increased his love for her. He felt such love for her that he treated her as if she were his wife, and not his mistress.

Thinking over her past misfortunes, the lady felt she was now happily situated. She felt quite consoled and cheerful again, so that all her beauties blossomed out, and nothing but her beauty was talked about in all Greece. The young and handsome Duke of Athens, a relative and friend of the Prince, greatly desired to see her; and sending notice of his visit, as he was accustomed to do, he arrived with a numerous company at Chiarenza, where he was honourably received with great joy.

Some days later, when the beauties of the lady were being discussed, the Duke asked if she were as wonderful as people said. To which the Prince replied: "Far more so. But you shall judge with your own eyes, not from my words!"

The Duke eagerly accepted, and the Prince conducted

him to her. Being warned of their visit, she received them
politely and with a cheerful visage, and sat down with
them; but as she understood little or nothing of their language, they could not enjoy the pleasures of conversation.
Therefore everyone gazed at her in wonderment, especially
the Duke, who could scarcely believe that she was a mortal
woman. Gazing at her, he failed to realise how the poison
of love was working upon him, and, thinking he was
merely satisfying his curiosity, he found he was deep in
love with her. When he had left her and the Prince, and
had time to think matters over, he concluded that the
Prince was the happiest man in the world to have such a
beautiful woman at his pleasure. Then, after a great many
agitated reflections, his love got the better of his honesty,
and he decided to deprive the Prince of this felicity and
to get it for himself.

Having a mind to accomplish this, he put aside all reason
and justice, and devoted his whole attention to deceit. One
day, in collaboration with one of the Prince's most confidential servants (whose name was Ciuriaci) he secretly
prepared his horses and everything else for departure. That
night, with an accomplice, he was let into the Prince's
apartment by the treacherous servant, and, since it was
very hot, he found the lady asleep and the Prince naked at
a window overlooking the sea, enjoying the faint sea
breezes. His accomplice, knowing what was to be done,
crept quietly to the window, stabbed the Prince in the back
with a dagger and threw him out of the window.

The palace overlooked the sea from a great height, and
the window where the Prince had been standing was directly above some small houses which had been destroyed
by the sea and were therefore rarely or never visited. Thus
things turned out as the Duke had expected, and the
fall of the Prince's body was not heard by anyone.

When the Duke's bravo saw that this murder was successful, he pretended to embrace Ciuriaci, but in fact threw
a rope (which he had concealed for the purpose) round
his neck so that he could not utter a sound. Then as the
Duke came in, he strangled Ciuriaci and threw his body
after the Prince's. When this had been done without arous-
ing the attention of the lady or of anyone else, the Duke
took a light in his hand and secretly examined all of the
charms of the sleeping beauty. He looked at everything
and was highly delighted; she had charmed him when
clothed, but when naked she delighted him beyond all expression. Therefore, heated with desire and caring nothing

for the crime he had just committed, although his hands were still bloody he got into bed and lay with her, while she was heavy with sleep and thought he was the Prince.

After he had lain with her in the greatest delight, he got up and let in some of his attendants. He warned the lady not to make any noise, led her out by the secret door through which he had entered, put her on horseback as quietly as possible, and set off full speed for Athens with all his train. But he had a wife, and therefore did not take Alatiel to Athens, but to a very handsome residence he had on the seashore not far from the town. There he secretly hid the grieving lady, and arranged for her to be served with every honour.

Next morning the Prince's courtiers waited until Nones for him to get up. Hearing nothing, they softly opened the doors of his apartments (which were not locked), but found no one there. But they felt no alarm, thinking that the Prince had gone off secretly somewhere to enjoy the lady all to himself for a few days.

The next day it happened that a madman wandered among the ruins where lay the bodies of the Prince and Ciuriaci, and came out dragging Ciuriaci behind him by the rope. The attendants were amazed at this sight and persuaded the madman to take them to the place where he had found the body; and there, to the great grief of the whole city, they found the body of the Prince, which they buried with all honours. They then enquired into the authors of this crime, and, seeing that the Duke of Athens was not there but had secretly departed, they realised that he had murdered the Prince and carried off the lady. They immediately elected the dead man's brother as their new Prince, and urged him to avenge the murder. Having collected further proofs of the crime, this new Prince called upon his friends, relatives and servants, and gathered together a large and powerful army to make war on the Duke of Athens.

Hearing of this, the Duke at once began to gather forces for his defence, and many gentlemen came to his aid, including Constantine and Manuel, son and nephew of the Emperor of Constantinople, with a large contingent. They were received with the greatest honour by the Duke and by the Duchess, who was their sister.

Day by day the war became more imminent. The Duchess invited both her relatives to her apartment and there, with many tears, told them the whole story and the reason for the war, and showed how she had been insulted by the

Duke who was keeping this woman secretly hidden somewhere. And in great grief she begged them to advise her
for the best, in regard to the Duke's honour and her own
satisfaction. The two young men already knew all about
the matter and therefore, without asking many questions,
comforted her as best they could and bade her be of good
cheer; they found out from her where the lady was concealed, and then departed. They had often heard praise of
the lady's marvellous beauty, which they desired to see,
and they asked the Duke to let them see her. Forgetting
what had been the Prince's fate through letting him see
her, he promised to do so. He ordered a magnificent dinner in a most beautiful garden, belonging to the house
where the lady was lodged, and next day took them and a
few companions to dine with her.

As Constantine sat beside her, he looked at her with
amazement, telling himself that he had never seen so beautiful a woman and feeling that there was every excuse
for the Duke or anyone else who committed any treacherous crime to get possession of her. And as he kept gazing at
her time after time, the same thing occurred to him as had
happened to the Duke. He fell hopelessly in love with
her, abandoned all thought of the war, and began to ponder over means of getting her away from the Duke, while
he carefully concealed his love from everyone.

While he was burning with desire, the time came to meet
the Prince's forces which were drawing near the Duke's
territories. So the Duke and Constantine and all the rest
left Athens and marched to the frontier to prevent the
Prince from advancing any further. While they were there,
Constantine's mind and thoughts were filled with the lady.
He thought that, since the Duke was away, he could easily
achieve his desire, and therefore pretended to be ill in
order to have an opportunity for returning to Athens. With
the Duke's permission he handed over his command to Manuel, and returned to his sister in Athens. A few days later
he turned the conversation on the insult done her by the
Duke in keeping a mistress, and told her that if she wished,
he was ready to help her by taking Alatiel away.

The Duchess thought Constantine was doing this for
love of her and not love of the lady, and told him that she
liked the idea greatly, if only it could be carried out in such
a way that the Duke would never know she had consented
to it. Constantine immediately gave her a promise, and
she consented that he should act as seemed best to him.

Constantine secretly equipped a fast ship and sent it

one evening to lie off the garden where the lady was living. He arranged with his friends on board what they were to do, and then went with other friends to call on the lady. There he was greeted by the attendants and by the lady herself, and they all went into the garden. Pretending that he had a private message from the Duke to Alatiel, he went alone with her through a gate which opened to the sea. One of his companions had already unlocked it and gave the signal to the boat; and Constantine immediately had the lady seized and carried on board. Then he turned to her attendants, and said:

"Let no man move or say a word, unless he wants to die. I am not robbing the Duke of a woman, but wiping out the shame he has put upon my sister."

Nobody was eager to reply to this, and Constantine and his attendants then went on board the ship. He sat beside the weeping lady, and ordered the rowers to start at once, which they did with such speed that the boat reached Aegina the next day. They landed there to rest, and Constantine enjoyed the lady, who wept over her unlucky beauty. They boarded the ship again, and in a few days reached Chios. Fearing his father's reproofs and also that the abducted lady might be taken from him, Constantine decided to remain there, and for many days Alatiel wept over her misfortunes. But Constantine comforted her, just as the others had, and she began to feel content with what Fortune had prepared for her.

While things were going on in this way, Osbech, King of Turkey, who was continually at war with the Emperor, happened to arrive at Smyrna. There he heard how Constantine was living a lascivious life with a lady he had abducted, and was quite unguarded. Osbech armed a number of small ships and sailed to Chios by night, where he silently landed his troops and surprised many of the Greeks in their beds, before they knew the enemy was upon them. The rest, who had rushed to arms, were slain. He burned the whole island, put the spoils and prisoners on the ships, and returned to Smyrna.

Osbech was a young man, and, as he was looking over the spoils, he came upon the woman who had been found sleeping in bed with Constantine, and was highly delighted with her. Without any delay he made her his wife, celebrated the marriage, and lay happily with her for several months.

Before this event occurred the Emperor had been treating with Basano, King of Cappadocia, for them both to at-

tack Osbech simultaneously from different quarters. But
they had not come to an agreement because the Emperor
would not grant some of Basano's demands, which he
thought excessive. However, when he heard what had happened to his son he was filled with grief, and immediately
did what the King of Cappadocia had required of him.
Urging him to attack Osbech with all his forces, the Emperor prepared to invade him from the other side.

Hearing of this, Osbech collected an army and, to avoid
being caught between the forces of two great monarchs,
he marched against the King of Cappadocia, leaving the
beautiful lady in Smyrna under the guardianship of a
trusted friend. Before long, Osbech gave battle to the King
of Cappadocia, but his army was defeated and scattered,
and he himself slain. The victorious Basano immediately
marched on Smyrna, and as he advanced everyone submitted to him as conqueror.

The name of Osbech's friend, who was looking after the
lady, was Antioco. Although he was elderly, he also fell
in love with her great beauty, forgetting the faith pledged
to his lord and friend. He could speak her language, which
was delightful to her, since for several years she had been
compelled to live as if she were a deaf-mute, for nobody
had understood her language nor she theirs. Urged by his
desire, Antioco became so familiar with her that in a few
days they both forgot their lord away at the war, and became intimate in an amorous as well as a friendly manner,
both taking great delight in each other between the sheets.
But when they heard Osbech was conquered and slain, and
that Basano was coming to pillage everything, they agreed
not to await his coming. Taking the greater part of Osbech's
treasure, they secretly fled to Rhodes; but they had not
been there very long, when Antioco fell mortally sick. A
merchant of Cyprus, his friend, whom he greatly loved, was
living there; and Antioco, feeling he was drawing near his
end, determined to leave this man his wealth and his dear
lady. Being come near to death, he called them both before
him, and said:

"I see I am certainly failing, which grieves me, for I
never enjoyed life so much as I have done recently. One
thing will make me die happy. Since I must die, at least
I shall die in the arms of the two persons I love most in the
world—in yours, my dear friend, and in those of this lady
whom I have loved more than myself ever since I have
known her. It grieves me to die and leave her here, a
stranger, without help and without advice. And it would

grieve me still more, if I did not know you are here and did not believe you would take the same care of her as of me. Therefore I beseech you, if I die, take my goods and her, and do with them both what you think will be a consolation to my soul. And you, dearest lady, after I am dead do not forget me, so that I may boast there that I am loved here by the most beautiful woman Nature ever created. If you will give me hope of these two things, I shall depart in peace."

The merchant friend and the lady both wept when they heard these words. They tried to comfort him, and solemnly promised they would do what he asked, if he should die. Very soon he did die, and they buried him honourably.

Soon after this the Cyprus merchant finished all his business in Rhodes, and determined to return to Cyprus on a Catalan ship making the voyage. He therefore asked the lady what she wanted to do, and whether she would return to Cyprus with him. The lady replied that she would gladly go with him and hoped that for Antioco's sake he would treat her as a sister. The merchant replied that this would give him the greatest pleasure; and so that he might protect her from any insult on the voyage, he gave out that she was his wife. They went on board ship and were given a small cabin in the stern, where they slept together in the same bed in order to keep up the pretence. In this way occurred something which neither of them had intended when they left Rhodes. They forgot their love and friendship to dead Antioco, and, stimulated by the darkness, convenience and warmth of bed, they began to feel excited with mutual desires, and before they had reached Baffa (where they were going) they were lying together. After they reached Baffa she remained for some time with the merchant.

There happened to come to Baffa on business one Antigono, a very elderly gentleman of great wisdom and little wealth. He had involved himself in the service of the King of Cyprus, and Fortune had been against him. One day, when the merchant had gone on a voyage to Armenia, this Antigono happened to pass by the lady's house just at the moment when she came to the window. As she was very beautiful, he gazed at her, and remembered that he had seen her somewhere before, though he could not recollect where.

The beautiful lady, who had long been Fortune's plaything, now saw the end of her misfortunes drawing near. As soon as she saw Antigono she remembered that she had seen him in an important position among her father's servants. A sudden hope came to her that through his advice she might return to her royal estate; and so, since the merchant was away, she sent for Antigono as soon as she could. When he arrived, she blushingly asked him if he were Antigono of Famagusta, as she believed. Antigono said "yes," and added:

"Madonna, I seem to recognise you but I can't remember where I saw you. If it is not displeasing to you, I beg you will recall yourself to my memory."

Hearing this, the lady wept, threw her arms round his neck (to his great amazement) and then asked him if he had never seen her in Alexandria. On hearing this question, Antigono immediately recognised that she was Alatiel, the Sultan's daughter, who was thought to be drowned. He wished to pay her the customary respect, but she refused, and asked him to sit down with her. Antigono did so, and then respectfully asked how, when and by what means she came there, since the whole of Egypt was convinced that she had been drowned at sea several years before. To this the lady replied:

"I wish I had been drowned, rather than go through the sort of life I have endured, and I think my father will wish the same, if he ever knows about it."

Whereupon she began to weep bitterly again. And Antigono said:

"Madonna, do not despair before it is time. Tell me, if you please, your misfortunes and the life you have led. Perhaps with God's help we may find some remedy."

"Antigono," said the beautiful lady, "when I see you, I seem to see my own father, and feel for you the love and tenderness I am bound to feel for him. I therefore spoke to you, when I could have concealed myself. There are very few persons whom it would give me as much pleasure to see as yourself. And so I shall tell you, as if you were my father, all the misfortunes which I have kept secretly to myself. If, when you have heard them, you can think of any means by which I can return to my former state, I beg you to make use of them; if not, I beg you will never tell anyone that you have seen me here or heard anything about me."

Having said this she then told him with many tears all that had happened to her from the time when she was wrecked in Majorca to that moment. Antigono wept with pity, and then, after some thought, said:

"Madonna, since you have always concealed your identity in your troubles, I can certainly restore you to your father, dearer than ever, and see you married to the King of Garbo."

She asked him how, and he carefully explained his plan to her in detail. And to prevent any delay, Antigono immediately returned to Famagusta, and went to the King, to whom he said:

"Sire, may it please your Majesty, you can do yourself great honour and be of great service to me, who am a poor man on your account, without much cost to yourself."

The King asked how, and Antigono then said:

"There has arrived at Baffa the beautiful young daughter of the Sultan, who for so long was thought to be drowned. To preserve her chastity she has suffered great hardships. She is now in poverty, and desires to return to her father. If you will send her to him under my protection, this will do you great honour and be of vast service to me. I think the Sultan will never forget such a service."

Moved by his royal virtue, the King at once consented. He sent for Alatiel and had her brought honourably to Famagusta, when she was received by himself and the Queen with the greatest festivity and magnificence. When the King and Queen questioned her about her adventures, she replied exactly as Antigono had advised her. A few days later, at her request, the King sent her with an honourable attendance of ladies and gentlemen, under the care of Antigono, to her father the Sultan. It is needless to ask whether he received her and Antigono and the rest with delight. After she had rested, the Sultan desired to know how she chanced to be still alive, and where she had been for so long without ever sending any news of herself. The lady had most carefully got into her mind what Antigono had advised her to say, and answered her father as follows:

"About the twentieth day after my departure from you, father, our ship was wrecked in a storm and driven on to the shores of a place in the West not far from Aiguesmortes. What happened to the men on board I have never known; all I know is that next day I seemed to return from death to life. The inhabitants had already seen the wrecked ship, and were hastening from every direction to rob it. I got down on to the shore with two of my women, who were immediately seized by young men and taken off in different directions. What happened to them I never learned. I was caught by two young men and dragged along by the hair, weeping loudly. They were dragging me along a track towards a large wood when four men on horseback passed that way, and when the men dragging me along saw them, they at once released me and fled.

"Seeing this, the four men, who appeared to me persons of authority, rode up to me and asked me many questions. I talked a great deal, but they did not understand my speech, nor I theirs. After a long discussion they set me on one of their horses and took me to a convent of women, living in accordance with their religious laws. There I was kindly received and always honourably treated, and together with them I served with great devotion the Holy Crescent in the Hollow Vale, which is much honoured by the women of that country. After I had been with them for some time and had learned something of their language, they asked me who I was and where I came from. Knowing where I was and fearing that if I told them the truth they might do me some injury as an enemy of their faith, I replied that I was the daughter of a great nobleman in Cyprus, who was sending me to Crete to be married when the ship was thus driven out of its course and wrecked.

"For fear of trouble I often followed their customs in many respects. The chief of these ladies, who was called Abbess, asked me if I wished to return to Cyprus, and I replied that I desired it above everything. But she was so tender of my honour that she would never entrust me to any person travelling to Cyprus until two months ago. At that time certain good men of France with their wives, among whom were relatives of the Abbess, passed through on their way to Jerusalem to visit the Sepulchre, where He whom they believe to be God was buried after the Jews had slain Him. She entrusted me to them and begged them to deliver me to my father in Cyprus.

"It would take long to relate how much these gentlemen honoured me and the joy with which their wives received me. We went on board ship and after many days arrived at Baffa. When we arrived there, of course I did not know anyone and did not know what to say to the gentlemen who were to hand me over to my father, as the venerable Abbess had instructed them. But God perhaps was sorry for me, since He brought Antigono to the shore at the very hour when we were disembarking. I called to him immediately and told him in our language (so that the gentlemen and their wives would not understand) that he must receive me as his daughter. He immediately understood, and greeted me with the greatest joy, showing every honour his poverty permitted to the gentlemen and ladies. He then took me to the King of Cyprus, who received me with honour such as I can never fully relate, and has now sent me to you. If there is anything more to know, Antigono will tell you, for he has often heard me tell the story of my adventures."

Antigono then turned to the Sultan and said:

"Sire, what she has now related she has several times told me, and the ladies and gentlemen with whom she returned said the same. She has only omitted one thing, because she did not think it fitting for her to speak of it. And this is what the gentlemen and ladies who accompanied her said of the virtuous life she led with the nuns, and her praiseworthy behaviour, and the tears and the regrets of the ladies and gentlemen when they handed her over to me and left her. If I tried to tell you all that they said about her, I should need all the rest of today and the night as well, and then not finish. It must be enough if I say that, according to what they told me and I have observed for myself, you may boast that you possess the most beautiful, the most chaste and most virtuous daughter of any living monarch."

The Sultan was marvellously delighted with all these things, and piously prayed God to grant him grace to reward fittingly everyone who had done her honour, particularly the King of Cyprus who had sent her to him so honourably. After a few days he presented Antigono with very great gifts, and gave him permission to return to Cyprus, returning the warmest thanks to the King both by letter and by special ambassadors for the kindness shown to his daughter. After this, he determined to carry out the original plan and marry Alatiel to the King of Garbo. He therefore wrote to that King all that had happened and said that if he still wished to marry Alatiel he must send for her. The King of Garbo was delighted, sent an honourable company for her, and received her with joy. And thus she, who had lain perhaps ten thousand times with eight different men, went to bed with him as if a virgin and made him think she was one. And thereafter she lived with him happily as Queen. Hence the saying: A kissed mouth loses no savour, but is renewed like the moon.

# EIGHTH TALE

*The Count of Antwerp is falsely accused, is exiled and leaves his two children in different parts of England. He returns in disguise, finds them well, joins the King of France's army as a groom, his innocence is proved, and he is restored to his rank*

The ladies sighed much over the adventures of the beautiful Alatiel, but who knows what was the cause of their sighs? Perhaps some of them sighed as much with longing for such frequent marriages as from pity for the lady. But I shall not enquire into this. When they had all laughed at Pamfilo's last words and the queen saw his tale was ended, she turned to Elisa and ordered her to tell the next story. And she began cheerfully as follows:

The field in which we are wandering today is a very wide one, and each of us could run, not one but ten courses, so wide are Fortune's strange and grievous changes. Since I am to tell one among these infinite happenings, it shall be this.

When the Empire of Rome passed from the French to the Germans, there was bitter enmity and continual war between the two nations. Therefore, to defend his country and attack his enemy's, the King of France together with his son and all his friends and relatives gathered all the forces of the kingdom into one large army. Before leaving he had to appoint a regent. He knew that Walter, Count of Antwerp, was a good and wise man, and a loyal friend and subject; and, although the Count was skilled in warfare, the King preferred to give him a more delicate task, and appointed him regent of the whole realm of France.

The Count entered upon his office in a wise and orderly way, consulting the queen and her daughter-in-law about everything. And although they had been left under his jurisdiction, he chose to honour them as his superiors. Walter was a very handsome man of about forty, as pleasant and as polite as any nobleman could be. In addition, he was the most graceful and delicate knight of that age, and the best dressed.

Now, while the King of France and his son were away at the war, the Count's wife died, leaving him with two young children, a boy and a girl. He spent much time with the two royal ladies discussing with them the affairs of the kingdom. The wife of the King's son gazed much at him, observing his person and manners with great affection, and fell passionately in love with him. Since she was young and fresh, and he had no wife, she thought her desires could be easily satisfied with no hindrance but the shame of confessing them to him, which she soon got rid of. And one day when she was alone and thought the time fitting, she sent for him as though she had some business to discuss.

The Count, who was very far from sharing the lady's passion, at once went to her. He found her lying on a couch alone, and she made him sit down beside her. He twice asked her why she had sent for him, and she made no reply. At length her love overcame her; she blushed scarlet with shame, trembled, and nearly wept, and she began to speak in broken words:

"Most dear and sweet friend and my lord, a wise man like you must know the frailty of men and women, how for different reasons it is greater in one than another. A just judge will not give the same punishment for the same sin in different persons. Who would not say that a poor man or woman, who should give all their energy to earning a living, should be more heavily reproved for feeling and following love's appetites than a rich and idle lady who lacked nothing that could please her desires? No one, I am sure.

"Therefore I think that these things do much to excuse a lady if by chance she allows herself to fall in love; and if the lover she chooses is wise and brave she may be wholly excused. Both these apply to me, and, in addition my youth and my husband's absence should serve to defend my ardent love in your sight. If these things have that weight with the wise which they ought to have, I beg you will give me the advice and help I am about to ask of you.

"Owing to my husband's absence I cannot withstand the force of love and the desires of the flesh, which are so powerful that every day they overcome the strongest men as well as weak women. The comfort and idleness in which I live assist the pleasures of love, and I have allowed myself to fall in love. I know that if such a thing were known it would not be modest, but if nobody knows about it I think it is scarcely immodest at all. And Love has been very gracious to me, for it has not deprived me of my good sense in choosing a lover but has rather enlightened it, by showing me that you are a person worthy to be loved by a woman like me. For, if I am not deceived, you are the most handsome, the most charming, the most attractive and the wisest knight in the whole realm of France. And just as I can now say that I have no husband, so are you now without a wife. I beg you, by the great love I feel for you, not to deny me your love, and to pity my youth which melts for you like ice at a fire."

At this point she was so overcome with tears that she could not say another word, although she had meant to implore him at much greater length. Overcome, weeping, ashamed, she could do nothing but let her head fall on the Count's shoulder.

The Count, who was a most loyal knight, reproved her wild love with severe reproaches, and repulsed her when she tried to throw her arms round his neck. He swore a solemn oath that he would rather be rent asunder than do such a wrong to the honour of his over-lord.

When the lady heard this, she forgot her love and fell into a rage.

"Base knight!" said she, "shall I let my desire be so scorned by you? God forbid! Since you would let me die, I will either have you killed or hounded out of the land!"

So saying, she pulled down her hair, tore open her clothes at her breasts, and shrieked:

"Help! Help! The Count of Antwerp is trying to rape me!"

The Count had more fear of the courtier's envy than of his own conscience and felt that more belief would be given to the lady's malevolence than to his innocence. He therefore left the room and the palace as quickly as he could, hurried to his own house, threw his two children on to a horse, mounted himself, and galloped towards Calais as fast as he could.

Many attendants rushed in when the lady screamed, and when they saw her and heard what she said, they believed her words. Moreover they thought that the Count's politeness and attentions in the past had simply been a means to this end. So they rushed in fury to the Count's house to arrest him. Not finding him, they first stole everything of value in it, and then pulled it down.

The news in its worst form reached the King and his son with the army; and in great anger they condemned him and his descendants to perpetual exile and offered a large reward to anyone who captured him dead or alive.

Regretting that flight made his innocence appear guilt the Count arrived at Calais with his children, unrecognised, took ship for England and set out for London dressed as a poor man. Before entering the city he talked to his children at great length principally on two subjects: first, he told them to endure patiently the poverty into which they and he had been thrown by Fortune through no fault of theirs; and, second, he warned them never to tell anyone where they came from or whose children they were, if they valued their lives.

The boy, named Louis, was about nine; and Violante, the girl, about seven. As far as their childish years allowed, they fully understood their father's warning, and proved it by deeds later on. To achieve this end the Count thought it best to change their names, and called the boy Perotto and the girl Giannetta. And coming poorly clothed into London, like French beggars, they went about asking alms.

One morning when they were outside a church, the wife of one of the King of England's generals came out and saw the Count and his two children begging. She asked him where he came from and if they were his children. He replied that he came from Picardy, that the misdeeds of his ne'er-do-well eldest son had forced him to go away with his other two children. The pious lady looked at the little girl and liked her greatly, because she was pretty and charming and attractive, and said:

"Worthy man, if you are willing to leave your little daughter with me I will look after her, for she looks a good child. And if she turns out a good girl I will marry her to someone suitable when the time comes."

This request pleased the Count, who immediately said "yes" and gave her the child with many tears and recommendations. Having thus provided for his daughter with someone he knew about, he decided to stay there no longer. So he and Perotto begged their way across the island and finally reached Wales, quite worn out, for they were unused to travelling on foot. Here, in great state, lived another of the King's generals with many attendants, and the Count and his little boy often went to his house to beg for food.

In this courtyard they found one of the general's sons and other boys of gentlemen's families who indulged in boyish sports, like running and jumping. Perotto mingled with them and at every game was the equal or the superior

of them all. The general happened to see this more than
once, liked the boy's manner and behaviour, and asked who
he was. The reply was that he was the son of a poor man
who sometimes came there to ask alms. The general thereupon asked him for the boy, and the Count, who prayed
God for nothing better, freely gave him, although it was
bitter to him to part from his son.

Thus the Count disposed of his son and daughter. He
then decided he would stay in England no longer, and
somehow or other managed to pass over to Ireland, and
came to Standford, where he took service with a knight who
was part of an earl's household, and did all the jobs of a
servant or groom. And there he remained, unknown to
anyone, for many years, in poverty and hard work.

Violante, now called Giannetta, stayed in London with
the lady, and grew in years and in body and in beauty, so
much delighting the lady and her husband and everyone
else in the house and all who knew her that it was marvellous to behold. And everyone who saw her manners and
behaviour said she was worthy of the highest honour and
wealth. And so the lady who had taken her from her father,
without knowing anything about him except what she had
heard from him, decided to marry the girl honourably, according to the station in life she believed the girl occupied. But God, the just observer of merits, knowing her
to be a noblewoman and guiltlessly bearing the burden of
another's sin, disposed otherwise. And we must believe
that His mercy permitted what happened, in order that
the noble girl should not fall into the hands of a man of
vile condition.

The lady with whom Giannetta lived had an only son,
greatly beloved by his father and mother, not only because
he was a son but because of his virtues and merits, for he
was well behaved and valiant and bold and handsome of
person. He was about six years older than Giannetta, and
seeing her most beautiful and graceful, he fell so deeply in
love with her that he had eyes for no one else. Since he imagined her to be of low condition he was unwilling to ask
her as his wife from his father and mother; moreover,
dreading lest he should be reproved for having set his love
so low, he kept it a secret to himself, whereby he increased
his love more than if he had spoken of it.

All this caused him so much distress that he fell seriously
ill. Doctors were called in, examined his water, but could
not discover what his illness was; so that they all despaired
of curing him. His father and mother felt inexpressible

pain and sorrow at this, and often begged him piteously to tell them the cause of his illness, to which he either replied by sighs or said that he felt wasting away.

One day a young but very learned doctor happened to be sitting beside him, holding his pulse, when Giannetta (who carefully nursed him out of her respect for his mother) came into the room. When the young man saw her, without saying or doing anything he felt the fire of love spring up more fiercely in his heart, which caused his pulse to beat more rapidly than usual. The doctor immediately noticed it with great surprise, and remained as he was to see how long this beating would last.

When Giannetta went out of the room, the beating of the pulse slackened, which suggested to the doctor the true cause of his illness. Therefore, while still holding the pulse, he called for Giannetta as if he wanted to ask her something. She immediately returned, and as soon as she came into the room, the young man's pulse beat higher; and when she left, it slackened. The doctor now felt certain, left the room, and, drawing the young man's mother and father aside, said to them:

"Your son's health does not depend upon the aid of doctors but lies in the hands of Giannetta. From certain signs I have discovered that your son ardently loves her, although, so far as I could see, she does not know it. You now know what you have to do if you value his life."

The gentleman and his wife were happy to hear this, since it showed one way to save their son's life, but greatly dreaded lest they might have to give him Giannetta as his wife. So when the doctor had gone, they went to the sick man, and the lady said:

"My son, I should never have thought you would have concealed any desire from me, especially when through not obtaining it you found yourself in a decline. You may be certain that I would do anything for you as I would for myself, even if it were less than virtuous. But, since you have done so, it happens that God has pitied you more than you yourself, and to prevent your dying of this illness He has showed us the cause of it, which is simply the extreme love you feel for some girl, whoever she may be. There is no reason for you to be ashamed to tell it, for it is natural at your age, and if you did not fall in love I should think the less of you. So, my son, do not be restrained with me but tell me all that you desire. Throw off the melancholy and pining which comes from this sickness, be comforted, and be certain that you can propose to me nothing for your satisfaction which I shall not do to the best of my ability, since I love you more than life itself. Away with shame and fear, and tell me if I can do something in aid of your love. And if you do not find me eager to do this and to carry it out, consider me the cruelest mother that ever bore child."

When the young man heard what his mother said, he was at first ashamed; but then he recollected that no one else was better able to satisfy his wishes. So he banished shame, and said:

"Madonna, nothing has caused me to conceal my love so much as the fact that I have noticed that most elderly people will not remember they were once young themselves. But since I see you are so considerate, I do not deny that what you say is true; moreover, I will tell you with whom I am in love, so that you may carry out your promise and thus make me well again."

The lady, trusting too much that she could achieve this end in a manner different from what he expected, told him cheerfully to make plain his desires and that she would act without delay in such a manner that he would be satisfied.

"Madam," said the young man, "the great beauty and praiseworthy behaviour of our Giannetta, and her not pitying me or even noticing it, and my unwillingness to tell anyone, have brought me to this state. And if you do not keep your promise in one way or another, be certain my life will be short."

The lady thought this was more a time for comforting than for reproving him, so she smiled and said:

"Ah, my son, have you let yourself get ill on this account? Be comforted and leave things to me, as soon as you are well."

Filled with new hope, the young man very soon showed signs of the greatest improvement, to the delight of his mother, who then attempted to carry out her promise. One day, talking with Giannetta, she asked her jestingly but courteously if she had a lover. Giannetta went very red and answered:

"Madam, to expect love is not befitting a poor girl like me, driven from her home and compelled to serve others."

To which the lady replied:

"If you haven't one, we wish to give you one with whom you will live joyously, and you will take more delight in your beauty. It is wrong that so handsome a girl as you should be without a lover."

Giannetta answered:

"Madam, you rescued me from the poverty of my father,

and brought me up as your own daughter, and therefore I ought to obey you in everything. But in this respect I think I shall be doing right never to obey you. If you are pleased to give me a husband I mean to love him, but otherwise not; for nothing is left me from the possessions of my ancestors except virtue, and that I mean to keep and to serve as long as my life endures."

This remark seemed to the lady a serious obstacle to what she had meant to say in order to carry out her promise to her son. But, being a clever woman, she inwardly approved of the girl, and said:

"What! Giannetta! Now suppose our lord the King, who is a young knight, while you are a very beautiful girl, should want to enjoy your love—would you refuse him?"

To this she replied immediately:

"The King might force me, but he would never make me consent to anything I did not think right."

The lady saw her determination and said no more, thinking she would put her to the proof. So she told her son that when he was well she would put him and Giannetta in the same room and he could do his best to have his pleasure of her; adding that she thought it unseemly that she should play the bawd to her own son, and ask her maidservant to lie with him.

This did not please the young man at all, and he suddenly grew worse. Whereupon his mother spoke openly to Giannetta, but found her more constant than ever. She then told her husband what she had done, and, although it was a grief to them, they agreed together to let him marry her, preferring that their son should live with a wife unbefitting him rather than die with no wife at all. This was carried out after all this talk. Giannetta was delighted, and with a devout heart gave thanks to God who had not forgotten her. And yet, for all this, she never claimed to be more than the daughter of a plain man of Picardy. The young man got better and married her most happily and began to enjoy life with her.

Meanwhile Perotto, who had remained in Wales with the King of England's general there, likewise grew in grace with his lord, and became very handsome, and no one in the whole island was his equal in tourneys and jousts and other feats of arms; wherefore he was famous and known to everybody as Perotto the Picard. And as God did not forget his sister, so likewise He showed that He remembered Perotto. For, there came a dreadful plague to that country which carried off nearly half the inhabitants, while the greater part of the remainder fled to other places in terror; so that the land seemed abandoned. In this plague there perished the general, his lord, and the general's wife and son and brothers and grandchildren and many other relatives. All that remained alive were a daughter just of age to marry and Perotto and a few other servants. When the plague was over, this girl, with the consent and advice of the few inhabitants left alive, took Perotto as her husband, since he was a brave and valiant man, and made him lord of all that she had inherited. Not long afterwards the King of England heard of the general's death, and, knowing Perotto's valour, made him general in the dead man's place. This, briefly, is what happened to the Count of Antwerp's two innocent children, whom he had left and lost.

Eighteen years had now passed since the Count fled from Paris. He had endured much during his miserable life in Ireland, and, feeling he was growing old, he thought he would like to find out what had happened to his children, if he could do so. He was quite changed from his former appearance and through long habit was stronger in body than when he lived in idleness in his youth. He set out poor and ill-furnished from the place where he had lived so long, and arrived in England. He then went to the place where he had left Perotto, and found him a general and a great lord, and saw he was healthy and strong and handsome. This greatly delighted the Count, but he would not make himself known until he had learned the fate of Giannetta.

He therefore set out, and did not rest until he reached London. There he prudently enquired about the lady with whom he had left his daughter, and found that Giannetta was married to her son. This greatly delighted him, and he counted all his former suffering a small thing since he had found both his children alive and successful. Since he wanted to see her, he began to hang about the house like a beggar. One day Giachetto Lamiens—such was the name of Giannetta's husband—saw and pitied him because he saw he was a poor old man, and therefore ordered one of the servants to take him into the house and give him something to eat; which the servant willingly did.

Giannetta and Giachetto already had several children, the eldest of whom was not more than eight, and they were the prettiest and most charming children in the world. When they saw the Count eating, they all gathered round him, and began to make merry with him, as if some secret virtue had told them he was their grandfather. Recognising his grandchildren, he showed them love and began to caress them, wherefore the children would not leave him, however much their tutor called them. Hearing this, Giannetta came out of her room to that where the Count was, and threatened to beat them if they disobeyed their tutor. The children began to cry, and said they wanted to stay with the kind man who loved them more than their tutor; at which the Count and the lady laughed. The Count had stood up, not like a father but like a poor man, to honour his daughter as a lady; and at seeing her he had felt great delight. But neither at that moment nor later did she recognise him, because he was quite changed from what he had been—old, white-haired, bearded, thin and sun-burned, so that he seemed a man quite different from the Count. Seeing that the children wanted to stay near him and cried when they were taken away, she told the tutor to let them remain.

While the children were standing round the old man, Giachetto's father happened to come in and heard about this from the tutor; and, as he disliked Giannetta, he said:

"Let them stay there, with the bad luck God gave them! They are only copying the person they are born from. By their mother they are descended from beggars—small wonder if they want to stay with beggars."

The Count heard these words and suffered at them; but he took the insult in silence, as he had taken many another.

Although Giachetto was displeased when he heard of the delight his children took in the old man (that is, the Count), still, he loved them so much that, rather than see them weep, he ordered that the old man should be received into the house as a servant, if he wished to remain. He replied that he would gladly stay, but that he could do nothing but attend to horses, to which he had been accustomed all his life. He was therefore allotted a horse, and when he had finished work he played with the children.

While Fortune had treated the Count of Antwerp and his children as I have related, the King of France died, after making many treaties with the Germans, and was succeeded by his son, whose wife had caused the Count's exile. The last truce with the Germans expired, and the new King began a very bitter war. His relative, the King of England, sent him the assistance of a large army, commanded by his General Perotto and by Giachetto Lamiens, the son of his other general. With him went the old man (that is, the Count) still unrecognised by anybody, and remained with the army for a considerable time as a groom. And, as he was a good soldier, he did more service both by his deeds and advice than was expected of him.

During this war the Queen of France fell seriously ill, and, finding she was dying, she repented of her sins and confessed to the Archbishop of Rouen, who was considered by all a good and most saintly man. Among other things she told him of the great wrong she had done the Count of Antwerp. Nor was she satisfied with telling him only, but related all that had happened in the presence of many men of worth, and besought them to intercede with the King so that the Count if living, or, if not, his children, might be restored to their rank. Soon after which she departed this life, and was honourably buried.

When the King was told of this confession, he sighed to think of the wrong done this good man. He then proclaimed throughout his whole army and in many other places that he would give a large reward to anyone who could give him information concerning the Count of Antwerp and his children, because he had now learned from the Queen's confession that the Count was innocent of the crime for which he had been exiled, and the King intended to restore him to his former or greater rank. When the disguised Count heard of this and found out that it was true, he went straight to Giachetto and begged him to come with him to Perotto, since he could give them the information the King wanted. And when they were all three together, the Count said to Perotto, who was just about to question him:

"Perotto, Giachetto here married your sister, and has never had any dowry with her. Therefore, so that your sister may not be dowerless, I intend that he and no one else shall receive the reward promised by the King, for yourself who are son to the Count of Antwerp, and for Violante your sister and his wife, and for me who am the Count of Antwerp and your father."

When Perotto heard this he gazed fixedly at him and suddenly recognising him, threw himself at the Count's feet, wept, embraced him and said:

"Father, you are indeed welcome."

When Giachetto heard what the Count said, and then saw what Perotto did, he was so amazed and delighted that he scarcely knew what to do. He felt ashamed of the insults he had given the Count when he was a groom, and threw himself weeping at the Count's feet, humbly asking his pardon for all past injuries, which the Count benignly granted and raised Giachetto to his feet. And when they had all three talked over their various adventures and wept and rejoiced much together, Perotto and Giachetto wanted to give the Count new clothes. But he utterly refused and said that Giachetto should first obtain the reward, and then present the Count to the King dressed as he was in order to shame him more.

Giachetto then went to the King with Perotto and the Count, and offered to bring him the Count and his children for the reward promised. The King immediately had the great reward placed before Giachetto's eyes, and ordered Giachetto to take it with him when he had truly told him where the Count and his children were living. Giachetto then turned round and, pointing to the Count his groom and to Perotto, said:

"Sir, there are the father and son; the daughter, who is my wife, is not here, but by God's grace you shall soon see her."

The King then gazed at the Count, and, after looking at him for some time, recognised him, although he was so greatly altered from what he had been. With tears in his eyes the King raised the Count from his knees, kissed and embraced him, and received Perotto affably. He then ordered that the Count should be furnished with clothes, servants, horses and equipment befitting his nobility; which was done at once. Beyond this, the King greatly honoured Giachetto, and asked to hear all about their adventures.

When Giachetto took the rich reward for having given information about the Count and his children, the Count said to him:

"Take these things from the munificence of my lord the King, and remember to tell your father that your children, his grandchildren and mine, did not have a beggar for their mother."

Giachetto took the gifts, and afterwards called his wife and mother to Paris, and Perotto's wife came also. There they rejoiced with the Count, whom the King had restored to all his estates and had made greater than ever. Then everyone returned to his own home, and the Count dwelt in Paris more gloriously than before until his death.

## NINTH TALE

*Bernabò da Genova is tricked by Ambrogiuolo, loses his money and orders his innocent wife to be murdered. She escapes and, dressed as a man, enters the Sultan's service.*

*She meets the trickster; brings Bernabò to Alexandria;
the trickster is punished; she returns to woman's clothes;
and they go home wealthy to Genoa*

With this piteous tale Elisa performed her task, and then
Filomena the queen, who was tall and beautiful, neat-
waisted, with a pleasant smiling face, said:

We must keep our promise to Dioneo, and since only
he and I are left to tell a tale, I will tell mine first, and then
he shall tell his last, as he wished. So saying, she began as
follows:

There is a common proverb among the people to the effect that the deceiver is at the mercy of the deceived. This
does not seem as if it could be proved true, if it were not
showed to be so by certain events. And so, most dear ladies,
I propose to show you that this is true, while keeping to the
subject proposed. And I think it should not be disagreeable
to you to hear this, for you may learn to be on your guard
against deceivers.

At a certain Parisian inn were gathered several important
Italian merchants, some on one errand, some on another,
according to their custom. One evening they had dined
merrily together, and then began to discuss various topics.
Passing from one subject to another, they began to talk of
their wives, whom they had left at home, and one of them
said jokingly:

"I don't know what my wife does, but I do know that
when I come across a girl I like, I put on one side the love
I have for my wife, and enjoy the girl as much as I can."

Said another:

"So do I, for whether I believe it or not, my wife takes
any chance she can get; so we act reciprocally. The ass receives what he gives at home."

A third was of much the same opinion; in short, all
seemed to agree that the wives they had left at home did
not waste their time. But one man there, named Bernabò
Lomellin da Genova, denied this, and asserted that by a
special grace of God he had a wife who possessed all the
virtues which a woman or even, to a great extent, a knight
or a young man should possess, so that perhaps in all Italy
there was not another like her. She was beautiful and still
young, straight and strong of body, while she was more skilful than other women at all feminine work, such as working in silk and the like. Moreover, he said that no squire or
gentleman's servant could better serve a gentleman's table
than she, since she was well bred, educated and discreet. In

addition he praised her because she could ride a horse, hold a hawk, read and write and argue as well as any merchant. After much other praise, he came to the topic under discussion, and asserted that no chaster or more modest woman could be found anywhere. Wherefore he certainly believed that if he remained away from home for ten years or forever, she would never have anything to do with another man.

Among the merchants talking thus was a young man named Ambrogiuolo da Piacenza, who laughed heartily when he heard the last praise Bernabò gave his wife, and jestingly asked if the Emperor had granted him this privilege more than to other men.

Bernabò, in some annoyance, replied that this grace had been given him, not by the Emperor, but by God, who was a little more powerful than the Emperor.

Then said Ambrogiuolo:

"Bernabò, I do not doubt for one moment that you think you are speaking the truth, but it seems to me that you have not closely considered the nature of things. If you had done so, I do not think you are so obtuse that you would have failed to perceive certain things which would make you talk more reasonably on this topic. I should like to discuss the matter a little further with you, so that you may not think that we, who have spoken freely of our wives, suppose they are made differently from yours, but that what we have said comes from our knowledge of their common nature.

"I have always heard that man is the most noble animal among the mortal beings created by God, and after him, woman. But, as we usually believe, and see from deeds, man is the more perfect. Since he is more nearly perfect, he must assuredly have more firmness and constancy, since women are universally more fickle; and this might be proved by many natural causes, which at present I do not intend to discuss. If man has more strength of mind and yet cannot prevent himself from yielding to any woman who asks him or even from desiring one who pleases him, and moreover from doing all he can to be with her, not once in a month but a thousand times a day; how can you expect a naturally fickle woman to resist the entreaties, the flatteries, the gifts, the thousand other methods used by a clever man who is in love with her? Do you think she can resist? However much you may assert it, I do not believe that you do believe it. You yourself say that your wife is a woman, that she is made of flesh and bones like other women. If this is so, she must have the same desires as other women and the same powers of resistance to her natural appetites. So it is quite possible that she may be most modest, and yet do what other women do; and when a thing is merely possible, you should not deny it so sharply or assert the contrary, as you do."

To this Bernabò replied:

"I am a merchant and not a philosopher, and I shall answer like a merchant. And I say I know quite well that what you say does occur with foolish women who are without any shame. But wise women are so careful of their honour that they become much stronger in guarding it than men, who do not trouble about it. And my wife is just such a one."

Said Ambrogiuolo:

"If every time they had to do with a different man there grew a horn on their heads to show what they had done, I think indeed that few would choose to do it. But, so far from a horn growing, there is neither trace nor track appears, if they are wise. Shame and loss of honour only occur, if things are talked about. So, when they can do it secretly, they do it; or else abstain out of stupidity. And you may take this as certain, that the only chaste woman is one who has never been asked, or was refused if she herself asked. And although I know such things must be so from natural and true reasons, yet I should not speak as fully as I do if I had not often proved them to be true with many women. And I maintain that if I were near your most chaste wife, I think I could very soon bring her to the point where I have already brought others."

Bernabò replied angrily:

"Wordy argument can go on forever; you will talk and I shall talk, and in the end nothing will be proved. But since you say all women are so yielding and that you have such a genius in this matter, while I want to show you that my wife is a chaste woman—I am ready to have my head cut off if you can ever bring her to commit this act with you. And if you can't, I will not make you lose more than a thousand gold florins."

Ambrogiuolo began to grow heated, and said:

"Bernabò, I don't know what I should do with your blood if I won. But if you want to test what I have said, put five thousand florins (which should be less valuable to you than your head) against my thousand. You set no time limit, but I will agree to go to Genoa and within three months from the day I leave here I will have my will of your wife, and as proof I will bring back with me something that she values most highly and will give you such proofs that you yourself will admit them, on condition, however, that during that period you do not go to Genoa and do not write her any information about this matter."

Bernabò at once agreed; and, although the other merchants present tried to break off the bet, since they knew that great ill might come of it, yet the two merchants were so heated that, against the will of the others, they set down their mutual agreement in fair script of their own handwriting.

When the agreement was drawn, Bernabò remained where he was, and Ambrogiuolo went to Genoa as quickly as he could. He remained there a few days cautiously enquiring about the street where the lady lived and about her behaviour, and what he heard was the same, or more than Bernabò had told him; which made him think that he had come on a fool's errand. However, he got into touch with a poor woman who often went to the lady's house and whom the lady liked. He was unable to persuade her to do anything else, but corrupted her with money to carry him hidden in a chest to the lady's house and into her bedroom. And then, in accordance with Ambrogiuolo's orders, the woman pretended that she had to go away, and left the chest there for several days.

The chest remained in the bedroom until night-time, and when Ambrogiuolo thought that the lady was asleep, he opened the chest by a secret device, and gently stepped out into the room where a light was burning. By means of this light he examined and firmly fixed in his memory the shape of the room, its frescoes and everything particularly worthy of note in it. He then went towards the bed where the lady was lying fast asleep with a little maid servant, turned back the bed clothes from her and perceived that she was as beautiful naked as when clothed. But he could find no special mark to report, except that under her left breast was a mole surrounded by a few downy hairs as bright as gold. After noting this he gently covered her up again, for when he saw she was so beautiful he was tempted to risk his life and get into bed beside her. But, since he had heard she was so cruel and sharp to lovers, he did not risk it. He spent the greater part of the night in the bedroom at his leisure, and took a purse and a gown from a wardrobe, and then a ring and a girdle, all of which he put into his chest, and then got in himself, and shut it as it had been before. And in this way he passed two nights, without the lady noticing anything unusual.

On the third day, the woman returned for the chest, as they had arranged, and had it taken back to the place whence it had been brought. Ambrogiuolo got out, satisfied the old woman in accordance with his promise, and returned to Paris before the expiration of the time agreed, taking with him the articles mentioned. There he called together the merchants who had been witnesses of their words and wager, and in the presence of Bernabò he claimed to have won the wager, because he had done what he had boasted he would do. To prove his words, he first described the bedroom and its frescoes, and then showed the things he had brought back with him, vowing that the lady had given them to him.

Bernabò admitted that the bedroom was such as he described and also recognised that these objects were really his wife's; but he said that Ambrogiuolo might have learned the description of the bedroom from one of the servants of the house, and might have obtained the articles in the same manner. Therefore, if Ambrogiuolo had nothing more to say, Bernabò did not think this sufficient to win the wager. Whereupon Ambrogiuolo said:

"Indeed this would not be sufficient, but since you wish me to give further proof, I will do so. And I say that Madonna Zinevra, your wife, has a rather large mole under her left breast, and round about it are perhaps six downy hairs as bright as gold."

When Bernabò heard this, he felt as much pain as if he had been stabbed in the heart with a dagger. Even if he had said nothing, the change in his countenance would have showed plainly that what Ambrogiuolo said was true. And after a little time he said:

"Gentlemen, what Ambrogiuolo says is true; therefore since he has won, let him come at any hour he chooses, and he shall be paid."

And the next day Ambrogiuolo was paid in full. Bernabò then left Paris and returned to Genoa, full of rage against his wife. When he came near the town, he would not enter it, but went to an estate he possessed about twenty miles away. He then sent a servant whom he trusted to Genoa with two horses and a letter, informing his wife that he had returned and telling her to come to him; but he secretly ordered the servant to kill the lady in some suitable place, and then to return to him. The servant reached Genoa and gave the letter and the message, which the lady joyfully received. Next morning, she and the servant mounted their horses and set out for the estate. As they rode along, talking of various matters, they came to a deep solitary valley, shut in with steep rocks and trees, which seemed to the servant a place where he could safely carry out his master's orders. So he drew his dagger, grasped the lady by the arm, and said:

"Madonna, recommend your soul to God, for you shall go no further; here you must die."

Seeing the dagger and hearing these words, the lady exclaimed in terror:

"Mercy of God! Before you kill me, tell me how I have offended you that you should want to murder me?"

"Madonna," said the servant, "you have in no wise offended me. How you have offended your husband I do not know, but he bade me kill you on this road without any pity; and if I did not do it, he threatened to hang me up by the neck. You know how much I am bound to him and how I can refuse nothing he commands me. God knows I am sorry for you, but I can do nothing else."

To this the lady replied, weeping:

"Ah! God's mercy! Do not murder a woman who never harmed you, only to serve another. God, Who knoweth all things, knows that I never did anything for which my husband should thus reward me. But never mind that now. If you are willing, you can please God, your lord and me, in this way: take my clothes, and give me your doublet and cloak; return with my clothes to your lord and say you have killed me; and in exchange for the life you give me, I swear to you I will disappear and go so far away that no news of me shall ever reach him or you or this country."

The servant did not want to kill her, and was easily persuaded to pity. So he took her clothes, gave her his doublet and cloak, allowed her to keep the money she had, begged her to disappear from that country, and left her on foot in the valley. He then returned to his master, and told him that he had not only carried out his orders but had left her dead body to several wolves.

Some time later Bernabò returned to Genoa, and was severely blamed when the affair became known.

The lady was left alone and disconsolate, and when night came on she disguised herself as well as she could and went to a little neighbouring village, and there obtained what she needed from an old woman. She shortened the doublet and altered it to fit her, made a pair of short drawers out of her chemise, cut off her hair, and thus made herself look like a sailor. She then walked to the sea and happened upon a Catalan gentleman, whose name was Segner Encararch; he had left his ship at a distance and had come to a fountain at Alba to refresh himself. She entered into conversation with him, giving the name of Sicuran da Finale, was taken into his service, and went on board ship. There she was supplied by the gentleman with better clothes, and served him so well and exactly that he was delighted.

Soon after this the Catalan sailed to Alexandria, taking with him some peregrine falcons which he presented to the Sultan. He dined several times with the Sultan, who noticed and was pleased by Sicuran's behaviour as he waited on his master, and therefore the Sultan asked for him as his own servant. And although this was a grief to the Catalan, he left Sicuran with the Sultan. And in a short time Sicuran acquired the affection and good graces of the Sultan by his good conduct, just as he had done with the Catalan.

Time passed by, and at a certain period of the year there was a fair and great gathering of Christian and Saracen merchants at Acre, which was under the Sultan's government. To protect the merchants and their goods, the Sultan was accustomed to send, along with other officials, certain important officers and sufficient soldiers to guard them. When the time came, the Sultan determined that this duty should be carried out by Sicuran, who was already thoroughly acquainted with the language.

Thus Sicuran came to Acre as lord and Captain of the Guard of merchants and their goods; and well and diligently performed everything connected with his office. As he went to and fro on his duties, he came upon many merchants from Sicily, Pisa, Genoa, Venice and other parts of Italy, and gladly became familiar with them for the sake of his memories of his own land. One day he went into a Venetian clothes shop and there to his amazement saw, among other trinkets, a purse and girdle he recognised as his own. Without showing any signs of surprise, he politely asked from whom they came, and if they were for sale. Now, Ambrogiuolo da Piacenza had come thither in his ship with much merchandise from Venice, and hearing the Captain of the Guard ask who was the owner of these things, he stepped forward and said laughingly:

"Messer, these things are mine, and are not for sale. But if they please you, I will gladly give them to you."

Seeing him laugh, Sicuran suspected that the man had recognised him by something he had done; but, keeping his countenance, he said:

"Perhaps you are laughing because you see a soldier like myself asking about such feminine things?"

Said Ambrogiuolo:

"I am not laughing at that, but at the manner in which I got them."

And Sicuran then said to him:

"Ah! God give you good luck; but if it is not unseemly, tell us how you got possession of them."

"Messer," said Ambrogiuolo, "these, with other things, were given me by a lady of Genoa, named Madonna Zinevra, wife of Bernabò Lomellin, one night when I lay with her, and I promised to keep them for love of her. I was laughing because I remembered what a fool Bernabò was to wager five thousand gold florins against one thousand that I should not bring his wife to serve my pleasure. But this I did, and won the wager. And he, who should have been punished for his stupidity rather than she for doing what all women do, returned from Paris to Genoa and killed her, according to what I have heard."

When Sicuran heard this, he saw at once the reason for Bernabò's anger, and plainly perceived that Ambrogiuolo was the cause of all the trouble. And Sicuran determined that he should not escape unpunished. However, he pretended to think the story an excellent one, and artfully established such close relations with the man that, when the fair was over, he persuaded him to come to Alexandria, bringing all his goods with him. There Sicuran secured him a shop and gave him a considerable sum of money. And Ambrogiuolo, perceiving how useful this would be to him, willingly remained there.

Sicuran was eager to prove his innocence to Bernabò, and did not rest until he had found an opportunity of bringing him to Alexandria, through the influence of certain great merchants of Genoa in that city. Bernabò arrived in poverty, and Sicuran secretly had him looked after by a friend until the time came to do what he meant to do. Now, Sicuran had already caused Ambrogiuolo to relate the story in the Sultan's presence and made him take pleasure in it. But when Bernabò arrived, he thought he would delay no further. So, at a suitable time, he besought the Sultan to order Bernabò and Ambrogiuolo into his presence, and there in the presence of Bernabò to compel Ambrogiuolo by gentle means—and if they failed, by force—to tell the truth about what had happened (as he boasted) with Bernabò's wife.

Ambrogiuolo and Bernabò arrived, and, in the presence of many witnesses, the Sultan sternly commanded Ambrogiuolo to tell truly how he had obtained the five thousand gold florins from Bernabò. Sicuran, in whom Ambrogiuolo had put his trust, was also present and with a very angry countenance threatened him with the direst torture if he did not confess. Ambrogiuolo, thus threatened on both sides, and to some extent compelled, related everything that had happened, in the presence of Bernabò and many others, expecting no greater punishment than having to return the five thousand florins and the other articles. And, when Ambrogiuolo had finished speaking, Sicuran, as the Sultan's officer, turned to Bernabò, and said:

"And what did you do to your wife through this trick?"

Bernabò replied:

"Overcome by anger at the loss of my money and by shame for the disgrace I felt my wife had brought upon me, I caused my wife to be killed by one of my servants. And, according to what he told me, she was immediately devoured by a number of wolves."

All these things were thus related in the presence of the Sultan, who could not yet understand what was Sicuran's reason for arranging the meeting and explanation. But Sicuran said to him:

"Sire, now you may clearly perceive how much that lady should rejoice in her husband and lover. In an hour the lover reft her of honour, blasted her fame with lies, and ruined her husband. And her husband, putting more faith in the lies of others than in her truth, which from long experience he ought to have known, had her killed and eaten by wolves. In addition to this, the lover and husband bear her so much love and good will that they do not recognise her, although they have long dwelt with her. But in order that you may fully understand what each of them deserves, and if, as a special grace to me, you will punish the deceiver and pardon the deceived, I will bring her into the presence of you and them."

The Sultan was willing to do anything to please Sicuran in this affair, and therefore granted his request and told him to bring in the lady. Bernabò was amazed, for he firmly believed his wife was dead. As for Ambrogiuolo, he began to suspect his misfortune, and feared worse things than having

to pay back money; he did not know whether to hope or
fear that the lady should appear there, but awaited her
coming in consternation.

When the Sultan had granted his request, Sicuran threw
himself weeping at the Sultan's feet, abandoned his mascu-
line voice and demeanour, and said:

"Sire, I am the wretched, unfortunate Zinevra, and for
six years I have wandered about the world disguised as a
man. That traitor Ambrogiuolo falsely and wickedly slan-
dered me; and that other cruel and wicked man gave me
to a servant to be murdered and eaten by wolves."

Tearing open her clothes and displaying her breasts, she
showed the Sultan and everyone else that she was a woman.
She then turned to Ambrogiuolo and scornfully asked him
when she had ever lain with him, as he had formerly
boasted. But he, having recognised her, was mute with
shame, and said not a word.

The Sultan, who had always believed her to be a man,
was so much amazed by what he saw and heard that he
thought it must be rather a dream than reality. But when
he recovered from his amazement, he recognised the truth,
and gave the highest praise to the life and constancy and
behaviour and virtue of Zinevra, who till that time he had
known as Sicuran. He gave her most handsome woman's
clothes and women to wait upon her; and, at her request,
pardoned Bernabò the hanging he deserved. When Bernabò
recognised her, he threw himself at her feet, weeping and
asking pardon, which, although he was unworthy of it, she
granted him and raised him to his feet, and tenderly embraced him as her husband.

The Sultan then commanded that Ambrogiuolo should
immediately be tied to a stake in the most conspicuous part
of the city, and smeared with honey and left there in the
sun, and never taken thence until he crumbled away. After
this he ordered that all Ambrogiuolo's riches should be
given to the lady; and this amounted to more than ten thousand double ducats. He then gave a most magnificent banquet, where he did honour to Bernabò as the husband of
Madonna Zinevra, and to Madonna Zinevra as the most
worthy of women. And he gave them more than another
ten thousand double ducats in jewels, and vessels of gold
and silver, and in money.

After the banquet, he had a ship prepared for them and
gave them leave to return to Genoa when they pleased.
Thither they returned with great wealth and in great joy,
and were received with very great honour, especially Ma-

donna Zinevra, who was thought to be dead by everybody. And ever after, as long as she lived, she had a reputation for great virtue.

The same day Ambrogiuolo was tied to a stake and smeared with honey, and, after enduring great agony, was killed and eaten to the bones by the multitudes of flies, wasps and gad-flies which swarm in that country. His white bones, strung together by the sinews, remained there a long time and bore witness of his wickedness to all who saw them. And thus the deceiver lay at the mercy of the deceived.

## TENTH TALE

*Paganino da Monaco steals the wife of Messer Ricciardo di Chinzica, who finds out where she is and follows her; he becomes friendly with Paganino and asks for his wife back. Paganino says she may return to him, if she wants to; but she will not do so, and, on the death of Messer Ricciardo, becomes the wife of Paganino*

Each member of the happy band highly praised the tale told by their queen, and, above all Dioneo, who was the only one left to tell a tale that day. After highly commending her story, he spoke as follows:

Fair ladies, part of the queen's tale has made me change my mind as to the story I shall tell, and forces me to tell another. I am thinking of the stupidity of Bernabò (although matters turned out well for him) and of all the other men who make us see that they believe what he believed; which is, that while they go to and fro in the world and take their pleasure here and there first with one woman and then with another, they imagine that their wives are sitting at home with their hands in their girdles, as if we who are born and grow up under their hands did not know the contrary. I shall show you the stupidity of all such men and especially of those who think themselves more powerful than Nature, and believe that fictitious arguments will achieve what they are unable to do themselves, forcing others to what they are themselves, however contrary to the nature of those who are thus compelled.

In Pisa there was once a judge, more endowed with mental ability than bodily strength, whose name was Messer Ricciardo di Chinzica. He was very rich and got it into his head, perhaps, that he could satisfy a wife with the same sort of work he gave his studies; in any case, he sought with great earnestness to get a young and beautiful woman as his wife. Whereas, if he had known how to advise himself as he advised others, he would have avoided both youth and beauty. And so it came about that Messer Lotto Gualandi gave him to wife his daughter, Bartolomea, one of the most beautiful and charming girls of Pisa, although most of the girls in that town are as thin as worm-eating lizards. . . . The judge brought her to his house with the greatest rejoicing and gave a magnificent wedding feast; and on the first night managed to consummate the marriage once with her, although he very nearly failed to do even that. Next morning, since he was thin and dry and out of spirits he had to cheer himself up with white wine and sweetmeats, and other restoratives.

The judge now formed a better estimate of his powers than he had done before, and began to teach his wife a calendar fit for boys who stand up to read, perhaps the calendar made at Ravenna. According to what he told her, each holiday was not only the feast day of some saint but of many; and he proved to her by numerous arguments that out of reverence to them a man and wife should abstain from carnal embraces. To these he added Fasts, Ember Days, vigils of the Apostles and a thousand other Saints, Friday and Saturday and the Lord's Sabbath, and the whole of Lent, certain phases of the moon and many other exceptions, thinking perhaps that there should be the same delays with women in bed as he often arranged in lawsuits.

He continued in this manner for a long time, not without grievous melancholy in the lady, whom he scarcely lay with once in a month; but he watched over her jealously in case someone else should teach her the working days, as he had taught her the holidays.

During the hot weather Messer Ricciardo happened to take it into his head to visit a beautiful property he possessed near Monte Nero, where he went to stay for several days with his wife to enjoy the cool air. While they were there he arranged a fishing expedition one day to provide her with some amusement; he went out in a small boat with some fishermen and she followed in another boat with other women to watch them. And in the excitement of fishing they went several miles out to sea, without realising it.

While they were all eagerly watching the fishermen there suddenly appeared a galley of Paganino da Mare, a very famous pirate of that time. Seeing the small boats, he came after them, and although they fled as swiftly as they could, Paganino captured the boat containing the women. When Paganino saw the beautiful lady, he wanted nothing more of them, but put her on his galley and sailed away, in full view of Messer Ricciardo who was already on shore.

No need to enquire whether the judge was infuriated when he saw this, since he was so jealous that he dreaded the very air itself. In Pisa and elsewhere he complained bitterly of the wickedness of pirates, although he did not know who had carried off his wife or where she had been taken.

As Paganino gazed upon her beauty, he felt all was well; and, since he had no wife, he determined to keep her with him, and therefore tried to comfort her as she wept bitterly. During the day words did not seem of much avail, but when night came the calendar fell from her girdle and every saint's day and holiday went out of her head when he began to comfort her with deeds. Long before they reached Monaco, she had forgotten all about the judge and his laws, and was living most happily with Paganino. And when they reached Monaco he not only gave her pleasure both day and night, but honoured her as his wife.

Some time later Messer Ricciardo heard where his wife was, and, feeling that no intermediary could do what was necessary, he set off to find her with the greatest impatience, quite prepared to spend any amount of money to get her back. He took ship and went to Monaco, where he saw her and she saw him; and that evening she told Paganino that her husband was there, and what she intended to do. The next morning Messer Ricciardo saw Paganino and accosted him, and in a short time struck up a warm acquaintance with him. Paganino pretended not to recognise the judge, and waited to see what he wanted to do. When Messer Ricciardo thought the right moment had arrived, he spoke to Paganino as politely and ably as he could, explaining why he had come there, and begging him to name any sum he pleased for the ransom of his wife. To this Paganino replied with a cheerful countenance:

"Messer, you are welcome, and I will give you an answer in few words. It is true I have a girl in my house, but I do not know whether she is your wife or anyone else's, because I don't know you, nor do I know her either, except that she and I have lived together for some time. If you

are her husband, as you say, I will take you to her, since
you seem to me a worthy gentleman, and I am sure she will
recognise you. If she admits that matters are as you say,
and if she wants to go away with you, then out of respect
for your worship I will accept any ransom for her you like
to give. But if this is not so, you are behaving basely in
trying to take her away from me, since I am a young man
and can look after a woman as well as anyone especially
a woman like her, for she is the loveliest I ever saw."

Then said Messer Ricciardo:

"Certainly she is my wife, and you will see it is so, if you
will take me to her. She will at once throw her arms round
my neck. And I ask nothing better than what you suggest."

"Very well," said Paganino, "let us go."

They then went to a room in Paganino's house, and he
sent for her. She was dressed and prepared, came out of
her room and went towards Ricciardo and Paganino, but
said nothing to Ricciardo which she would not have said
to any other stranger Paganino had brought to the house.
The judge, who had expected her to receive him with the
greatest delight, was amazed at this, and said to himself:
"Perhaps the melancholy and long suffering I have endured
since I lost her have so altered me that she does not recognise me." So he said:

"Lady, it cost me dear to take you fishing, for I never
felt such grief as I have suffered since I lost you; and now
you greet me so shyly that you appear not to recognise me.
Do you not see that I am Messer Ricciardo, come to pay
anything required by this gentleman, in whose house we
are, in order to get you back and take you away? And he
has graciously offered to restore you to me for any sum I
choose to name."

The lady turned to him with a slight smile, and said:

"Messer, are you speaking to me? Beware lest you are
making a mistake about me, for I do not remember that I
ever saw you before."

Said Messer Ricciardo:

"Beware what you are saying! Look closely at me. If you
will recollect, you will see that I am your husband, Ricciardo di Chinzica."

The lady said:

"Pardon me, Messer, it is perhaps not so modest for me
to look closely at you as you suppose; however, I have
looked at you sufficiently to know that I never saw you
before."

Messer Ricciardo imagined that she was afraid to confess

in Paganino's presence that she knew him. So he asked Paganino to allow him to speak privately with her alone in a room. Paganino gave permission, but said he was not to kiss her against her will. And he ordered the lady to go into a room with Ricciardo, to listen to what he had to say, and to reply as she wished. The lady and Messer Ricciardo then went alone into the room, and, when they had sat down, he said:

"Ah! Heart of my body, my sweet soul, my hope, do you not recognise Ricciardo who loves you more than he loves himself? How can this be? Am I so much altered? Ah! Beautiful apple of my eye, look at me a moment."

The lady began to laugh, and, without allowing him to go any further, said:

"You know quite well that I am not so forgetful as not to know that you are Messer Ricciardo di Chinzica, my husband. But when I lived with you, you showed that you knew little of me; for, if you had been as wise or eager as you claimed to be, you ought to have been wise enough to see that I was a young, fresh, vigorous girl, and consequently you should have known that young women require something else beside food and clothes, although they are too modest to say so. And you know quite well how you performed this.

"If you preferred the study of the law to a wife, you should not have married. However, you did not seem to me to be a judge, but a town-crier of holy days and fasts and vigils, so thoroughly did you know them. And I tell you that if you had given as many holidays to the peasants on your land as you gave the worker who should have ploughed my little field, you would not have reaped one grain of wheat. God has beheld my youth with pity, and has allowed me to meet a man with whom I lie in this room, where nothing is known of holidays (I mean the sort of holiday so much praised by you, who are more devoted to God than the service of ladies), and through that door never come Saturdays or Fridays or vigils or Ember Days or Lent (which is so long), but we work and beat our wool day and night. And since matins rang this morning I had one more experience of this work. Therefore I intend to remain with him and to work while I am young; and saints' days and pardons and fasts I shall keep for when I am old. So go away, and good luck to you, as quickly as you can, and keep as many saints' days as you like, but without me."

When Messer Ricciardo heard this, he was filled with grief, and as soon as she was silent, he said:

"Alas, my sweet soul, what words are these? Have you no thought for your honour and the honour of your family? Will you stay here in mortal sin as this man's whore, when you are my wife in Pisa? When you grow tiresome to him, he will turn you out of the house with great disgrace to yourself; whereas you will always be dear to me, and, even if I did not wish it, you would always be mistress of my house. Shall this inordinate and immodest appetite cause you to abandon your honour and me, who love you more than life itself? Ah! My dear hope, do not say so, but come away with me. Now that I know your desires, I shall henceforth try to satisfy them. And so, my sweet, change your mind and come away with me, for I never felt at ease since you were taken from me."

To this the lady replied:

"I do not want anyone to be more tender of my honour than I am myself. My parents should have done that when they gave me to you; but since they were unconcerned about my honour then, I shall be unconcerned about theirs now. If I am in mortal sin here, I should also be so with a cold pestle. So don't be more tender of my honour than I am. And I tell you this—here I feel I am Paganino's wife, whereas in Pisa I seemed to be your whore when I remember what phases of the moon and what geometrical quadratures were needed for a conjunction of my planet and yours. Here Paganino holds me all night in his arms and embraces me and bites me, and if you want to know how often he mounts me, God will tell you for me. You say you will try to satisfy me—but how? Will you do it three times and then stand up erect again like a club? Have you become a bold cavalier since I last saw you? Go away and try to live, for you seem to me so consumptive and pale that you must be hanging on to life by the skin of your teeth. And I tell you this also—even if this man does leave me (which he does not seem likely to do if I want to remain) I do not intend to return to you, for however much you were squeezed you would not make a single drop of sauce. I stayed with you once to my own sorrow, and I should seek my living somewhere else. Once more I tell you that there are no saints' days and vigils here, and so I mean to stay. Therefore, in God's name go away, for, if you don't, I shall scream and say you are trying to rape me."

Messer Ricciardo saw he was in a bad way, and now perceived his folly in having married a young wife. Sadly and dolefully he left the room in exhaustion, and had a long talk with Paganino, all to no avail. Finally, having achieved nothing, he left his wife and returned to Pisa, where his grief brought him to such a state of insanity that whenever anyone greeted him or asked him something as he went about the city, his only answer was: "The vile thief has no holidays." And not long afterwards he died. Hearing of this and knowing how much the lady loved him, Paganino took her as his lawful wife; and as long as their legs would carry them they worked together and enjoyed themselves, without ever observing saints' days or vigils or Lent. And so, my dear ladies, when Bernabò argued with Ambrogiuolo I think he was putting the cart before the horse.

This tale made them all laugh until their jaws ached, and all the ladies unanimously agreed that Dioneo was right and that Bernabò was a fool. But when the tale was done and the laughter had died down, the queen saw that the hour was late, that everyone had told a tale, and that the end of her reign was at hand. So, in accordance with their agreement, she took the garland from her hair, set it upon Neifile's head, and said gaily:

"Now, my dear, you are the ruler of this little nation." And then sat down again.

Neifile blushed slightly at the honour, and her face was like a fresh rose of April or May when morning begins to glow; her eyes were bright and lovely as the morning star, though she kept them a little lowered. But when she had collected herself and the congratulations of the others to their queen had subsided, she sat up a little more erect than usual and said:

"Since I am your queen I shall not depart from the customs of those who went before me, as you have approved them by obeying them; and I shall tell you in a few words what I think, and, if you agree, we will carry it out.

"As you know, tomorrow is Friday and the next day is Saturday, which are somewhat tedious days to most people on account of the fasting. Since He who died that we might live suffered His Passion on Friday, that day is worthy of all reverence; wherefore it would be considered far more right and fitting that we should spend the day in prayers to the honour of God than in telling of tales. On Saturday women are accustomed to wash their heads and get all the dust out of their hair and all the dirt caused by the work of the preceding week. And many people are accustomed to fast on Saturday out of reverence to the Virgin Mother of the Son of God, and thereafter to rest from all work in honour of the ensuing Sunday. Therefore, since we cannot fully carry out the life we have planned on those days, I think we should do well to refrain from telling stories on those two days.

"Moreover, we shall then have been here four days, and, if we wish to avoid other people coming here, I think we should do well to change and go somewhere else. I have already thought of a place and have made all arrangements. When we meet together there, after our siesta on Sunday, in order to give you more time to think (for today we have spent a long time in talk) and because it is perhaps better to restrict the subject of our tales, we will talk about one of the many acts of Fortune. What this shall be I have already thought; we will tell tales of those who have acquired by their wits something they wanted or recovered something they had lost. Let everyone think of something to say on this subject which will be useful or at least amusing to the whole band, excepting always Dioneo's privilege."

All commended the queen's speech and plan, and agreed to them. After this, she called for her steward and discussed with him where the tables should be placed that evening and everything else which would be done during the period of her reign. Then she and all her subjects stood up, and she gave them permission to do anything they chose.

The ladies and men walked towards a little garden, and when dinner time came after they had enjoyed themselves there, they dined joyfully together. After dinner, the queen ordered Emilia to dance, and Pampinea sang the following song, in which the others joined:

*What lady should sing, if I do not sing, since I am contented in all my desires?*

*Come then, Love, the cause of all my joy, of every hope and every happy thing. Together let us sing, not of sighs nor of the bitter pain which now makes sweeter for me your delight, but of that clear flame wherein I burn and live and do rejoice, adoring you as very God to me.*

*The first day when I came within your flame, O Love, you brought into my sight a man whose youth and beauty, ardour and valour could never be surpassed or even equalled. He so enflamed me that henceforth gaily I sing with you, my Lord.*

*And this to me is the supreme delight—that he loves me even as I love him, thanks be to you, O Love. In this world I possess what I desire, and in the next I trust to rest in peace through that unbroken faith I bear to him. God, who sees this, will bring me to His Kingdom.*

After this they sang other songs and danced more dances and played various musical instruments. And when the queen thought it was time to go to bed, each one went to his room with torches borne before him. The two next days they busied themselves with the matters of which the queen had spoken, and eagerly awaited the Sunday.

**END OF THE SECOND DAY**

# THE THIRD DAY

# THE THIRD DAY

*Here begins the third day of the* Decameron, *wherein, under the rule of Neifile, tales are told of those who by their wits obtained something they greatly desired or regained something they had lost*

The rising sun had already turned the crimson dawn to orange when the queen arose on Sunday, and had the whole band awakened. The steward had already sent on ahead to the place they were going many necessary things and servants to prepare what was needed. When he saw the queen had started, he immediately had everything else packed up, struck camp, and followed the ladies and gentlemen with the baggage and remaining servants.

Accompanied and followed by her ladies and the three young men, the queen struck off slowly in a westerly direction along a not very frequented path, full of plants and flowers, which were beginning to open to the rising sun, where they were led by the song of some twenty nightingales and other birds. She went along jesting and laughing with her band, and, between Prime and Tierce, when they had not gone more than two miles, she brought them to a rich and beautiful mansion, set above the plain on a little hill. They entered, and went all over it; and when they had seen the great hall and the fine decorated rooms filled with everything befitting, they greatly praised the house and said its owner must be a man of great magnificence. They then went down and saw its vast cheerful courtyard, its cellars filled with the finest wines, and the great plenty of very cool water there; all of which made them praise the place still more.

They then sat down to rest in an open loggia overlooking the courtyard, where boughs and the flowers in season had been thickly strewn. Thither came the discreet steward, and served them with the most exquisite sweetmeats and the finest wines as refreshment. After this they went into a walled garden beside the mansion, which at a first glance seemed to them so beautiful that they began to examine it more carefully in detail. On its outer edges and through the centre ran wide walks as straight as arrows, covered with pergolas of vines which gave every sign of bearing plenty of grapes that year. These were in full flower, and filled the garden with a perfume which mingled with the scents of many other flowers, and made them feel they were among all the spicery of the East. The sides of these walks were almost closed in with jasmin and red and white roses, so that it was possible to walk in the garden in a perfumed and delicious shade, untouched by the sun, not only in the early morning, but when the sun was high in the sky.

It would take long to tell how many plants there were and of what sort and how they were arranged; but there was an abundance of every pleasant plant which grows in our climate. In the midst of this garden was something which they praised even more than all the rest; this was a lawn of very fine grass, so green that it seemed nearly black, coloured with perhaps a thousand kinds of flowers. This lawn was shut in with very green citron and orange trees bearing at the same time both ripe fruit and young fruit and flowers, so that they pleased the sense of smell as well as charmed the eyes with shade. And in the midst of this lawn was a fountain of very white marble most marvellously carved. A figure standing on a column in the midst of this fountain threw water high up in the air, which fell back into the crystal-clear basin with a delicious sound; and, whether this water was conveyed by natural or artificial means, a mill could have been turned with less. The water which overflowed from the fountain basin ran out of the lawn by some hidden way, where it reappeared again in cunningly made little channels which surrounded the lawn. It then ran all through the garden in many similar canals which all finally met in one place where the water emerged from the garden, though before it ran down to the plain it turned two millwheels at great speed, which was of no small utility to the owner.

The sight of this garden, of its beautiful plan, of the plants and the fountain and the little streams flowing from it, so much pleased the ladies and the three young men that they said, if Paradise could be formed on earth, it could be given no other form than that of this garden, nor could any further beauty be added to it. As they walked in delight about the garden, weaving most beautiful garlands from various tree branches and listening to the song of some twenty different kinds of birds who seemed to be singing one against another, they came upon a new delightful beauty which they had not thought of. They found that the garden contained about a hundred kinds of beautiful animals, and began pointing them out to each other. In one direction rabbits emerged, in another hares were running, elsewhere goats were lying down and young deer were grazing. In addition, many other kinds of harmless animals were running gaily about as if they were tame. All of which added a greater pleasure to all the other pleasures.

When they had walked about enough, looking at one thing and another, they had tables set round the beautiful fountain, and there, at the queen's command, they sang six songs and danced several dances. After this they sat down to eat and were excellently and attractively served with fine, delicate food. Enlivened by this, they rose from the table and gave themselves up once more to music and singing and dancing, until the heat increased so far that the queen thought it was time for a siesta for those who wanted it. Some went to their siesta, but others, charmed by the beauty of the garden, would not leave it, but remained there, either reading romances or playing chess or checkers while the others were asleep. After Nones they got up and refreshed their faces with cool water and, at the queen's command, sat down on the lawn near the fountain in their usual order, waiting to begin to tell stories on the subject suggested by the queen. The first to whom the queen allotted this task was Filostrato, who began as follows:

## FIRST TALE

*Masetto da Lamporecchio pretends to be deaf and dumb in order to become gardener to a convent of nuns, where all the women eagerly lie with him*

Most fair ladies, there are many men and women so stupid that they think when a girl has put a white veil over her forehead and a black cowl on her back, she ceases to be a woman and to feel a woman's desires, as if making her a nun had turned her to stone. If they hear anything contrary to this belief they become as angry as if some huge and wicked crime against nature had been committed. They forget that they themselves are unsatisfied although they have full liberty to do as they please, nor will they take into account the great influence of idleness and solitude. Similarly, there are many people who think that the hoe, the spade, coarse food and poverty take away all carnal desires from those who work on the land, and make them heavy in mind and understanding. Now the queen has ordered me to tell a tale, and, without departing from the subject allotted, I shall be glad to show by a little tale how much such persons are deceived.

In our countryside there was, and still is, a convent of nuns, renowned for their sanctity, the name of which I shall not mention to avoid diminishing that fame. Not long ago it contained only eight nuns and an abbess, all young women. And it happened that the fellow who looked after their very beautiful garden became discontented with his wages, made up his accounts with the steward, and returned to Lamporecchio, whence he had come. Among others who welcomed him was a robust young working man, handsome enough for a peasant, whose name was Masetto. He asked the gardener, whose name was Nuto, how long he had been there, and Nuto told him. Then Masetto asked him what he did at the convent. And Nuto replied:

"I worked in their fine large garden, sometimes went to get wood in the forest, drew water, and did other jobs for them. But the nuns gave me such small wages that I could scarcely afford to buy shoes. Besides, they were all young and seemed to have the very devil in them, for I could do nothing to please them. Once, when I was working in the garden, one of them said: 'Put this here,' and another said: 'Put that here,' and another took the hoe out of my hand, and said: 'That's not right.' They were such a nuisance that I gave up working, and went out of the garden. So, what with one thing and another, I wouldn't stay there any longer, and came back here. The steward there asked me to send him someone from here when I arrived, and I promised I would; but God make him the saint of buttocks before I find or send him anyone."

Nuto's words gave Masetto such a desire to be with these nuns that he felt quite faint, for he saw by what Nuto said that he would be able to do what he desired. He also saw that it would be better to say nothing about it to Nuto, so he remarked:

"Ah! You did well to come away. What can a man do with women? He had much better be with devils. Six times out of seven they don't know what they want themselves."

When their conversation was over, Masetto began to ponder how he should go about getting taken on by the nuns. He knew quite well that he could do the jobs Nuto had told him about, but he was afraid he might not be taken because he was too young and good looking. So after much inward debate he thought: "The place is a long way from here and no one there knows me. If I pretend to be dumb they will certainly take me on." With this plan in mind, he took an axe on his shoulder, and set out for the convent dressed as a poor man, without telling anyone where he was going. On his arrival, he went in and by chance found the steward in the courtyard. He feigned that he was dumb, and by signs asked for food for the love of God, and offered to split logs if needed.

The steward gave him some food, and then took him to some logs which Nuto had not been able to split, but which Masetto, who was very strong, split up in a very short time. The steward then had to go into the forest, and took Masetto with him, and there made him cut wood, load it on an ass, and then signed to him to drive the animal back. All this he did very well, and the steward kept him there several days to help with certain work. One day it happened that the abbess saw him, and asked the steward who he was. And the steward replied:

"Madonna, he is a poor deaf-mute who came here begging one day, and I gave him food, and have made him do what work was needed. If he knows how to work in the garden and wants to stay, I think he would make a good servant, and we can do what we like with him. Moreover, there is no need to fear that he would start joking with your young ladies."

Said the abbess:

"God's faith, you speak truly. Find out if he is a gardener, and try to keep him. Give him a pair of shoes and an old gown, flatter him, and give him plenty to eat."

The steward said he would do so.

Meanwhile, Masetto had not been far off, and had heard everything they said while he was pretending to sweep the courtyard; and he said to himself in great delight: "If you put me in there, I'll work your garden in a way it was never worked before."

The steward, who had seen how well Masetto worked, asked him by signs if he would stay there, and Masetto made signs that he would do what he wanted; so the steward took him on, ordered him to work in the garden, and showed him what he had to do. The steward then left him, and went to do other tasks in the convent. As he worked there day after day the nuns began to tease him and to sing songs about him, as often happens to deaf-mutes, and said the most naughty words they knew to him, never dreaming that he could hear them. The abbess paid little or no attention to this, thinking perhaps that he lacked a tail in front as well as speech. One day he was resting after he had been hard at work, when two very young nuns came into the garden. They approached him as he lay pretending to be asleep, and began to look at him. One of them, who was a little more daring than the other, said:

"If I thought you would keep it a secret, I would tell you something I have often thought of, which might be pleasant to you also."

The other replied:

"Speak out, I shall certainly never speak of it to anyone."

Then the bolder one said: "I don't know if you have ever thought how we are imprisoned here, where no man ever dares to enter except the old steward and this deaf-mute. I have often heard from many women who come to see us here that all the other pleasures in the world are hollow in comparison with that a woman feels with a man. I have often thought I would try it with this deaf-mute, since I can do so with nobody else. He is the best person possible for it, because, even if he wanted to, he could not hold us up to scorn. You see he is a great stupid youth, grown up except in mind. I should like to know what you think about this."

"Oh!" said the second, "what are you saying? Don't you know we have promised our virginity to God?"

"Bah!" said the first, "how many promises are made every day, and never kept? We may have promised, and no doubt others will keep the promise."

Then her companion said:

"And what shall we do if we become pregnant?"

The first replied:

"You think of trouble before it comes to you. When that happens, we'll begin to think about it. There are a thousand ways of keeping it secret, if we ourselves do not speak of it."

The second nun was already more eager than the first to find out what kind of an animal man is, and said:

"Well, how shall we go about it?"

The first answered:

"You see it is now Nones, and I think all the sisters are asleep, except ourselves. Let us search the garden to see if there is anyone in it, and, if not, all we have to do is to take him by the hand into that little hut, where he shelters from the rain. While one is with him, the other can keep watch. He is so stupid that he will do anything we want."

Masetto heard everything they said, and, being perfectly willing to obey them, only waited to be taken by one of them. When they had searched all about, and found that there was nowhere from which they could be observed, the nun who had started the project went up to Masetto and woke him, whereupon he immediately stood up. She took him by the hand with flattering caresses, while he uttered a foolish laugh, and led him into the little hut, where Masetto did what she wanted without waiting for an invitation. When she had had what she wanted, she gave place to her companion, like an honest friend, and Masetto, pretending to be simple-minded, did what she wanted. And, before they departed, they each wanted to find out again how the deaf-mute could ride them. Afterwards, when they talked it over, they agreed that it was even more pleasant than they had heard. So henceforth, at suitable times, they enjoyed themselves with the deaf-mute.

One day it happened that another nun saw what they were doing from the little window of her cell, and showed them to two others. At first they proposed to denounce them to the abbess, but then changed their minds and came to an understanding with the first two, whereby they became sharers in Masetto's farm. Later on, three more nuns joined them, owing to various occurrences.

Finally the abbess, who had not noticed anything of what had been going on, was walking alone in the garden one day when she came upon Masetto. Through riding so hard at nights he was now soon tired by a little work in the day, and was lying fast asleep in the shade of an almond tree. The wind had blown up the skirts of his shirt and left him quite exposed. The abbess gazed at him and was taken with the same desires as the nuns. She woke Masetto, and took him to her room and kept him there several days, enjoying and re-enjoying those pleasures which she had formerly condemned in others, while the nuns complained bitterly that the gardener did not come to work in the garden.

At last she sent him back to his own room but often wanted him again and took more than her share, so that Masetto was not able to satisfy so many. He saw that it would be troublesome to him if he pretended to be mute any longer; so, one night, when he was with the abbess, the ligament of his tongue broke and he said:

"Madonna, I have heard that one cock can satisfy ten

hens, but that ten men can scarcely satisfy one woman.
I have to satisfy nine women, and cannot keep going
much longer. So I have reached such a state through what
I have done that I can no longer do anything. You must
either let me go away, or find some remedy."

When the abbess heard the dumb man speak, she was
stupefied, and said: "What is this? I thought you were
dumb?"

"Madonna," said Masetto, "I was dumb, but not born
so. My dumbness came from an illness which deprived me
of speech, and I have only recovered it tonight, for which
I give thanks to God."

The abbess believed him, and asked him what he meant
by saying he had to satisfy nine women. Masetto told her
the truth. When the abbess heard it, she perceived that every
one of her nuns knew more than she did. She discreetly
would not allow Masetto to leave, and determined to make
some arrangement with the nuns so that Masetto would
not bring contempt on the convent.

It was made plain to all what they all had done behind
each other's backs, and it was unanimously agreed (with
Masetto's consent and complete belief on the part of the
people in the district) that they should give out that Masetto's speech had been restored to him after many years by
their prayers and the merits of the Saint to whom the convent was dedicated. And, as the old steward happened to
die shortly after, Masetto was made steward in his place.
Thus his labours were shared out in such a way that he
could perform them. In the said labours he begot a large
quantity of little nuns, but things were so carefully concealed that nothing was known about them until after the
abbess' death, when Masetto was getting old and eager to
return home with the money he had saved. And, when the
whole thing came out, he easily obtained permission.

Thus Masetto, who had left home with nothing but an
axe on his shoulder, returned old, rich and a father without having the expense and trouble of rearing his children,
because he had been smart enough to make good use of his
youth. And he often used to say that he had treated Christ
in such a fashion that he had put many a horn on His head.

# SECOND TALE

*A groom lies with the wife of King Agilulf and the King secretly discovers it. He finds the man and cuts off some of his hair; but the groom cuts off the hair of all the others and so escapes punishment*

Sometimes the ladies blushed and sometimes laughed at Filostrato's tale; when it was ended the queen ordered Pampinea to speak next, and so, with a laughing face, she began as follows:

There are some persons so indiscreet in showing they know what they had better not know, that sometimes, when they think they are concealing their own shame by reproving the hidden faults of others, they merely increase it extremely. That this is true, fair ladies, I intend to show you by its contrary, in the cunning of a man of even lower station than Masetto, and in the wisdom of a great King.

Agilulf, King of the Lombards, established his throne in Pavia, a city of Lombardy, as his predecessors had done. He took as his wife Teudelinga, widow of Autari, formerly King of the Lombards, a modest and educated woman of the greatest beauty, but unfortunate in her lovers. Through the courage and wisdom of this King Agilulf, the affairs of Lombardy were in a state of peace and prosperity, when it happened that one of the Queen's grooms—a man of the lowest birth but in other respects far above his station in life, rather like the King in height and good looks—fell violently in love with the Queen.

His humble station in life did not prevent his realising the indecency of his love, and, like a wise man, he spoke of it to nobody, nor even did he express it to her by his eyes. Although he lived without any hope of finding favour in her sight, yet he felt proud to think that he had set his desires so high; and, as he was burned up with the fire of love, he was far more eager than any of his fellow-servants to do everything which he thought might please the Queen. Thus it happened that when the Queen rode, she more often chose the horse looked after by this groom than any other. Whenever this happened, the man considered it a very great favour, and never left her stirrup-side, thinking himself blessed whenever he could touch her skirts.

But, as we often see, the less hope there is, the greater the love becomes; and so it was with this poor groom, the more so since it was most painful for him to go about with this great desire concealed within him, when he had no hope to support him. Many times he determined to kill himself, since he could not get free from this love. Pondering on this, he decided to die in such a way that it would be known he did it for love of the Queen; and, moreover, he determined that he would risk his life in trying to satisfy his desire wholly or in part. He did not attempt to speak to the Queen or to tell her of his love by letter, for he knew that it would be useless to say or write anything; but he meant to try to lie with her by a trick. The only way he could think of, was to personate the King—who, as he knew, did not lie with her every night—and in this way enter her room and get at her.

During several nights he hid himself in a great hall of the King's palace, which was midway between the King's apartments and the Queen's, so that he might see how the King was dressed and how he behaved when he went to her. One night he saw the King come out of his apartments, wrapped in a large mantle, carrying a small lighted torch in one hand and a small rod in the other. Without saying a word, the King knocked once or twice with the rod at the Queen's apartment, the door was immediately opened, and the torch taken from his hand. Having observed this and that the King returned in the same way, the groom thought he would do likewise. He contrived to get hold of a mantle like that he had seen the King wearing and a small torch and a rod; and then he carefully bathed himself so that the smell of the horse manure should not be offensive to the Queen or lead her to suspect the deceit. After which, he hid himself with these objects in the great hall.

When everyone was asleep, he thought it time either to succeed in his desire or to go to a longed for death in a high cause; he therefore lighted his torch with a flint and tinder he had brought for the purpose, wrapped himself in the mantle, went to the door of the apartment and knocked twice with the rod. The door was opened by a sleepy chamber-maid, who took the light and put it aside. Without saying a word, he took off the mantle, opened the curtains of the Queen's bed where she was asleep, and got in beside her. He pretended to be angry, because he knew that when the King was angry, he would not hear a word from anybody; and so, without saying a word to her, or her saying anything to him, he took her lustfully in his arms and knew her carnally several times. Although it was bitter to him to leave, yet, since he was afraid that by staying there too long the delight he had had would be turned to woe, he got up, took the mantle and the light, went off without saying a word, and returned to his own bed as quickly as possible.

The groom had scarcely gone when the King arose and went to the Queen's room, greatly to her surprise. When he got into bed with her and merrily greeted her, she took courage from his good humour, and said:

"What is the meaning of this novelty tonight, Sire? You have only just left me, after taking your pleasure of me more than usual, and now you return immediately! Be careful of what you are doing."

When the King heard these words he immediately guessed that the Queen had been deceived by a similarity of person and dress; but, as he was a wise man, he also thought that he would pretend to notice nothing, since neither the Queen nor anyone else had perceived it. Many a foolish man would not have done this, but would have said: "I wasn't here. Who was here? Where did he go? How did he get in?" Such remarks would have given rise to many things, which would have grieved the lady unnecessarily and would have given her occasion to desire at other times what she had just felt. Thus by keeping silent, he avoided shame, whereas by exclaiming he would have brought it on them. So, far more angry within than appeared by his face or words, the King replied:

"Do you think I am incapable of being with you once and then coming back to you again?"

Said the Queen: "No, Sire; but I beg you will consider your health."

To this the King replied: "I will follow your advice; and I will leave, without troubling you any further."

Filled with anger and fury on account of what he saw had been done to him, he took up his mantle and left the room, intending to find secretly the person who had done it. He knew the man must be some person of his own household and that, whoever he was, he could not have got away. So he lighted a very dim lantern and went to a long room in the palace built over the stables, where most of his servants slept in different beds. He considered that the man who had done what his wife had told him, would still have a beating heart and a rapid pulse; so, beginning at one end of the room, he went along feeling their hearts, so find out which was beating.

Everyone in the room was asleep, except the groom who had been with the Queen. He saw the King come into the room and that he was looking for somebody; and this created such fear in the groom that his heart beat faster than ever. He plainly saw that if the King perceived this, he would infallibly be killed without delay. Several possible things to do flashed through his mind, but when he noticed that the King was unarmed he determined he would pretend to be asleep, and would wait and see what the King did.

The King had touched many of them, but had found no one he thought was the man; but as soon as he came to the groom and felt the beating of his heart, he said to himself: "This is the man." But, as he did not want anyone to know about what he intended doing, the King did nothing to the man but took a pair of scissors he had with him, and cut off one side of his hair—which at that time was worn very long—so that he might recognise him next morning. After which, the King returned to his own room.

The cunning groom had noticed everything and at once perceived why he was marked. Without the least delay, he arose, found a pair of shears—of which there were several lying about in the room for use on the horses—went softly along to all those asleep in the room, and cut off part of the hair of each man in exactly the same way, just above the ear. After which, he went back to sleep, without anyone having noticed him.

Next morning the King arose and ordered all his servants to come into his presence before the gates of the palace were opened. When all were standing bare-headed before him, he began to look at their heads to find the man whose hair he had cut; but he was amazed to find that nearly all of them had their hair cut in exactly the same way. Whereupon the King said to himself: "The man I am looking for is of base condition, but he has his wits about him." The King saw that he could not get hold of the man he was looking for without a great disturbance, and, since he did not want to purchase a small revenge with a great shame, he determined to give him a word of warning and to show him that he was observed. So the King turned to them all and said:

"Let the man who did it never do it again, and go all of you in peace."

Another man would have racked them, tortured them,

questioned them, made investigations; and by doing so he would only have revealed what every man should try to keep secret. And, suppose he had discovered the man and taken full vengeance on him, he would not have wiped out his shame but would have greatly increased it, and would have damaged his wife's good name.

Those who heard what the King said were greatly surprised, and for a long time tried to discover what he had meant; but nobody understood it, except the one man for whom it was meant. And the groom, like a wise man, never revealed the secret during the King's lifetime, and never again risked his own life in such a bold deed.

## THIRD TALE

*Under pretence of confession and purity of conscience, a lady, who is in love with a young man, deceives a holy and unsuspecting friar into arranging the complete satisfaction of her pleasure*

After Pampinea was silent, several of the band praised the groom's courage and prudence as well as the King's wisdom; the queen then turned to Filomena and ordered her to follow next, whereupon Filomena began gracefully to speak as follows:

I intend to tell you of a trick played by a fair woman on a stupid friar, which will be the more pleasing to laymen since most of these monks are fools and men unpractised in manners and yet think themselves wiser and better than everyone else, whereas in fact they are far less so. You may see how stupid-minded they are by the fact that they cannot get on in the world like other men, but find out a refuge where they can obtain food, like pigs. This I shall tell you, charming ladies, not only to carry out our plan but to show you how the monks—in whom we credulously put too much faith—can be and sometimes are cleverly tricked, not only by men, but even by one of us women.

Not many years ago in our city—which contains more tricks than love or faith—there lived a gentlewoman endowed by nature with beauty and fine manners and high spirits and keen wits. Her name has no importance in this tale, and, although I know it, I do not intend to tell it, because there are still some people alive who would then be offended, whereas they will otherwise let it pass with a laugh.

This lady was of high birth, but married to a wool merchant. She despised him for being a merchant, because she thought that no man of low birth, however rich he might be, was worthy of a gentlewoman. Moreover, when she saw that, with all his wealth, he could do nothing but design a wool mixture pattern or weave cloth or argue about thread with a spinning-girl, she determined to accept no more of his embraces than she was compelled. For her own satisfaction she decided to find somebody whom she thought more worthy of her than the wool merchant; and thus she fell in love with a gentleman in the prime of life, to such an extent that if she did not see him during the day she could not sleep at night. But the gentleman did not notice it, and so paid no attention to her. She, on the other hand, was extremely cautious, and would not let him know either by letter or some female messenger, for fear of possible danger. Then she discovered that this gentleman frequented a friar who was considered a most worthy friar by everybody on account of his holy life, although he was a gross fat man; and she felt he would make an excellent go-between for her and her lover. After much thought as to how she should proceed, she went at a convenient hour to the church where he lived, sent a message to him, and told him that she wished to make her confession to him. The friar guessed she was a gentlewoman, and willingly listened to her. After she had made her confession, she said:

"Father, I have come to you for help and advice in the matter I am about to tell you. Since I have told you about them, you know my parents and my husband, who loves me more than life itself. He is a very rich man and can do what he likes, and always gives me immediately anything I want; for which reason I love him more than I love myself. Apart from anything I might do, I should deserve to be burned alive more than any other woman, if I even thought anything contrary to his honour and pleasure.

"Now, there is a man whose name I don't know, but he seems to be a gentleman and (if I am not mistaken) a great friend of yours, a tall handsome man, dressed in good brown clothes. Perhaps he does not understand my intentions, but he seems to have laid siege to me. If I go to the door or window or leave the house, he immediately appears; in fact, I am greatly surprised that he is not here now. This greatly distresses me, because such behaviour often brings unmerited disgrace on virtuous women.

"I have sometimes thought that I would speak of it to my brothers; but then I recollected that men sometimes deliver messages in such a way as to bring a sharp answer, which leads to words, and words lead to blows. To prevent misfortune and scandal I have kept silence and decided rather to speak to you about it, both because you are his friend and because it is your duty to reprimand such things even in strangers, as well as in friends. I beg that you will reprove him for this, and ask him not to continue in this way. There are enough other women quite ready for such things, who would be delighted to have him gaze at them and court them, which to me is most displeasing since I am entirely averse to such matters."

So saying, she lowered her head as if she were crying. The holy friar at once guessed rightly of whom she was speaking, and fully believed that what she said was true. He highly praised the lady for her virtuous intentions, and promised to act in such a way that she should have no further annoyance from the man. Then, as he now knew she was rich, he praised charity and alms-giving, and told her of his necessities. To which the lady said: "If he denies the thing, I beg you will let him know that I myself told you about it, and that I am distressed by it."

Having thus confessed and made her penitence, she recollected the friar's praise of alms-giving and deftly filled his hand with money, asking him to say masses for the souls of her dead relatives. After which, she arose and made her way home.

Not long afterwards the gentleman came to see the friar, as he was accustomed to do, and after they had talked about several different matters, the friar drew him to one side and courteously reproved him for his designs on the lady, as she had made the friar believe. The gentleman was greatly surprised, since he had never stared at her and very rarely passed her house. He began to justify himself, but the friar would not listen to him, and said:

"Don't pretend to be surprised and don't waste words in denying it, because you cannot do so. I did not hear about this from neighbours, but she told me herself, in great distress. Such nonsense is most unseemly in you; moreover, I can tell you that if ever a woman scorned such follies, she does. So, for your own honour and her satisfaction, stop, and leave her in peace."

The gentleman, who was smarter than the holy friar,

was not long in seeing the lady's shrewd device. He therefore pretended to be ashamed and said he would not meddle with her again. Leaving the friar, he walked towards the lady's house, where she was standing at a little window to see him if he passed by. When she saw him coming, she looked at him so graciously and gaily that he knew he had rightly understood the friar's words. From that day onwards, under pretext of other business, he continually but prudently went up and down the street, to his own pleasure and the great delight and satisfaction of the lady. But when the lady had found out that he liked her as much as she liked him, she was anxious to give him more proof of the love she felt for him; so, she returned to the holy friar, and, kneeling down at his feet, began to weep. The friar pityingly asked her what was the matter, and she replied:

"Father, the matter is that man accursed of God, your friend, of whom I complained the other day. I think he was born to be a thorn in my flesh, and to make me do something which will destroy my happiness, and make me unworthy ever to lay myself at your feet again."

"What!" said the friar. "Has he not stopped annoying you?"

"No, indeed," said the lady, "and since I complained to you, which perhaps he took in ill part, he seems to continue out of spite, and now every day passes the house at least seven times where he used to pass once. Would to Heaven that passing by and staring would suffice him, but he is so ardent and so impudent that yesterday he sent a woman to my house with a message and trinkets—a purse and a girdle, as if I needed purses and girdles! I took it so ill that if I had not considered the sin and also your friendship I should have raised an outcry, but I controlled myself and determined to do nothing about it until I had consulted you.

"Moreover, I had at first immediately given back the purse and girdle to the woman who brought them, and harshly dismissed her, telling her to take them back. But then I felt afraid that she would keep them for herself and tell him that she had given them to me, as I have heard such women sometimes do; so I called her back, and angrily snatched them out of her hand. I have brought them to you, so that you can return them to him, and tell him that I don't need such things, for, thanks to God and my husband, I have enough purses and girdles to suffocate him. You will pardon me, Father, but if he does not cease, I shall tell my husband and brothers, and let come what may. And if he must suffer, I had much rather he did, than that I should be blamed on his account. So there you are!"

She said all this with much weeping, and then from under her petticoat drew a rich, handsome purse and a fine, valuable girdle, and threw them into the friar's lap. The friar, believing all she said, was exceedingly angry, and said:

"Daughter, I am not surprised that these things anger you, nor can I reprove you, but highly praise you for having followed my advice. I reprimanded him the other day, and he has not carried out what he promised me. So, what between that and his new offence to you, I shall so warm his ears that he will annoy you no more. But, by the blessing of God, do not let yourself be so carried away with anger that you speak of this to any of your relatives, for great ill might come of it. And never fear that any blame will fall upon you; in the presence of God and man I shall always bear witness to your chastity."

The lady pretended to be a little comforted, and, knowing his avarice and that of others, turned to different topics, saying:

"Messer, last night I saw the spirits of several of my dead relatives, and it seemed to me that they were in great anguish and asked for alms, especially my mamma who seemed so afflicted and miserable that it was pitiful to see her. I think she suffers great pain at seeing me so distressed by this enemy of God, and therefore I wish you to say prayers and the forty masses of Saint Grigorio for their souls, so that God will remove them from penal fire."

So saying, she put a florin into his hand, which the holy friar most willingly took, and approved her devotion with many good words and devout examples. Then he gave her his blessing, and sent her away.

After she had gone, he failed to perceive that she had hoodwinked him, and sent for his friend. When the gentleman saw the friar was angry, he immediately guessed that he had a message from the lady, and so waited to hear what the friar would say. The friar repeated what he had said before, and added new and stronger reproofs, reprimanding him harshly for what the lady had said he had done. The gentleman, who did not yet see to what point the friar was coming, faintly denied having sent the purse and girdle so that the friar would not lose all faith in him if, by chance, the lady had given them to the friar. But the friar flew into a rage, and said:

"O wicked man! How can you deny it? Here they are, just as she returned them to me, with tears. See whether you recognise them."

The gentleman pretended to be greatly ashamed, and said:

"Yes, I do recognise them, and confess that I did wrong. But since I see what her intentions are, I swear to you that you shall never hear another word about this."

Then followed many words, and finally the silly friar gave his friend the purse and girdle. After many admonitions and requests that he would refrain from these things, the friar sent the gentleman away on receiving his promise.

The gentleman was delighted both by the certainty he felt that the lady loved him, and by the handsome gift. After he had left the friar he went to a place where he could prudently show his lady that he had received both gifts. This greatly pleased the lady, especially since she felt that her plot would succeed. To crown her labours she only needed her husband to go away; and not long afterwards it happened that her husband had to go to Genoa on business. The morning that he got to horse and rode away, the lady went to the holy friar, and after much weeping and wailing, said:

"Father, I tell you I can no longer endure this, but since I promised you the other day that I would do nothing without telling you, I have come to justify myself. You will see what reason I have to weep and complain when I tell you what your friend, that devil from hell, did to me a little before dawn this morning.

"I don't know by what ill luck he heard that my husband went yesterday morning to Genoa, but this morning at the time I mentioned your friend came into my garden and climbed up a tree to my bedroom window which looks over the garden. He had already opened the window and was getting into the bedroom when I awoke and jumped out of bed. I was about to scream for help when he besought my mercy for the love of God and yourself, telling me who he was. Whereupon, out of my friendship for you, I hearkened to him, and ran to the window as naked as when I was born and slammed it in his face. I think he then went away, for I heard no more of him. See for yourself whether such things are to be endured. For my part, I shall put up with them no longer, and I have already suffered too much out of my friendship for you."

When the friar heard this, he was as angry as a man can be, and did not know what to say, except that he several times asked her if she was quite certain it was not someone else. The lady replied:

"Praised be God, I can distinguish him from another. I tell you it was he and if he denies it, do not believe him."

Then said the friar:

"Daughter, there is nothing to say except that this is too much impudence and a most wicked attempt. You did your duty in sending him away as you did. But, since God has twice saved you from disgrace when you have followed my advice, I beg that you will once more do so, and allow me to act without complaining to your relatives. Let me see if I can curb this devil unchained, whom I thought a very saint. If I can manage to withdraw him from this vileness, all is well. If I cannot do so, I now give you permission, with my blessing, to do whatever your conscience tells you is right."

"Well," said the lady, "this time I will not anger or disobey you. But take care that he annoys me no more, for I promise you I shall never come to you again on this matter."

So saying, she left the friar abruptly, as if she were angry. She had scarcely left the church when the gentleman appeared and was called aside by the friar, who began to abuse him violently, calling him perfidious, perjurer and traitor. The gentleman, who had twice before learned whither the friar's reprimands tended, waited attentively and tried by ambiguous answers to make him speak out plainly, saying:

"Why this anger, Messer? Have I crucified Christ?"

Said the friar:

"O impudence! Hear what he says! He talks as if a year or two had passed and the lapse of time had made him forget his villainy and baseness. Have you forgotten how you outraged somebody this morning? Where were you a little before dawn?"

The gentleman replied:

"I don't know where I was. The news has soon reached you."

"It is true," said the friar, "that the news has reached me. I hear that you think that the lady ought to take you straight into her arms because the husband is away. Look, gentlemen, here's an honest man! What! So you've become a night-walker, a scaler of gardens and a tree-climber. Do you think that your importunity will overcome this saintly woman, and so climb up to her window by a tree at night? Nothing in the world is so displeasing to her as you, and yet you persist. Truly, apart from the fact that she has plainly showed it, you might have been reformed by my reproofs. Now, listen to me. Hitherto, not out of love for you but in consideration of my requests, she has kept silence about what you have done, but she will do so no longer. I have given her permission to do whatever she likes if you ever displease her again. What will you do if she tells her brothers?"

The gentleman now saw what he was to do, and soothed down the friar as best he could with many fair promises. The next night he entered the garden, climbed up the tree, found the window open, and was in his lady's arms as quickly as possible. She had been awaiting him with extreme desire and received him gaily, saying:

"Many thanks to messer friar, who showed you so well how to get here!"

After they had enjoyed each other, they talked and laughed over the stupidity of the silly friar, and spoke scornfully of wool-combers and carders and weavers, and gave each other mutual delight. And they so arranged matters that, without having to return to messer friar, they spent many another night together with the same joy. Unto which I pray God in His mercy soon to bring me and all other Christian souls who desire it.

## FOURTH TALE

*Don Felice shows Brother Puccio how to become a saint by carrying out a certain form of penance. This Brother Puccio does, and at the same time Don Felice enjoys himself with Brother Puccio's wife*

Filomena finished her tale, and Dioneo with honied words praised the lady's device and also the prayer uttered by Filomena herself at the end. The queen laughed, and looking at Pamfilo, said:

"And now, Pamfilo, continue our amusement with some pleasant tale."

Pamfilo immediately replied that he was quite willing, and began:

Madonna, there are many people who strive to go to

Heaven, and, without meaning to, send others there. And this, as you are about to hear, happened to a woman neighbour of ours not long ago.

According to what I have heard, there lived near San Pancrazio a good, rich man named Puccio di Rinieri, who, being given wholly to spiritual things, joined the Third Order of Saint Francis, and was called Brother Puccio. His whole household consisted of his wife and a maid servant and he had no need to work at any trade; for which reason, and because he cultivated the spiritual life, he was frequently at church. He was a foolish, thick-witted man, said his prayers, went to sermons, attended mass, never failed to be at Lauds where laymen sing, and fasted and whipped and pricked himself as if he had belonged to the flagellant orders.

His wife, Monna Isabetta, was a young woman of about twenty-nine or thirty, fresh and pretty and plump as a ripe apple. Owing to her husband's saintliness, and perhaps his age, she was often condemned to much more abstinence than she liked. When she wanted to go to sleep or perhaps to be a little jocose with him, he would tell her about the life of Christ and the sermons of Friar Nastigo or the lamentations of Mary Magdalen and similar things.

About this time there returned from Paris a monk named Don Felice, a brother of San Pancrazio, a handsome young man both intelligent and very learned, with whom Brother Puccio struck up a close friendship. Since the monk was able to remove easily all his doubts and, moreover, seemed to be a man of most holy life, Brother Puccio often brought him home to dinner or supper, as the case might be. And the wife was friendly to him and entertained him out of love for Brother Puccio.

As the monk continued to frequent Brother Puccio's house and saw how fresh and plump his wife was, he perceived what it was she lacked, and determined, if he could, to supply her with it, to spare Brother Puccio the trouble. He made cunning play with his eyes at her, and in a short time she felt the same desires that he felt; and, at the first opportunity after he was sure of this, the monk spoke to her. But, although he found her quite ready to complete the good work, they could discover no way to do it, because she would trust herself with the monk nowhere but in her own house, and there it was impossible because Brother Puccio never left the place. This made the monk very melancholy. But after much thought he hit upon a way to lie with the lady in her own house, without any suspicion, even though Brother Puccio was there all the time. So, one day, when he went to call on Brother Puccio, he said:

"I have often perceived, Brother Puccio, that your greatest desire is to become a saint. But it seems to me that you are taking the longest road, when there is a much shorter one used by the Pope and the great prelates, which they do not permit to be taught. The reason for this is that the clergy, who live chiefly upon alms, would be ruined, because the laymen would not then need to give them alms or anything else. But you are my friend and have done me much honour, I believe you would follow this rule and tell it to nobody else, and so I will teach it to you."

Brother Puccio immediately became most interested, and earnestly besought the monk to teach it to him, swearing that he would not tell anyone about it without the monk's consent, and promising that he would at once carry out the rule, if he could.

"Since you make this promise," said the monk, "I will tell you about it. Now, you must know that the holy Doctors of the Church hold that those who wish to become saints must perform the penance I am about to describe to you. But understand this correctly—I do not say that after this penance you will not be a sinner as you are now; but all the sins you have committed up till the time of this penance will be purged away and forgiven you, and the sins you commit afterwards will not be recorded to your damnation, but will be washed away with the holy water, as your venial sins are now.

"When a man begins this penance he must first of all confess his sins with the greatest diligence. After which he must start upon a severe fast and abstinence of forty days, during which time you must abstain, not only from other women, but even from your own wife. In addition to this, you must have some place in your house from which you can see the sky, and retire there at the hour of Complines. You must have a large table there, arranged so that you can rest your buttocks against it while your feet are on the ground and your arms stretched out as if on a crucifix. If you like to rest your arms on some support, you may do so. In this way you must remain gazing at the sky, without moving, until daylight. If you were a man of learning, you would need to repeat certain prayers which I would tell you; but, since you are not learned, you must say three hundred Paternosters and three hundred Ave Marias in honour of the Holy Trinity. And, as you gaze at the sky, you must ever keep God in mind, the Creator of heaven and earth, and think upon the Passion of Christ as you stand in the position He hung upon the cross.

"Then, when Matins ring, you can leave this place if you wish, and lie down on your bed in your clothes, and sleep. After that, you must go to church and hear at least three masses, and say fifty Paternosters and as many Ave Marias. After that you may go about any business you have with simplicity, dine, and remain in church until Vespers, when you must recite certain prayers which I shall give you in writing, without which the penance is worthless. And then at Complines, you must start all over again. If you do this, as I once did, I hope that when you come to the end of the penance you will feel a marvellous sense of eternal beatitude, if you have carried out the penance devoutly."

Then said Brother Puccio:

"This is neither too severe nor too long, and can easily be carried out. I shall begin on Sunday, in the name of God."

Brother Puccio went home, and, with the monk's permission, related everything to his wife. The lady at once understood the monk's intention in keeping Brother Puccio fixed all night in one place. It seemed to her a good plan, so she said she was glad of this and anything else he did for the sake of his soul, and added that, in order that God might make his penance profitable, she would fast with him, but not attempt the remainder.

They were thus all in accord, and when Sunday came Brother Puccio began his penance, and messer monk went to the lady as soon as it was too dark for him to be seen, and spent most of the night with her. They dined together, eating and drinking well, and then he lay with her until morning, when he got up and left, and Brother Puccio went to bed.

The place which Brother Puccio had chosen for his penance was beside the lady's bedroom, and only divided from it by a very thin wall. One night as messer monk was frolicking unrestrainedly with the lady, and she with him, Brother Puccio thought he felt the floor of the house shaking. So, having come to the end of his first hundred Paternosters, he halted, and without moving called to his wife and asked what she was doing. The lady was witty, and, as she was then riding the ass of San Benedetto, or rather of San Giovanni Gualberto, she replied:

"Faith, husband, I am tossing about as much as I can."

Said Brother Puccio:

"Why are you tossing about? What do you mean by tossing about?"

This excellent woman, who was laughing—and no doubt had excellent reasons for laughing—then said:

"How is it you don't know what I mean? I have heard you say a thousand times that those who have no supper toss about all night."

Brother Puccio believed that it was fasting which kept her from sleeping and made her toss about in bed, so in all good faith he said:

"Wife, I told you not to fast; but since you would do it, stop thinking about it and try to go to sleep. You are leaping about in bed so much that you make everything shake in here."

Then said the lady:

"Don't you trouble about that. I know quite well what I'm doing. You attend to what you are doing, which I would do if I could."

Brother Puccio was then silent, and went on with his Paternosters. But after that night the lady and messer monk made up a bed in another part of the house, wherein they lay together with the greatest delight as long as Brother Puccio's penance lasted.

Early each morning the monk went away, and the lady returned to her own bed, and a little later Brother Puccio came to the same bed from his penance. In this way the brother went on with his penance and the lady continued her pleasures with the monk, to whom she often said laughingly:

"You made Brother Puccio do the penance, and we have gone to Heaven!"

From the good food which the monk gave her, the lady perceived that her husband had long kept her on a meagre diet; so, when Brother Puccio's penance was over, she found means to dine with the monk elsewhere, and for a long time discreetly took her pleasure with him. And thus, to make my last words agree with my first, it came about that while Brother Puccio thought he was going to Heaven by doing penance, he sent to Heaven the monk who had showed him the way, and his own wife who had lived with him in great want of that substance which the monk in pity most abundantly gave her.

# FIFTH TALE

*Zima gives Messer Francesco Vergellesi one of his horses, on condition that he is allowed to speak in private to Messer Francesco's wife. She says not a word, but Zima answers himself for her; and things turn out in accordance with his replies*

Pamfilo finished the tale of Brother Puccio, with much laughter from the ladies; and then the queen ordered Elisa to follow next. She immediately began to speak sharply, not from malice but from long custom:

Many people who know a great deal think that other people know nothing at all; and often when they think they are hoodwinking others they afterwards discover that they have themselves been hoodwinked. Therefore I think it very foolish of anyone to match himself unnecessarily with another person's wits. But since everyone may not share my opinion I shall relate, since it is now my turn, what happened to a knight of Pistoia.

Among the family of the Vergellesi in Pistoia there was a knight named Messer Francesco, a very rich man, both wise and shrewd, but exceedingly mean. He had been named podestà of Milan, and had furnished himself with everything necessary for his journey, except that he could not find a horse good enough for him, and was in some perplexity.

At that time there was living in Pistoia a young man named Ricciardo. He was of humble birth but very rich, and went about so neatly and handsomely dressed that most people called him "Zima," or the Beau. For a long time he had been in love with Messer Francesco's most beautiful and virtuous wife, whom he had courted in vain. Now he happened to possess one of the finest horses in Tuscany, which he greatly valued for its beauty. Everyone knew that he was courting Messer Francesco's wife, and told Messer Francesco that if he asked for the horse, Zima would let him have it out of the love he bore the lady. Drawn by his avarice, Messer Francesco sent for Zima and offered to purchase the horse in the hope that Zima would give it to him. Zima was glad to hear of this, and said to the knight:

"Messer, if you gave me everything you have in the world, you could not purchase my horse from me. But, if you wish, you shall have him as a gift, on condition that before you take him I may say a few words to your wife, with your permission and in your presence, but at such a distance from anyone else that nobody can overhear what I say."

Urged on by his avarice and hoping to make a fool of the other man, Messer Francesco replied that he might say as much as he liked. Leaving Zima in the great hall of his palace, he went up to his wife's room, told her how easily he was obtaining the horse, and ordered her to come and hear what Zima had to say, but to take care that she made no reply whatever to anything he said. The lady greatly disapproved of all this, but as she was bound to carry out her husband's wishes, she said she would do so; and then went with her husband to the great hall to hear what Zima had to say. After confirming the bargain with the knight, Zima sat down with the lady in another part of the hall, at a distance from everyone else, and said:

"Most fair lady, I feel sure that you are keen enough to have known for a long time how much love I bear you, compelled to this by your beauty, which is certainly beyond that of any woman I ever saw. I say nothing of your noble manners and the singular virtues you possess, any one of which is sufficient to match the high spirit of any man. There is no need for me to tell you in words that my love is the greatest and most ardent that ever a man felt for any woman, and will continue as long as my wretched life supports these limbs, and even longer. And if you loved me as I love you, we should love for eternity. And therefore you may rest assured that you possess nothing, however vile or precious, which you can hold and count upon in every respect as upon me, whatever I may be worth, and upon everything I possess. To give you full proof of this, I tell you now that I should think it the greatest of favours if you would be pleased to command anything I can do to please you; for, I am sure that when I ordered it, the whole world would swiftly obey me.

"Therefore, since I am all yours as you hear me say, not undeservedly do I yearn to offer up my prayers to you on high, from whom alone and from no other can come all my peace, all my happiness and all my salvation. As your most humble servant I beseech you, my dear delight and the one hope of my soul, which, hoping in you, is nurtured in the fire of love, that your mercifulness may be so great and your former harshness to me (who am yours) so much softened that I may be comforted by your pity so that I may say that, since I fell in love with your beauty, so through your beauty do I receive life. If your lofty spirit does not bow to my prayers, my life will fade away, and I shall die, and you may be called my murderess. Apart from the fact that my death would do you no honour, I believe that your conscience would sometimes prick you for having done this, and that sometimes you would feel more kindly towards me, and say to yourself: 'Alas! How wrong I was not to pity my Zima!' And, as this repentance would be useless, it would but cause you the more pain.

"Wherefore, in order that this should not happen, I beseech you, while you can still help me, to have pity upon me rather than to let me die, for you alone can make me the happiest or most wretched of mankind. I hope that your graciousness will not permit me to receive death as the reward for so great a love, but that you will revive my spirits (now trembling with terror in your presence) with a gentle and favourable reply."

He was then silent, heaving several deep sighs and shedding a few tears, and waited for the lady's reply. The lady, who had hitherto been quite unmoved by the long courtship, the striving, the serenades and other such things which Zima had done for her sake, was now touched by the ardent words of her eager lover, and began to feel what she had never felt before—love. In obedience to her husband's order, she remained silent, yet she could not check a little sigh which showed what she would gladly have replied to Zima. He was surprised to find, after waiting a short time, that she made no answer, and then began to realise the trick played upon him by the knight. But as he gazed into her face he saw a light in her eyes as she looked at him from time to time; moreover he noticed the sighs which gently came from her breast, and so took hope again. Hope made him resourceful, and so, while the lady listened, he began to answer himself, as if she were speaking, as follows:

"Dear Zima, of course I have long perceived that your love for me is great and perfect, and your words to me today make it plainer than ever. I am glad of your love, as I ought to be. Yet, however harsh and cruel I have been to you, you must not think that what I feel for you in my heart is what appeared in my face. I have always loved you and held you dearer than any other man. But I have had to behave as I have done, from fear of others and to keep my reputation. But the time has now come when I can plainly show you that I love you, and reward you for the love you bore and bear me. So, cheer up, and be of good hope, since Messer Francesco is going as podestà to Milan in a few days, as you know, for you have given him your beautiful horse for love of me. When he has gone away, I promise you faithfully, by the love I bear you, that in a few days you shall be with me, and we will enjoy a complete and delicious fulfillment of our love.

"I shall not be able to speak to you about this again, so when you see two towels hanging out my bedroom window, which looks over the garden, come that night to me at the entrance to the garden, and take good care you are not seen. You will find me there waiting for you, and we will spend the whole night together in delight and pleasure with each other, as we desire."

When Zima had spoken in this way on behalf of the lady, he replied in his own person:

"Most dear lady, my whole soul is so filled with supreme joy at your gracious answer that I am scarcely able to give you fitting thanks. If I could speak as I wish, no amount of speech would suffice for me to thank you fully as I should like and as I ought to do. So I leave it to you to imagine all that I am unable to express in words. This only I will say, that I shall certainly carry out what you have ordered me to do. Perhaps I shall then be more emboldened by the great favour you have granted me, and I shall try as much as I can to return you the greatest thanks possible. Now there is nothing more to be said at present. And so, my dearest lady, God grant you happiness and the good things you most desire; and so I commend you to God."

For all this, the lady said not a word. Zima then arose and walked towards the knight, who, seeing him advancing, also stood up and came towards him laughing, and said:

"Well? Have I kept my promise?"

"No, messer," said Zima, "you promised I should speak with your wife, and you brought me to talk to a marble statue."

These words greatly pleased the knight, and gave him an even higher opinion of his wife's virtue than he had had before. He said:

"Well, the horse that was yours is now mine."

"Yes, messer," replied Zima, "but if I had known that the

favour I asked was to bring such meagre fruit, I would have given you the horse without asking for the favour in return. But God willed that I should do so, and thus you have bought the horse while I have not sold him."

The knight only laughed at this. Being thus fitted with a horse, he set out for his governorship of Milan a few days later.

The lady was left alone in the house, and kept thinking about what Zima had said to her and about his love for her and the horse he had given for love of her. And as she saw him continually passing by the house, she said to herself: "What am I about? Why should I waste my young years? My husband has gone to Milan and will not be back for six months, and when will he ever make up for them? When I am an old woman? Besides, when shall I ever find such a lover as Zima? I am alone, and there is nobody to be afraid of. I don't know why I don't enjoy this good time while I can. I shall never again have such an opportunity. Nobody will ever know it. And if it ever should come out—better to do it and repent of it, than not do it and repent."

After this discussion with herself, she one day hung two towels at the window overlooking the garden, as Zima had said. And when Zima saw them, he was overjoyed. That night he came secretly and alone to the entrance into the lady's garden, and found the gate open. From there he went on to another door which opened into the house, where he found the lady awaiting him. When she saw him, she arose and greeted him with the greatest delight, and he went with her up the stairs, embracing and kissing her a hundred thousand times. Without any delay they went to bed, and enjoyed the last limits of love. Nor was this first time the last, for, as long as the knight was in Milan, and after his return, Zima came to her many and many a time, with the greatest pleasure to them both.

## SIXTH TALE

*Ricciardo Minutolo falls in love with the wife of Filippello Fighinolfi. He discovers she is jealous of her husband and tells her that Filippello is going to lie with Ricciardo's wife in a bagnio. She goes there, thinks she is lying with her husband, but finds it was Ricciardo*

Elisa had no more to say; and the queen, after praising Zima's cleverness, ordered Fiammetta to tell the next tale. She smilingly replied: "Willingly, Madonna," and so began:

Sometimes it will be good to get away from our own city, although it has abundance of everything and produces types of every subject, and, as Elisa has done, to relate what has happened in other parts of the world. Therefore I shall shift the scene to Naples, and tell you how one of these prudes—who are so rebellious to love—was led by her lover's cunning to taste the fruit of love before she knew its flowers. And this will warn you of things which might happen and give you pleasure in those which have occurred.

The very ancient city of Naples is perhaps the most delightful of all Italian towns. There once lived in it a young man named Ricciardo Minutolo, renowned for the nobility of his blood and the splendour of his wealth. Although his wife was a charming and most beautiful girl, Ricciardo fell in love with another woman who, in everyone's opinion, was far more beautiful than any of the other Neapolitan ladies. She was named Catella, the wife of a gentleman named Filippello Fighinolfi, whom she most chastely loved beyond everything else.

Ricciardo Minutolo, being in love with this Catella, did everything which can be done to gain the love and favour of a lady; but since all this failed to gain him the least part of what he desired, he fell into despair. He could not get free from his love, and could neither die nor take any pleasure in life. While he was in this state of mind, certain ladies among his relatives urged him to abandon this love, telling him he laboured in vain because Catella cared for nobody but Filippello, of whom she was so jealous that she feared every bird of the air would take him away from her.

When Ricciardo heard of Catella's jealousy, he suddenly thought of a way to satisfy his desires. He began to pretend that he despaired of getting Catella's love and that he had fallen in love with another lady, for whom he gave serenades and jousts and did everything which he had formerly done for Catella. Before very long almost all the Neapolitans, including Catella, believed that he had ceased to love her and was deep in love with the other lady. He persevered so much, and everyone was so thoroughly convinced, that even Catella abandoned the frigidity she had opposed to his love, and greeted him as a neighbour in a friendly way when they happened to meet, just as she greeted other men.

In the hot weather many knights and ladies made up groups, according to the Neapolitan custom, to make holiday at the sea shore, and to dine and sup there. Ricciardo, knowing that Catella had gone to the seaside with her friends, also went with his friends, and was invited to join the group of Catella and her women friends, after he had first let himself be urged as if he did not particularly want to stay. The ladies, including Catella, soon began to jest with him about his new love, which he pretended was very great, and so gave them the more chance to talk. At length, some of the ladies went one way and some another, as usually happens in such places, and Catella was left with Ricciardo and a few ladies. Ricciardo then let drop a jest about some love affair of her husband, which immediately aroused Catella's jealousy, and made her burn with desire to know what Ricciardo meant. In a little time her self-restraint gave way, and she begged Ricciardo, by his love for the other lady, to make clear to her just what he meant about Filippello. Said Ricciardo:

"You have implored me in the name of a person for whose sake I cannot refuse anything you ask me. I am ready to tell you, but you must promise me never to say a word about it to him or anyone else until you have seen for yourself that what I say is true. And, whenever you like, I will show you how you can see it."

The lady agreed to this request which made her believe more than ever that what he said was true, and swore that she would never speak of it. Ricciardo then took her aside, so that the others could not overhear them, and spoke as follows:

"Madonna, if I still loved you as I once did, I should not be eager to tell you something which I feel must give you pain; but, since that love is over and gone, I do not mind telling you the whole truth. I do not know whether Filippello was ever annoyed by my love for you or whether he thought you were in love with me—in any case, I myself never showed him anything—but now, having perhaps bided his time until I was less likely to be suspicious, he is trying to do to me what I think he feared I did to him; which is, to have his pleasure of my wife. According to what I hear, he has been very secretly urging her to this by messages for some time, all of which I have been showed by my wife who has returned him the answers I have dictated.

"This morning, just before I started out, I found my wife in close consultation with a woman, whom I immediately guessed to be what she was. I called my wife, and asked her what the woman wanted of her, and she said: 'This woman is Filippello's go-between, whom you made

to carry my replies and give him hopes; and she says that
he wants to know what I mean to do, and that, whenever I
like, I can meet him secretly in a bagnio here. He begs and
worries me to do this. If you had not made me keep up
this correspondence—I don't know why—I would have got
rid of him in such a way that he would never have looked
at me again.' I then thought that this was going too far and
could no longer be endured, and I felt I must tell you about
it, so that you might know how he rewards your fidelity,
which was nearly the cause of my death.

"In order that you might not think all this empty words
and fables, and to give you the chance of seeing and touching the truth whenever you wanted, I made my wife answer
the waiting messenger that she was ready to come to the
bagnio tomorrow, at Nones, when everyone is asleep. The
messenger went off, delighted with this answer. Now, I do
not suppose you think I shall let my wife go; but if I were
you, I should arrange for him to find you there instead of
her. When he has lain with you, let him know with whom he
has been, and honour him in a befitting way. If you do this,
I think he will be so much ashamed that you will avenge
at one and the same time the injuries he is trying to do
both you and me."

Catella listened eagerly to all this, without considering
who was talking to her or noticing his deceits, and like all
jealous people immediately believed what he said, and began
to twist certain things which had happened to fit in with
this tale. In a rage she said she would certainly do what he
suggested, since it was no great trouble, and that if he did
come she would make him so much ashamed that he would
always remember it whenever he saw another woman. Ricciardo was delighted at this, and felt his plot was a good one
and proceeding well. He urged her on with much more talk,
and, to strengthen her belief, begged her never to say that
she had heard about it from him, which she faithfully promised.

The next morning Ricciardo went to the woman who kept
the bagnio he had mentioned to Catella, told her what he
intended to do, and asked her to help him as much as she
could. The woman, who was under great obligations to
him, said she would gladly do so, and arranged with him
what she was to do and say. In this bagnio she had a room
which was very dark, since it had no window to let in the
light. In accordance with Ricciardo's instructions, she prepared this room and made up a bed in it as well as she

could; and after he had dined, Ricciardo got into this bed and waited for Catella.

The lady, who had listened to Ricciardo and believed what he said more than she ought to have done, returned home full of anger. It happened that Filippello came home in a preoccupied mood, and did not treat her as affectionately as usual. She noticed this, and became more suspicious than ever, saying to herself: "He is thinking about that woman, with whom he thinks he shall have delight and pleasure tomorrow, but he shall certainly not have it." With this in her mind, she lay awake nearly all night, wondering what she should say to him in the bagnio.

What more? At Nones, Catella took her attendant, and, without changing her plan, went to the bagnio Ricciardo had told her about. There she found the woman, and asked her if Filippello had been there that day. Following Ricciardo's instructions, the woman said:

"Are you the lady who was to come here to speak to him?"

Catella replied:

"I am."

"Then," said the woman, "go to him in there."

Catella, who was looking for something she would not be glad to find, let herself be taken to the room where Ricciardo was lying, entered with her head wrapped in a veil, and locked the door. Seeing her come in Ricciardo sprang to his feet joyfully, clasped her in his arms, and said softly:

"How good that you have come, my delight!"

To pretend that she was the other woman, Catella embraced and kissed him and caressed him, without uttering a word, for fear he would recognise her if she spoke. The room was very dark, which pleased both parties; nor did they remain gazing at each other for long. Ricciardo led her to the bed and there, not speaking in such a way that she would recognise his voice, lay with her for a very long time with the greatest delight and pleasure to them both. But when Catella thought the time had come to show her fury, she began to speak angrily, as follows:

"Ah! How wretched is the fate of women, and how illplaced is the love of many of them in their husbands! Alas! Alas! I have loved you more than my life for eight years; and you, as I have just felt, are burned and consumed with love for another woman, vile and wicked man that you are. Whom do you think you have been lying with? You have lain with her whom you have deceived with false flatteries, pretending love to her when you are in love with another.

"Faithless betrayer, I am not Ricciardo's wife, I am Catella. Listen, and you will recognise my voice, and know I am she. It seems to me a thousand years until we can be in the light and I can shame you as you deserve, you filthy disgraceful hound. Oh! Alas! Whom have I loved all these years with such love? You, you treacherous hound, who, thinking you held another woman in your arms, have given me more caresses and amorous pleasures in this short time than in all the rest of the time we have been together.

"You were ardent enough here today, you renegade hound, while in your own home you are weak and tired and impotent. Thank God, you have been ploughing your own field and not another man's field, as you thought. I am not surprised that you didn't come near me last night. You were waiting to unload yourself elsewhere, and you wanted to come into battle a very fresh soldier. Thanks to God and my wits, the water has flowed into the right channel. Why don't you say something, vile man? Why don't you answer? Have you become dumb listening to me? By God's faith, I don't know what keeps me from thrusting my fingers into your eyes, and tearing them out. You thought you were very secret in carrying out this betrayal. Ah! God! One person is as wise as another. It didn't turn out as you thought. I had better arms round your neck than you thought."

Ricciardo was inwardly greatly amused by these words, but made no reply; he kept embracing and kissing her and caressing her more than ever. So, continuing her denunciations, she went on:

"Oh! Yes! You now think you can deceive me with your feigned caresses, you importunate hound, and console and pacify me. I shall never be consoled for this until I have denounced you in the presence of all our relatives and friends and neighbours. You wicked man, am I not as beautiful as Ricciardo Minutolo's wife? Am I not as much a lady? Why don't you answer, filthy hound? What has she got more than I have? Move over there, don't touch me, you have done enough feats of strength for one day. Now that you know me, I am quite sure everything you did to me would be forced. But, by God's grace, I will yet make you starve for it. I don't know what keeps me from sending for Ricciardo, who loved me more than himself, and could never boast that I even looked at him once. I don't know what ill there would be in it. You thought you had his wife here, which is as good as if you had had her, since it was your intention. If I had him, you could not blame me."

Many were her words, and great was the lady's complaining. At last Ricciardo began to think that if he allowed her to go away with these beliefs, great ill might follow; he therefore decided to speak and undeceive her. So, taking her tightly in his arms and holding her so that she could not escape, he said:

"My sweet soul, do not be angry. What I was unable to achieve by simply loving you, Love has taught me to obtain by guile—I am Ricciardo."

Recognising his voice as he spoke, Catella immediately tried to throw herself out of bed, but could not. She then tried to scream, but Ricciardo clapped one of his hands on her mouth, and said:

"Madonna, it is now too late to alter what has happened if you were to scream for the rest of your life. If you scream or if in any way you ever allow anyone to know about this, two things will happen. The first (which is of some importance to you) is that your honour and reputation will be destroyed, because when you say that I got you here by guile, I shall say that it is not true and that I got you here by promising you money and gifts, and that you became angry and made this disturbance and invented your story because I did not give you as much as you hoped. You know quite well that people are more ready to believe evil than good, and so they will more easily believe me than you. In addition to which, there would be mortal enmity between your husband and me, and matters might so turn out that I should kill him or he me; and thus you would never be happy or contented again.

"And so, heart of my body, do not at one and the same time injure yourself and put your husband and me into mortal danger and dispute. You are not the first woman and will not be the last who has been tricked; I did not deceive you to rob you of your reputation, but from the sovereign love I have for you; and I am prepared always to have for you the same love and to become your most humble servant. For a long time, I and everything I possess or can do or am worth have been yours and at your service; and I mean that henceforth they shall be yours more than ever. Now, you are a wise woman in other matters, and I am certain you will be wise in this."

While Ricciardo was talking, Catella wept bitterly and uttered many reproaches in her anger, but reason gave so much weight to the true words spoken by Ricciardo that she saw that what he said might possibly happen. So she said:

"Ricciardo, I do not know how God will help me to bear the injury and deceit you have done me. I will not scream here, where I have been brought by my own simplicity and extreme jealousy. But be certain that I shall never be happy until in one way or another I have revenged myself for what you have done to me. You have had what you desired, and you have ill-treated me as much as you liked. It is now time to leave me. Leave me, I beg you."

Ricciardo, who saw how angry she was, had determined not to leave her until he had made his peace with her. So with the most honied words he humbled himself before her, and said so much and begged her so hard and besought her until at last she was overcome and made her peace with him. And with equal good will on both sides they lay together again for a long time with the greatest delight. The lady then found how much more savoury a lover's kisses are than those of a husband, and her harshness towards Ricciardo was changed into tender love for him. From that time forward she loved him most tenderly and by skilful arrangement they often enjoyed their love together. God grant that we may enjoy ours!

## SEVENTH TALE

*Tedaldo quarrels with his mistress and leaves Florence. Some time later he returns disguised as a pilgrim; he talks with his mistress and shows her how she was in error, liberates from death his mistress' husband who was condemned for having killed Tedaldo, and reconciles him with his brothers. Thereafter he wisely enjoys himself with the lady*

Fiammetta was silent as they all praised her, when the queen, anxious to lose no time, gave the word to Emilia, who began thus:

It pleases me to return to our city, whereas the last two tale-tellers were pleased to depart from it, and to tell you how one of our fellow citizens regained his lost mistress.

In Florence there lived a noble young man, named Tedaldo degli Elisei, deeply in love with a lady named Monna Ermellina, the wife of Aldobrandino Palermini; and on account of his eminent virtues he fully deserved to enjoy his desires. But Fortune, the enemy of the happy, soon opposed this pleasure. Whatever the reason may have been, the lady for a time was charmed with Tedaldo, and then suddenly turned round and refused to listen to any messenger he sent her and even to see him at all. Consequently Tedaldo fell into deep melancholy and disgust, but this love of his was so much concealed that nobody knew it was the cause of his melancholy.

He laboured hard in different ways to regain the love which he had lost through no fault of his, but, finding all his efforts vain, he determined to leave the country and not give her—the cause of his woes—the satisfaction of seeing him waste away. He got together what money he could and, without saying a word to any of his friends and relatives except one intimate companion who knew the whole story, he secretly went to Ancona under the name of Filippo di Sanlodeccio. There he met with a rich merchant, whose service he entered and with whom he sailed to Cyprus. Tedaldo's manner and behaviour so much pleased this merchant that he not only paid him a good salary, but made him his partner and left a large part of his business to Tedaldo's care; and Tedaldo worked so hard and so skilfully that in a very few years he became a rich and famous merchant. During these occupations he often remembered his cruel lady and was pierced with love and greatly desired to see her again; but such was his strength of mind that for seven years he conquered in this battle.

One day in Cyprus he heard someone singing a song he had himself made in the past, telling of the love he felt for his lady and her love for him and the delight he had in her, and he felt that she could not have forgotten him. And there came upon him so great a desire to see her again that he could not withstand it, and made ready to return to Florence. He set all his affairs in order and went to Ancona with only one servant. There he collected all his wealth and sent it to a friend of his partner in Florence, while he followed with his servant, disguised as a pilgrim returning from the Sepulchre. When he reached Florence, he went to a small inn kept by two brothers, which was near his mistress' house. The first place he went to was her house, in order to see her if possible. But he found all the doors and windows shut, which made him suspect that she was dead or had moved away. He returned pensively to the inn, and there to his great surprise saw four of his own brothers in mourning. Knowing that he was so greatly changed from what he had been when he went away that he was not easily recognisable, he went confidently to a shoemaker and asked him why these men were dressed in black. The cobbler replied:

"They are dressed in black because one of their brothers named Tedaldo was murdered about a fortnight ago. I have been told that they have proved in Court that he was murdered by one Aldobrandino Palermini (who is in prison) because this brother was in love with his wife and had returned in disguise to be with her."

Tedaldo was greatly surprised that anyone should so much resemble him as to be mistaken for him, and he was grieved at Aldobrandino's misfortune. He learned also that the lady was alive and well. It was now night, and he returned to his inn, full of various thoughts; and, after he had dined with his servant, he was given a bedroom at the top of the house. Either he was kept awake by his thoughts or by the uncomfortable bed or perhaps by the bad supper he had eaten, but half the night had worn away and still Tedaldo had not fallen asleep. As he lay awake he heard some people enter the house under the roof, and then saw a light through the crack of the door. He went softly up to the door and peeped through the crack to find out who they were, and saw a handsome girl holding the light, and three men coming down from the roof towards her. After they had greeted her, one of the men said:

"Thank God, we can now feel safe, for we now know for certain that the death of Tedaldo Elisei is proved against Aldobrandino Palermini by Tedaldo's brothers. He has confessed it, and the sentence is recorded. But we must keep quiet, for if it were known that we are here, we should be in the same danger as Aldobrandino."

After saying this to the girl, who seemed delighted to hear it, they came down and went to bed. Tedaldo, after hearing this, began to think of the many errors which may come into men's minds, reflecting first on his brothers who had wept over and buried a stranger in his place, and then on the innocent man accused of a false suspicion and condemned to death by false witnesses. He then thought of the blind severity of the laws and their administrators, who in their eager investigation of the truth, often by their cruelty, prove something which is false, and while they call themselves ministers of justice and God are the workmen of iniquity and the devil. He then turned his thoughts towards saving Aldobrandino, and decided what he would have to do there.

He got up in the morning, left his servant behind, and

went alone to his mistress' house. By chance he found the door open, went in, and found his mistress sitting on the floor of a little room weeping and bewailing, which almost made him weep with pity. He went towards her, and said:

"Madonna, do not lament; your peace is at hand."

Hearing this, the lady raised her head and said in tears:

"Good man, you seem to me to be a foreign pilgrim; what do you know of peace or of my woe?"

The pilgrim replied: "Madonna, I am from Constantinople, and I have just arrived as a messenger sent by God to change your tears into mirth and to rescue your husband from death."

"If you are from Constantinople," said the lady, "and have only just arrived, how can you know about me and my husband?"

The pilgrim then told her the whole story of Aldobrandino's suffering, informed her who she was, how long she had been married, and many other things which he knew perfectly well. The lady was so much surprised by this that she took him for a prophet and fell at his feet, beseeching him in God's name to hurry if he had come to save Aldobrandino, for time was short. The pilgrim, pretending to be a very holy man, said:

"Madonna, arise and do not weep, pay attention to what I am about to say, and take care not to speak of it to anyone. God has revealed to me that your present tribulation is due to a sin you committed, which God has willed that you should purge in part by this trouble, and that you should wholly amend. If not, you will fall into even worse distress."

Then said the lady:

"Messer, I have committed many sins, and I do not know which of them I should amend rather than another. If you know, tell me, and I will do what I can to make amends."

"Madonna," said the pilgrim, "I know quite well which sin it is, and I ask you about it, not to be informed myself, but to make you remember it. But let us come to the point. Tell me, do you remember ever to have had a lover?"

When the lady heard this, she heaved a deep sigh and was greatly amazed, for she thought nobody had ever known about it, although since the murder of the man who had been buried as Tedaldo there had been some talk about it, owing to certain words incautiously let drop by the friend of Tedaldo who knew about it. And so she replied:

"I see that God has revealed all men's secrets to you, and so I am ready not to conceal my own from you. It is true that in my youth I loved the unfortunate young man whose death has been laid upon my husband. His death has grieved me so much that I have bitterly wept for it; for, although I was harsh and cruel to him before he went away, yet neither his departure nor his long absence nor his unhappy death could remove him from my heart."

Said the pilgrim:

"You never loved the unfortunate young man who is dead, but you did love Tedaldo Elisei. But tell me—why were you angry with him? Had he ever offended you?"

To this the lady replied:

"Indeed, he never did anything to offend me, and the reason for my harshness was the talk of a cursed friar to whom I once made my confession. When I told him of my love for this young man and of the intimacy between us, the friar made such a hubbub about it that I was terrified. He told me that if I continued I should go straight into the devil's mouth in the depths of hell, and be burned in penal fire. This frightened me so much that I determined to be intimate with him no longer. To avoid all temptation, I refused his letters and messages. I suppose he went away in despair, but if he had persevered a little longer I think I should have changed my harsh resolution towards him as I saw him wasting away like snow in the sun, for I desired nothing more than to be friends with him again."

Said the pilgrim:

"Madonna, this is the sin which now torments you. I know certainly that Tedaldo never forced you to anything. When you fell in love with him, you did so of your own free will, and he was glad of it. At your request, he came to you and was intimate with you, wherein you showed him so much affection both by words and deeds that, if he loved you first, you increased his love a thousandfold. If that was so (and I know it was) what could induce you to withdraw your love so harshly? Such things should be considered beforehand, and when you think you might repent of them, as of ill doing, you should not do them. Thus, even as he became yours, so you became his. When he was not yours you could do anything you pleased, since it only concerned yourself; but to take yourself away from him when you were his was an unseemly thing, a robbing of him, for it was against his will.

"Now, you must know that I am a friar and so know all about their habits; since it is for your good, I shall speak openly and not deny what I should deny to others. I am glad to speak of them to you, so that henceforth you may know them better, which you do not seem to have done in the past. At one time the friars were good and holy men, but those who call themselves friars today and wish to be esteemed as such have nothing of the friar about them but their gowns. And even their gowns are not friarly, because the founders of the friars ordered their gowns to be scant and poor and made of poor stuff, to show that in their spirit they despised all temporal goods by clothing their bodies in such base garb, whereas the friars of today have ample, full glossy gowns of the finest stuffs, which they have developed into an elegant and pontifical shape. Dressed in these gowns they are not ashamed to strut about like peacocks in churches and squares, showing off their clothes like laymen. Just as the fisherman tries to catch as many fish from the stream as possible with one cast of his net, so these friars give their greatest attention to snaring and entangling in the wide folds of their robes all the bigots and widows and other silly men and women they can get hold of. To speak truth, they do not even wear friars' gowns, but only the colour of their gowns. Where their predecessors desired men's salvation, the friars today want wealth and women. They give their whole thought to frightening the minds of silly people with noise and paintings and to telling them that sins are purged by almsgiving and masses. They say all this because they became friars, not out of devotion, but from baseness of soul and to avoid working, and because some people send them bread and others wine and others their portion of meat, for the souls of their deceased relatives.

"It is certain that sin is purged away by prayer and almsgiving; but if those who give alms saw or knew the persons they were giving to, they would much rather keep the money themselves or throw it to pigs. Because they know how inferior the possessors of great wealth are to other men (for they live in greater comfort), every friar labours with sermons and terrifying threats to isolate a rich man from others, so that he alone may be intimate with the wealthy. The friars denounce men's lust, so that when the denounced are cleared away the women will be left to the denouncers. They condemn usury and ill-gotten gains, so that when restitution is made to them, they can make larger gowns and procure bishoprics and other possessions greater than those which they asserted would lead their owners to damnation.

"When they are reproved for these and many other indecent actions, they reply: 'Do as we tell you, and not as we do,' thinking this a complete discharge of the most grievous charges, as if the sheep could be more constant and steadfast than the shepherds! And a large number of the friars know quite well that many of those to whom they make this reply do not understand it in the sense they mean it. When the friars of today tell you to do what they say, they want you to fill their purses, let them know your secrets, be chaste and patient, forgive injuries and refrain from evil-speaking—all good, honourable, holy things. But what is their motive? Simply that they may do those things which they could not do if the laymen did them. Who does not know that laziness cannot exist without money? If you spent your money on your own pleasures, the friar could not be idle in his Order. If you lay with the women you know, the friars would not have them. If you were not patient and forgiving of injuries, the friar would not be so anxious to come to your house to corrupt your family. But why do I go into all these details? Every time the friars make the excuse, 'Do as we tell you, not as we do,' they condemn themselves in the sight of all intelligent people. If they think they cannot be virtuous and abstain from wrong, why do they not stay in their cloisters? Or if they wish to be virtuous, why do they not follow the holy words of the Gospel: 'Then Christ began to act and to teach'? Let them first do good actions, and then admonish others. With my own eyes I have seen hundreds of them who were visitors, lovers, seducers, not only of lay women, but of nuns. And yet these friars make the greatest noise about this in the pulpits. Are these the men to whom we should confess? Those who do so, do as they please, but God knows if they act wisely.

"But, let us grant that the friar who denounced you was right when he said it was a most deadly sin to break matrimonial faith. Is it not much worse to rob a man? Is it not much worse to murder him or to send him wandering about the world in exile? Everyone will grant that. For a woman to lie with a man is a natural fault; to rob or kill or drive him away comes from wickedness of spirit.

"I showed you just now how you robbed Tedaldo by depriving him of yourself after you had become his of your own free will. I tell you moreover that, as far as you are concerned, you killed him; when you were so cruel to him it was not your fault that he did not kill himself with his own hands. And the law declares that he who is the cause of wrong is as guilty as he who actually commits wrong. You cannot deny that you were the cause of his exile and of his wandering about the world for seven years. Thus, by every one of these three things, you committed a far greater sin than by lying with him. But let us look more closely— perhaps Tedaldo deserved these things? He certainly did not. You yourself have confessed it, and I know that he loved you more than himself.

"No one was ever so much honoured, praised, commended as you were, above all other women, by him whenever he could do so honourably and without creating suspicion. He placed in your hands all his possessions, all his honour, all his liberty. Was he not a young noble? Was he not as handsome as any of his fellow citizens? Was he not accomplished in all things appertaining to young men? Was he not beloved? Was he not held dear? Was he not welcomed by all men? You will not deny all this.

"How then could you take such a cruel resolution against him, simply through the talk of a silly, stupid, envious friar? What is this error in women which makes them reject men and hold them in slight esteem? Whereas, women should remember what they themselves are, and how God has given man more nobility than any other animal, and should be proud when any man loves them, and hold him most dear, and take the greatest pains to please him, so that they may always be beloved. You know what you did at the instigation of a friar, who must certainly have been some fat-witted glutton, trying to worm himself into the place from which he strove to eject another.

"Divine justice, which weighs everything in exact scales and brings all things to a fitting end, would not allow this sin of yours to go unpunished. Without reason you withdrew yourself from Tedaldo; and therefore your husband is in danger without any fault in him and you are in great grief, on account of Tedaldo. If you desire to be freed from this, you must make me a promise and keep it. You must promise that if ever Tedaldo returns here from his long exile, you will restore to him your favour, your love, your kindness and your intimacy, and set him back exactly in the position he was in before you so foolishly listened to that raving friar."

The lady listened most attentively to the pilgrim's words, for his reasoning seemed to her most exact, and she felt convinced that she was now in trouble on account of the sin he described. So she said:

"O friend of God, I know that what you say is true, and I perceive from your explanation what these friars are, whom I have hitherto thought to be so saintly. I frankly admit that my fault was great in what I did to Tedaldo, and if I could, I would gladly make amends in the manner you say. But how can I do so? Tedaldo can return here no more. He is dead. Therefore, I do not see why I should promise to perform something which cannot be done."

Said the pilgrim:

"Madonna, Tedaldo is not dead, as God has revealed to me, but is alive and safe and sound, if only he may recover your favour."

Then said the lady:

"Beware what you are saying. I saw him lying dead at my door stabbed through and through; I held him in these arms and shed many a tear on his dead face, which perhaps caused the malicious talk about all this."

Said the pilgrim:

"Madonna, in spite of what you say, I assure you Tedaldo is alive. And when you make the promise I demand, I hope you will soon see him."

The lady replied:

"This I do and will do gladly. Nothing could make me so happy as to see my husband released without harm, and Tedaldo alive."

Tedaldo then thought it time to give the lady some comfort by speaking out, and more certain hope for her husband. So he said:

"Madonna, to give you some hopes for your husband I must tell you a secret, which you must be careful never to reveal."

They were alone in a remote room, and the lady had the fullest confidence in the sanctity of the man she thought was a pilgrim. Tedaldo then produced a ring which he had most zealously kept, because the lady had given it to him the last night he had lain with her; and said:

"Madonna, do you know this ring?"

The lady recognised it as soon as she saw it, and said:

"Yes, Messer, I gave it to Tedaldo in the past."

The pilgrim then stood up, swiftly threw off his hat and gown, and, speaking in Florentine dialect, said:

"And do you know me?"

As soon as she saw him, the lady recognised Tedaldo, but was as much terrified as if she had seen dead men walking about like the living. She did not greet him as Tedaldo returned from Cyprus, but in her fear turned to flee as if he were Tedaldo returned from the grave. But Tedaldo said:

"Have no fear, Madonna, I am your Tedaldo, alive and well. I was never dead, as you and my brothers thought."

The lady was partly reassured, partly frightened by his

voice, but after looking more closely at him and finding
that he really was Tedaldo, she threw herself weeping on
his shoulder, and kissed him, exclaiming:

"My sweet Tedaldo, how glad I am you have come back!"

After embracing and kissing her, Tedaldo said:

"Madonna, this is not the time for more intimate greetings. I must go and see that Aldobrandino is released safe
and sound, of which I hope you will hear good news before
tomorrow evening. If, as I hope, I have good news of his
safety, I shall come to see you tonight, and can then tell you
all about myself more fully than I can now."

Putting on his pilgrim's hat and gown, he kissed the lady
once more and cheered her with hopes, and then departed.
He then went to the prison where Aldobrandino was sadly
thinking more of his imminent death than of any hopes of
safety. With the permission of the gaolers, Tedaldo was allowed to give Aldobrandino spiritual comfort. He sat
down beside him, and said:

"Aldobrandino, I am a friend, sent to save you by God,
Who has had pity upon your innocence. Therefore, if in reverence to God you will grant me a small gift I ask of you,
I promise you without fail that tomorrow evening you shall
hear your acquittal, instead of the sentence of death you
expect."

Aldobrandino replied:

"Worthy man, since you are earnest to save me, you must
be a friend, as you say, although I do not know you and
do not remember ever to have seen you. Indeed I never
committed the crime for which men say I should be condemned to death. I have committed other sins, which perhaps have brought me to this pass. But in all reverence to
God I say that, if He now is merciful to me, I will both
promise and perform, not only a small thing, but a great
thing. If I escape, I will do anything you please to ask of
me."

Then said the pilgrim:

"The only thing I want is that you will forgive Tedaldo's
four brothers for having brought you to this pass, in the
belief that you had murdered their brother, and that you
will receive them as brothers and friends when they come
and ask your pardon."

Said Aldobrandino:

"Only he who has been injured knows how sweet a thing
is revenge and with what ardour it is desired. Nevertheless,
since God designs my escape, I will gladly pardon them,
and do now pardon them. If I escape alive and free from

here, I will act in such a way in this matter that you shall be satisfied."

This delighted the pilgrim, who, without revealing anything more to him, urged him to be of good heart because he would undoubtedly hear certain news of his safety before the next day was over. Leaving Aldobrandino, Tedaldo then went to the Signoria, and went secretly to a knight who was in charge, and said:

"My lord, every man should labour for the truth to be made known, above all those who hold the position you hold, in order that those who have not sinned may go free and that sinners may be punished. In honour of you and in hatred of those who have deserved punishment, I have now come to you that justice may be done. As you know, you have proceeded with rigour against Aldobrandino Palermini, you think you have proved that he murdered Tedaldo Elisei, and you are about to condemn him to death. I believe this to be entirely false, and before midnight I think I can put into your power the men who murdered the young man."

The worthy man, who was sorry for Aldobrandino, gladly lent an ear to what the pilgrim said. After they had discussed the matter together, by Tedaldo's means the two inn-keepers and their servant were arrested without resistance while in their first sleep. When threatened with torture to get at the truth of the matter, the prisoners could not face it, but each separately and all together confessed that they were the murderers of Tedaldo Elisei, who was personally unknown to them. When asked the reason, they said:

"Because when they were absent from the inn he had insulted the wife of one of them and had tried to force her to lie with him."

After this, with the knight's permission, the pilgrim departed, and went secretly to Madonna Ermellina's house. There he found everyone had gone to bed except his mistress, who was equally anxious to hear good news of her husband and to be fully reconciled with her Tedaldo. When he arrived, he said with a cheerful face:

"My dearest lady, be happy, for tomorrow you will certainly have your Aldobrandino here safe and sound."

And then he related fully what he had done, in order to convince her thoroughly. The lady was wildly happy at these two events which had happened so close together, for she once more saw Tedaldo alive after she had wept him as dead, and she saw Aldobrandino set free from danger when she believed that in a few days she would have to weep his death also. She embraced and kissed Tedaldo affectionately, and then they went to bed together, and in all good will made a merry and gracious peace pact, each enjoying delicious pleasure with the other. When morning came, Tedaldo arose and told his mistress what he intended to do, and once more warned her to keep everything secret. Then he left the lady's house in his pilgrim's garb, so that he could be present when Aldobrandino was released.

When day came the Governor, who had obtained full information about the case, immediately set Aldobrandino at liberty, and shortly afterwards hanged up the malefactors by their necks in the place where they had committed the murder. Aldobrandino, being set free, to his own great joy and the delight of his wife and all his friends and relatives, recognised that this was the work of the pilgrim, and therefore took him home to stay with them as long as he chose to remain in the city. And once there, they could not sufficiently honour him, especially the lady who knew who he really was. After a few days he thought it was time to reconcile his brothers with Aldobrandino, for he heard they were not only scorned on account of his escape, but were in arms for fear of him. And so he asked Aldobrandino to carry out his promise, which he said he was perfectly ready to do. The pilgrim therefore arranged a great banquet for the next day and told Aldobrandino that he wished him and his relatives and all their wives to receive the four brothers and their wives, adding that he himself would go to them immediately and invite them on his behalf to this banquet and peace pact.

Since Aldobrandino fell in with everything the pilgrim suggested, the latter immediately went to the four brothers and urged upon them the natural reasons which would occur to anyone in such a situation, so that at least he had little difficulty in persuading them to ask Aldobrandino's pardon and to request his friendship. He then invited them and their wives to dine with Aldobrandino the next day. And, having the security of his pledged word, they freely accepted the invitation.

Next day at dinner time, Tedaldo's four brothers, all dressed in black, came with their friends to the house where Aldobrandino was awaiting them. There, in the presence of all those whom Aldobrandino had invited, they cast their weapons on the floor and placed themselves in Aldobrandino's hands, beseeching his pardon for what they had wrought against him. Aldobrandino received them with tears, kissed each one on the mouth and spoke a few words to each, and so pardoned all injuries they had done him. After them came their sisters and wives, all dressed in brown, and were graciously received by Madonna Ermellina and the other ladies. Both men and ladies were magnificently served in the banquet, wherein everything was praiseworthy, save only one thing—the silence which resulted from the recent mourning still represented by the dark clothes of Tedaldo's relatives. Indeed, some people on this account blamed the pilgrim's arrangement and banquet, of which he was quite aware. Therefore, when he thought the time had come to remove this mourning, he stood up while they were still eating dessert, and said:

"One thing only is lacking to the gaiety of this feast— the presence of Tedaldo. He has been with you the whole time, although you have not recognised him, and I shall now show him to you."

He threw off his gown and all his pilgrim's garb, and appeared in a suit of fine green silk. Everyone gazed long at him in amazement, before they could really believe that he was Tedaldo. Seeing their incredulity, Tedaldo related to them many things concerning family affairs, and what had happened to them and to him. This convinced his brothers and the other men, who ran to embrace him with tears of joy, and so did all the ladies, whether they were his relatives or not, save only Monna Ermellina. Aldobrandino noticed this, and said:

"Ermellina, what does this mean? Why do you not greet Tedaldo like the other ladies?"

To this the lady replied so that all could hear:

"There is no one I would greet more willingly, for I am more indebted to him than to any other man, since it was he who saved you for me. But I am restrained by the malicious words spoken in the days when we wept over the man we thought was Tedaldo."

Said Aldobrandino:

"Away! Do you think I believe in such yappers? By labouring to save me, Tedaldo has proved that this was false, although I never at any time believed it. Get up at once, and embrace him."

The lady, who asked nothing better, was not slow to obey her husband. She got up, as the others had done, and embraced and thanked him. Aldobrandino's generosity delighted Tedaldo's brothers and every man and woman present; and any suspicion created in their minds by the things which had been said in the past was entirely swept away. When everyone had thus made much of Tedaldo, he

himself stripped the mourning garments from his brothers
and sisters and other relatives, and ordered other clothes to
be brought for them. When these arrived, they sang and
danced and amused themselves, so that the banquet, which
had begun in silence, ended in merry noise. Then they all,
just as they were, accompanied Tedaldo to his own house
with the greatest joy, and dined there that evening. And in
this way they kept up their rejoicings for several days.

For some time the Florentines looked upon Tedaldo as a
man risen from the dead and a nine days' wonder. Many of
them, including even his brothers, still felt a tiny doubt in
their minds as to whether he really was Tedaldo, and perhaps this might have lingered a long time if something had
not occurred to bring to light the identity of the man who
had been murdered. It happened in this way. One day some
men from Lunigiana passed by their house and saw Tedaldo;
whereupon they immediately went up to him and said:

"Good health to Faziuolo."

Tedaldo, in the presence of his brothers, said to them:

"You have made a mistake."

They were confused when they heard him speak and
asked his pardon, saying:

"Indeed, no two men ever resembled each other so
closely as you resemble a friend of ours, named Faziuolo da
Pontremoli, who came to Florence about a fortnight ago
or more, and of whom we have heard no news whatever. It
is true that we were surprised by your clothes, for he was
only a soldier of fortune, as we are."

When Tedaldo's elder brother heard this he immediately
asked them how Faziuolo had been dressed. They told
him, and it turned out that the dead man had been dressed
exactly as they said. What with this and other proofs, it was
fully recognised that the murdered man was Faziuolo and
not Tedaldo. And after this all suspicion vanished from his
brothers and everyone else.

Tedaldo, who was now a very rich man, persevered in his
love. The lady was never angry with him again, and, as they
acted most discreetly, they long enjoyed their love together. May God so allow us to enjoy ours!

# EIGHTH TALE

*Ferondo eats a certain powder and is buried as if dead. The Abbot, who is in love with his wife, takes Ferondo out of his grave, puts him in prison and makes him believe he is in Purgatory. He is resurrected and brings up as his own a child begotten on his wife by the Abbot*

When Emilia came to the end of her long tale—which displeased nobody by its length, but was considered by them all to have been told very briefly considering the quantity and variety of events treated—the queen made a sign to Lauretta, who began as follows:

Most dear ladies, I wish to tell you about a true event, which seems much more like fiction than what we have just heard. It has come into my mind through hearing about a man who was bewailed and buried in mistake for another man. I shall tell you, then, how a living man was buried for dead, and how he himself and many others believed that he was resurrected from the grave and not alive all the time; and how a man was adored as a saint in consequence, when he ought rather to have been punished.

There was in Tuscany a certain monastery, such as we see many to this day, in a place unfrequented by men. A certain monk was made Abbot, and he was a most holy man in every respect, except the usage of women. But he acted so cautiously in this respect, that nobody knew or even suspected it; so that he was held to be a most holy and just man in all things.

It happened that this Abbot was very friendly with a rich farmer, named Ferondo, a heavy and very stupid man, whose company was only pleasing to the Abbot because he sometimes amused himself with the man's stupidities. This Ferondo had a very beautiful wife, with whom the Abbot fell so much in love that he could think of nothing else day or night. But he almost fell into despair when he discovered that Ferondo, although simple-minded and stupid in other respects, was most alert in loving his wife and guarding her from others. The Abbot went to work so skilfully, however, that he persuaded Ferondo to come with his wife to sit in the abbey garden. There the Abbot talked to them most devoutly of the blessedness of eternal life and the holy works of divers men and women, so much so that the wife wished to have him as her confessor, and got permission from Ferondo to do so. The woman therefore came to make her confession to the Abbot, to his great delight, and sat down at his feet as if she had come to say something else, and began thus:

"Messer, if God had given me a different husband or had not given me one at all, perhaps it would be easy for me to enter, under your instruction, upon that path which you told us leads other people to eternal life. But when I think how stupid Ferondo is, I feel I may call myself a widow; and yet I am a married woman, and can take no other husband while he is alive. Fool as he is, he is so unreasonably and excessively jealous of me that I can only live with him in trouble and misfortune. So, before I come to confession, I beg you in all humility to give me your advice about this, because it will be of small avail for me to confess or perform other good works unless I can do something about my husband."

This speech filled the Abbot's soul with joy, for he felt that Fortune had opened up the way to his greatest desire; so he said:

"My daughter, I consider it a great misfortune that a beautiful and delicate woman like you should have a fool for a husband, and still more so a jealous man. Since your husband is both, I can easily believe what you say. To speak briefly, the only advice or remedy I can see is that Ferondo shall be cured of his jealousy. I know quite well what medicine will cure him, but you must keep quite secret what I shall tell you."

Said the lady:

"Have no hesitation, Father; I would rather die than say anything you told me not to say. But how can this be done?"

The Abbot replied:

"If we want him to be cured, it is absolutely necessary for him to go to Purgatory."

"And how can he go there alive?" said the lady.

Said the Abbot:

"He will have to die and so go to Purgatory, and when he has endured sufficient punishment to be cured of his jealousy, we shall make certain prayers to God to bring him back to life, and this God will do."

"Then," said the lady, "I shall have to remain a widow?"

"Yes," replied the Abbot, "for a certain time, during which you must not marry anyone else, for God would be angry, and when Ferondo came back you would have to return to him, and he would be more jealous than ever."

Said the lady:

"If only he is cured and I do not have to stay always in prison, I am content. Do as you please."

"I will do so," said the Abbot, "but what reward shall I have from you for this service?"

"Father," said the lady, "anything you please that is in my power. But what can a woman like me do for such a man as you?"

"Madonna," said the Abbot, "you can do as much for me as I am about to do for you. Just as I am ready to do what will be for your good and comfort, so you can do something to save my life."

"If that is so," said the lady, "I am quite ready."

"Well," replied the Abbot, "will you give me your love and make me happy with you, for I am burning with love for you?"

The lady replied in great amazement:

"Oh! Father! What is this you ask for? I thought you were a saint! Is it seemly that holy men should ask such things of women who come to ask their advice?"

Said the Abbot:

"My sweet soul, do not be surprised. Sanctity is not diminished by this, because sanctity resides in the soul, and this is a sin of the body. But in any case, your delicious beauty has such power over me that love compels me to do this. You should be more proud of your beauty than other women, because it delights holy men who are accustomed to see the beauties of Heaven. Besides, although I am an Abbot, I am a man like other men, and you can see I am not yet old. You should not find any difficulty in doing this, but you should rather desire it, because while Ferondo is in Purgatory, I shall come to you at night and give you the pleasures he ought to give you. Nobody will ever know about it, for everyone thinks I am as holy as you thought until just now. Do not refuse the favour which God sends you, for many a woman would eagerly desire what you may have and will have, and would wisely listen to my advice. Besides, I have some beautiful and valuable jewels which I mean shall be yours. So, my dear hope, do for me what I gladly do for you."

The lady hung her head and did not know how to refuse and yet thought it wrong to accept. The Abbot, seeing she had listened to him and hesitated to reply, went on talking to her and before he finished had convinced her that it was right to do what he asked. At last she said shamefacedly that she was ready to do what he wanted, but that she could not do anything until Ferondo was in Purgatory. To this the Abbot joyfully replied:

"We will arrange for him to go there immediately. See that tomorrow or the next day he comes to me."

And so saying, he nimbly put a most beautiful ring into her hand, and dismissed her. The lady, delighted with this gift and in full expectation of others, returned to her companions and told them marvels about the Abbot's sanctity, as they went home together.

A few days later Ferondo went to the abbey, and as soon as the Abbot saw him he determined to send him to Purgatory. He possessed a powder of marvellous virtue which he had received from a great Prince of the Levant, who asserted that this powder was used by the Old Man of the Mountain when he wished to put anyone asleep and send him to Paradise and then bring him back. According to the quantity administered, the person who took it slept a shorter or longer period without any harm, and as long as its virtue lasted everyone would swear the person who took it was dead. The Abbot measured out enough powder to make a man sleep three days and mixed it in a glass of rather cloudy wine in his cell. Ferondo drank this, without noticing anything amiss, and the Abbot then took him to the cloister, where he and his monks began to amuse themselves with Ferondo's foolish sayings. He had not been there long when the powder began to work and there came upon him so sudden and irresistible a desire to sleep that he began to sleep as he stood, and suddenly fell down in a deep sleep.

The Abbot pretended great distress at this accident, made them loosen his clothes, called for cold water to throw on his face, and attempted other remedies for bringing him out of his swoon, as if he thought Ferondo was suffering from a disturbance of the stomach or some other illness. When the Abbot and the monks saw that nothing brought him to, they felt his pulse and found it motionless, so that they all believed him to be dead. They sent to tell his wife and relatives, who all came immediately; and, when the wife had bewailed him for a time, the Abbot had him put into a tomb dressed in all his clothes. The lady returned home, and declared that she would never leave a little boy she had had by Ferondo, and took over the control of Ferondo's child and possessions.

There was a Bolognese monk who had come from Bologna that day and was deep in the Abbot's confidence. That night they got up secretly and together lifted Ferondo out of his grave and carried him to a large, completely dark tomb which was used as a prison for erring monks. There they undressed him and reclothed him as a monk, laid him on a heap of straw and left him until he should regain consciousness. The Bolognese monk, informed by the Abbot of what had to be done, waited there for Ferondo's recovery, without anyone else knowing anything about what was going on.

The next day the Abbot and some of his monks paid a visit of condolence to the lady, whom they found all dressed in black and lamenting. After cheering her up, the Abbot boldly asked her to keep her promise. The lady, who was now free and without the hindrance of Ferondo, said she was ready, especially as she saw another valuable ring on the Abbot's finger, and agreed that he should come to her that night. The Abbot accordingly dressed himself in Ferondo's clothes and went to her, accompanied by the Bolognese monk. He lay with her until dawn in the greatest delight and pleasure, and then returned to the abbey; and often repeated the journey on a similar errand. As he went to and fro, he sometimes met one or other of the inhabitants, who thought he was Ferondo's ghost haunting the countryside as a penance. There was much talk of this among the common people of the village, and more than once news of it was brought to the wife, who knew better what the apparition was.

When Ferondo recovered his senses and began to wonder where he was, the Bolognese monk went into the tomb, exclaiming in a terrifying voice, seized him and beat him with a birch. Ferondo yelled and wept, and kept shrieking:

"Where am I? Where am I?"

"You are in Purgatory," replied the monk.

"What!" exclaimed Ferondo. "Am I dead, then?"

"Of course you are," said the monk.

Ferondo then began to lament for himself and his wife and his child, uttering the most absurd things imaginable. The monk then brought him something to eat and drink, whereupon Ferondo said:

"Oh! Do the dead eat?"

"Yes," said the monk, "what I bring you was yesterday brought to the church by the woman who was your wife, for masses to be said for your soul; and God has willed that it should be handed on to you."

Then said Ferondo:

"God be good to her! I bore her such good will before I died that I held her all night in my arms and did nothing but kiss her, and did something else to her whenever I wanted."

Then, as his appetite was sharp set, he began to eat and drink. But, as he thought the wine rather bad, he said:

"God punish her for not giving the priest the wine from the cask next the wall!"

When he had eaten, the monk seized him again and gave him another severe thrashing with the same birch. Ferondo yelled again, and asked.

"But why do you do this to me?"

Said the monk:

"God has commanded that it shall be done to you twice a day."

"But why?" said Ferondo.

"Because you were jealous," said the monk, "although your wife was the best woman in the district."

"Alas! You say truly," said Ferondo, "and the sweetest. She was as sweet as honey, but I never knew that God did not like a man to be jealous, or I shouldn't have been jealous."

"You ought to have known it before," said the monk, "and have amended your life. If you ever happen to return to life, remember what I am now doing to you, and never be jealous again."

"Do those who die ever return to life?" said Ferondo.

"Yes," said the monk, "if God wills it."

"Oh!" said Ferondo. "If I ever return to life, I shall be the best husband in the world. I'll never beat her, I'll never say anything unkind to her—except about the wine she sent me yesterday, and because she didn't send me a candle, so that I had to eat in the dark."

"She did send one," said the monk, "but it was burned at the mass."

"Oh!" said Ferondo. "You say truly. Certainly, if I ever return, I will let her do what she likes. But tell me, who are you?"

Said the monk: "I also am dead. I came from Sardinia, and because I praised my lord and master on account of his jealousy, God has condemned me to this punishment. I am to give you food and drink and beat you, until God decides what next shall be done with us."

"Is there nobody here but us?" asked Ferondo.

"Thousands," said the monk, "but you cannot see or hear them, nor can they see and hear you."

"How far are we from the village?" asked Ferondo.

"Ho!" said the monk. "Hokey-pokey abracadabra thousands of miles!"

"Faith," said Ferondo, "that's a long way. We must be right out of the world, it's so far."

With these and similar conversations, with eating and beating, Ferondo was kept in prison ten months, during all which time the Abbot continued to visit the lady scot-free, and enjoyed himself thoroughly with her. But, as misfortune would have it, the lady became pregnant, and as soon as she found it out, told the Abbot. They both decided that Ferondo must be brought back from Purgatory to life as soon as possible and return to her, and that she must say she was pregnant by him. Next night the Abbot called to Ferondo in his prison, and said in a counterfeited voice:

"Ferondo, be of good cheer. It has pleased God that you shall return to the earth. When you get back, you will have a son by your wife, and you shall call his name Benedetto, because this favour is granted you on account of the prayers of your holy Abbot and of your wife, and for love of San Benedetto."

Ferondo was overjoyed to hear this, and said:

"Glad indeed am I. God be good to the Lord God and to the Abbot and to San Benedetto and to my dear, sweet, honey wife!"

The Abbot mixed in the next wine he sent Ferondo enough of the powder to make him sleep for about four hours, dressed him in his own clothes again, and then with the monk's help secretly put him back in the tomb where he had first been buried. At dawn next morning, Ferondo awoke and saw, through a crack in the tomb, a ray of light, which he had not seen for ten months. He thought he had come to life again, and began to shout: "Let me out! Let me out!", beating his head so hard against the lid of the tomb that he moved it, for it was not very heavy, and began to climb out. The monks who were saying matins ran up and recognised Ferondo's voice, and saw him climbing out of the tomb. They were so terrified by the unexpectedness of the event that they fled in horror, and went to tell the Abbot. He pretended to have just risen from prayer, and said:

"Fear not, my sons; take the cross and the holy water, and come with me, and let us see what God's omnipotence has to show us."

Ferondo was very pale when he got out of the tomb, since he had not seen the light for ten months. When he saw the Abbot, he ran to his feet, and said:

"Father, it was revealed to me that your prayers and the prayers of San Benedetto and my wife have released me from the pains of Purgatory and brought me back to life; wherefore I pray that God may be good to you now and every day and always."

Said the Abbot:

"Praised be the omnipotence of God! Go, my son, since God has sent you back to life, and console your wife who, ever since you departed this life has dwelt in tears; and henceforth be the friend and servant of God."

"Messer," said Ferondo, "leave it to me; when I get at her, I'll kiss as much as I want!"

When the Abbot was left alone with his monks, he pretended to be greatly amazed by all this, and made them devoutly sing the Miserere. Ferondo returned to his house, and everyone who met him fled from him as a thing of horror, but he called out to them and vowed he was risen from the dead. His wife was also afraid of him. But when people were a little reassured about him and saw that he was alive, they kept asking him questions, as if he had come back a wise man. He answered everything, gave them news of the souls of their departed relatives, and told them the most marvellous tales of what had happened to him in Purgatory, and then before everyone he related the revelation made to him through the mouth of the "Hangel Gubriel" before he was resurrected. He returned home with his wife and took possession of all his property, and, as he thought, made her pregnant. As chance would have it, at exactly the right time according to the opinion of those fools who think a woman carries a child exactly nine months, the lady produced a boy baby, who was named Benedetto Ferondi.

Ferondo's return and the things he said made nearly everyone believe that he was resurrected from the dead; which greatly increased the fame of the Abbot's sanctity. Ferondo, who had received many a beating for his jealousy, was cured of it, and, as the Abbot had promised the lady, was never jealous any more. The lady was so pleased that she lived chastely with him as of old, but in such a manner that, whenever she could, she rejoined the holy Abbot who had served her so well and diligently in her greatest need.

# NINTH TALE

*Giletta di Nerbona heals the King of France of a fistula.
In reward she asks for Beltramo di Rossiglione as her
husband, who marries her against his will, and goes off
to Florence in contempt of her. There he falls in love
with a girl, whom Giletta impersonates, and in this way
lies with him and has two children by him. Whereby she
becomes dear to him and he recognises her as his wife,
to the great joy of everyone*

When Lauretta's novel was over, only the queen was left to
tell a tale, if Dioneo's privilege was to be respected. So,
without waiting to be urged by her subjects, she began to
speak as follows:

Who can ever tell a tale to equal Lauretta's? It was an
advantage to the others that she was not first, for then few
would have been pleased with them; yet I hope that those
which remain to be told today will also give pleasure. But,
however that may be, I shall tell you the story which I have
thought of, to illustrate the given subject.

In the realm of France there lived a gentleman, named
Isnardo, Count of Rossiglione, who, because he was sickly,
always retained near him a doctor named Master Gerardo
di Nerbona. The Count had an only son named Beltramo,
a handsome and charming boy, who was brought up with
other children of his age, among whom was the Doctor's
daughter, Giletta. This girl felt an infinite love for Beltramo, far beyond her tender years. When the Count died,
Beltramo was left as the King's ward, and had to go to
Paris; which left the girl very disconsolate. Not long afterwards her own father died, and, if she could have found
any plausible pretext for going to Paris, she would most
willingly have gone there to see Beltramo. But since she
was rich and alone in the world, she was most strictly
guarded, and could find no reasonable pretext. When she
reached marriageable age, Beltramo still remained in her
memory and she refused many men to whom her relatives
would have liked to marry her, without ever saying why.

Thus, as she was more than ever consumed with love for

Beltramo, who (she heard) had become a most handsome young man, news arrived that the King of France was afflicted with a fistula, which had resulted from unskilful treatment of a tumour on his chest. The fistula caused him the greatest annoyance and pain, and no Doctor had been found to treat it properly; for, although many Doctors had tried, not one had been able to cure it, and all had made it worse. So the King in despair refused all further advice and treatment. This news greatly pleased Giletta, who thought that it not only gave her a reasonable pretext for going to Paris but that, if the illness were what she thought, she might easily obtain Beltramo as her husband.

She had learned much about such things from her father, and therefore made a powder from certain herbs which cured the disease she believed the King to be suffering from; and then took horse and rode to Paris. The first thing she did was to devise means of seeing Beltramo, after which she managed to get admittance to the King and asked him as a favour to allow her to see his fistula. Since she was a young and charming girl, the King could not refuse, and showed it to her. When she had examined it, she knew at once that she could cure it, and said:

"Sire, whenever you are pleased to permit it, I am sure I can cure you of this illness in a week (with God's help), and you will have neither pain nor trouble."

The King inwardly was amused at her words, and said to himself: "How can a young woman know what the greatest Doctors in the world do not know?" He thanked her for her good intentions, and replied that he had determined never to follow a Doctor's advice again. Then said Giletta:

"Sire, you scorn my skill, because I am young and a woman. But I must tell you that I am not a Doctor from my own knowledge, but with the aid of God and the knowledge of Master Gerardo Nerbonese, my father, a famous Doctor when he was alive."

Then the King said to himself: "Perhaps she is sent me by God. Why should I not try what she can do, since she says she can cure me without pain in a short time?" And, being ready to give her a trial, he said:

"Young lady, suppose you do not cure me and thus break our agreement, what penalty will you agree to?"

"Sire," replied the girl, "put me under guard. If I do not cure you in a week, have me burned. But if I cure you, what reward shall I have?"

"You seem to me unmarried," replied the King, "if that is so, I will marry you well and nobly."

Said the girl: "Sire, I am happy that you should marry me, but I want the husband I shall ask for, except that I shall not ask for one of your sons or any of the royal family."

The King immediately gave her his promise. The girl then began her treatment, and in a short time the King was perfectly cured. And when the King saw he was well again, he said:

"Young lady, you have well earned your reward."

"Then, Sire," she replied, "I have earned Beltramo di Rossiglione, whom I began to love in my childhood and have loved deeply ever since."

The King felt this was a great gift to make her, but since he had promised and would not break his word, he sent for Beltramo and said to him:

"Beltramo, you are now grown up and your education complete. I now wish you to return home and to oversee your district, and to take with you a young lady whom I have chosen as your wife."

"And who is the lady, Sire?" said Beltramo.

"The girl who cured me of my illness," replied the King.

Beltramo, of course, knew her well, and when he had recently seen her had thought her beautiful, but scorned marrying her since he knew her family was not noble like his. He said:

"Sire, then you give me a she-Doctor as a wife? Please God, such a woman shall never be my wife."

Then said the King:

"Then you wish me to break the faith I pledged to the girl if she cured me? She has asked for you as her reward."

"Sire," said Beltramo, "I am your man, and you can take from me all I have, and give me to whomsoever you please; but I tell you plainly that I shall never be satisfied with such a marriage."

"Yes, you will," said the King, "because the girl is beautiful and sensible and loves you deeply Therefore I hope you will live a much happier life with her than you would have with a woman of nobler family."

Beltramo was silent, and the King gave orders to make great preparations for the wedding feast. When the appointed day came Beltramo married her against his will, and in the presence of the King married the girl, who loved him more than herself. After this, he did what he had made up his mind to do—he took leave of the King, saying that he intended to return to his home and there consummate the marriage. But, when he got to horse, he did not return home, but went to Tuscany. There he heard that the Florentines were at war with the Sienese, and determined to join them. The Florentines received him honourably and joyfully, made him captain of a certain number of troops and paid him well, so that he remained for some time in their service.

The new wife was not much pleased with all this, but, hoping to bring him home by her good behaviour, she went to Rossiglione, where she was received by all as their lady. When she arrived she found everything ruined and in disorder, owing to the long period when there had been no Count there; and, like a sensible woman, she set everything in order with great diligence. Her subjects were greatly pleased by this, and held her very dear and in great esteem, condemning the Count because he was not satisfied with her. When the lady had thus set the whole estate in order, she sent two knights to the Count to inform him of it, and to say that if he did not wish to return home he begged he would tell her so and that she would come to him wherever he wished. To this Beltramo returned the following harsh reply:

"Let her do as she likes about that. I will never return to her until she can show me this ring on her finger and my child in her arms."

He prized the ring highly and never parted from it, because he had been told that it contained some occult virtue.

The knights saw the impossibly hard conditions he imposed and found that nothing they could say would shift him; so they returned to their lady and gave her the message. She was greatly grieved by this and after much thought determined to find out whether and where these two conditions could be satisfied, so that she might have her husband back. Having decided what she would do, she called together the best and most important men of the district, and in piteous words related to them what she had done for love of the Count, and what had been the result. She finally said that she did not intend to keep the Count in perpetual exile, by living on his estate herself, and that therefore she meant to pass the remainder of her life in pilgrimages and good works for the salvation of her soul. She begged them to take over the guard and governorship of the district and to inform the Count that she had gone away and left him in free possession, and intended never to return to Rossiglione again.

As she spoke, the good men shed tears, and then earnestly besought her to change her mind and stay with them.

But they entirely failed. She commended them to God, furnished herself with money and valuable jewels and, without knowing where she was going, set out with a cousin and a waiting-maid in the dress of pilgrims, and never paused until she reached Florence. There she chanced upon a little inn, kept by a good widow, and lived there quietly as a poor pilgrim, eager to hear news of her husband. It happened that the very next day she saw Beltramo and his company pass by the inn on horseback, and although she easily recognised him, she asked the good woman of the inn who he was. The inn-keeper replied:

"He is a foreign gentleman, named Count Beltramo, a courteous pleasant man, much beloved in this town. He is wildly in love with a neighbour of mine, who is a gentlewoman but poor. She is a most chaste girl and is not yet married on account of her poverty, but lives alone with her good, prudent mother. Perhaps, if the mother were not there, she would before now have done the Count some pleasure."

The Countess listened most carefully to all this, and after thinking over every detail and grasping firmly the whole situation, she made up her mind what she would do. She found out the house and the name of the lady whose daughter was beloved by the Count, and one day went there secretly in her pilgrim's garb. She found the lady and her daughter in very poor circumstances, and after greeting them, she told the mother that she wished to speak to her at her convenience. The gentlewoman rose, and said she was ready to listen to her. They then went into a room alone together and sat down, and the Countess began as follows:

"Madonna, it seems to me that you are among Fortune's foes. So am I. But, if you wish, you may be able to help both yourself and me."

The lady replied that she desired nothing better than to be able to aid herself honestly. The Countess went on:

"I must have your pledged word. And if I put my trust in you and you deceive me, you will ruin yourself and me too."

"Tell me with confidence anything you wish to say to me," replied the lady, "and you will never be betrayed by me."

The Countess then told her who she was, and beginning from the time when she first fell in love, related everything that had happened down to the present day in so moving a manner that the gentlewoman fully believed her, especially as she had already heard part of the story from others, and began to pity her. After telling her all this, the Countess went on:

"You have heard among all my other troubles, what are the two things I must have if I am to have my husband. And I do not know anyone who can help me to get them except yourself, if what I hear is true—that the Count, my husband, is deeply in love with your daughter."

"Madonna," said the gentlewoman. "I do not know whether the Count loves my daughter, but he makes a great show of doing so. But what can I do to help you to obtain what you want?"

"Madonna," replied the Countess, "I will tell you. But first of all I want to tell you what will happen if you do me this service. I see that your daughter is beautiful and of marriageable age, and according to what I am told and observe for myself, the reason you keep her at home is that you have no dowry for her. In repayment of the service you do me I intend to give you from my own money the dowry which you yourself consider fitting to marry her honourably."

The poor lady was delighted with the offer, but as her spirit was above the vulgar, she said:

"Madonna, tell me what I can do for you, and if I can do it honestly, I will gladly do it for you, and you shall then do what pleases you to do."

Then said the Countess: "By means of somebody in whom you can trust you must inform the Count, my husband, that your daughter is ready to do his pleasure when she can be sure that he loves her as much as he pretends; but that she will never believe him until he sends her the ring he wears on his finger, which she has heard he prizes so highly. If he sends her the ring, you will give it to me. Then you will send to tell him that your daughter is ready to pleasure him, and then you will bring him quietly here and secretly let him lie with me in place of your daughter. Perhaps God will so favour me that I shall become pregnant. And thus, with your help, I shall have his ring on my finger and his child in my arms, and shall thus win him back and live with him as a wife should live with her husband."

This seemed a great request to the lady, who feared that dishonour might fall upon her daughter. But then she thought that it was a virtuous deed to help the good lady to have her husband again and that she would be working towards a virtuous end. Confiding in her virtuous love, she not only promised to help the Countess but a few days later (with the utmost secrecy, as they had arranged) she got possession of the ring despite the Count's reluctance, and skilfully put the Countess to bed with the Count in place of her own daughter. In these first embraces, most eagerly sought by the Count, it pleased God that the Countess should become pregnant with two male twins, which was made manifest when the time came for her to bring them forth. Nor did the gentlewoman pleasure the Countess once only with her husband's embraces, but many times; and she arranged everything so skilfully that not a word was known about it, for the Count never dreamed he was with his own wife, but thought he was lying with the other girl. When the Count left in the morning he gave her valuable and beautiful jewels, all of which the Countess carefully preserved. But when she found she was pregnant, she was unwilling to impose this service on the gentlewoman any longer, and said to her:

"Madonna, thanks be to God and you, I now have what I desired. It is time for me to do what will please you, so that I can depart."

The gentlewoman replied that she was glad she had what pleased her, but that she had not done this service for a reward, but because she felt she ought to do it for a virtuous object. Said the Countess:

"Madonna, this gives me great pleasure, and so I do not mean to give you what you ask as a reward, but to do good, as I feel I ought to do."

Constrained by necessity, the gentlewoman then most shamefacedly asked for a hundred pounds to marry her daughter. Perceiving her bashfulness and hearing her courteous demand, the Countess gave her five hundred pounds and as many valuable jewels as amounted to the same sum. The gentlewoman was more than satisfied with this, and most warmly thanked the Countess, who then left her and returned to her inn.

To prevent Beltramo from sending to her any more and coming to the house, the gentlewoman and her daughter went away to the country house of their relatives. And a little later Beltramo was called home by his tenants and, having heard that the Countess had gone away, he returned home.

When the Countess learned that he had left Florence and gone home, she was very glad, and remained in Florence until the time of her delivery, when she brought forth two male children exactly like their father; and had them most carefully nursed. When she thought the right time had come, she set forth and, without being recognised by anyone, came to Montpellier. There she rested a few days, and made enquiries about the Count. She learned that on All Saints Day he was to give a great entertainment in Rossiglione for his knights and ladies; and she made her way there in her customary pilgrim's garb. At the moment when the knights and ladies were about to sit down to table, she entered the great hall in her pilgrim's robe, carrying her two children in her arms, and made her way to the Count. Throwing herself at his feet, she said weeping:

"My lord, I am your unhappy wife, who have been wandering about the world far and wide to allow you to return home. I beg you that you will observe the conditions brought me by the two knights I sent to you. See, here in my arms, not one of your children, but two. And, look, here is your ring. It is now time for me to be received as your wife, in accordance with your promise."

The Count was amazed to hear this, for he recognised his ring and even the children, for they were so like him. But he said: "How can this have happened?"

Then, to the great surprise of the Count and all present, she related in order everything that had happened. The Count knew that what she said was true and saw her perseverance and her wisdom and the two beautiful children. Therefore, to keep his promise and to please all his men and the ladies, who all begged him to recognise and honour her as his legitimate wife, he threw aside his obstinate prejudice, lifted the Countess to her feet and kissed and embraced her and recognised her as his legitimate wife and the children as his own sons. Then he had her dressed in garments befitting her, and to the great joy of all there present and of all his vassals when they heard of it, he held high festival, not only that day but during many days. And from that day onwards he honoured her as his wife and spouse, and loved her and held her very dear.

## TENTH TALE

*Alibech becomes a hermit, and the monk Rustico teaches her how to put the devil in hell. She is afterwards taken away and becomes the wife of Neerbale*

Dioneo had listened closely to the queen's story, and, when it was over and only he remained to tell a story, he did not wait to be commanded, but smilingly began as follows:

Most gracious ladies, perhaps you have never heard how the devil is put into hell; and so, without departing far from the theme upon which you have all spoken today, I shall tell you about it. Perhaps when you have learned it, you also will be able to save your souls, and you may also discover that although love prefers to dwell in gay palaces and lovely rooms rather than in poor huts, yet he sometimes makes his power felt among thick woods and rugged mountains and desert caves. Whereby we may well perceive that all of us are subject to his power.

Now, to come to my story—in the city of Capsa in Barbary there lived a very rich man who possessed among other children a pretty and charming daughter, named Alibech. She was not a Christian, but she heard many Christians in her native town crying up the Christian Faith and service to God, and one day she asked one of them how a person could most effectively serve God. The reply was that those best serve God who fly furthest from the things of this world, like the hermits who had departed to the solitudes of the Thebaid Desert.

The girl was about fourteen and very simple minded. Urged by a mere childish enthusiasm and not by a well ordered desire, she secretly set out next morning quite alone, without saying a word to anyone, to find the Thebaid Desert. Her enthusiasm lasted several days and enabled her with great fatigue to reach those solitudes. In the distance she saw a little hut with a holy man standing at its entrance. He was amazed to see her there, and asked her what she was seeking. She replied that by God's inspiration she was seeking to serve Him, and begged the hermit to show her the right way to do so. But the holy man saw she was young and pretty, and feared that if he kept her with him he might be tempted of the devil. So he praised her good intentions, gave her some roots and wild apples to eat and some water to drink, and said:

"Daughter, not far from here dwells a holy man who is a far greater master of what you are seeking than I am; go to him."

And so he put her on the way. When she reached him, she was received with much the same words, and passing further on came to the cell of a young hermit named Rustico, to whom she made the same request as to the others.

To test his spiritual strength, Rustico did not send her away, but took her into his cell. And when night came, he made her a bed of palm leaves and told her to sleep there.

Almost immediately after this, temptation began the struggle with his spiritual strength, and the hermit found that he had greatly over-estimated his powers of resistance. After a few assaults of the demon he shrugged his shoulders and surrendered. Putting aside holy thoughts and prayers and macerations, he began to think of her beauty and youth, and then pondered how he should proceed with her so that she should not perceive that he obtained what he wanted from her like a dissolute man. First of all he sounded her by certain questions, and discovered that she had never lain with a man and appeared to be very simple minded. He then saw how he could bring her to his desire under pretext of serving God. He began by eloquently showing how the devil is the enemy of the Lord God, and then gave her to understand that the service most pleasing to God is to put the devil back into hell, to which the Lord God has condemned him. The girl asked how this was done, and Rustico replied:

"You shall soon know. Do what you see me do."

He then threw off the few clothes he had and remained stark naked, and the girl imitated him. He kneeled down as if to pray and made her kneel exactly opposite him. As he gazed at her beauty, Rustico's desire became so great that the resurrection of the flesh occurred. Alibech looked at it with amazement, and said:

"Rustico, what is that thing I see sticking out in front of you which I haven't got?"

"My daughter," said Rustico, "that is the devil I spoke of. Do you see? He gives me so much trouble at this moment that I can scarcely endure him."

Said the girl:

"Praised be God! I see I am better off than you are, since I haven't such a devil."

"You speak truly," said Rustico, "but instead of this devil you have something else which I haven't."

"What's that?" said Alibech.

"You've got hell," replied Rustico, "and I believe God sent you here for the salvation of my soul, because this devil gives me great trouble, and if you will take pity upon me and let me put him into hell, you will give me the greatest comfort and at the same time will serve God and please Him, since, as you say, you came here for that purpose."

In all good faith the girl replied: "Father, since I have hell in me, let it be whenever you please."

Said Rustico: "Blessings upon you, my daughter. Let us put him in now so that he will afterwards depart from me."

So saying, he took the girl to one of their beds, and showed her how to lie so as to imprison the thing accursed of God. The girl had never before put any devil into her hell and at first felt a little pain, and exclaimed to Rustico:

"O father! This devil must certainly be wicked and the enemy of God, for even when he is put back into hell he hurts it."

"Daughter," said Rustico, "it will not always be so."

To prevent this from happening, Rustico put it into hell six times, before he got off the bed, and so purged the devil's pride that he was glad to rest a little. Thereafter he returned often and the obedient girl was always glad to take him in; and then the game began to give her pleasure, and she said to Rustico:

"I see that the good men of Capsa spoke the truth when they told me how sweet a thing is the service of God. I certainly do not remember that I ever did anything which gave me so much delight and pleasure as I get from putting the devil into hell. I think that everyone is a fool who does anything but serve God."

Thus it happened that she would often go to Rustico, and say:

"Father, I came here to serve God and not to remain in idleness. Let us put the devil in hell."

And once as they were doing it, she said:

"Rustico, I don't know why the devil ever goes out of hell. If he liked to remain there as much as hell likes to receive and hold him, he would never leave it."

The girl's frequent invitations to Rustico and their mutual pleasures in the service of God so took the stuffing out of his doublet that he now felt chilly where another man would have been in a sweat. So he told the girl that the devil must not be chastened or put into hell except when pride made him lift his head. "And we," he said, "have so quelled his rage that he prays God to be left in peace." And in this way he silenced the girl for a time. But when she found that Rustico no longer asked her to put the devil in hell, she said one day:

"Rustico, your devil may be chastened and give you no more trouble, but my hell is not. You should therefore quench the raging of my hell with your devil, as I helped you to quell the pride of your devil with my hell."

Rustico, who lived on nothing but roots and water, made a poor response to this invitation. He told her that many devils would be needed to soothe her hell, but that he would do what he could. In this way he satisfied her hell a few times, but so seldom that it was like throwing a bean in a lion's mouth. And the girl, who thought they were not serving God as much as she wanted, kept murmuring.

Now, while there was this debate between the excess of desire in Alibech's hell and the lack of potency in Rustico's devil, a fire broke out in Capsa, and burned Alibech's father with all his children and servants. So Alibech became heir to all his property. A young man named Neerbale, who had spent all his money in riotous living, heard that she was still alive and set out to find her, which he succeeded in doing before the Court took over her father's property as that of a man who had died without heirs. To Rustico's great relief, but against her will, Neerbale brought her back to Capsa and married her, and together they inherited her large patrimony. But before Neerbale had lain with her, certain ladies one day asked her how she had served God in the desert. She replied that her service was to put the devil in hell, and that Neerbale had committed a great sin by taking her away from such service. The ladies asked:

"And how do you put the devil in hell?"

Partly in words and partly by gestures, the girl told them. At this they laughed so much that they are still laughing, and said:

"Be not cast down, my child, they know how to do that here, and Neerbale will serve the Lord God with you in that way."

As they told it up and down the city, it passed into a proverb that the service most pleasing to God is to put the devil into hell. And this proverb crossed the seas and remains until this day.

Therefore, young ladies, when you seek God's favour, learn to put the devil in hell, because this is most pleasing to God and to all parties concerned, and much good may come of it.

Dioneo's tale moved the chaste ladies to laughter hundreds of times, so apt and amusing did they find his words. When he had finished, the queen knew that the end of her reign had come, and therefore took the laurel wreath from her head and placed it upon Filostrato's saying pleasantly:

"We shall soon find out if the wolf can guide the flock, as well as the flock has guided the wolves."

Filostrato laughingly replied:

"If my advice were followed, the wolves would have showed the flock how to put the devil in hell, as Rustico taught Alibech; and so they would not be called wolves, where you would not be the flock. However, since the rule now falls to me, I shall begin my reign."

Said Neifile:

"Filostrato, in trying to teach us, you might have learned wisdom, as Masetto da Lamporecchio learned it from the nuns, and you might have regained your speech when your bones were rattling together from exhaustion!"

Filostrato, finding the ladies' sickles were as good as his shafts, ceased jesting, and occupied himself with the government of his kingdom. Calling the steward, he made enquiries into everything, and gave orders to ensure the well being and satisfaction of the band during his kingship. He then turned to the ladies and said:

"Amorous ladies, to my own misfortune—although I was quite aware of my disease—I have always been one of Love's subjects owing to the beauty of one of you. To be humble and obedient to her and to follow all her whims as closely as I could, was all of no avail to me, and I was soon abandoned for another. Thus I go from bad to worse, and believe I shall until I die. Tomorrow then it is my pleasure that we tell tales on a theme in conformity with my own fate—that is, about those persons whose love ended unhappily. In the long run I expect a most unhappy end for myself, and the person who gave me the nickname of Filostrato, or the Victim of Love, knew what she was doing."

So saying, he rose to his feet, and gave them all leave to depart until supper time.

The garden was so delightful and so beautiful that they all chose to remain there, since no greater pleasure could be found elsewhere. The sun was now not so hot, and therefore some of them began to chase the deer and rabbits and other animals which had annoyed them scores of times by leaping in among them while they were seated. Dioneo and Fiammetta began to sing the song of Messer Guglielmo and the Lady of Vergiu. Filomena and Pamfilo played chess. Thus, with one thing and another, time

passed so quickly that supper time arrived long before
they expected. The tables were set round the fountain,
and there they ate their evening meal with the utmost
pleasure.

When they rose from table, Filostrato would not depart from the path followed by the preceding queens, and
so ordered Lauretta to dance and sing a song. And she
said:

"My lord, I do not know any songs of other persons,
and I do not remember any of my own which are fitting
for this merry band. But if you wish to have one of those
I remember, I will gladly sing it."

"Nothing of yours could be anything but fair and pleasing," said the king, "so sing it just as it is."

Then to the accompaniment of the others, Lauretta sang
as follows in a sweet but rather plaintive voice:

*No helpless lady has such cause to weep as I, who
vainly sigh, alas, for love.*

*He who moves the heavens and all the stars made
me for His delight so fair, so sweet, so gracious and
so lovely that I might show to every lofty mind some
trace of that high Beauty which ever dwells within
His presence. But a weak man, who knew not Beauty,
found me undelightful and scorned me.*

*Once there was one who held me dear, and in my
early years took me into his arms and to his thoughts,
being quite conquered by my eyes. And time, that
flies so swiftly, he spent in serving me; and I in courtesy made him worthy of me. But now, alas, he is
taken from me.*

*Then came a proud, presumptuous man, who thought
himself both noble and valourous, and made me his,
but through false belief became most jealous of me.
And then, alas, I came near to despair, for I saw that
I, who came into the world to pleasure many, was
possessed by one alone.*

*I curse my luckless fate that ever I said "yes" to man,
and changed to a wife's garb. I was so gay in my old
plain maiden's dress! Now in these finer clothes I
lead so sad a life, reputed less than chaste. O hapless*

*wedding feast! Would I had died before I knew the*
*fate it held for me!*

*O my first love, with whom I was so happy, who now*
*in Heaven do stand before Him who created it, have*
*pity on me. I cannot forget you for another. Let me*
*feel that the flame wherewith you burned for me is*
*not extinct, and pray that I may soon return to you.*

Here ended Lauretta's song, which was noted carefully
by them all, but interpreted differently. Some understood
it in the Milanese sense—that it is better to be a good pig
than a pretty girl. Others were of a better, more sublime
and truer understanding, but of this I shall not now speak.

After this the king had many torches brought and made
them sing other songs as they sat on the grass and flowers,
until the rising stars began to turn towards the west. Then,
thinking it time for sleep, he said good night and sent each
one to his room.

**END OF THE THIRD DAY**

# THE FOURTH DAY

# THE FOURTH DAY

*Here begins the fourth day of the* Decameron, *wherein, under the rule of Filostrato, tales are told of those whose love had an unhappy ending*

Most dear ladies, both from the words I have heard from learned men and from the things I have often seen and read, I conceived that the swift impetuous wind of envy smote only high towers and the topmost branches of trees. But I was deceived. I flee and have ever striven to flee the fierce attacks of that raging spirit by seeking my way, not only in the plains, but in the deepest valleys. This may be perceived by all who read these tales, which I have written without signing, and in the vulgar tongue of Florence and in prose, and in addition have composed them in the most humble and modest style I could. Yet I have not desisted, though fiercely shaken by this wind until almost uprooted, and lacerated by the fangs of envy. Whereby you may easily see the truth of what wise men are wont to say—that in this world only misery is safe from envy.

Some who have read these tales, discreet ladies, have said that you are too pleasing to me and that it was not modest that I should take delight in pleasing and comforting you and—others have said worse than this—in commending you, as I do. Others, speaking more deliberately, said that at my age it was not good to indulge in such things as talking about ladies or trying to please them. And many, showing themselves most tender of my fame, say that I should be wiser to remain with the Muses on Parnassus than to thrust myself among you with such nonsense.

There are others again who, speaking more spitefully than wisely, say that I should act more discreetly by thinking of where I shall earn my bread than by "feeding on wind" with such twaddle. And there are others who have laboured to prove, in depreciation of my work, that the things I have related happened otherwise. Thus, worthy ladies, while I fight in your service, I am thrust at, harmed and wounded in life, by these and like blasts, and sharp fierce teeth. God knows I have listened to these things with a tranquil mind, and although my defence entirely belongs to you, yet I do not intend to spare my own strength. Therefore, without making any formal reply, I intend to make without any delay some slight answer to reprimand them. For, if I have so many presumptuous enemies before I have completed a third of my labours, I see that long before I reach the end they will so multiply, if they are not confuted, that they will very easily overcome me; and even your power, great as it is, would be unable to resist them.

Before I come to my reply to them, I want to tell, not a whole story (because I would not seem to include my tales with those told by the laudable company I have described), but part of a story, so that its very defect may show that it is not one of theirs. And so I address this fable to my detractors:

A long time ago there dwelt in our city a man named Filippo Balducci. He was a man of low birth, but rich and expert in those things appertaining to his state of life. He had a wife whom he greatly loved, and who loved him, and they spent a happy life together, each striving to do what would please the other.

As happens to all of us, the good woman departed this life, leaving to Filippo nothing of herself but an only child of about two, whom he had begotten on her. Filippo was more disconsolate at the death of his wife than any other man at the loss of what he most loved. Seeing that he was deprived of the companionship he most loved, he made up his mind to renounce the world and to devote himself to the service of God, and to do the same for his little boy. He gave away to charities all he had, and straightway departed to Mount Senario where he found a little hut for himself and his child, and lived upon alms, in fasting and prayer. He was most careful never to speak to his son of temporal matters, so that he might not be withdrawn from God's service, but always spoke of the glory of eternal life and of God and the Saints, and taught him nothing but holy prayers. Many years they spent in this kind of life, where the son was never allowed out of the hut and never allowed to see anyone but his father.

This worthy man was accustomed to go occasionally to Florence, whence, after receiving the aid of God's friends in accordance with his needs, he returned to his hut. One day when Filippo was an old man and the boy about eighteen, he asked his father where he was going. Filippo told him, and the young man said:

"Father, you are now an old man, ill able to endure fatigue. Why do you not take me to Florence with you, and there make me known to the friends and devotees of God and yourself, so that I, who am young and far more able to work than you, may go to Florence for what you need, whenever you wish, and you can stay here?"

The worthy man, thinking that his son was now grown up and so accustomed to God's service that worldly things would have little effect on him, said to himself: "He is right." And so he took his son with him the next time he went. The young man had never seen anything like the palaces, houses, churches and other things with which Florence is filled, was astounded, and kept asking his father what they were and what they were called. The father told him; and when one question was satisfied, the son asked another. As they went along, the son questioning and the father answering, they chanced to meet a band of well dressed and handsome young women, returning from a couple of weddings. As soon as the son saw them, he asked his father what they were. And the father said:

"My son, cast your eyes upon the ground, look not upon them, they are evil."

"But what are they called?" asked the son.

The father did not want to tell him they were women, for fear of awakening some useless and mischievous desire in his carnal appetites, and therefore said:

"They are called Geese."

Wonderful to relate! He who had never seen a woman, indifferent to palaces, oxen, horses, asses, money and all the other things new to him, immediately said:

"Father, do let me have one of those geese."

"O my son!" said the father. "Be silent, they are wicked things."

"Are wicked things always made like that?" the son asked him.

"Yes," said the father.

Then said the son: "I do not know what you are talking about nor why they are wicked. For my part, I have never seen anything so beautiful and so lovely as they are. They are more beautiful than the painted angels you have often showed me. Ah! Let us take one of these geese home with us, and I'll feed it."

"I won't allow it," said the father; "you do not know how they are fed."

But he felt at once that Nature was stronger than his teaching, and regretted having brought his son to Florence. . . . But I do not mean to tell any more of this story, and so come back to those for whom I meant it.

Some of my censors, youthful ladies, say that I do ill by striving too much to please you, and that I take too much pleasure in you. This I most openly confess, viz., that you please me, and that I strive to please you. I should like to ask them if this is to be marvelled at? Quite apart from the amorous kisses and pleasant embraces and delicious couplings which are so often enjoyed with you, sweet ladies, they are to consider the pleasure of merely seeing you continually, your fine manners and your exquisite beauty and your charming dresses and, in addition, your womanly virtues. Thus we see that a youth bred up on a wild solitary mountain with no companion but his father, only asked for you, ladies, only desired you, only gave his affection to you. If you were above everything else pleasing to a young hermit, a youth without feelings, a sort of wild animal, will my critics blame me if I, whose body was by Heaven made most apt to love you and whose soul has been disposed thereto since my childhood, should feel the power of the light of your eyes, the sweetness of honied words and the flame lighted by piteous sighs? Will they blame me if you are pleasing to me, and if I strive to please you? I care little indeed if I am condemned by those who do not love you and have no desire to be loved by you, for they are persons who neither know nor feel the pleasures and strength of natural affection.

Those who go about talking of my age simply show that they do not know a leek may have a white head and a green tail. But, jesting apart, I reply seriously that I do not see why I should be ashamed of delighting in these things until the end of my life, since they and the pleasures they give were highly prized by Guido Cavalcanti and Dante Alighieri in their old age, and by Messer Cino da Pistoia in extreme old age.

If it were not a departure from the customary method of argument, I would here turn to history and show them many examples of the valiant men of old who strove eagerly to please ladies in their age. And if my critics do not know about them, let them go and look for them. I admit it is good advice to tell me to remain with the Muses on Parnassus, but we cannot always dwell with the Muses, nor they with us; and when a man leaves them he is not to be blamed if he delights to look upon those who resemble them. The Muses are women, and although women are not so much to be esteemed as the Muses, yet in their aspect they resemble the Muses. So, if they delighted me for no other reason, yet for this reason they ought to delight me. Moreover, women have been the cause of my writing thousands of verses wherein the Muses were in no wise the cause of my writing them. They aided me and showed me how to compose these verses. And perhaps when I wrote them, however feeble they may have been, the Muses visited me, perhaps in honour of the likeness which women have to them. Thus, when I composed these verses, I was not so far distant from Parnassus and the Muses as some people think.

But what shall we say to those who feel such compassion for my hunger that they advise me to get bread? Indeed, I do not know. But yet when I wonder what they would reply if in my need I asked them for bread, I feel they would answer: "Go, seek your bread among fables." Yet the poets of the past have found more bread in their fables than many a rich man in his treasures. And some by their fables have done honour to their time, while many who sought to have more bread than they needed have perished in bitterness.

What more? Let these persons drive me from them when I ask them for bread, which, thank God, I do not now lack. And if that need comes to me, I can, like the Apostle, endure both abundance and poverty. And, after all, this concerns me more than anyone else. As for those who say that these tales did not happen as I say—I should be very glad if they would show me the originals, and if what I have written should prove to be different, I would admit their reproof to be just and would strive to amend. But so long as they can produce nothing but words, I shall leave them to their opinion and follow my own, saying of them what they say of me.

At present, I think I have said enough by way of retort, and so, most gentle ladies, I shall go on, armed with the help of God and yourselves and with patience, and turn my back to this blast of envy, and let it blow. For I do not see that anything worse can happen to me than happens to the dust in a storm of wind—either it is not moved from the ground or it is carried up into the air and often falls upon men's heads, upon the crowns of Kings and Emperors, and sometimes is left lying upon lofty palaces and high towers. And if it falls from them, it can fall no lower than the place whence it come.

If ever I were disposed to serve you in anything with all my power, I am more than ever so disposed now; because I know that anyone who speaks reasonably will say that I and others who love you are thereby acting naturally. And to thwart the laws of Nature requires too much strength, especially as those who labour to do so, not only labour in vain, but to their own great harm. I confess I do not possess that strength and do not want it. If I had it, I would rather lend it to another than use it for myself. Therefore let my censors be silent; and if they cannot warm themselves let them live cold, and, driving away corrupt appetite, let them live in their pleasure and me in mine for that short space of life which is granted me.

But we have wandered far enough, fair ladies, and it is time to return to the point from which we started, and to continue on our appointed way.

Already the sun had driven every star from heaven and the damp shadow of night from the earth, when Filostrato arose and with him all his company. They went into the fair garden, and there took their delight. When the time to eat came, they dined in the place where they had supped the evening before. They took their siesta when the sun was at its highest, and then arose and, in their wonted manner, went and sat down by the fountain.

Filostrato then ordered Fiammetta to tell the first tale, and she, without waiting to be told again, in womanly fashion began as follows.

## FIRST TALE

*Tancred, Prince of Salerno, murders his daughter's lover and sends her the heart in a gold cup. She pours poison on it, which she drinks; and so dies*

Our king has given us a sad theme for tale-telling today, thinking that as we came here to enjoy ourselves it is befitting to speak of the tears of others, which cannot be heard without pity either by the teller or the listeners. Perhaps he did this to temper the happiness we have had in the past few days. But, whatever his motive, it is not for me to change his good pleasure, and so I shall tell you a piteous story of misadventure, worthy of your tears.

Tancred, Prince of Salerno, was a humane and kindly man, except that in his old age he stained his hands with the blood of lovers. In the whole of his life he had no child but one daughter, and it would have been happier for him if he had not had her. This girl was as much beloved by her father as any daughter ever was, and long after she had reached marriageable age this tender love of his prevented him from marrying her to anyone. At length he gave her to a son of the Duke of Capua, who died soon after the marriage; and she returned home a widow. In face and body she was most beautiful, and young and merry and perhaps cleverer than a woman should be. She lived with her father in great luxury like a great lady, and, when she saw that her father loved her so much that he cared little about marrying her again, while she thought it immodest to ask him to do so, she determined that if she could she would secretly have a valiant lover.

Many men, both nobles and others, frequented her father's Court. She observed the manners and behaviour of many of these men, among them a young servant of her father's named Guiscardo, a man of humble birth but whose virtues and noble bearing pleased her so much that she fell secretly in love with him, and the more she saw him the more she admired him. The young man, who was no novice, soon perceived this and took her so deep into his heart that he could think of scarcely anything but his love for her.

Since they both were secretly in love with each other, the young widow desired nothing so much as to be alone with him, and, as she would trust nobody in this love affair, she thought of a new device for telling him where to meet her. She wrote him a letter telling him what he had to do the next day in order to be with her, and then put it into a hollow stick, which she laughingly gave him, saying:

"Make a bellows of this tonight for your servant to blow the fire."

Guiscardo took it, and realised that she would not have given it to him and have spoken these words without some reason. When he got to his lodging he looked at the stick, saw it was hollow and found her letter, which he read. When he discovered what he was to do, he was the happiest man alive, and prepared to meet her in the way she had arranged.

Near the Prince's palace was a cave, hollowed out of a hill in the remote past, and dimly lighted by a small opening cut in the hill-side. The cave had been so long abandoned that this opening was almost covered over with brambles and other plants. A secret stairway, secured by a very strong door, led to the cave from one of the rooms in the palace where the lady had her apartments. This stairway had been disused so long that scarcely anyone remembered its existence. But Love, from whose eyes nothing secret can be hidden, brought it to the remembrance of this enamoured lady.

To avoid anyone's knowing about all this, she exerted her wits for many days until she had succeeded in opening the door. Having opened it, she entered the cave alone and saw the outer entrance, and afterwards told Guiscardo to find some means of entering it, telling him about how far it was from the ground. Guiscardo immediately prepared a rope with knots and loops so that he could climb up and descend. The next night he wrapped himself in a leather skin as protection against the brambles and, without allowing anyone to know about it, went to the cave entrance. There he fitted one of the rope loops round a strong tree stump which had grown up in the mouth of the cave entrance, and so let himself down into the cave, and waited for the lady.

Next day, under pretence of taking a siesta, she sent away her women and shut herself up alone in her room. Then, opening the door, she got into the cave where she found Guiscardo; and together they made much of one another. They afterwards went to her room and remained together with the greatest delight for a large portion of that day. They made the necessary arrangements to keep their love secret: Guiscardo returned to the cave, she locked the door, and returned to her waiting women. When night came Guiscardo climbed up his rope and got out by the same opening he had come in, and returned home. Having thus learned this way, he returned often in the course of time.

But Fortune, envious of this prolonged and deep delight, changed the lovers' joy into piteous lament by a grievous happening.

Tancred was sometimes accustomed to go alone to his daughter's room to talk to her for a time, and then depart. One day he went there while his daughter (whose name was Ghismonda) was in a garden with all her women. Unwilling to disturb her pleasure he went into the room unseen and unheard, and finding the windows of the room shut and the bed-curtains drawn, sat down at the foot of the bed on a low stool. He leaned his head on the bed, drew the curtain round him, as if he had been hiding himself, and went to

sleep. As misfortune would have it, Ghismonda had bidden
Guiscardo come that day, and therefore left her women in
the garden and softly entered the room where Tancred was
asleep. She locked the door without noticing that he was
there, and opened the other door for Guiscardo, who was
waiting for her. They went to bed together, as usual, and
while they were playing together and taking their delight,
Tancred awoke and saw and heard what his daughter and
Guiscardo were doing. In his distress he nearly made an
outcry, but then determined to remain silent and hidden if
he could, so that he could carry out with less shame what he
had already determined to do.

The two lovers remained a long time together, as they
were accustomed to do, without noticing Tancred; and
when they thought it was time they got out of bed, Guiscardo returned to the cave, and she went out of the room.
Tancred, although he was an old man, climbed out of a
window into the garden, and returned to his own apartment
almost dead with grief.

That night, by Tancred's orders, Guiscardo was arrested
by two men as he came out of the cave opening still wrapped
in the leather skin, and was secretly taken to Tancred. And
when Tancred saw him, he said almost in tears:

"Guiscardo, my kindness to you has not merited the outrage and shame you have done me, as this day I saw with my
own eyes."

But to this the only reply Guiscardo made was:

"Love is more powerful than either you or I."

Tancred then ordered that he should be closely guarded
in a neighbouring room; which was done. The next day,
while Ghismonda was still ignorant of what had happened,
Tancred went to his daughter's room as usual after dinner, having turned over all kinds of thoughts in his mind.
He had her called, locked himself in with her, and said to
her in tears:

"Ghismonda, I thought I knew your virtue and modesty
so well that, whatever had been said to me, it would never
have come into my mind (if I had not seen it with my own
eyes) that you would have yielded to any man who was not
your husband, or even have thought of doing so. Whenever I think of it I shall always grieve during that short
space of life left me in my old age.

"Since you had to come to this disgrace, would to God
that you had taken a man who was worthy of your noble
blood. But among all the men in my Court you chose Guiscardo, a young man of the basest extraction, bred in my

Court from childhood, almost out of charity. You have plunged my mind in the greatest perplexity, and I do not know what to do. Last night I had Guiscardo arrested when he came out of the cave opening, and I have him in prison; and I know what I shall do with him. But God knows what I am to do with you. On the one hand, I am urged by the love I feel for you, which is greater than any father ever felt for a daughter. On the other hand, I am urged by my indignation at your folly. The one urges me to forgive you, the other to punish you against my natural feeling. But before I make up my mind, I should like to hear what you have to say."

So saying he bowed his head, and wept like a beaten child. As Ghismonda listened to her father, she saw that her secret love was discovered, and that Guiscardo was in prison. This caused her inexpressible grief, which she was very near to showing by tears and shrieks, as most women do. But her lofty love conquered this weak feeling, she kept her countenance with marvellous strength of mind, and made up her mind that before she made any prayer for herself, she would not remain alive since she saw Guiscardo was already as good as dead. So she faced her father, not like a weeping woman detected in a fault, but like a brave and unconcerned one, and replied to him unperturbed, with a clear and open visage:

"Tancred, I am not prepared either to deny or to supplicate, because the former would not avail me and I do not want to avail myself of the latter. Moreover, I do not mean to make your love and gentleness of service to me, but to confess the truth, to defend my fame with good reasons and then with deeds to follow boldly the greatness of my soul. It is true that I have loved and do love Guiscardo. As long as I live—which will not be long—I shall love him. And if there is love after death, I shall continue to love him then. I was not drawn to this love so much by my womanish weakness as by your neglecting to marry me and by his virtues.

"Since you are flesh and blood, Tancred, you should know that you begot a daughter of flesh and blood, not of stone or iron. You should have remembered now and earlier, although you are now an old man, what and how powerful are the laws of youth. Although you spent the best years of your manhood in warfare, yet you should know the power of idleness and luxury upon the old as well as upon the young.

"Now, I was begotten by you and so am of flesh and blood, and I have not lived so long that I am yet old. My youth and my flesh are the reasons why I am filled with amorous desires; and they have been greatly increased by my marriage, which showed what pleasure there is in satisfying these desires. I could not resist them, but yielded to them, as a young woman would do; and fell in love. As far as I could, I endeavoured to avoid shame to you and to me in doing what I was drawn to do by natural sin. Compassionate Love and kindly Fortune found and showed me a secret way to reach my desires, without anyone else knowing. Nor do I make any denial of all this, however you may have learned it or whoever told you.

"I did not take Guiscardo at a venture, as many women would have done, but I chose him above all others deliberately and with forethought, and he and I have long enjoyed our desires. Whereby it appears from your bitter reproof that, in addition to my sin of loving, you think (following, in this, rather common opinion than the truth) that I have erred in addition by choosing a man of low birth, as if you thought you need not be angry if I had chosen a nobleman. Here you should not reprove my error but that of Fortune, who often lifts the unworthy on high and casts down the most worthy.

"But let us leave all this, and look at the principles of things. You will see that we all have the same flesh, and that all souls were created by the same Creator with equal powers, equal strength and equal virtues. It was virtue which first introduced differences among us who were born and are born equal. Those who were most virtuous and most devoted themselves to virtue were called noble, and the others remained commoners. And although this law has been glossed over by contrary custom, yet it is neither repealed nor broken by Nature and good manners. Therefore, he who lives virtuously manifests himself noble; and if such a man is called other than noble, the fault rests not with him but with those who call him ignoble.

"Consider all your nobles, examine their virtues, their manners, their behaviour; and then look upon Guiscardo. If you will pass judgment without prejudice, you will see that Guiscardo is most noble, and that all your nobles are peasants. Concerning the virtue and valour of Guiscardo I shall trust nobody's judgment save that of your words and my own eyes. Whoever praised him so much as you have praised him for all worthy deeds befitting a valiant man? And certainly you were not wrong. If my eyes did not deceive me, you never praised him for anything which I did not see him perform better than your words could express. If I was deceived here, I was deceived by you.

"Will you now say that I chose a man of base condition? You would speak falsely. You may say he is a poor man, and that is granted—to your shame, since you left one of your bravest servants in such a state. Poverty takes away nobleness from no man, but wealth does.

"Many Kings, many great Princes, were once poor. Many of those who plough and watch herds were once rich.

"Now, concerning your doubt as to what you should do to me—hesitate no further, if you are determined to be cruel, to do in your old age what you did not do in your youth. Wreak your cruelty upon me, for I will use no supplication to you, and it was I who was the real cause of this sin, if sin there is. And I tell you that if you do not do to me what you have done or may do to Guiscardo, my own hands shall perform it upon myself.

"Go, weep with women, and if you must be cruel and think we have deserved death, kill him and me with the same stroke."

The Prince saw his daughter's greatness of soul, but he did not believe she was as resolute as her words sounded. So he departed from her, and determined to use no cruelty upon her person but to cool her hot love with other punishment. He therefore commanded the two men who were guarding Guiscardo to strangle him the next night without any noise, to cut out his heart and send it to him. And they did as they were ordered.

Next day, the Prince sent for a large handsome gold cup and put Guiscardo's heart into it. This he sent to his daughter by a trusted servant, with orders to give it to her and to say: "Your father sends you this to console you for what you most loved, even as you consoled him for what he loved most."

When her father left her, Ghismonda did not abandon her desperate resolution, but sent for poisonous herbs and roots and distilled them with water, to have poison ready in case what she feared should happen. When the servants came with the Prince's present, and repeated his words, she took the cup with a firm countenance, opened it, saw the heart, and knew for certain that it was Guiscardo's heart. She turned her face to the servant, and said:

"Gold alone is a fitting burial place for such a heart. Herein my father has done wisely."

So saying, she carried it to her mouth and kissed it and then said:

"Always, in every respect my father's love has been most tender towards me, and herein more than ever. For this princely present I render him the highest thanks, as I ought to do."

And then, holding the cup tightly, she gazed upon the heart, and said:

"Ah! Thou most sweet dwelling-place of all my delight, cursed be the cruelty of him who has made me look upon you with the eyes of my head! It was enough for me to gaze upon you hourly with the eyes of my spirit. You have run your race, you are now free from all that Fortune imposed upon you. You have reached that bourn to which all men run. You have left the labours and miseries of the world, and from your enemy have you received that burial your valour deserved. Nothing is lacking to your funeral rites, save only the tears of her you loved so dearly in your life. That you might have them, God inspired my pitiless father to send you to me. Those tears I shall give you, although I had determined to die dry-eyed and with a calm face. And when I have wept for you, I shall straightway act in such a way that my soul shall be joined with yours, and do you accept that soul which of old was so dear to you. In what company could I go more gladly or more securely to an unknown land than with your soul? I am certain that it is yet here, and looks upon the place of its delight and mine. And since I am certain your soul loves me, let it wait for mine by which it is so deeply beloved."

So saying, she bowed weeping over the cup, and with no womanish outcries shed as many tears as if she had had a fountain of water in her head, kissing the dead heart an infinite number of times, so that it was a marvel to behold. Her women did not know whose heart it was, and did not understand her words, but all were filled with pity and began to weep, and pityingly but in vain asked her the cause of her lamentations, and strove to comfort her as best they could. But when she felt she had lamented long enough, she raised her head and dried her eyes, and said:

"O most beloved heart, I have performed all my duties to you; nothing now remains for me to do, save to come with my soul to bear company with yours."

So saying, she took the phial containing the poison she had made, and poured it into the cup where the heart was wet with her tears. Fearlessly she lifted it to her mouth and drank; and having drunk, she lay down on her bed and arranged her body as modestly as she could, and placed the heart of her dead lover upon her heart, and thus awaited death without uttering a word.

Her women, having heard and seen these things, sent word of them to Tancred, although they did not know that she had drunk poison. Dreading what might happen, Tancred came at once to his daughter's room, and reached it just as she had laid herself down upon the bed. He tried to comfort her with sweet words too late; and seeing to what extremity she was come, he began piteously to weep. And the lady said:

"Tancred, spare your tears for a fate less longed for than this of mine; give them not to me, for I do not want them. Whoever saw anyone but you weep over what he willed should happen. And yet, if any of the love you once felt for me is still alive grant me one last gift—although it displeased you that I lived secretly and silently with Guiscardo, let my body lie openly with his in the place where you have cast it."

The agony of his weeping prevented the Prince from replying. Then she felt her end was come, and holding the dead heart to her bosom, she said:

"God be with you, and let me go."

She veiled her eyes and all sense left her and she departed this sad life.

Such, as you have heard, was the sad end of the love of Guiscardo and Ghismonda. Tancred wept much and repented too late of his cruelty; and, amid the general grief of all Salerno, buried them both honourably in the same grave.

## SECOND TALE

*Frate Alberto persuades a lady that the Angel Gabriel is in love with her and thus manages to lie with her several times. From fear of her relatives he flies from her house and takes refuge in the house of a poor man, who next day takes him to the Piazza as a wild man of the woods. He is recognised, arrested and imprisoned*

The tale told by Fiammetta many times drew tears from her

companions' eyes, but when it was ended the king said with a stern face:

"I should value my life little in comparison with half the joy Ghismonda had with Guiscardo. Nor should you marvel at this, since while I am alive I suffer a thousand deaths hourly, and yet not one particle of delight is granted me. But, putting aside my life and its fate, it is my will that Pampinea should continue with a tale in part similar to my own fate. If she continues as Fiammetta has begun, doubtless some drops of dew will fall upon my amorous fire, and I shall feel them."

Pampinea felt the wishes of the company more through her own affection than through the king's words, and, being more willing to amuse them than to please the king, she determined to tell an amusing tale without departing from the subject given, and so began.

They say commonly in proverbial style: A wicked man who is thought to be good can do evil and yet not have it believed. This gives me ample material to speak on the subject proposed, and at the same time to show the hypocrisy of the monks. Their gowns are long and wide, their faces artificially pale, their voices humble and pleading when they ask something, loud and rude when they denounce their own vices in others, and when they declare how they obtain salvation of themselves and others by their gift. Not as men who seek Paradise, like ourselves, but as if they were its owners and lords, they allot a more or less eminent place there to everyone who dies, in accordance with the amount of money he leaves them; and thereby they first deceive themselves—if they really believe it—and then deceive those who put faith in their words. If I were permitted to do so, I could soon show many simple minded persons what is hidden in their ample gowns. Would to God that all their lies had the same fate as befell a minor friar, who was no paltry fellow, but was considered one of the best casuists of Venice. It gives me the greatest pleasure to tell this tale, so that perhaps I may divert your minds with laughter and amusement from the pity you feel for Ghismonda's fate.

In Imola, most worthy ladies, there lived a man of wicked and corrupt life, named Berto della Massa. His evil deeds were so well known to many people of Imola that no one in Imola would believe him when he spoke truth, let alone when he lied. Seeing, then, that his tricks were useless there, he moved in despair to Venice, that welcomer of all wickedness, thinking that in that town he might make a different use of his vices than he had done before. As if conscience-stricken for his wicked deeds, he gave signs of the greatest humility. He became not only the most Catholic of men, but made himself a minor friar, and took the name of Friar Alberto da Imola. In this guise he began to pretend to a severe life, praising penitence and abstinence, and never eating flesh or drinking wine when he could not get them good enough for him.

Never before had a thief, a ruffian, a forger, a murderer turned into a great preacher without having abandoned those vices, even when he had practised them secretly. And after he had become a priest, whenever he was celebrating Mass at the altar in the presence of a large congregation, he always wept over the Saviour's Passion, for he was a man who could shed tears whenever he pleased. In short, what with his sermons and his tears, he so beguiled the Venetians that he was trustee and guardian of nearly everyone's will, the keeper of many people's money, the confessor and adviser of most men and women. Thus, from wolf he became shepherd, and in those parts the fame of his sanctity was greater than San Francesco's ever was at Assisi.

Now, it happened that a silly stupid young woman, named Madonna Lisetta da ca Quirino, the wife of a merchant who was away in Flanders with the galleys, went with other women to confess to this holy friar. As she knelt at his feet like the Venetian she was—and they are all fools—he asked her half way through her confession if she had a lover. And she tartly replied:

"Why, messer friar, have you no eyes in your head? Do you think my beauties are no more than these other women's? I could have as many lovers as I wanted. But my beauty is not to be yielded to the love of anybody. How many beauties do you see like mine, for I should be beautiful in Paradise?"

And she went on to say so many things about her beauties that it was tedious to listen to her. Friar Alberto at once saw her weakness, and, feeling that she was ready made to his hand, he fell in love with her. But, reserving his flatteries for another time, he put on his saintly air and began to reprove her, and to say this was vain-glory and other things of the kind. So the lady told him he was a fool, and did not know how to distinguish one beauty from another. And Friar Alberto, not wanting to anger her too much, finished off the confession and let her go with the others.

A few days later he went with a trusted friend to Madonna Lisetta's house and took her aside into a room where they could not be seen. There he fell on his knees before her, and said:

"Madonna, I beseech you for God's sake to forgive me for what I said to you on Sunday when you spoke of your beauty, because I was so severely punished that night I have not been able to get up until today."

Then said Madonna Pot-stick: "And who punished you?"

"I will tell you," said Friar Alberto. "While I was praying that night, as I always do, I suddenly saw a bright light in my cell. Before I could turn to see what it was, I beheld a most beautiful young man with a large stick in his hand, who took me by the cowl, dragged me to my feet and beat me as if to break my bones. I asked him why he did this, and he replied: 'Because you presumed today to reprove the heavenly beauty of Madonna Lisetta whom I love more than anything except God himself.' And I asked: 'Who are you?' And he said he was the Angel Gabriel. 'O my lord,' said I, 'I beg you will pardon me.' And he said: 'I will pardon you on condition that you go to her as soon as you can and obtain her forgiveness. And if she does not forgive you I shall return here, and so deal with you that you will be miserable for the rest of your days.' What he afterwards said to me I dare not tell you until you have pardoned me."

Donna Windy-noddle, who was as sweet as salt, was enchanted at these words, and thought them all true.

"I told you, Friar Alberto," said she, "that mine were heavenly beauties. But, so help me God, I am sorry for you, and to spare you any further trouble I forgive you, if only you will tell me truly what the Angel then said."

"Madonna," replied Friar Alberto, "since you have pardoned me, I will tell you willingly. But, you must not repeat a word of what I tell you to anyone in the world, if you do not want to destroy your happiness, you who are the luckiest woman in the world.

"The Angel Gabriel told me to tell you that he loves you so much he would often have come to spend the night with you, but for his fear of terrifying you. He now sends a message through me to say that he wants to come to you one night and to spend part of it with you. But he is an Angel, and if he came to you in the form of an Angel you could not touch him; and so he says that for your delight he will come in a man's shape and bids you tell him when you want him to come and in whose shape, and he will come. And so you ought to think yourself more blessed than any other woman living."

Madonna Silly then said she was very glad to have the Angel Gabriel in love with her, because she loved him and always put up a fourpenny candle to him wherever she saw him painted. Whenever he liked to come to her he would be welcome and he would find her alone in her room, on one condition, which was that he would not abandon her for the Virgin Mary whom he was said to be very fond of; and she was inclined to believe this since whenever she saw his picture he was kneeling before the Virgin. In addition, she said that the Angel should come in any shape he pleased—she would not be afraid.

Then said Friar Alberto:

"Madonna, you speak wisely, and I will arrange with him as you say. But you can do me a great favour, which will cost you nothing. The favour is that you will allow him to come in my body. This will be a very great favour because he will take the soul from my body and put it in Heaven, and he will enter into me, and my soul will be in Paradise as long as he remains with you."

Then said Madonna Little-wit:

"I am content. I want you to have this consolation for the stripes you received on my account."

Said Friar Alberto:

"Tonight leave the door of your house open, so that he can come in. Since he is coming in a human body, he can only enter by the door."

The lady replied that this should be done. Friar Alberto departed, and she remained in such a state of delight that her chemise did not touch her backside, and the time she had to wait for the Angel Gabriel seemed like a thousand years.

Friar Alberto thought it better to be a good horseman than an Angel that night, so he fortified himself with all sorts of good cheer, in order not to be unhorsed too easily. He obtained permission to be out that night, and went with his trusted friend to the house of a woman friend, which he had made his starting point more than once before when he was going to ride the mare. From there he went in disguise to the lady's house, and having transformed himself into an Angel with the fripperies he had brought with him, he went upstairs into the lady's bedroom. When she saw something white come in, she kneeled down. The Angel gave her his benediction, raised her to her feet, and signed to her to get into bed. She did so immediately in her willingness to obey, and the Angel got into bed with his devotee.

Friar Alberto was a robust and handsome man and in excellent health. Donna Lisetta was fresh and pretty and found him a very different person from her husband to lie with. That night he flew many times with her without wings, which made her call herself blessed; and in addition he told her a great many things about heavenly glory. Just before dawn, he collected his trappings and returned to his friend, who had kept friendly company with the other woman so that she should not feel afraid by sleeping alone.

After the lady had dined, she went with a woman friend to see Friar Alberto, and gave him news of the Angel Gabriel, telling him how the Angel looked and what he had said about the glory of eternal life, to which she added all sorts of marvellous fables.

"Madonna," said Friar Alberto, "I know not how you were with him, all I know is that last night he came to me, and when I had delivered him your message, he suddenly took my soul to a place where there were more flowers and and roses than ever I saw, one of the most delicious places that ever existed, where my soul remained until dawn this morning. But what happened to my body I do not know."

"Didn't I tell you?" said the lady. "Your body lay all night in my arms with the Angel Gabriel. And if you don't believe me, look under your left breast, where I gave the Angel such a kiss that the mark will remain for several days."

Then said Friar Alberto:

"I will do something today which I have not done for a very long time. I shall undress myself to see if what you say is true."

After a lot more chatter, the lady returned home. And Friar Alberto thereafter visited her many times in the guise of an Angel, without the slightest difficulty. But one day Madonna Lisetta was with one of her gossips, and as they were discussing their beauties, she said like the empty-pated fool she was, in order to show off:

"If you knew who was in love with my beauty you would not speak of anyone else's."

The gossip was anxious to hear about it, and knowing Lisetta well, said:

"Madonna, you may be right, but as I do not know whom you mean I shall not change my opinion so easily."

The lady, who had very little sense, then said:

"Gossip, he does not want it talked about, but the person I mean is the Angel Gabriel, who loves me more than himself, so he says, because I am the most beautiful person in the world or the Maremma."

The gossip felt like laughing outright, but restrained herself to keep the conversation going, and said:

"God's faith, Madonna, if you mean the Angel Gabriel and say so, it must be true, but I did not think the angels did such things."

"Gossip," said the lady, "you are wrong. By God's favour, he does it better than my husband, and he tells me they do it up above. But, because he thinks me more beautiful than anyone in Heaven, he has fallen in love with me, and often spends a night with me. So you see!"

As soon as the gossip had left Madonna Lisetta, it seemed like a thousand years to her before she had got into a company where she could laugh at all this. She went to a gathering of women, and told them the whole tale. These women told their husbands and other women, and they told others, and so in less than two days the story was all over Venice. Among others who heard it were the lady's cousins, and, without saying anything to her, they made up their minds to find this Angel and see whether he could fly. So they watched for him every night.

Some rumours of all this came to the ears of Friar Alberto, who went to the lady one night to scold her for it. He was scarcely undressed when her cousins, who had seen him come in, were at the door. Friar Alberto heard them, and guessed what they were. He jumped up, and, having no other means of escape, opened a window overlooking the Grand Canal, from which he threw himself into the water.

The water there was deep; he was a good swimmer, and so did himself no harm. He swam to the other side of the canal and immediately entered an open house there, begging the goodman for the love of God to save his life, and told him all sorts of lies to explain why he was there naked at that hour of night.

The goodman, who was just setting off on his business, pitied Friar Alberto and put him into bed, telling him to stop there until he came back. He then locked the friar in, and went about his business.

When the lady's cousins entered her room, they found the Angel Gabriel had left his wings behind and flown away. They abused the lady indignantly, and, leaving her very disconsolate, returned home with the Angel's trappings.

Meanwhile, soon after dawn, the goodman was on the Rialto and heard how the Angel Gabriel had gone to lie with Madonna Lisetta the night before, how he had been discovered by her relatives and had thrown himself into the canal, and nobody knew what had become of him. So he immediately realised that this was the man in his own house. He went home and after much discussion arranged that the Friar should pay him fifty ducats not to hand him over to the cousins; and this was done. Friar Alberto then wanted to leave, but the goodman said:

"There is only one way of doing this. There is a festival today where one man leads another dressed like a bear or a wild man of the woods or one thing or another, and then there is a hunt in the Piazza di San Marco, and when that is over the festival ends. Then everyone goes off where he pleases with the person he has brought in disguise. Now, you may be spied out here, and so, if you like, I will lead you along in some disguise and can take you wherever you like. Otherwise I don't see how you can leave here without being recognised. The lady's relatives know you must be in some house in the neighbourhood, and have posted guards everywhere to catch you."

Friar Alberto did not at all like the idea, but he was so much afraid of the lady's relatives that he agreed to it, and told the man where he wanted to go, and how he should be led along. The goodman smeared him all over with honey and then covered him with feathers, put a chain round his neck and a mask on his face. In one hand he gave him a large stick and in the other two great dogs which he had brought from the butcher; and then he sent someone to the Rialto who announced that everyone who wanted to see the Angel Gabriel should go to the Piazza di San Marco. That was true Venetian good faith!

Having done this, he took the Friar out, and, walking before him, led him along on a chain; and everybody came round saying: "What's this? What's this?" And thus he took the Friar to the Piazza, where there was a great crowd of people, made up of those who had followed them and those who had come from the Rialto on hearing the announcement. He then led his wild man of the woods to a column in a conspicuous and elevated place, pretending that he was waiting for the hunt. The poor friar was greatly plagued by flies and gad-flies, because he was smeared all over with honey. And when the good man saw that the Piazza was full of people, he pretended that he was going to unchain his wild man; but instead he took off Friar Alberto's mask, and shouted:

"Gentlemen, since the pig has not come to the hunt and since the hunt is off, I don't want you to have gathered here for nothing, and so I want you to see the Angel Gabriel who came down from Heaven to earth last night to console the ladies of Venice."

As soon as the mask was off, Friar Alberto was recognised by everybody, and there went up a great shout against him, everybody saying the most insulting things that ever were said to any scoundrel. And first one and then another threw all sorts of filth in his face. There he was kept a long time until the news reached the other friars of his convent. Six of them came down to the Piazza, threw a gown on his back and bound him, and then in the midst of a great tumult took him back to the monastery, where he was imprisoned. And it is believed that he soon died there after a life of misery.

Thus a man who was thought to be good and acted evilly without being suspected, tried to be the Angel Gabriel and was turned into a wild man of the woods, and, in the long run, was insulted as he deserved and came to weep in vain for the sins he had committed. Please God that this may happen to all like him.

## THIRD TALE

*Three young men are in love with three sisters and fly with them to Crete. The eldest kills her lover out of jealousy; the second sister yields to the Duke of Crete to save her from death, but is murdered by her own lover who runs away with the first sister. The third sister and her lover are involved in the affair, and, when arrested, confess to it; they bribe the guard, and escape to Rodi where they die in poverty*

At the end of Pampinea's tale, Filostrato remained silent for a time and then said to her:

"One good thing which pleased me in your tale was the ending. But there was too much mirth in it, which I should have preferred not be to there."

He then turned to Lauretta and said:

"Lady, do you now follow with a better tale, if that may be."

"You are too cruel to lovers," said Lauretta, laughing,

"since you want them to come to a sad end. To obey you, I shall tell you about three lovers who all came to a bad end after a very short enjoyment of their love."

So saying, she began as follows:

As you may easily perceive, youthful ladies, every vice can easily do the greatest harm to those who practise it and to others as well. I think that anger is one of the vices to which we give rein with most danger to ourselves. Anger is nothing but a sudden and unreflecting emotion aroused by the grief we feel, which expels our reason, blinds the eyes of the spirit with darkness, and consumes our souls with burning rage. This often occurs in men, and more often in one than another, but is far more dangerous in women, because they blaze up more easily, burn with a sharper flame and restrain it less. This should not surprise us, because, if we look carefully, we shall see that fire naturally kindles light and delicate things more rapidly than those which are hard and weighty. And—let the men not take it in ill part —we women are more delicate and much more fickle than they are.

Therefore, since we are naturally inclined to this, and since our gentleness and kindness are most restful and pleasing to the men whom we frequent, and since anger and rage are dangerous and troublesome, and with a desire to make you guard against it more strictly, I shall tell you a tale of three young men and as many women, as I said before, to show you how their love fell from happiness to great misery on account of anger.

As you know, Marseilles is on the sea coast of Provence. It is an ancient and most noble city, and formerly contained more rich men and great merchants than it does now. Among them was one Narnald Cluada, a man of low birth but a true and honest merchant extremely rich in goods and money, who had several children by his wife, among them three girls who were older than the boys. The two eldest were twins aged fifteen, and the third was fourteen. Their marriage was only delayed until Narnald returned from Spain, where he had gone on a trading expedition.

The names of the two twins were Ninetta and Maddalena, and the third was named Bertella. Ninetta was beloved by a poor young gentleman named Restagnone, and she was in love with him. They had acted in such a way that they had enjoyed their love unknown to anyone; and they had enjoyed it for some time when two very rich young men named Folco and Ughetto, whose fathers were dead, fell in love respectively with Maddalena and Bertella.

When Restagnone learned of this through Ninetta he thought that he would be able to supply his poverty through their love. So he struck up a close friendship with them, and often accompanied them both when they went to visit their mistresses and his. And when he thought he had become sufficiently friendly with them, he invited them one day to his house and said:

"My dear friends, our familiarity together must have proved to you my friendship for you and that I would do for you what I would do for myself. Since I am so fond of you, I intend to tell you what has occurred to my mind, and then we will do together whatever seems best to you. If your words do not deceive me, and so far as I can judge from your acts both day and night, you are deeply in love with two of the sisters, as I am with the third. If you agree, I think I have found a sweet and pleasant remedy for your passion. You are very rich young men; I am not rich. If you will put all our wealth together and give me a third share of the whole and decide upon which part of the world we shall go to and live happily with these girls, I promise that the three sisters will take a large part of their father's money and come with us wherever we want to go. It is now for you to decide whether you will join in this, or not."

The two young men were so much in love that when they heard they should have their mistresses they were not long in making up their minds, and said they were ready to do it wherever it might lead. A few days after Restagnone had the young men's answer he was with Ninetta, whom he could only meet with the greatest difficulty. After he had spent some time with her he told her what he had discussed with the young men, and laboured with many arguments to persuade her to this enterprise. But he had very little difficulty, because she wanted to be with him undisturbed far more than he did. So she replied that she liked the plan and that her sisters would do whatever she wanted, especially in this matter; and told him to prepare everything necessary as quickly as possible.

Restagnone returned to the young men who urged him to do what he had discussed with them; and he told them that as far as their mistresses were concerned the matter was settled. They decided to go to Crete. Under pretext of setting up in trade, they sold the possessions they had, and turned everything they could into money. They then bought a swift ship, fitted it out secretly with a powerful armament, and awaited the event.

Ninetta, for her part, knowing her sisters' desire, so

worked upon them with honied words that they felt they could not live until they had carried out the plan. So, when the night came for them to go on board the ship, the three sisters opened a large chest of their father's and took out a great quantity of jewels and money, and with this went softly out of the house, as had been arranged, and met their three lovers who were waiting for them. They went on board ship without delay, ordered out the oars, and were off. They stayed nowhere and reached Genoa the next evening, where the new lovers took the first joy and pleasure of their love.

Having taken the rest they needed, they went on from one port to another, and eight days later reached Crete without any hindrance. There they bought large and fine estates, and built very handsome and delightful houses near Candia. There, like the happiest men in the world, they lived like barons with their wives and many servants and dogs and hawks and horses, in banqueting and feasting and merriment. Thus they lived, when it happened (for we see every day that, although certain things are pleasant, too much plenty leads to disgust) that Restagnone, who had been very much in love with Ninetta, began to dislike her when he could have her whenever he wanted without any hindrance, and so his love for her diminished. One day at a feast he was charmed by a beautiful young woman of the island, and, pursuing her with the utmost eagerness, began to give entertainments for her. Ninetta found it out, and became so jealous that he could not take a step without her knowing about it, and then was always nagging at him about it.

But, as surfeit begets disgust, so thwarted desire increases appetite; and thus Ninetta's reproaches fanned the flame of Restagnone's new love. Whether Restagnone did or did not get the love of his new lady, Ninetta in the course of time was convinced that he had, in spite of everything he said. This plunged her into such grief and then into such anger and consequently into such a rage that her love for Restagnone changed into bitter hatred, and, embittered by her anger, she determined to avenge the insult she thought she had received, by killing Restagnone.

There was an old Greek woman who was very skilful in preparing poisons, and Ninetta persuaded her with gifts and promises to brew her a mortal poison. One evening, when Restagnone was very hot and therefore not very careful about what he was drinking, she gave him the poison. It was so powerful that before morning he was dead. Folco

and Ughetto and their wives, not suspecting that he had
died of poison, wept bitterly for him with Ninetta, and
buried him honourably.

Not long afterwards the old woman who had made the
poison for Ninetta was arrested for some other crime, and
under torture confessed this among her other wicked deeds,
thus making plain what had happened. Without saying anything about it, the Duke of Crete one night entered Folco's
mansion and arrested Ninetta, and took her away without
any noise or opposition. And without any torture she very
soon told the Duke all he wanted to hear about Restagnone's death.

Folco and Ughetto heard privately from the Duke why
Ninetta had been arrested, and told their wives, who were
greatly distressed. They exerted all their wits to think of
some way of saving Ninetta from being burned, to which
they knew she would be condemned since she had fully
deserved it. But it all seemed useless, since the Duke was
determined that justice should be done.

Maddalena, who was a very beautiful girl, had long been
courted by the Duke, but had never consented to do his
pleasure. She thought that if she yielded to him she would
save her sister from burning. She therefore sent him a message secretly to say that she was at his disposal on two conditions: first, that her sister should come back to her safe
and free, second, that the whole matter should be kept a
secret. The message came to the Duke and pleased him.
After a long debate with himself, he agreed to do it, and
told her he was ready. One night therefore, with the lady's
consent, the Duke had Folco and Ughetto arrested, as
if he wanted to get information from them, and went to
spend the night secretly with Maddalena. Before this he
had pretended to have Ninetta sewed up in a sack to be
thrown into the sea that same night, but instead took her
back to her sister to whom he gave her as the price of that
night. When he left in the morning he told Maddalena that
this, their first night together, must not be the last. He also
insisted that the guilty woman should be sent away so that
no blame might fall upon him or he be compelled to proceed against her.

The next morning Folco and Ughetto were set at liberty,
and heard that Ninetta had been drowned in a sack that
night, which they believed. They returned home to console
their wives for the death of their sister, but although Maddalena did all she could to conceal Ninetta, Folco discovered she was there. This greatly amazed him, and he sud-

denly became suspicious, for he had noticed that the Duke was in love with Maddalena. So he asked her how Ninetta came to be there.

Maddalena tried to tell him a long story, but he was too wily to believe it and compelled her to tell him the truth, which after much talk she did. Folco flew into a rage, drew his sword and killed her as she begged in vain for mercy. Then, dreading the Duke's anger and justice, he left her dead in the room, went to the room where Ninetta was, and very cheerfully said to her:

"Your sister has just decided that I shall take you away at once, so that you may not fall into the Duke's hands."

Ninetta believed him, and, being in a fright, was anxious to go. As it was already night, she started off at once with Folco, without taking leave of her sister. They went to the coast with the little money Folco could lay his hands on, went on board a small ship, and nobody ever heard where they went.

The next day Maddalena was found murdered, and certain persons who envied and hated Ughetto, immediately informed the Duke. He had loved Maddalena very much, and rushed immediately to the house and arrested Ughetto and his wife who knew nothing about the flight of Folco and Ninetta. And the Duke compelled them to confess that they were guilty of the murder of Maddalena.

They naturally feared that this confession would mean their death, so they bribed the guards set over them with a certain sum of money, which by chance they had concealed in the house. Without having time to take anything with them, they fled with their guards and went on board a ship, and fled by night to Rhodes where they lived only a short time longer in poverty and misery.

Such was the fate brought upon themselves and others by Restagnone's mad love and Ninetta's anger.

## FOURTH TALE

*Contrary to the treaty made by his grandfather, King Guglielmo, Gerbino joins battle with a ship of the King of Tunis in order to capture his daughter; she is killed by those on board; he kills them; and he is executed*

When Lauretta had finished her tale, the different members of the party lamented one with another the lovers' sad fate. Some blamed Ninetta's anger, others said other things, when the king, as if roused from deep thought, turned to Elisa and signed to her to speak. She began modestly as follows:

Fair ladies, there are many people who think that Love speeds his shafts solely through the eyes, and scorn those who think that some people may fall in love by hearsay. That they are wrong will appear from the tale I am about to tell you. You will see from it how mere report can create love without the beloved person having ever been seen, and also how it can lead several people to a miserable end.

According to the Sicilians, Guglielmo the Second, King of Sicily, had two children, one a boy named Ruggieri, the other a girl, Gostanza. Ruggieri died before his father, leaving a son named Gerbino, who was carefully brought up by his grandfather, and became a most handsome young man, renowned for his prowess and courtesy. His fame was not confined to the limits of Sicily, but was noised throughout various parts of the world, and especially in Barbary which at that time was tributary to the King of Sicily. Among others who heard the magnificent fame of Gerbino's virtue and courtesy was a daughter of the King of Tunis, who, according to what we are told by those who saw her, was one of the most beautiful creatures ever formed by Nature, and the most accomplished, with a great and noble spirit. She liked to hear talk of valiant men, and listened so eagerly to what one person and another said of Gerbino's valiant deeds that she tried to imagine what he was like and fell deeply in love with him, so that she liked to talk and to hear about him better than anything else.

On the other hand, the fame of her beauty and worth came to Sicily, and, not in vain and not without delight to him, reached Gerbino's ears. So he was as eager for the girl as she was for him. Wherefore, being most desirous to see her, while awaiting some reasonable pretext for getting his grandfather's permission to go to Tunis, he charged some of his friends to go there and to let her know as well as they could his great and secret love for her, and to bring him back news of her. One of these friends, taking women's jewels as if he were a merchant, most skilfully succeeded in seeing her. He told her all about Gerbino's love and offered the Prince and all he had to her. She received message and messenger with a cheerful face, and replied that she felt a like love; in witness whereof, she sent him one of her most precious jewels. Gerbino received this with all the joy which can be felt on receiving a most precious gift, and wrote to her several times and sent her most valuable gifts, and made a pact with her to see and touch her, if Fate should permit.

Things went on in this way a little further than they should, each being very ardent towards the other, when the King of Tunis married his daughter to the King of Granada. This filled her with distress when she thought how she would be taken so far from her lover, and almost wholly deprived of him. To prevent this, she would gladly have fled from her father and have gone to Gerbino, if she had seen any way to do it. Similarly, when Gerbino heard of this marriage, he was immeasurably distressed, and determined that, if he could, he would carry her off by force if she went to her husband by sea.

The King of Tunis heard a rumour of Gerbino's love and intention, and was in some dread of his power and valour. So, when the time came to send his daughter away, he informed King Guglielmo of what he intended to do, and asked for a pledge that he should not be intercepted either by Gerbino or anyone else on his behalf. King Guglielmo was now an old man, and had heard nothing of Gerbino's love. He did not suspect that this pledge was asked on Gerbino's account, and so freely granted it; and, as a sign of good faith, he sent his glove to the King of Tunis. As soon as he had received this pledge, the King of Tunis prepared a large and handsome ship in the port of Carthage, furnished it with everything needed by those who were to travel in it, ornamented and arranged it, and only waited for good weather to send his daughter to Granada.

The young princess saw and knew all about this, and sent secretly one of her servants to Palermo, ordering him to salute Gerbino from her and to tell him that she was sailing for Granada in a few days; whereby it would be known whether he was as brave a man as people said and if he loved her as much as he had often declared.

The message was exactly delivered, and the messenger returned to Tunis. When Gerbino received it, he did not know what to do; for he knew that King Guglielmo had pledged his faith to the King of Tunis. But he was urged by love, and, after hearing his mistress's words, he could not be a poltroon; so he went to Messina, rapidly armed and manned two swift galleys, and set off in the direction of Sardinia, since he knew the lady's ship would pass that way.

It turned out as he had supposed. A few days later the

ship appeared, sailing before a light breeze, close to the
place where he was waiting. When he saw it, Gerbino said
to his friends:

"Gentlemen, if you are as valiant as I suppose, there is
not one of you who has not felt or now feels love, without
which in my opinion no mortal can attain virtue or happiness. If you have been or are in love, you will easily understand my desire. I am in love, and love urged me to undertake this adventure. She whom I love is in the ship you see
before you, which, together with the person I most desire,
contains great wealth; and, if you fight like valiant men,
we can obtain it all with little difficulty. For my share of
the spoils of victory I ask only one woman, for love of
whom I am under arms; all the rest I freely give to you.
Let us go forward, and boldly attack the ship. God favours
our enterprise, for he keeps them there without a wind."

Fair Gerbino had no need of so many words, for the men
of Messina, eager for spoil, were panting to do what Gerbino exhorted them to do. They greeted the end of his
speech with a great shout, the trumpets sounded, they
grasped their arms, the oars beat the sea, and they bore
down upon the ship.

When those who were in the ship saw the galleys coming
towards them, they prepared to defend themselves, since
they could not escape. When the fair Gerbino came up
with them, he ordered that the ship's commanders should
come on board the galleys if they did not want to fight. As
soon as the Saracens found out who had summoned them,
they said they were being attacked in violation of King
Guglielmo's faith, in proof of which they displayed his
glove, and said they would never yield themselves or anything on board their ship except by force. Gerbino saw the
lady on the ship's poop and thought her more beautiful than
he had been told; and so, more inflamed with love than ever,
he replied that there was no need of gloves since there were
no falcons there. And he added that they must either yield
up the lady, or prepare for battle. Without further parley
they straightway began to shoot arrows and stones at each
other, and the battle lasted a long time with heavy casualties
on both sides. Finally, when Gerbino saw he was making
little progress, he made a fire-ship of a small boat he had
brought with him from Sardinia, and with the two galleys
brought it alongside the ship. When the Saracens saw it,
they knew they must either yield or die; they brought up
the lady from the under to the upper deck and took her

to the ship's prow. They called to Gerbino and before his eyes cut her veins as she shrieked for help and mercy, and threw her into the sea, shouting:

"Take her, we give her to you such as we can and as your good faith deserves."

Seeing their cruelty, Gerbino boarded them as if he cared not for death or arrows or stones. In spite of those on board, he rushed on to the ship like a raging lion which gluts its rage before its hunger, now upon one now upon another of a herd. With a sword in his hand Gerbino cut down one Saracen after another, and killed many of them. As the fire increased in the burning ship, he ordered his sailors to take what spoils they could, and then left it after a very joyless victory over his enemies.

Afterwards, he recovered the lady's body from the sea, and wept many tears over it for a long time. He then returned to Sicily, and buried her honourably on a tiny island almost opposite Trapani, called Ustica; and from there went home in the greatest sorrow.

When the King of Tunis heard the news, he sent ambassadors dressed in black to King Guglielmo, to complain of the breach of faith and to relate what had happened. King Guglielmo was greatly angered, and, seeing no other way of doing the justice they asked of him, he arrested Gerbino. And although every one of his barons begged him not to do so, the King himself condemned Gerbino to death, and had his head cut off in his own presence; preferring to be left without a-grandson rather than be held a faithless King.

Thus, as I said, within a few days the two lovers died a violent death without enjoying any fruit of their love.

## FIFTH TALE

*Isabetta's brothers murder her lover. He appears to her in a dream, and tells her where he is buried. She secretly digs up the head and puts it in a pot of basil. For a long time she weeps over it every day; her brothers take it away, and soon after she dies of grief*

When Elisa had finished her tale, the king praised it, and then ordered Filomena to follow next. After a piteous sigh of compassion over the fate of the hapless Gerbino and his lady, she began as follows:

Gracious ladies, my tale will not be of persons so noble in rank as those Elisa has told us about, but perhaps the tale will be no less piteous. The mention of Messina brought it to my mind, for there it happened.

In Messina, then, were three brothers, merchants, who became rich men after the death of their father (a man from San Gimignano); and with them lived their sister, Isabetta, a beautiful and accomplished girl, who for some reason had not married. Besides the three brothers there was a young man named Lorenzo in their shop, who overlooked all their business. He was handsome and graceful, and when Isabetta had seen him a few times she fell in love with him. And Lorenzo likewise, after meeting her a few times, put aside his other love affairs, and gave himself up to loving her. And, as they each pleased the other, it was not long before they were certain of it, and did what each of them desired above everything.

This went on for some time with pleasure to them both, but one night when Isabetta was going to the room where Lorenzo slept, she was seen by the eldest of the three brothers, although she did not see him. He was a prudent young man, and although the affair angered him, he restrained himself and said and did nothing then, but waited until the morning, turning over various plans in his mind. When the day came he told his brothers what he had observed between Isabetta and Lorenzo the previous night. After long debate, they agreed to pass it over in silence and to pretend that they had seen and knew nothing, in order that no shame might fall upon them or their sister, until a time came when without harm or inconvenience to themselves, they could wipe away the shame before it went further.

With this view, they went on joking and laughing with Lorenzo as usual, and one day, under pretext of recreation, they all three rode out of the city, taking Lorenzo with them. When they came to a very remote and solitary place which was suitable, they murdered the unsuspecting Lorenzo and buried him in such a way that no one would notice it. They then returned to Messina, and gave out that they had sent Lorenzo away on business, which was easily believed since they had often before sent him away in such a manner.

When Lorenzo did not return, Isabetta often and earnestly asked after him (for his absence was very grievous to her) and one day when she was asking eagerly after him, one of the brothers said to her:

"What do you mean? What business have you with Lorenzo that you keep asking about him? If you ask about him again, we'll give you a fitting answer."

This grieved and saddened Isabetta, who dreaded and did not know what might have happened. She asked no more questions, but at night she often called piteously upon Lorenzo and begged him to come to her; sometimes she would lament his absence with tears and then suddenly become more cheerful and await his return. One night she had wept bitterly because Lorenzo did not return and after her tears, fell asleep, and then Lorenzo appeared to her in a dream, his face all pale and disordered and his clothes ragged and torn. And she thought he said:

"O Isabetta, you do nothing but call upon me and grieve for my long absence and accuse me with your tears. But I cannot return to you, because I was murdered by your brothers the last day you saw me."

He then told her the place where he was buried, and said she must not call upon him nor wait for him longer, and so disappeared.

When the girl awoke, she believed in the vision, and wept bitterly. She got up in the morning, but said nothing about it to her brothers, for she had determined to go to the place mentioned and to see whether her dream was true. She had permission to go out of the town, for recreation, with a woman who had lived with them and knew all her affairs, and so set out for the place as soon as she could. Putting aside the dry leaves there, she dug where the ground seemed softer. She had only dug a little way when she came upon the body of her unhappy lover, which was not yet corrupted or rotten; and thereby knew that her vision was true. Sadder than any woman living, she realised that this was not the time to weep. If she had been able, she would have taken away the whole body to give it fitting burial. But, seeing she could not do this, with a knife she severed the head from the shoulders as well as she could. She reburied the rest of the body and wrapped the severed head in a cloth and gave it to the woman to carry. Then she returned home, without anyone having seen her.

She shut herself up in her room with the head, weeping over it long and bitterly until she had washed it all over with her tears, and kissed every part of it a thousand times. She then took a large handsome pot, the kind used to grow marjoram or basil, and put the head in it wrapped in fine cloth. She covered it with earth and planted several sprigs of the finest Salerno basil, which she watered only with her tears or rose water or orange water. She then spent all her time near it, and wooed it with her desire since it contained her Lorenzo. And when she had looked at it a long time, she bent over it and wept until all the basil was wet with her tears.

From long and continual care and from the richness of soil resulting from the decaying head, the basil grew thickly and very scented. And, as the girl went on in this way, she was observed by several neighbours. They went to the brothers, who themselves had been surprised by the alteration in her looks and had noticed how her eyes seemed to be escaping from her head, and said to them:

"We are certain that she does the same thing every day."

The brothers several times reproved her to no avail, and then secretly had the pot taken away from her. When she found it gone, she kept asking for it insistently. It was not given back to her, and with weeping and tears she at last fell ill, and throughout her illness asked for nothing but her pot of basil.

The brothers were greatly surprised by this, and so wanted to see what was in the pot. They took out the earth and saw the cloth and the head, which had not so rotted away but that they recognised it as Lorenzo's by the curled hair. This amazed them still more, and made them fear that the murder might be discovered. They therefore buried the head, and withdrawing their money, left Messina and went to Naples. The girl continued to weep and to ask for her pot of basil, and so weeping, died. And this was the end of her hapless love. But after a certain time the whole affair became known to many people, one of whom made the song which is still sung:

"Wicked was he that took away my pot of flowers."

# SIXTH TALE

*Andreuola loves Gabriotto. She tells him a dream, and he tells her another. He suddenly dies in her arms, and while she and her servant are carrying him to his house they are arrested by the police, and she relates what had happened. The magistrate wants to lie with her; she will not allow it. Her father hears about it, establishes her innocence and gets her released. She refuses to remain in the world and becomes a nun*

Filomena's tale delighted the ladies, because they had often heard the song sung, but had never been able to find out, for all their questioning, what was the occasion of its being written. But, when the king heard the end, he ordered Pamfilo to follow in his turn, who spoke thus:

The dream related in the previous tale gives me the opportunity to tell one which contains two dreams relating to future happenings, as the dream in the former tale related to the past. And scarcely had the two dreams been told by the persons who saw them, than they both came true. And yet, amorous ladies, you must know that everybody living sees various things in dreams which seem quite true when he is asleep, but when he wakes he thinks some true, some probable and some quite beyond the truth; and yet many are found to come true.

Wherefore many people pay as much attention to a dream as they would to anything they saw when awake; and so are depressed or made happy by their dreams, according to whether they are favourable or not. On the other hand, some people have no faith in dreams until they find themselves in the danger of which their dreams had warned them. I praise neither of these sorts of people, because all dreams are not true, neither are they all false. Everyone of us can see for himself that they are not all true; but Filomena's tale shows, and I intend by my tale to show, that all dreams are not false. Therefore I think we should not fear any dream which is contrary to virtuous life and actions, and should not let it divert us from good intentions. But nobody should believe or take comfort from dreams which favour perverse and wicked deeds; yet give complete faith to dreams which are contrary to such things. But let me come to my tale.

In the city of Brescia there was formerly a gentleman named Messer Negro da Ponte Carrao, who among other children had a daughter named Andreuola. She was young and beautiful and unmarried, and fell in love with a neighbour called Gabriotto, a man of low estate but excellent behaviour, handsome and a pleasant man. By the help of a servant in the house, Gabriotto not only learned that Andreuola was in love with him, but many times met her in her father's garden to their great mutual delight.

So that nothing but death might separate them from their delicious love, they secretly became man and wife, and so carried on their love affair in secret. One night when the girl was asleep, she had a dream. She thought she was in the garden with Gabriotto and held him in her arms, to the joy of them both. While they were there she saw something dark and terrible, whose shape she could not distinguish, come out of his body. She thought this shape seized Gabriotto and clasped him violently in its arms against his will, and plunged with him underground; after which she saw neither of them again. This caused her such inexpressible anguish that she awoke, and although on awakening she was happy to find it was only a dream, yet it made her afraid.

When she found that Gabriotto wanted to come to her the next night, she did all she could to persuade him from coming that evening; but, finding that he wanted to come and being unwilling to make him feel suspicious, she received him that night in the garden. It was summer time, and after picking red and white roses, they went to sit down by a clear and beautiful fountain which was in the garden.

After they had taken their delight, Gabriotto asked her why she had not wanted him to come there. The girl then told him the dream she had had the night before and how it had made her anxious. When Gabriotto heard this, he laughed, and said it was great folly to put any faith in dreams, because they were the result of excess or lack of food, while every day showed how false they were.

"If I followed dreams," he went on, "I should not have come here, less on account of your dream than of one I had myself a few nights ago. I dreamed I was in a beautiful and delightful forest hunting, and there I caught the most beautiful and charming little she-goat you ever saw. She was white as snow, and very soon she became so fond of me that she would never leave me. And I thought she was so dear to me that, to prevent her leaving me, I put a gold ring round her neck and held her by a chain of gold.

"After this I dreamed that I was resting beside the she-goat with my head against her, when suddenly there appeared a coal-black greyhound, hungry and terrifying to look at, which came towards me. I made no resistance, and I thought the greyhound thrust its muzzle into my left side and gnawed at it until it reached the heart, which it tore out of me to carry away. This made me feel such anguish that my dream broke, and as I awoke I clapped my hand to my side to make sure that nothing had been torn from it. But, as I found nothing wrong, I laughed at myself for looking.

"But what, after all, is the meaning of all this? I have seen similar and more terrible things before now, without the slightest thing different happening to me. So let them go, and let us enjoy ourselves."

The girl had been frightened by her own dream but was much more frightened when she heard his. But she hid her fear as well as she could, in order not to annoy Gabriotto. As they kissed and embraced each other, she felt a vague anxiety, and kept looking into his face more often than usual and gazing about the garden to see if something black was coming. And as they were doing this, Gabriotto heaved a deep sigh, clutched her and said:

"Ah, my soul! Help me, I am dying."

And so saying, he fell down on the grass. Andreuola lifted him on to her lap as he lay there and exclaimed, almost weeping:

"*O* my sweet lord, what is it you feel?"

Gabriotto made no reply, but gasped and broke out into perspiration all over, and very soon died. Everyone can imagine how grievous and painful this was to the girl, who loved him more than herself. She wept over him and called to him in vain. She touched him all over his body, and found every part was cold; and so knew he was dead. Not knowing what to do or say, she went all in tears and agony of mind to call the maid servant who was her confidante in this love affair, and told her of this misfortune. After they had wept pitifully together for some time over Gabriotto's death, Andreuola said to the servant:

"Since God has taken him away from me, I do not intend to remain alive. But before I kill myself we must act in such a way as to save my honour and to conceal the secret love between us; and we must also bury the body from which the gracious soul has departed."

"My child," said the maid servant, "do not talk of killing yourself. You have lost him here and if you kill yourself you will lose him in the next world, because you will go to hell, and I am sure his soul is not there, for he was a good young man. It is much better to take comfort and to think of helping his soul with prayers and other pious deeds, in case he needs them for any sin he has committed. The quickest way to bury him is in this garden, which nobody will ever know, because no one knew he came here. If you do not want to do that, let us put him outside the garden and leave him; someone will find him tomorrow morning and take him home, and his relatives will bury him."

Although the girl was full of bitterness and continued

weeping, yet she listened to the servant's advice. The first part she rejected, and replied to the second as follows:

"God forbid that a man so dear to me, my beloved husband, should be buried like a dog or left in the street. He has had my tears and he shall have those of his relatives, if possible. I have thought already what we must do."

She immediately sent the servant for a roll of silk stuff she had in a chest. She stretched it on the ground and laid Gabriotto's body on it with a pillow under his head. With many tears she closed his eyes and mouth, and made a garland of roses for his head and covered him with the roses they had plucked together, and then said to the servant:

"It is not far from here to the door of his house. You and I can carry him there as we have arranged him, and we can leave him at the door. It will soon be day, and then he will be taken in. And although this will be no consolation to his relatives, it will be some small pleasure to me, in whose arms he died."

So saying, she once more shed abundant tears on his face, and for a long time wept for him. The day was then near; and at the servant's urgent entreaties, she stood up, took from her finger the ring with which Gabriotto had wedded her and put it on his finger, saying plaintively:

"My dear lord, if your soul now sees my tears, or if any feeling or consciousness remains in your body after the departure of your soul, receive kindly this last gift from her whom you loved so much when you were alive."

So saying, she fell down swooning beside him. After she had recovered, she stood up, and she and the servant took the piece of silk on which the body was lying, went out of the garden, and made their way towards his house. As they went along, it chanced that they were met and arrested with the dead body by some of the watch who happened to be going that way. Andreuola, who was more eager to die than to live, recognised the police, and said frankly to them:

"I know who you are, and I know it is useless for me to try to fly. I am ready to go with you before the Magistrate, and to tell him all about it. But, if I obey you, let none of you dare to touch me nor remove anything from this body, if he does not want to be accused by me."

So nobody touched her, and they all went to the palace with Gabriotto's body. When the Magistrate was informed, he got up and had her brought into his room, and questioned her about what had happened. He had some doctors examine the body to see if the man had died of poison or otherwise, and they all said he had not, but that a tumour near the heart had burst and suffocated him. Hearing this and realising that she was guilty of a small offence, he tried to make her give him what she could not sell, and told her he would set her free if she would yield to his desires. But his words were of no avail, and, contrary to all decency, he tried to force her. But Andreuola, aroused and strengthened by anger, defended herself vigorously, and rebuffed him with high scornful words.

Next day, Messer Negro was told about it. Grieved to the point of death he went to the palace with many of his friends, and there made enquiries about it of the Magistrate, and sadly asked that his daughter might be returned to him. The Magistrate wanted to confess that he tried to force her, before she accused him. So he praised the girl's constancy, and then admitted what he had done. Wherefore, seeing she was so virtuous, he had fallen in love with her, and was willing to marry her, if it pleased her father and herself, although she had been married to a man of low estate. While they were talking in this way, Andreuola came to her father, and threw herself weeping before him, saying:

"Father, it is not necessary for me to tell you the story of my love and its sad fate, for I am certain you have heard all about it. With all humility I ask your pardon for the fault I committed in taking as my husband the man I loved, without your knowledge. I do not ask this favour of you that my life may be saved, but so that I may die as your daughter and not as your enemy."

So saying, she fell at her father's feet. Messer Negro was old, and a man of gentle and kindly nature; and when he heard these words he began to weep, and tenderly raised his daughter to her feet, and said:

"Daughter, I should have been happier if you had taken a husband I thought fitting for you; but if you took a man whom you loved, he ought to have pleased me too. But it grieves me that from lack of confidence in me you concealed him from me, and still more that you have lost him before I knew about him. But, since this is as it is, to please you I will honour him as my son-in-law now he is dead, as I would gladly have honoured him in his lifetime."

Turning then to his sons and relatives, he bade them prepare great and honourable obsequies for Gabriotto. Meanwhile, the young man's relatives and nearly all the other men and women of the town had heard the news, and had gathered there. So the body was laid out in the courtyard on Andreuola's silk cloth and with all the roses, and was bewailed not only by her and his women relatives but by almost all the women of the town and many men. He was then taken from the courtyard like a lord, not like a common man, on the shoulders of the noblest citizens, and carried to his grave with the utmost honour.

A few days later the Magistrate followed up his proposal, but when Messer Negro spoke of it to his daughter, she would not hear of it. But, desiring in all things to please her father, she and her servant became nuns in a convent famous for its sanctity, and there lived virtuously for many years.

## SEVENTH TALE

*Simona loves Pasquino. They are together in a garden, and Pasquino rubs a leaf of sage on his teeth and falls dead. Simona is arrested and, while explaining to the judge how Pasquino died, she rubs one of the same leaves on her teeth, and dies too*

Pamfilo finished his tale, and the king, showing no compassion for Andreuola, looked at Emilia and signed to her that it was his pleasure she should continue next after those who had spoken. Without any delay, she began as follows:

My dear friends, Pamfilo's tale induces me to tell one which is in no respect like his, except that the person I shall speak of lost her lover in a garden, like Andreuola. She was arrested also like Andreuola, but escaped from the Court, not by force or virtue, but by an unexpected death. As we have often said, love frequently inhabits the houses of noblemen and yet does not scorn the dwellings of the poor, and there displays his power just as he makes himself dreaded by the rich as a most powerful lord. This will be seen to some extent from my tale. In telling it I shall return to our own city, from which we have departed today in relating different events in different parts of the world.

Not long ago there lived in Florence a girl named Simona, quite beautiful and charming for her state of life. Although she had to earn her own bread by spinning wool, she was not so poor in spirit but that she longed to receive love into her soul. Love was born in her from the words and deeds of a young man, of the same state of life as herself, who was sent by his master to bring her wool to spin.

Love entered her soul through the pleasing aspect of this young man, who was named Pasquino; she greatly desired yet did not expect that it would go further, and, with every thread of wool she span she breathed a thousand sighs hotter than fire as she thought of the young man who had brought her the wool to spin. On the other hand he became very solicitous that his master's wool should be well spun, and came to see her more often than any other worker, as if she and nobody else were spinning all his master's cloth.

Thus, as he was always coming and she was anxious to have him come, it naturally happened that he became more ardent and she got rid of her accustomed shame and fear; and so they came together for their mutual pleasure. They liked each other so much that they contrived to meet each other without waiting to be invited. And as this went on from day to day increasing, Pasquino happened to say to Simona that above all things he wanted her to come with him to a garden, where they could be together more freely and with less suspicion.

Simona agreed to this. And one Sunday after dinner she told her father that she wanted to go to the festival of San Gallo, but instead went with a friend named Lagina to the garden Pasquino had mentioned. He was there with a friend named Puccino, who was nicknamed Stramba. A love affair was quickly struck up between Stramba and Lagina, who remained in one part of the garden, while the other two went off by themselves.

In that part of the garden where Pasquino and Simona were walking, there was a large and beautiful head of sage. They sat down beside it and talked gaily together, especially about a picnic they were planning to have in the garden. As they talked, Pasquino turned to the sage plant and picked off one of its leaves, with which he began to rub his teeth and gums, saying that sage cleaned them wonderfully from everything which might remain after eating. And while he was rubbing his teeth, he went back to the picnic which they had been discussing before. He had not been talking long when his countenance altered, and soon after that he lost sight and speech, and in a short time died.

Simona then began to weep and scream and call for Stramba and Lagina. They came running up, and when Stramba saw that Pasquino was dead and already swollen up with dark patches on his face and body, he screamed out:

"You wicked woman, you've poisoned him!"

And he made such a disturbance that many of the people living near the garden heard him. They came running towards the noise, and found Pasquino dead and swollen up, and Stramba lamenting and accusing Simona of having poisoned him, and Simona almost beside herself with grief at the sudden death of her lover and quite unable to defend herself, so they all believed what Stramba said. They therefore seized the weeping Simona, and took her to the Magistrate's palace.

There Stramba and two other friends of Pasquino's, named Atticciato and Malagevole, preferred the accusation; and the judge immediately began to examine the case. He could not see how Simona could have committed a crime or be guilty, and, as he could not understand her explanations, he wanted to see the dead body and the place and manner of death in her presence, and there hear what she had to say. So without any disturbance he went with her to the place where Pasquino's body still lay, swollen up like a tub, and went up to it marvelling at his death, and asked her how it had happened. She went up to the sage bush and there related the whole story, and to demonstrate what she was saying she copied Pasquino, and rubbed her teeth with a leaf of sage.

Stramba and Atticciato and the other friends and companions of Pasquino scoffed at all this in the judge's presence, and continued urging her guilt and clamouring for nothing less than that she should be burned alive as a punishment for her crime. The poor girl in her confusion and distress at the death of her lover and with fear at the punishment asked for by Stramba, went on rubbing her teeth with the sage; and the same misfortune happened to her as to Pasquino, to the amazement of everybody present.

O happy spirits, whose ardent love and mortal life ended on the same day! And yet more happy if you went together to the same place! And happiest of all, if there is love in that place, and you love there as you did here! But in the judgment of us who remain here alive, most happy of all was the soul of Simona, whose innocence Fortune would not allow to suffer from the accusations of Stramba, Atticciato and Malagevole (no doubt wool-carders or even baser men), nor could find any better way of saving her from infamy than to involve her in the same fate as her lover, and to let her follow the beloved spirit of her Pasquino!

The judge was stupefied by this accident, as indeed were all those present, and, not knowing what to say, was silent for a long time. At last, recovering his wits, he said:

"Plainly this sage is poisonous, which is not usual with sage. Pull it up by the roots and burn it so that it cannot harm anyone else in the same way."

Those who had charge of the garden immediately did this in the judge's presence. And they had no sooner plucked up this head of sage than the reason for the death of the two poor wretches became apparent. Under the sage was a huge toad whose venomous breath had poisoned the sage. Nobody was anxious to go near the toad, so they built a large brushwood fire all round and burned the toad and the sage. Thus ended the judge's enquiry into poor Pasquino's death. Stramba, Atticciato, Guccio Imbratta and Malagevole took up the swollen bodies of Pasquino and Simona and buried them in the church of San Paolo, of which perhaps they were parishioners.

### EIGHT TALE

*Girolamo is in love with Salvestra. Compelled by his mother's entreaties, he goes to Paris. When he returns, he finds her married; he secretly enters her house and dies there. His body is taken to a church, and Salvestra dies beside him, and both are buried in the same grave*

When Emilia had finished, Neifile began at the king's command. Most worthy ladies, in my opinion there are some persons who think they know more than other people, and in fact know less. They oppose their opinions not only to the advice of other men but even to the nature of things; and through their presumptuousness great evils have occurred, but never any good. Among all natural things, love least of all will endure contrary advice or action, for its nature is such that it can more quickly consume itself than be removed by foresight. So it occurs to me to tell you the tale of a woman who tried to be wiser than she was or than was befitting her or than the case in which she tried to show her wisdom needed; she attempted to expel love from an enamoured heart (a love set there perhaps by heavenly influence), and succeeded in driving out love and life at one and the same time from her son's body.

As old stories tell, there lived long ago in our city a very great and rich merchant, named Leonardo Sighieri, who had by his wife one son, named Girolamo, after whose birth he departed this life, leaving all his affairs in order. The child's guardians and mother brought him up well and scrupulously. The boy grew up with other children of the neighbourhood, and became attached to a girl of his own age, the daughter of a tailor. When he was older this familiarity developed into such love that Girolamo was never happy unless he saw her, and she loved him as much as he loved her.

The boy's mother of course noticed it, and often scolded and punished him for it; and as Girolamo could not be restrained she complained to the guardians. And on account of her son's wealth she behaved like someone trying to turn a plum into an orange, and said to them:

"Our boy, though only just fourteen, is so much in love with a tailor's daughter, named Salvestra, that if we do not take him away from her, he may one of these days marry her without anyone's knowledge, and then I shall never be happy again. Or else he will pine away when he sees her married to someone else. So I think that to avoid this you should send him to some distant place on business among our factors, and when he gets away from her he will get her out of his mind, and we can then find him some well-born girl as a wife."

The guardians agreed, and said they would do what they could. They called the boy into the counting-house, and one of them talked kindly to him as follows:

"My boy, you are now grown up, and it is right that you should begin to learn something about your affairs. We should be very glad if you would go to Paris for a time, where a great part of your wealth is employed in trade; moreover, you will become more polished and accomplished than you can here, for you will frequent lords and barons and gentlemen and learn their habits, and then you can come back here."

The boy listened carefully, and replied that he did not want to go because he thought he would be as well off in Florence as anyone else. The good men then reproved him, but being unable to get any other reply from him, went and told his mother. She was extremely angry, not because he would not go to Paris, but on account of his love, and attacked him violently.

Then, soothing him down with soft words, she flattered him and begged him to do what his tutors wanted, to please her. And at last he agreed that he would go away for one year only.

So Girolamo went to Paris deeply in love, and by being put off from time to time was kept away two years. He then returned home more in love than ever, and found his Salvestra married to a young man who made tents, which filled him with grief. But, seeing that there was nothing else to do, he tried to possess his soul in peace. He discovered where her house was, and, as young men do when they are in love, he began to pass to and fro in front of it, thinking that she had no more forgotten him than he her.

However, it turned out otherwise. She no more remembered him than if she had never seen him; or if she did recollect anything, she did not show it, but rather the contrary. In a very short time the young man discovered this, to his great grief. He nevertheless did everything he could to recall himself to her; but as he seemed to achieve nothing, he determined to speak to her himself, even at the risk of his life.

He found out the arrangement of her house from a neighbour, and one evening when she and her husband were out on a pleasure trip with their neighbours, he secretly went in and hid himself behind some rolls of canvas. There he waited until they came home and went to bed; and when the husband was asleep, he crept to the place where he had seen Salvestra lie down, and, putting his hand on her breast, said softly:

"O my sweet, are you asleep?"

The girl, who was not asleep, was about to scream, but the young man said quickly:

"For the love of God, don't scream, I am your Girolamo."

Hearing this, she began to tremble, and said:

"For God's sake, go away, Girolamo. The time is gone when in our childhood we could be lovers. I am married, as you see, and it is wrong for me to think of any man but my husband. So in the name of God I beg you will go away. If my husband heard you, even suppose nothing worse happened, I should never live in peace and quiet with him again, whereas now he loves me, and we live happily together."

The young man felt a sharp pang at these words; and he reminded her of past times and his love which had not been quenched by absence, and mingled entreaties with promises;

but yet obtained nothing. So, longing for death, he finally asked as a reward for his great love that she would let him lie beside her until he was warm, since he was frozen with waiting for her. He promised her he would say nothing about it and not touch her and go away as soon as he was a little warmer. Salvestra was a little sorry for him, and on these conditions agreed to what he asked.

The young man then lay down beside her without touching her. He gathered into one fixed thought his long love for her and her coldness and his lost hopes, and made up his mind to die. Without saying a word, he clenched his fists, held his breath, and died beside her.

After some time, the girl began to wonder at his stillness, and, fearing that her husband might awake, she said:

"Now, Girolamo, why don't you go away?"

Not getting any reply, she thought he must have gone to sleep. So she stretched out her hand to wake him up and began to shake him, but she found him as cold as ice, which greatly amazed her. She touched him again, and, finding he did not move, realised that he was dead. So there she lay in great distress, not knowing what to do.

At last she determined to find out what her husband would say ought to be done if this had happened to someone else. So she woke him up, and told him what had just happened to her as if it had happened to somebody else, and then asked him what he would do if it had happened to her. The good man replied that he thought the dead body should be secretly carried home and left there, without any blame falling on the woman, who in his opinion had committed no sin. Then the young woman said:

"That is what we must do."

She then took his hand, and made him feel the dead man. The husband jumped up in amazement and lighted a light; and without entering into any explanation with his wife he dressed the body in its own clothes and, aided by his innocence, at once lifted it on to his shoulders and carried it to the door of Girolamo's house, where he left it.

Next morning when Girolamo was found lying dead before his own house, there was a great disturbance, and much uproar from the mother. He was carefully examined, and no wound or bruise was found upon him; so the doctors agreed that he had died of grief, as indeed he had.

The dead body was then carried to a church, and the grieving mother and many other women, both relatives and neighbours, began to weep and lament over him, as is customary with us. And while they were bewailing him, the good man in whose house Girolamo had died, said to Salvestra:

"Throw a cloak over your head, and go to the church where they have taken Girolamo. Mingle with the women, and find out what they are saying about all this, and I will do the same among the men, so that we can find out if anything is being said about us."

The girl had become compassionate too late; and this proposal pleased her, because she wanted to see the dead man to whom she would not give one kiss in his lifetime; and so she went.

It is a marvellous thing to think how difficult it is to examine into the power of love! The heart, which Girolamo's good fortune could not move, was touched by his misery. When, hidden under her cloak among the women and girls, she saw his dead face, the old flame flared up and such pity came suddenly upon her that she did not rest until she got close to the body. There she uttered a shrill scream and threw herself on the young man, whose face she did not drench in tears, because no sooner had she touched him than grief took away her life as it had taken away the young man's life.

But, as the women crowded round to comfort her and to tell her to get up (although they did not know who she was), and still she did not get up, they tried to lift her and found her motionless. And when they did lift her up they discovered at one and the same time that she was Salvestra and that she was dead. And all the women who were there were overcome with pity and began to lament more loudly than before. The news ran through the church to the men outside and came to the husband's ears. He wept a long time without listening to comfort or consolation from anyone, and then related to those about him the story of what had happened the night before between his wife and the young man. Thus, everyone discovered the reason for the death of the two young people, and grieved for it.

They then took the dead girl and dressed her as dead bodies are customarily decked out, and laid her on the same bier with Girolamo. After long lamentation they were both buried in the same grave; and thus they whom love could not join together became inseparable companions in death.

## NINTH TALE

*Messer Guglielmo Rossiglione makes his wife eat the heart of Messer Guglielmo Guardastagno, her lover, whom he had slain. When she finds it out, she throws herself from a high window and kills herself, and is buried with her lover*

Neifile finished her tale, which aroused pity in the hearers, and then the king who had no intention of taking away Dioneo's privilege, began his tale, since he was the only one left to speak.

Pitiful ladies, since you are so much moved by sad happenings to lovers, you will feel as much pity at the tale I have prepared as at that we have just heard, because those I shall speak of were of nobler rank and their misfortune more terrible.

You must know then, that, according to the Provençals, there were once two noble knights of Provence, both with castles and vassals, one of whom was named Messer Guglielmo Rossiglione and the other Messer Guglielmo Guardastagno. Both were valiant men at arms and therefore loved each other; and they were wont always to go together to jousts and tourneys and other feats of arms, bearing the same device.

As each dwelt in his castle, about ten miles apart, it happened that Messer Guglielmo Guardastagno—despite the brotherhood of arms and friendship between them—fell deeply in love with Messer Guglielmo's beautiful and charming wife. He behaved in such a way that the lady found it out, and, as she knew him to be a most valiant knight, she fell in love with him too, so much so that there was nothing she desired nor loved more, and above all wished to be wooed by him. This very soon happened, and, as they loved each other very much, they often came together.

But they were not sufficiently discreet in their behaviour, and the husband found it out. He was so much enraged that his old love for Guardastagno changed to mortal hatred; but he kept his hatred better concealed than the

lovers had kept their love, and determined to kill Guardastagno.

While Rossiglione was in this mood a great tournament
was proclaimed in France, which Rossiglione immediately
announced to Guardastagno, asking him to come and discuss whether they should go to it and how. To which
Guardastagno cheerfully replied that he would come to sup
with him the next day without fail.

Rossiglione then thought that the time had come to kill
him. Next day he armed, and went to horse with some of
his followers, and laid an ambush in a wood about a mile
from his castle, through which he knew Guardastagno had
to pass. After waiting for a time they saw the knight riding
towards them unarmed with two unarmed attendants, like
a man who suspected no danger. When he came up to the
ambush, Rossiglione rushed at him furiously, lance in hand,
shouting: "You are a dead man," and so saying thrust his
lance through the knight's chest.

Guardastagno was pierced by the lance before he could
make any defence or utter a word, and fell dead. His two
servants, without recognising the enemy who had done
this, turned their horses' heads and galloped back to their
lord's castle as fast as they could. Rossiglione dismounted,
cut open Guardastagno's breast with a dagger, tore out his
heart with his own hands, and, wrapping up the heart in a
lance pennon, gave it to one of the attendants to carry. He
ordered them not to dare to speak a word of what had occurred and then remounted his horse and returned to his
castle as night fell.

The lady had heard that Guardastagno was to sup there
that evening, and was awaiting him with the greatest desire.
She was greatly surprised when she found he did not come,
and said to her husband:

"How does it happen, Messer, that Guardastagno has
not come?"

"Lady," replied the husband, "I have heard from him
that he cannot get here until tomorrow."

The lady was a little angry at this. Rossiglione dismounted, and called for the cook, to whom he said:

"Take this boar's heart and make the best and most delicious dish of it you can; and when I am at table, send it
to me in a silver dish."

The cook expended all his art and care on the dish,
minced up the heart and spiced it, and made it into a most
delicious dish.

At the usual time Messer Guglielmo and his wife sat

down at table. Food was served, but he ate little, for his thoughts were occupied by the crime he had just committed. The cook sent him up the dressed heart and he had it set before his wife, praising the dish to her while he pretended to be a little out of sorts himself. The lady had a good appetite, tasted the dish, and thought it good; and therefore ate it all up. When the knight saw that his wife had finished the heart, he said:

"Lady, what did you think of that dish?"

"My lord," she replied, "In good faith, it pleased me greatly."

"God be my helper," said the knight, "I can easily believe you; nor do I marvel that what gave you so much pleasure when alive should please you when dead."

At this the lady was silent for a moment, and then said:

"How? What is it you have made me eat?"

"What you have eaten," said the knight, "is verily the heart of Messer Guglielmo Guardastagno, whom you, like a faithless woman, loved so dearly. And you may be certain that it is he, because I tore the heart from his breast with these hands, a short time before I returned home."

No need to ask whether the lady was in anguish when she heard this about the man whom she loved so much. After a little time she said:

"You have acted like a base and treacherous knight. If I, under no compulsion from him, made him lord of my love and thereby did you wrong, I should have borne the penalty, and not he. But, please God, no other food shall ever follow a food so noble as the heart of a knight so courteous and valiant as Messer Guglielmo Guardastagno."

And jumping to her feet she ran to a window which was behind her and threw herself out of it without the slightest hesitation. This window was high above the ground so that the lady was not only killed by her fall but smashed to pieces.

Messer Guglielmo was stunned by this event and felt he had done wrong, and, dreading the revenge of the Count of Provence and the peasants, he saddled his horses and fled. Next day the whole countryside heard what had happened. The two bodies were taken up by the inhabitants of Messer Guglielmo Guardastagno's castle and by the inhabitants of the lady's castle. With great grief and lamentation they were buried in the church of the lady's own castle and laid in the same grave, and over them were written verses telling who they were and the manner and the reason of their death.

## TENTH TALE

*A doctor's wife thinks her lover is dead and puts him into a chest which is carried off by two usurers. He wakes up and is arrested as a thief. The lady's servant tells the Magistrate how she had put him into the chest, unknown to the usurers; he escapes hanging, and the money-lenders are fined for stealing the chest*

When the king had finished his tale, Dioneo alone was left to speak, so, at the king's command, he began thus:

The miseries told of unfortunate lovers, ladies, have so saddened my eyes and breast (and yours) that I have longed for the end to come. Now, thank God, they are done with—unless I should add another tale on this dreary topic, which God forbid—so without entering on such painful subjects, I shall begin on a better and more cheerful topic, which perhaps will serve as a guide to the tales we tell tomorrow.

You must know, fairest ladies, that not long ago there lived in Salerno a very great surgeon named Maestro Mazzeo della Montagna. Although he had reached extreme old age, he married a beautiful and noble girl of his city, whom he kept supplied with rich clothes and jewels and everything which could please a woman, beyond any other woman in the town. True, she was rather cold most of the time, since she was not well covered in the doctor's bed.

You remember Messer Ricciardo di Chinzica and how he taught his wife to keep holiday. Well, in the same way, this doctor told his wife that very many days were needed to recover from the strain of lying with a woman and the like twaddle; so that she lived in the greatest discontent. She was a prudent and high-minded woman, so, to save the household goods she determined to turn highwayman and spoil others. She looked at many young men, and at last one so occupied her mind that she set all her hopes and soul and possessions upon him. This the young man perceived, and, as she pleased him mightily, he returned her love.

This young man was named Ruggieri da Jeroli, of noble birth but of such a vicious life and blameworthy behaviour that he had not one friend or relative left who wished him well or ever wanted to see him again. He was ill-famed throughout Salerno for robberies and other vile deeds, about which the lady cared little since he pleased her for other reasons. And so she arranged with one of her maid servants in such a way that he and she could be together. After they had taken their delight, the lady began to deplore his past life and begged him for love of her to refrain from such things. To help him to do this she gave him sums of money from time to time.

They went on in this way very prudently for some time, when it happened that there came into the doctor's hands a patient with a diseased leg. After examination the doctor told the relatives that if a certain decayed bone were not taken out he would either lose his leg or his life; if the bone were removed he might recover, but he could only consider him as in a desperate condition. And his relatives acquiesced in this.

The doctor saw that the patient would not allow the operation and would be unable to endure the pain unless he had an opiate. He decided to perform the operation in the evening, and that morning he had distilled a certain preparation of his which when drunk would put a man to sleep for as long a period as he thought necessary for the operation. The preparation was brought to the house, and the doctor put it in his bedroom, without telling anybody what it was.

That evening, just as the doctor was going to this patient, there came a message from certain of his closest friends in Amalfi to say that nothing must stop him from going there immediately, because there had been a big riot and many people had been wounded. The doctor postponed the operation on the leg until the next morning, went on board a small boat, and set out for Amalfi. His wife, knowing he would not be back home that night, had Ruggieri brought in secretly as usual, put him in her bedroom and there locked him in until such time as the other persons in the house should have gone to bed.

While Ruggieri was waiting for the lady in her bedroom, there came upon him a violent thirst, either from the exercise he had taken that day or from eating salt meat or perhaps from habit. He saw on the window-sill the bottle of opiate which the doctor had prepared for the sick man, and, thinking it was drinking water, he lifted it to his lips and drank it off. In a very short time a deep slumber came over him, and he fell fast asleep.

As soon as she could, the lady went to her bedroom, and, finding Ruggieri asleep, she shook him and in a low voice told him to get up; but nothing happened, he neither replied nor stirred. The lady then became rather annoyed and shaking him more roughly said:

"Get up, sleepy-head. If you want to sleep, you should go home and not come here."

The push she gave Ruggieri made him fall off the chest on which he was lying, but he gave no more signs of life than a corpse. The lady now became frightened, tried to lift him up, shook him harder, pulled his nose, tweaked his beard; but all to no effect. He was sleeping like a log. She then began to fear that he was dead, and pinched him and burned his flesh with a lighted candle, still with no result. So she, who was no doctor, although her husband was one, felt certain he was dead. No need to ask if she was in distress, since she loved him as much as she did. Not daring to make a noise, she wept over him silently, and lamented this misfortune.

After some time the lady began to remember that she might be publicly shamed in addition to her loss, and thought that some means must be found of getting him out of the house without delay. Not knowing what to do, she quietly called up the maid servant, told her what had happened and asked her advice. In great amazement the servant pulled and shook him, and, finding he was without feeling, she agreed with the lady that he was dead, and advised that he should be put out of the house.

Then said the lady:

"But where can we take him so that when he is found tomorrow nobody will suspect that he has been brought from here?"

"Madonna," replied the servant, "late this evening I saw a fairly large chest outside the shop of the carpenter next door. If he has not taken it into his house, it will suit us perfectly, because we can put him inside, give him two or three slashes with a knife, and leave him there. I don't see why the person who finds him there should think he comes from here rather than from anywhere else. Since he is such a disorderly young man it will be thought that he was murdered by one of his enemies while on some dirty business, and then put in the chest."

The lady agreed to the servant's advice, except that relating to knife slashes, saying that she could not possibly allow it. She then sent the servant out to see if the chest were still there; and she came back and announced that it was.

The servant was young and strong, and, with the lady's help, raised Ruggieri on to her shoulders. The lady went in front to see if anyone was coming, and the servant carried Ruggieri to the chest, into which they put him and closed the lid and left him.

At that time two young men had recently returned home. They lent out money at usury and liked to make a lot of money and spend little. They needed household goods, and the day before had noticed this chest, and had planned together to steal it away to their house if it were left out that night. About midnight they left their house, found the chest, and without looking further into it (although it seemed rather heavy), took it home and put it into the room where their wives were asleep, without troubling to take it anywhere else. There they left it, and went to bed.

After sleeping a long time Ruggieri digested the potion and exhausted its strength; and towards dawn he awoke. Although he had come out of his sleep and had recovered his senses, yet his brain was still stupefied, and he remained deaf that night and for several days afterwards. He opened his eyes, but saw nothing. He fumbled about with his hands, and finding himself in the chest, said to himself:

"What's all this? Where am I? Am I asleep or awake? Now I begin to remember—this evening I went to my mistress's bedroom, and I seem to be in a chest. What does it all mean? Has the doctor come home or something else happened so that the lady had to hide me here while I was asleep? I believe so; it must be that."

He then lay silent, and listened whether he could hear anything. He remained still a long time, but being uncomfortable in the small chest and feeling stiff in the side on which he was lying, he tried to turn over on the other side. He did this so nimbly that he knocked his buttocks against one side of the chest which was standing unevenly, and so made it wobble and then fall over. It went down with a crash and woke the sleeping women, who were so terrified that they lay in silence.

Ruggieri was also frightened by the fall, but, finding the chest had opened, he thought that if anything happened he would be better off outside than in. And what between his not knowing where he was and one thing and another he began to fumble about the room, trying to find whether there was a door or a staircase by which he could escape.

The women heard him fumbling as they lay awake, and said: "Who's there?" Ruggieri, not recognising the voice, made no reply. Then the women called to the two young men who were in a deep sleep, because they had sat up late, and heard nothing.

The women were still more frightened then, jumped out of bed, ran to the window and began to shriek: "Thieves! Thieves!" Several of the neighbours got into the house by way of the roof or otherwise and rushed into the room, and at the same time the two young men were awakened by the noise. When Ruggieri saw them all appear he was beside himself with amazement and did not know how or if he could escape. He was captured and handed over to the watch, who had also run up at the noise. He was taken before the Magistrate and, being known as a bad character, was immediately put to the torture, and confessed that he had entered the usurers' house as a thief. So the Magistrate thought he would string him by the neck as soon as possible.

Next day the news ran through Salerno that Ruggieri had been arrested while robbing a usurer's house. When the lady and her servant heard it they were so amazed that they were not far from believing that they had not really done what they did the night before, but had only dreamed it. In addition, the lady was nearly mad with grief when she thought of the danger Ruggieri was in.

About the middle of Tierce the doctor returned from Amalfi, and asked where his potion was, because he wanted to operate on his patient. When he found the bottle was empty, he made a great fuss, so that everything in the house was upside down. The lady, who had other things to trouble about, said to him angrily:

"Why do you make such a fuss, Doctor, as if the upsetting of a bottle of water was so important? Isn't there plenty more water in the world?"

"Woman," said the doctor, "you think it was pure water. It was not, it was a sleeping potion."

He then told her the reason why it had been prepared. As soon as the lady heard this, she guessed that Ruggieri had drunk it, and so had seemed dead to them. And she said:

"We did not know it. You'll have to make some more."

Seeing there was nothing else to do, the doctor ordered another potion. Soon afterwards, the maid servant went out to find what was being said about Ruggieri, and when she returned, said:

"Madonna, everyone speaks ill of Ruggieri, and as far as

I could discover, he has not one friend or relative who will lift a finger to help him. Everyone thinks the judge will have him hanged tomorrow. In addition to this, I have one piece of news for you, for I think I have found out how he came to be in the usurers' house. You know the carpenter outside whose shop we found the chest to put Ruggieri in—well, he has had a long wrangle with a man who claims that the chest was his, and when the man asked for the value of the chest in money, the carpenter replied that he had not sold the chest, and that it had been stolen the night before. Then the other man said: 'That's not true, because you sold it to two young usurers, as they themselves told me last night when I saw it in their house at the time Ruggieri was arrested.' Said the carpenter: 'They're liars. I never sold it to them, but they stole it from me last night. Let us go to them.' And so they went off together to the usurers' house, and I came back here. It is easy to see how Ruggieri was carried to the place where he was found, but how he got out of the chest, I don't see."

The lady now perfectly understood how it had all happened. She told the servant what she had heard from the doctor, and begged her to help Ruggieri to escape, for she wanted both to save Ruggieri and to keep her own reputation.

"Madonna," said the servant, "tell me what to do, and I will gladly do anything."

The lady realised that she must be quick off the mark, and had already decided what had to be done. This she told the servant in proper order. The servant first went weeping to the doctor, and said:

"Messer, I have come to ask your forgiveness for a great fault I have committed towards you."

"What's that?" said the doctor.

Shedding copious tears, the servant said:

"Messer, you know what a young man Ruggieri da Jeroli is, and he likes me, and what between being in love with him and being afraid of him I had to go with him this year. He knew you wouldn't be home last night, and got round me to let him come into my bedroom to sleep with me. And he got thirsty, and as there was nowhere I could get wine or water quickly, and I didn't want the mistress to see me in the parlour, I remembered I had seen a bottle of water in your bedroom. So I went and got it, and gave it to him to drink, and put the bottle back where I had found it, and you afterwards made such a fuss about it. I do confess I did wrong, but then who doesn't do wrong sometimes? I am very sorry I did it, not only for this but because Ruggieri may lose his life in consequence. So I beg you to forgive me and to give me permission to go and try to help Ruggieri as far as I can."

Although the doctor was angry, he replied jokingly:

"You have forgiven yourself—you thought last night you were going to have a young man who would warm your fur for you, and you had a sluggard instead. Be off with you, and try to save your lover, but don't you bring him into this house again, or I'll make you pay for that time and this!"

The girl felt she had brought off the first coup very well; and then went straight off to Ruggieri's prison, where she so worked upon the gaoler that he allowed her to speak to Ruggieri. Then, as soon as she had told Ruggieri what answers he had to make the judge, she got herself taken before him. Before the judge would listen to her, he wanted to grapple with such a fresh, buxom young Christian woman; and she, wanting a favourable audience, made no objection. When the milling was over, she said:

"Messer, you have arrested Ruggieri da Jeroli as a thief, and the charge is false."

Then, beginning at the beginning, she told him the whole story, how she, his mistress, had brought him into the doctor's house, and how she had given him the opiate to drink, and how she had thought he was dead and put him in the chest. After that she told him the conversation she had heard between the carpenter and the owner of the chest to show him how Ruggieri had got into the usurers' house.

The judge saw that it would be easy to find out if this story were true. So he first questioned the doctor about the potion, and found that was true; after that he sent for the carpenter and the owner of the chest and the usurers, and after much talk found that the usurers had stolen the chest the night before. Finally he sent for Ruggieri, and asked him where he had lodged the night before. Ruggieri replied that he did not know, but he remembered that he had gone to sleep with Doctor Matteo's servant, and that he had drunk some water in her bedroom because he was very thirsty; but he did not know what happened afterwards until he awoke and found himself in a chest in the usurers' house.

The judge was greatly amused at hearing all this, and made the servant and Ruggieri and the carpenter and the usurers repeat their tales several times. Finally, he recognised that Ruggieri was innocent and set him at liberty, and fined the usurers ten florins for stealing the chest. No need to ask whether Ruggieri was glad, and his mistress also was delighted. So the lady and the lover continued their loves and pleasures better than before, and laughed over it all with the invaluable servant who had wanted to give him two or three slashes with a knife. May I have the same success in love—but not to be put in a chest!

If the earlier tales had saddened the ladies' bosoms, this last tale of Dioneo's made them laugh so much, especially when the judge wanted to grapple with the servant, that they quite recovered from their sadness.

But the king now saw that the sun was turning yellow, and that the end of his reign was at hand. In a few graceful words he begged the ladies' pardon for having chosen as the topic of their tales a matter so sad as the misfortunes of lovers. After this he stood up, took the laurel wreath from his head, and as the ladies waited eagerly to see whom he would bestow it upon, he gracefully set it on the golden head of Fiammetta, saying:

"I give you this crown, since you better than anyone else can console the band for the harshness of today by what you will order tomorrow."

Fiammetta's hair was curled, long and golden, and fell about her delicate white shoulders; her oval face was the true colour of white lilies, mingled with all the splendour of red roses; her eyes were like a falcon's; she had a plump little mouth, with lips like twin rubies; and she smiled as she answered:

"Filostrato, I take it willingly; and, in order that you may perceive what you have done, I will and command that you all prepare yourselves to tell tales tomorrow of those lovers who have attained happiness after grief or misfortune."

This proposal pleased everyone. She then called the steward and made all necessary arrangements with him; after which the whole band stood up, and she gave them permission to do as they liked until supper time.

Some of them went into the garden, whose beauty was such that it could not soon pall; some went down to the mills which were turning outside the garden; and others went elsewhere, according to their whims, to amuse themselves until supper. They all gathered at supper as usual, and supped with great pleasure near the beautiful fountain. Then they arose and sang and danced, and after Filomena had danced the queen said:

"Filostrato, I do not intend to alter the customs of my

predecessors. Just as they did, I order that someone sing a song. Now I am quite sure your songs are like your tales, and as we don't want to have another day disturbed by your woes, I order you to sing any song you like."

Filostrato replied that he would willingly do so, and immediately began to sing the following song:

> *By tears I show how much, how rightly, the heart grieves when love's faith is betrayed.*
>
> *Love, when first you placed within my heart her for whom I sigh without hope, you showed her to me so full of virtue that I should have held all torture light that came through you into my mind, which now remains in grief! But now I know my error, and know it to my cost.*
>
> *I learned to know Love's cheat when she, in whom alone I hoped, abandoned me; for, when I thought myself more forward in her favour, more her servant, and did not see the coming of my future pain, I found she had given welcome to another's worth, and driven me forth.*
>
> *How great my comfortless grief is, Love, you know, and even so much I call upon you with my plaints; I burn so fiercely that I crave for death, as for a lesser pain. Come then, and end my madness and my cruel harsh life with death's blow—for, wherever I may go, my suffering must be less.*
>
> *No other way, no other comfort to my woe, remains, save death. Grant it me then. End my calamities with death, O Love, and take the heart from such a wretched life. Ah, I err, since wrongfully are joy and pleasure taken from me. Yet when I die, O Lord, make her happy as you have made her love anew.*
>
> *My song, if none should sing you, what care I, for none can sing you as I sing. One task alone I charge you with—go, seek out Love, and unto him alone reveal how tedious to me is my sad and bitter life, and pray him by his worth to bring me to a better port.*

The words of this song clearly expressed Filostrato's state of mind, and the reason for it. Perhaps the face of one of the ladies dancing would have made it even plainer, if the darkness of oncoming night had not hidden the blushes on her cheeks.

When he had ended, many other songs were sung until it was time to go to bed, when, at the queen's command, each went to his room.

### END OF THE FOURTH DAY

# THE FIFTH DAY

# THE FIFTH DAY

*Here begins the fifth day of the* Decameron, *wherein, under the rule of Fiammetta, tales are told of those lovers who won happiness after grief or misfortune*

The eastern sky was already white, and the rising rays had lightened all our hemisphere when Fiammetta was aroused by the sweet songs of birds which were singing gaily from the bushes. She arose, and had the other women and the three young men called. She then walked slowly in the fields talking with her companions, and passed over the dewy grass of the open plain until the sun was fully risen. When they felt the sun's rays grow hot, they turned their steps towards their rooms; and having refreshed themselves there with excellent wines and sweetmeats, they went out to amuse themselves in the garden until dinner time.

After they had sung a song and one or two ballads, the time for dinner soon arrived; and, as everything had been prepared by the steward, they sat down to eat when the queen wished. After dinner, which passed off merrily, they did not forget their custom of dancing, and danced to songs and the music of instruments. The queen then gave them permission to depart until after the siesta; so some went to bed, and others remained in the beautiful garden.

A little after Nones they all gathered together as usual near the fountain. The queen occupied her throne, looked smilingly at Pamfilo and ordered him to tell the first of these merry tales, to which he willingly agreed, and thus began.

## FIRST TALE

*Through love Cimone becomes civilised and captures his lady on the high seas. He is imprisoned in Rhodes, and liberated by Lisimaco, and the two of them once more*

*carry off their mistresses on their wedding day and fly
with them to Crete. They marry the ladies and return
home to live happily on their estates*

I thought of many tales, delightful ladies, each of which
might have been told as the first on this happy day. But one
especially pleased me because it will not only show you
that happy ending which is to be the subject of our stories,
but will also display how holy, how weighty and how full
of good are love's powers, which many people wrongly
condemn and insult, for they know not what they are saying. If I mistake not, this story will please you, because I
think you are in love.

As I have read in the ancient chronicles of Cyprus, there
lived once in the island a nobleman whose name was Aristippo, who possessed more wealth than any of the other
inhabitants. And, but for one misfortune, he might have
thought himself the happiest of men. Among his other children he had a son called Galeso, who was taller, and more
beautiful than all the others, but almost stupid and beyond
hope. Now, neither the labours of his tutor nor the entreaties or floggings of his father could beat any knowledge
or good manners into his head. Moreover, his voice was
loud and uncouth, more like an animal's than a man's. And
so everyone contemptuously nicknamed him "Cimone,"
which means in their language the same thing as "Brute" in
ours. This waste of his life caused his father the greatest
distress. He lost all hope in his son, and, in order to avoid
having the cause of his trouble continually before him, he
ordered Cimone to his country house to live among the
labourers there. Cimone liked this very much, because the
habits and behaviour of rough people were more to his taste
than those of citizens.

So Cimone went to the country and there occupied himself with matters appropriate to that life. One day a little
after noon he was going from one estate to another with a
staff on his shoulder, and entered a small wood—they are
very beautiful in that country—and since it was May the
wood was in full leaf. As he went along, chance brought
him to a little glade surrounded with tall trees, in one corner of which was a beautiful cool brook. On the green grass
beside it he saw a beautiful girl lying asleep. Her dress was
so thin that it concealed scarcely any of her white body,
and from her waist downwards she was covered only by a
very fine white garment. Two women and a man, her servants, were also lying asleep at her feet.

When Cimone saw her, he leaned upon his staff and gazed intently at her with the greatest admiration, as if he had never before seen a woman's form. In that rough bosom of his, which could not be made to feel any civilised pleasures no matter how much he was exhorted, there awoke a thought which whispered to his coarse material soul that she was the most beautiful thing ever seen by any living being. Then he began to notice her different beauties, admiring her hair, which he thought pure gold, her forehead, her nose, her mouth, her throat and her arms, and above all her yet undeveloped breasts. From a peasant he had suddenly become a judge of beauty, and longed to see her eyes which were closed in a deep sleep; and he was several times tempted to wake her so that he might see them. But, since he felt she was more beautiful than any other woman he had ever seen, he wondered whether she were not a Goddess. He yet had enough good sense to feel that divine things are more to be reverenced than worldly things, and therefore restrained himself, and waited for her to wake up of herself. Though the waiting seemed very long to him, yet he was so taken with this new delight that he could not leave her.

After a long time the girl, whose name was Efigenia, awoke before her servants, and as she opened her eyes and lifted her head she saw Cimone standing before her, leaning on his staff. So in great amazement she said:

"Cimone, what are you looking for in the wood at this time of the day?"

(Cimone was known to almost everyone in the whole country-side, for his handsomeness, his brutality, and his father's nobility and wealth.)

He made no answer to Efigenia's words, but began to gaze fixedly into her now open eyes, and felt within himself such sweetness coming from them that he was filled with a delight he had never known before. So she called to her women, and stood up, saying:

"God be with you, Cimone."

To which he replied:

"I will come with you."

Although the girl excused herself from his company, for she was afraid of him, he was unable to leave her until he had accompanied her to her home. He then went to his father's town house, saying that he had determined never to return to the country. This was very troublesome to his father and other relatives, but they let him alone, waiting to see what was the reason for his change of mind.

Cimone's heart, which no teaching could ever enter, was

pierced by love's dart through Efigenia's beauty; and in a
very short time he passed from one way of thinking to another so that he amazed his father, his relatives, and everyone who knew him.

First of all he asked his father to allow him clothes and
other refined things, such as his brothers had; which his
father very gladly did. He then frequented worthy young
men and listened to the ways befitting gentlemen and especially lovers; and in a very short time, to everyone's amazement, he not only learned the elements of literature but became esteemed among philosophers. Moreover—and the
cause of all this was the love he felt for Efigenia—he not
only changed his rough, rustic voice into one more civilised
and pleasant, but became a master of singing and music
and most expert and daring in horse-riding and fighting by
land and sea.

In short (to avoid mentioning every detail of his accom-
plishments), within four years of his first falling in love,
he came forth the gayest, most accomplished and most
virtuous of all the young men in the island of Cyprus.

What are we to say of Cimone, most charming ladies?
Indeed, nothing else than that the high virtues infused in
his noble spirit by Heaven were driven back and bound by
envious Fortune in the smallest portion of his heart; and
all these bonds were broken by love, which is the more powerful of the two. Love, the awakener of sleeping genius, by
its power drew them forth into the light from their cruel
overshadowing darkness, plainly showing whence it draws
the minds which are subject to it and whither it leads them
with its rays.

Now although Cimone in his love for Efigenia passed reasonable bounds in some things, as young men are wont to
do, yet when Aristippo reflected that love had changed him
from a sheep to a man, he not only endured them patiently
but urged his son to follow his own pleasure. Cimone, who
now refused the name of "Brute" and remembered that
Efigenia had called him this, wished his desire to have a
virtuous end, and so often asked Cipseo, the father of Efigenia, to give her to him as his wife. But Cipseo always replied that he had promised her to Pasimunda, a young
noble of Rhodes, whom he did not mean to disappoint.

When the time came for this arranged marriage to be
fulfilled, and the husband sent for her, Cimone said to himself:

"Now is the time to show you, O Efigenia, how much you
are beloved by me. Through you I became a man; and if I

can have you I do not doubt that I shall become more famous than any god. I will certainly have you or die."

Having said this, he quietly gathered together certain young men who were his friends, secretly armed a ship with everything necessary for giving battle, and put to sea where he waited to intercept the ship taking Efigenia to her husband in Rhodes. After Efigenia had done all honour to her husband's friends, she went on board ship, the prow was turned towards Rhodes, and away they went. Cimone was not napping, and the next day overhauled them in his ship. He went up on the prow and shouted to those on Efigenia's ship.

"Stop, lower your sails, or you may expect to be boarded and thrown into the sea."

Cimone's opponents had drawn their arms under cover, and prepared to defend themselves. Wherefore, after he had spoken, Cimone took a grappling iron, threw it on the prow of the Rhodians as they sped along, and by main force attached it to the prow of his own ship. Then, bold as a lion, he leapt on board the Rhodians' ship with no one following him, so that almost all gave him up for lost. But love spurred him on. With a sword in his hand he dashed impetuously upon his enemies, wounding now one, now another, and bringing them down like cattle. The Rhodians then threw down their arms, and almost with one voice yielded themselves prisoners.

Cimone said to them:

"Young men, neither desire of spoil nor any hatred I have for you made me leave Cyprus to attack you on the high seas. What impelled me is something which to me would be a very great thing to possess, and is very easy for you to yield up peacefully. That is Efigenia, whom I love above all things; and since I could not obtain her from her father in friendship and peace, love has compelled me to take her from you as an enemy by force of arms. I mean to be to her what your Pasimunda was to have been. Give her to me, and depart with God's grace."

The young men, compelled more by force than generosity, yielded up the weeping Efigenia to Cimone. And he, seeing her weep, said:

"Noble lady, be not disconsolate; I am your Cimone, and I deserve you far more through my long love than Pasimunda from a promise."

Cimone took her on board his own ship without touching any of the Rhodians' possessions and, turning to her companions, permitted them to depart. Delighted above all men to have obtained so precious a prey, Cimone spent some time in trying to console the weeping lady, and then decided with his young friends not to return immediately to Cyprus. By unanimous consent they turned the ship's prow towards Crete, where almost all of them, especially Cimone, thought they would be in safety, on account of ancient and recent family ties and friendships.

But Fortune, which had gaily yielded Cimone the possession of the lady, suddenly changed the young man's extreme joy into sad and bitter lamentation.

Not four hours had passed since Cimone had left the Rhodians when night came on, which was more welcome to Cimone than any other he had ever awaited. But with night there came a very fierce storm, which covered the sky with clouds and the sea with dangerous winds. It was so dark they could not see what they were doing or where they were going, nor could they carry out any of the ship's duties.

No need to ask whether Cimone was distressed by this. It seemed to him that God had granted him his desire so that he would feel more agony in death, for without this he would have cared little about dying. His companions likewise lamented, but above all Efigenia, who wept loudly and dreaded the shock of every wave. In her lamentation she bitterly cursed Cimone's love and his ardour, asserting that the only cause of this tempest was that God would not allow him to enjoy his presumptuous desire which had made him want her as his wife against their wills, but intended that he should see her die first and then himself die miserably afterwards.

Such and greater were their lamentations. The sailors did not know what to do, the wind grew stronger every hour, and, without knowing where they were going they came to Rhodes. Not knowing it was Rhodes, they exerted themselves to the utmost to reach land to save their lives. In this, Fortune was favourable to them and led them to a small bay, to which the Rhodians whom Cimone had released had brought their ship a little time before. They did not know they had anchored off Rhodes until dawn, when the sky became a little clearer, and they saw about a bow-shot from them the very ship they had set free. Cimone was much distressed by this and feared that the same thing would happen to him as had happened to them; so he gave orders to use every effort to get away and to go wherever Fortune took them, since they could not be in a worse place. They used every effort to get away, but in vain. The wind blew so strongly against them not only were they unable to get out of the little bay but were driven willy-nilly on the shore.

They were recognised by the Rhodian sailors who had left their ship. Some of them immediately ran to a neighbouring town to which the noble young Rhodians had gone, and told them that Cimone and Efigenia in their ship had by chance arrived there, as they had done. They heard this news with delight, gathered together all the men of the town, and hurried to the sea. Cimone and his friends had landed and had made up their minds to take to the woods, but they and Efigenia were all captured and taken to the town. Lisimaco, for that year chief magistrate of the Rhodians, came out with a great force of men-at-arms, and took Cimone and all his companions off to prison, as Pasimunda (who had heard the news) had arranged after complaining to the Senate.

In such wise the luckless and love-lorn Cimone lost his Efigenia soon after winning her, without having had anything from her but a few kisses. Efigenia was received and consoled by many noble ladies of Rhodes both for the anguish of being captured at sea and for the hardships she had endured in the tempest; and she remained with them until the day appointed for her marriage.

The lives of Cimone and his friends were spared (although Pasimunda did his utmost to have them condemned to death) because they had released the Rhodians the day before, but they were condemned to perpetual imprisonment. And, as you may well believe, they lay in prison miserably with no hope of any pleasure again. But Pasimunda urged the wedding as quickly as he could.

Fortune, as if repenting the injury done to Cimone, brought about a new event in his favour.

Pasimunda had a brother who was younger but no less brave than he, by name Ormisda. He had long been in treaty to take as wife a beautiful young woman of the city, named Cassandra, who was deeply beloved by Lisimaco; and the marriage had several times been delayed by different accidents.

When Pasimunda saw he was on the point of celebrating his marriage with great rejoicings, he thought it would be excellently done if Ormisda could be married at the same time, and so spare the expense of another marriage feast. So he reopened negotiations with Cassandra's parents, and they were successful; he and his brothers agreed with them that Ormisda should marry Cassandra on the same day that Pasimunda married Efigenia.

As soon as Lisimaco heard of this he was deeply annoyed, for he saw himself thwarted in his hopes; he firmly believed that if Ormisda did not marry Cassandra, he would get her. But like a wise man he kept his anger to himself. He then began to think how he could prevent this marriage from being carried out, and saw no way but to carry her off.

This he thought would be easy on account of the office he held, but he considered it would be far more dishonourable than if he had not held this office. But after long consideration, honour gave way to love, and he made up his mind to carry off Cassandra, come what might. Thinking over what assistance he would need and how he would go about it, he remembered Cimone, whom he held in prison together with his companions; and he came to the conclusion that he could have no better or more faithful ally than Cimone in such an affair. So next night he had Cimone brought secretly to his room, and spoke to him as follows:

"Cimone, even as the Gods are good and liberal givers of things to men, so they are most acute testers of men's virtues. Those men whom they find firm and constant under all trials they make worthy of higher rewards, since they are more valorous. They desired a more certain test of your virtue than you could have shown of yourself within the limits of your father's house, which I know abounds in riches. First, as I have been told, they changed you from a senseless beast to a man, by the sharp solicitude of love. Then with ill luck and your present tedious prison they wished to see whether your soul was changed from what it was, after you had for a brief time enjoyed the prize you won. Now, if your spirit is what it was, nothing will ever make you so happy as what they are preparing to give you. This I shall show you, so that you may regain strength and become bold-hearted.

"Pasimunda, delighted by your misfortune and the urgent solicitor of your death, is hastening to celebrate his marriage with your Efigenia, so that he may enjoy the prize which Fortune first granted you in a merry mood and then in anger snatched away. How much this must grieve you—if you love as I believe—I myself realise, because his brother Ormisda is preparing to do the same thing to me on the same day with Cassandra, whom I love before everything else in the world. No other way is left open by Fortune to escape this injury and misfortune save the strength of our spirits and of our right hands. We must take our swords in our hands and cut a way, you to the second, I to the first, carrying-off of our ladies. I do not ask if your liberty is dear to you, because I know you care little for it without your lady, but if you wish to have her again the Gods have given her into your hands, if you will follow me in my attempt."

These words brought back his lost spirits to Cimone, and without taking much time to reply, he said:

"Lisimaco, you can have no stronger or more faithful companion than I in such a deed, if I shall obtain what you tell me. So let me know what you want me to do, and you will see yourself followed with the greatest energy."

Said Lisimaco:

"In two days' time the new wives will enter their husbands' houses for the first time. You, armed, with your companions, and I with some of mine in whom I can trust, will enter the houses towards evening. We will carry off the women in the middle of the banquet, and take them to a ship which I have secretly made ready, cutting down anyone who dares to oppose us."

Cimone liked the plan, and until the time came remained quietly in prison.

When the wedding day arrived, great and magnificent was the pomp, and every part of the two brothers' house was filled with merry-making. Lisimaco had prepared everything needed. Cimone and his friends and Lisimaco's companions were all armed under their clothes, and Lisimaco first gained them over to his cause by a long speech. He then divided them into three parts, one of which he sent quietly down to the port so that no one could prevent them from boarding the ship when it became necessary, and with the other two he went to Pasimunda's house. He left another party at the door, so that no one could shut it or hinder them from coming out; and he and Cimone went up the stairs with the remaining party. They came to the hall where the two brides were at table with many other ladies, rushed in and threw the tables on the floor; each took his own lady and put her in the arms of his followers, and commanded that they should at once be taken to the waiting ship.

The brides began to weep and shriek, and so did all the other ladies and servants; and suddenly everything was in an uproar and laments everywhere. Cimone, Lisimaco and their followers drew their swords, and made their way towards the outer stairway, with none to oppose them. As they went down, along came Pasimunda who had picked up a large stick when he heard the noise; but Cimone vigorously struck him in the head and split it in halves, so that he fell dead at his feet. The wretched Ormisda rushed to his aid, but was killed by another blow from Cimone. A few others who tried to approach were wounded and driven off by the followers of Cimone and Lisimaco.

Leaving the house full of blood, uproar, lamentation and grief, they made their way, unopposed, to their ship with their prizes. They put the women on board and followed with all their companions. The shore was filled with armed men coming up to the rescue of the women, but the conspirators put out their oars and departed, delighted with their deed. They reached Crete, where they were gladly welcomed by their many friends and relatives; they married the ladies and made a great feast, and enjoyed their prizes in happiness.

The uproar and tumult in Cyprus and Rhodes over this lasted a long time. Finally, after their parents and friends had interceded in one place and another, it was arranged that after a certain period of exile Cimone and Efigenia should return to Cyprus, and Lisimaco return to Rhodes with Cassandra. And each lived happily with his wife on his estate.

## SECOND TALE

*Gostanza loves Martuccio Gomito. She hears he is dead; in despair she gets into a boat which is carried by the wind to Susa. She finds him alive at Tunis, makes herself known to him, and, he, who had become the King's favourite on account of his advice, marries her, and they return rich to Lipari*

The queen, after highly praising Pamfilo's tale, ordered Emilia to follow with the next, and she began as follows:

Everyone should take delight in those things wherein he sees recompenses follow affections; and since love more deserves happiness than affliction in the long run, I shall obey the queen in speaking of the present subject with much greater pleasure than I obeyed the king on the subject which went before.

You must know then, delicate ladies, that near Sicily is a little island called Lipari, wherein not long ago lived a very beautiful girl named Gostanza, the daughter of very common people in the island. There was a young man on the island named Martuccio Gomito, gay, well mannered and skilled in his occupation, who fell in love with her. And she likewise fell so much in love with him that she was never happy except when she saw him. Martuccio therefore wished to marry her, and asked her of her father; but he replied that Martuccio was poor and would not let him have her.

Martuccio was enraged to find himself refused on account of poverty, and swore with certain of his relatives and friends never to return to Lipari unless he were rich. He went away and coasted the shores of Barbary as a pirate, robbing everyone weaker than himself. Fortune was favourable to him if only he had known how to be moderate in his good luck. But it was not enough for himself and his companions that they had become very rich in a short time; they wanted to be extremely rich, and so it happened that after a long battle certain Saracen ships captured and robbed him and his companions, most of whom were massacred by the Saracens. The ship was sunk, and Martuccio was taken to Tunis, put in prison, and for a long time was in misery.

The news came to Lipari, not through one or two persons but by many, that all who were on the ship with Martuccio had been drowned. The girl had grieved very much at Martuccio's departure, but when she heard he was dead with the others, she wept long and made up her mind to die. Her heart lacked strength for her to slay herself in some violent way, and she thought of a different way of death. One night she secretly left her father's house and went to the port, where she found a small fisherman's boat a little apart from the other ships. She found the mast, sail and oars in it, because its owners had only just left it. She immediately went on board and rowed out to sea. She had some knowledge of seafaring ways, like all the women in the island; so she hoisted the sail, threw away the oars and the rudder, and let the wind carry her along. She felt it was inevitable either that the rudderless and unballasted boat would capsize in the sea, or that it would strike on a rock and sink, so that even if she tried to save herself, she would fail, and would of necessity be drowned. She wrapped her head in a cloak, and lay down weeping in the bottom of the boat.

But it all turned out very differently from what she had imagined. The wind that carried her along was northerly and gentle, the sea was slight, the boat stout, and so the next day towards evening she was carried ashore near a city named Susa, about a hundred miles above Tunis.

The girl did not know whether she was on land or sea, because she had made up her mind to lie there without raising her head, whatever happened. When the boat ran ashore, a poor woman happened to be on the beach, rolling up the fishermen's nets. When she saw the boat she was surprised to see it run on shore under full sail. Thinking the fishermen might be sleeping on it, she went to the boat and saw no one in it but the girl, who was fast asleep. She called to her several times, and at last made her hear. She realised from the girl's clothes that she was a Christian, and asked her in Italian how it happened that she had arrived there all alone in the boat. Hearing Italian, the girl thought the wind must have driven her back to Lipari. She started to her feet and looked around, and finding she was in a country she did not recognise, she asked the woman where she was. And the woman replied:

"You are near Susa in Barbary, my child."

At this the girl felt sorry that God had not sent death to her, hesitated in shame, and did not know what to do; and so sat down beside the boat, and began to cry. The woman took pity on her, and after much entreaty managed to take her to a little hut, and there after much wheedling persuaded her to tell how it had happened. This made the woman see that she must be hungry, so she prepared fish and dry bread and water, and persuaded her to eat a little.

Gostanza then asked the woman who she was that she spoke Italian so well; and she replied that she came from Trapani, was named Carapresa (good omen) and was there the servant to some Christian fishermen. Hearing the name Carapresa, the girl felt it was a good omen, and although she was still very unhappy and herself did not know why, she began to hope she knew not what and ceased to desire death. Without saying why or wherefore, she earnestly begged the woman for the love of God to have pity on her youth and to advise her how she could escape any harm being done her. At this Carapresa, like a good-hearted woman, left her in the hut, quickly collected her nets, returned to the girl, and wrapping her up in her own cloak took her to Susa. Arrived there, she said:

"Gostanza, I am taking you to the house of a very kind Saracen lady, for whom I have often worked. She is old and gentle. I shall recommend you to her as well as I can, and I am sure she will gladly take you in and treat you like a daughter. Stay with her, and try to get into her good graces by serving her as well as you can, until God sends you better luck." The old lady listened to the tale, gazed at the girl's face, and began to weep. She kissed her forehead and then led her by the hand into her house, where she lived with several other women but no men, and where they all worked at handicrafts, some in silk, some in palm and some in leather. In a few days the girl learned one of these crafts and worked with them. She won the favour and good liking of the old lady and the others to such an extent that it was amazing, and in a very short time she learned their language from them.

Now while the girl was in Susa and had already been lamented at home as lost and dead, it happened that the King of Tunis, by name Mariabdela, was attacked by a young man of great family and power in Granada, who claimed the kingdom of Tunis, and came with a great multitude of men to drive the King out of his realm. The news of this came to the ears of Martuccio Gomito in prison, for he knew the Barbary tongue well; and hearing that the King of Tunis was making great preparations for defence, he said to one of the men who kept guard over him and his companions:

"If I could speak to the King, I have it in my heart that I could give him a piece of advice whereby he would win this war."

The guard mentioned this to his commander, who at once informed the King. And the King ordered Martuccio to be brought before him, and asked him what his advice was. To which he replied:

"Sire, if I well observed your manner of battle in the time when I frequented your country, I believe that battles are won more by the archers than by any other troops. And if some means could be found whereby the enemy archers lacked ammunition while your own were abundantly provided, I believe you would win the battle."

"Doubtless," said the King, "I believe I should win, if that could be done."

"Sire," said Martuccio, "if you wish, it can be done, and in this way. You must make your archers' bow-strings much thinner than those commonly used. Then you must manufacture arrows, whose notches will be useless except on thin strings. And this must be done so secretly that your enemy knows nothing about it, and is unable therefore to find any remedy. My reason for saying this is as follows: When the enemy archers have shot their arrows and your own archers theirs, you know that during the battle the enemy will have to collect the arrows your men have shot, while your men will have to pick up theirs. But the enemy will not be able to use your arrows, because the notches will be too small for the bow-strings; while the opposite will happen with your men and the enemy's arrows, because the thin string will easily fit the large notch. And so your men will have an abundance of arrows, while the enemy will be short of them."

The King was a wise lord, and took Martuccio's advice which he followed exactly; and thus won the war. And so Martuccio was high in his favour, and consequently in a great and rich estate. The news of this went through the country, and it came to Gostanza's ears that Martuccio Gomito whom she had long thought to be dead, was alive. So that her love for him, which had already become cooler in her heart, blazed up again in a sudden flame and became greater, and revived her dead hopes. She told the good lady with whom she was living everything that had happened to her, and said she desired to go to Tunis to see with her eyes the man of whom report had spoken to her ears. The lady praised her desire, and, as if she were her mother, took her in a boat and went to Tunis, where she and Gostanza were honourably received in the house of a relative. Carapresa went with them, and they sent her out to get information about Martuccio. She came back and reported that he was alive and in great estate. So the lady thought it a pleasure to be the person to tell Martuccio that his Gostanza had come to him. One day she went to Martuccio and said:

"Martuccio, in my house lives captive a servant of yours from Lipari, who wants to speak to you in private. I was unwilling to trust anyone else, and so I came to tell you myself, as he wished."

Martuccio thanked her, and went after her to her house. When he saw Gostanza, she nearly died of joy, and unable to restrain herself, she threw her arms round his neck and kissed him; she could not utter a word, but pity for past misfortunes and present joy made her weep softly. Martuccio gazed at her silently in astonishment, and then said with a sigh:

"O my Gostanza, then you are alive? Long ago I heard you were lost, and that nothing had been heard of you in your home."

So saying, he embraced and kissed her, weeping tenderly.

Gostanza told him all her adventures, and the kindness she had received from the gentlewoman with whom she was living. After much talk, Martuccio left her and went to the King his master, and told him the whole story, all that had happened to him and to the girl. And he added that, with the King's permission, he intended to marry her in accordance with our law. The King marvelled at all this. He sent for the girl, and she confirmed everything that Martuccio had said.

"Then," said the King, "you have well earned him as your husband."

He then sent for great and noble gifts, part of which he gave to her and part to Martuccio, and gave them permission to do together whatever they wished. Martuccio did honour to the lady with whom Gostanza had lived, thanked her for taking the girl into her service, gave her such gifts as were suitable, recommended her to God and departed, not without many tears from Gostanza. Then, with the King's permission, they went on board a ship together with Carapresa, and returned to Lipari with a favourable wind, where there was such rejoicing that it cannot be described.

There Martuccio married her and gave a large and handsome wedding feast; and thereafter they long enjoyed their love together in peace and quietness.

### THIRD TALE

*Pietro Boccamazza runs away with Agnolella. They fall among thieves; the girl flees to a wood and is taken to a village. Pietro is captured and escapes from the robbers. He is taken to the place where Agnolella is, marries her, and returns with her to Rome*

There was not one of them but praised Emilia's tale. The queen turned to Elisa when it was finished, and ordered her to follow next. And she gladly obeyed, and began thus:

I have in mind, charming ladies, an unfortunate night which befell two imprudent young people, but as it was followed by many happy days, the tale I want to tell falls within our subject. In Rome, which was once the world's head as it now is its tail, there lived not long ago a young man named Pietro Boccamazza, belonging to an honourable Roman family, who fell in love with a charming and very beautiful girl, named Agnolella, the daughter of one Gigluozzo Saullo, a plebeian, but beloved by the Romans. And he went to work in such a manner that the girl came to love him no less than he loved her. Urged by his burning love, and unable to endure longer his desire for her, Pietro asked for her as his wife.

When his relatives heard of it, they all went to him and sharply blamed him for what he wanted to do. Moreover they sent word to Gigluozzo Saullo not to pay any heed to Pietro's words, because if he did they would never consider him a friend or a relative.

When Pietro saw the only road blocked by which he had hoped to attain his desire, he wanted to die of grief. If Gigluozzo would have consented, he would have married his daughter, against the wishes of all his relatives. Then he thought of a way in which this could be done, if the girl consented. He sent her a message to say that he wanted her to fly from Rome with him, and she agreed. Having made arrangements, Pietro got up very early one morning, and she and he mounted horses and set out for Anagni, where Pietro had some friends in whom he had great confidence. They had no time to get married because they were afraid of being pursued, and as they rode along they talked together of their love, and from time to time kissed each other. It happened that Pietro was none too familiar with the way, and when they were about eight miles from Rome, he took a road to the left, when he should have gone to the right.

They had not ridden on for more than two miles when they came near a little fortified place, whence they were espied, and twelve men suddenly came out of it towards them. As they drew near the girl saw them, and shrieked:

"Pietro, we must fly, we are being attacked."

She turned her horse towards a large wood, struck spurs into him and, clinging to the saddle, was carried into the wood by the horse when it felt the spur. Pietro had been looking more at her face than the road, and had not seen the men coming so soon as she had. While he went on looking for them without seeing them, they came upon him, captured him, and made him dismount from his horse. They asked him who he was, and when he told them, they discussed it among themselves, and said:

"He is one of the friends of our enemies. What else are we to do except take away his clothes and horse, and hang him up on one of these oaks in scorn of the Orsini?"

They all agreed to this, and told Pietro to undress. He

had already done so with a premonition of his fate, when suddenly an ambush of about twenty-five men came upon them, shouting: "Death! Death!" In their surprise they left Pietro and thought of their own defence; but finding themselves greatly outnumbered by the attackers they began to flee while the others pursued them.

When Pietro saw this he at once picked up his clothes, jumped on his horse, and fled as fast as he could in the direction where he had seen the girl going. But he saw no road or path in the wood and saw no horse track, and could not find the girl; so as soon as he felt safe and out of reach of those who had attacked him, he gave way to his grief, and began to weep as he went to and fro in the wood calling to her. But no one answered him.

He did not want to turn back, and if he went forward he did not know where he would arrive; moreover, he was afraid of the wild beasts in the wood both for himself and the girl, whom he kept thinking he saw mangled by a wolf or a bear.

So Pietro went wandering all day through the wood, shouting and hallooing and going back over the same ground when he thought he was going forward. And what with shouting and weeping and fear and fasting he was so weary that he could not go one step further. Not knowing what else to do when night came on, he dismounted from his horse and tied it to a large oak, and then climbed up into it himself to avoid being eaten by wild animals during the night. Soon after, the moon rose. The weather was very fine and Pietro was anxious not to go to sleep in case he fell out of the tree, although even if he had wanted to sleep, his grief and thinking about the girl would have kept him awake; so he remained awake, sighing and weeping and cursing his misfortune.

When the girl fled, she did not know where to go except by letting her horse take her where he wanted; and she went so deep into the wood that she could no longer see the opening by which she had entered. So she spent the day, like Pietro, wandering about the wild wood, sometimes going forward and sometimes waiting, weeping and calling to him and lamenting her woes. At last towards evening, when Pietro still was not to be seen, she came upon a little path. The horse followed it and when she had gone about two miles she saw a little house in the distance, to which she hastened as quickly as she could. There she found an aged man living with his old wife. And when they saw her alone they said:

"My child, what are you doing, going about the country alone at this hour?"

The girl replied weeping that she had lost her companions in the wood, and asked how far it was to Anagni.

"My child," replied the old man, "this is not the way to go to Anagni, and it's more than twelve miles from here."

"Is there any inn near," she asked, "where I can stay?"

"There is no inn near enough for you to reach today," he replied.

Then said the girl: "Since there is nowhere else I can go, will you shelter me here tonight for the love of God?"

"We are glad to have you stay the night with us," said the old man, "but I must tell you that in this country day and night there are robber bands, both friends and enemies, who often commit great outrages and havoc. If by ill luck any of them came while you were here and saw you so young and pretty, they might do you despite and shame, and we could not help you. I wanted to tell you, so that if it should happen, you could not reproach us."

Although the girl was frightened by the old man's words, it was so late at night that she said:

"Please God, He will guard both you and me from this misfortune; and if it happens to me, it is far worse to be mangled in the woods by wild beasts than to be slain by men."

So saying, she dismounted from her horse and entered the poor man's cottage, where she supped sparsely with them on what they had. Afterwards she lay down fully clothed with them on their low bed, and spent the whole night sighing and weeping her misfortune and Pietro's, for whom she dreaded the worst.

Towards dawn she heard a great tramping. She got up and went into a large courtyard behind the little house, where she saw a quantity of hay in which she hid, so that the men would not find her if they came there. Hardly had she hidden herself when a large band of thieves came to the door, made them open it, went in and found the girl's horse standing in its saddle. So they asked who was there. The old man, not seeing the girl about, replied:

"Nobody is here but ourselves. We caught the horse last night, when it must have run away from someone, and we took it into the house so that the wolves should not eat it."

"Well then," said the leader of the band, "it'll do for us, since it has no other owner."

They scattered all through the little house, and some went in to the courtyard and laid down their spears and wooden shields. One of them, not having anything better to do, thrust his lance into the hay and came near to killing the girl and she to crying out. The spear came so close to her left breast that it ripped open her clothes, and she was about to utter a shriek for fear of being wounded; but she remembered where she was, and lay still and silent. The band cooked their kids and other meat in various places, ate and drank, and then went about their business, taking the girl's horse with them. When they were some distance away, the old man said to his wife:

"What has happened to the girl we took in last night? I didn't see her here when we got up."

The wife replied that she did not know, and went to look for her. Realising that the robbers had gone, the girl emerged from the hay, to the old man's delight, since she had not fallen into their hands. It was now daylight, and he said to her:

"Now the day is here, we will take you, if you wish, to a village about five miles away where you will be safe. But you will have to go on foot, since the thieves who have just left took away your horse."

Making the best of it, the girl begged them in God's name to take her to the village. So they set out and reached it about the middle of Tierce. This place belonged to one of the Orsini named Liello di Campo di Fiore, and by chance his wife was there, a very good and saintly woman. She at once recognised the girl when she saw her, received her joyously, and wanted to know everything that had happened to her, which the girl related in full. The lady also knew Pietro, who was a friend of her husband's, and grieved over his plight. When she heard he had been captured, she thought he must be dead. So she said to the girl:

"Since you don't know what has happened to Pietro, stay here with me until I am able to send you safely to Rome."

Pietro remained on his oak in the greatest distress. Early in the night he saw at least twenty wolves, which all went for the horse as soon as they saw it. The horse jerked its head, broke the bridle and began to rush away. But the wolves surrounded it and made this impossible. The horse killed several of them with its teeth and hoofs, but at last they brought it down and killed it, tore it to pieces and finally went away after eating everything but the bones. Pietro, who felt his horse was a companion and a support in his troubles, was dismayed, and imagined he would never be able to get out of the wood.

Just before daylight, as he sat in his oak, dying of cold,

he saw a large fire about a mile away. When it was full day he got down fearfully from his oak, and went towards the fire which he finally reached. There round about it he found some shepherds eating and making merry, and they took pity upon him and let him join them. After he had eaten and warmed himself, he told them all his misfortunes and how he came to be there alone, and asked them if there were any country house or fortified place near, where he could go.

The shepherds said that about three miles away was the stronghold of Liello di Campo di Fiore, whose wife was then living there. Pietro in delight begged that one of them would guide him to the place, which two of them gladly did. When Pietro arrived, he found nobody he knew, but went about trying to find means for seeking the girl in the wood. The lady then sent for him, and he went to her at once; and when he saw Agnolella with her, there was never any joy like his.

He longed to go and kiss her, but refrained out of modesty in front of the lady. And if he was happy, the girl's happiness was no less. The lady welcomed him warmly and listened to his adventures. Then she sharply reproved him for wanting to act contrary to the wishes of his relatives. But seeing that he was determined and that the girl liked him, she said to herself:

"Why do I take this trouble? They are in love, they know each other. Each is a friend of my husband, and their desires are chaste. I think God approves of them since He saved one of them from the gallows and the other from a spear, and both of them from wild beasts. Therefore, so let it be."

And turning to them, she said:

"It is in your minds, as in my own, for you to be husband and wife; let us do it and make the wedding here at the expense of Liello. I will make peace between you and your relatives."

Pietro was delighted and Agnolella even more so. They were married, and the lady made them as honourable a wedding as possible in a mountain town; and there most delightfully they enjoyed the first fruits of their love. A few days later they and the lady went to horse well guarded, and returned to Rome. There she found Pietro's relatives very angry at what he had done, but succeeded in making the peace with them. And he lived in peace and happiness with his Agnolella until their old age.

# FOURTH TALE

*Ricciardo Manardi is discovered by Messer Lizio da Valbona with his daughter, whom Ricciardo marries, and remains on good terms with the father*

After Elisa was silent the queen listened to the praise given to her tale by the company, and then ordered Filostrato to tell one; and he began laughingly as follows:

I have been condemned so often by so many of you because I imposed upon you subjects of cruel tales and tears that I think I am obliged—in order to try to repair the trouble I have caused—to tell you something to make you laugh a little. So I intend to tell you a short little tale about a love affair which came to a happy ending after no more woe than a few sighs and a brief fear mingled with shame.

Not long ago, worthy ladies, there lived in Romagna a wealthy and accomplished knight, named Messer Lizio da Valbona. On the verge of old age a daughter was born to him by his wife, Madonna Giacomina, and this daughter as she grew up became more beautiful and charming than any girl of that country. Since she was the only child she was greatly beloved by her father and mother, and watched over with the greatest care, for they hoped to make a great match of her.

Now it happened that Messer Lizio's house was much frequented by a handsome and comely young man named Ricciardo, belonging to the family of the Manardi of Brettinoro, whom Messer Lizio and his wife treated as if he were their son. As the young man was continually seeing this very beautiful and charming girl, who was so accomplished and delightful and already of marriageable age, he fell deeply in love with her, and concealed his love with the greatest care. But the girl noticed it, and without making any resistance, began to love him too, which naturally delighted Ricciardo. He often made up his mind to speak to her, but was silent from fear of offending her; however, one day he found the opportunity and courage to say:

"Caterina, I beseech you not to let me die of love."

And the girl promptly answered:

"I hope to God you will not let me die of it."

This answer gave Ricciardo great pleasure and eagerness, and he said:

"I shall never refuse anything which pleases you, but you must find some means of saving your life and mine."

"Ricciardo," said the girl, "you see how carefully I am watched, and for that reason I do not see how you can come to me, but if you can see anything I can do without shame to myself, tell me, and I will do it."

After thinking for a time, Ricciardo said abruptly:

"My sweet Caterina, I can see no other way unless you can sleep or manage to be on the balcony overlooking your father's garden. If I knew you would be there at night, I would find some means of getting there, however high it might be."

"If you have the courage to come there," said Caterina, "I think I can arrange to sleep there."

Ricciardo said he had; and so they hastily kissed once, and parted.

It was about the end of May, and next day the girl began to complain to her mother that she had not been able to sleep on account of the excessive heat. Said the mother:

"What heat do you mean, my child? It was not hot at all."

"Mother," said Caterina, "you ought to add 'in my opinion,' and then perhaps you would be right. But you should remember how much warmer girls are than elderly women."

"That's true, my child," said the mother, "but I cannot make it hot and cold at will, as you perhaps might like. You must endure the weather the season brings. Perhaps it will be cooler tonight, and you will sleep better."

"God grant it," said Caterina, "but it doesn't usually happen that the nights get cooler as the summer comes on."

"Well," said the mother, "what do you want done?"

"If my father and you are willing," replied Caterina, "I should like to have my bed on the balcony beside the bedroom overlooking the garden; and there I could sleep, and listen to the nightingales, and be in a cooler place, and be much more comfortable than in your bedroom."

"Well," said the mother, "cheer up, my child. I will speak to your father, and we will do what he wishes."

Now Messer Lizio was an old man and therefore perhaps a little cross grained; so when he heard about this, he said:

"What's this about a nightingale and wanting to sleep to its singing? I'll make her sleep to the cricket's song too."

The night after Caterina was told this, she not only did not sleep herself—more from annoyance than from the heat

—but did not allow her mother to sleep, and kept complaining of the great heat.

So next morning the mother went to Messer Lizio, and said:

"Messer, you cannot care much for the child; what does it matter to you which balcony she sleeps on? She could not keep still all night for the heat. Besides, why should you wonder that she wants to hear the nightingale singing, when it's a girl's whim? Young people like those things which are like them."

Hearing this, Messer Lizio said:

"Go, make her up whatever bed will go there, and hang it round with some serge, and let her sleep there and listen to the nightingale's singing as much as she wants."

As soon as the girl heard this, she had a bed made up at once. And, since she was to sleep there that night, she so arranged matters that she saw Ricciardo, and made him a sign agreed upon between them, whereby he understood what he had to do.

When Messer Lizio heard the girl go to bed he locked a door which led from the bedroom to the balcony, and went to bed also. And when Ricciardo saw that everything was quiet, he climbed on to a wall with the help of a ladder, and then clinging to the brick projections of another wall, he reached the balcony—with great difficulty, and great danger if he had fallen—and was greeted softly but with the greatest delight by the girl. After many kisses they lay down together, and took delight and pleasure of each other almost the whole night, making the nightingale sing many times.

Nights are short and their delight was great, and already the day was at hand, though they did not know it. They were so warm with the weather and their play that they both went to sleep almost at once, Caterina with her right arm round Ricciardo's neck and her left hand holding the thing you are ashamed to mention among men.

Thus they slept without waking until dawn came and Messer Lizio got up. Remembering that his daughter was sleeping on the balcony, he softly opened the door, saying to himself:

"Let us see how the nightingale made Caterina sleep last night."

He crept up and gently lifted the serge curtain round the bed, and saw Ricciardo and Caterina sleeping naked and uncovered in the embrace I have just described. He recog-

nised Ricciardo, and then departed to his wife's bedroom,
and called to her:

"Get up at once, wife, and come and see how your daughter is so fond of the nightingale that she has caught it and
is still holding it in her hand."

"How can that be?" said the lady.

Said Messer Lizio:

"You will see if you come at once."

The lady dressed hurriedly, and softly followed Messer
Lizio. When they came to the bed and the serge was lifted,
Madonna Giacomina could plainly see how her daughter
had caught and was holding the nightingale, which she had
so much wanted to hear sing. Whereat the lady, considering
herself basely deceived by Ricciardo, wanted to scream and
insult him; but Messer Lizio said:

"Wife, if you value my love, say nothing of this. In truth,
since she has caught him, he shall be hers. Ricciardo is a
gentleman and a rich young man. We can have nothing
but good from an alliance with his family. If he wants to
escape from me, he must first marry her. So he'll find he has
put the nightingale in his own cage, and not in anyone
else's."

This consoled the lady; and when she saw that her husband was not angered by what had happened, and when she
considered that her daughter had spent a good night and
had rested well and caught the nightingale, she was silent.

They had scarcely spoken these words when Ricciardo
awoke and saw it was bright day; thinking himself certain
of death, he woke Caterina and said:

"Alas, my heart, what shall we do? The daylight has come
and caught me."

At these words Messer Lizio stepped forward, lifted the
serge, and replied:

"We shall do well."

When Ricciardo saw him, he felt as if the heart had been
torn from his body. He sat up in the bed, and said:

"Sir, I beg you mercy for God's sake. I know I have
merited death, as a wicked and treacherous man, and therefore do with me as you will. But, if it may be, I beg you will
have pity on my life, and not have me die."

"Ricciardo," said Messer Lizio, "this is not the reward
I should have had for my love of you and my trust in you.
But, since it is so, and since youth has made you commit
this fault, take Caterina as your legitimate wife to save
yourself from death and me from shame, so that, as she has

been yours this night, she may be yours so long as she lives. In this way my peace and your safety may be achieved. And if you will not do this, recommend your soul to God."

While all this was being said, Caterina loosed her hold of the nightingale, and covering herself over began to weep and to beg her father to forgive Ricciardo. And, on the other hand, she begged Ricciardo to do what Messer Lizio wanted, so that they might long and securely enjoy such nights.

But there was no need of many entreaties. On the one side shame for the fault committed and desire to amend it, on the other side the fear of dying, the desire to escape, and moreover ardent love and the desire to possess the beloved, made him say freely and without hesitation that he was ready to do what Messer Lizio wanted. So Messer Lizio borrowed one of Madonna Giacomina's rings, and without getting out of bed Ricciardo took Caterina as his wife in their presence. After which, Messer Lizio and his wife went away, saying:

"Rest for a while, perhaps you need it more than to get up."

When they had gone, the two young people embraced each other, and, since they had not travelled more than six miles that night, they went on another two; and so ended the first day.

When they got up, Ricciardo made more definite arrangements with Messer Lizio, and a few days later, as was fitting, he again wedded the girl in the presence of friends and relatives, and took her home with great rejoicing, and honourably made a great wedding festival; and afterwards for a long time in peace and quietness hunted birds with her day and night as much as he pleased.

## FIFTH TALE

*Guidotto da Cremona bequeaths his daughter to Gia-comino da Pavia and dies. Giannole di Severino and Minghino di Mingole both fall in love with her in Faenza and quarrel over her; the girl is discovered to be Gian-nole's sister and is given to Minghino as his wife*

Each of the ladies laughed so much as they listened to the tale of the nightingale that although Filostrato had ended his tale they could not stop laughing. But when everyone had done laughing, the queen said:

"Certainly, if you distressed them yesterday, you have tickled them so much today that no one can reasonably complain."

And as it was Neifile's turn to speak, she ordered her to tell a tale, which she began merrily as follows:

Since Filostrato went to Romagna for his tale, I also want to go somewhat afield with my story telling. In the city of Fano dwelt two Lombards, one of whom was named Guidotto da Cremona and the other Giacomino da Pavia, old men who had spent almost all their youth as soldiers in feats of arms. When Guidotto was at the point of death, having no son or any friend or relative whom he trusted more than Giacomino, he bequeathed him his daughter (who was about ten years old), and his possessions; and, after settling all his affairs, he died.

About this time the city of Faenza, which had long been at war and in disasters, returned to a better frame of mind, and permission was freely given to all who wished to return there. And so Giacomino, who had lived there in the past and liked the place, returned there with all he had and took with him the child Guidotto had bequeathed him, whom he loved and treated as his own daughter.

When the child grew up she was as beautiful a girl as any in the town; and she was as modest and well behaved as she was beautiful. So, many began to court her, but two handsome and excellent young men especially fell deeply in love with her, so much so that through jealousy they began to hate each other extremely. One of them was named Giannole di Severino and the other Minghino di Mingole. As she was now fifteen years old, either of them would gladly have taken her as his wife, if his relatives had permitted. But, seeing that honest means were forbidden, each of them began to look for some other way of getting her.

Giacomino had in his household an old woman servant and a man servant named Crivello, a pleasant and friendly man. Giannole was very familiar with him and, when he thought the time ripe, confessed his love to him and begged him to give aid in attaining his desire, promising him great things if he succeeded. Said Crivello:

"The only thing I can do for you is to take you to her when Giacomino has gone out to dinner, because she would not listen to me if I spoke to her on your behalf. If that pleases you, I promise to do it; do then what you think is best."

Giannole said that he wanted nothing better, and so they agreed.

Minghino on the other hand had become familiar with the old woman, and had gone so well to work with her that she had several times carried messages from him to the girl and had almost inflamed her with love for him. Moreover, she had promised to bring him to the girl when Giacomino happened to be away from home in the evening.

Not long after this, through Crivello's arrangements, Giacomino went out to sup with a friend. He informed Giannole, and arranged with him that on a given signal he was to come, and would find the door open. On the other hand, the old woman servant, knowing nothing about this, sent to tell Minghino that Giacomino would not sup at home, and told him to remain near the house so that when he saw her signal he could come in.

Evening came, and the two lovers, knowing nothing about each other but mutually suspicious, went with some armed friends to get possession of the girl. Minghino and his friends awaited the signal in a friend's house close to the girl's; Giannole and his companions remained at a little distance.

When Giacomino had gone, Crivello and the servant each tried to get the other out of the way.

"Why don't you go to bed?" said Crivello. "What are you wandering about the house for?"

"Why don't you go for your master?" replied the woman. "What are you waiting here for, now you've had supper?"

Thus they each tried to make the other go away. But Crivello saw that the time arranged with Giannole had come, and said to himself: "Why do I bother about her? If she doesn't keep quiet she may have a rough time." He made the signal, opened the door, Giannole immediately went in with two of his friends, found the girl in the great hall and seized on her to carry her off. The girl resisted and screamed loudly, and so did the old woman. Hearing this, Minghino and his friends immediately rushed up. Seeing the girl already being dragged out of the door, they drew their swords and shouted:

"Ah! Traitors, you are dead men! This shall not be. What do you mean by this violence?"

So saying, they began the fight. The neighbours also came out with arms and lights at the noise, and condemning the violence began to help Minghino. After a long contest, Minghino rescued the girl from Giannole, and took her back to Giacomino's house. Before the riot was over the sergeants of the police force arrived and arrested many of them. Among the captured were Minghino, Giannole and Crivello, who were taken to prison. Things quieted down, and Giacomino returned home. He was greatly depressed by the occurrence and made enquiries as to how it had happened; but finding that the girl was entirely blameless he became calmer, and determined to marry her off as quickly as possible to prevent any repetition of the event.

Next morning, the relatives of both parties, having learned the truth and knowing what disaster might fall on the two imprisoned young men if Giacomino proceeded against them as he might reasonably have done, went to him and begged him with soft words not to be too angry at the injury he had received from the two young men's lack of common sense, but rather to consider the friendship and good will which they believed he bore to them. And they proposed that they themselves as well as the young men should make any amends he liked to ask. Giacomino, who had seen much of the world and was a kindly man, replied briefly:

"Gentlemen, if I were in my own country as I am in yours, I hold myself so much your friend that I would do what I could to please you either in this or in other matters. In this case, I ought especially to bow to your wishes since here you have done an injury to one of yourselves—the girl is not from Cremona or Pavia, as many people perhaps think, but from Faenza. And neither I nor she nor the man who bequeathed her to me knows whose daughter she is. So what you ask shall be done, as far as I am concerned."

The worthy men were astonished to learn that she came from Faenza, and, after thanking Giacomino for his generous answer, they begged him to tell them how she had come into his hands, and how he knew she came from Faenza. Said Giacomino:

"Guidotto da Cremona was my friend and brother in arms, and at the point of death he told me that when this city was captured by the Emperor Frederick, he went after spoils and entered a house with his friends which he found full of property but abandoned by its inhabitants except for this girl, who was then about two years old and came down the stairs calling him 'father.' This aroused his pity, and he took her and everything in the house to Fano. When he died, he left me all he had and the girl, on condition that in due time I should marry her to someone and give her what rightfully belonged to her as a dowry. She has reached marriageable age, but I have not been able to find anyone to whom I should like to give her. I should be glad to do it so that what happened last evening may not be repeated."

Among those present was one Guglielmino da Mudicina, who had been with Guidotto at that time, and knew whose house it was Guidotto had robbed. Seeing the man there, he went up to him and said:

"Bernabuccio, do you hear what Giacomino says?"

"Yes," replied Bernabuccio, "and I was thinking the more about it because I remember that in the confusion of that day I lost a little girl about the age Giacomino speaks of."

"She certainly is the same," said Guglielmino, "because I was there and heard Guidotto speaking of the spoil he had made, and knew it was your house. Try to think if there is any mark by which you can recognise her, and look for it, for you will certainly find she is your daughter."

Bernabuccio pondered, and then remembered that over her left ear she had a cross-shaped scar, the result of a tumour which had been cut out a little before the accident. So, without any hesitation he went up to Giacomino, who was still there, and asked to be taken to his house to see the girl. Giacomino gladly took him along, and had the girl brought before him. As soon as Bernabuccio saw her, he seemed to be looking at the face of her mother who was still a handsome woman. But, not relying on this, he asked Giacomino's permission to lift the hair above her left ear; to which Giacomino consented.

Bernabuccio went up to her as she stood there modestly, lifted her hair with his right hand, and saw the cross. He then knew she was his daughter, and began to weep and to embrace her tenderly; and, as she resisted, he turned to Giacomino, saying:

"Brother, this is my daughter. The house robbed by Guidotto was mine, and in the confusion this child was forgotten in the house by my wife and her mother. Hitherto we have always thought that she was burned that day along with the house."

When the girl heard this and saw he was an old man, she believed him and, moved by secret impulses, accepted his embraces and began tenderly to weep with him. Bernabuccio immediately sent for her mother and other relatives and her sisters and brothers, and showed her to them and related what had happened. After great rejoicing and a thousand kisses, he took her off to his house, to Giacomino's

great content. The city magistrate, who was a very worthy
man, heard about this, and knowing that Giannole (whom
he had in prison) was Bernabuccio's son and the girl's
brother, he determined to pass lightly over the crime he had
committed. He intervened, together with Bernabuccio and
Giacomino, and made peace between Giannole and Minghino. With the consent of Minghino's relatives, he made
a match between him and the girl, whose name was Agnesa.
At the same time he liberated Crivello and the others who
had been arrested in this concern. Minghino very happily
made a great wedding feast, and took the girl to his home,
and thereafter lived many years with her in peace and content.

## SIXTH TALE

*Gianni di Procida is found with a girl he loves and is
handed over to King Federigo to be bound to a stake
and burned; he is recognised by Ruggieri dell' Oria, escapes, and marries the girl*

When Neifile's tale, which pleased the ladies, was finished,
the queen ordered Pampinea to prepare to tell the next; and
she at once raised a smiling face and began:

Fair ladies, very great is the power of love, which brings
lovers to great exertions and into excessive and unsuspected
dangers, as we may perceive for many events related today
and earlier; but still it pleases me once more to show it with
the tale of a young man in love.

Ischia is an island near Naples, where among others was
a very beautiful and gay girl whose name was Restituta,
the daughter of a gentleman on the island, named Marin
Bolgaro. This girl was deeply in love with a young man
called Gianni from an island named Procida, near Ischia;
and he with her. He not only came from Procida to Ischia
to see her during the day, but often came by night; and
when he could not find a boat he would swim from Procida
to Ischia to see at least the walls of her house, if nothing
more.

While this eager love affair was going on, the girl happened to be alone one day on the sea shore, going from

rock to rock, getting the shell fish with a knife. She came to a place among the rocks which was shady and near a stream of cool water, where certain young Sicilians from Naples had landed in their boat. When they saw how beautiful the girl was and that she was alone and had not seen them, they determined to seize her and to carry her off; which they accordingly did. In spite of her screams, they caught her, put her on the boat, and made off. When they reached Calabria, they began to discuss which of them should have her; and each of them wanted her. Since they could not agree and were afraid that they might quarrel and ruin their affairs, they decided to give her to Federigo, King of Sicily, at that time a young man who took great delight in such things. And this they did when they came to Palermo.

The King was charmed with her beauty; but since he was rather sickly, he ordered that until he was stronger she should be placed in certain handsome apartments in his garden, which had the name Cuba, and there be waited upon. And this was done.

The carrying off of the girl caused a great uproar among the people of Ischia, and what was particularly annoying to them, they could not find out who had done it. But Gianni, who was more deeply interested in it than anyone, did not wait to hear news in Ischia, but having found out in which direction the boat had gone, he armed one himself, went on board, and as rapidly as possible scoured the whole coast from the Minerva to Scalea in Calabria. He enquired everywhere among the young men, and was told at Scalea that she had been taken to Palermo by Sicilian sailors. Gianni made his way there as swiftly as possible, and after much seeking he there found that the girl had been given to the King and was lodged in the Cuba. This greatly distressed him, and made him lose nearly all hope, not only of getting her back, but even of seeing her again.

But love kept him there; and seeing that no one knew him, he sent away his ship, and remained alone. He was always passing by the Cuba, and one day he happened to see her at a window, and she saw him, which was a great delight to both. Gianni saw it was a solitary place, managed to approach and speak to her, and discovered what he must do if he wanted to speak to her again. He then departed, after having carefully studied the arrangement of the building. He waited until nightfall and allowed part of the night to pass, and then returned. Climbing up a wall where a tree climber would not have found anything to hold, he entered the garden, where he found a plank, which he placed against the girl's window, and by that means easily got to her.

The girl felt she had lost her honour, which in the past she had guarded most jealously, and thought she could give it to no more worthy man; so she had determined to satisfy all his desires, to induce him to take her away. And therefore she had left the window open, so that he could quickly get in. Finding the window open, he softly got in and lay down beside the girl, who was not asleep. Before proceeding further, the girl told him her whole intention, and begged him to get her out of the place and away. Gianni said that nothing would please him better, and that after he had left her he would without fail make such arrangements that the next time he returned there, he would take her away with him. After this, they embraced each other with great delight and took that pleasure beyond which love can give no more. And when they had repeated it several times, they unawares fell asleep in each other's arms.

The King, who had been pleased with her first appearance, recollected her, and, feeling better, decided to go and spend some time with her, although it was nearly morning. So he went secretly to the Cuba with some of his attendants. He went to her apartments and ordered that the room in which he knew the girl was sleeping should be quietly opened; and went in with a large candlestick borne alight before him. Looking at the bed, he saw her and Gianni lying asleep naked and embraced. This annoyed him so much and put him into such a rage that he very nearly killed them both with a knife lying near at hand, without saying a word. But, recollecting that it is a most vile thing in any man, above all in a King, to slay two naked people asleep, he restrained himself and determined they should be burned alive in public. Turning to one of his attendants, he said:

"What do you think of this guilty woman, in whom I once put my hopes?"

He then asked if he knew who the young man was who had had such impudence to come into his house and commit such an outrage and displeasure to himself; and the man replied that he did not ever remember to have seen him.

The angry King then went back to his room, and ordered that the two lovers should be taken and bound, naked as they were, and as soon as it was day they should be taken to the market place of Palermo, bound back to back to a stake, kept there until the hour of Tierce so that all might see them, and then burned as they had deserved. After giving these orders, he returned to his room in Palermo in deep anger.

As soon as the King had gone, a number of men set upon the lovers, awakened them, and immediately seized and bound them without pity. When the two young people found what had happened, they were woeful and feared for their lives and wept and lamented, as you may well suppose. In accordance with the King's orders, they were taken to Palermo, bound to a stake in the market place, and faggots and fire were prepared before their eyes to burn them at the hour the King had fixed.

All the people of Palermo, both men and women, flocked to see the two lovers. The men drew to one side to look at the girl, and just as they all praised her as beautiful and well-made, so all the women, who had run to look at the young man, commended him as a handsome and well-built young man. The unfortunate lovers, consumed with shame, stood with their heads hanging down, and wept for their misfortune, every moment expecting cruel death by fire.

While they were kept there until the hour fixed, the crime they had committed was bawled about by everyone and came to the ears of Ruggieri dell' Oria, a man of the greatest valour and at that time the King's admiral. He went to the place where they were bound, to see them; and having arrived he first looked at the girl and praised her beauty, and then went to look at the young man whom he recognised without much difficulty. He went nearer, and asked if he were Gianni di Procida. Gianni lifted his head, and recognising the admiral, said:

"Sir, I was once he whom you name, but I am now about to be nothing."

The admiral then asked him what had led him to that plight, and Gianni replied:

"Love and the King's wrath."

The admiral then made him tell the tale more fully. And when he had heard how everything had happened, and was about to depart, Gianni called him, and said:

"Sir, if it may be, beg me one favour from him who has sent me here."

Ruggieri asked what that was, and Gianni said:

"I see that I must soon die. Now, since I am bound back to back with this girl whom I have loved more than my life, and she me, I ask as a favour that we may be turned face to face, so that I may gaze at her face as I die, and depart in peace."

Said Ruggieri laughing:

"Willingly. And I will so act that you will see her so much you will be weary of it."

As the admiral left he ordered those who had been appointed to carry out this execution, not to proceed any further without express orders from the King. And then he hastened to the King without further delay. And although he saw the King was angry he did not fail to speak his mind, and said:

"King, how have you been injured by the two young people whom you have commanded to be burned in the market place?"

The King told him, and Ruggieri went on:

"The fault they committed deserved punishment, but not from you. As faults deserve punishment, so benefits deserve reward, apart from favour and pity. Do you know who they are whom you want to burn?"

The King said he did not; and Ruggieri then said:

"I wish you to know so that you may see how wisely you allow yourself to be carried away by a fit of anger. The young man is the son of Landolfo di Procida, the brother of Messer Gianni di Procida, by whose aid you are King and lord of that island. The girl is the daughter of Marin Bolgaro, whose power alone prevents your rule from being driven out of Ischia. Moreover, these two young people have long been in love, and they committed this sin (if what two young people do in love can be called a sin) because they were compelled by love and not because they wished to insult your majesty. Why then will you have them die, when you ought to honour them with the greatest pleasure and gifts?"

When the King heard this and was certain that Ruggieri was telling the truth, he not only felt ashamed to proceed to further cruelty, but regretted what he had done. He at once ordered that they should be unbound from the stake and brought before him. And having enquired into their condition, he decided to compensate for the injury he had done with honours and gifts. He had them honourably garbed, and knowing they were both consenting, married the girl to Gianni, gave them magnificent gifts, and sent them happily home, where they were received with the greatest rejoicing, and long lived together in peace and joy.

# SEVENTH TALE

*Teodoro falls in love with Violante, the daughter of Messer Amerigo, his master, makes her pregnant, and is condemned to the gallows. While he is being whipped to execution, he is recognised by his father and set free, and afterwards marries Violante*

The ladies were trembling with suspense to know whether the lovers would be burned, but when they heard of their escape, they praised God and became cheerful again. The queen, having listened to the end of the tale, imposed the task of the next upon Lauretta, who began merrily as follows:

Fairest ladies, in the reign of good King Guglielmo of Sicily, there lived on the island a gentleman named Messer Amerigo Abate da Trapani, who, among other worldly possessions, was well furnished with children. He therefore needed servants, and when certain Genoese galleys of the Levant arrived with a cargo of children they had captured along the coast of Armenia, he bought some of them in the belief that they were Turks. They all seemed to be peasants, except one, who looked of better blood and appearance, and was named Teodoro.

Although as this boy grew up he was treated as a slave, yet he was bred along with Messer Amerigo's children. He inclined more to his own nature than to his present state, and became so well-bred and well-behaved and thereby pleased his master so much that he was made a free man. Amerigo thought he was a Turk, and so had him baptised under the name of Pietro, set him in charge of his affairs, and had great confidence in him.

Along with Messer Amerigo's other children there grew up a daughter named Violante, a beautiful and delicate girl. As her father was slow in marrying her off, she fell in love by chance with Pietro; but though she loved him, and thought highly of his manners and actions, she was ashamed to let him know it. But love eased her of this trouble. Pietro had often looked covertly at her, and had fallen so much in love with her that he was only happy when he saw her.

But he was afraid lest somebody should find this out, for he thought it a wrong thing to have done. But the girl, who liked to watch him, discovered this; and, to give him more confidence, showed herself delighted with it, as indeed she was. And in this way some time passed, neither attempting to say anything to the other, although both desired it. But while they were both equally burning in the flames of love, Fortune, as if she had determined that it should be so, found a way for them to get rid of the fear which impeded them.

About a mile outside Trapani, Messer Amerigo had a fine estate, which his wife and daughter with other girls and women often visited for recreation. One very hot day when they had gone there, taking Pietro with them, the sky suddenly became overcast with dark clouds, which we often see occurs in the summer. To avoid being caught there, the lady and her companions set out for Trapani as quickly as they could. But Pietro and the girl, both being young, got far ahead of the mother and her friends, urged no doubt as much by love as by fear of the weather. When they were so far ahead of the lady and the others that they were almost out of sight, there came several claps of thunder followed by thick and very large hail. The lady and her friends took refuge in a workman's cottage. Pietro and the girl, having no nearer shelter, ran to an old, almost ruined hut, where nobody lived. They both huddled under the little piece of roof yet remaining, compelled to touch each other by the narrowness of the shelter. This contact was sufficient to strengthen their spirits a little and enable them to reveal their amorous desires. Pietro began first:

"If I could stay where I am, I would to Heaven that this hail would never cease."

"I should like it too," said the girl.

From these words they came to holding and squeezing hands, and from that to putting their arms round each other, and then to kissing, while the hail continued. Not to relate everything in detail—the weather did not clear up until they had tasted the last delights of love, and had arranged to meet each other secretly again for their delight. The bad weather ceased, they waited for the lady at the entrance to the town, which was near at hand, and returned home with her.

They met several times secretly in the same place, to their mutual pleasure. The good work proceeded so well that the girl became pregnant, which was highly displeasing to them both. She tried many means to procure an abortion, contrary to the course of nature, but could not succeed. So

Pietro, in fear of his life, determined to run away, and told her so. But when she heard this, she said:

"If you go away, I shall certainly kill myself."

Pietro, who was greatly in love with her, said:

"How can you want me to remain, lady mine? Your pregnancy will reveal our fault. You will easily obtain pardon, but the penalty for your sin and mine will have to be borne by wretched me."

"Pietro," replied the girl, "my sin will indeed become known. But unless you speak of it, be sure that yours never will."

"Since you make me the promise," said Pietro, "I will stay, but be careful not to break it."

The girl concealed her pregnancy as much as she could, but when she saw from the swelling of her body that it could be concealed no longer, she confessed it one day with great lamentations to her mother, begging for her help. In her distress the mother said very sharp things to her, and wanted to know how it had happened. The girl made up a story, revealing the truth in a different form, in order to protect Pietro.

The mother believed her, and sent her to one of their farms to conceal her daughter's slip. Now, when the time of birth came, the girl was screaming as women are wont to do. The mother never thought that Messer Amerigo would come there, since he scarcely ever did so; but it just happened that as he was returning from hawking he passed close by the room where his daughter was shrieking, and in his astonishment suddenly entered and asked what was the matter. When the lady saw her husband come in, she rose up sadly and told him what had happened to her daughter. But he was less credulous than his wife, said it was false that she did not know by whom she was pregnant, and that he meant to know. Only by revealing it could she obtain his pardon; otherwise he would let her die without pity.

The lady did her best to make her husband satisfied with what she had said, but failed completely. He flew into a rage, rushed with a drawn sword in his hand to his daughter (who had borne a male child while her mother was holding him in talk), and said:

"Either tell me the name of this child's father or you shall die at once."

In fear of her life the girl broke her promise to Pietro, and revealed all that had happened between him and her.

When the knight heard it, he was fiercely vindictive, and could scarcely refrain from killing her. But when he had said to her what anger dictated, he mounted his horse, rode to Trapani, and related the injury done him by Pietro to one Messer Currado, who was then governor for the King. The unsuspecting Pietro was immediately arrested, and, when put to the torture, confessed everything.

A few days later he was condemned by the governor to be whipped through the town and then hanged by the neck. So that the same hour should remove from the earth the two lovers and their child, Messer Amerigo (whose anger was not satiated by having brought Pietro to death) mixed poison with wine in a cup and gave them, together with an unsheathed dagger, to a servant, saying:

"Take these two things to Violante and tell her for me that she is immediately to choose death either by poison or steel. If not, tell her I will have her burned in the sight of all her townsmen, as she has deserved. After that, take the child she bore recently, dash its head against the wall, and throw its body to the dogs."

The servant departed, being one more disposed to evil than to good, after receiving this cruel sentence of an angry father on his daughter and grandchild.

The condemned Pietro was whipped on his way to execution, and those who were conducting him chanced to take him past an inn where lodged three noblemen of Armenia. They had been sent as ambassadors to the Pope by the King of Armenia, to treat of most important matters concerning a crusade which was planned; they had dismounted there to rest and refresh themselves for a few days, and had received great honours from the noblemen of Trapani, particularly from Messer Amerigo. When they heard the executioners passing by with Pietro, they went to the window to look at them. Pietro was naked to the waist and his hands were tied behind his back. Among the ambassadors was an old man of great authority, by name Fineo. As he gazed at Pietro, he saw on his breast a large red mark, not dyed but naturally imprinted in the skin, like those which women call "strawberry marks." Looking at it, he suddenly remembered his son who fifteen years before had been carried off by pirates on the coast of Laiazzo, of whom he had never been able to get any news. He estimated the age of the captive being whipped, and knew that if his son were alive he would be about the age this man appeared to be. He began to suspect from the birthmark that this was his son, and thought that if he were he must still remember his name and his father and the Armenian language. So when Pietro came near, he called out:

"Teodoro!"

On hearing the voice, Pietro immediately lifted his head, and Fineo, speaking in Armenian, said:

"Where do you come from? Whose son are you?"

Out of respect for this worthy gentleman the soldiers halted, and Pietro replied:

"I was from Armenia, the son of one Fineo, and I was brought here when a child by men I did not know."

By this Fineo knew for certain that this was his lost son. So he descended, weeping, with his companions and ran among the soldiers to embrace him. Fineo threw on his shoulders a cloak of the richest material from his own back, and begged those who were leading him to execution to wait there until they received orders to take him back. And they replied that they would do so willingly.

Fineo already knew the reason why he was condemned to death, for the story was about everywhere. So he went at once with his friends and their followers to Messer Currado, and said to him:

"Messer, the man you have condemned to death as a slave is a free man and my son, and he is ready to take as his wife the girl he is said to have devirginated. Be pleased to delay the execution until we know whether she will take him as her husband, for if she will, you cannot then break the law which sets him free."

Messer Currado was amazed when he heard that Pietro was the son of Fineo. He was ashamed of his mistake, confessed that what Fineo said was true, and hurrying back to his house, sent for Messer Amerigo and told him what had happened. Messer Amerigo, who believed his daughter and grandchild were already dead, was the unhappiest man alive because of what he had done, for he realised that if she were not dead everything could be happily mended. But nevertheless he sent posthaste to his daughter countermanding what he had ordered. The man who took the message found the servant sent by Messer Amerigo had put the knife and the poison before her; and because she would not choose quickly, he was abusing her and trying to force her to take one or the other. But when he heard his master's orders, he left her, returned to him, and told him how matters stood. Messer Amerigo was glad to hear it, and hastened to Fineo. In the best terms he knew, he apologised almost in tears for what had happened, begged his pardon, and said that if Teodoro would take his daughter to wife, he would be glad to give her. Fineo gladly accepted the apology, and said:

"I mean that my son shall take your daughter. If he will not, let the sentence against him be carried out."

Fineo and Messer Amerigo being thus in agreement, they went to Teodoro who was still in fear of death, yet glad to have found his father; and asked him what he wanted to do. And when Teodoro heard that Violante would be his wife if he wished, he was so happy that he felt as if he had leaped from hell to heaven, and said that this would be the greatest of all favours to him, provided it pleased both of them.

They then sent to the girl to find out her wishes. When she heard what had happened and would happen to Teodoro she ceased to be a wretched woman awaiting death, and, after a time, putting trust in their words, became a little more cheerful, and replied that if she could follow her own desire nothing would make her happier than to be Teodoro's wife; but that nevertheless she would do what her father commanded.

Thus the girl was betrothed in concord, and a great feast was made, to the delight of all the citizens. The girl became happier and put her child out to nurse; and not long afterwards returned more beautiful than ever. She went to meet Fineo, whose return from Rome was expected, and greeted him with the reverence due to a father. He was happy to have so beautiful a daughter-in-law, and celebrated the wedding with great pomp and rejoicing, accepting and always holding her as his daughter. A few days later he went on board ship with her, his son and his little grandson, and took them to Laiazzo, where the two lovers remained in peace and quietness for the rest of their lives.

## EIGHTH TALE

*Nastagio degli Onesti is in love with one of the Traversari and spends all his possessions without obtaining her love. At the request of his relatives, he goes to Chiassi, and there sees a horseman hunting a girl who is killed and devoured by two dogs. He invites his relatives and the lady he loves to dine with him, and she sees the girl torn to pieces. Fearing the same fate, she marries Nastagio and lives happily with him*

When Lauretta was silent, Filomena, at the queen's command, began thus:

Charming ladies, as pity is commended in us, so divine justice rigidly punishes cruelty in you. To display this to you and cause you to drive it wholly from you, I desire to tell you a tale no less full of compassion than of delight.

In Ravenna, that most ancient city of Romagna, there were of old many nobles and gentlemen, among whom was a young man named Nastagio degli Onesti, who became exceedingly rich on the death of his father and an uncle. As happens to young men without a wife, he fell in love with a daughter of Messer Paolo Traversaro, a girl of far more noble birth than he, whom he hoped to win by his actions. But however fair and praiseworthy they were, they not only failed to please her but actually seemed to displease her, so cruelly, harshly, and unfriendly did the girl behave, perhaps on account of her rare beauty, perhaps because her lofty and disdainful nobility of birth made her despise him and everything he liked.

This was so hard for Nastagio to bear that for very grief he often desired to slay himself. But, dreading to do this, he very often determined to leave her or, if he could, to hate her as she hated him. But in vain, for it seemed that the less hope he had, the more his love grew.

As the young man continued to love and to spend money recklessly, his friends and relatives felt that he was wasting both himself and his possessions. So they often advised and begged him to leave Ravenna, and to go and live somewhere else for a time, to diminish his love and his expense. Nastagio several times made mock of this advice; but unable to say "No" to their repeated solicitations, he agreed to do it. He made great preparations, as if he were going to France or Spain or some other far off land, mounted his horse, and left Ravenna accompanied by many of his friends. He went to a place about three miles from Ravenna, called Chiassi; and having set up tents and pavilions there, told his friends he meant to stay there and that they should return to Ravenna. There Nastagio led the most extravagant life, inviting different parties of people to dine or sup, as he had been accustomed to do.

Now, in very fine weather about the beginning of May, he began to think of his cruel lady, and ordered his attend-

ants to leave him alone so that he could dream of her at his
ease; and in his reverie his footsteps led him into the pine
woods. The fifth hour of the day was already spent, and he
was a good half mile inside the woods, forgetful of food
and everything else, when suddenly he thought he heard a
loud lamentation and the wild shrieks of a woman. Breaking
off his sweet reverie, he raised his head to see what it was,
and to his surprise found himself in the pine forest. But, in
addition, as he looked in front of him he saw coming towards him a very beautiful girl, naked, with disordered
hair, and all scratched by the thorns and twigs of the brambles and bushes in the wood. She was weeping and calling
for mercy. Beside her he saw two very large, fierce mastiffs,
savagely pursuing her, and frequently snapping cruelly at
her; and behind her on a black horse was a dark knight,
with grief and anger in his face, with a sword in his hand,
who often threatened her with death in dreadful and insulting terms.

This aroused astonishment and terror in his soul, and
finally compassion for the unfortunate lady, from which was
born the desire to set her free from such agony and such a
death, if he could. But, finding himself unarmed, he ran to
tear off a tree bough in place of a cudgel, and began to advance towards the dogs and the knight. But the knight saw
him, and called to him from a distance:

"Nastagio, don't meddle here, let me and these dogs do
what this wicked woman has deserved."

As he spoke the dogs seized the girl by the thighs, bringing her to the ground, and the knight dismounted from his
horse. Nastagio went up to him, and said:

"I do not know who you are, though you seem to know
me; but I tell you it is baseness in an armed knight to want
to kill a naked woman, and to have set dogs at her, as if
she were a wild beast. I shall certainly defend her as far as
I can."

Then said the knight:

"Nastagio, I am of the same country as yourself, and
you were still a little child when I, whose name was Messer
Guido degli Anastagi, was more deeply in love with this
woman than you now are with your Traversaro. Owing to
her cruelty and pride, my misfortune caused me in despair
to kill myself with the sword you see in my hand, and I am
damned to eternal punishment. Not long afterwards, she,
who had rejoiced exceedingly at my death, died also, and
died unrepentant, believing that she had not sinned but done
well; but for the sin of her cruelty and of her rejoicing at

my torments, she too was and is damned to the punishments of hell. When she descended into hell, the punishment imposed upon us was that she should fly from me and that I, who once loved her so much, should pursue her as a mortal enemy, not as a beloved woman. As often as I catch her I kill her with the very sword with which I slew myself, and split her open, and drag out (as you will soon see) that hard cold heart, wherein love and pity could never enter, together with her entrails, and give them to these dogs to eat.

"After no long space of time, in accordance with the justice and the will of God, she rises up again as if she had not been dead, and once more begins her anguished flight, and I and the dogs pursue her. Every Friday at this hour I catch up with her here and slaughter her as you will see. And do not think that we rest on other days. I catch her in other places where she thought or wrought cruelly against me. Having changed from a lover to an enemy, as you see, I am condemned in this way to pursue her for as many years as the months she was cruel to me. Now let me execute divine justice, and strive not to oppose what you cannot prevent."

Nastagio was terrified by these words, and there was scarcely a hair of his body which did not stand on end. He drew back and gazed at the miserable girl, awaiting fearfully what the knight would do. When the knight had done speaking, he rushed like a mad dog at the girl with his sword in his hand, while she, held on her knees by the mastiffs, shrieked for mercy. But he thrust his sword with all his strength through the middle of her breast until it stood out behind her back. When the girl received this thrust, she fell forward still weeping and shrieking. The knight took a dagger in his hand, slit her open, took out her heart and everything near it, and threw them to the mastiffs who hungrily devoured them at once.

But before long the girl suddenly rose to her feet as if nothing had happened, and began to run towards the sea, with the dogs continually snapping at her. The knight took his sword, remounted his horse and followed; and in a short time they were so far away that Nastagio lost sight of them. After seeing these things, Nastagio hesitated a long time between pity and fear; but after some time it occurred to him that it might be useful to him, since it happened every Friday. So having marked the place, he returned to his servants, and in due course sent for many of his relatives and friends, to whom he said:

"You have long urged me to refrain from loving my fair enemy and to cease my expense. I am ready to do so, if you will do me one favour—which is that next Friday you will come and dine with me, and bring Messer Paolo Traversaro, his wife, his daughter, all their women relatives, and any other women you like. Why I want this you will see later."

They thought this a small thing to do. So they returned to Ravenna, and invited those whom Nastagio wanted. And although it was hard to get the girl whom Nastagio loved, still she went along with the rest. Nastagio made preparations for a magnificent feast, and had the tables set among the pines near the place where he had seen the massacre of the cruel lady. He placed the men and women at table in such a manner that the girl he loved was exactly opposite the place where this would happen.

The last course had arrived when they all began to hear the despairing shrieks of the pursued lady. Everyone was astonished and asked what it was. Nobody knew. They stood up to look, and saw the agonised girl and the dogs and the knight. And in a very short time they all arrived in front of them. Great was the uproar against knight and dogs, and many started forward to help the girl. But the knight, speaking to them as he had spoken to Nastagio, not only made them draw back, but filled them with astonishment and terror. He did what he had done before; and all the women, many of whom were relatives of the suffering girl and of the knight, and remembered his love and death, wept as wretchedly as if it had been done to themselves.

When the massacre was over, and the lady and the knight had gone, those who had seen it fell into different sorts of discourse. But the most frightened was the cruel lady beloved by Nastagio, who had distinctly seen and heard everything, and knew that these things came nearer to her than to anyone else, for she remembered the cruelty with which she had always treated Nastagio. So that in her mind's eye she already seemed to be flying from his rage and to feel the mastiffs at her sides.

Such fear was born in her from this that, to avoid its happening to her, she could scarcely wait for that evening to change her hate into love and to send a trusted maid-servant secretly to Nastagio, begging him to go to see her, because she was ready to do anything he pleased. Nastagio replied that this was a happiness to him but that he desired his pleasure with honour, which was to take her as his wife, if she would agree. The girl knew that she herself had been the only obstacle to this hitherto, and replied that she was willing. So making herself the messenger, she told her father and mother that she was willing to marry Nastagio, which greatly delighted them. Next Sunday Nastagio married her and made a wedding feast, and lived happily with her for a long time.

Nor was this the only good which resulted from this terrifying apparition, for all the ladies of Ravenna took fear, and became far more compliant to the pleasures of the men than they had ever been before.

## NINTH TALE

*Federigo degli Alberighi loves, but is not beloved. He spends all his money in courtship and has nothing left but a falcon, and this he gives his lady to eat when she comes to visit him because there is nothing else to give her. She learns of this, changes her mind, takes him as her husband, and makes him a rich man*

Filomena had ceased speaking, and the queen, seeing that nobody was left to speak except Dioneo (who had his privilege) and herself, began cheerfully as follows:

It is now my turn to speak, dearest ladies, and I shall gladly do so with a tale similar in part to the one before, not only that you may know the power of your beauty over the gentle heart, but because you may learn yourselves to be givers of rewards when fitting, without allowing Fortune always to dispense them, since Fortune most often bestows them, not discreetly but lavishly.

You must know then that Coppo di Borghese Domenichi, who was and perhaps still is one of our fellow citizens, a man of great and revered authority in our days both from his manners and his virtues (far more than from nobility of blood), a most excellent person worthy of eternal fame, and in the fullness of his years delighted often to speak of past matters with his neighbours and other men. And this he could do better and more orderly and with a better memory and more ornate speech than anyone else.

Among other excellent things, he was wont to say that in

the past there was in Florence a young man named Federigo, the son of Messer Filippo Alberighi, renowned above all other young gentlemen of Tuscany for his prowess in arms and his courtesy. Now, as most often happens to gentlemen, he fell in love with a lady named Monna Giovanna, in her time held to be one of the gayest and most beautiful women ever known in Florence. To win her love, he went to jousts and tourneys, made and gave feasts, and spent his money without stint. But she, no less chaste than beautiful, cared nothing for the things he did for her nor for him who did them.

Now as Federigo was spending far beyond his means and getting nothing in, as easily happens, his wealth failed and he remained poor with nothing but a little farm, on whose produce he lived very penuriously, and one falcon which was among the best in the world. More in love than ever, but thinking he would never be able to live in the town any more as he desired, he went to Campi where his farm was. There he spent his time hawking, asked nothing of anybody, and patiently endured his poverty.

Now while Federigo was in this extremity it happened one day that Monna Giovanna's husband fell ill, and seeing death come upon him, made his will. He was a very rich man and left his estate to a son who was already growing up. And then, since he had greatly loved Monna Giovanna, he made her his heir in case his son should die without legitimate children; and so died.

Monna Giovanna was now a widow, and as is customary with our women, she went with her son to spend the year in a country house she had near Federigo's farm. Now the boy happened to strike up a friendship with Federigo, and delighted in dogs and hawks. He often saw Federigo's falcon fly, and took such great delight in it that he very much wanted to have it, but did not dare ask for it, since he saw how much Federigo prized it.

While matters were in this state, the boy fell ill. His mother was very much grieved, as he was her only child and she loved him extremely. She spent the day beside him, trying to help him, and often asked him if there was anything he wanted, begging him to say so, for if it were possible to have it, she would try to get it for him. After she had many times made this offer, the boy said:

"Mother, if you can get me Federigo's falcon, I think I should soon be better."

The lady paused a little at this, and began to think what

she should do. She knew that Federigo had loved her for a long time, and yet had never had one glance from her, and she said to herself:

"How can I send or go and ask for this falcon, which is, from what I hear, the best that ever flew, and moreover his support in life? How can I be so thoughtless as to take this away from a gentleman who has no other pleasure left in life?"

Although she knew she was certain to have the bird for the asking, she remained in embarrassed thought, not knowing what to say, and did not answer her son. But at length love for her child got the upper hand and she determined that to please him in whatever way it might be, she would not send, but go herself for it and bring it back to him. So she replied:

"Be comforted, my child, and try to get better somehow. I promise you that tomorrow morning I will go for it, and bring it to you."

The child was so delighted that he became a little better that same day. And on the morrow the lady took another woman to accompany her, and as if walking for exercise went to Federigo's cottage, and asked for him. Since it was not the weather for it, he had not been hawking for some days, and was in his garden employed in certain work there. When he heard that Monna Giovanna was asking for him at the door, he was greatly astonished, and ran there happily. When she saw him coming, she got up to greet him with womanly charm, and when Federigo had courteously saluted her, she said:

"How do you do, Federigo? I have come here to make amends for the damage you have suffered through me by loving me more than was needed. And in token of this, I intend to dine today familiarly with you and my companion here."

"Madonna," replied Federigo humbly, "I do not remember ever to have suffered any damage through you, but received so much good that if I was ever worth anything it was owing to your worth and the love I bore it. Your generous visit to me is so precious to me that I could spend again all that I have spent; but you have come to a poor host."

So saying, he modestly took her into his house, and from there to his garden. Since there was nobody else to remain in her company, he said:

"Madonna, since there is nobody else, this good woman,

the wife of this workman, will keep you company, while I go to set the table."

Now, although his poverty was extreme, he had never before realised what necessity he had fallen into by his foolish extravagance in spending his wealth. But he repented of it that morning when he could find nothing with which to do honour to the lady, for love of whom he had entertained vast numbers of men in the past. In his anguish he cursed himself and his fortune and ran up and down like a man out his senses, unable to find money or anything to pawn. The hour was late and his desire to honour the lady extreme, yet he would not apply to anyone else, even to his own workman; when suddenly his eye fell upon his falcon, perched on a bar in the sitting room. Having no one to whom he could appeal, he took the bird, and finding it plump, decided it would be food worthy such a lady. So, without further thought, he wrung its neck, made his little maid servant quickly pluck and prepare it, and put it on a spit to roast. He spread the table with the whitest napery, of which he had some left, and returned to the lady in the garden with a cheerful face, saying that the meal he had been able to prepare for her was ready.

The lady and her companion arose and went to table, and there together with Federigo, who served it with the greatest devotion, they ate the good falcon, not knowing what it was. They left the table and spent some time in cheerful conversation, and the lady, thinking the time had now come to say what she had come for, spoke fairly to Federigo as follows:

"Federigo, when you remember your former life and my chastity, which no doubt you considered harshness and cruelty, I have no doubt that you will be surprised at my presumption when you hear what I have come here for chiefly. But if you had children, through whom you could know the power of parental love, I am certain that you would to some extent excuse me.

"But, as you have no child, I have one, and I cannot escape the common laws of mothers. Compelled by their power, I have come to ask you—against my will, and against all good manners and duty—for a gift, which I know is something especially dear to you, and reasonably so, because I know your straitened fortune has left you no other pleasure, no other recreation, no other consolation. This gift is your falcon, which has so fascinated my child that if I do not take it to him, I am afraid his present illness will grow so much worse that I may lose him. Therefore I beg you, not by the love you bear me (which holds you to nothing), but by your own nobleness, which has shown itself so much greater in all courteous usage than is wont in other men, that you will be pleased to give it me, so that through this gift I may be able to say that I have saved my child's life, and thus be ever under an obligation to you."

When Federigo heard the lady's request and knew that he could not serve her, because he had given her the bird to eat, he began to weep in her presence, for he could not speak a word. The lady at first thought that his grief came from having to part with his good falcon, rather than from anything else, and she was almost on the point of retraction. But she remained firm and waited for Federigo's reply after his lamentation. And he said:

"Madonna, ever since it has pleased God that I should set my love upon you, I have felt that Fortune has been contrary to me in many things, and have grieved for it. But they are all light in comparison with what she has done to me now, and I shall never be at peace with her again when I reflect that you came to my poor house, which you never deigned to visit when it was rich, and asked me for a little gift, and Fortune has so acted that I cannot give it to you. Why this cannot be, I will briefly tell you.

"When I heard that you in your graciousness desired to dine with me and I thought of your excellence and your worthiness, I thought it right and fitting to honour you with the best food I could obtain; so, remembering the falcon you ask me for and its value, I thought it a meal worthy of you, and today you had it roasted on the dish and set forth as best I could. But now I see that you wanted the bird in another form, it is such a grief to me that I cannot serve you that I think I shall never be at peace again."

And after saying this, he showed her the feathers and the feet and the beak of the bird in proof. When the lady heard and saw all this, she first blamed him for having killed such a falcon to make a meal for a woman; and then she inwardly commended his greatness of soul which no poverty could or would be able to abate. But, having lost all hope of obtaining the falcon, and thus perhaps the health of her son, she departed sadly and returned to the child. Now, either from disappointment at not having the falcon or because his sickness must inevitably have led to it, the child died not many days later, to the mother's extreme grief.

Although she spent some time in tears and bitterness, yet, since she had been left very rich and was still young, her brothers often urged her to marry again. She did not want to do so, but as they kept on pressing her, she remembered the worthiness of Federigo and his last act of generosity, in killing such a falcon to do her honour.

"I will gladly submit to marriage when you please," she said to her brothers, "but if you want me to take a husband, I will take no man but Federigo degli Alberighi."

At this her brothers laughed at her, saying:

"Why, what are you talking about, you fool? Why do you want a man who hasn't a penny in the world?"

But she replied:

"Brothers, I know it is as you say, but I would rather have a man who needs money than money which needs a man."

Seeing her determination, the brothers, who knew Federigo's good qualities, did as she wanted, and gave her with all her wealth to him, in spite of his poverty. Federigo, finding that he had such a woman, whom he loved so much, with all her wealth to boot, as his wife, was more prudent with his money in the future, and ended his days happily with her.

## TENTH TALE

*Pietro di Vinciolo goes out to sup. His wife brings a lover into the house; Pietro returns, and she hides the lover under a chicken coop. Pietro tells her how, while he was supping with Ercolano, a young man whom the wife had hidden was discovered. She blames Ercolano's wife, but an ass unhappily treads on the lover's finger as he is under the coop, and he gives a shriek; Pietro runs out, sees him, and perceives how his wife has tricked him; but in the end he pardons her fault*

The queen finished her tale, and they all praised God for having worthily rewarded Federigo; and then Dioneo began, without waiting to be ordered.

I know not whether it be an accidental vice and the result of the corruption of men's manners, or whether it be a natural failing to laugh at bad things rather than at good deeds, especially when we are not directly concerned. Now since the task I undertook before and am about to carry out again, has no other object but to drive away melancholy from you and to raise mirth and merriment, I shall tell you this tale, enamoured ladies, although its matter in part be less than chaste, because it may amuse you. While you listen to it, do as you do when you enter a garden and, stretching out your delicate hands, pluck the roses and avoid the thorns. In so doing, leave the bad man in his misfortune with his woes, and laugh at the amorous tricks of the wife, and feel compassion for the misfortunes of others, where it is needed.

Not long ago in Perugia there was a rich man named Pietro di Vinciolo, who took a wife, more to deceive others and to avoid the general opinion of himself among the Perugians, than for any desire he had of her. And Fortune was so far conformable to his wish that the wife he took was a robust wench with lively red hair, who would rather have had two husbands than one, whereas she had chanced upon a man who would rather have had to do with another man than with her.

In process of time she found this out. And since she was fresh and pretty, and felt herself friskish and robust, she got angry and often exchanged sharp words with her husband; and they led a miserable life together. But, seeing that this exhausted her without improving her husband, she said to herself:

"This man leaves me in sorrow and goes off in his vice in wooden shoes through the dry,[1] while I am trying to carry someone else in a ship through the rain.[2] I took him as my husband and gave him a good large dowry, knowing him to be a man, and thinking he wanted what men do and ought to want; and if I had not thought he was a man, I would never have taken him. He knew I was a woman; why did he marry me if he didn't like women? This is unendurable. If I had not wanted to live the life of the world, I should have become a nun. If I wait for delight and pleasure from him, I might perhaps wait in vain until I am an old woman, and then vainly regret my lost youth. He himself is an example to me, that I should find some consolation, and some pleasure as he does. In me this pleasure will be commendable, whereas in him it is blameworthy; for I only offend the laws, whereas he offends the laws and Nature too."

Having thought this over a good many times, the good

---

[1] I.e., is a sodomist.
[2] I.e., I am a normal woman.

woman, with an idea of carrying out her plan secretly, became familiar with an old woman, who yet seemed more like a pious old thing than a bawd, always going to church services with beads in her hand and never talking about anything but the lives of the Fathers or the stigmata of St. Francis, so that almost everybody thought she was a saint. And when she thought it a fitting time, the wife told her everything she intended.

"My child," said the old woman, "God, who knows everything, knows that in this you will do well. And if you did it for no reason, yet you and every other young woman should do it, in order not to waste the time of your youth, because to those who have any understanding there is no grief like having wasted time. What the devil good are we when we are old, except to watch the supper on the hearth? If anyone knows it and can bear witness to it, I can. Now I am an old woman I realise with bitter soul-prickings how I wasted my time. And although I did not lose it all (for I don't want you to think I was a simpleton), still I did not do what I could have done. When I remember it, and see what I now am, and think how nobody would kindle up a spark of desire for me, God knows what grief I feel.

"The same thing does not happen to men. They are born fitted for a thousand things and not for this only, while the larger number of them are much better old than young. But women are only born to do it and make children, and so are esteemed. And if you haven't noticed anything else, you ought to have noticed this—that we are always ready for it, which does not happen with men. Moreover, one woman would tire out many men, whereas many men cannot tire one woman. Now, since we are born for this, I say once more you will be doing well to give your husband tit for tat, so that in your old age your mind will not have any reproach to bring against your flesh.

"Everyone gets from this world what he takes from it, especially women, who have far more necessity to make use of time while they have it than men, because, as you can see for yourself, when we get old, neither husband nor anyone else wants to see us, so we're chased in the kitchen to tell tales to the cat, and scour the pots and pans. Worse than that even, they make songs about us, saying: 'The best morsels for the girls, and quinsies to the old women'; and they say lots of other similar things.

"To keep you no longer in talk, I say now that you could not have spoken to anyone in the world who can be more useful to you than me; for however haughty a man may be

I am not afraid to say what is necessary to him, and however harsh or boorish, I can smooth him down and bring him to the point I want. Tell me the one you want, and leave the rest to me. But remember, my child, that I am poor, and that you will be remembered in all my church-goings and all the paternosters I say; and I shall pray God for the souls of all your departed dead."

Thus ended the old woman. And the young woman came to an agreement with the old one that, if she saw him, she was to bring her a young man who often passed through the district; and she described him in such a way that the old woman knew who he was. Then she gave her a piece of salt meat, and sent her away.

Not many days afterwards the old woman brought the young man described to her room, and soon afterwards another, according as the young woman wanted. And, although in fear of her husband, she did not miss the opportunity.

One evening her husband was going out to supper with a friend of his, named Ercolano, and so the girl arranged with the old woman to bring her a young man, who was one of the handsomest and pleasantest in Perugia. Which was quickly done. The young woman and the young man were just sitting down to supper, when they heard Pietro at the door, shouting to her to open it. When she heard it, the wife gave herself up for dead. Wanting to hide the young man if she could, and not having the cunning to get him out of the house or hide him elsewhere, she hid him under a chicken coop in a shed next to the room in which they were supping, and threw over it a piece of straw sacking she had emptied that day. After which, she quickly opened the door to her husband. When he came into the house, she said:

"You've guzzled up that supper pretty quickly."

"We never even tasted it," said Pietro.

"How did that happen?" asked his wife.

"I'll tell you," said Pietro. "Ercolano and his wife and I were sitting down to table when we heard somebody sneeze near us, to which we paid no attention the first and second times. But the person sneezed a third, a fourth, a fifth and many other times, which greatly surprised us. Ercolano was already a little annoyed with his wife because she had kept him waiting a long time at the door, and said to her in a rage: 'What does this mean? Who is it sneezing like this?' He got up from the table, and went to the staircase near at hand, under which was a cupboard to store things away, as we see arranged in houses every day.

"It seemed to him that the sound of the sneezing came from this cupboard, so he opened a little door in it, and as soon as this was opened there suddenly came out the worst stink of sulphur imaginable, which he had noticed before and had complained of, whereupon his wife had said: 'I am whitening my veils in there with sulphur, and the pots too, which I sprinkled with sulphur so that they would get the fumes, and put them under the staircase, and the smell still comes from them.' And after Ercolano had opened the door and the fumes had cleared off a little, he looked inside and saw the person who had sneezed and was still sneezing owing to the sulphur fumes. And as he sneezed, the sulphur had got such a hold on his chest, that he was not far from never sneezing or doing anything else again.

"As soon as Ercolano saw him, he shouted: 'Now I see, wife, the man for whose sake you kept us waiting at the door so long without opening when we came. But may I never have anything please me again, if I don't make you pay for this!' The wife, hearing this and seeing that her fault was discovered, fled from the table without attempting any excuse; and I don't know where she went. Ercolano, not noticing that his wife had fled, told the sneezing man to come out; but he was beyond all power of moving, and did not stir for anything Ercolano said.

"Thereupon Ercolano took him by one of his feet and dragged him out and ran for a knife to kill him. But, fearing the police on my own account, I jumped up and prevented him from killing the man or doing him any harm. My shouting and defending him aroused the neighbours who came in and took the almost swooning young man, and carried him somewhere—I don't know where—out of the house. So our supper was quite spoiled by all this, and I not only haven't guzzled it but never even tasted it, as I said."

At this tale, the wife perceived that there were others who knew as much as she did, although some had bad luck. She would have been glad to defend Ercolano's wife with words, but as blaming the faults of others seemed to her to make things easier for her own, she said:

"Here's fine doings! Here's a good and saintly woman! Here's the faith of a modest woman, who seemed to me so saintly that I would have confessed my sins to her. And, what's worse, she gives a mighty good example to the young, since she's getting old already. Cursed be the hour when she came into the world and the hour which allowed her to live, the wicked deceitful woman that she must be, the universal shame and scorn of all women on this earth! Curse her for leaving her chastity and the faith promised to her husband and the honour of the world, he that is such a good man and an honourable citizen and treated her so well, for another man, and not being ashamed to bring him to scorn and herself with him! So help me God, I'd have no pity on such women. They ought to be killed. They ought to be thrown into the fire and burned to ashes."

Then, recollecting that her lover was near at hand, hidden under the hencoop, she began to urge Pietro to go to bed, as it was then bedtime. But Pietro was more anxious to have something to eat than to go to bed, and asked if there were not something for supper.

"Ah!" said the wife, "yes, indeed, there's supper! We're quite accustomed to have supper when you're not here! Yes, I'm Ercolano's wife, am I? Why don't you go to bed? Go to sleep this evening!"

Now, it happened that during the evening some of Pietro's workmen had brought certain things in from the country, and had stalled their asses without giving them any water to drink, in a little stable next to the shed. One of the asses was very thirsty indeed, and, managing to get his head out of the halter, walked out of the stable and went snuffing at everything, trying to find some water. And so he came up to the hen-coop where the young man was hidden.

He was on his hands and knees, and one of his fingers was outside the hen-coop. Now, as luck or ill luck would have it, the ass trod on his finger; whereupon, in his anguish, he uttered a yell. Pietro was astonished to hear it, and knew that someone must be in the house. He went out of the room and heard the young man moaning, for the ass had not yet taken its hoof off his finger and was still pressing heavily on it. Said Pietro: "Who's there?" He ran to the hen-coop, lifted it up, and saw the young man who, in addition to the pain he felt from the ass treading on his finger, was trembling with fear lest Pietro should do him an injury.

Pietro recognised him as a young man he had long been prowling after for his vicious pleasures, and asked him: "What are you doing here?" but the youth made no answer, and only begged him for the love of God to do him no harm.

"Get up," said Pietro, "I won't do you any harm; but tell me, how do you happen to be here, and why?"

The young man confessed everything. Pietro, no less joyous than his wife was distressed at the discovery, took him by the hand and led him into the room, where the wife was waiting in the greatest terror imaginable. Pietro made her sit down opposite and said:

"So you cursed so hard Ercolano's wife, and you said she ought to be burned and that she was the shame of you all —why didn't you say it of yourself? Or, if you didn't want to confess that, how could your conscience endure to say it of her, when you knew you had done the same thing as she had? Nothing, indeed, induced you to do it; except that all you women are alike, and you hope to hide your own sins under the failings of others. May fire come down from heaven and burn you all, vile generation that you are!"

The wife, seeing that at the first onslaught he had hurt her with nothing worse than words, and noticing that he was in high glee at holding such a handsome youth by the hand, plucked up heart and said:

"I am very sure that you would like fire to come from heaven and burn up all us women, since you are as fond of us as a dog is of sticks. But, God's Cross! You won't see it happen. I should like to have a little discussion with you, to find out what you complain of. It is indeed well to compare me with Ercolano's wife, a hypocritical, snivelling old woman, who gets what she wants out of him, and he treats her as well as a wife can be treated, which doesn't happen to me. For, granted that I am well clad and shod, you know how I fare in other matters and how long it is since you lay with me. I'd go with rags on my back and broken shoes and be well treated by you in bed, rather than have all these things and be treated as you treat me. Understand plainly, Pietro, I'm a woman like other women, and I want what they want. So, if I go seeking for what I can't get from you, there's no need to abuse me. At least I do you so much honour that I don't go with boys and scrubby fellows."

Pietro saw that she could go on talking all night, and so, as he cared nothing about her, he said:

"That's enough, wife. I'll be content with that. Will you be so gracious as to get us some supper, for I rather fancy this boy has had no more supper than I have."

"No, indeed," said the wife, "he has had no supper; for when you arrived in an ill hour, we were just sitting down to table to sup."

"Go along then," said Pietro, "and get us some supper, and afterwards I will arrange this affair in such a way that you will have nothing to complain of."

Finding her husband so agreeable, the wife jumped up and re-laid the table, brought out the supper she had prepared, and supped merrily with her bad husband and the young man. What Pietro arranged after supper to satisfy all three of them has entirely gone out of my head. But I know that next morning the young man found himself in the piazza, not quite knowing whether the night before he had been with the wife or the husband. And so, dear ladies, I want to tell you: "He who does it to you, you do it to him." And if you can't, keep it in mind while you can, so that the ass may receive what he gets at home.

Dioneo's tale was now ended, and the ladies' laughter was restrained less from lack of amusement than from shame. The queen, seeing that the end of her reign was at hand, stood up and took off her garland, and gracefully placed it on Elisa's head, saying:

"Madonna, it is now for you to give orders."

Having received the honour, Elisa followed the adopted routine and first arranged with the steward for what was needed during the period of her rule; after which she said to the satisfaction of the company:

"We have already heard how many people by means of good sayings and prompt retorts and quick wits have been able to turn the teeth of others on themselves with a sharp nip or have averted threatened dangers. And since this is a good topic and may be useful, my will is that tomorrow, with God's help, we tell tales within these limits—that is, of such persons who have retorted a witticism directed at them, or with a quick retort or piece of shrewdness have escaped destruction, danger or contempt."

This was highly commended by them all. Whereupon the queen rose to her feet, and gave them all to do as they chose until supper time. The merry company arose as the queen arose, and according to custom, each of them gave himself up to what pleased him most. But when the cicadas ceased their song, everyone was called, and they all went to supper. After this had been festively served, they went to singing and music. Emilia danced at the queen's command, and then Dioneo was ordered to sing a song. He immediately began: "Old mother Hale, lift up your tail, and see the good news I bring you." Whereat all the ladies burst out laughing, especially the queen, who ordered him to abandon that song and start another.

"Madonna," said Dioneo, "if I had cymbals, I would

sing: 'Up with your petties, Monna Lapa,' or 'Under the olive tree springs the grass,' or would you like me to sing: 'The waves of the ocean make me ill with their motion'? But then I haven't any cymbals, so see which of these others you would like. Do you like: 'Out you go to be chopped to shreds, like a melon down in the garden beds'?"

"No," said the queen, "sing something else."

"Well," said Dioneo, "shall I sing: 'Monna Simona, put it up in the cask, it isn't the month of October'?"

"No, no," said the queen laughing, "sing a nice song, if you like, but not that one."

"Don't get angry, Madonna," said Dioneo. "Which do you like best? I know over a thousand. Would you like: 'If I don't tickle my little prickle,' or 'Gently, gently, husband dear,' or 'I'll buy a cock for a hundred dollars'?"

"Dioneo," said the queen rather angrily, although all the others were laughing, "cease joking, and sing a pleasant song. If you don't, you will discover how angry I can be."

At this Dioneo left his jests, and began to sing as follows:

*Love, the fair light that issues from her eyes has made me slave to thee and her.*

*The splendour of her lovely eyes, passing through mine, moved me before your flame was kindled in my heart. However great your worth, I learned it through her beauteous face; imagining which, I found myself gathering every virtue and yielding them to her—another cause of sighs in me.*

*Now, dear my Lord, I have become one among your followers, and in obedience await your grace; but yet I know not if the high desire which you have set within my breast and my unshaken faith are wholly known to her, who so possesses all my mind that save from her I would not and I do not hope for peace.*

*Therefore I pray you, sweet my love, to show them to her, and make her feel a little of your flame, in grace to me who, as you see, am all consumed with love, and bit by bit worn down with pain. And then, when it is time, commend me to her, as you should, and gladly would I come with you to do it.*

When Dioneo by his silence showed that his song was ended, the queen, after having highly praised it, had others sung. And when part of the night was spent and the queen felt that the heat of day was quenched in night's coolness, she ordered everyone to rest as he chose until the following day.

**HERE ENDS THE FIFTH DAY**

# THE SIXTH DAY

# THE SIXTH DAY

*Here begins the sixth day of the* Decameron, *wherein, under the rule of Elisa, tales are told of those who have retorted a witticism directed at them or with a quick retort or piece of shrewdness have escaped destruction, danger or contempt*

The moon in the middle sky had lost its radiance and already the whole hemisphere was bright with the new day, when the queen arose and the company was awakened. They strolled slowly down the hillside, talking on various topics, arguing about the merits of the various tales and laughing again over the different events related, until the rising sun grew hot and everyone saw it was time to return to the house, which accordingly they did.

There the tables were laid and the whole house strewn with scented plants and exquisite flowers; and the queen ordered them to eat before the day became too hot. After they had merrily dined, they sang several pleasant and amusing songs before doing anything else, and then some went to sleep, some to chess and some to draughts. Dioneo and Lauretta sang a song about Troilus and Cressida.

When the time came to return to their usual gathering, the queen had them all warned, and they sat down by the fountain. The queen was just about to order someone to tell the first tale, when something unusual occurred—the queen and all of them heard a great uproar among the servants and attendants in the kitchen. The steward was sent for and asked who was screaming and what was the cause of the uproar; and he replied that there was a dispute between Licisca and Tindaro, but he did not know the reason for it, since he had been trying to calm them down when he was sent for. So the queen ordered that Licisca and Tindaro should at once appear before her and when they came, the queen asked what was the cause of their dispute.

Tindaro tried to answer, but Licisca, who was rather elderly and very conceited, and warmed up with the dispute, interrupted him, saying:

"See what a brute of a man you are, trying to speak before I do! Let me speak."

She then turned to the queen, and said:

"Madonna, he wants to tell me about Sicofante's wife. And, as if I didn't know her well, he does nothing more nor less than try to make me believe that the first night Sicofante lay with her, Messer Mazza had to force his way into the Black Mountain with an effusion of blood. And I say it isn't true, but that he entered calmly and with the greatest ease. And the man is so foolish that he thinks girls are such idiots they waste their time attending to the warnings of their fathers and brothers, when six times out of seven they know all about it three or four years before they have to get married. God, they'd be in a pretty plight if they had to wait that long. By the faith of Christ (who knows what I'm saying when I swear), I never had a neighbour who was a virgin when she married. And the married ones too—I know what tricks they play on their husbands. And this great ox tries to tell me about women, as if I was born yesterday!"

While Licisca was talking the ladies laughed so heartily you could have pulled all their teeth out. Six times did the queen command silence, all to no avail—she wouldn't stop until she had said all she wanted to say. When she had finished her say, the queen turned laughingly to Dioneo, and said:

"Dioneo, this is a question for you. And so, when we have ended our tales, you shall pass sentence on it."

But Dioneo immediately replied:

"Madonna, the sentence is passed without hearing any further. I say that Licisca is right and I believe things are as she says, and Tindaro is an ass."

Licisca burst out laughing at hearing this, and said to Tindaro:

"Didn't I tell you? Go along with you. Do you think you know more than I do, when you haven't washed the sleep out of your eyes? Thank you, I haven't lived for nothing."

If the queen had not bidden them be silent with a stern face, and ordered them not to quarrel any more and sent Tindaro and the woman away, under threat of reprimands, there would have been nothing else to do all day but attend to them. But when they had gone, the queen ordered Filomena to tell the first tale; and she began merrily as follows:

# FIRST TALE

*A knight asks permission to carry Madonna Oretta on his pillion and promises to tell her a tale; he does it so badly that she asks him to set her down*

Youthful ladies, even as the stars in the pure screen are the ornaments of heaven and the flowers of the green meadows in the spring and the trees of the hills, so witty sayings are to good manners and amusing conversation; and they are the more excellent in women since much speech is more befitting women than men. True it is, whatever the reason be, either the poorness of our genius or the singular enmity of the heavens to this our age, that few or no ladies now remain who can speak at the right moment, or, if they do so, say the right thing, which is a scandal to all of us. But since Pampinea has already enlarged on this topic, I shall say no more about it. However, to show you the beauty of the right thing said at the right moment, I intend to tell you of a courteous retort of a lady which imposed silence on a knight.

Many of you may have known by sight or have heard about a gentle and accomplished lady of our city whose merit was such that her name must not be concealed—she was then called Madonna Oretta, and was the wife of Messer Geri Spina. She was once in the country, as we now are, going for her amusement from one house to another in the company of ladies and knights who had dined at her own house that day; and since the road they had intended to traverse on foot was rather long, one of the knights in the party said:

"Madonna Oretta, I will tell you one of the finest stories in the world, if you like, which will make the way seem as short as if you were riding on a pillion."

"Messer," said the lady, "I beg you will do so, it will be most pleasant for me."

Our knight, who told a tale no better than he wore his sword, began his tale, which was indeed a very good one. But he kept repeating the same things three or four or six times, and then going back to the beginning, and saying: "No, I'm not telling it right," and then going wrong about names, putting one in place of another, so that he spoiled the tale nicely. Moreover, he articulated very badly in reproducing personalities and events. And so, as Madonna Oretta listened to him, she felt a sweat come over her and a sinking of the heart, as if she had been ill and about to die. And when she could endure it no longer, and saw that the knight had got into such a tangle he could not get out of it, she said:

"Messer, your horse trots too roughly. I beg you will allow me to go on foot."

The knight, who happened to have a quicker wit in understanding hints than in telling tales, saw the jest, and took it in the right spirit. He turned the conversation to other things, and left unfinished the tale which he had begun and continued so badly.

## SECOND TALE

*The baker Cisti makes a jest and shows Messer Geri Spina that he had made an unreasonable request*

Each of the ladies and men highly praised Madonna Oretta's remark, and the queen then commanded Pampinea to follow next. And she began thus:

Fair ladies, I do not know which is worse—to see Nature joining a noble spirit to a vile body or Fortune giving a base occupation to a body endowed with a noble soul, as you may observe in our fellow citizen, Cisti, and many others. This Cisti, who had a most lofty spirit, was made by Fortune a baker. Certainly I should curse both Nature and Fortune, if I did not know that Nature is most prudent and that Fortune has a thousand eyes, although fools figure her as blind. I think they behave as we often see mortals do, who, when dubious of the future, as opportunity serves, bury the most precious things they have in the vilest parts of their houses (as being the least likely to be suspected); and when in their necessity they take them out, they find a base hiding place has served them better than a fair room would have done. And so the two ministers of this world often hide their most valued possession under the shadow of the occupations reputed base, so that when they are drawn forth at the fitting moment, their splendour will be the more apparent. The story of Madonna Oretta, the wife of Geri Spina, puts me in mind of how Cisti the baker showed what he was in a little affair which I shall relate to you in a short tale.

In the time of Pope Boniface, who held Messer Geri Spina in high esteem, certain of his noble ambassadors came to Florence on important business. They stayed at the house of Messer Geri and discussed the Pope's affairs with him. Whatever the cause may have been, it happened that almost every morning Messer Geri and these ambassadors passed by Santa Maria Ughi, where Cisti the baker had his oven and personally attended to his business.

Now, although Fortune had bestowed a humble occupation upon him, she had been so far kindly to him that he had become very rich. He would never abandon his trade for another, but lived extremely well; and among other good things he had the best white and red wine of Florence or the district. When he saw Messer Geri and the Pope's ambassadors pass his shop every day during the very hot weather, he thought it would be courteous to offer them some of his good white wine. But then, reflecting on his own station in life and that of Messer Geri, he felt it would not be fitting in him to presume to invite him. So he thought of a way to make Messer Geri invite himself.

Wearing a white doublet and a clean apron over it, which showed him to be rather a miller than a baker, every morning at about the time he expected Messer Geri and the ambassadors to pass, he placed at the shop door a tin pail of fresh water and a small Bolognese jug of his good white wine, and two glasses which looked like silver, they were so bright. As they passed, he would be sitting beside these things, and after rinsing his mouth once or twice, he drank off some of the wine with such gusto that it would have made the very dead want to taste it. Messer Geri noticed this on one or two mornings, and the third time he said:

"What is it, Cisti? Is it good?"

Cisti sprang to his feet, and said:

"Messer, yes. But how can I make you understand it, unless you taste it?"

Messer Geri happened to be thirsty, either because of the weather or his fatigue or the gusto with which he saw Cisti drinking, so he turned smilingly to the ambassadors, and said:

"Gentlemen, let us taste this worthy man's wine. Perhaps we shall not repent of it."

And so he turned with them towards Cisti, who had a handsome bench brought from his shop, and begged them to sit down. Their servants came forward to wash the glasses, but Cisti said:

"Stand back, my friends, and leave that service to me. I can pour out wine as well as I can bake bread. And don't you expect to taste a drop." ·

So saying, he washed four handsome new glasses, and called for a small jug of his good wine, which he gave Messer Geri and his friends to drink. They thought the wine was better than any they had tasted for a long time, and highly praised it; and as long as the ambassadors were there Messer Geri went there to drink it with them nearly every morning. When they were about to leave, Messer Geri gave a magnificent banquet to which he invited all the most honourable citizens, including Cisti, who, however, refused to go. Messer Geri ordered one of his servants to go for a flask of Cisti's wine, and to fill half a glass to every guest at the supper table. The servant, who was perhaps irritated because he had never been allowed to taste the wine, took a huge flask; but when Cisti saw it, he said:

"My son, you weren't sent to me by Messer Geri."

The servant kept assuring him that he was so sent, but he could get no other answer and so returned to Messer Geri, and told him. Said Messer Geri:

"Go back to him, and say you are sent from me. And if he says anything else, ask him to whom I have sent you."

The servant returned, and said:

"Cisti, Messer Geri did mean to send me to you."

"No, my boy, he did not," replied Cisti.

"Well," said the servant, "who did he send me to?"

"The Arno," replied Cisti.

The servant reported this to Messer Geri, whose eyes were suddenly opened to the truth; and he said to the servant:

"Show me the flask you took to him."

And when he saw it, he said:

"Cisti was right."

And he scolded the servant, and made him take a proper sized flask. And as soon as Cisti saw it, he said:

"Now I know that you come from him."

And Cisti willingly filled the flask. Soon after he had a cask filled with the same wine and tenderly carried to Messer Geri's house. And he followed it, and said:

"Messer, I don't want you to think that I was frightened by the large flask this morning. But, thinking that you had forgotten what I showed you with my small jugs—that this is not servants' wine—I thought I would remind you. But since I do not mean to hoard it any longer, I have brought it all to you. Do what you please with it."

Messer Geri was charmed with Cisti's gift, and made him what he thought were suitable thanks; and ever afterwards esteemed him highly as a friend.

### THIRD TALE

*Monna Nonna de' Pulci imposes silence on the less than modest remarks of the Bishop of Florence*

When Pampinea had finished her tale and they had all highly praised Cisti's generosity and retort, the queen was pleased to order Lauretta to speak next; and she began cheerfully as follows:

Charming ladies, Pampinea and Filomena have both touched with truth upon our small merit and the happiness of retorts. There is no need then for me to return to them, but I should like to remind you that the nature of repartee is such that it should nip like the sheep, not snap like the dog. For if the retort bites like a dog, it is not a retort, but an insult. And this is admirably brought out by the retorts of Madonna Oretta and Cisti. True, if the person who retorts has at first been snapped at like a dog, he is not to be blamed for retorting in the same way, as he would otherwise be. And so we should always observe how and when and with whom and where we are jesting. One of our prelates, who failed to notice these rules, received back as good a bite as he gave, which I shall show you in a short tale.

Messer Antonio d'Orso, a learned and worthy prelate, was Bishop of Florence; and there came to Florence a Catalan gentleman, Messer Dego della Tata, general to King Roberto. He was a very handsome man and a great ladies' man, and he happened to be specially in love with a very pretty Florentine woman, who was niece to the Bishop's brother. He discovered that her husband was a base and miserly fellow, although of good family, and arranged to give him five hundred gold florins on condition that he (Dego) should spend a night with the wife. He had penny pieces gilded and, after lying with the wife against her will, gave the husband this false money. This became known to everyone, and the harm and the joke were on the bad husband. The Bishop, like a wise man, pretended to know nothing about it.

The Bishop and the General were great friends, and one St. John's day as they were riding along together, they saw the ladies going through the streets to the horse race. The Bishop saw a young woman, who has since died in the present plague, whose name was Monna Nonna de' Pulci, a cousin of Messer Alessio Rinucci, whom you must all have known. She was then a fresh, handsome, well-spoken, high-spirited girl and not long before had married in Porta San Pietro. The Bishop pointed her out to the General and, putting his hand on the General's shoulder, said:

"Nonna, what do you think of him? Do you think you could make a conquest of him?"

Nonna felt that these words were a reflection on her chastity and would do her harm in the minds of the numerous people who heard the remark. So, determined not to endure the slight, but to give tit for tat, she retorted:

"Messer, perhaps he would not make a conquest of me, but I should want good money."

The General and the Bishop both felt themselves hit by this remark, the former because he had played this dishonest trick on the niece of the Bishop's brother, the latter as receiving the shame on behalf of his own brother's niece. Silently and ashamed they went away, without looking at each other, and spoke no more that day.

So, as the girl was snapped at, she did right to snap back with another jest.

## FOURTH TALE

*Chichibio, cook to Currado Gianfigliazzi, changes Currado's anger to laughter, and so escapes the punishment with which Currado had threatened him*

Lauretta was silent, and they all praised Nonna; whereupon the queen ordered Neifile to follow next. And she said:

Amorous ladies, although quick wits often provide speakers with useful and witty words, yet Fortune, which sometimes aids the timid, often puts words into their mouths which they would never have thought of in a calm moment. This I intend to show you by my tale.

As everyone of you must have heard and seen, Currado Gianfigliazzi was always a noble citizen of our city, liberal and magnificent, leading a gentleman's life, continually delighting in dogs and hawks, and allowing his more serious affairs to slide. One day near Peretola his falcon brought down a crane, and finding it to be plump and young he sent it to his excellent cook, a Venetian named Chichibio, telling him to roast it for supper and see that it was well done.

Chichibio, who was a bit of a fool, prepared the crane, set it before the fire, and began to cook it carefully. When it was nearly done and giving off a most savoury odour, there came into the kitchen a young peasant woman, named Brunetta, with whom Chichibio was very much in love. Smelling the odour of the bird and seeing it, she begged Chichibio to give her a leg of it. But he replied with a snatch of song:

"You won't get it from me, Donna Brunetta, you won't get it from me."

This made Donna Brunetta angry, and she said:

"God's faith, if you don't give it me, you'll never get anything you want from me."

In short, they had high words together. In the end Chichibio, not wanting to anger his lady-love, took off one of the crane's legs, and gave it to her. A little later the one-legged crane was served before Currado and his guests. Currado was astonished at the sight, sent for Chichibio, and asked him what had happened to the other leg of the crane. The lying Venetian replied:

"Sir, cranes only have one leg and one foot."

"What the devil d'you mean," said Currado angrily, "by saying they have only one leg and foot? Did I never see a crane before?"

"It's as I say, Sir," Chichibio persisted, "and I'll show it you in living birds whenever you wish."

Currado would not bandy further words from respect to his guests, but said:

"Since you promise to show me in living birds something I never saw or heard of, I shall be glad to see it tomorrow morning. But, by the body of Christ, if it turns out otherwise I'll have you tanned in such a way that you'll remember my name as long as you live."

When day appeared next morning, Currado, who had not been able to sleep for rage all night, got up still furious, and ordered his horses to be brought. He made Chichibio mount a pad, and took him in the direction of a river where cranes could always be seen at that time of day, saying:

"We'll soon see whether you were lying or not last night."

Chichibio, seeing that Currado was still angry and that he must try to prove his lie, which he had not the least idea how to do, rode alongside Currado in a state of consternation, and would willingly have fled if he had known how. But as he couldn't do that, he kept gazing round him and thought everything he saw was a crane with two legs. But when they came to the river, he happened to be the first to see a dozen cranes on the bank, all standing on one leg as they do when they are asleep. He quickly pointed them out to Currado, saying:

"Messer, you can see that what I said last evening is true, that cranes have only one leg and one foot; you have only to look at them over there."

"Wait," said Currado, "I'll show you they have two."

And going up closer to them, he shouted: "Ho! Ho!" And at this the cranes put down their other legs and, after running a few steps, took to flight. Currado then turned to Chichibio, saying:

"Now, you glutton, what of it? D'you think they have two?"

In his dismay Chichibio, not knowing how the words came to him, replied:

"Yes, messer, but you didn't shout 'ho! ho!' to the bird last night. If you had shouted, it would have put out the other leg and foot, as those did."

Currado was so pleased with this answer that all his anger was converted into merriment and laughter, and he said:

"Chichibio, you're right; I ought to have done so."

So with this quick and amusing answer Chichibio escaped punishment, and made his peace with his master.

## FIFTH TALE

*Messer Forese da Rabatta and Master Giotto, the painter, returning from Mugello, laugh at each other's mean appearance*

The ladies were delighted by Chichibio's reply, and when Neifile had finished, Pamfilo then spoke by the queen's command.

Most dear ladies, it often happens, as Fortune hides great treasures of virtue under base occupations, as Pampinea just now showed us, that the marvellous minds of Nature are to be found in very ugly men. This will appear from two of our citizens, of whom I mean to tell you a short tale.

One of these was Messer Forese da Rabatta, small and deformed in his person, with a flat ugly face, as if he were worse than one of the nasty Baronci family; and yet he was so skilled in the laws that many worthy men considered him a repository of Civil Law. The other was Giotto, whose genius was of such excellence that with his art and brush or crayon he painted anything in Nature, the mother and mover of all things under the perpetual turning of the heavens, and painted them so like that they seemed not so much likenesses as the things themselves; whereby it often happened that men's visual sense was deceived, and they thought that to be real which was only painted.

Now he who brought back to light that art which for many centuries had lain buried under errors (and thus was more fitted to please the eyes of the ignorant than the minds of the wise), may rightly be called one of the shining lights of Florentine glory. And the more so since he performed it with the greatest humility, and, although the master of all painters living, always refused to be called master. This title he refused shone the brighter in him, in that it was eagerly usurped by his disciples or by those who were less skilled than he. But although he was a very great artist, he was no more handsome in his person or aspect than Messer Forese. But let us come to the tale.

Messer Forese and Giotto had estates in Mugello. Messer Forese had gone to visit his in the summer time when the law courts have their vacation; and as he rode along on a poor hack of a horse he fell in with Giotto who was also returning to Florence, after visiting his own estate. He was no better dressed or horsed than the other. And the two old men rode along gently together.

As often happens in the summer, a sudden shower of rain came on. As quickly as possible they took shelter in the cottage of a workman, who was a friend to them both. But, as the rain showed no signs of abating and they wanted to reach Florence that day, they borrowed two old serge cloaks from the labourer and two hats all rusty with age, because he had no better, and set out on their way again. They had gone a long way, were wet through, and splashed with mud from their plodding horses (which is not wont to improve anyone's appearance), when the weather cleared up a little, and they began to talk after having been silent for a long time.

As Messer Forese rode along listening to Giotto, who was an admirable talker, he began to look at him from head to foot and, noticing how shabby and unkempt he was, he began to laugh, without remembering his own appearance, and said:

"Giotto, suppose we met a stranger who had never seen you before; do you think he would believe you are the greatest painter in the world, as you are?"

But Giotto immediately replied:

"Messer, I think he would believe if, when he looked at you, he could believe that you know your A B C."

Messer Forese at once recognised his error, and found himself paid back in the same coin for which he had sold the goods.


## SIXTH TALE

*Michele Scalza proves to certain young men that the Baronci are the greatest gentlemen in the world or the Maremma and wins a supper*

The ladies were still laughing at Giotto's quick retort when the queen ordered Fiammetta to follow next, who began as follows:

Young ladies, Pamfilo's mention of the Baronci—whom

you perhaps do not know as well as he does—reminds me of a tale which proves their nobility without deviating from our subject. And so I shall tell it to you.

Not long ago in our city was a young man named Michele Scalza, who was a most charming and amusing fellow, always with a handful of stories ready. So he was very popular with the young Florentines who liked to have him in their gatherings. One day when he was at Mount Ughi with some of them, there arose a discussion as to which was the oldest and most aristocratic family in Florence. Some said the Uberti, others the Lamberti, some this and some that, as the humour moved them. Scalza began to laugh at this, and said:

"Get along with you, you idiots, you don't know what you're talking about. The oldest and most aristocratic family, not only of Florence, but of the world or the Maremma, are the Baronci. All philosophers are agreed upon this, and every man who knows them as I do. And to avoid all mistake, I mean the Baronci our neighbours, near Santa Maria Maggiore."

When the young men, who had expected him to say something very different, heard this, they all laughed at him and said:

"You're joking—as if we didn't know the Baronci as well as you do."

"I'm not joking," said Scalza, "but telling the truth, and if anyone here would like to make a wager on it of a supper for six, I'll take him. And I'll do more, I'll abide by the judgment of anyone you like."

One of them, named Neri Manini, said:

"I'm ready to win that supper."

They agreed to take as their judge Piero di Fiorentino, in whose house they were. They went to him, accompanied by all the others to see Scalza lose his bet and to make fun of him; and related the whole thing to Piero. Piero was a sensible young man, and after hearing what Neri had to say, he turned to Scalza, and said:

"And how will you prove what you assert?"

"How?" said Scalza. "I'll prove it in such a way that not only you, but my opponent, will admit that I am right. You know that the more ancient a family is, the greater its nobility, which is commonly admitted among nobles. Now, the Baronci are an older family than any in the world, and consequently more noble. If I can prove that they are the oldest family, I shall have won the wager.

"You must know that the Lord God made the Baronci

when he was still a prentice hand at painting; but the remainder of mankind were made when God had learned to paint. To judge whether I am speaking the truth, consider the Baronci and the rest of mankind. You will see that all other men have well-composed and proportioned faces, whereas you will see some of the Baronci with long narrow faces, others with disproportionately wide faces, some with huge long noses and others with very short ones, some without any chins, and jaw-bones like an ass. You'll see some of them with one eye larger than the other and bulging out further, like the faces made by children when they're learning to draw. So, as I said, it is plain that the Lord God made them when he was learning to paint; therefore they are the oldest family in the world, and consequently the most noble."

Piero the Judge, Neri who had laid the wager, and all the rest of them, having heard Scalza's argument and remembered the Baronci, burst out laughing, and vowed that Scalza was right, that he had won the supper, and that undoubtedly the Baronci were the oldest and most aristocratic family, not only in Florence, but in the world or the Maremma.

And so Pamfilo was right when, trying to describe the ugliness of Messer Forese, he said he was uglier than one of the Baronci.

## SEVENTH TALE

*Madonna Filippa is discovered with a lover by her husband and taken before the judge; she escapes scot-free by a quick retort and has the law altered*

Fiammetta finished her tale, and everybody laughed at Scalza's new argument to prove that the Baronci were more noble than any other family. The queen then turned and ordered Filostrato to speak next, and he began thus:

Most worthy ladies, it is always a good thing to know how to speak well, but I think it best of all when it is called for by necessity. This was well done by a lady, of whom I intend to tell you, for she not only provided merriment and laughter to those who heard her, but saved herself from the snare of a shameful death, as you shall hear.

In Prato there was once a law, no less blameworthy than harsh, which without any distinction condemned to be burned alive any woman whose husband found her in adultery with a lover, just like a woman who lay with any other man for money.

While this law was in force a beautiful woman, named Madonna Filippa, who was very much in love, was found one night in her room by her husband, Rinaldo de' Pugliesi, in the arms of Lazzarino de' Guazzagliotri, a noble and handsome young man of that country, whom she loved beyond her own self. Rinaldo was exceedingly angry when he saw this, and could scarcely refrain from rushing at them and killing them. And if he had not feared the consequences to himself in following his anger, he would have done so.

He restrained himself from this, but could not refrain from claiming from the law of Prato what was forbidden him to take himself—his wife's life. He produced sufficient evidence, and the next day he brought the accusation against his wife and had her cited before the court, without consulting anyone.

The lady was a great-hearted woman, as usually happens with women who are really in love; and although she was advised against it by her numerous friends and relatives, she determined to appear before the Court and rather die bravely confessing her fault than to live in exile by basely fleeing, and thus showing herself unworthy of such a lover as the man in whose arms she had lain the night before. She appeared before the judge accompanied by many men and women, who urged her to deny the fault; and asked him in a clear voice and with a firm countenance what he wanted of her.

The judge looked at her, saw she was beautiful and accomplished, and, as her speech showed, a woman of high spirit. He felt compassion for her, suspecting that she would make the confession which, for his honour's sake, would force him to condemn her to death. But, since he could not avoid putting the question to her, he said:

"Madonna, as you see, here is Rinaldo your husband, and he lays a plaint against you that he has found you in adultery with another man. And therefore he demands that in accordance with the law I punish you for it by death. But this I cannot do unless you confess it, and so beware of what you say in answer, and tell me if your husband's accusation is true."

The lady, without the slightest fear, replied in a pleasant voice:

"Messer, it is true that Rinaldo is my husband, and that last night he found me in the arms of Lazzarino, wherein I have often lain, through the deep and perfect love I have for him. Nor shall I ever deny it. But I am certain you know that the laws should be equal for both sexes and made with the consent of those who are to obey them. That is not so in this case, for it only touches us poor women, who are yet able to satisfy many more than men can; moreover, no woman gave her consent or was even consulted when this law was passed. And so it may reasonably be called an inequitable law.

"If, to the harm of my body and your own soul, you choose to carry out this law, it is for you to do so. But before you proceed to judgment, I ask one little favour of you—ask my husband whether or not I have not always wholly yielded him my body whenever and howsoever often he asked it."

Rinaldo, without awaiting the judge's question, immediately replied that beyond all doubt she had always yielded to his pleasure whenever he required it.

"Then," said the lady swiftly, "I ask you, Messer Judge, if he has always had from me what he needed and pleased, what should and shall I do with what remains over? Should I throw it to the dogs? Is it not far better to give it to a gentleman who loves me beyond himself than to let it spoil or go to waste?"

The case concerning so well known a lady had attracted to the Court almost all the inhabitants of Prato. When they heard this amusing question they laughed heartily, and then almost with one voice shouted that the lady was right and spoke well. Before they separated, with the judge's consent they modified this cruel law, and limited it only to those women who were unfaithful to their husbands for money.

So Rinaldo departed in confusion, and the lady returned home free and happy and in triumph, like one escaped from the flames.

# EIGHT TALE

*Fresco advises his niece not to look in the mirror if it was unpleasant to look at disagreeable people*

Filostrato's tale at first touched the ladies' hearts with a slight feeling of shame, and the appearance of modest blushes in their faces gave evidence of it; but then, as they glanced at each other, they could scarcely refrain from laughing, and listened to the tale with demure smiles. When it was ended, the queen turned to Emilia, and ordered her to follow next. She started as if awakened from sleep, took a deep breath, and began thus:

Fair ladies, a long train of thought has for some time carried me far away from here; and so I shall make shift to obey our queen with a much shorter tale than I should have told if I had had my wits about me, and shall tell you of the foolish error of a girl, which was reproved by an amusing remark from her uncle—if she had had sense enough to understand it.

A man named Fresco da Celatico had a niece nicknamed Ciesca, who, although handsome enough in face and body (yet she was not one of those angels we often see), thought herself so important and so noble that she fell into the habit of sneering at all men and women and everything she saw, without examining herself. And yet she was so tedious, annoying and irritating that nothing could be done to please her. Moreover, she was so conceited that it would have been quite superfluous for her to have been one of the Royal Family of France. When she walked in the streets she pretended such haughty disgust that she did nothing but turn up her nose, as if a stink had come from everybody she saw or met.

We will not dwell on her other disagreeable and irritating habits, but come to the point. One day she returned to the house and sat down beside Fresco with a great display of affectation, and did nothing but sniff.

"Ciesca," asked Fresco, "why have you come home so early on a fête day?"

To which she replied with her fade-away airs: "It is true I have come home early, and that is because I think that the world never held such unpleasant and disgusting men and women as there are today. Everyone of them who passes by displeases me like ill luck itself. I don't think there is a woman in the world who is more distressed by seeing horrible people than I am. I came home early to avoid looking at them."

Fresco, who had had enough of his niece's disgusting airs, said: "My girl, since you find it so trying to look at unpleasant people, you ought never to look in the mirror if you want to be happy."

But she, who was as empty as a hollow cane, although she thought herself another Solomon in wisdom, understood Fresco's real meaning no more than a sheep would have done, and said she intended to look in the mirror like anyone else. And so she remained in her clownishness, and does to this day.

## NINTH TALE

*Guido Calvalcanti with a jest politely insults certain Florentine gentlemen who came upon him unawares*

Emilia finished her tale, and the queen realised that if Dioneo's privilege was to be kept there was no one left but herself to tell a tale; and so she began:

Fair ladies, although you have deprived me beforehand of more than two of the tales I meant to tell, yet I still have one left whose conclusion contains a jest perhaps more stinging than any related.

You must know that in the past our city maintained many good and praiseworthy customs which have disappeared today, thanks to the avarice which has grown up with our wealth and driven them away. Among them was a custom for groups of gentlemen to meet together in different places in Florence, taking care to include only those who could afford the expense; and for each in turn to entertain the rest on his appointed day. In this way they entertained foreigners, when they were there, and their own fellow citizens. Similarly at least once a year they all dressed alike and rode through the city and jousted on notable days, especially during the great fête days or when the news of some victory or something of the kind came to the city.

Among these groups was that of Messer Betto Brunelleschi; and he and his friends made great efforts to obtain the company of Guido Calvalcante de' Calvalcanti, not without reason, for apart from the fact that he was one of the greatest logicians then in the world and an excellent philosopher (for which they cared little), he was also a most accomplished and charming and eloquent man, and better able to perform everything befitting a gentleman than anyone else. He was also very rich, and could reward beyond all expression those whom he thought deserved it. But

Messer Bruno was never able to obtain his company, and he and his friends thought this was because Guido, who sometimes meditated, had become very much cut off from mankind. And because he held some of the opinions of Epicurus, the common run of mankind said that his speculations were solely directed to discovering (if he could) that God does not exist.

One day Guido set out from Or' San Michele and made his way along the Corse degli Adimari to San Giovanni, which he often did. At that time all round San Giovanni were large tombs of marble and many others, now in Santa Reparata; and Guido was walking among the porphyry columns there and the tombs and the door of San Giovanni, which was locked, when Messer Betto and his friends arrived on horseback by way of the Piazza di Santa Reparata. Seeing Guido among the tombs, they said:

"Let us go and tease him."

Spurring their horses, as if to a playful attack, they were upon him before he noticed them; and one of them said:

"Guido, you refuse to be one of our group. But suppose you do find that God does not exist, what good will that be?"

Guido, seeing that they had caught him, retorted promptly:

"Gentlemen, you may say what you please of me in your own house."

And putting his hand on one of the large tombs he vaulted over it (for he was a very active man) and so escaped from them. They remained staring at each other, and saying that he was out of his wits, and that what he had said had no meaning, since the place where they were standing had no more to do with them than any other of the citizens, and least of all with Guido. But Messer Betto turned to them, and said:

"It is you who are witless if you have failed to understand his words. In a few words he has politely insulted us extremely. If you consider, you will see that these tombs are the house of the dead, because the dead are laid there and dwell in them; and he calls them our house to show that we and other foolish and illiterate men are worse than dead in comparison with him and other men of learning, and so therefore we are in our own house."

Then each of them understood what Guido had meant, and was filled with shame, and never tried to tease him again, and henceforth considered Messer Betto as a quick-witted and clever knight.

# TENTH TALE

*Friar Cipolla promises certain peasants that he will show them a feather of the Angel Gabriel. Instead of which he finds only some charcoal, which he tells them is some of that which roasted Saint Lorenzo*

Every other member of the party had now told a tale, and Dioneo knew it was his turn. So, without waiting for a formal command, he began as soon as silence had been imposed on those who were praising Guido's retort.

Charming ladies, although I have the privilege of speaking of any subject I like, today I do not intend to depart from the subject on which you have all spoken so admirably. Following in your footsteps I mean to show you how skilfully one of the friars of Saint Antonio escaped with quick resource from the trap which two young men had prepared for him. You will not mind if I take some time in telling the tale, for if you will look at the sun you will see it is still in mid-heaven.

As you may have heard, Certaldo is a small town in the Val d'Elsa, and although it is small was in the past inhabited by noblemen and wealthy families. Now, one of the friars of Saint Antonio was for a long time accustomed to go there once a year for the excellent pasture he found, gathering alms which fools give such people. His name was Friar Cipolla (Onion); and perhaps was welcomed as much for his name as his devotion, for that country produces onions famous throughout Tuscany.

This Friar Cipolla was a little, red-haired, merry-faced fellow, and the biggest rogue in the world. He was quite uneducated, and yet was such a prompt and able speaker that anyone who did not know him would have thought him not only a great scholar but another Cicero or perhaps Quintilian. He was gossip or friend or acquaintance to nearly everyone in the district.

Now one day in the month of August he went there, as was his custom, and on Sunday morning when all the good men and women of the surrounding villages had gathered there for Mass at the canonical hour, he turned to them and said:

"Ladies and gentlemen, as you know you are every year accustomed to send some of your wheat and oats to the poor of my lord Messer Saint Antonio, some little and some more, according to their ability and devotion, so that the blessed Saint Antonio will protect your cows and asses and pigs and flocks. In addition you—and especially those of you who are written down as members of our confraternity —are wont to pay the little debt which is paid once a year. Now I am sent by Messer Abbot to collect these things to the best of my ability. And so, with God's blessing, when you hear the bells ring after Nones, you will gather outside the Church and I will preach to you as usual and you shall kiss the Cross. Moreover, since I know you are all most devoted to my lord Messer Saint Antonio, as a special favour I shall show you a beautiful and most holy relic, which I myself have brought overseas from the Holy Land. This is nothing less than one of the feathers of the Angel Gabriel, which he dropped in the bedroom of the Virgin Mary when he came to make the Annunciation to her in Nazareth."

So saying, he ended his speech, and returned to the Mass.

When Friar Cipolla was saying this there happened to be along with many others in the church two smart young fellows, named Giovanni del Bragoniera and Biagio Pizzini. After they had laughed heartily together over Friar Cipolla's relic, they determined to play a trick on him over this feather, although they were close friends of his. They knew that Friar Cipolla was going to dine in the town that day, and when they thought he was at table they went into the street and made their way to the inn where the Friar was staying. Their plan was that Biagio should hold the Friar's servant in talk, while Giovanni searched through his traps for the feather and took it away, to see what he would say to the people when he found it out.

Friar Cipolla had a servant, called by some Guccio Whale, by others Guccio Dauber, and by others Guccio Pig. He was such an artful fellow that Lippo Topo himself never did as much, while Friar Cipolla often joked about him with his friends, saying:

"My servant has nine qualities, and if one of them had existed in Solomon or Aristotle or Seneca, it would have been sufficient to ruin all their virtue, wisdom and holiness. Think what sort of a fellow he must be then, when he has nine such qualities, and neither virtue, wisdom nor holiness."

And when he was asked what these nine qualities were, he would reply as follows:

"I'll tell you. He's lazy, lying and lousy; negligent, disobedient and evil-speaking; reckless, heedless and bad mannered. In addition he has several other little faults not worth mentioning. But the most amusing thing about him is that wherever he goes he wants to have a wife and set up house. Since he has a large, black, greasy beard, he thinks himself so handsome and charming that all the women who see him must fall in love with him. If he were allowed, he would be after them and think of nothing else. True, he is a great help to me, for however secretly anyone wants to speak to me, he must hear his share of it; and if I am asked a question he's so much afraid that I shall not know what to answer that he immediately replies 'Yes' or 'No,' as he thinks fitting."

Friar Cipolla had left this servant behind at the inn, and had ordered him to take great care that nobody touched his possessions, especially his knapsacks which contained the sacred matters. But Guccio Dauber liked to be in a kitchen more than a nightingale among green boughs, especially when he knew there was a servant girl there. He had seen the host's servant, a fat, round, stumpy, ugly girl with a pair of breasts like two baskets of dung, and a face like one of the Baronci, all sweaty, greasy and smoky. Leaving Friar Cipolla's room and abandoning all his traps, Guccio slipped into the kitchen like a vulture after carrion; and although it was August he sat down by the fire and began to talk to the girl, whose name was Nuta. He told her he was a gentleman by procuration, that he had an incredible number of florins, apart from those he had to give other people which were considerable, and that he could do and say so many things that it was abracadabra marvellous. Without considering his hood which had enough grease on it to suffice the great cauldron of Altopascio, or his torn and patched doublet all sweat-stained round the collar and armpits, with more spots and colours in it than ever were in a Tartar or Indian garment, or his burst-out shoes, or his rent hose, he talked to her as if he had been the Lord of Castiglione and said he meant to set her up with new clothes and take her out of her wretched service to be with someone else, and that in addition to having his great possessions she might hope for even better fortune. These and a great many other things which he most amorously told her came to nothing, like most of his undertakings of this sort.

Meanwhile the two young men discovered that Guccio Pig was occupied with Nuta, which delighted them, for half their errand was thus already accomplished. With no one to stop them they walked into Friar Cipolla's open room, and the first thing they took up to search was the knapsack containing the feather. Opening the knapsack they found a little casket wrapped up in a large piece of silk; and, opening the casket, they found it contained a feather from a parrot's tail, which they guessed at once was the feather he had promised to show the people of Certaldo.

Certainly in those times it was easy for him to impose on their credulity, for the luxuries of Egypt had not then entered Tuscany, except to a very small extent, as they have since done so widely to the grave harm of all Italy. But even if these feathers had been known to a few people, they were not known at all to the inhabitants of Certaldo. Thus, while the rough virtues of our ancestors endured, not only had they never seen a parrot, but had never even heard one mentioned.

The young men were delighted to find the feather, and took it out. In order not to leave the casket empty, they picked up some charcoal they saw in a corner of the room, and filled the casket with that. They then shut it, and replaced everything as they had found it. They then went off merrily with the feather, without anyone seeing them, and waited to hear what Friar Cipolla would say when he found the charcoal in place of the feather.

The simple-minded men and women who were at church returned home from Mass, after hearing that they were to see a feather of the Angel Gabriel after Nones. One neighbour told another, one gossip another, and when everyone had had dinner, so many men and women flocked to the town to see the feather that the place could scarcely hold them.

After a good dinner and a little nap Friar Cipolla got up a little after Nones. Hearing that a great multitude of peasants had come to see the feather he ordered Guccio Dauber to come along at once to the bells and to bring the knapsacks with him. Although it was hard to tear Guccio away from the kitchen and Nuta, he went along with the required things. Drinking water had inflated his body so much that Friar Cipolla at once sent him inside the church door, where he began to ring the bells loudly.

When all the people were assembled, Friar Cipolla began his sermon without noticing that his effects had been tampered with; he said a great deal about his own deeds, and when he came to the point of showing the Angel Gabriel's feather, he first made them recite the general confession, then had two candles lighted, and having first put back his cowl he unwrapped the silk and brought out the casket.

After saying a few words in praise of the Angel Gabriel and his relic, he opened the casket. When he saw it full of charcoal, he did not at all suspect that it had been done by Guccio Whale (whom he knew to be incapable of such an effort of imagination) nor did he even blame him for not having prevented others from doing it; but he silently cursed himself for having allowed his property to be looked after by Guccio whom he knew to be negligent, disobedient, reckless and heedless. But yet he did not change colour, but lifted up his hands and face to Heaven, and said in a voice heard by all:

"O Lord, for ever let Thy power be praised!"

He then closed the casket and, turning to the people, said:

"Ladies and gentlemen, you must know that when I was still very young I was sent by my superior to the lands of the rising sun, with the express charge to find out the secrets of Porcelain, which although they cost nothing to mark, are more profitable to others than to us.

"So I set out from Venice and went along Greek Street, and thence by road through the kingdom of Garbo and through Baldacca, thence reaching Parione, and afterwards at some expense of thirst,—Sardinia. But why do I name all these countries I passed through? Passing the inlet of St. George I came to Truffia and Buffia, lands thickly inhabited with many people. From thence I came to the land of Falsehood where I found a great many friars and other religious, who all scorned poverty for the love of God, took little account of others' troubles, followed their own interests and spent none but uncoined money in those lands. I then came to the country of the Abruzzi, where the men and women walk over the mountains in clogs and dress up pigs in their own guts. A little further on I found people who carry bread in sticks and wine in bags. And thence I came to the mountains of the Bacchi, where all the water runs backwards.

"In short, I travelled so far that I came to Turnip India, and I swear to you by my sacred gown that I saw pens fly, a thing incredible to those who have not seen it. Witness will be borne to this by the great merchant, Maso del Saggio, whom I found there cracking nuts and selling the husks retail.

"But since I could not find what I sought there, and since

I should have had to proceed by water thereafter, I turned back to the Holy Land where in summer a cold loaf is worth four cents and a hot one nothing. There I found the Reverend Father Nonmiblasmete Sevoipiace, the most worthy patriarch of Jerusalem. He, from reverence to the habit of my lord Messer Saint Antonio which I wore, showed me all the relics he had about him. And there were so many of them that if I told you everything I should never get to the end. But not to disappoint you, I shall tell you of some of them.

"First of all he showed me the finger of the Holy Ghost, as entire and sound as it ever was, and the forelock of the Seraph which appeared to Saint Francesco, and a nail of one of the Cherubim, and a rib of the Verbum Caro made at the factory, and clothes of the Holy Catholic Faith, and some of the rays of the Star which appeared to the wise men in the East, and a phial of Saint Michael's sweat when he fought with the Devil, and the jaw-bones of Saint Lazarus, and many others.

"Now, since I freely gave him some of the eminences of Monte Morello in the vulgar tongue and certain chapters of the Caprezio which he had long been seeking, he also shared his holy relics with me, and gave a tooth of the Holy Cross, and a little bottle containing some of the noise of the bells in Solomon's Temple, and the feather of the Angel Gabriel which I spoke of to you, and one of the clogs of Saint Gherardo da Villamagna which not long ago in Florence I gave to Gherardo di Bonsi who holds it in extreme reverence; and he also gave me some of the coals over which the most blessed martyr Saint Lorenzo was roasted. Which things I most devoutly brought back with me, and have them all.

"My superior indeed would never allow me to exhibit them until they proved to be genuine. But now that certain miracles have been performed by them and letters received from the Patriarch, which both make them certain, I am permitted to show them. But I always carry them with me, for I am afraid to trust them to anyone else.

"I carry the Angel Gabriel's feather in a small casket to prevent it from being harmed, and the charcoal of roasted Saint Lorenzo in another. These caskets are so much alike that I often mistake one for the other, and that is what has happened to me today. For, while I thought I had brought the casket containing the feather, I find I have brought the casket with the charcoal. And I cannot consider this an error but rather the will of God, Who Himself placed that casket in my hand, thereby reminding me that the anniversary of Saint Lorenzo occurs a couple of days hence.

"Thus God, desirous that I should show you the charcoal, to reawaken in your minds the devotion you ought to feel for Saint Lorenzo, caused me to take up, not the feather I meant to show you, but the blessed charcoal sprinkled with the sweat of that most holy body. And, my blessed children, remove your hoods and come forward devoutly to behold them.

"But first of all I wish you to know that whosoever has the sign of the cross made on him with this charcoal may live for a whole year secure from fire, and may touch it without feeling it."

After saying this he sang the lauds of Saint Lorenzo, opened the casket, and displayed the charcoal. When the foolish multitude had gazed at the charcoal for a time, they pressed round Friar Cipolla in crowds, giving him larger offerings than usual and begging him to touch them with the charcoal. So Friar Cipolla took the charcoal in his hand and made huge crosses on their white shirts and doublets and on the women's veils, vowing that, as he had often proved, the charcoal miraculously recovered in the casket the weight it lost in forming the crosses.

Thus, having made crusaders of all the people of Certaldo, to his own benefit, Friar Cipolla turned the tables on those who thought they had put him in a quandary by stealing his feather. The two young men were present at his preaching, and when they heard his new trick and how farfetched it was and what he said, they laughed until their jaws ached. After the mob had departed, they went up to him and told him what they had done with the utmost merriment, and then gave him back his feather, which next year brought him in as much as the charcoal had done that year.

This tale pleased and amused the whole party, and there was much laughter at Friar Cipolla, and especially at his pilgrimage and the relics he saw and brought back with him.

When the tale ended, the queen's reign ended with it; so she stood up, took the garland from her head and laughingly placed it on Dioneo's, saying:

"Dioneo, it is time for you to see what a burden it is to rule and direct women. Do you be king and rule in such a way that when your government is over we are able to praise it."

Dioneo took the garland, and replied laughingly:

"I dare say you have often seen better kings than I am

among the chessmen; and certainly if you will obey me as a king should be obeyed, I will make you enjoy that without which no entertainment is really merry. But enough of words; I shall reign as well as I can."

He then called the steward, as usual, and made arrangements for what needed to be done during his reign. After which he said:

"Worthy ladies, we have discussed human nature and its different adventures in so many ways that if Licisca just now had not suggested a new topic to me for tomorrow's tales, I should have had to think a long time before I found us a new theme. As you heard, she said she never had a woman neighbour who was a virgin when she married, and she added that she knew all about the tricks which wives play on their husbands. Setting aside the first part, which is child's play, I think that the second should make a pleasant subject for discourse. Therefore, since Donna Licisca has provided the opportunity, I desire that tomorrow we tell tales of the tricks played by wives on their husbands, either for love's sake or for their own safety, whether found out or not."

Some of the ladies thought that this was a subject ill-befitting them, and asked that it should be altered. But the king replied:

"Ladies, I know what I have ordered you, as well as you do. What you point out is powerless to make me change my command, in view of the fact that the times are such that any kind of talk is allowed, provided men and women abstain from wrongdoing. You know that, owing to the misery of the times, the judges have deserted the tribunals, the laws both human and divine are silent, and full license is granted everyone to save his own life. So, if you enlarge your chastity a little in talk, not to follow it with immodest actions but to amuse yourselves and others, I do not see how anyone in the future can find any plausible reason for condemning you.

"Moreover, from the very first day until now your gathering has been most chaste, whatever may have been said here, and I do not think it has been stained (or, with God's help, ever will be stained) by any act. Who does not know your chastity? Why, in my opinion it would not fail at the threat of death, let alone from a few merry tales.

"To tell you the truth, if anyone heard that you refrained sometimes from talking of these trifles, they might suspect that the reason you would not talk of them was that you were guilty of them. In addition, it is a small honour to me, who have obeyed you in everything, that when you have made me your king you want to take the law out of my hands and not talk on the subject I have determined. So put off a suspicion more befitting evil minds than yours, and let everyone think of a good tale to tell."

When the ladies heard this, they said it should be as he pleased. And the king then gave everyone permission to do as he pleased until supper time. The sun was still high, because the tales told had been brief; and when Dioneo and the other young men had sat down to play games, Elisa called the women to one side, and said:

"Since we are here, I want to take you to a place not far from here which I believe you have never seen. It is called the Ladies' Valley, and I have never had time to take you there before today, when it is still early. So, if you like to come, I have no doubt that you will enjoy the place when you get there."

The ladies said they were ready. Without saying anything to the young men, they called one of the maids, and set out. They had not much more than a mile to go before they came to the Ladies' Valley. They entered it by a narrow path, on one side of which ran a clear brook; and you may imagine how happy they were to see it so delicious and so beautiful, especially in that hot weather. According to what I heard from some of them, the hollow of the valley was as smooth as if it had been made with compasses, although it appeared to be the work of Nature, not of human hands. It was a little more than half a mile in circumference, with six moderately sized hills about it, on the summit of each of which was a country house built like a fine castle. The sides of the hills sloped down to the plain like the tiers in a theatre, which we see from above diminishing gradually in circumference. The slopes looking towards the south were full of vines, olives, almonds, cherries and other fruit-bearing trees, without the waste of a hand's breadth of land. The slopes facing north were covered with straight and very green woods of dwarf oaks, ashes and other trees. The smooth ground at the foot had no more entrances than that by which the ladies had come in, and was full of firs, cypresses, laurels and pines, as well ordered and arranged as if they had been planted by the best gardener. When the sun was high, little or none of its rays reached the ground through them, while underneath was fine turf sprinkled with purple and other coloured flowers.

What delighted them no less was a stream which issued from the valley dividing two of the hills, and fell with a sound delightful to hear over a ledge of natural rock and seemed to sprinkle everything with quicksilver. When it reached the small plain, it ran swiftly through a fair channel to the middle, and there formed a tiny lake, such as is made as a fishing pool by citizens who have the right to do so.

This lake was no deeper than a man's chest. It was untroubled and its clear waters showed the bottom to be formed of fine gravel, which could have been counted by anyone who wished to do so. Not only could you see the bottom when you looked in but quantities of fish moving hither and thither, that it was a wonder as well as a pleasure to see them. Its border was the turf of the meadow, which was the more beautiful there since it was kept moist by the lake. The overflow fell into another little channel and thus ran out of the lower end of the valley.

The ladies went to this lake and after looking at everything and praising the place, they decided to bathe since it was so hot and the lake was in front of them and there was no chance of their being seen. They told their servant to go and stand in the path by which they had entered, and to warn them if anyone came; and then all seven undressed and entered the water which veiled their white bodies as thin glass would a red rose. Their movements did not muddy the water, and so they pursued and tried to catch the fishes, which had much ado to conceal themselves. After they had caught some in this merriment, they came out and dressed, unable to praise the place more than they had praised it. Then, as it was time to return, they set out home at a gentle pace, talking of the beauty of the valley. It was still early when they got back, and found the young men playing as they had left them. Said Pampinea laughingly:

"Well, we've deceived you today."

"And how?" asked Dioneo. "Are you freer in your acts than you wanted to be in words?"

"Yes," said Pampinea; and then told them where they came from, what the place was, how far distant, and what they had done there. Hearing of the beauty of the place, the king was anxious to see it, and therefore ordered supper immediately. And when it had been served to the content of all, the three young men and their servants left the ladies and went to the valley. None of them had ever been there before, and after they had looked at it all they declared it to be one of the most beautiful spots in the world. When they had bathed and dressed, they returned home, since it was getting late. There they found the ladies singing a song by Fiammetta in which they bore their part; and then they discussed the Ladies' Valley with them.

The king then called the steward, and ordered several beds to be prepared and carried there next morning, in case anyone wished to rest or sleep there in the afternoon. He ordered lights, wine and sweetmeats, and commanded every man to dance. When Pamfilo had obeyed him with a dance, the king turned to Elisa and said gaily:

"Fair lady, today you honoured me with the crown, and I mean to honour you this evening by asking for a song. So sing one you like."

Elisa smilingly replied that she was happy to do so, and began in a soft voice as follows:

> *Love, if I escape your clutch, I do not think that any other grasp could hold me.*
>
> *I was but a girl when I entered Love's battle, thinking it sweet and deepest peace, and laid my weapons on the ground, as one who yields him in good faith. But you, O treacherous tyrant, harsh and fierce, were swiftly upon me with your arms and clutch.*
>
> *You bound me in your chains to him who was born to cause my death. He seized me, filled as I was with bitter tears and woes, and holds me in his prison. So cruel is his lordship that no sigh nor piercing plaint of mine can move him.*
>
> *All my laments are scattered to the winds; none hears or cares to hear them. From hour to hour my torment grows, and life is weary to me—yet I cannot die. Ah, Lord, have pity on my woe, and do what I can never do—give him to me, bound captive in your chains.*
>
> *If this you will not do, at least take from me the knotty bonds of hope. Ah! this I beg of you, my lord; if you will do it, I trust I shall be beautiful again, and throw off grief, and deck myself with white and scarlet flowers.*

Elisa ended her song with a piteous sigh, and although they marvelled at the words none of them could think what was the cause of her singing them. But the king, who was in a good humour, called for Tindaro, and bade him bring his bagpipes, to the sound of which they danced. But when the night was far advanced he bade them all go to rest.

**HERE ENDS THE SIXTH DAY**

# THE SEVENTH DAY

# THE SEVENTH DAY

*Here begins the seventh day of the* Decameron, *wherein, under the rule of Dioneo, tales are told of the tricks played by wives on their husbands, for love's sake or for their own safety, whether found out or not*

Every star had vanished from the eastern sky except only that star we call Lucifer which still shone in the whitening dawn, when the steward arose and went to the Ladies' Valley with much baggage, and there arranged everything as his master had ordered. Very soon after his departure the king arose too, awakened by the noise of the baggage train and the horses, and had the ladies and the other two men called. The sun's rays had scarcely begun to dart forth when they all set out. Nor had the nightingales and other birds ever sung so gaily as they seemed to sing that morning, to whose accompaniment they went to the Ladies' Valley, where they were greeted by yet more birds which seemed to rejoice at their coming.

As they explored it once more and gazed at it anew, it seemed more beautiful to them even than before, since the time of day was even more favourable to its beauty. When they had broken their fast with good wine and delicate food, they began to sing (for they would not allow the birds to outdo them in song) while the valley echoed back the sounds they uttered; and the birds, determined not to be beaten, added new and sweet notes to the songs.

But when the dinner hour arrived the tables were set under the gay and beautiful trees near the lake, and at the king's pleasure they sat down and ate and watched the shoals of fish in the water, which they discussed as they watched them. And when dinner was over, the tables were removed; and they sang more songs even more lively than before. Beds were then set out in different parts of the little valley, and each was enclosed in curtains and canopies of French stuffs. The king then gave permission for anyone who chose to go and rest on them. Those who did not want to sleep could choose any other amusement they liked. But when they were all afoot again, and it was time to begin tale-telling, the king had carpets laid on the grass not far from where they had dined near the lake, and then ordered Emilia to begin. And she began smilingly as follows:

## FIRST TALE

*Gianni Lotteringhi hears a knock at his door by night; he wakes his wife and she makes him think it is a ghost. They go and exorcise it, and the knocking ceases*

It would have pleased me better, Sir, if such had been your pleasure that some other person than I should have begun on the excellent topic of which we are to speak. But since you wish me to set an example to the others, I shall gladly do so. And I shall endeavour, dearest ladies, to say something which may be useful to you in the future; for if other women are as timorous as I am, especially of ghosts— though God knows I don't know what they are and never found anyone who did, and yet we all equally fear them— by carefully listening to my tale you will learn a good and holy prayer which will be most useful in driving them away when they come to you.

In the district of San Brancazio in Florence there lived a wool-comber named Gianni Lotteringhi, a man who was more skilled in his art than wise in other matters. Being a simple sort of man he was often made leader of the singers of Santa Maria Novella, and had to oversee their school. He filled many other such trivial offices, which gave him a high opinion of himself. This came about because he was a fairly wealthy man, and frequently made presents to the good friars. Now since he gave some of them hose, and some hoods, and some scapularies, they taught him useful prayers and the Paternoster in the vulgar tongue and the song of Saint Alesso, and the lament of San Bernardo, and the lauds of Madonna Matelda, and the like idiocies, which he esteemed greatly, and made much use of for the salvation of his soul.

His wife was a very beautiful, clever and charming woman, by name Monna Tessa, the daughter of Mannuccio da la Cuculia. Perceiving that her husband was a simpleton, and having fallen in love with a handsome young man named Federigo di Neri Pegolotti who was also in love with her, she arranged with her maid servant that Federigo should come to speak with her in a house which her husband had in Camerata. She spent the whole summer in this place; and Gianni sometimes came to stay there, and next morning returned to his business and his church singing.

Federigo, who desired her greatly, went there one evening by arrangement when Gianni was away, and with great delight dined and slept with the lady; and as she lay in his arms that night she taught him six of her husband's psalms. But, since neither she nor Federigo intended this to be the last time they were together, and since they did not want to send the servant for him each time, they made the following arrangement: every day when he visited or returned from a house he owned near there, he was to look into a vineyard near her house where he would see the skull of a donkey on one of the poles in the vineyard, and when the skull was turned in the direction of Florence he could come to her that evening in all security, and if he did not find the door open, he was to knock softly three times and she would open it for him; but when he saw the donkey's skull turned towards Fiesole, he was not to come, because Gianni would be here. And in this way they often managed to see each other.

But on one occasion when Federigo was to sup with Monna Tessa it happened that Gianni arrived late at night, after saying that he would not come. The lady was greatly distressed, and he and she supped on a little salted meat which she had had cooked separately; she ordered the servant to put into a white napkin two boiled fowls and a number of new laid eggs and a flask of good wine, and to lay them down at the foot of a peach tree which stood beside a lawn in the garden, that could be reached without going through the house—a place where she had more than once supped with Federigo. And she was so upset about all this that she quite forgot to tell the servant to wait until Federigo came and to tell him that Gianni was there, and that he was to take the things she had put in the garden. She and Gianni and the servant had not been long in bed when along came Federigo and tapped gently at the door, which was so near the bedroom that Gianni heard it at once, and so did the lady; but she feigned sleep to prevent any suspicion of herself in Gianni's mind. After waiting a little, Federigo tapped a second time, and Gianni in surprise poked his wife, and said:

"Tessa, can you hear what I hear? Someone seems to be knocking at our door."

The lady, who had heard it better than he had, pretended to wake up, and said:

"What? Eh?"

"I say," persisted Gianni, "that someone seems to be knocking at our door."

"Knocking?" said the lady. "Why, dear Gianni, don't you know what it is? It's the ghost which has terrified me so much these last nights that as soon as I hear it I put my head under the clothes, and haven't dared to look out again until it was broad daylight."

"Come now," said Gianni, "don't be afraid. Before we went to bed I said the *Te lucis* and the *Intemerata* and other prayers, and blessed the bedposts in the name of the Father, the Son and the Holy Ghost; so there's no need to fear that it can do us any harm, whatever power it has."

The lady did not want Federigo to feel any suspicions about her and be angry, so she determined to get up and let him know that Gianni was there. She therefore said to her husband:

"Your words may have made you safe, but I shall never think myself safe and sound until we have exorcised it while you are here."

"But how can it be exorcised?" said Gianni.

"I know how to exorcise it," said the lady, "for when I went to the special church service at Fiesole the other day, one of those woman hermits—who is the most holy woman in the world, Gianni—seeing me so much terrified, taught me a holy and efficacious prayer; and she said she had made use of it more than once before she became a hermit, and had always found it worked. But God knows I never dared to go and test it by myself; but now that you are here, let us go together and exorcise it."

Gianni said he was quite ready; so they got up and went softly to the door where Federigo, already rather suspicious, was waiting. Said the lady to Gianni:

"Spit when I tell you to."

"Right!" said Gianni.

The lady then began the exorcism, and said:

"Spirit, spirit, who goest by night, by the path you came here, depart. Go to the garden, and there at the foot of the peach tree you will find a filthy dirty thing and a hundred droppings of my hen. Put a cork in the wine flask and depart, and do no harm to me and my Gianni."

She then said to her husband: "Spit, Gianni"; and Gianni spat. Federigo outside the door heard all this, and immediately recovered from his jealousy and consequent illtemper; indeed he was bursting with laughter and when Gianni spat he said softly:

"Your teeth!"

When the lady had exorcised the ghost three times in this way, she returned to bed with her husband.

Federigo, who had been expecting a supper and had none, understood the words of the exorcism perfectly well. He went into the garden, found the two fowls, the wine, and the eggs, at the foot of the large peach tree, took them home, and supped heartily. And afterwards, when he was with the lady, he often laughed over the exorcism with her.

True it is that some people say that the lady had turned the donkey's skull in the direction of Fiesole but that a workman passing through the garden gave it a knock with his stick, and turned it round in the direction of Florence, so that Federigo thought she had given the signal, and therefore came, and that lady's exorcism was after this fashion:

"Spirit, spirit, depart in God's name, for I didn't turn the donkey's skull, someone else did, God punish him, and I'm here with my Gianni."

And so Federigo had to go away without supper or bed. But a neighbour of mine, a very old lady, tells me that both versions are true, according to what she heard when a child. But the second did not happen to Gianni Lotteringhi but to a man named Gianni di Nello, who lived by the Porta San Piero, and was as big a fool as Gianni Lotteringhi.

And so, dear ladies, it is for you to choose which of the two you like best, or both of them. They are most useful in such cases, as you have just heard. Try them, and you may yet be glad of them.

## SECOND TALE

*Peronella hides her lover in a butt when her husband comes home; and when the husband sees it, she says that she has sold it to a man who is inside it seeing whether it is sound. The lover jumps out, makes the husband clean it, and then carries it home*

Emilia's tale was listened to with great mirth, and the exorcism was commended by them all as both efficacious and holy. And when the tale was ended, the king ordered Filostrato to follow next, and he began as follows:

Dearest ladies, men, and especially husbands, play so many tricks upon you that whenever a woman plays one on her husband you should not only be glad that it has occurred and that you are hearing it talked of, but you should go about repeating it to everyone, so that men may know that women know as much about such things as they do. This cannot but be useful to you, for when any person knows that another is aware of such things he does not lightly attempt to deceive him. Who then can doubt that, when what we say on this topic today is known to men, it can fail to restrain them from such deceits, since they will discover that you too can play tricks when you wish? So I intend to tell you what a young woman—although of base extraction—did to her husband almost in a twinkling, to save herself from his anger.

Not long ago in Naples a poor man married a pretty and charming girl named Peronella. He was a bricklayer and she a wool-comber, and together they earned enough to live moderately well. One day a handsome young man saw this Peronella, and liked her so much that he fell in love with her; and he made up to her so successfully in one way and another that he became familiar with her. They agreed upon the following arrangement for meeting: that when her husband got up each morning to go to work or to find work the lover should hide somewhere to see him depart, and when he had gone the lover was to come into the house, since Avorio, the place where they lived, was very little frequented. And this they often did.

But one day when the husband had gone out for the whole day and Giannello Strignario (this was the young man's name) had gone into the house and was with Peronella, the husband unexpectedly returned, and, finding the house barred from within, knocked; and, as he knocked, said to himself:

"O Lord, praise be to Thee for ever, for although Thou hast made me a poor man, Thou hast consoled me with a good chaste young wife who bars the door from inside while I am away, so that nobody can enter and do her harm."

Peronella knew it was her husband from his way of knocking, and said:

"Alas, Giannello, I am as good as dead! Here is my husband—bad luck to him—and I don't know what his com-

ing back means, for he never returns at this hour. Perhaps
he saw you when you came in. But in any case, for the love
of God get into this butt and be silent, and I will go and
open the door, and find out what brings him back home so
early today."

Giannello quickly got into the butt, and Peronella went
down and opened the door to her husband, and said sharply:

"What new idea of yours is this to come home so early
today? From what I can see, you don't intend to do any
work today, since you've brought back your tools. If you
go on like this, how are we to live? How shall we get our
bread? Do you think I'll let you pawn my petticoat and
other clothes? I do nothing but spin day and night and
work my fingers to the bone to earn at least enough oil to
keep our lamp burning. Husband, husband, every woman
in the place is amazed and mocks at me for all my labour,
and you come back here with your hands dangling when
you ought to be at work."

Then she began to weep, and went off again:

"Alas, poor me, unhappy me, what an unlucky hour I
was born in! I could have married such a good young man
and I wouldn't have him for the sake of a man who thinks
nothing of the woman he has brought into his house. Other
women enjoy themselves with their lovers, and there's not
one of them but has two or three, and has a good time, and
makes her husband think the moon is the sun. But poor
me! because I'm good and pay no heed to such things, life
goes wrong and I have bad luck. I don't know why I don't
have lovers like other women. Understand me, husband. If
I wanted to do wrong I could easily find someone to do it
with, for there are plenty of gay young men in love with
me, and they've offered me money or dresses or jewels if I
preferred, but I'd never take anything of the kind, for I'm
not the daughter of a woman of that sort; and here you
come back home when you ought to be at work."

"Wife," said the husband, "don't be angry, for the love
of God. You must believe that I know your value, and indeed only this morning I partly realised it. I did indeed
start out to work this morning, but all this shows that you
did not know, any more than I did, that today is the festival
of Santo Galeone, and as there's no work to be done I've
come home at this early hour. And yet I've found a way to
provide us with bread for more than a month, for the man
you see here with me has bought the butt, which, as you
know, has been littering up the house, and he's giving me
five florins for it."

"And all that's the more woe to me," said Peronella, "you're a man, and go about the world and should know things, and you've sold the butt for five florins, while a little woman like me who hardly ever goes out of the door and knew what a nuisance the butt was in the place, has sold it for seven florins to a man who, when you returned, had just got inside to see if it were sound."

The husband was more than delighted when he heard this, and said to the man who had come for the butt:

"God be with you, good man. You hear how my wife has got seven florins for the butt which you would only pay five for."

"Very well," said the man, and went away.

Then Peronella said to her husband:

"Come along, since you are here, and attend to our affairs."

Giannello had kept his ears pricked up to know if he had to fear or invent anything, and since he had heard what Peronella said he jumped quickly out of the butt, and pretending to know nothing about the husband's return said:

"Where are you, good woman?"

The husband came up to him, and said:

"Here I am, what do you want?"

"Who are you?" said Giannello. "I want the lady with whom I made the bargain for this butt."

"You can do what you want with me," said the good man, "I'm her husband."

Then Giannello said:

"The butt seems quite sound to me, but I think you must have kept wine lees in it, for it's all encrusted with some dry matter which I can't scrape off with my nails. But I won't take it unless I first see it cleaned."

"The bargain shan't be called off for that," said Peronella. "My husband will clean it all."

"Yes, indeed," said the husband.

He put down his tools, stripped himself to his shirt-sleeves, got a light and a scraper and, getting into the butt, began to scrape it. Peronella, as if she wanted to see what he was doing, put her head and shoulder and one arm into the large opening of the butt, and kept saying:

"Scrape here, scrape there, and there too. A little bit's left there."

As she stood there pointing things out to her husband, Giannello, who had scarcely satisfied his appetite that morning when the husband returned, saw that he could not do so, as he wanted, and determined to do it as he could. He went up behind her as she stood over the mouth of the butt, and, even as the unbridled and love-heated stallions of Parthia assail the mares, so did he satisfy his young desire, which was brought to its summit and himself removed precisely at the moment when the scraping of the butt was ended, and Peronella drew her head out, and the husband climbed out. And so Peronella said to Giannello:

"Take the light, good man, and see if it's cleaned as you want."

Giannello looked in, said it was all right, and that he was content. He paid the seven florins, and had the butt taken to his house.

### THIRD TALE

*Friar Rinaldo lies with his godchild's mother. The husband finds him with her, and they make him believe that the friar is charming away the child's worms*

Filostrato's reference to the Parthian mares was not so obscure that the ladies failed to laugh at it, although they pretended to be laughing at something else. When the king saw the tale was ended, he ordered Elisa to speak next, and she began obediently as follows:

Charming ladies, the exorcism of Emilia's ghost reminds me of another exorcism about which I shall tell you, for although it is not so good as hers, I cannot at present think of any other tale on our subject.

You must know that there was in Siena a pleasant young man of honourable family, by name Rinaldo. He was deeply in love with the beautiful wife of a rich neighbour. He hoped that if he could manage to speak with her he could obtain what he desired from her, but could find no way of doing it. However, as the lady was pregnant, he thought it a good idea to become the child's godfather; so he made up to the husband, presented his request in the best way he could, and was accepted.

Rinaldo thus became the godfather of Madonna Agnesa's child, and so had a better pretext for seeing her, and speaking to her. He therefore told her in words what she had long before known by the language of his eyes. But this was very little help to him, although the lady was not displeased to hear his declaration.

Not long afterwards, for some reason or other, Rinaldo became a friar; and whatever may have been the satisfaction he found in that profession, he persevered in it. Now, although at the time when he became a friar he put aside his love for this lady along with other vanities, yet in the course of time he returned to them all, without however putting off his gown. He delighted to dress himself in fine cloth and to be handsome and well furnished in everything about him, and to make songs and sonnets and ballads, and to sing, and to occupy himself with many similar things.

But why do I say so much of this Friar Rinaldo? Are they not all alike? Ah! shame of this wicked world! These friars do not blush to appear fat and florid, curious in their garments and all their possessions. They strut along, not like doves, but like cocks with their crests up. Their cells are full of boxes of ointments and creams, boxes of various sweetmeats, phials and bottles of distilled waters and oils, flasks of Malvoisie and Greek wine and other very expensive wines, so that they look less like friars' cells than the shops of apothecaries and perfumers. What is worse, they are not ashamed to let it be known that they are gouty, and think that other people do not know that fasting, plain and scanty fare, sober living, make thin, meagre and more healthy men. And if such men fall ill, it is not with the gout, which is medicined by chastity and all the other abstinences befitting a friar's life. They think that other people do not know that a strict life, long vigils, prayers and scourgings should make men look pale and sad, and that San Domenico and San Francesco never had four cloaks for one, and never dressed themselves in fine cloth but with coarse undyed wool, to keep out the cold and not to make a display. May God dispose of these things and enlighten the simple souls who provide them!

Thus, Friar Rinaldo returned to his former desires, and began to visit the lady frequently. As his boldness grew, he began to urge her more insistently than ever to satisfy his desires. The lady, being thus solicited and perhaps finding Friar Rinaldo a more handsome man than she had thought at first, one day when she was more stiffly urged had recourse to what all women do when they want to yield what is asked of them, and said:

"What! Friar Rinaldo, do friars do such things?"

"Madonna," replied Friar Rinaldo, "when I take this gown off my back—which I should be very glad to do—I am a man like other men, and not a friar."

The lady pretended to laugh, and said:

"Ah! But you are my child's godfather. How could it be, then? It would be very wrong; and I have often heard it said that this is a great sin. Otherwise, I would certainly do what you want."

"You are very foolish," said Friar Rinaldo, "if you let that stop you. I don't say it isn't a sin, but God pardons the greatest sins to those who repent. But tell me, who is more nearly related to your child, I who held him at the font, or your husband who begat him?"

"My husband," replied the lady.

"You are right," said the friar, "and does not your husband lie with you?"

"Why, yes," said the lady.

"Very well," said the friar, "I am less nearly related to your child than your husband is, and so I ought to be able to lie with you like your husband."

The lady knew nothing of logic and required little persuasion; so she believed or pretended to believe that what the friar said was true, and replied:

"How can I reply to your learned arguments?"

And immediately, without any regard for their spiritual relationship, she prepared to do him pleasure. Nor was this the only time, for under cover of their spiritual relationship —which gave them more opportunity, since the suspicion was less—they often lay together. One day Friar Rinaldo came to the lady's house and found no one else there except a pretty and very agreeable maid-servant. He sent his companion off to the dove-cote with the maid-servant, to teach her the Lord's Prayer, and himself went with the lady and her little child to her bedroom, locked the door, and began to enjoy himself with her on a day-bed. While they were in this posture, the husband came into the house without any of them hearing him, went to the bedroom door, knocked, and called to his wife. When Madonna Agnesa heard him, she said:

"I am as good as dead, here's my husband! He'll now see the reason for our familiarity."

Friar Rinaldo was undressed—he was in his tunic, without gown or scapulary.

"You say truly," said he, "if I were dressed, we might find a way out. But if you open the door, and he finds me here like this, no excuse is possible."

A sudden idea flashed on her mind, and she said:

"Put on your clothes. As soon as you're dressed take your godchild in your arms, listen carefully to what I say to my husband, so that your tale tallies with mine, and leave the rest to me."

The husband was still knocking, and the wife called out: "I'm coming."

She got up, and went and opened the door and said cheerfully:

"Husband, Friar Rinaldo, the child's godfather is here; and indeed he was sent by God. If he had not come, we should certainly have lost our child."

The silly man was amazed to hear this, and said: "What? What?"

"O husband," said the lady, "he fell into a swoon, and I thought he was dead, and did not know what to do or to say. But Friar Rinaldo, the child's godfather, happened to come in, picked the child up, and said: 'Gossip, there are worms in his body which oppress his heart, and they would have killed him; but don't be afraid, I will speak a charm and kill them all, and when I go away you will find the child as healthy as ever.' We wanted you to say certain prayers, but the girl could not find you; so he made his companion say them in the highest part of the house, and he and I came to this room. Only the child's mother could do him this service; and we locked the door to prevent anyone else from disturbing us. He still has the child in his arms, and I think he is only waiting for his companion to finish his prayers, which I think must be done, for the child has already regained his senses."

The silly man was so occupied with love for his child that he believed it all and did not see his wife's deceit. He heaved a deep sigh, and said:

"I want to go and see him."

"Don't go yet," said the wife, "or you will spoil what has been done. Wait. I'll see if you can come in, and I'll call you."

Friar Rinaldo by now was dressed. He had heard everything, had taken the child into his arms, and arranged matters as he wished.

"Gossip," said he, "do I not hear your husband?"

"Yes, Messer," replied the silly man.

"Then come here," said Friar Rinaldo.

The silly man went in, and Friar Rinaldo said:

"Take your son, who by God's grace is in good health, although just now I thought you would not see him alive at sundown. You must make a wax statue of the child's size to the glory of God and place it in front of the figure of Santo Ambrugio, through whose merits God has granted you this favour."

Seeing his father, the child ran to him affectionately, as little children do. The father picked him up, weeping as if he had snatched the child from the grave, and kissed him, and thanked the godfather for having saved his life.

Friar Rinaldo's companion had taught the maid-servant four Lord's Prayers instead of one, and had given her a purse of white thread which a nun had given to him, and had made the girl his devotee. He had heard the silly husband calling at the wife's door, and had gone down softly to see and hear what was going on.

Seeing things had turned out well, he came forward, entered the room, and said:

"Friar Rinaldo, I have said all four of the prayers you told me to recite."

"Brother," said Friar Rinaldo, "you have good wind, and did well. For my part, when the child's father arrived, I had only said two. But God has rewarded your labours and mine and has granted the grace that the child should be healed."

The silly husband then sent for good wines and sweetmeats, and entertained the godfather, and his companion, who needed it more than the former. Then he left the house with them, and took leave of them, and went immediately to have the wax statue made, which was fastened in front of the figure of Santo Ambrugio, but not the one at Milan.

## FOURTH TALE

*One night Tofano shuts his wife out of the house and, since he will not let her in for all her entreaties, she throws a large stone into the well and makes him think she has drowned herself. Tofano rushes out of the house to the well. She runs in and locks the door and screams insults at him*

When Elisa's tale was ended, the king turned immediately to Lauretta to show it was his pleasure she should speak next; and accordingly she began as follows:

O Love, how great and varied are your powers! What resources and shrewdness you have! What philosopher, what artist ever could or will be able to show the sagacity, the shrewdness, the skill which you suddenly bestow upon those who follow your footsteps! Indeed the knowledge of all others is tardy compared with yours, as we may perceive from the tales which have already been told. To these, amorous ladies, I shall add one concerning what was accomplished by a simple woman who could have been taught by none save Love.

In Arezzo there lived a rich man named Tofano. His wife was a very beautiful woman named Ghita, of whom he very soon became jealous for no special reason. She was angry when she observed this, and often asked him what was the reason for his jealousy. But since he could give only poor and general reasons, the lady made up her mind to make him die of the sickness which he dreaded without any reason.

She had noticed that she was courted by a young man, whom she considered attractive, and cautiously began to come to an understanding with him. Things advanced so far between them that they needed only to transform their words into acts, and the lady thought of a way to do this. Among her husband's other bad habits was drinking, and she not only commended it, but often artfully urged him to it. She went about it so well that she was able to make him drunk nearly every time she wished; and when she saw he was drunk, she put him to bed, and went to her lover, and this not once but many times. And she felt such confidence in the drunkenness of her husband that she not only brought her lover to her own house, but often went and spent most of the night in his house, which was not far distant.

The amorous lady went on in this way for some time when the husband noticed that although she encouraged him to drink, she hardly ever drank herself. So he suspected that the lady made him drunk so that she could do what she wanted while he was asleep. He determined to test whether his suspicions were justified, and so, one evening, after having drunk nothing at all, he pretended in speech and behaviour to be completely drunk. The lady was deceived, and thinking he needed no more drink quickly put him to bed. After which, as she had often done before, she left the house and went to her lover's house, and remained there until midnight.

When Tofano found the lady had gone, he got up and

locked the door from the inside, and went and sat at one of the windows so that he could see his wife when she returned and let her know that he had found her out. At last she came home, and found herself locked out. In great distress she tried to force her way in, but Tofano, after letting her try for a time, called to her:

"Woman, you labour in vain, for you cannot enter here again. Go back to the place whence you come, and be sure you shall never return until, in the presence of your relatives and neighbours, I have done you the honour befitting this affair."

The lady begged him to let her in for the love of God, saying that she did not come from where he thought but from sitting up with a woman neighbour because the nights were so long she could not sleep all through them, and could not sit up alone in the house. Her entreaties were of no avail, because the fool was in a mood to let all the people of Arezzo know his shame, when none of them knew it. Finding her prayers useless, the lady began to threaten, and said:

"If you don't let me in, I'll make you the unhappiest man alive."

"And what can you do to me?" retorted Tofano.

The lady, whose wits were sharpened by love, replied:

"Before I will endure the shame you are determined wrongfully to inflict on me, I'll throw myself into the well here, and when my body is found everyone will think that you threw me in when you were drunk. So you will either have to fly and lose all you have and become a thief, or your head will be cut off for murdering me, which indeed you will have done."

But these words had no effect on Tofano's silly determination. And so the lady said:

"Ah! I can't endure your scorn; may God forgive you; leave my spindle here for you to take up."

The night was so dark that people could scarcely see one another in the street; so the lady went to the well, took up a large stone lying beside it and let the stone fall into the well, shrieking, "God forgive me!" The stone fell into the water with a loud splash; and when Tofano heard it, he thought that she had thrown herself in. Seizing the bucket and the rope, he rushed out of the house to the well to rescue her. The wife had hidden herself near the door, and ran into the house and locked the door as he rushed out to the well. She went to the window, and said:

"You should drink water when you're drinking other things, and not the night afterwards."

At this mockery Tofano ran back to the door, but not being able to get in, told her to open the door. The lady now ceased talking in the low tones she had hitherto used, and almost shrieked at him:

"By God's Cross, you foul drunkard, you shall not come in tonight! I can't endure your habits any longer—everyone must see the sort of man you are and at what hours you come home."

Tofano in his rage also began to shout insults at her, so that the neighbours, hearing the noise, got up and went to their windows, and asked what it was all about. The lady began to cry, and said:

"It's this wicked man, who comes home drunk at night or else sleeps in taverns and comes home at this hour. I've put up with it for a long time, but I can't stand it any longer, so I've shamed him by locking him out of the house to see whether that will not amend him."

The fool Tofano, on the other hand, told them what had really happened, and threatened her violently. Then the lady said to the neighbours:

"See what kind of a man he is! What would you say if I were in the street as he is, and he in the house as I am? God's faith, I doubt you will believe what he says. You can now judge of his wits. He says I have done what I think he must have done himself. He thought he would frighten me by throwing something into the well. Would to God he had thrown himself in and been suffocated, and then the wine he had drunk too much of would have been well watered."

All the neighbours, both men and women, then began to reprove Tofano, and laid the blame on him, and abused him for what he said against his wife. In short, the noise spread from neighbour to neighbour until it reached the lady's relatives. Hearing of the affair from different persons, they rushed up and beat Tofano until he was bruised all over. They then entered the house, took the lady's property, and returned home with her, threatening Tofano with worse to follow. Seeing things had turned out ill and that his jealousy had led him astray, and having still some affection for his wife, he employed his friends as intermediaries, and managed to arrange that she should come back to him in concord, promising her that he would be jealous no longer. Moreover, he gave her permission to do anything she chose, but so discreetly that he should know nothing about it. Thus, after strife was peace. Long life to love, and death to jealousy and all cuckolds!

## FIFTH TALE

*A jealous husband disguises himself as a priest and hears his wife's confession; she gives him to understand that she loves a priest who comes to her every night. While the husband watches at the door, she brings her lover in through the roof and lies with him*

When Lauretta had finished her tale and everyone had praised the lady for having done what was right and befitting such a fellow, the king, not to lose time, turned to Fiammetta, and gaily laid upon her the task of telling the next tale. Accordingly she began thus:

Most noble ladies, the preceding tale induces me to tell another of a jealous husband, for I think that whatever their wives do to them—especially when they are jealous without cause—is well done. And if the lawmakers had well considered the matter I think that they should have imposed no further penalty upon women who thus defend themselves than they impose upon those who have committed no fault; for jealous husbands are plotters against the lives of young women and most diligent seekers after their death.

Women pass the whole of the week shut up in the house, attending to domestic and family affairs, hoping—like everyone else—for a little rest and amusement on feast days, such as are enjoyed by field labourers, town artisans and the rulers of courts. Thus God did when he rested the seventh day, and thus we are required to do by civil and canon laws which, considering the glory of God and the common weal, have laid down distinctions between working days and feast days. But jealous husbands will in no wise consent to this; and by keeping their wives more closely shut up they make the days, which for others are happy days, more miserable and more painful than other days for their wives. How wretched this is for the poor women, only those who have endured it can know. Therefore in conclusion I say that the wrnog which a woman does a jealous husband is not to be condemned but rather commended.

In Armenia there was a merchant, rich both in money and goods, whose wife was a most beautiful woman. He became madly jealous of her, for no other reason than this —that he loved her greatly and thought her very beautiful and knew that she did all she could to please him, and so he thought every other man must love her and think her beautiful, and that she also tried to please them—which is the reasoning of a silly man with little feeling. Being thus jealous, he kept such watch over her and restrained her so closely that many a man who is condemned to death is less jealously watched by his warders.

The lady was not allowed to go to marriages or to feasts or to church or to set foot out of the house; nor did she even dare go to the window or look out of the house for any reason. Thus her life was miserable, and she endured it the more impatiently since she knew she was guiltless. Therefore, seeing herself wrongfully harmed by her husband she determined (if she could) to give him some reason for it. Since she could not go to the window and thus have an opportunity of showing herself pleased with the love of any man who attracted her as he passed through the countryside, and since she knew there was a handsome and pleasing young man in the house next door, she thought that if there were any crack in the wall dividing the two houses she would look through it so often that she would see the young man and be able to speak to him and to give him her love if he wanted it. Moreover she determined that, if it were possible, she would sometimes be with him and in this way endure her wretched life until the devil of jealousy left her husband. When her husband was out, she searched up and down the wall, and at last found a fissure in an unfrequented part of the house. Looking through it, although she had difficulty in seeing plainly, she was able to make out that the fissure looked into a room; and she said to herself: "If this is Filippo's room, my task is half completed." (Filippo was the name of the young man.) And so she made her servant—who was sorry for her—look cautiously through the fissure, and thus found that the young man did indeed sleep there alone.

She therefore went frequently to the crack in the wall and, when she heard the young man there, dropped in gravel and splinters until he came up to see what the noise was. She then called softly to him, and he, recognising her voice, answered her. She soon told him what was in her mind, and the young man in great delight widened the fissure on his side of the wall, but in such a way that nobody would notice it. There they often talked together and touched hands, but could advance no further owing to the close watch kept by the jealous husband.

Christmas was approaching, and the lady told her husband that, with his permission, she would go to church and confess and take the sacrament like other Christians. But the jealous husband said:

"What sins have you committed that you need to confess?"

"What!" said the lady. "Do you think I am a saint, because you keep me so closely mewed up? You know well enough that I commit sins like every other living person. I shan't tell them to you, but to a priest."

These words aroused the jealous husband's suspicions, and he thought he would try to find out what sins she had committed, and hit upon a way of doing so. He replied that she might do as she wished, but that she was not to go to any other church save their own private chapel, that she was to go there in the morning, and confess either to the chaplain or to a priest whom the chaplain would bring there, and not to anybody else; and that then she was to return to the house. The lady half guessed his plan, but without saying anything further replied that it should be done in this way.

On Christmas morning the lady got up at dawn and dressed herself and went to the church selected by her husband. The jealous husband also got up and went to the same church before she got there. He had already arranged with the priest there to be allowed to do what he wanted, so he put on one of the priest's gowns with a large falling hood such as we see priests wear, and having pulled the hood over his face he sat down in the choir. When the lady came to the church, she asked for the priest, who came, and in response to the lady's request for a confessor said that he could not hear her confession himself but that he would send her a brother priest. And so he departed, and sent the jealous husband to her. He came to her highly pleased with himself; but although the day was not very bright and he had pulled the cowl far over his eyes, his disguise was not so good as to prevent the lady from recognising him at once. As soon as she saw who he was, she said to herself:

"Praised be God, the jealous man has turned priest; but let him go, I'll give him what he's looking for."

She pretended not to know him, and kneeled at his feet. Master Jealous had put some little stones in his mouth to impede his speech and prevent his wife from recognising his voice, and thought he had disguised himself so well in other respects that she could not possibly recognise him. When they came to the confession, the lady among other things told him that she was married and in love with a priest, who came and lay with her every night. To hear this was a dagger in the heart of the jealous husband; and if he had not wanted to hear more, he would have abruptly ended the confession and gone away. But he remained seated, and asked the lady:

"What? But does not your husband lie with you?"

"Yes, messer," replied the lady.

"Well then," said the jealous husband, "how can the priest lie with you too?"

"Messer," said the lady, "I don't know what arts the priest uses, but however closely a door is locked, it opens as soon as he touches it. And he also tells me that when he comes to the bedroom door, he repeats certain words which throw my husband into a deep sleep; and when he knows my husband is asleep, he opens the door and comes in and lies with me, and this never fails."

"Madonna," said the jealous husband, "this is ill done, and must not continue."

"Messer," said the lady, "I think that is impossible, because I love him too much."

"Then," said the jealous husband, "I cannot absolve you."

"That grieves me," said the lady. "I did not come here to tell you lies. If I thought I could do what you require, I would say so."

"In truth, Madonna," said the jealous husband, "I am sorry for you, for I see you are damning your soul by this. To help you I will labour on your behalf with special prayers to God which may assist you. From time to time I will send you one of my acolytes, and you will tell him whether the prayers have aided you or not; if they have helped you, we will proceed further."

"Messer," said the lady, "do not send anyone to the house, for if my husband knew it, it would not go out of his head for anyone in the world but that the man came for some ill purpose, he is so jealous, and I should have no peace with him for a year."

"Madonna," said the jealous husband, "have no fear; I can certainly arrange it in such a way that you will never have a harsh word from him about it."

"If that is what you can do," said the lady, "I am content."

She ended her confession and received her penance; then arose and went to hear Mass. The jealous husband, suffocating at his misfortune, threw off the priest's robe and returned home, eager to find some means of catching his wife and the priest together so that he could play a shrewd trick on them both.

The lady returned from church, and saw by her husband's face that she had given him something to think about; but he tried to conceal from her what he had done and what he thought he had found out. He determined to wait for the priest that night at the street door, and said to the lady:

"Tonight I must go out and sup. I shall sleep away from home. So lock the street door and the door on the stairway and the bedroom door, and go to bed when you like."

"Very well," replied the lady.

As soon as she had time she went to the crack in the wall and made the accustomed signal, and as soon as Filippo heard it he came towards her and the lady told him what she had done that morning, and what her husband had said after dinner, and added:

"I am certain he will not leave the house, but will stand guard over the doorway; therefore do you find some way of getting into the house tonight by the roof, so that we can be together."

"Leave that to me, Madonna," said the young man, delighted at all this.

When night came the jealous husband armed himself and hid in a ground floor room, while the lady locked all the doors, particularly that on the stairway so that the husband could not get in. And when the young man thought it a fitting time he cautiously came into the house from his side; the two then went to bed together and gave each other pleasure and a good time, and when it was day the young man returned to his own house.

The jealous husband, supperless and afflicted and dying of cold, spent almost the whole night, weapon in hand, waiting for the priest to come to the door. Towards daytime he fell asleep, unable to watch any longer. He got up about the hour of Tierce when the outer door of his house was open, and pretended to come from somewhere outside, entered his house and breakfasted. A little later he sent a small boy, disguised as if he were the acolyte of the priest who had heard her confession, to ask if the person she knew of had been to her again. The lady, who saw quite well from whom the messenger was, replied that he had not come that night, and that if he acted in this way she might come to forget him, although she did not want to do so.

What more need I tell you? The jealous husband wasted many nights waiting for the priest at the entrance, and the lady continued to enjoy herself with her lover. Finally, the husband could endure it no longer and angrily asked his wife what she had said to the priest the morning she had gone to confession. The lady replied that she would not tell him, since it was neither right nor proper that she should do so.

"You vile woman," said the jealous husband, "despite you, I know what you said to him. And it is perfectly fitting that I should know who is the priest with whom you are so much in love and who lies with you every night by enchantment; otherwise I shall cut your veins."

The lady replied that it was not true that she was in love with any priest.

"What!" said the jealous husband. "Did you not say this and that to the priest who confessed you?"

"Not for him to tell it you," said the lady, "but it suffices if you were present; and yes, I did say so."

"Then," said the jealous husband, "tell me who the priest is, and quickly."

The lady smiled and said: "It pleases me when a wise man is led by a simple woman as a sheep is led to the slaughter by its horns, although you are not a wise man and have not been since the hour when you allowed the evil spirit of jealousy to enter you without knowing why. And the more foolish and stupid you are, the less is my glory.

"Do you think, husband, that I am as blind in the eyes of my head as you are in the eyes of your mind? Indeed no. When I saw you I knew you were the priest who confessed me, and I decided to give you what you were looking for, and did give it you. But if you had been as wise as you think you are, you would not have attempted to know your good wife's secrets that way; moreover without nourishing useless suspicions, you would have perceived that what I confessed was the truth, and yet there was no sin in it.

"I told you I loved a priest; and you, whom I love so unwisely, had you not made yourself into a priest? I said that no door of my house could remain locked when he wanted to lie with me; and what door of your house has ever been locked against you when you wanted to come in where I was? I said that the priest lay every night with me; and when did you not lie with me? Every time you sent the messenger to me when, as you know, you had not been with me, I replied that the priest had not been with me.

"Who but you, who have allowed yourself to be blinded with jealousy, would have been so foolish as to misunderstand this? You spent the night watching the house door, and thought you had persuaded me that you had gone out to supper and to spend the night.

"Repent now, and become a man as you used to be, and do not allow yourself to be duped by those who know your ways as I do, and give up this tedious watch you have been keeping. I swear to God that if I wanted to give you horns, you might have a hundred eyes instead of the two you have, and yet I should find means to have my pleasure without your knowing it."

The jealous husband, who had thought himself very clever in finding out his wife's secret, found he had been mocked at, and without making any further reply felt convinced that his wife was a wise and chaste woman. He put away his jealousy at the very moment when he ought to have taken it on, just as he had been jealous when there was no necessity. So the clever woman, having now permission to do as she liked, no longer brought her lover in over the roof like a tom-cat, but through the door, and by acting prudently often enjoyed herself with him and lived a happy life.

## SIXTH TALE

*Madonna Isabella is with Leonetto and at the same time is visited by one Messer Lambertuccio. Her husband comes home; she sends Messer Lambertuccio out of the house with a drawn sword in his hand, while her husband guards Leonetto home*

Fiammetta's tale pleased them all greatly, and they all said the lady had acted quite rightly and had done what such a man deserved. The king then ordered Pampinea to speak next, and she began as follows:

Many people, speaking unthinkingly, say that love destroys good sense and makes a lover a fool. To me this seems a foolish opinion. It has been proved so by the tales already told, and I intend to prove it once more.

Our city, so well provided with all good things, contained a young and beautiful woman who was the wife of a valiant and worthy knight. It often happens that a man grows tired of one sort of food, and desires variety. Thus, the lady was not content with her husband, and fell in love with a young man named Leonetto, who was pleasant and well behaved, although not of noble birth; and he similarly fell in love with her. As you know it rarely happens that there is no result when both of the parties want the same thing, so no long time elapsed before their love was fulfilled.

But as she was a fair and charming woman, a knight named Messer Lambertuccio fell in love with her also; and as she thought him a displeasing and tedious man, nothing could induce her to like him. He sent many messages to her which profited him not at all; but since he was a man of power, he then threatened to destroy her reputation if she did not do what he wanted. So the lady, knowing and fearing him, made up her mind to do what he desired.

As our custom is in the summer, the lady (whose name was Isabella) went to spend some time on a handsome estate she had in the country; and one morning when her husband had gone somewhere on horseback for several days, she sent a message to Leonetto to come and stay with her. And he gladly did so.

When Messer Lambertuccio heard that her husband had gone away, he mounted his horse and went and knocked at her gate. The lady's maidservant saw him and went at once to the bedroom where she was lying with Leonetto, and called to her:

"Madonna, Messer Lambertuccio is here quite alone."

At this the lady was grievously distressed, but in great fear she begged Leonetto not to mind if she hid him behind the bed curtains until Messer Lambertuccio had gone away. Leonetto hid himself, for he was just as much afraid as the lady, who ordered the maid to go down and open the door to Messer Lambertuccio. He dismounted from his horse in the courtyard, tied it to a ring, and went inside. The lady went to meet him at the stair-head with a smiling face, and greeted him as cheerfully as she could, asking him for what purpose he had come. The knight embraced and kissed her, saying:

"My love, I heard your husband was not here, and so I have come to spend a little time with you."

After these words, they entered her bedroom and locked the door; and Messer Lambertuccio began to enjoy her. Just at this point the husband returned, quite contrary to the lady's expectations. When the servant saw him coming to the house, she ran to the bedroom and said:

"Madonna, here's the master coming back! I think he's in the courtyard already."

When the lady heard this she gave herself up for dead, knowing that she had two men in the house, and that the presence of the knight could not be concealed on account of his horse in the courtyard. But she immediately leaped out of bed and, making up her mind as to what she should do, said to Messer Lambertuccio:

"Messer, if you have the slightest love of me and wish to save me from death, do as I tell you. Take your drawn sword in your hand, and rush down the stairs with an angry and threatening face, saying as you go: 'I vow to God I'll get him somewhere else.' And if my husband tries to stop you or asks you any question, say nothing but what I've told you to say, mount your horse; and on no account stay with him."

Messer Lambertuccio said he would gladly do so. He drew his sword and did as the lady commanded, while his face was aflame with his recent exercise and anger at the return of the lady's husband. The husband, already dismounted in the courtyard, was amazed to see the other horse, and then he saw Messer Lambertuccio coming out of the house just as he was about to enter. Surprised by his visage and words, the husband said:

"What does this mean, Messer?"

Messer Lambertuccio put his foot in the stirrup and mounted, saying not a word except: "By God's body, I'll meet him somewhere else." And so rode away.

The gentleman went in and found his wife at the head of the stairs, in dismay and alarm, and said to her:

"What is all this about? Whom is Messer Lambertuccio threatening so angrily?"

The lady took him to the bedroom so that Leonetto could hear her words, and said:

"Messer, I was never so much afraid before. A young man whom I do not know came rushing in here followed by Messer Lambertuccio with a drawn sword. The young man found this room open and said trembling all over: 'Madonna, for God's sake help me, and let me not be killed in your arms.' I jumped up at once, and as I was about to ask him who he was and what was the matter, in came Messer Lambertuccio, saying: 'Where are you, traitor?' I ran to the door and when he tried to enter I opposed him, and he was so courteous that when he saw I did not wish him to enter he talked to me and then went away as you saw."

"You did well," said the husband. "It would have been a great misfortune if anyone had been killed here; and Messer Lambertuccio behaved very badly by following someone who had taken refuge in the house."

He then asked where the young man was, and the lady replied:

"I don't know where he hid, Messer."

"Where are you?" said the knight. "You can come out in safety."

Leonetto who had listened to all this in terror, as if fear had been a duty for him, came out of his hiding place.

"What is your quarrel with Messer Lambertuccio?" asked the knight.

"Messer," replied the young man, "I do not know at all. I think he must be out of his senses or has mistaken me for somebody else. He saw me in the street not far from your house, drew his sword and said: 'Traitor, you shall die!' I did not stay to enquire why, but fled as swiftly as I could and came in here, where, thank God and this lady, I escaped him."

Then said the knight:

"Have no further fear; I will take you back safe and sound to your own house, and you can then find out what it is all about."

So, after they had supped, he lent the young man a horse, and took him back to Florence to his house. In accordance with the lady's instructions, Leonetto saw Messer Lambertuccio that same evening in secret, and so arranged matters with him that although there was much talk about the affair, the knight never found out the trick played upon him by his wife.

# SEVENTH TALE

*Lodovico tells Madonna Beatrice of his love for her. She sends her husband into the garden disguised as herself and lies with Lodovico who afterwards goes and beats Egano, the husband*

Madonna Isabella's readiness of wit, as related by Pampinea, was thought wonderful by the whole company. But Filomena, whom the king ordered to speak next, said:

Amorous ladies, if I am not deceived I think I can now tell you a better. You must know that in Paris there lived a Florentine merchant who through poverty had become a merchant, and who had prospered so well in trade that he became very rich. By his wife he had an only son, whom he named Lodovico. Since the boy inclined rather to his father's nobility than to trade, the merchant would not put him into any business but placed him along with other gentlemen in the service of the King of France where he learned good manners and other excellent things.

While he was at Court, certain knights just returned from the Holy Land came to a gathering of young men, among whom was Lodovico. They were discussing the fair women of England and France, and other parts of the world. One of the knights said that in all the parts of the world he had visited and among all the ladies he had seen, none could equal in beauty the wife of Egano de' Galluzzi of Bologna, by name Beatrice. And all his companions who had been to Bologna agreed with him.

When Lodovico, who had never been in love, heard this, he was taken with such a desire to see her that he could think of nothing else. Making up his mind to go to Bologna to see her and to stay there for some time if she pleased him, he told his father that he wanted to go to the Holy Land. And with great difficulty he obtained permission to go.

Assuming the name of Anichino, he went to Bologna; and as luck would have it, the very next day he saw the lady at a feast and thought her more beautiful than he had ever imagined. He fell violently in love with her, and determined never to leave Bologna if he could not gain her love. He pondered upon what means to adopt and, putting all others aside, decided that if he could become familiar with her husband—who kept her closely guarded—he might be able to achieve what he wanted. He therefore sold his horses and arrayed his servants, whom he ordered to pretend that they did not know him. He then entered into conversation with his host and told him that he would be glad to enter the service of some lord, if such could be found. Said the host:

"You are just the man who would suit a gentleman of these parts named Egano, who thinks much of his attendants and would wish them all to be like you. I will speak to him."

This he did, and before leaving Egano the host arranged for him to employ Anichino, who pleased him greatly. He remained with Egano and had plenty of opportunity for seeing his wife; moreover, he served Egano so well that Egano became extremely fond of him and could do nothing without him and gave him the overseeing not only of his person but of all his property.

One day when Egano had gone hawking without Anichino, the latter was playing at chess with Madonna Beatrice. She had not yet become aware of his love, although from observing his behaviour she had inwardly come to think highly of him and to like him. Anichino, who wished to please her, very skilfully allowed himself to be beaten, which greatly delighted the lady. All the other ladies of the party went away and left them playing alone, whereupon Anichino heaved a deep sigh. The lady looked at him, and said:

"What is the matter, Anichino? Are you grieved because I beat you at chess?"

"Madonna," replied Anichino, "a much greater matter than that was the cause of my sighing."

"If you have any liking for me, tell about it," said she.

When Anichino heard himself requested by his liking for her—from the woman he loved above everything—he heaved a deeper sigh than before. And so the lady again begged him to tell her the reason for his sighs.

"Madonna," said Anichino, "I fear it may annoy you if I tell you; and then I fear you may reveal it to someone else."

"It will certainly not annoy me," said the lady, "and you may be quite sure that I shall not repeat what you tell me to anyone unless you wish me to do so."

"Since you make me this promise," said Anichino, "I will tell you about it."

Then with tears in his eyes, he told her who he was, what he had heard about her, how and why he had fallen in love with her, and why he had taken service with her husband. He then humbly besought her to have pity upon him, if she could, and to keep his secret and gratify his desire. If she could not do this, he begged her to allow matters to remain as they were and to let him go on loving her.

Strange softness of Bolognese blood! How greatly you are to be praised in these matters! Never do you desire tears and sighs, but ever yield to soft entreaties and amorous desires! Had I worthy praise to bestow upon you, my voice would never be weary of commending you!

The lady gazed at Anichino as he talked and believed his words. His entreaties impressed his love so forcibly upon her mind that she too began to sigh, and after several sighs, she said:

"My sweet Anichino, be of good heart. Neither gifts nor promises nor the courtship of gentlemen, lords and others (for I have been, and still am, courted by many men) could ever move my heart to love them. But in the short space of time while you were speaking you have made me more yours than mine. I think you have well earned my love, and so I give it you, and promise you that you shall enjoy it before tonight has passed.

"To effect this, come to my bedroom at midnight. I will leave the door open. You know on which side of the bed I sleep; come there, and if I am asleep touch me until I awake, and I will console you for your long desire. To make you quite sure of me, I will give you the first fruits of a kiss."

And she threw her arms about him and kissed him amorously, and he her.

After this, Anichino departed from the lady to perform his duties, awaiting the night with the greatest joy imaginable. Egano returned from hawking and, since he was tired, went to bed after supper. The lady soon followed him, and left the bedroom door open as she had promised.

At the appointed hour Anichino came and softly entered the room, locking the door behind him. He went to the side where the lady slept and, placing his hand on her breasts, found that she was awake. She took Anichino's hand in both hers and held it tightly, and turned so sharply in the bed that Egano awoke, and she said to him:

"I said nothing about it last night because I thought you

were tired, but tell me truthfully, Egano, among all your servants who is the best and the truest and the one you love most?"

"Why do you ask me that?" asked Egano. "Don't you know? I never had any friend or confidant whom I loved and trusted as much as Anichino. For what reason do you ask?"

When Anichino found that Egano was awake and that they were talking about him, he tried several times to withdraw his hand and go away, fearing that the lady had deceived him. But she held him so tightly that he could not get away.

"I will tell you why," said the lady to Egano. "I thought it was as you say and that he was more faithful to you than anyone. But he has undeceived me, for when you were away hawking and he remained here, he was not ashamed to ask me to yield to his desires. To convince you of it and to avoid having to bring all sorts of proofs, I replied that I consented, and that after midnight tonight I would go into the garden and wait for him at the foot of the pine. I have no intention of going; but if you wish to know your servant's loyalty you can easily do so, by putting on one of my gowns and a veil over your face and going there to see if he will come, which I am sure he will do."

"I will certainly go to the rendezvous," said Egano. And getting up he put on one of the lady's dresses and a veil over his head, as well as he could in the dark; and then went down into the garden to wait for Anichino at the foot of the pine.

As soon as he had gone, the lady got out of bed and locked the bedroom door. Meanwhile Anichino had been in the greatest fear he had ever felt in his life, and had struggled hard to escape from the lady's grasp, a hundred thousand times cursing her and her love, and himself for trusting her. But when he saw why she had done all this, he was the happiest man in the world. And when the lady got back into bed, he undressed and got in with her, and together they took their joy and pleasure for a long time.

Finally, the lady thought that Anichino should stay no longer, and so made him get up and dress, and said to him:

"My sweet love, take a stout stick and go down into the garden. Pretend that you made love to me to test me, and abuse Egano as if you thought him to be me, and give him a good thrashing, from which will result marvellous delight and pleasure."

Anichino went down into the garden with a good willow stick in his hand, and when Egano saw him coming to the foot of the pine tree he got up as if to greet Anichino with delight. But Anichino said:

"You wicked woman, so you've come, and you thought I would do such a wrong to my lord? A thousand curses on you!"

And lifting his stick he began to beat Egano, who without uttering a word tried to escape when he heard these words and saw the stick. But Anichino went after him saying:

"God punish you, you wicked woman; tomorrow I shall tell Egano."

Egano, after receiving a good beating, got back to his bedroom as quickly as he could; and his wife asked him if Anichino had come to the garden. Said Egano:

"I wish he hadn't, because, thinking I was you, he beat me all over with a stick, and said the most insulting things ever said to a bad woman. I was certainly surprised that he should have said such things to you with the idea of doing what would shame me; but he wanted to put you to the test, since he saw you so merry and open."

"Praised be God," said the lady, "that he tested me with words and you with acts. I think he will be able to say that I bore his words more patiently than you his deeds. But since he is so faithful to you, you should value and cherish him."

"You say truly," replied Egano.

Convinced by what had happened, he believed he had the truest wife and the most faithful servant that ever a gentleman had. And so, though Anichino and the lady often laughed over the scene together, they had much more liberty than they would otherwise have had, to take their delight and pleasure together for as long as Anichino chose to remain in Bologna.

## EIGHTH TALE

*A man becomes jealous of his wife. She ties a thread to her toe at night so that she can know when her lover comes. The husband finds it out; but while he is pursuing*

*the lover, the wife puts another woman in bed in her*
*place. The husband beats this woman and tears her hair*
*and then goes for his wife's brothers; finding what he says*
*to be false, they upbraid him*

They all thought that Madonna Beatrice had been extremely cunning in tricking her husband, and everyone said
that Anichino must have been in great fear when he found
the lady grasping him tightly and telling her husband that
he had made love to her. But after Filomena had finished,
the king turned to Neifile, and said:

"Speak next."

Smiling a little, she began thus:

Fair ladies, it is a heavy task for me to tell you a tale
which will please you as much as those already related, but
with God's help I hope to accomplish it.

You must know that in our town there was once a very
rich merchant named Arriguccio Berlinghieri, who, as we
still see merchants doing every day, foolishly thought to
ennoble himself by marrying a lady of quality. So he married a suitable girl, whose name was Monna Sismonda.
Now, since her husband—like other merchants—was often
away and spent little time with her, she fell in love with a
young man named Ruberto, who had long courted her.

She became familiar with him, and perhaps acted im-
prudently through her great delight in him, but Arriguccio
either heard something about the affair or had some other
reason, for he became exceedingly jealous. He gave up his
journeys abroad and almost the whole of his business, and
gave practically all his attention to watching over her. He
would never go to sleep until she had first got into bed;
and this was very grievous to the lady, because she now
could never be with Ruberto.

Ruberto earnestly urged her to find a means of meeting,
and after much thought she hit upon a plan. The bedroom
was distant from the street, and she had noticed that although Arriguccio took a long time in going to sleep, he
slept very soundly; so she decided to make Ruberto come
to the door of the house in the middle of the night, when
she would go down and open it, and spend some time with
him while her husband slept. In order to know when
Ruberto arrived and yet allow no one else to know, she arranged to lower a thread out of the bedroom window so
that one end touched the ground, while she brought the
other end along the bedroom floor to her bed, and when
she was in bed tied it to her big toe under the clothes. She

let Ruberto know about this plan, and told him when he
came to pull the thread. If her husband were asleep, she
would let the thread go, and come down and open the door;
but if he were not asleep she would hold the thread tight
and pull it towards her, which would mean that Ruberto
was not to wait. Ruberto liked the plan, and thus when he
came they were sometimes able to meet, and sometimes not.

This plan was successful for some time; but one night
when the lady was asleep Arriguccio stretched himself in
bed and touched the thread with his foot. He put his hand
down and found the thread was attached to his wife's toe,
whereupon he said to himself: this must be some trick.
When he discovered that the thread passed out through the
window, he was convinced of it. He therefore gently untied
it from his wife's toe and fastened it to his own, and waited
to see what would happen. Not long afterwards along came
Ruberto and pulled the thread as usual. Arriguccio felt it,
but as he had tied the thread loosely and Ruberto had
pulled it hard, the thread remained in Ruberto's hand, and
so he thought he was to wait. Arriguccio immediately got
up, armed himself, and ran to the street door to see who
it was and to fight him, for although Arriguccio was only
a merchant, he was a fierce, powerful man. He did not open
the door gently as the lady did, and so Ruberto, who was
listening outside, guessed that the door was being opened
by Arriguccio. He therefore took to flight at once, with Arriguccio after him. Finally, after Ruberto had fled for some
distance with the other man after him, he drew his sword
and turned round, and they began to fight, one attacking
and the other defending.

The lady was awakened by Arriguccio's opening the bedroom door, and when she found that the thread had gone
from her toe she immediately realised that her trick had
been found out. She heard Arriguccio running after Ruberto, and immediately made up her mind what she ought
to do. She jumped out of bed, and called to her maid-servant
who knew all about the affair, and persuaded her with many
entreaties to take her mistress' place in the bed and to endure Arriguccio's blows without making herself known,
telling her that she (Sismonda) would be so grateful that
she would see the maid had no reason to regret doing it.
She extinguished the light in the bedroom and went and hid
in another part of the house, awaiting the event.

The neighbours heard the fight going on between Arriguccio and Ruberto and, getting out of bed, began to abuse
them. Arriguccio was afraid of being recognised and had

to let the young man go without having discovered who he was or doing him any injury; and so returned home full of anger and fury and burst tempestuously into the bedroom, saying:

"Where are you, vile woman? You've put out the light so that I shan't find you, but you've made a mistake!"

He went over to the bed, seized the servant (whom he thought to be his wife) and kicked and beat her with his hands and feet until her face was black with bruises. Finally he tore her hair, all the time abusing her as the vilest of women. The servant maid cried shrilly, as well she might; and although she screamed: "Oh, mercy, for God's sake; oh, no more!" her voice was so broken with sobs and Arriguccio was so blinded with rage, that he did not notice she was not his wife. After beating her and cutting off her hair in this way, he said:

"Vile woman, I won't touch you any further, but I shall go for your brothers and tell them of your fine doings. After that let them come for you and do with you what they think their honour requires, and take you away, for you shall certainly stay no longer in this house."

So saying, he went off, locking the room behind him. Monna Sismonda had heard everything, and, as soon as Arriguccio had gone, she came into the room, lighted the lamp, and found the poor maid-servant weeping bitterly. She consoled her as well as she could, and put her in her own room, where she had her waited on and looked after and gave her enough of Arriguccio's money to make her quite contented. When she had put the servant in her room, she quickly re-made the bed and put the whole room in order and re-lighted the lamp, as if no one had been to bed there that night. She then dressed herself, as if she had not been to bed, lighted a lamp, took some sewing, and sat down to sew at the head of the stairs and to wait for what would happen.

Arriguccio rushed out of the house and went to his wife's brothers as quickly as he could, and there beat at the door until they heard him and let him in. The lady's mother and three brothers all got up when they heard Arriguccio was there, and went down to him with lights, and asked him why he came to them alone at that time of night. Arriguccio then told them the whole story, beginning with the thread which he had found tied to Monna Sismonda's toe, down to the end. And to prove the truth of what he said, he showed them the hair which he cut (as he thought) from his wife's head, adding that they were to come back with him and do what their honour demanded, because he would no longer have her in his house.

The lady's brothers, who naturally believed him, were greatly annoyed, and full of anger against her, called for torches and set out with Arriguccio for his home, intending to deal harshly with her. The mother followed them in tears, beseeching first one and then another not to believe this too quickly without further enquiry, because the husband might have been angry with her and have harmed her for some other reason, and have accused her to clear himself. She also said that she was amazed that such a thing could have happened, since she knew her daughter well and had brought her up from a baby, and many such words.

Finally they reached Arriguccio's house and, entering, began to ascend the stairs. When Monna Sismonda heard them, she said:

"Who's there?"

"You'll soon know, you vile woman," answered one of the brothers.

"What does this mean?" said Monna Sismonda. "Lord help me!"

She then stood up, and said:

"My brothers, you are welcome; what do you seek at this hour?"

As soon as they saw her seated there sewing, with not a mark on her face which Arriguccio had told them he had bruised all over, they were amazed, and curbed the first impulse of their anger. They then asked her what was the affair of which Arriguccio had complained to them, threatening her savagely if she did not tell everything. Said the lady:

"I don't know what I have to say or why Arriguccio should have any reason to complain of me."

Arriguccio gazed at her as if out of his senses, remembering how he had beaten her in the face and scratched her and hurt her, whereas now he saw her quite unscathed, as if nothing had happened. The brothers then related everything Arriguccio had told them, about the thread and the beating and all the rest. The lady turned to Arriguccio, and said:

"Why, husband, what is this I hear? Why do you make me out a vile woman to your own shame, when I am not one, and make yourself out a cruel and harsh man, which you are not? When were you here in the house with me to-night? When did you beat me? I don't remember anything about it."

"What!" said Arriguccio, "you vile woman, did we not go to bed together? Didn't I beat you and cut off your hair?"

"But you didn't go to bed in this house tonight," replied the lady. "Let us leave that, for I can bring no other proof of it save my true words, and let us come to the other things you say—that you beat me and cut off my hair. You never beat me, and everyone here present, including yourself, may see whether I have any marks of a beating on my person. And I warn you not to be so bold as to lay a hand upon me, for, by God's Cross, I'd give you back as good as you gave. Nor did you ever cut off my hair, as you can feel or see. But perhaps you did it when I was unaware; let me see whether my hair is cut off or not."

And, lifting the veil from her head, she showed that she had all her hair, uncut.

When the mother and the brothers heard and saw these things, they turned to Arriguccio, and said:

"What do you mean, Arriguccio? This is not what you came and told us you had done—how will you prove the remainder?"

Arriguccio stood like a man in a dream, trying to speak. But, seeing that what he had thought he could show was otherwise, he remained silent. The lady then turned to her brothers, and said:

"Brothers, I see he has gone about seeking for me to do what I never wished to do—which is to tell you his baseness and cruelties. But now I shall do it. I quite believe that what he told you he did has happened, and I will tell you how.

"This worthy man, to whom you gave me as wife in an ill hour, calls himself a merchant and would like to be in good repute. Such a man should be more temperate than a monk and chaster than a virgin, and yet there are few evenings when he does not go drinking in taverns, sometimes going with one bad woman, sometimes with another. And I have to sit up for him, in the way you found me, until the middle of the night, and sometimes till dawn. I am certain that in his drunkenness he lay with some woman, and then woke up and found the thread tied to her toe. He then performed the bold feats of which he tells us, came back to her, beat her and cut off her hair. Not having come to himself, he believed (and I am sure, still believes) that he did these things to me. But still whatever he may have said of me, I don't want you to look upon him as anything but a drunkard. And since I forgive him, you also must pardon him."

At this the lady's mother took up the tale, and said:

"By God's Cross, daughter, this cannot be endured. This ungrateful and beastly cur should be killed; he's not worthy to have a girl like you. Why, look you! It would have been too much if he had taken you out of the gutter. The foul fiend run away with him if you are to be at the mercy of the words of a little donkey's dung tradesman, who comes from a pig-sty in the country dressed in shoddy, with hose like a bell-tower and a feather in his backside, and when he has three cents wants to marry the daughter of gentle people, and takes a coat of arms and says: 'I belong to such a family, and my people do this and that.' I wish my sons had followed my advice, for they could have married you into the house of the Counts of Guidi with a hunk of bread as a dowry; but they would marry you to this pearl among men. If you were the best daughter in Florence and the most chaste, he would not be ashamed to call you a whore, as if we did not know you. God's faith, if they did what I wanted, they would beat him until he stank!"

She then turned to her sons, and said:

"My sons, I told you this could not be so. Have you heard how your good brother-in-law treats your sister? The little four-cent tradesman that he is! What! If I were you, after he has said what he has about her and done what he has done, I should never think myself content or repaid until I had despatched him from this earth. And if I were a man I would not let anyone else prevent me from doing it. God punish him! The foul drunkard! And he isn't even ashamed!"

The young men then turned upon Arriguccio, and gave him the worst abuse that ever fell upon a criminal, and said finally:

"We forgive you this because you are drunk. But, as you value your life, don't ever let us hear anything of the kind again; for if anything like it comes to our ears, be sure we will pay you for both!"

So saying, they departed. Arriguccio was like a man dazed; and, not knowing whether what he had done was true or a dream, he said not another word, and left his wife in peace. And she, by her cunning, not only escaped the immediate danger but prepared the way to do anything she wanted in the future, without the least fear of her husband.

## NINTH TALE

*Lidia, the wife of Nicostrato, is in love with Pirro who asks of her three things (all of which she performs) to test her sincerity. Moreover, she lies with him in the presence of Nicostrato and makes Nicostrato believe that what he saw was not true*

Neifile's tale was so much liked that the ladies could not stop laughing and talking about it, although the king several times imposed silence on them and ordered Pamfilo to tell his tale. Finally, when they were silent, Pamfilo began thus:

Revered ladies, I believe that those who are deeply in love are prepared to do anything, however doubtful and troublesome. Although this has been showed in several tales, yet I think I can prove it to you still further with the tale I intend to tell, wherein you will hear of a lady whose luck was better than her common sense. Nor do I advise you to take the risk of following in her footsteps, because luck is not always favourable and all men cannot be blinded in the same way.

In Argos, that most ancient city of Achaia, much more renowned for its dead kings than for its size, there lived a nobleman named Nicostrato. When he was on the verge of old age, Fortune bestowed upon him as wife a noble lady, no less ardent than beautiful, named Lidia. Nicostrato, being a rich nobleman, possessed numerous servants and dogs and hawks, and took the greatest delight in hunting. Among his servants was a charming young man named Pirro, accomplished, handsome and skilled in everything he had to do; and Nicostrato loved and trusted him above all men.

Now Lidia fell in love with this young man, so that day and night she could think of nothing else. Pirro either did not perceive, or did not want, her love, for he gave no sign that he cared about her, which filled the lady's spirit with intolerable woe. Determined that he should know about it, she called a maid-servant named Lusca, in whom she had great confidence, and said:

"Lusca, the benefits you have received from me ought to make you faithful and obedient. Therefore take care that what I am about to tell you shall be known to nobody except the person whom I shall order you to tell.

"As you see, Lusca, I am a fresh young woman, abounding in all those things which any woman would desire. In short, I can make no complaint, save of one thing, which is that my husband is too old in comparison with me, so that I am not well contented in that which is most pleasing to young women. Yet, like other women, I desire it, and for some time I have determined that since Fortune has been so much my foe as to give me an old husband I will not be my own enemy by refusing to discover some means of obtaining my delight and salvation. After estimating these as well as other things I have made up my mind that Pirro is more worthy than any other to supply this want with his embraces; and I am so much in love with him that I am never happy except when I see him or am thinking about him. And I think I shall die if I do not have him soon.

"Therefore, if you value my life, make known my love to him in whatever way you think best, and beg him for me that he will come to me when you send for him."

The maid-servant replied that she would gladly do this. Choosing a suitable place and time, she drew Pirro aside, and gave him her lady's message in the best terms she could. Pirro was greatly surprised to hear this, for he had never noticed anything of the kind and feared that the lady had sent the message to test his fidelity. So he replied abruptly and rudely:

"Lusca, I cannot believe that these words come from my lady, so beware what you say. If they do come from her, I do not believe she meant you to speak to me. And even if she did mean you to do so, my lord honours me more than I deserve and I will not for my life do him such an outrage. Therefore take care never to speak to me of such matters again."

Undismayed by these austere words, Lusca persevered:

"Pirro, I shall speak of these or any other matters ordered by my lady as often as she chooses to command me, whether it pleases you or not. But you're a fool."

And, being rather angry at Pirro's words, she returned to her lady, who wanted to die when she heard them. A few days later, however, she spoke again to the maid-servant:

"Lusca, you know the oak does not fall at the first blow. So I want you to go again to the man who has chosen so curious a way of fidelity, to my harm; and at a fitting time tell him of my desire and do all you can to achieve success. If things are left as they are, I shall die and he will think himself mocked, and I shall only receive his hatred when I seek his love."

The servant consoled her lady, and went to look for Pirro, whom she found in a cheerful mood, and said to him:

"Pirro, a little time ago I told you how my lady and yours was burning with love for you; and once more I tell you that if you remain as hostile as you were the other day, you may be certain that she will not live long. Therefore I beg you to console her in her desire. If you remain in this obstinacy, I shall think you a gross fool when I had thought you to be a wise man. What can be more flattering for you than to be loved by so beautiful, so charming a lady as she is? Moreover, how much you should think yourself indebted to Fortune when you realise that she has prepared such a thing for you, fitting the desires of your youth and forming such a remedy for your material needs? Which of your equals do you know who will be better off than yourself, if only you are wise? If you give her your love, what other man will equal you in arms, horses, possessions and money?

"Open your mind to my words and reflect. Remember that generally Fortune comes only once to a man with gay face and open bosom. And when such a man fails to receive her and then becomes a poor beggar, he can only blame himself and not Fortune. Moreover, in these matters there is no need of the same fidelity between servants and masters as there is between friends and relatives. Thus, servants are wont to treat their masters—as far as they can—just as their masters treat them. If you had a fair wife or mother or daughter or sister, and Nicostrato was in love with her, do you think he would feel the sense of loyalty to you that you think you have about his wife? More fool you, if you believe it. Whatever you may think, you can be sure that he would use force, if flattery and prayers failed. Let us treat them and their affairs as they treat us and ours. Take the chance Fortune brings you. Don't drive her away, but go to meet her as she comes to you. Be sure that if you don't do so, not only will my lady inevitably die but you will repent it so often that you will want to die yourself."

Pirro had many times reflected on the words which Lusca had first spoken to him, and had made up his mind that if she came to him again he would make a different reply and would do all he could to please the lady, if he could be certain that she was not merely making a test of him. So he said:

"Lusca, I know that everything you say is true. But, on

the other hand, I know my lord to be a very wise and careful man who has full control of all his affairs; I am afraid
that Lidia is doing this to test me with his knowledge and at
his request. But if she will do three things to reassure me,
certainly she can command nothing of me that I will not
promptly perform. The three things I ask are these: first,
that she will kill Nicostrato's best falcon before his eyes;
second, that she will send me a lock of Nicostrato's beard;
third, one of his best teeth."

These things seemed difficult to Lusca and most difficult
to the lady. But love, who is a good comforter and a great
master of skilful devices, determined her to attempt them;
and so she sent the maid to tell Pirro that what he required
should be done, and soon. Moreover (she added), whereas
he thought Nicostrato such a wise man, she promised to
lie with Pirro in his presence and yet to make Nicostrato believe it had not happened.

Pirro therefore waited to see what the lady would do.

A few days later Nicostrato gave a big dinner, as he often
did, to certain gentlemen. When the tables were drawn,
Lidia came out of her room dressed in a green velvet robe
and her jewels. She came into the room where they were
assembled and, in the presence of Pirro and them all, went
to the perch where sat the falcon which Nicostrato prized so
highly, took up the bird as if she wanted it to perch on her
hand, and then holding it by the jesses dashed it against the
wall and killed it.

"Why, wife, what have you done?" exclaimed Nicostrato.

"Nothing," she answered him, and then turning to the
gentlemen who had dined there, she said: "Gentlemen, I
could ill revenge myself upon a King who injured me if I
could not take my revenge on a falcon. You must know that
this bird has deprived me of much of the time which men
usually give up to ladies' pleasures, for as soon as the dawn
appears Nicostrato is up and out on horseback with his
falcon on his wrist, to watch it fly over the broad plains.
And I, such as you now see me, must remain alone and discontented in bed. Therefore, I have often desired to do what
I have now done, and my only reason for waiting was that
I wanted to do it in the presence of men who would judge
my quarrel justly, as I believe you will."

The gentlemen thought her affection for Nicostrato was
such as her words pretended, and so they turned laughingly
to the angry husband, and said:

"Why! The lady was right to avenge her wrong by killing
the falcon!"

After the lady had returned to her room, they made so many jokes about it all that they changed Nicostrato's annoyance to laughter. And Pirro said to himself: "The lady has made a lofty beginning to my fortunate love—pray God she may persevere."

Not many days after Lidia had killed the hawk she was in her room with Nicostrato caressing him and jesting with him. He in jest pulled her by the hair, which gave her an opportunity to carry out the second test imposed by Pirro. She quickly grasped a littie lock of his beard and laughingly pulled it so hard that it came away from his chin. And when Nicostrato complained, she said:

"What makes you put on such a look? Because I have pulled about six hairs from your beard? You didn't feel what I felt when you pulled my hair just now."

So from one speech to another they continued their love-play, and the lady carefully preserved the lock from the beard and sent it that same day to her dear lover.

The third thing caused the lady more thought. But as she was of a high spirit and love gave her wits, she thought out a way of achieving it. Nicostrato had two pages, whose fathers had given them to him so that they might be bred up in his house and learn the manners befitting gentlemen, which they were. When Nicostrato sat at table, one of them carved before him and the other served him with drink. She sent for them both and told them that they had bad breath, and commanded them to turn away their heads when they were serving Nicostrato, and never to speak of the matter to anyone. The boys believed her, and thereafter behaved as the lady had told them. So one day she said to Nicostrato:

"Have you noticed what those boys do when they are waiting on you?"

"Yes," said Nicostrato, "and I mean to ask them why they do it."

"Don't do that," said the lady, "for I can tell you why. I have kept silence about it a long time in order not to annoy you. But now that I see other people are beginning to notice it, I shall conceal it no longer. The only reason for their behaviour is that your breath smells so badly. I don't know what the cause can be, for it is not customary with you. But it is a vile thing, since you consort with gentlemen; we must find some means of curing it."

"What can it be?" said Nicostrato. "Has one of my teeth gone rotten?"

"Perhaps that's it," said Lidia.

She took him over to the window, made him open his mouth, and after looking here and there, she said:

"Oh! Nicostrato, how could you endure it so long? Why, you've a tooth there which looks to me not only eaten away but quite rotten. If you keep it any longer in your mouth it will infect those beside it. I advise you to have it out, before the harm goes any further."

"Since you think so," said Nicostrato, "I am content. Send for a chirurgeon at once to take it out.

"In God's name," said the lady, "don't send for any chirurgeon. It seems to me to be in such a state that I can draw it myself without the help of any doctor. Moreover, these doctors are so heartless in performing such services that I could not bear to see you in their hands. So I'll do it all myself. For, if it's too painful, I'll stop at once, which no doctor would do."

She then sent for the necessary implements and ordered everyone out of the room except Lusca. She locked the door and made Nicostrato lie down on a table. She then put the forceps in his mouth round one of his teeth, and, in spite of his yells, one of the women held him down while the other pulled out a tooth by main force. She hid the good tooth at once and took another rotten tooth which she had held concealed and showed it to him as he lay there half dead with pain, saying:

"Look what you've had in your mouth for so long."

Although Nicostrato had suffered great pain and complained bitterly of it, he believed her, and since the tooth was out thought himself cured. They comforted him with one thing and another, and, when the pain was assuaged, he left the room.

The lady immediately sent the tooth to her lover; and he, being now certain of her love, said he was ready to do her pleasure. The lady wished to give him further assurance while every hour seemed like a thousand hours until she could be with him. She wanted to carry out what she had promised him herself, and so pretended to be ill. One day Nicostrato, attended only by Pirro, came to visit her after dinner; and she begged him to help her into the garden as some diversion to her sickness. So Nicostrato on one side and Pirro on the other carried her into the garden, and sat her down on a lawn at the foot of a large pear tree. After sitting there a little time, the lady—who had already informed Pirro of what he had to do—said:

"Pirro, I very much want to have one of those pears; so climb up the tree and throw some of them down."

Pirro climbed nimbly up and began to throw pears down; and then he said:

"Messer, what are you doing? And you, Madonna, are you not ashamed to allow it in my presence? Do you think I'm blind? Just now you were very ill; how can you be cured so quickly that you are able to do such things? And if you want to do them, you have plenty of bedrooms—why don't you go and do it there, which would be more chaste than to do it in my presence."

The lady turned to her husband, and said:

"What's Pirro talking about? Is he raving?"

"I'm not raving, Madonna," said Pirro, "do you think I can't see?"

Nicostrato was amazed, and said:

"Why, Pirro, I think you must be dreaming."

"My lord," replied Pirro, "I'm not dreaming at all, nor are you dreaming. You're moving so hard that if this pear tree moved in the same way, not a pear would be left on it."

"Whatever can this be?" said the lady. "Can it really be that what he says seems to be true to him? God help me, if I were as well as I used to be I would climb up to see the marvels which he says he sees."

Pirro remained in the tree and went on in the same strain. Then said Nicostrato: "Come down." And he came down. Then Nicostrato asked:

"What do you say you saw?"

"You must think me out of my mind or wandering," said Pirro. "I saw you lying on your lady, and had to tell you so. And as I came down I saw you get up and sit down where you now are."

"You certainly were out of your mind," said Nicostrato, "for we have not moved from where we are since you climbed up the pear tree."

"Why do we argue about it?" said Pirro. "I saw you. And if it's true I see you now, I then saw you on your wife."

Nicostrato was more and more amazed, and finally said:

"I should like to see whether this pear tree is bewitched, and what are the wonders seen by those who climb it."

And he climbed up the tree. As soon as he was in it, the lady began to make love with Pirro; and as soon as Nicostrato saw them, he shouted:

"You vile woman, what are you doing? And you too, Pirro, in whom I had such trust!"

So saying, he began to climb down the tree. The lady and Pirro said:

"We're sitting still."

As he came down, they returned to the places where they had been sitting. As soon as Nicostrato was on the ground and saw them in the positions where he had left them, he began to denounce them. But Pirro said:

"Nicostrato, I confess that you were right in what you said, and that I saw wrongly when I was in the pear tree. I know it from this—that I see and know that you also saw wrongly. No further proof is needed that I speak truth save only for you to consider that if your lady, who is most chaste and wise, desired to outrage your honour, she would certainly not do it before your eyes. I say nothing of myself, for I would rather be torn in pieces than even think of it, let alone perform it in your presence. The error of this vision must therefore necessarily come from the pear tree, for the whole world would not have convinced me that you were not carnally lying with your wife here if I had not heard you say that you believed I was doing what I know I have never thought of, nor ever have done."

Thereupon, the lady rose to her feet as if in anger, and said:

"You must be crazed if you think I am so stupid as to commit this folly before your very eyes, supposing I wanted to do what you say you saw. You may be sure that if I wanted to do it I should not come here; I should have sense enough to do it in one of our rooms in such a way that I think it improbable you would ever know about it."

Nicostrato believed both of them when they said they would never do such a thing in his presence, and therefore ceased his upbraiding and began to talk about the strangeness of the fact and the miracle of the vision, which so changed things for everyone who climbed the tree. But the lady pretended to be angry at Nicostrato's suspicions of her, and said:

"This pear tree shall never again cause such shame to me or any other lady, if I can prevent it. Pirro, go and get an axe, and avenge yourself and me at once by cutting it down, although it would be better to knock Nicostrato on the head with the axe for having allowed the eyes of his intellect to be blinded so easily. For, however much the eyes in your head might believe what you say, yet your judgment ought never to admit that it is so."

Pirro immediately went for an axe and cut down the pear tree. And when the lady saw it fall, she said to Nicostrato:

"Now I have seen the fall of my honour's enemy, my anger has departed."

And, at his earnest entreaty, she forgave Nicostrato,

commanding him never to assume that such a thing could happen, since she loved him more than herself. So the poor deceived husband returned to the house with her and her lover; and Pirro and Lidia often took delight and pleasure of each other at their ease. May God grant the like to us!

# TENTH TALE

*Two Sienese are in love with the same woman, and one of them is godfather to her child. The godfather dies and, as he had promised, his spirit returns to his friend and tells him his state in the next world*

The king alone was now left to tell a tale; and when the ladies—who were regretting the pear tree which was cut down for no fault of its own—were silent, he began thus:

'Tis most manifest that every just king ought to be the first to observe the laws he himself has made; and if he does otherwise he should be considered a slave worthy of punishment, and not a king. Now I, your king, am almost compelled to fall into this fault and censure. It is true that yesterday when I made the law for our tale-telling today, I had no intention of making use of my privilege, but intended to speak on the same subject as yourselves. But what I intended to say has been said, and moreover so many other and finer things have been related that however much I ransacked my memory I cannot think of anything to say on this topic which equals the tales already told. Therefore, since I must break the laws I made myself, I confess myself worthy of punishment and ready to make any amends you impose upon me, and so fall back upon my privilege.

The tale Elisa told about the godfather and the child's mother and also the stupidity of the Sienese suggest that I shall depart from the theme of the tricks played on foolish husbands by their wives and shall tell you, dearest ladies, a tale of the Sienese; for although it contains certain matters contrary to faith, yet in part you will be amused to hear it.

There lived in Siena two young men of the people, one named Tingoccio Mini and the other Meuccio di Tura. They lived by the Porta Salaia and hardly frequented anybody but each other, which leads one to suppose that they were very fond of each other. They went to church and to sermons, as people do, and often heard of the glories and the miseries which are allotted to the souls of the dead in the next world according to their deserts. Desirous of obtaining sure information of all this and seeing no other means, they promised each other, and confirmed it with a solemn oath, that whichever of them died first would, if he were able, return and give the other the information he desired.

After they had made this promise, and continued their familiarity, Tingoccio became godfather to the child of Ambruogio Anselmini, who lived with his wife Monna Mita in Campo Reggi. Tingoccio, accompanied by Meuccio, often visited his godchild's mother, who was a most beautiful and charming woman, and fell in love with her, despite their spiritual kinship. And Meuccio, who liked her very much and often heard Tingoccio praise her, also fell in love with her. Neither spoke of his love to the other, though not for the same reason. Tingoccio refrained from speaking of it to Meuccio because he himself thought it wrong to love his godchild's mother and would have been ashamed for anyone to know it. Meuccio, on the other hand, was silent, because he had noticed how much Tingoccio liked her. And he said to himself: "If I reveal it to him, he will be jealous of me; and since he can speak to his godchild's mother whenever he wants, he would be able to prejudice her against me, and thus I should not obtain anything I want from her."

The two young men being thus in love, it happened that Tingoccio, who had more opportunity of showing the lady his desire, laboured so well by word and deed that he had his pleasure of her. Meuccio soon noticed this, and although it annoyed him, yet he pretended not to see it, and the hope of one day obtaining his desire determined him to give Tingoccio no chance to thwart him. One of the two young men was thus more fortunate in love than the other; and Tingoccio, having found the happy land, dug and ploughed it so hard that he fell ill. And in a few days the illness became so serious he could not rally from it, and departed this life.

The third day after his death (for perhaps he could not come sooner) he kept his promise and appeared in Meuccio's bedroom while he was in a deep sleep, and called to him. Meuccio awoke and said:

"Who are you?"

"I am Tingoccio," replied the other, "and in accordance with my promise I have returned to give you news of the other world."

Meuccio was rather terrified to see him, but pulled himself together, and said:

"You are welcome, my brother."

And then asked him if he were lost. Said Tingoccio:

"The things which cannot be found are lost; and how could I be here if I were lost?"

"I don't mean that," said Meuccio. "I ask whether you are among the damned souls in the penal fires of hell."

"No, not there," answered Tingoccio, "but for the sins I have committed I am in great pain and anguish."

Meuccio then asked Tingoccio what punishments were allotted in the next world for each sin which is committed here, and Tingoccio told him. Meuccio then asked him if there were anything he could do for him. Tingoccio said there was, and asked him to have Masses and prayers said for him and to give alms, since these things are a great comfort to the dead. Meuccio said he would gladly do so and, as Tingoccio was leaving, Meuccio remembered the mother of the child to whom Tingoccio was godfather, and lifting his head, said:

"I remember something, Tingoccio. What punishment has been allotted you for lying with the woman to whom you were spiritually akin?"

Said Tingoccio:

"Brother, when I arrived there, 'I found a man who seemed to know all my sins by heart, and he ordered me to go to a place where I bewail my faults in very great pain, along with many companions who are condemned to the same punishment. As I stood there among them, I remembered what I had done with my godchild's mother, and trembled with fear, for I expected some much greater punishment would be inflicted on me for that, although I was then in a large burning fire. Someone who was beside me, said: 'What woe have you more than the others here that you tremble so much in the fire?' And I said: 'My friend, I am afraid of the judgment which will be passed upon me for a great sin I have committed.' He then asked me what the sin was. And I replied: 'The sin was that I lay with my godchild's mother, and lay with her so much that I exhausted myself.' He then mocked at me, saying: 'Away, you fool, have no fear; no one troubles about spiritual kinship here.' And this completely reassured me."

And then, as the day was at hand, he said:

"Meuccio, God be with you; I can stay no longer."

And so departed in haste.

Meuccio, hearing that in the next world no account was

made of spiritual kinship, began to laugh at his own folly for having respected such things. So, abandoning his ignorance, in this matter he became wise. If Friar Rinaldo had known this, there would have been no need for him to use syllogisms when he converted his godchild's mother to his desires.

The West Wind arose as the sun drew nearer to setting, and when the king had finished his tale and no one else remained to speak, he took the garland from his head and placed it on Lauretta's head, saying:

"Madonna, I crown you queen of our company with your namesake leaf; now command, as Sovereign Lady, what you think will please and divert us all."

Lauretta, being made queen, sent for the steward, and ordered him to set the tables in the beautiful valley earlier than usual, so that they might return home at more leisure. And then discussed with him what needed to be done during her reign. She then turned to the gathering, and said:

"Yesterday Dioneo desired us to tell tales of the tricks which wives play upon their husbands. But for the fact that I don't want to show myself one of the race of snarling dogs, I should say that tomorrow we ought to tell tales of the tricks which men play upon their wives. And so I say that everyone must think of a tale about the tricks played every day by women upon men, by men upon women and by men upon men. I think this will be as pleasant a theme for tale-telling as today's."

So saying, she arose, and left the company at liberty until dinner time. The men and women therefore arose also, and some of them waded barefoot in the clear water, while others amused themselves by wandering among the tall beautiful trees above the green lawns. Dioneo and Fiammetta sang together a long piece about Palemon and Arcite. And so in various ways they passed the time delightfully until supper. They then supped merrily and at ease from tables set at some distance from the lake, untroubled by flies, sung to by a thousand birds, and cooled by a soft wind which breathed from the little hills about them.

The tables were drawn while the sun was yet in the sky, and at the queen's desire they walked about the beautiful valley, and then slowly turned their footsteps homeward. Laughing and jesting at a thousand things, both from the tales told that day and others, they came to the mansion a little before nightfall. There they refreshed themselves after the short walk with cool wine and sweetmeats, and then began to dance near the fountain to the sound of Tindaro's Sicilian bagpipes or to other instruments. Finally the queen ordered Filomena to sing a song, and she began thus:

*Ah! Luckless life! Shall I ever be able to return whence I was reft by bitter parting?*

*So fierce is the desire within my breast, and yet I know not if ever I shall be again where once, alas, I was. O my dear love, my only peace, who hold my heart in duress, ah! tell me—for I dare not ask another and know not whom to ask—alas! my love, alas! give me some hope, give me some comfort for my wandering spirit.*

*I cannot tell what was the delight which set this fire in me so that by day and night I have no rest, for hearing, seeing, feeling, each with unwonted force lights stronger fire wherein I burn; and none but you can comfort me or give me back my shaken courage.*

*Tell me if this shall be, and when—that I shall be where I can kiss those eyes that murdered me. Tell me, my heart, my love, when you will come, and tell me soon, to comfort me. Let Time until you come be short, and long your staying, for Love has wounded me so deeply.*

*If ever once again I hold you, I shall not be so foolish as I was, and let you go again. I shall hold you in my arms, and let come what may; and on your lovely mouth let my desire feed full. I say no more of all the rest—only come soon, for but to think of it invites my singing.*

This song made the whole company feel that Filomena was held by some new and pleasant love; and since it appeared from her words that she had gone further than mere looking, those who were present thought her fortunate and envied her. But when the song was over the queen remembered that the next day was Friday, and so said cheerfully:

"Noble ladies, and you young men, you know that tomorrow is the day consecrated to the Passion of Our Lord; and if I remember aright we devoutly commemorated it during the reign of Neifile, and ceased our pleasant tale-telling, as also upon the ensuing Saturday. Therefore, being desirous to follow the example set by Neifile, I consider it would be right for us to do tomorrow and the day after what we did formerly and that we should abstain from telling of tales, and consecrate our thoughts upon what was done on those days for the salvation of our souls."

This devout speech of the queen pleased them all; and as a good portion of the night was ready spent she set them at liberty, and all went to their rest.

**HERE ENDS THE SEVENTH DAY**

# THE EIGHTH DAY

# THE EIGHTH DAY

*Here begins the eighth day of the* Decameron, *wherein, under the rule of Lauretta, tales are told of the tricks played every day by men upon women or women upon men or men upon men*

It was Sunday morning, and the rays of rising light already appeared on the tips of the highest hills. The shadows departed and all things became clear to see. The queen and her companions arose and walked over the dewy grass, and about the midst of Tierce visited a little church near at hand, where they heard divine service. Returning home they dined merrily, sang and danced, and then the queen gave them permission to rest. But when the sun had passed mid-heaven they all by the queen's command gathered together and sat down by the beautiful fountain for their wonted tale-telling; and Neifile, being ordered by the queen, began thus:

## FIRST TALE

*Gulfardo borrows money from Guasparruolo and then gives his wife the same sum of money to lie with her. In the presence of Guasparruolo and his wife he claims to have paid her back the sum and she has to admit it*

God has ordained that I should tell the first tale today, and I am content it should be so. We have said much, amorous ladies, of the tricks played upon men by women, and so I mean to tell you of a trick played upon a woman by a man; not that I mean to blame the man or to say that the woman did not deserve it, on the contrary I mean to commend the man and to blame the woman and to show that men can trick those who trust in them even as they are tricked by those in whom they trust. Properly speaking, this should not be called a trick but a merited reproof. The reason is this:

A woman should be wholly modest and guard her chastity as her life, and on no account allow it to be corrupted. But our fragility does not always permit us to do this. I assert therefore that the woman who yields for money is deserving of the stake and fire, whereas she who submits to love, whose very great power is known, deserves pardon from a judge who is not too austere—as Filostrato told us a few days ago happened in the case of Madonna Filippa at Prato.

There was once in Milan a German soldier named Gulfardo, a bold man and faithful to those he served, which rarely happens with Germans. And since he most honestly repaid any sums of money lent him, he could always find merchants ready to lend him any quantity of money at a low rate of interest. This soldier fell in love with a beautiful woman named Madonna Ambruogia, the wife of a friend of his, a wealthy merchant named Guasparruolo Cagastraccio. He was so prudent that his love was perceived neither by the merchant nor by anyone else; and one day he spoke to her, begging her that she would be pleased to be gracious to his love, and saying that he for his part was ready to do anything she commanded him.

After much discussion the lady came to this decision—she was ready to do what Gulfardo wanted on two conditions, the first of which was that nobody should ever hear anything about the affair, while the second was that she needed two hundred gold florins for certain needs and that if he, who was a rich man, would give her that sum, she would always be at his service.

When Gulfardo, who had thought her a high-spirited woman, saw her avarice, he felt deep scorn at her baseness, and his fervent love was changed to hate. He determined to play a trick upon her, and told her he would gladly do that and anything else he could to please her. Therefore, she was to let him know when she wanted him to go to her and he would bring her the money; nobody should ever hear about it except a friend of his, in whom he had great confidence and who always accompanied him whatever he did.

The lady, like the bad woman she was, felt glad when she heard this, and sent back word that her husband Guasparruolo would have to go to Genoa on business a few days later, that she would let him know the time, and send for him.

Gulfardo thereupon went to Guasparruolo and said:

"I need two hundred gold florins for a certain affair, and I want you to lend them to me at the same rate of interest you lend to others."

Guasparruolo said he would gladly do so, and counted him out the money at once. A few days later he went to Genoa, as his wife had said; and so she sent to Gulfardo and told him to come, bringing the two hundred gold florins with him. Gulfardo, taking his friend with him, went to the lady's house, and found her waiting for him. The first thing he did was to put the two hundred gold florins in her hand in the presence of his friend, saying:

"Madonna, take this money, and give it to your husband when he returns."

The lady took the money and did not see why Gulfardo used those words. On the contrary, she thought he spoke thus so that his friend would not know that he was giving her the money as the price of her person. And so she said:

"I will gladly do so, but I must count them first."

She emptied them out on to a table and found there were two hundred. She put them away in a great delight, and took Gulfardo to her bedroom, where she let him satisfy himself on her person, not only that night but many others, until her husband returned from Genoa.

When Guasparruolo returned from Genoa, Gulfardo at once went to him, and finding him with his wife, said in her presence:

"Guasparruolo, I did not need the two hundred gold florins you lent me, because I was unable to carry out the affair for which I borrowed them. I brought them back at once to your wife and gave them to her. So you must cancel my debt."

Guasparruolo turned to his wife, and asked if this were true. And she, seeing the witness present, could not deny it, and had to say:

"Yes, I had the money, and forgot to tell you about it."

"Gulfardo," said Guasparruolo, "I am satisfied; good-bye; I will cancel your debt."

Gulfardo departed, and the tricked woman gave her husband the dishonest price of her wickedness; and thus the cunning lover enjoyed his mercenary lady for nothing.

# SECOND TALE

*The priest of Varlungo lies with Monna Belcolore and leaves her his cloak as a pledge. He borrows a mortar of her and, when she asks for it, he claims his cloak which he says he had left as a pledge for the mortar, and so the good woman is left grumbling*

Both the men and the ladies commended the trick which Gulfardo played on the greedy Milanese lady. The queen then turned smilingly to Pamfilo and ordered him to follow next; and so he began thus:

Fair ladies, I mean to tell you a little tale about those who are constantly injuring us without our being able to injure them in the same way—I mean the priests, who have declared a Crusade against our wives, and seem to think that when they can get on one of them they have obtained forgiveness of their sins as much as if they had brought the Sultan captive from Alexandria to Avignon. We poor men of the world cannot do the like to them, although we should avenge ourselves by attacking no less eagerly the mothers, sisters, female friends and daughters of priests. So I mean to tell you about a pleasant love affair, which is not long but amusing from its conclusion; and you may at least learn from it that priests are not to be believed in everything.

In Varlungo, a village which is not far from here (as each of you knows or has heard) there was a worthy priest, most valiant of person in the service of ladies. Although he could not read much, every Sunday at the foot of an elm he comforted his parishioners with good and holy discourses. And when the male parishioners were absent, there never was a priest who more willingly visited their wives, taking them fairings and holy water and a few candle-ends, and giving them his blessing.

Now, among all his female parishioners one especially charmed him. This was one Monna Belcolore, the wife of a labourer, who went by the name of Bentivegna del Mazzo. She was a pleasant, fresh, brown-skinned, buxom peasant-girl, who knew how to grind the mill better than anyone. Moreover, she was a skilled performer on the cymbals and could sing: "The water flows in the cleft," and, waving a pocket handkerchief in her hand, dance Sellinger's Round better than any of her neighbours. All these things so charmed our priest that he was frantic about her, and rambled about all day trying to catch a glimpse of her. When he knew she was in church on Sunday morning, he lifted up his voice with a *Kyrie* or a *Sanctus* to show her what a fine singing voice he had, and brayed like an ass; whereas, if she were not there, he passed over them very hurriedly. But yet he acted in such a way that neither Bentivegna del Mazzo nor any other man observed him.

In order to become more familiar with Monna Belcolore, he was continually sending her gifts. At one time he sent her a bunch of fresh garlic bulbs, for he grew the best of anyone in the district in his garden, which he dug with his own hands; then a little basket of peas in their pods or a bunch of fresh onions or shallots. Choosing his time, he would gaze at her in a gloomy way and heap amorous reproaches on her, while she with rustic awkwardness pretended not to notice and went her way disdainfully; so that messer priest could not come to the point.

One afternoon when the priest was sauntering along he met Bentivegna del Mazzo with a laden ass; and after joking with him, asked him where he was going. Bentivegna replied:

"Why, father, I'm going into the city on business and I'm taking these things to Ser Bonacorri da Ginestreto, who is helping me about some lawsuit where I've got to appear before the clerk to the justice of the 'Sizes."

Said the priest:

"Well done, my son, go, with my blessing, and come back soon. And if you see Lapuccio or Naldino don't forget to tell them to bring the straps for my harness."

Bentivegna said it should be done, and as he went off in the direction of Florence the priest thought that now was the time to go to Belcolore and try his luck. So, putting his best foot forward, he made no pause until he reached her cottage, which he entered, saying:

"God bless this house—who is within?"

Belcolore, who was in the hay shed, heard him and said:

"O father, you're kindly welcome. But what are you doing out in this heat?"

"So God be good to me," replied the priest. "I came to spend a little time with you, for I met your good man going into the town."

Belcolore came down and took a seat and began to sift some cabbage seed which her husband had gathered.

"Ah, Belcolore," said the priest, "must you always make me die in this way?"

Belcolore giggled, and said:

"Why, what do I do?"

"You don't do anything," said the priest, "but you won't let me do to you what I want to do and what God commands."

"Get away with you!" said Belcolore. "Priests don't do such things."

"Yes, we do," said the priest, "and better than other men. Why not? And we are better workers than other men. Do you know why? Because we only grind at harvest time. But you'll find it out for yourself if you'll only lie still and let me go."

"What good would it do me," said Belcolore, "when all you priests are as mean as you can be?"

"I don't know," said the priest. "Ask what you want. Do you want a pair of shoes or some ribbons or a piece of fine cloth, or what do you want?"

"Right you are, brother!" said Belcolore. "I don't want any of those things, but if you are so fond of me will you do me a service, and I'll do what you want?"

"Say what you want," said the priest, "and I'll gladly do it."

Then said Belcolore:

"On Saturday I have to go to Florence, to hand in the wool I have spun and to have my spinning-wheel mended. If you'll lend me five lire, which I know you have, I can take out of pawn my dark petticoat and my best girdle which I had to take to uncle, and you know that without them I can't go to church or anywhere else; and then I'll always do what you want."

"So help me God," said the priest. "I haven't them with me; but trust me, and you shall have them gladly before Saturday."

"Yes," said Belcolore, "you're all great promisers, and keep your word not at all. Do you think you can treat me like Biliuzza, who went away with nothing but promises? God's Faith, it was that sent her on the streets. If you haven't got them, go and get them."

"Ah!" said the priest, "don't make me go back home now. I see that my luck has been so good that no one else is here, and perhaps when I came back someone would be here and interrupt us. I don't know when there will be such a good chance as now."

"Ah well!" said she. "If you want to go, go; if not, stay as you are."

The priest saw that she would not do what he wanted unless she were *salvum me fac,* and would do nothing *sine custodia;* so he said:

"I see you don't believe I would get them; to convince you I'll leave with you my cloak of Turkish cloth."

Belcolore lifted her head, and said:

"Yes? And what is your cloak worth?"

"What's it worth?" said the priest. "Why, it comes from Douai in Touai and some of our people would call it Fourai. Not a fortnight ago I paid seven lire for it to Lotto the old clothes man and made five soldi on the bargain, according to what Buglietto told me, and you know he's an expert in all such cloths."

"Oh, is it?" said Belcolore. "God help me, I should never have thought so; but give it me first."

Messer priest, who had shot his bolt, took off his cloak and gave it to her. And when she had put it away, she said:

"Father, come along to the hayloft. Nobody ever goes there."

There the priest gave her the sweetest flopping kisses and enjoyed her for a long space of time, making her a relative of the Lord God. He then departed in his cassock, as if he had been to a wedding; and returned to his church.

But when he reflected that all the candle-ends he collected in a whole year were not worth one half of five lire, he felt he had made a mistake, regretted having left his cloak behind, and began to think of some means of getting his cloak back for nothing. And since he was a very cunning fellow, he thought of a way of getting it back, which succeeded. The next day was a festival, and he sent a little boy to Monna Belcolore's house to ask her to lend him her stone mortar, because that morning Binguccio dal Poggio and Nuto Buglietti were going to dine with him and he wanted to make sauce. Belcolore sent him the mortar. And at dinner time when the priest knew Bentivegna del Mazzo and Belcolore would be eating, he sent for the parish clerk, and said:

"Take this mortar to Belcolore and say: 'The parson thanks you and will you send him back the cloak which the little boy left as a pledge?' "

The clerk went off to Belcolore's cottage with the mortar and found her at table with Bentivegna. He laid down the mortar and delivered his message. When Belcolore heard him ask for the cloak she tried to speak, but Bentivegna interrupted her angrily:

"So you take pledges from the parson, do you? By Christ, I'd like to give you a good wipe in the nose. Give it back at once, and a pox on you. And henceforth if he wants anything of ours, even the ass, don't you say 'No' to him!"

Belcolore got up grumbling and went to the chest under the bed, took out the cloak, and as she gave it to the clerk, she said:

"Say to the priest: 'Belcolore says that she prays God you may never again grind sauce in her mortar, not having done her any honour in this.' "

The clerk went off with the cloak and delivered the message to the priest, who said, laughing:

"When you see her, tell her that if she won't lend the mortar, I won't lend the pestle—tit for tat."

Bentivegna supposed his wife said these words because he had scolded her, and thought no more about them. But Belcolore was furious with the parson, and would not speak to him until vintage time. Then, after threatening to send the priest into the biggest devil's mouth, she made it up with him over new wine and hot chestnuts, and thereafter they often gorged together. Instead of the five lire the priest mended her cymbals and hung her up a large bell; and she was well satisfied.

## THIRD TALE

*Calandrino, Bruno and Buffalmacco go about Mugnone looking for the magic stone, Heliotrope, and Calandrino thinks he has found it. He returns home laden with stones and his wife scolds him; in anger he beats her and tells his companions what they know better than he*

The ladies laughed extremely at Pamfilo's tale, and the queen then ordered Elisa to follow next. Still laughing, she began thus:

Fair ladies, I do not know if my little tale, which is as true as it is amusing, will make you laugh as much as Pamfilo's; but I shall do my best.

Our city has always abounded in strange and various odd customs. Not so long ago there lived in it a painter called Calandrino, a simple-minded man of eccentric habit who spent much of his time with two other painters, named Bruno and Buffalmacco. They were very amusing men, but in other respects alert and sensible, and passed their time with Calandrino because they found his habits and simple-minded ways very funny.

At the same time there lived in Florence a young man named Maso del Saggio, who had an exceptional charm in everything he did, and who moreover was very astute and clever. Hearing of Calandrino's simplicity, he determined to amuse himself by playing some trick on the man or by making him believe some fantastic thing.

One day this young man saw Calandrino in the church of San Giovanni, looking at the paintings and the inlay work of the canopy which is over the high altar in that church, not long before erected there; and he thought this was a good place and time to carry out his idea. He informed the person with him of what he intended to do, and together they halted near the place where Calandrino was seated; pretending not to see him, they began to talk about the occult qualities of certain stones, of which Maso talked as confidently as if he had been some great and famous jeweller. Calandrino listened to what they were saying, and, perceiving after a time that their talk was not intended to be secret, joined them, much to Maso's delight. Calandrino, following up their talk, asked Maso where these magic stones could be found. Maso replied that they occurred in Nomansland, a country of the Baschi, in a district which is called Bengodi, where they tie the vines with sausages and you can buy a goose for a cent and have the gosling with it. Moreover, in that country there was a mountain of grated Parmesan cheese, inhabited by people who did nothing but make macaroni and ravioli, which they cooked in chicken broth and then threw on the ground, and those who can pick up most get most. Nearby there was a stream of white wine, the best ever drunk, without a drop of water in it.

"Oh," said Calandrino, "that sounds a great country. But what do they do with all the chickens they cook?"

"All the Baschi eat them," replied Maso.

"Were you ever there?" asked Calandrino.

"Was I ever there?" said Maso. "I've been there thousands of times."

"How many miles away is it?" asked Calandrino.

"More than a thousand, going night and day," replied Maso.

"It must be further off than the Abruzzi," said Calandrino.

"Ah! indeed," replied Maso, "that it is."

The simple-minded Calandrino, observing that Maso made these remarks with a sober face and without laughing, believed them as the most manifest truth, and said:

"It's too far off for me. But if it were nearer, I should like to go there once with you to see the macaroni tumbling down, and get a bellyful of it. But tell me, are there none of those occult stones in that country?"

"Yes," replied Maso, "it contains two stones of the greatest occult powers. One is the grinding-stone of Settignano and Montisci, by whose virtue flour is made; and so they say in that country that favours come from God and the millstones from Montisci. But there are so many of these stones here that we think as little of them as they do of emeralds, of which they have a mountain higher than Mount Morello which shines by night, good Lord! And you must know that anyone who embellishes millstones and sets them in a ring before a hole is bored in them, and takes them to the Sultan, may have anything he asks for. The other is a stone which we jewellers call Heliotrope, a stone of the greatest powers, for whoever carries it about on him is invisible to others."

"These are great virtues," said Calandrino, "but where is the second stone found?"

Maso replied that they could be found in the district of Mugnone.

"How large are they?" asked Calandrino. "And what colour?"

"They're of different sizes," replied Maso, "some large and some small, but they're all of a blackish colour."

Calandrino noted all these things and then left Maso, pretending that he had business, but determined to look for these stones. But he made up his mind to do nothing without the knowledge of Bruno aond Buffalmacco, who were his special friends. So he went looking for them at once, and wasted the whole morning doing so, in order that they might go and look for the stones before anybody else. Finally, when it was already past Nones, he remembered that they were working in the monastery of the nuns of Faenza, and in spite of the great heat he abandoned his own work and almost ran there. He called them down, and spoke to them thus:

"My friends, if you will trust in me, we can become the richest men in Florence, for I have heard from a man worthy of belief that in Mugnone there exists a stone which makes everyone who wears it invisible. Therefore I think that we ought to go and look for it before anyone else goes. We shall certainly find it, because I know it. When we've got it, all we have to do is to put it in our pockets and go up to the tables of the money-changers (which, as you know, are always covered with crowns and florins) and take as many as we want. Nobody will see us. And so we shall suddenly get rich, without having to spend the whole day daubing walls like snails."

Bruno and Buffalmacco laughed inwardly when they heard this, and, after exchanging glances, pretended to be greatly surprised and praised Calandrino's plan. Buffalmacco asked what was the name of the stone. Calandrino, who was a stupid fellow, had already forgotten the name, but he replied:

"What does the name matter when we know its powers? I think we ought to go and look for it at once."

"Well," said Bruno, "but what is its shape?"

"They're of no particular shape," said Calandrino, "but they're all blackish. So I think we simply have to pick up all the black stones we see until we come upon it. Don't let's waste any more time, but start now."

"Wait a moment," said Bruno; and turning to Buffalmacco, he added: "I think Calandrino speaks well. But I don't think this is the time to go, because the sun is high over Mugnone and has dried all the stones, so that the stones there now look white whereas in the morning, before the sun has dried them, they look black. Moreover, there are a lot of people now working in the Mugnone who would see us and might guess what we were after and do the same themselves and perhaps find the stones, so that we should have our labour for nothing. If you agree, I think we should go in the early morning when it is easier to distinguish the black from the white, and on a feast day when there will be nobody to see us."

Buffalmacco praised Bruno's idea, and Calandrino agreed to it. They arranged that they would all meet on Sunday morning, and go to look for the occult stone. But above everything Calandrino besought them not to speak of the matter to anyone, because he was sworn to secrecy. And when they had promised this, he told them what he had heard about the country of the Bengodi, vowing on his oath that it was all true.

After Calandrino left them, they arranged together what they would do. Calandrino looked forward eagerly to Sunday morning; and when it came he got up very early, called his friends, and set out for Mugnone by way of the Porta San Gallo to look for the stone. Calandrino in his eagerness went on ahead of them, darting to one side and the other, and whenever he saw a black stone he fell upon it and put it in the fold of his gown.

His friends followed after him, occasionally picking up a stone, but Calandrino had not gone far before he had already filled his bosom with stones. Therefore he tucked up the skirts of his tunic (which was not in the narrow Flemish style) and fastened them to his girdle to make a large bag, which he soon filled; and after that he made another bag of his cloak which he also filled.

Buffalmacco and Bruno saw that Calandrino was laden with stones and that it was near dinner time, and so, in accordance with their plan, Bruno said:

"Where's Calandrino?"

Buffalmacco could see him close at hand but turned round, looking in every direction, and said:

"I don't know. But he wasn't far away just now."

"Well," said Bruno, "I think he's now at home having dinner, and has left us like idiots to go looking for black stones all over Mugnone."

"He was quite right," said Buffalmacco, "to play a trick on us and leave us here, since we were so silly as to believe him. Bah! Who but ourselves would have been so stupid as to believe that such a valuable stone could be found in Mugnone?"

Hearing their talk, Calandrino imagined that he had found the stone and that its magic virtue prevented them from seeing him, although he was near at hand. Delighted at his luck, he said not a word but made up his mind to go home, and turned his steps in that direction. Seeing this, Buffalmacco said:

"What shall we do? Shall we go home?"

"Let us go," said Bruno, "but I vow to God that Calandrino shall never catch me again. If he were here, as he was all morning, I'd give him such a knock on the heel with this stone that he'd remember this trick for a month."

As he spoke he lifted his arm and gave Calandrino a whack on the heel. At the pain Calandrino lifted his foot and gasped, but yet was silent, and went on his way. Buffalmacco then took one of the stones he had picked up, and said:

"Look at this stone. I wish I could hit Calandrino in the back with it."

And he threw the stone so that it hit Calandrino full in the back. In short, with one thing and another, they pelted Calandrino all the way from Mugnone to Porta San Gallo. There, they threw down the stones they had been carrying, went over to the customs guards and let them into the joke. And, pretending not to see Calandrino, the guards let him pass through amid shouts of laughter. Without halting, Calandrino went straight to his home, which was in the Canto alla Macina. And Fortune so favoured the jest that nobody spoke to him while he was going through the streets, for hardly anyone was about, and they were all at dinner. And so Calandrino entered his house with his burden. His wife, a handsome and worthy woman named Tessa, happened to meet him at the head of the stairs; and, being angry at his long absence, said to him scoldingly:

"What the devil brings you back when everyone else has finished dinner?"

At these words Calandrino saw that he was visible to her, and full of rage and grief said:

"Ah! You vile woman, are you there? You've ruined me, but by God's faith I'll pay you back!"

Whereupon he ran into a little room and got rid of all the stones he had brought with him, and then rushed at his wife in beastly wise, took her by the hair, threw her on the ground, kicked and beat her all over with his fists and feet, and left no cap on her head and not a bone unbruised, in spite of all her begging for mercy with clasped hands.

Buffalmacco and Bruno laughed over the joke with the guards for a time, and then slowly followed at some distance behind Calandrino. When they reached his door they heard the fierce beating he was giving his wife, and called to him as if they had only just met him. Calandrino came to the window, all breathless and red-faced and sweaty, and told them to come up. Pretending to be a little annoyed, they went upstairs and found the room full of stones, and in one corner the wife pitifully weeping, all ruffled and torn and bruised and pale, and Calandrino sitting unbuttoned in the other, panting like a man exhausted. After gazing at him, they said:

"What's all this, Calandrino? Are you going to build a wall with all these stones?" And then they added: "And what's the matter with Monna Tessa? You seem to have beaten her. What's it all about?"

Calandrino, wearied with the weight of the stones and by

the rage with which he had beaten his wife and by grief at having lost (as he thought) his good luck, could not fetch up breath enough to form words for an answer. And so Buffalmacco went on:

"Calandrino, if you were angry with someone else, you shouldn't make a fool of us in this way. You took us out to look for precious stones and then without a word left us in Mugnone and came home, which displeases us very much. But this shall be the last time you do such a thing to us."

Calandrino made an effort and replied:

"Don't be angry, my friends, it all happened differently from what you think. Unlucky that I am! I found the stone! Do you want me to prove it? When you first asked each other where I was, I was standing not ten yards from you; and when I saw you start home and that you could not see me, I went on a little ahead, and so reached here just before you."

Then, beginning at the start, he told them everything they had said and done, and showed them the marks made on his back and heel by the stones; and then went on:

"I came in the town gate with all these stones and no one said a word to me, though you know how annoying and fussy those customs guards are about seeing everything. Moreover, I met several of my friends in the streets who always have a joke for me and offer me a drink, and not one of them said a word to me, but passed without seeing me. Finally I got home, and that devil of a cursed woman appeared before me and saw me, because, as you know full well, women deprive all things of their virtue. And so I, who might have called myself the luckiest man in Florence, became the most unlucky. So I beat her as hard as I could, and I don't know why I didn't slit her veins for her. Cursed be the hour when first I saw her and when she came into this house!"

And, his anger rising up again, he was about to get up and beat her once more.

As Buffalmacco and Bruno listened to him, they pretended to be greatly amazed and confirmed all Calandrino said; and wanted so much to laugh that they nearly burst. But when he got up in a fury to beat his wife again, they restrained him, saying that it was no fault in her, but rather in him, for, since he knew that women make things lose their virtue, he ought to have told her not to come near him that day. This piece of foresight God had not vouchsafed him, either because the luck was not to be his or because he had it in mind to cheat his friends, whom he should have told as soon as he discovered that he had found the stone.

After many words and much trouble they reconciled the weeping wife with him and departed, leaving him all melancholy in a house full of stones.

## FOURTH TALE

*The Canon of Fiesole falls in love with a widow who does not love him. He lies with her maid, thinking it is she; the lady's brothers bring the Bishop to see him*

Elisa told her tale to the great delight of the company, and when she had brought it to an end the queen turned to Emilia and thus showed her that she was to follow Elisa. Accordingly, she began thus:

Worthy ladies, several of the tales we have told have showed how priests, friars and other clerics torment our minds. But since whatever we may say, more will remain to say, I mean to tell you a tale of a Canon who, despite the whole world, determined to have a certain lady, whether she wanted him or not. And she, like a wise woman, treated him as he deserved.

As you all know, Fiesole, whose hilltop we can see from here, is a very ancient city and was once very large. Now it has fallen into ruins, but still has its Bishop. Near its chief church, a widowed lady, named Monna Piccarda, had a farm with a small house. Since she was a wealthy woman, she spent most of the year there with her two brothers, who were courteous and pleasant young men.

The lady was still young and pretty and attractive, and as she frequented his church the Canon fell violently in love with her. After some time his passion reached such a height that he told the lady how much he loved her, and begged her to content his love, and to love him as he loved her.

This Canon was a man old in years, but very young in wits, offensive and haughty, thinking himself capable of anything. His manners and behaviour were so ungainly and displeasing, and he himself so tedious and boring that nobody liked him. There was nobody who liked him less than this lady, who hated him more than a headache. And so, being a wise woman, she replied:

"Messer, it should be very dear to me to have your love, and I ought to love you and will gladly love you; but there should never be any unchastity in the love between us. You are my spiritual father and a priest, and close upon old age, all of which things ought to make you modest and chaste. Moreover, I am no longer a girl, to whom such love affairs are suitable, but a widow. You know yourself what modesty is demanded of widows, and therefore you must excuse me if I never love you in the way you request, nor ever wish to be loved in that way by you."

The Canon could get no more out of her at that time, but did not allow himself to be cast down or overcome at the first attack. With his wonted impudence he solicited her by letter and message, and by word of mouth when he saw her come to church. This courtship became so annoying to the lady that she made up her mind to get rid of him in the way he deserved, since she could do so in no other way. But she did nothing until she had first informed her brothers. She told them what the Canon had proposed to her and what she intended to do, and obtained full permission from them to proceed. A few days later she went to church; as soon as the Canon saw her he came to meet her, and as usual entered into familiar talk with her. When the lady saw him coming, she looked at him kindly, and let him draw her to one side. After the Canon had talked a great deal in his usual style, the lady heaved a deep sigh and said:

"Messer, I have heard it said that if any castle is attacked every day it is bound to be taken at last; and I see the same thing has happened to me. You have attacked me at one time with soft words, and then with one charming thing and another, until you have broken down my determination, and I am ready to be yours since you care so much for me."

The Canon in great joy replied:

"Madonna, all my thanks! To tell you the truth, I have marvelled how you held out so long, since this never happened to me with any woman before. I've often said to myself: 'If women were silver, they would not be coined into money, since none of them can resist the hammer.' But never mind that—when and where can we be together?"

"My sweet lord," replied the lady, "the 'when' may be whenever you please, since I have no husband to whom I must render an account of my nights; but I don't know where."

"Why not," said the Canon, "in your house?"

"Messer," replied the lady, "you know I have two young brothers, who go in and out of the house day and night with their friends. My house is not very large and so it cannot be there, unless you will be quite mute without saying a word or making any noise, and act in the dark like the blind. If you agree to this, it may be in my house, for they never come into my room; but their room is so near mine that you cannot utter a word without being overheard."

"Madonna," said the Canon, "never mind that for one or two nights, until I can think of somewhere we can be together more comfortably."

"Messer," said the lady, "it is for you to decide. But I beg you that all this may be secret, and no word of it ever breathed."

"Madonna," replied the Canon, "have no fear about that; and if possible, let us be together tonight."

"It shall be so," said the lady; and then after arranging with him how and when he should come, she returned home.

The lady had a maid-servant, who was not very young and had the ugliest and most deformed face you ever beheld. She had a large snub nose and a wry mouth and thick lips and large irregular teeth, and squinted; her eyes were always running, and her colour was green and yellow; so she looked as if she had lived in an unhealthy place like Sinigaglia, instead of in Fiesole. Moreover, she had hip disease and was deformed on one side. Her name was Ciuta, but everyone called her Ciutazza, on account of her yellow complexion. Although she was deformed in person, she was rather mischievous. The lady sent for her, and said:

"Ciutazza, if you will do me a service tonight, I shall give you a fine new chemise."

"Madonna," said Ciutazza at the mention of the chemise, "I would throw myself into the fire for a new chemise."

"Well," said the lady, "I want you to lie with a man tonight, in my bed, and to caress him. Take care not to speak a word, so that you are not heard by my brothers who sleep in the next room, as you know. And then I'll give you the chemise."

"Oh!" said Ciutazza. "If necessary, I'd sleep with six men, let alone one."

That evening the Canon came along as arranged, and the two young brothers in concert with the lady were in their room and made themselves heard. So the Canon entered the lady's room very quietly in the dark and went to bed as she had told him to do; and Ciutazza, who had been well coached by the lady in what she was to do, also got into bed. Messer Canon, thinking he had the lady beside him, took Ciutazza in his arms and kissed her without saying a word, and she kissed him. The Canon then began to take his pleasure of her, enjoying the possession of what he had so long desired.

After this, the lady made her brothers do the remainder of what she had arranged, and so they softly left their room and went out to the public square. Here Fortune was more favourable to them than they expected; for, since it was very hot, the Bishop had asked for the two young men so that he might rest and drink with them at their house. But when he saw them, he told them what he wished; and so they went into a small cool courtyard with many lights round them, and drank their good wine in peace. After drinking, the young men said:

"My lord, you have done us the favour of visiting our little house, to which we meant to invite you when we met you. And now you are here we should like you to look at a little thing we want to show you."

The Bishop replied that he would gladly do so. One of the brothers took a torch and went ahead, followed by the Bishop and all the others; and led them to the bedroom where Messer Canon was lying with Ciutazza. To make up time he had ridden posthaste and before they arrived he had already ridden more than three miles. But being consequently a little tired, he was resting with Ciutazza in his arms, in spite of the heat.

The young man entered the room with the torch in his hand, and then the Bishop and all the others; and they were showed the Canon lying with Ciutazza in his arms. This awoke Messer Canon; and when he saw the light and so many people about him, he plunged his head under the bedclothes in great shame and terror. But the Bishop reproved him sternly, and made him look out from the clothes and see with whom he had been lying.

The Canon saw the lady's deceit, and was in the deepest distress at this and at the insult which he felt had been offered him. At the Bishop's command he was forced to dress himself, and was sent off to his own house under a guard to endure severe punishment for the sin he had committed.

The Bishop then wished to know how this had come about, and why he had come there to lie with Ciutazza. The two brothers then told him the whole story; and when the Bishop had heard it he greatly commended the lady and the two young men who, being unwilling to stain their hands with a priest's blood, had treated him in the way he deserved.

The Bishop made the Canon bewail his sin for forty days, but love and shame made him bewail it more than forty-nine days. Moreover, for a long time he could never go out in the street without the little boys pointing at him and screaming:

"Look at the man who lay with Ciutazza!"

Which angered him so much that it nearly sent him crazy. Thus the worthy lady rid herself of the impudent Canon, and Ciutazza earned a chemise and a good night.

## FIFTH TALE

*Three young men take the breeches from a judge of the Marches in Florence while he is on the bench*

When Emilia finished her tale, the widow was praised by them all; the queen then looked at Filostrato, saying:

"It is now your turn."

He immediately replied that he was ready, and began thus:

Delightful ladies, the young man named Maso del Saggio, mentioned just now by Elisa, has caused me to abandon the tale I meant to tell you for another one about him and his friends; for although it is immodest, since it contains words which you blush to use, yet it is so amusing that I shall tell it.

As you all know, there often come to our city, Rectors from the Marches, who are usually mean-spirited men of such wretched and poverty-stricken lives that they seem mere lousy fellows. In their wretched avarice they bring along with them a train of judges and notaries, who seem to have come from the plough and the last rather than from the law schools.

Well, one of these men came to us as Governor, and among the many judges he brought with him was one named Messer Niccola da San Lepidio who looked more like a locksmith than anything else; and this man sat with the other judges to hear criminal cases.

Although the citizens may have nothing whatever to do in the Court, yet they often go there; and so one morning Maso del Saggio happened to be there, looking for a friend of his. He saw Messer Niccola as he sat there and thought him a queer looking bird, and so gazed more closely at him. He saw that Messer Niccola had a dirty judge's cap on his head and a pen-case at his girdle, and a waistcoat longer than his coat, and a number of other things unbefitting a respectable man. But the most notable thing of all in Maso's opinion was the judge's pair of breeches, for as he sat there his robes were so narrow that they opened in front while the seat of his breeches came halfway down his legs. Without spending more time in gazing, Maso abandoned his search for the first friend and went to look for others. He found two, named Ribi and Matteuzzo, who were just as merry fellows as Maso himself, and said to them:

"Come along to the Court with me, I want to show you the strangest scarecrow you ever beheld."

So he took them to the Court, and showed them the judge and his breeches. They laughed long at the sight, and then going nearer to the bench where the judge sat, they saw they could easily get underneath it. Moreover, they saw that the plank on which the judge's feet rested was so rotten that they could easily get a hand and an arm through it. Thereupon Maso said to his friends:

"Let's pull his breeches off—it can easily be done."

Each of the friends saw at once how it could be done. So, having arranged what they would do and say, they returned there next morning. When the Court was full of people Matteuzzo, without letting anyone see him, got under the bench and placed himself just under the point where the judge's feet rested. Maso went up to the judge on one side and Ribi on the other, and each of them took hold of part of his garments. Said Maso:

"Messer, O messer! I beg you, in God's name, before that great thief on the other side of you escapes, make him give me back the pair of my gaiters he's sneaked from me, and he says he didn't, and not a month ago I saw him repairing them."

Ribi, on the other side, protested loudly:

"Messer, don't believe him, he's a low glutton, and because he knows I came to claim a bag he stole from me, he brings up this business of gaiters which I've had in my house for ages. And if you don't believe me I can bring my witnesses, Trecca my neighbour, and Grassa the tripe-woman, and a man who sweeps up the dirt from Santa

Maria a Verzaia who saw him when he came back from the country."

Maso kept interrupting Ribi, and he yelled and Ribi yelled. As the judge stood up nearer to them to hear them better Matteuzzo chose his time and, putting his hand through the rotten board, grasped the seat of the judge's breeches, and pulled hard. The breeches came off at once because the judge was a very thin man. As soon as he felt them go, in his bewilderment he tried to draw the folds of his robe about him and then sit down. But Maso and Ribi kept pulling at his robe, and shouting:

"Messer, you do basely not to right me here and not to listen to me and to try to send me away. In this country such small matters as this are dealt with summarily."

And they continued pulling at his robes until everyone in Court saw that he had no breeches on. As for Matteuzzo, he dropped them as soon as he got them, and went off without being seen by anyone. Ribi, thinking matters had gone far enough, said:

"I vow to God I'll appeal to the higher Court."

And Maso, dropping the robe, said:

"No, I shall keep coming back here until I find you less perplexed than you seem to be today."

And then they both got away as quickly as they could. The judge, whose breeches had been pulled off in everyone's presence, then seemed to awake from sleep and discovered the trick played on him. He asked what had become of the men who were disputing about the gaiters and the bag. When they could not be found, he swore by God's guts that he would know whether it was a custom in Florence to pull off a judge's breeches when he was seated on the bench of justice.

The Governor made a great uproar about the matter when he heard of it. But when his friends pointed out to him that this had only been done to show him that the Florentines knew he had brought ploughmen instead of judges with him, for cheapness' sake, he said no more, and the affair went no further.

## SIXTH TALE

*Bruno and Buffalmacco steal a pig from Calandrino. They persuade him to try to discover the thief with ginger pills and white wine; they give him two pills made of aloes, whereby it appears that he stole the pig. They make him pay under threat of telling his wife*

As soon as Filostrato's tale—which aroused much laughter —was finished, the queen ordered Filomena to speak next, and she began thus:

Graceful ladies, Filostrato was led by Maso's name to tell the story you just heard, and in the same way I am led by Calandrino's name to tell you a tale about him and his friends which I think will amuse you.

There is no need for me to tell you who Calandrino, Bruno and Buffalmacco were, for you have already heard. So, proceeding, I say that Calandrino had a little farm not far from Florence, which came to him as his wife's dowry. Among the things he derived from it he had a pig every year, and in December he and his wife always went to the country to kill and salt down the pig.

On one occasion, when his wife was unwell, Calandrino went down alone to kill the pig. When Bruno and Buffalmacco heard of it and knew that his wife would not be with him, they went and stayed with a priest, a great friend of theirs, who was a neighbour of Calandrino's. On the morning of the day they arrived, Calandrino had killed the pig; and when he saw them with the priest, he said:

"You are very welcome. I'd like you to see what a good farmer I am."

So he took them to his house, and showed them the pig. They saw the pig was a very fine one, and heard from Calandrino that he intended to salt it down for his family. Then said Bruno:

"Bah! What a fool you are! Sell it and let us enjoy the money, and you can tell your wife it was stolen."

"No," said Calandrino, "she wouldn't believe me, and she'd drive me out of the house. Don't bother me, I won't do it."

They talked to him a great deal, but unavailingly. Calandrino asked them to supper, but so grudgingly that they refused and went away. Said Bruno to Buffalmacco:

"Shall we steal the pig tonight?"

"How can we?" asked Buffalmacco.

"I can see how to do it," said Bruno, "if it is not moved from where it is now."

"Very well," said Buffalmacco, "we'll do it. Why shouldn't we? And then we can make merry over it with the priest."

The priest said he liked the idea, and Bruno said:

"We must make use of a little art here. Buffalmacco, you know how mean Calandrino is, and how much he likes to drink when other people pay. Let us go and take him to the tavern, and there the priest will pretend to pay for us all to do him honour and will refuse to let him pay anything. He'll get drunk, and it will then be easy to steal the pig since he's alone in the house.

And they did as Bruno suggested. When Calandrino saw that the priest would not allow him to pay, he went at the drink, and although he didn't need a great deal he tanked himself up well. It was already late when they left the tavern and without eating any supper, Calandrino went home to bed. He thought he had locked the door, but in fact left it open.

Buffalmacco and Bruno went and supped with the priest, and after supper they took certain tools to break into the house as Bruno had planned, and set out quietly. But when they found the door open, they went straight in, took down the pig and carried it to the priest's house. There they hid it, and went to bed.

Next morning, when the wine had cleared from Calandrino's head, he got up; and as soon as he went downstairs he found his pig gone and the door open. So he went about asking first one and then another if they had got his pig, and when he could not find it, he began to make a great uproar—oh! alas! his pig was stolen!

Bruno and Buffalmacco got up and went to Calandrino's house to hear what he would have to say about the pig. As soon as he saw them, he called to them, almost in tears, and said:

"Alas, my friends, my pig has been stolen!"

Bruno went up and whispered to him:

"A wonder that you've been wise once in your life!"

"Alas," said Calandrino, "I'm speaking the truth."

"That's the way," said Bruno, "make a fuss, and it'll look as if it were true."

Calandrino yelled louder at him:

"By God's body, I say it really has been stolen from me!"

"That's right, that's right," said Bruno, "that's the way to do it, shout, make a noise, and it'll look as if it were true."

"You'll make me wish my soul to the devil!" said Calandrino. "I say you don't understand me. May I be hanged if the pig hasn't really been stolen."

"Why!" said Bruno, "how can that be? I saw it here last night. Do you want to make me believe it has flown away?"

"It's as I say," said Calandrino.

"Bah!" said Bruno. "Can it really be?"

"It certainly is," said Calandrino. "I've been robbed, and I don't remember how I came home last night. My wife will never believe me, and even if she does I shall never get any peace again."

"God help me," said Bruno, "this is a misfortune, if it's true. But you know, Calandrino, that last night I told you to behave in this way. I don't want you to deceive your wife and us at the same time."

Calandrino then shrieked:

"Why do you put me in despair, and make me curse God and the Saints and those with them? I tell you the pig was stolen from me last night."

"If that's so," said Buffalmacco, "we must try to find some way to get it back, if possible."

"And what way can be found?" asked Calandrino.

"Well," said Buffalmacco, "the person who stole your pig did not come from India to do it. It must have been one of your neighbours. If you can get them together, I could make the test of bread and cheese on them, and we should see at once who has it."

"Yes," said Bruno, "you could easily make some of the gentry round here take bread and cheese! I'm certain one of them has it, and they would guess what we were about, and refuse to come."

"Then what's to be done?" said Buffalmacco.

"You will see me do it," said Bruno, "with ginger pills and white wine, which you must invite them to drink. They won't suspect that and will come. We can have the ginger pills blessed, like bread and cheese."

"You're right," said Buffalmacco. "What do you think about it, Calandrino? Do you want us to do it?"

"I beg you to do it for the love of God," said Calandrino. "I feel I should be half consoled if I knew who has the pig."

"Very well," said Bruno, "I'm ready to go to Florence

to get you the necessary things, if you will give me the money."

Calandrino had about forty soldi, which he gave to Bruno, who went off to a special friend of his in Florence and bought a pound of ginger pills and got his friend to make him up two strong aloe pills. He then made him cover them with sugar like the other pills, and put a certain mark on them so that he might recognise them and not lose or mislay them. In addition he bought a flask of good white wine, and returned to Calandrino in the country, and said:

"Tomorrow, invite everyone you suspect to come and drink with you. Tomorrow is a festival, so everyone will come. Tonight Buffalmacco and I will put the right spell on the pills and bring them to your house tomorrow. For love of you I myself will administer them, and I'll say and do everything necessary."

Calandrino invited them, and the next morning collected together under the elm near the church a large gathering of young Florentines (who were in the country), and of peasants. Bruno and Buffalmacco came along with their box of pills and the flask of wine, and when they had arranged everyone in a circle, Bruno said:

"Gentlemen, I must tell you the reason why you are here, so that if you are displeased you may have no reason to complain of me. Last night Calandrino here had his pig taken from him, and cannot find who has it. Now, nobody can have taken it except one of us here present, and so, to find out who took the pig, I am going to give a pill to each of us and a drink of wine. You must know that whoever has the pig will not be able to chew the pill but will find it more bitter than poison and will spit it out. Therefore, to avoid this shame falling on one of you in public, it would perhaps be better for the man who took the pig to confess it to the priest, and I will refrain from this test."

But everyone present said he was willing to eat a pill. So Bruno ranged them up, Calandrino among them, and beginning at one end gave each of them a pill. When he came to Calandrino he took one of the bitter pills and put it in his hand. Calandrino at once lifted it to his mouth and began to chew it, but as soon as his tongue tasted the aloes he could not endure the bitterness, and spat it out. Everyone was watching everyone else to see who would spit out the pill. Bruno had not finished handing them out, and pretended not to notice; but when he heard them saying: "Why, Calandrino, what does this mean?" he turned round, and, seeing that Calandrino had spat out his pill, said:

"Wait a minute, perhaps something else made him spit it out; take another one."

And he put the second bitter pill in his mouth, and went on handing out the others. Calandrino found this pill far more bitter than the first. But, being ashamed to spit it out, he kept it in his mouth after chewing it a little, and the bitterness made him shed tears as big as hazel-nuts. Finally, unable to endure it any longer, he spat it out like the first pill.

Buffalmacco was giving drinks to Bruno and the rest of the company; and when they saw this they all said that Calandrino must certainly have stolen his own pig. And some of those present sharply reproved him. When they had all gone, and only Bruno and Buffalmacco were left with Calandrino, Buffalmacco said:

"I was certain all along that you had it, and that you pretended you were robbed so that you wouldn't have to stand us a drink."

Calandrino, who had not yet got rid of the bitterness of the aloes, swore that he had not got the pig, but Buffalmacco said:

"How much did you get for it, you dirty fellow? Six florins?"

At this Calandrino was in despair, and Bruno said:

"Now look here, Calandrino, there was a fellow here that ate and drank with us and who told me that you have a little girl here whom you keep and give what you can. He was certain that you had sent her this pig. You are very skilled at taking people in. You once took us out to Mugnone to collect black stones, and after sending us on a fool's errand you left us in the lurch and tried to make us believe that you had found the stone. Now, with all your vows you try to make other people believe that the pig was stolen, when you've given it away or sold it. We have had enough of your tricks and know them. You can't play them any longer. Now, we spent a lot of time and trouble in saying spells over the pills, and either you must give us a couple of brace of capons or we shall tell Monna Tessa the whole story."

Calandrino saw they would not believe him, and felt that he had had enough trouble without having his wife's scoldings into the bargain; so he gave them the two brace of capons. After they had salted the pig, the pair of them returned to Florence, leaving Calandrino with the loss and the laugh against him.

## SEVENTH TALE

*A scholar is in love with a widow who loves someone else and makes him wait for her a whole winter's night in the snow. By a device of his he makes her spend a whole July day naked on a tower in the sun, exposed to flies and gadflies*

The ladies laughed greatly at poor Calandrino, and would have laughed still more if they had not been sorry to see him lose the capons as well as the pig. When the tale was ended, the queen ordered Pampinea to tell her tale; and she immediately began thus:

Dearest ladies, it often happens that the trickster is tricked, and so it is not very wise to delight in such games. In several tales we have laughed at the tricks played, but no one has told us of vengeance taken for a trick. Now, I intend that you shall feel some sympathy for the just retribution which fell upon a woman of our town, whose trick recoiled on her own head and put her in danger of death. It will not be useless for you to hear this, because it will make you cautious in playing tricks on others; and thus will make you wise.

Not many years ago in Florence there was a young woman named Elena, beautiful in person, haughty in spirit, well born, and suitably provided with this world's goods. She was a widow, but would never remarry, for she was in love with a handsome and pleasant young man of her choice. Being free from all other cares, she frequently enjoyed herself with him, by the assistance of a maid-servant whom she greatly trusted.

About this time a young nobleman of our city named Rinieri returned to Florence, after studying for a long time in Paris, not to peddle out his learning again for money as so many do, but to know the reason of things and their causes, a thing most befitting gentlemen. And there he lived decently, much honoured for his noble birth and learning.

But as often happens, those who have most intelligence in these deep matters are most swiftly snared in love. Thus

it befell with Rinieri. One day as he was going along the
street to a feast, this Elena appeared before his eyes, dressed
in black as our widows are wont to be; and in his judgment
she was more beautiful and charming than any woman he
had ever seen. He thought to himself that the man to whom
God granted the favour of holding her naked in his arms
might indeed call himself blessed. He gazed at her secretly
time and again; and, knowing that great and precious things
are not to be acquired without labour, he determined to
give all his attention and care to pleasing her, so that by
pleasing her he might obtain her love and thereby enjoy her.

The young lady did not keep her eyes fixed on the ground,
but esteeming herself as much as (and indeed more than)
she was worth, gazed about her with artful glances; and
soon noticed the delight with which he looked upon her. She
said laughingly to herself about Rinieri: "I shall not have
come here in vain today, for, if I am not mistaken, I have
caught a simpleton by the nose." She then began to glance
at him out of the corners of her eyes, and as far as she
could, strove to show him that she was interested in him.
Moreover, she thought that the more men were taken with
her beauty the more highly it would be prized, especially by
the man to whom she had given her love.

The learned scholar put aside all his thoughts of philosophy, and turned his mind wholly upon her. Thinking to
please her he began to pass to and fro before her house,
under various pretexts. The lady, who was vainglorious of
this conquest for the reasons before mentioned, often allowed him to see her. The scholar therefore found means to
speak with her maid-servant, and, telling her of his love,
begged her to use her influence with the lady to obtain him
her favours. The servant made large promises, and told
everything to the lady, who heard it all with shrieks of
laughter, and said:

"Did you see where he lost the wisdom he brought back
from Paris? Well, let us give him what he wants. The next
time he speaks to you, tell him I love him much more than
he loves me, but I must guard my chastity so that I may
go about among other women with an open countenance;
and he, if he is as wise a man as they say, ought to think
the more of me for it."

Ah, the bad silly woman! She did not know, ladies, what
it is to contend with a scholar.

The happy scholar then proceeded to more urgent entreaties, to writing letters and sending gifts. They were all
accepted, but only general answers were returned. And in

this way he was kept dangling for a long time. Finally, she told her lover all about it, and he was a little angry with her and rather jealous; so, to show him that he was wrong to suspect her, she sent her servant to the scholar (who was becoming more urgent) to say to him that she had never had time to do anything to please him since he had told her of his love, but that she hoped to be with him at Christmas, which was then near at hand. Therefore, if he wished, he should come to her courtyard on the evening after Christmas, and she would meet him there as soon as she could.

The scholar was the happiest of men at this, and went to the lady's house at the appointed time. The servant took him to a courtyard and locked him in, and he there awaited the lady. She had sent for her lover that evening, and, after supping merrily with him, told him what she had planned to do that night, adding:

"And you will be able to see how much I love the man of whom you have been so foolishly jealous."

The lover heard this with great satisfaction, and was eager to see carried out what the lady had told him she meant to do. The day before there had been a heavy fall of snow and everything was covered with it, so that the scholar had not been long in the courtyard when he began to feel colder than he would have wished. But he put up with it patiently, expecting speedy comfort.

After some time the lady said to her lover:

"Come into this room and let us look through the little window and see what the man you are jealous of is doing, and hear what he says to the servant whom I have sent down to talk to him."

They therefore went to the little window where they could see without being seen, and heard the servant talking to Rinieri, and saying:

"Rinieri, my mistress is in the greatest trouble. One of her brothers has arrived here tonight and has been talking to her for a long time, and after that had supper with her, and still has not gone. But I think he'll go soon. That is why she could not come to you before, but she'll soon be coming. She begs that you will not be angry at having to wait."

Believing this to be true, the scholar replied:

"Say to my lady that she must have no thought of me until it is convenient for her to come, but let her do so as quickly as she can."

The servant returned to the house, and went to bed. The lady then said to her lover:

"Well, what have you to say? Do you think that if I cared for him as you fear, I would allow him to remain there freezing all this time?"

The scholar tried to keep warm by walking up and down the courtyard. He had nowhere to sit down and no shelter from the sky, and cursed the brother for staying so long with the lady. At every noise he thought the lady was coming to open the door for him, but he hoped in vain. About midnight, when the lady had taken her pleasure with the lover, she said:

"My love, what do you think about our scholar? Which do you think the greater—his wisdom or my love for him? Will the cold I am causing him to suffer make you get rid of the jealousy which came into your breast the other day from my jests?"

"Heart of my body," replied the lover, "yes! I know that you are my happiness and my peace and my delight and all my hope, even as I am yours."

"Then," said the lady, "kiss me a thousand times to see whether you speak the truth."

So the lover held her close to him and kissed her, not a thousand, but a hundred thousand times. And when some further time had elapsed in these dalliances, the lady said:

"Let us get up for a while, and see if there is any diminishing of that fire in which my new lover writes me he burns all day long."

They got up and went to the same little window; and looking into the courtyard saw the scholar hopping about in the snow with teeth chattering so fast owing to the cold, that the like has never been seen.

Then said the lady:

"What say you to this, my sweet? Do you think now that I can make men dance without the noise of trumpets or Sicilian bagpipes?"

"Yes, dear love," replied the lover laughingly.

"Let us go down to the door," said the lady; "you will remain quiet and I will speak to him, and we'll hear what he has to say. Perhaps that will be as amusing as watching him."

They went softly out of the room down to the door, and there, without opening it at all, the lady called to him through a crack in a low voice. When the scholar heard her call to him, he gave thanks to God, believing too hastily that he was to be let in; and, going over to the door, he said:

"Here I am, madonna; open the door, for God's sake, I'm dying of cold."

"Oh, yes," said the lady, "I know you're chilly, and the cold is very great because there happens to be a little snow! I happen to know that it's much worse in Paris. I can't let you in yet because that cursed brother, who came to sup with me last evening, has not yet gone. But he will soon go, and I'll come down at once and let you in. With great difficulty I've managed to get away from him a moment to come down and cheer you up, so that you are not weary with waiting."

"Ah! madonna," said the scholar, "I beg you to let me in, for God's sake, so that I can wait under shelter, because it began to snow heavily just now, and is still snowing. I'll wait as long as you wish."

"Alas, my sweet," said the lady, "I can't; this door makes such a noise when it's opened that my brother would easily hear it if I opened it; but I will go and tell him to leave so that I can come down and let you in."

"Go quickly then," said the scholar, "and I beg you will have a good fire made for me to warm myself when I come in, for I am so cold I have hardly any sensation left."

"That cannot be," said the lady, "if what you have often written to me is true—that you are burning up with love of me. But I'm sure you make fun of me. Now I must go. Wait, and be of good heart."

The lover was delighted to hear all this, and went back to bed with her, where they slept little that night but spent most of it in pleasure and in making fun of the scholar.

The poor scholar (whose teeth chattered so hard that he seemed like a crane) at last realised that he had been tricked. He made several attempts to open the door and tried to find some other means of escape; but finding none he raged up and down like a lion in a cage, cursing the weather, the lady's malice, the length of the night and his own stupidity. In his rage with her, the long and ardent love he had felt for her was suddenly changed to sharp and bitter hatred, and he kept revolving different means of vengeance in his mind, for he now more desired to be revenged than he had formerly desired to be with the lady.

After long and dreary waiting the night drew towards day, and the dawn began to appear. The lady's maid-servant, acting on her instructions, then came down and opened the courtyard, and, pretending to pity him, said:

"The devil take the man who came here last night! He kept her in suspense all night and made you freeze. But you know how it is! Go in peace, and be sure that another night will give you what you could not have last night. I knew that nothing could have happened to displease my mistress more."

The angry scholar, who knew that threats are simply weapons to the person threatened, like a wise man kept to himself everything which his unrestrained passion would have expressed; and, without showing his anger, said in a low voice:

"Indeed I spent the worst night I ever knew, but then I know your mistress was not to blame, because in her pity for me she came down herself to explain and to comfort me. And, as you say, what did not happen last night will happen another night. Commend me to her, and so good-bye."

He then returned home as best he could, almost paralysed with cold. Weary and dying of sleep he threw himself down on his bed, and awoke to find that he had almost lost the strength of his arms and legs. So he sent for a doctor and told him the chill he had suffered, and asked him to look after his health. The doctor applied prompt remedies and in a very short time cured him of his cramps, and enabled him to stretch his limbs. If he had not been young and if the warm weather had not soon arrived, he would have died. But, having regained his health and strength, he pretended to be more in love with the lady than ever, in order to gratify his hatred.

Now, some time later, Fortune gave the scholar an opportunity of satisfying his desire. The young man whom the widow loved, disregarding the love she bore him, fell in love with another woman and would say and do nothing to please her, so that she wasted away in tears and bitterness. But her servant, who was very fond of her, finding no means of distracting her mistress from the grief caused by the loss of her lover, formed a most foolish plan. And this was that the lady's lover might be brought to love her again by the arts of black magic, of which the scholar must be a great master. This plan she told her mistress, and the foolish lady, not stopping to think that if the scholar knew black magic he would have employed it on his own behalf, listened to the servant's words and immediately told her to find out if the scholar would do it and to promise him that she would do anything he wanted in return.

The servant well and truly delivered the message, and

when the scholar heard it, he said exultantly to himself: "Praised be God! The time has come when, with Thy aid, I may punish the wicked woman for the injury she did me in exchange for the great love I bore her." And to the servant he said:

"Say to my lady that she must not be troubled any longer about this. If her lover were in India I could make him come to her at once and ask her pardon for what he has done to displease her. But I must wait for her to fix the time and place when I can tell her what she must do in this matter. Tell her this from me, and bid her be of good cheer."

The maid took back the answer, and arranged that they should meet in Santa Lucia del Prato. There the lady and the scholar met. Forgetting that she had brought him almost to the point of death, she openly told him everything and what she wanted, and begged him to help her. Said the scholar:

"Madonna, true it is that black magic is among the arts which I learned in Paris, and I am certain I understand it. But since it is highly displeasing to God, I had sworn never to make use of it for myself or for another. But the love I feel for you is so great that I cannot deny you anything you wish me to do. Therefore, even if I should go to hell for this only, yet I am ready to do it, if you want it. But I must warn you that this is a more difficult thing to do than you perhaps realise, especially when a woman wishes to regain a man's love or a man a woman's, because it must be carried out by the person interested. The person who does it must be of firm mind, because it must be carried out at night in a solitary place without company. I do not know whether you are ready to accept these conditions."

The lady, who was more amorous than wise, replied:

"Love spurs me so much that I would do anything to get back the man who has wrongfully abandoned me; but, if you please, tell me how I must show firmness of mind."

"Madonna," said the artful scholar, "I must make a tin image of the man you wish to recapture. When I send it to you, at the waning of the moon you must go naked and alone at night and seven times bathe with it. After that you must climb naked upon a tree or an uninhabited house; then turning to the north with the image in your hand, you must seven times repeat certain words I shall give you in writing. When you have recited them, there will come to you the two loveliest girls you ever saw, who will greet you and ask you what you wish them to do for you. Then you must tell them plainly what you desire, taking care not to give one person's name to another. When you have done this, they will depart and you can return to the place where you left your clothes, dress, and return home. And, of a certainty, half the next night will not have elapsed before your lover comes to you weeping and asking for your mercy and pity; and thereafter he will never again leave you for another woman."

The lady implicitly believed all this, and felt she already had her lover in her arms again. So, already half happy, she said:

"Doubt not, I will do all these things, and I have a most fitting place for them. In the Val d'Arno I have a farm which is close to the river bank; and it is now July, when bathing is delightful. I also remember that not far from the river is an uninhabited tower, where there is a ladder of chestnut wood, by which the shepherds climb to an earthen platform to look for their lost sheep. The place is solitary and out of the way, and I shall climb up on it and I hope I can perfectly execute what I have to do."

The scholar knew all about the lady's farm and tower, and was delighted to know her intention, but he said:

"Madonna, I never visited that district, and so I know neither the farm nor the tower. But if they are as you say, nothing could be better. So, when the time comes, I will send you the image and the prayer. But when you have what you desire, and know that I have served you well, I beg that you will remember me and keep your promise."

The lady said she would do so without fail, and, taking her leave of him, returned home. The scholar, delighted that his plan seemed to be succeeding, made the image and wrote out a fanciful incantation, which he sent to the lady when he thought the time ripe. He informed her that she was to carry out what he had told her the next night without any delay. He then secretly went with his servant to the house of a friend which was not far away from the tower, in order to carry out his plan.

On her side, the lady set out with her maid and went to the farm. When night came, she pretended to go to bed, and sent her maid to bed also. Then in the night she quietly went out of the house and walked down to the bank of the Arno, near the tower. She gazed about her, and, seeing and hearing nobody, undressed herself and hid her clothes under a bush. She then dipped seven times with the image and, holding it in her hand, went naked to the tower.

At nightfall the scholar had hidden with his servant among the willows and other trees near the tower, and saw everything. When she passed naked before him and he saw how the whiteness of her body overcame the shadows of night and then gazed at her breasts and other parts of her body and saw how beautiful she was, he felt pity for her, thinking of what would soon happen to them. Moreover, he was suddenly assailed by the desires of the flesh, which made that which was lying down stand up, and urge him to leave his hiding place and go and take her, and have his pleasure of her. And between pity and desire he was nearly overcome. But then he remembered who he was and the injury she had done him and why and for whom; and so his anger was rekindled and he drove away pity and desire, and held to his plan, and let her go.

The lady climbed up the tower, turned to the north, and began to repeat the words which the scholar had given her. Very soon he went softly into the tower and gradually removed the ladder leading up to the platform on which the lady was standing. He then waited to find what she would say and do.

Having repeated the incantation seven times, the lady waited for the two girls. It was much colder than she would have liked, and she waited so long that the dawn began to appear. Sad that things had not happened as the scholar had foretold, she said to herself: "I fear he has tried to give me a night such as I gave him; but he has avenged himself but poorly, for this has not been a third as long as his night, and the cold very different." She then turned to come down from the tower, to avoid being caught in daylight, but found the ladder had gone. She felt as if the ground had failed beneath her feet, and her spirit deserted her, and she fell down on the platform of the tower. When her strength returned, she began to weep and lament. She perceived that this must be the scholar's work, and regretted having offended him and then having trusted him, when she ought to have known he was her enemy. And thus a long time passed away. She then looked about for some other means of descending, but found none, and began to lament once more, for bitter thoughts came to her, and she said to herself: "O luckless woman, what will be said of you by your brothers and relatives and friends and all the Florentines, when it is known that you were found naked here? Your modesty will be discovered to be false; and even if you could think of lies to excuse yourself, they would be useless, for this cursed scholar who knows all about you would unmask your lies. Wretched woman! In the same hour you have lost the man you loved too well and your honour!"

And then she fell into such agony of mind that she was tempted to throw herself down from the tower.

The sun was now risen, and she got up on to one of the walls of the tower to look for a shepherd boy with his flock whom she could send for her servant. The scholar, who had been asleep under a bush, then awoke and saw her and she saw him. And the scholar said:

"Good morning, madonna. Have the beautiful girls come yet?"

At this the lady began to weep bitterly again, and begged him to come to the tower and speak to her. And the scholar was so courteous as to do this.

The lady, lying down on the platform so that only her face appeared at the trap-door, said weeping:

"Indeed, Rinieri, if I made you spend a bad night, you have been well avenged. Although it is July, I thought I should freeze, for I'm naked. And I have wept so much for the deceit I practised on you and my own folly in trusting you that it is a marvel my eyes are still in my head. I beg you—not for love of me, whom you cannot now love—but for love of yourself as a gentleman, that this may suffice you as vengeance for the injury I did you, that you will bring me my clothes and let me down from here, and that you will not take from me what you could never give me back if you wanted to—my honour. I did indeed deprive you of a night with me, but whenever you please I can give you back many nights for that one. Let this suffice you, and like a gentleman, be content that you have avenged yourself and made me know it. Do not abuse your strength upon a woman. It is no glory for an eagle to overcome a dove. Therefore, for the love of God and your own honour, have pity upon me."

The scholar, remembering the injury she had done him and seeing her weep and entreat him, felt both pleasure and pain—pleasure at his vengeance which he had desired above everything; pain because his humanity was moved to pity by her suffering. But humanity could not overcome the savagery of his love of vengeance, and he replied:

"Madonna Elena, if my prayers, which in truth I was unable to mingle with tears and to make honied as you now make yours, had so far availed me on the night when I was dying of cold in your snowy courtyard that you had given me a little shelter, it would now be easy for me to grant your request. If now you have more concern for your honour than in the past and find it grievous to stay here naked, make your entreaties to the man in whose arms you lay naked on the night you remember, when I went trampling up and down your courtyard in the snow with chattering teeth. Let him help you, let him bring you your clothes, let him put the ladder for you to come down; strive to make him tender for your honour, since now and a thousand other times you have not hesitated to put it in peril for his sake.

"Why do you not call upon him to help you? And who indeed ought to help you more than he? You are his. Whom indeed should he protect and aid, if he does not aid and protect you? Call to him, foolish woman that you are, and find whether his love for you and his wisdom added to yours can free you from my foolishness. For you remember that when you lay with him you asked him which he thought greater—my stupidity or your love for him. Do not now offer me what I do not want and what you could not refuse me if I desired it. Reserve your nights for your lover, if you happen to get away from here alive. Let them be yours and his. I had enough of one of them, and it is enough for me to have been duped once.

"Again, using your cunning in words, you strive to gain my kindness by praising me and calling me a worthy gentleman, and you secretly labour to withdraw me from punishing your malice by flattering my magnanimity. But your flatteries shall no longer darken the eyes of my intellect as your false promises did in the past. I know myself, and I did not learn so much about myself all the time I was in Paris as I learned of you in a single night.

"But, supposing I were magnanimous, you are not the person to whom magnanimity should be shown. The end of penitence and of vengeance with wild beasts like you should be death, whereas with men it should be as you say. I am no eagle and you no dove, but a poisonous serpent; and so, like a very old enemy I mean to persecute you with all my hatred and strength. Indeed, what I do to you cannot fittingly be called vengeance but is rather a punishment, because vengeance should exceed the offence whereas this does not equal it. Considering what you did to me, my vengeance (if I wanted it) would not be satisfied by taking away your life or that of a hundred women like you; for I should only be killing a vile, base and wicked woman.

"Setting aside your slight beauty of face, which a few years will ruin by covering it with wrinkles, what the devil are you more than any other poor creature? No thanks to you that a 'worthy gentleman' (as you called me just now) did not die, one whose life might be more useful to the world in a single day than a hundred thousand like you could be as long as the world endures. The pain you are suffering may teach you that it is one thing to dupe men of no understanding, and a very different thing to dupe a scholar. And if you escape, let this teach you never to fall into the same folly again.

"But if you want to come down so much, why don't you throw yourself down? With God's aid you would break your neck and escape from the pain you feel, and at the same time make me the happiest of men. I shall say no more. I managed to make you climb up there; do you contrive to get down, as you contrived to trick me."

While the scholar was saying all this the poor woman wept continually, and time passed by, and the sun rose higher and higher. But when at last he was silent, she said:

"Ah! Cruel man, if that cursed night angered you so much and my fault seems to you so great that you can be moved to pity neither by my young beauty nor bitter tears nor humble entreaties, at least you should be touched and your austere harshness softened by the fact that I trusted you and let you know all my secrets, whereby I enabled you to gratify your desire to make me conscious of my sin. For if I had not trusted you, there would have been no way for you to take that vengeance which you show me you desired so eagerly.

"Ah! Curb your anger, and forgive me. If you will forgive me and let me come down, I am ready to abandon that faithless man and to take you only as my lord and lover, although you despise my beauty, and call it brief and worthless. It is indeed so, like the beauty of other women; and yet I know that, though it should be valued for no other reason, it is the delight and pleasure and charm of men's youth. You are not an old man. You have treated me cruelly, and yet I cannot believe that you wish to see me suffer so base a death as to have me cast myself in despair from this tower before your very eyes, which I should delight so much if you had not become so false as you are. Ah! For God's sake, have pity upon me. The sun grows hot and the heat begins to pain me, even as the cold distressed you that night."

The scholar was delighted to keep her in talk, and said:

"Madonna, you put your trust in my hands, not for any love you bore me, but to regain the man you had lost. So it deserves nothing but a worse return. And you think foolishly if you believe that this was the only way in which I could have the vengeance upon you I desired. I had a thousand others. By pretending to go on loving you I had set a thousand snares for your feet; and if this had not occurred, you must inevitably have been caught in one of them before much time had elapsed. Whichever I had caught you in, you would have fallen into greater pain and shame than this now gives you. I chose this way, not to let you off more easily, but to be happy sooner. If all these had failed, I still have my pen, wherewith I should have written such things about you and in such a manner that when you heard them (as you would have done) you would have wished a thousand times a day that you had never been born.

"The power of the pen is greater than is supposed by those who have not personally endured it. I swear by God (and may He make me as happy at the end of this vengeance I am taking on you as He has made me in the beginning) that I would have written such things of you that you would have been made ashamed in yourself, as well as on account of other people, and you would have torn out your eyes so as not to see yourself any more. Therefore, don't blame the sea for having made the little river overflow.

"As I said before, I care nothing for your love or for having you mine. Be his whose you were formerly, if you can! I once hated him, but I now love him when I think of what he has done to you. You go about falling in love, and desire the love of young men, because you see they have fresher skins and blacker beards than others, and go about dancing and jousting. Those who are older possess all these qualities, and know moreover what these young fellows have yet to learn. Moreover, you think them better riders and able to go more miles in a day than older men. I admit that they caper along more rapidly, but older men with more experience know where the ticklish places are. Short and sweet is far better and more enjoyable than long and tasteless. Hard trotting soon tires another, however young; whereas gentle going may bring you later to the inn, but at least brings you there comfortably.

"Senseless creatures, you don't see how much evil is concealed under a little good appearance. Young men are not content with one woman, but want as many as they see, and think themselves worthy of them. Therefore, their love cannot be constant, and you yourself can bear witness to prove it. They think they should be honoured and caressed by their women, and think nothing is finer than to boast of the women they have had. This causes many women to lie with friars, who never wish to speak of it. You say that your love affairs are known only to me and your servant, but you are wrong and believe falsely if you believe that. His part of the country and yours hardly talk of anything else; but as usually happens, the person concerned in such matters is the last to hear of them. Moreover, young lovers take gifts from you when older men pay you.

"You made a bad choice, so remain his to whom you gave yourself and leave me whom you scorned. I have found a woman much better than yourself, who knows me far better than you did. If you would be more certain of the desire of my eyes in the next world than you seem to feel in my words in this world, cast yourself down; I am convinced that your soul would be received in the devil's arms and you would see whether my eyes were distressed or not by seeing you dismally fall. But I do not believe that you will give me this happiness, and so I say: if the sun begins to scorch you, remember the cold you made me suffer; mix that with the heat and you will certainly find the sun cooled down."

The unhappy lady, finding that the scholar's words tended to a cruel end, began to weep again and said:

"Since nothing in me can move you to pity, be moved by the love you bear that other lady whom you have found to be wiser than I, and by whom you say you are beloved. Forgive me for the love of her, and bring me my clothes so that I can dress, and let me down from here."

The scholar laughed at this, but seeing it was past Tierce, he replied:

"I cannot now say 'No,' since you have besought me by my lady. Tell me where they are, and I will go for them, and let you down."

Believing him, the lady took some comfort, and told him where she had left her clothes. The scholar left the tower, and ordered his servant to stay there and to take care that nobody else entered until he returned. So saying, he returned to his friend's house, where he dined at leisure and then went to his siesta.

The lady was thus left on the tower, a little comforted by false hopes but still in great distress; she went and sat down by that part of the wall which threw a small shadow, and began to wait, a prey to the bitterest thoughts. Now thinking, now hoping for and now despairing of the scholar's return with her clothes, she passed from one thought to another, and at last fell asleep, overcome with grief and the fatigue of a sleepless night. The sun was now in mid-heaven and very hot, and beat down directly and fiercely on her tender delicate body and uncovered head with such power that her body was not only burned all over but her skin began to split. So fierce was the burning that it awakened her from a profound sleep. She moved slightly when she felt the burning, and when she moved it seemed as if all the burning skin opened and tore apart, as we see happens when someone pulls a piece of burnt parchment. Moreover she had such a pain in her head that it seemed splitting asunder; which was no wonder. The platform on the tower was so hot that she could not bear to touch it with her feet or anything else for long; so she kept shifting about in tears and could not keep still. There was not a breath of wind, and so quantities of flies and gadflies came and settled on her cracked skin and stung her so sharply that each sting seemed like the stab of a spear-point. Therefore she kept perpetually waving her hands about her, cursing herself, her life, her lover and the scholar.

Being thus agonised, stung and pierced by the terrible heat of the sun, by flies and gadflies, and by hunger and still more by thirst, she got to her feet and began to look and listen for any person to whom she could call for aid, for she was now prepared to risk any consequences. But her ill luck deprived her even of that. The workmen had all left the fields on account of the heat, and it so happened that nobody was working near the tower that day, but they were all threshing their wheat near their cottages. So she heard nothing but the cicadas and saw nothing but the Arno, which made her want its water, and thus increased her thirst. She saw woods and shade and houses, and they also were anguish to her, since she longed for them.

What more need be said of this unhappy lady? The sun over-head, the heat from the platform beneath her, the stings of flies and gadflies all over her, had tanned her to such an extent that whereas the night before her whiteness had conquered the darkness, she had now become as red as madder and all bloody, so that she would have seemed the most ugly thing imaginable to anyone who saw her. In this state she remained, without any plan or hope, rather expecting death than anything else, until Nones were half sped. The scholar then awoke and remembered his lady. He therefore returned to the tower to see about her, and sent his servant off to get his food. The lady heard him, and came to the battlements, weak and suffering from pain, and sat down weeping, and spoke thus:

"Rinieri, you are over-vengeful. I did indeed make you freeze by night in my courtyard, but you have made me roast and burn by day on this tower and, in addition, make me die of hunger and thirst. I beg you in God's name to come up here and, since I have not the courage to kill myself, do you kill me; I desire death above all things, so great is the torment I endure. If you will not do me this favour, at least bring me a glass of water for me to moisten my mouth, for my tears do not suffice, so great are the dryness and heat within me."

Her voice showed the scholar how weak she was and he could see part of her body all burned by the sun. These things and her humble entreaties awoke some pity in him for her, and yet he replied thus:

"Wicked woman, you shall never die by my hands but by your own, if you want to die. You shall have as much water from me to soothe your heat as you gave me fire to comfort my cold. I greatly regret that the illness caused by my cold had to be cured by the warmth of stinking dung, whereas yours will be cured by the cold of rose water. Whereas I nearly lost my strength and person, you will only be skinned by this heat, and will become beautiful again like the snake when it sheds its skin."

"Wretched me!" replied the lady. "May God give beauty acquired in such a way to my worst enemies! But you, crueler than a wild beast, how can you bear to torture me thus? What worse could I expect from you or anyone else if I had slain all your family with the cruelest tortures? I know not what greater cruelty could be used against a traitor who had delivered up a whole city to the sword than that you have practised upon me, by roasting me in the sun and having me devoured by flies. And you refuse me even a glass of water, when condemned murderers going to their death are often given wine to drink if they ask for it. But, since I see you resolute in your harsh cruelty and that no suffering on my part can move you, I shall patiently await death, so that God may have mercy upon my soul, Whom I pray to look upon these deeds with just eyes!"

So saying, she dragged herself in great pain to the middle of the platform, despairing of ever escaping alive from such heat. In addition to her other sufferings she thought she would swoon with thirst, not once but a thousand times, and yet continued weeping bitterly and bewailing her misfortune.

It was now Vespers, and the scholar thought he had done sufficient. He wrapped her clothes in his servant's cloak and went to the lady's house, and there found her maid-servant sitting disconsolate and sad and resourceless at the door. And he said to her:

"Good woman, what has happened to your mistress?"

"Messer," replied the servant, "I do not know. This morning I expected to find her in the bed where I thought she went last night. But I could not find her there or anywhere else, and I do not know what has become of her, and so I am in great grief. Can you tell me nothing of her, Messer?"

The scholar replied:

"Would I had had you with her so that I could have punished you as I have punished her! But you shall not escape me, and I will so repay you for your deeds that you will never again play tricks on any man without remembering me."

He then turned to his servant, and said:

"Give her the clothes and tell her where to go for her, if she wants."

The servant obeyed. And when the maid took and recognised the clothes and heard what they said, she was afraid they had murdered her mistress, and could hardly restrain a scream. The scholar then departed, and she went at once with the clothes to the tower.

Now, one of the lady's workmen had lost two of his pigs that day and was looking for them. Just after the scholar's departure he came to the tower, and as he looked about for his pigs he heard the unfortunate lady's wretched lamentations. So he climbed into the tower and shouted:

"Who is crying there?"

The lady recognised her workman's voice, and, calling to him by name said:

"Ah! Go for my maid, and bring her up to me here."

The workman recognised who it was and said:

"Alas! Madonna, who took you up there? Your servant has been looking for you all day. But who ever would have thought that you were here?"

He took the sides of the ladder, placed them in position, and began to bind on the cross-pieces with osiers. Meanwhile the maid-servant arrived and entered the tower. Unable to keep silent longer, she clapped her hands and screamed:

"My sweet lady, where are you?"

The lady heard her and said as loudly as she could:

"My sister, I am here. Do not weep, but bring my clothes to me here at once."

When the maid heard her speak she was greatly comforted. She climbed up the ladder which the labourer had now mended, and with his assistance reached the platform. But when she saw her mistress, looking less like a human being than a burned log, lying on the floor naked and exhausted, she tore her face with her nails and began to weep over her as if she had been dead. But the lady begged her in God's name to be silent and to help her to dress. Having learned from the maid that nobody knew where she had been except those who had brought her clothes and the labourer, she took a little comfort from that, and begged them for God's sake never to speak of it to anyone.

After much talk, the labourer carried the lady, who was unable to walk, down from the tower. The poor maid, who had remained behind, came down less skilfully; her foot slipped and she fell from the ladder to the ground, breaking her thigh, and began to moan so much with the pain that it sounded like a lion. The labourer laid the lady on the grass and went back to see what was the matter with the maid; finding she had broken her thigh he took her to the same lawn, and laid her beside the lady. When the lady saw this added to her other woes and that the person from whom she most expected help had broken her thigh, she began to lament so piteously that not only was the labourer unable to console her, but himself began to weep.

The sun was now low, and they did not want night to come upon them there. So, at the lady's wish, he went to his cottage and called his wife and his two brothers, and returned with them and a table, on which they laid the maid and so carried her home. He then comforted the lady with a little cold water and encouraging words, and carried her to her bedroom on his shoulders. The labourer's wife gave her soft bread to eat, and then undressed her and put her to bed; after which she made arrangements for the lady and her maid to be taken to Florence. There the lady, who was furnished with a great store of wiles, invented a tale quite different from what had really happened, and with the aid of her maid-servant persuaded her brothers and sisters and everyone else that all this had happened through the Devil's spells. The doctors were sent for, and with great pain and agony to the lady who several times lost the whole of her skin, they finally cured her of a severe fever and her other ills; and they also healed the maid's thigh. Wherefore the lady put her lover out of her mind, and thereafter was very careful neither to have lovers nor to play tricks on men. And when the scholar heard that the

maid had broken her leg, he thought that sufficient vengeance; and so went on his way rejoicing, without saying anything more.

Thus it befell a foolish young woman and her tricks
when she thought she could dally with a scholar as with
any other man, not knowing that most of them know where
the Devil keeps his tail.

Therefore, ladies, beware of playing such tricks, especially
upon scholars.

## EIGHTH TALE

*Two men are close friends, and one lies with the other's
wife. The husband finds it out and makes the wife shut
her lover in a chest, and while he is inside, the husband
lies with the lover's own wife on the chest*

Elena's misfortunes were both pleasant and painful to the
ladies to hear. But since they thought she had partly deserved them, they listened with less pity, although they considered the scholar harsh, fiercely determined and cruel.
But when Pampinea had finished, the queen ordered Fiammetta to follow next, and, being ready to obey, she said:

Charming ladies, I think you are a little wounded by the
severity of the offended scholar, and so I think I should
soothe your irritated minds with something more amusing.
I therefore intend to tell you a little tale about a young man
who received an injury more gently and revenged it more
moderately,—whereby you may learn that it should be
enough for anyone if the ass receives as much in fodder
as it gives in work, without desiring to inflict injury beyond
the bounds of just vengeance when a man sets out to avenge
an injury he has received.

You must know then that, as I have heard, there were
in Siena two young men of the people in pretty good circumstances, named Spinelloccio Tanena and Zeppa di Mino.
They lived near each other in the Cammollia, and each
had a pretty wife. These two young men were always together and apparently loved each other like brothers, or
even more.

Now, as Spinelloccio was always in Zeppa's house, sometimes when Zeppa was there and sometimes when he was not, he became so familiar with his friend's wife that he got to lying with her; and this went on for some time without anyone finding it out. But one day Zeppa happened to be in the house when his wife thought he was out, and Spinelloccio came to call for him. The wife said Zeppa was out, so Spinelloccio at once went in and found the wife in the main room. Seeing nobody else about, he embraced and kissed her, and she him. Zeppa saw all this and said nothing, but remained hidden to see where this game would lead; and, in short, he saw his wife and Spinelloccio go arm in arm to the bedroom and there lock themselves in, which greatly enraged him. But knowing that if he created a disturbance he would not lessen his injury and would only increase his shame, he started to think out some way of avenging himself and so satisfying his mind, without it being known all round. After much thought, he believed he had found a way, and therefore remained hidden as long as Spinelloccio was with his wife.

When Spinelloccio had gone, Zeppa entered the bedroom where he found his wife still re-arranging her head-veils, which Spinelloccio had pulled off in their play. And he said: "What are you doing?"

"Can't you see?" said the wife.

"Yes, indeed yes," said Zeppa, "and I saw something else I did not want to see."

He then began to talk to her about what had happened, and after much talk she in great fear made a confession of it all, since she could not deny her familiarity with Spinelloccio; and then entreated his forgiveness with tears. Said Zeppa:

"Wife, you have done wrong, and if you want me to forgive you, be careful to do what I tell you. I want you to tell Spinelloccio that tomorrow about Tierce you want him to find some means of leaving me and coming to you here. When he is here, I shall return; and as soon as you hear me, make him get into that chest and lock it. When you have done that, I will tell you what else you have to do. And don't be afraid, I promise you I will not do him any harm."

To satisfy him, the wife promised to do this. Next day about the hour of Tierce, Spinelloccio and Zeppa were together, and Spinelloccio, who had promised the lady to go to her about that time, said to Zeppa:

"I'm going to have dinner with a friend today and don't want to keep him waiting; so good-bye."

"But it's a long time until dinner," said Zeppa.

"No matter," said Spinelloccio, "I have to talk to him about some business of mine, so I must get there early."

Spinelloccio then left Zeppa, took a turn, and went to the wife. They had not long been in the bedroom when Zeppa arrived. When the wife heard him, she pretended to be very much afraid, and made Spinelloccio get into the chest her husband had showed her, and locked him in. She then left the bedroom. Zeppa then said:

"Wife, is it time for dinner?"

"Yes," said she.

"Spinelloccio has gone out to dine with a friend," said Zeppa, "and has left his wife alone. Go to the window and call her, and tell her to come and have dinner with us."

The wife, still in fear for herself and therefore very obedient, did what her husband bade her. Spinelloccio's wife, urgently invited by Zeppa's, came in when she heard that her husband would not be dining at home. When she came in, Zeppa greeted her very affectionately and took her familiarly by the hand and whispered to his wife to go into the kitchen. He then took her into the bedroom, and as soon they were inside, he turned round and locked the door. Finding herself locked in the bedroom with him, she said:

"Zeppa, what is the meaning of this? So you got me in here for this? Is this your love and loyal friendship for Spinelloccio?"

Zeppa took her to the chest in which her husband was locked, and holding her tightly, said:

"Lady, before you begin to complain, listen to what I have to say. I have loved and love Spinelloccio like a brother; yesterday, without his knowing it, I discovered that my trust in him had come to this—that he was lying with my wife as he lies with you. Now, since I love him, I mean to exact no worse revenge than the offence itself. He has had my wife, and I mean to have you. If you refuse, I shall have to take it; and since I do not intend to let this offence go unpunished, I shall otherwise play such a trick on him that neither you nor he will ever be happy again."

After many reiterations by Zeppa, she finally believed what he asserted, and said: "Zeppa, since this revenge must fall upon me and I consent to it, do you remain at peace with your wife, as I intend to do, in spite of what she has done to me."

"Certainly I shall do so," replied Zeppa, "and, moreover, I will give you a jewel so valuable and beautiful that you have no other like it."

So saying, he embraced and kissed her and laid her upon

the chest in which her husband was locked, and there took his fill of pleasure with her, and she with him.

Spinelloccio in the chest heard all Zeppa's words and his wife's answers and then the dance which went on over his head; and for a long time he felt such rage that he almost died of it. If he had not been afraid of Zeppa he would have shouted insults at his wife, closed in though he was. But then, remembering that the wrong had begun with him and that Zeppa was right in doing this and was behaving humanely and like a true friend to him, he vowed to himself that he would be more Zeppa's friend than ever if he wanted it. When Zeppa had taken his fill of pleasure with the lady, he got off the chest. She then asked for the jewel; and he called for his wife, who came in saying only with a laugh:

"Madonna, you have given me tit for tat."

Zeppa then said: "Open this chest."

She did so, and Zeppa then showed the lady her Spinelloccio. It would take long to say which of the two was more ashamed: Spinelloccio when he saw Zeppa and knew that he knew what Spinelloccio had done, or the wife when she saw her husband and realised that he had heard and felt what she had been doing above his head. Then said Zeppa:

"Here's the jewel I give you."

Spinelloccio got out of the chest and without too much beating about the bush, said:

"Zeppa, we are quits. Therefore it is good, as you said to my wife just now, that we should remain friends. Since nothing divides us but our wives, let us have them in common."

Zeppa agreed, and all four dined together in the most peaceful way imaginable. Henceforth each of the two women had two husbands and each of the two men had two wives; and no quarrel or dispute ever arose between them.

# NINTH TALE

*Master Simone, the doctor, is persuaded by Bruno and Buffalmacco to join an imaginary gathering and when he goes out to the rendezvous at night Buffalmacco throws him into a ditch of foulness*

When the ladies had chatted a little over the community of wives between the two Sienese, the queen, who was the only person left to speak except Dioneo, began thus:

Amorous ladies, Spinelloccio well deserved the trick which was played upon him by Zeppa; and, in spite of what Pampinea said, I do not think we should condemn those who play tricks either upon those who ask for it or who deserve it. Spinelloccio deserved it, and I mean to tell you about a man who asked for it, considering that those who tricked him are not to be blamed but praised.

The man I mean was a doctor who went to Bologna a cow and returned to Florence clothed in fur. As we see frequently, our fellow-citizens return from Bologna as judges, doctors, or notaries, dressed in large ample robes with scarlet and fur and other impressive displays,—with results which we see daily. Among them was Master Simone da Villa, a man more wealthy in his inheritance than in learning, who returned not long ago dressed in scarlet with a large mantelet, calling himself a doctor of medicine, and took a house in the street we now call the Via del Cocomero.

Among the other notable habits of this newly returned Master Simone, was a custom of asking the person who happened to be with him about whomever he saw passing in the street. And he observed and noted everything as if the medicines he had to give his patients were to be composed from men's actions. Among those whom he cast eyes upon most fruitfully were two persons of whom we have already spoken twice today, the painters Bruno and Buffalmacco, who were his neighbours and always together. They seemed to him to care less about the world than other people and to live more gaily; so he asked a number of persons about them. Everyone told him they were poor painters, but he took it into his head that they could not possibly live so happily in poverty, and, as he had heard that they were clever fellows, he decided that they must have some source of large profit unknown to other men. So he wanted to become acquainted with both or at least one of them if possible; and he managed to strike up a friendship with Bruno. It did not take Bruno long to find out that this doctor was an ass, and Bruno had a good time with his stupidities while the doctor took marvellous delight in Bruno. After inviting Bruno to dinner several times, and thereby conceiving that he might speak familiarly with him, the doctor told him how much he was surprised that poor men like Bruno and Buffalmacco could live so merrily, and begged him to say how they did it. Bruno thought the request one of the doctor's wonted stupidities, and, laughing to himself, determined to reply in a way suitable to such a cow, and said:

"Master, I would not tell many persons what we do, but since you are a friend and I know you will not tell anyone else, I shall not refrain. It is true that my friend and I live as well and as merrily as you think, and even more so. Neither our art nor any possessions we have would furnish us enough money to pay even for the water we consume. But you must not suppose that we steal it, but we go on expeditions, and from these we derive everything for our needs and pleasures with no harm to others; and that is the reason why we live so merrily, as you have noticed."

The doctor believed him without in the least understanding. He immediately had the greatest desire to know what this going-on-expeditions meant, and earnestly begged to be told, swearing that he would never tell anyone.

"Oh! Master," said Bruno, "what are you asking me? You want to know a very great secret, and if anyone else came to know it I might be ruined and lose my life and fall into the mouth of the Lucifer of San Gallo. But so great is my love for your supreme Woodenness and the trust I have in you that I cannot possibly deny you anything you want; so I will tell you on condition that you swear by the Cross of Montisoni never to tell anyone."

The Master said he would not tell, and Bruno said:

"You must know then, sweet Master, that not long ago there dwelt in this city a great master of black magic named Michael Scott (because he came from Scotland), who was greatly honoured by many gentlemen, of whom few are now alive. When he was about to depart he yielded to their earnest entreaties and left behind two competent disciples, ordering them always to be ready to carry out the desires of the gentlemen who had entertained him.

"These two served the gentlemen aforesaid in certain love affairs and other slight matters. Finding that they liked the city and the manner of life in it, they determined to remain here permanently and formed close friendships with certain men, not considering whether they were gentle or common, poor or rich, but only whether they were men of their own sort. To please their friends they instituted a club of about twenty-five men who were to meet at least twice a month in some place determined by them. When they met, each one declared what he needed, and the two magicians quickly provided it that night.

"Buffalmacco and I were close friends of these two, and thus became and still remain members of their band. When we are gathered together, I tell you it is a marvel to see the hangings round the hall where we eat, and the tables royally spread, and the quantity of handsome servants both male and female subject to the whim of each person present, and the basins and jugs and flasks and cups and other gold and silver vessels from which we eat and drink, and the many varied dishes of food according to each man's desire which are set before us in due course.

"I could never describe to you the sweet sounds of infinite musical instruments and the songs full of melody which we hear; nor could I tell you all the wax candles which are burned at these feasts nor the quantity of sweetmeats consumed nor how precious are the wines we drink. And, by the pumpkin, I would not have you suppose that we wear the same clothes there as you see us in; the poorest of us seems an emperor, so rich are we in rare and beautiful garments.

"But above all our other pleasures is that of beautiful women, who are immediately brought to us at our pleasure from any part of the world. There you will see the lady of the Barbanicchi, the queen of the Baschi, the Sultan's wife, the Empress of Osbech, the Ciancianfera of Nornieca, the Semistante of Osbech, and the Scalpedra of Narsia. How can I enumerate them? Why, we have all the queens in the world, down to the Schinchimurra of Prester John's Land who has a horn in the middle of her backside. You see! And then when they have taken a drink and sweetmeats, each of them goes off to a room with the man at whose request they were fetched.

"You must know that these bedrooms are so beautiful they look like paradise. They are as scented as the spiceboxes in your shop when you pound cummin, and the beds we lie in would seem to you finer than those of the Doge of Venice. I leave you to imagine how the spinning girls handle the threads and draw the spindles to them to make thick cloth! But in my opinion the luckiest among us are Buffalmacco and I, because Buffalmacco nearly always sends for the Queen of France and I for the Queen of England, who are the two most beautiful women in the world. And we have so contrived it that they have eyes for no man but us. So you yourself can see how and why we live and go about more merrily than other men, since we possess the love of two such Queens; especially since, when we want a thousand or two gold florins from them, we immediately get them. All this we commonly call 'going on an expedition,' because we take things as people do on pirate expeditions, with this difference—that they never pay back, whereas we return everything after using it.

"Thus, most excellent Master, you have heard what we mean by going on expeditions; but you can see how necessary it is to keep this a secret, so I need not say any more about that or beseech you further."

The doctor, whose science probably went no further than curing babies of milk-sickness, believed every word that Bruno told him was true; and wanted to join this band more than anything else in the world. So he told Bruno that it was no wonder they were so merry; and with great difficulty restrained himself from asking to be one of them, but postponed this until his entreaties would acquire more weight by his having done Bruno more favours.

Having thus restrained himself, he cultivated the acquaintance more closely, invited Bruno to meals morning and evening, and displayed the greatest affection for him. And they were so continually together that it seemed as if the doctor could not live without Bruno.

Bruno was very well content, and since he did not want to seem ungrateful for the doctor's entertainment he painted the Passion in his dining-room and a Lamb of God over the entrance, and outside the shop door he painted a chamber-pot so that those who needed the doctor's advice should know where to look for it. And in a little loggia he painted the battle of the mice and cats, which the doctor thought extremely beautiful. And sometimes, after he had not supped with the doctor, he would say:

"Last night I was with the club, and since I'm a little tired of the Queen of England, I sent for the Grumeda of the Grand Khan of Tarisi."

"What does Grumeda mean?" asked the doctor. "I don't understand these names."

"O Master," said Bruno, "I don't wonder, for I've heard that neither Porcograsso nor Vannacenna mention them."

"You mean Hippocrates and Avicenna," said the doctor.

"Very likely," said Bruno. "I don't know, but I understand your names as little as you understand mine. But in the language of the Grand Khan the word Grumeda means Empress. Ah! You'd think her a pretty little woman! I know she'd make you forget your medicines and clysters and plasters!"

Bruno often talked in this way to whet his appetite, and one evening when he was holding the light for Bruno to paint the battle of the mice and cats, he felt that he had sufficiently involved Bruno with obligations, and determined to speak to him. And since they were alone, he said:

"Bruno, God knows there is no person alive for whom I would more willingly do anything than for you. Why, if you told me to go from here to Peretola I believe I would go; so you cannot be surprised that I have become so intimate with you. As you know, you told me not long ago about the doings of your merry band, which gave me such a desire to belong to it that I never wanted anything so much. This is not without reason, as you will see if I ever become a member. You can laugh at me for the rest of time if I don't bring there the prettiest maid-servant you ever saw, a girl I came across last year at Cacavincigli and think the world of. I offered her ten Bologna pieces to lie with me, but she wouldn't. So I entreat you to tell me what I must do to become a member and that you will do all you can to get me in. Indeed you'll find me a true and loyal companion. You've seen from time to time what a handsome man I am and how well I stand on my legs and how I have a face like a rose; moreover, I'm a doctor of medicine, such as I think you have none equal to me, and I know many good things and songs. I'll sing you one."

And he immediately began to sing. Bruno wanted to laugh so much that he could scarcely restrain himself, but he managed to do so; and when the song was over, the doctor said:

"Well, what do you think of it?"

"Why," said Bruno, "you bawl so artistically that you beat the mandolins and the rest of the band."

"I'm sure you'd never have believed it if you hadn't heard me," said the doctor.

"You say truly," replied Bruno.

"I know lots of others," said the doctor, "but never mind them now. Such as you see me, my father was a gentleman although he lived in the country, and my mother came from Vallecchio. You've seen for yourself that I have the finest books and the handsomest gown of any Doctor in Florence. God's faith, I have goods which cost hundreds of cents ten years ago. So I beg you'll do all you can to get me in. God's faith; if you do that I'll never charge you a farthing for my services when you're ill."

Bruno thought him a poor tool of a fellow in this as in other matters, and replied: "Master, hold the light this way, and don't be angry if I don't answer until I have finished the tails of these mice."

When the tails were done, Bruno pretended to be greatly embarrassed by the request, and said:

"Master, I know that you have done great things for me, but still, the thing you ask of me, although small in comparison with the greatness of your brain, is very great to me. There is nobody in the world for whom I would rather do my utmost than for you, because I love you dearly, and on account of your words which are so wise they would draw two souls from one weaver as well as persuade me. The more I am with you, the wiser you seem to me. Moreover, if nothing else made me love you, I should love you because you are enamoured of the beautiful girl you mention. But I must tell you this—in this affair I have not the power you suppose and so I cannot do what is needed on your behalf. But if you will promise me on your true and Catholic faith to trust in me, I can show you what you have to do, and since you have such fine books and other things as you told me just now, I think it can certainly be done."

"Speak out," said the doctor, "I see you don't really know me, and don't know how well I can keep a secret. When Messer Guasparruolo da Saliceto was judged for the podestà of Forlimpopoli there were few things he did which he did not send and tell me about, so good at keeping secrets did he find me. Shall I tell you the truth? I was the first man he told that he was going to marry Bergamina —what do you think of that?"

"Very well," said Bruno, "if he could trust in you, so can I! This is what you must do. In our gathering we always have a captain and two advisers, who are changed every six months. On the first of next month Buffalmacco will be captain, and I shall be adviser. The captain can do much to get you in and to have anyone he wants brought in, so I think that you should do your best to become intimate with Buffalmacco and to do him honour. He is a man who, when he sees how wise you are, will at once be taken with you; and when you have charmed him a little with your good sense and the fine things you have, you can ask him, and he won't be able to refuse you. I have already mentioned you to him, and he is very well disposed towards you. When you have done what I suggest, leave the rest to me."

"What you say delights me," said the doctor, "and if he is one who delights in wise men, let him talk with me a little and I will act in such a way that he will always be after me, for I am so wise I could furnish a whole city and yet remain most wise."

After this Bruno told Buffalmacco the whole story, and Buffalmacco thought it a thousand years until he could do what Master Fool was asking for. The doctor who wanted so much to go on expeditions had no rest until he became the friend of Buffalmacco, which was easily done. He then began to give excellent dinners and suppers to him and Bruno. And they flattered him like those gentlemen who smell out good wines and fat capons and other good things and get near them without having to be pressed, and yet always keep saying that they would not do it for anyone else. But when the doctor thought the time had come he made his request of Buffalmacco, as he had done with Bruno. Buffalmacco pretended to be very angry and made a scene with Bruno, saying:

"I vow to the high God of Passignano that I'm tempted to give you such a crack on the head that your nose would hit your heels, traitor that you are, for none but you could have revealed these things to the doctor!"

But the doctor defended Bruno warmly, saying and swearing that he had learned of it from someone else; and after many of his wise words Buffalmacco calmed down, and said:

"Master, it is plain that you have been to Bologna and that you have come home with a shut mouth; moreover I can see you did not learn your A B C on the block, as many fools do, but on the block-head which is very long; and if I'm not deceived you were christened on Sunday. Although Bruno tells me you went there to study medicine, it seems to me that you learned to captivate men, which you are able to do better than any man I ever saw with your wisdom and your tales."

Whereupon the doctor, interrupting him, said to Bruno:

"What a thing it is to converse and move with wise men! Who would have understood every particular of my feeling so quickly as this worthy man? You did not perceive my worth nearly so quickly as he has done. But tell him now what I said to you a while ago when you said that Buffalmacco delighted in wise men. Do you think I have done it?"

"Better than I expected," said Bruno.

"If you had seen me at Bologna," said the doctor to Buffalmacco, "you would have said more, since there was no man great or small, doctor or student, but wished me well, so much did they all learn from my talk and wisdom. I will go further, and tell you I never spoke a word without everyone laughing, so much did I please them. When I went away they all lamented and wanted me to stay; and the matter went so far that they were willing to let me alone and read medicine to all the students. But I would not do it, for I had decided to return to a great inheritance I have here which has always been in my family; and this I did."

Then said Bruno to Buffalmacco:

"What do you think? You wouldn't believe me when I told you. By the Holy Scriptures, in this country there is not another doctor who can cast asses' water as he does, and you wouldn't find another like him from here to the gates of Paris. Now see if you can refuse to do what he wants!"

"Bruno speaks truly," said the doctor, "but I am not properly appreciated here. You are all ignorant people, and I should like you to see me among doctors."

"Truly, Master," said Buffalmacco, "you know far more than I should ever have believed. Wherefore, speaking to you as one should speak to wise men like you, I tell you bombastically that I shall so endeavour that you shall become one of our group."

After this promise the doctor redoubled his civilities to them. And they made him believe the most absurd things, promising him that his mistress should be the Lady Watercloset, who was the fairest thing in all the arsey-versy of the human race. The doctor asked who this Lady was, and Buffalmacco said:

"O pumpkin full of seed, she is a very great lady, and there are few houses in the world where she has not some jurisdiction. Even the minor friars honour her to the sound of castanets. And I can tell you that when she is about she makes her presence known, although she remains shut up. But it was not long ago that she passed your door, going down to the Arno to wash her feet and get a breath of air. But her usual dwelling is in Latrina. Many of her officers go about there, carrying a staff and plumb-line in sign of her majesty. Many of her barons may be seen, such as the Tamagnin of the Gate, Don Meta, Manico di Scopa, the Squacchera and others, who were I think your familiar friends, but you no longer remember them. If we succeed, you can abandon the girl at Cacavincigli, and we will place you in the arms of this great lady."

The doctor, who was born and bred at Bologna, did not understand that all these were words for the jakes, and so was delighted with his lady. And soon after all this the two painters assured him that he would be received. The day before the evening on which they were to assemble, the doctor invited them both to supper, and after supper asked them how he should go to the gathering.

"Master," said Buffalmacco, "you must be very bold, for if you are not very bold you might be thwarted, and great harm would result to us. You shall hear how you must be bold. You must find some means after nightfall this evening to be on one of the raised tombs recently made outside Santa Maria Novella, wearing one of your best gowns, so that you may appear before the club for the first time in honourable wise, and also because you, being a gentleman (in case it might be said that we are not), the Lady intends to make you a knight of the bath at her expense. There you must await the person we shall send for you.

"To tell you everything, there will come for you a horned black creature, not very large, which will go whistling and leaping round the square near you to frighten you. But when it sees you are not afraid it will come up gently to you. And when it is close at hand, you must get down from the tomb without any fear and without thinking of God or the Saints, and when you have got onto it, you must fold your arms and hands on your chest and not touch the creature any further. It will then move gently along and bring you to us. But if you remember God or the Saints or feel afraid, I warn you it may throw you off or dash you somewhere which will hurt you stinkingly. So, if you have not the heart to be bold, do not come, for you will only harm yourself and do no good to us."

"You don't yet know me," said the doctor. "You hesitate, because you see I wear gloves and long robes. If you knew the things I did in Bologna when I went after women with my friends, you would marvel. God's faith, there was one night when a woman wouldn't come with us (what's worse, she was a little creature not a palm high), and I first punched her, and then, catching her up, I think I threw her a cross-bow shot, and made her come along with us.

"Another time I remember that, alone except for my servant, I was passing about dusk beside the churchyard of the minor friars where a woman had been buried that day; and I was not a bit afraid. So have no doubt, I am bold and stout enough. To come in all honourable wise I shall wear the scarlet robe in which I received my doctorate, and you'll see whether the company will not be glad to see me and if I'm not nearly made your captain right away. See how things will go when I'm there, since the Lady without ever having seen me wants to make me a knight of the bath! Perhaps knighthood won't befit me, perhaps I shan't know how to maintain my rank—and perhaps I shall! You leave it to me."

"Well said," replied Buffalmacco, "but see you don't play a trick on us and fail to come or to be there when we send for you. I say this because it is cold, and you doctors guard carefully against it."

"Please God," said the doctor, "I'm not one of your chilly ones. I don't mind the cold. I often get up in the night for the necessities which take men out of bed, and I never put anything but a fur coat over my doublet. So I'll certainly be there."

They then separated, and when night came on the doctor made an excuse to his wife, secretly got his fine gown and put it on, and went to one of the tombs. He got up on to the marble and waited for the creature, in the great cold. Buffalmacco, who was tall and active, managed to obtain one of those masks which used to be worn in certain games no longer in fashion, and put on a black fur coat inside out, so that he looked like a bear except that the mask was horned and had a devil's face. Thus disguised he went to the new square of Santa Maria Novella, and Bruno came along to see what would happen. When Buffalmacco found the doctor was there he began to leap about and make a great noise in the square, and to whistle and scream and yell as if he had gone mad.

When the doctor saw and heard him, the hair stood up on his flesh and he began to tremble all over like a man who was more timorous than a woman; and he then began to wish that he had stayed at home. But since he had come, he tried to hearten himself, so much was he conquered by his desire to see the marvels they had told him about. After Buffalmacco had raged around in this way for some time, he pretended to calm down, and going towards the tomb on which the doctor was lying, stood still.

The doctor, who was trembling all over with terror, did not know whether to stay where he was or to get down. Finally, fearing he might be hurt if he did not get down, he let his second fear drive out the first, got down from the tomb saying softly, "God help me," mounted the creature, and trembling all over folded his hands as he had been told. Buffalmacco then began to move slowly toward Santa Maria della Scala, and going on all fours took him near the nunnery of Ripole.

In that part of the country there were ditches, in which

the field labourers made their offerings to the Lady Water-closet to enrich their fields. When Buffalmacco got near them, he went close alongside one of them, put his hand on one of the doctor's feet with which he lifted him from his back and threw him into the ditch. He then began to snarl and leap and rage and went away alongside Santa Maria della Scala in the direction of Ognissanti, where he found Bruno who had run away because he could not restrain his laughter. They both laughed heartily together, and watched from a distance to see what the ditched doctor would do.

Master Doctor, finding himself in such an abominable plight, strove to stand upright and to get out of it. Plastered from head to foot, falling backward time and again, wretched and miserable, he finally got out after having swallowed a few drams, leaving his hood behind. He cleaned himself down with his hands as well as he could, and, not knowing what else to do, returned home and knocked until the door was opened. Scarcely was the door locked behind him as he entered in this stinking plight, when Bruno and Buffalmacco arrived to learn how the doctor had been received by his wife. As they listened, they heard the wife abusing him violently:

"Now, what a pickle you're in! You've been after some woman, and wanted to appear very fine in your scarlet gown. Am I not sufficient for you? My boy, I'd be enough for a whole nation, let alone you! Now they've ducked you by throwing you where you ought to be thrown. You're a fine Doctor, to have a wife and go about by night after other men's wives!"

And as she washed the doctor down, the wife did not cease tormenting him with these and similar words until midnight.

Next morning along came Bruno and Buffalmacco, having painted their skin beneath their clothes with dark patches, as if they had been beaten, and found the doctor already risen. As they entered, they smelled the stink, for it had not yet been possible to clean everything so that there was no smell. The doctor went to meet them and bade them good morrow. But Bruno and Buffalmacco, as they had arranged beforehand, replied angrily:

"So do we not say to you, but pray God that He may so deal with you that you die stabbed as the vilest traitor who ever lived! We were trying to do you honour and to please you, and it's no virtue in you that kept us from being murdered like dogs. Through your treachery we got enough bangs last night to drive a donkey to Rome, as well as running the risk of being expelled from the club where we were trying to get you received. If you don't believe us, look at our bodies."

They opened their clothes for an instant and showed him their chests all painted with bruises, and then covered them up at once. The doctor attempted to excuse himself, and to tell them about his misfortunes and where he had been thrown. But Buffalmacco said:

"I wish he had thrown you from the bridge into the Arno. Why did you think of God and the Saints? Weren't you told not to beforehand?"

"God's Faith, I didn't think of them," said the doctor.

"What!" said Buffalmacco, "you didn't think of them! You don't think much! Our messenger said you trembled like a bough and didn't know where you were. You've done well; But nobody shall ever do it again, and we shall henceforth honour you as you deserve."

The doctor then asked their pardon and begged them in God's name not to abuse him, and tried to pacify them with the softest words in his power. For fear lest they should talk of his disgrace he honoured and entertained them thereafter far more even than he had done before.

Thus, as you have heard, is wisdom taught to those who have not learned sufficient in Bologna.

## TENTH TALE

*A Sicilian woman artfully swindles a merchant of all the goods he had brought to Palermo. He pretends to return with more merchandise than before, borrows her money, and leaves nothing but water and hemp*

It is needless to ask whether the queen's tale made the ladies laugh at different times. There was not one of them but laughed so hard that the tears came into her eyes a dozen times. But when she had ended, Dioneo, whose turn it now was, said:

Gracious ladies, these tricks are the more pleasing when the person artfully tricked is more cunning. Now, although the tricks already related were all excellent, I intend to tell you of one which should please you more than any yet told, because the person tricked was a greater mistress in the art of tricking others than any of the victims of trickery you have heard about.

There was and perhaps still is an arrangement in all ports that when merchants arrive and unload their cargo, the goods are all carried to a warehouse, which in many places is called the Customs House, belonging to the government of the country. Those in charge must be furnished with a written account of all the goods and their value, and they then provide the merchant with storage room where he can deposit his goods under lock and key. The Customs officers then enter in their books all the goods credited to the merchant, and as he withdraws part or all his goods from the Customs, he has to pay them their dues. This Customs House book is often consulted by the brokers to find out the quantity and quality of the goods deposited and also the names of the merchants who hold them; and afterwards the merchants and brokers discuss exchange, barter, sale and other transactions, as the case may be.

This arrangement was in force at Palermo in Sicily, as in many other places; and there likewise lived many women, very lovely of body but foes to chastity, who would be and are thought noble and most honest ladies by those who do not know them. Being accustomed not to shave, but to flay men of all they have, these ladies, as soon as they see a foreign merchant, find out from the Customs book what he has and what his credit is. Then with soft words and their pleasing and amorous acts they strive to allure the merchant and to draw him into love. Many a merchant has been so beguiled, some of whom have lost part of their goods thereby, and some all. Some of them even have left behind their goods and ship and flesh and bones, so skillfully has the she-barber wielded the razor.

Well, not long ago a young man arrived there, sent by his masters. He was a Florentine, by name Nicolo da Cignano, otherwise known as Salabaetto; and he brought with him woollen goods worth five hundred gold florins, bought at the fair of Salerno. Having paid the Customs fees, he placed these goods in store, and, displaying no great haste to sell them, went about amusing himself on land.

He was white-skinned, golden-haired and very handsome, and life went well with him. It happened that one of these female barbers, who called herself Madonna Jancofiore, heard about him and cast an eye upon him. He thought she was a great lady, and when he discovered this he thought she had fallen in love with his good looks, and determined to manage the affair very prudently. So, without saying a word to anyone, he began to pass to and fro in front of her house. After having fired him with her glances for several days, pretending to be greatly in love with him, she secretly sent him a woman servant who was highly skilled in pandering. After much talk this woman told him with tears in her eyes that his charm and beauty had so taken her mistress that she could not rest day or night. Wherefore she desired above everything to meet him whenever he pleased secretly at a bagnio. After which she took a ring from her purse and gave it to him on behalf of her mistress.

Salabaetto was as happy as a man can be when he heard this. He took the ring, gazed at it, kissed it, put it on his finger, and replied to the good woman that if Madonna Jancofiore loved him she was well repaid, for he loved her more than his own life and was ready to go wherever she wished and at any time.

The go-between returned to the lady with this answer, and Salabaetto was immediately informed of the bagnio where he was to await her the next day after vespers. Without saying a word to anyone, he went there at the appointed time, and found the bagnio engaged by the lady. He had not been there long when in came two slaves with burdens. One of them carried a fine large cotton mattress on her head, and the other a very large basket filled with various things. They placed this mattress on a bed in one of the rooms, and laid over it a pair of sheets most delicately worked in silk, and then a coverlet of whitest Cyprus stuff, with two marvellously decorated pillows. They then undressed, got into the bath, and washed and cleaned it thoroughly.

Very soon the lady came to the bath with two more female slaves. As soon as she could, she greeted him lovingly, embraced and kissed him many times, and then, after several deep sighs, said:

"I don't know anyone but you who could have brought me to this. You have set fire to my soul, you Tuscan dog!"

After this they both entered the bath together naked, and the two slaves with them. Without permitting anyone else to lay a hand on him, the lady herself washed Salabaetto all over with soap scented with musk and cloves. She then had herself washed and rubbed down by the slaves. This done, the slaves brought two fine and very white sheets, so scented with roses that they seemed like roses; the slaves wrapped Salabaetto in one and the lady in the other and then carried them both on their shoulders to the bed. When they had ceased perspiring, the slaves took away these two sheets and left them naked between the others. They then took from the basket silver vases of great beauty, some of which were filled with rose water, some with orange water, some with jasmine water, and some with lemon water, which they sprinkled upon them. After which they refreshed themselves from boxes of sweetmeats and the finest wines.

Salabaetto felt he was in paradise, and gazed at her a thousand times, for she was indeed very beautiful. He thought it a hundred years until the slaves would go away and leave him in her arms. At last the lady ordered them to go, and they departed, leaving a small light burning in the room. The lady then embraced Salabaetto and he her, and they spent a long hour together to the immense joy of Salabaetto, who thought she was melting away with love for him.

When the lady thought it time to get up, she called in the slaves, who dressed them. Once more they refreshed themselves with drink and sweetmeats, and their hands and faces were washed in the scented waters. As the lady was going, she said to Salabaetto:

"If it pleased you, it would be a very great favour to me if you came and supped with me this evening and spent the night."

Salabaetto, who was already snared with her beauty and cunning allurements and thought she loved him as the heart of her body, replied:

"Madonna, every wish of yours is to me the greatest of pleasures. This evening and for ever I mean to do what pleases you, and to be commanded by you."

The lady then went home and decorated her bedroom with her best possessions and hangings, and arranged a magnificent supper. As soon as it was dark, Salabaetto went there, was joyously welcomed, and supped in great plenty and gaiety. Entering the bedroom, he perceived a wonderful scent of wood and aloes, and saw the bed was decked with bird ornaments of Cyprus and that there were many handsome things on the walls. All these things, taken separately and together, made him think she must be a very great and rich lady. And whatever he might have heard trumpeted against her life, he would not have believed it. And even if he had believed that she had deceived other men before, nothing in the world would have made him think that it could happen to him. That night he lay with her in the greatest pleasure, more and more in love with her.

Next morning she fastened on him a handsome girdle of silver with a beautiful purse attached, and said:

"My sweet Salabaetto, I commend me to you. My person is at your disposal and all I have here; and whatever I can do is at your command."

Salabaetto joyfully kissed and embraced her, departed from her house, and went to the merchants' gathering place. He went with her several times without any expense to himself, and fell ever deeper in love. And when he sold his woollen goods at a profit for cash, the lady at once heard of it, not from him but from others.

That evening when Salabaetto was with her, she began to jest and play with him, to kiss and embrace him, and pretend to be so much in love with him that it seemed as if she must die of love in his arms. She then tried to give him two beautiful silver gobiets she had, but Salabaetto would not take them, because at one time and another he had taken from her gifts which must have been worth thirty gold florins, without having been able to make her accept even a shillingsworth. Finally, having well warmed him up by pretending to be so excited about him and so liberal, she was called out by one of her slaves, as she had arranged. Having left the room and remained away for some time, she returned weeping, threw herself on the bed and began the most piteous lamentation ever made by woman. The amazed Salabaetto took her in his arms, and wept with her, saying:

"Heart of my body! What has happened to you so suddenly? What is the reason for this grief? Ah! My love, tell me."

The lady refused to tell him at first, and then said:

"Alas, my sweet lord, I don't know what to do or what to say. I have just received letters from Messina, and my brother writes to me that I must sell and pawn everything I have here and without fail send him a thousand gold florins within eight days, otherwise he will lose his head. I don't know what to do in order to get the money so quickly. If I had a fortnight or so, I would find means to collect it from places where I must have much more; or I would sell some of our lands. But, as I can't do that, I wish I had died before this bad news came to me."

So saying, she pretended to be in the greatest distress, and kept on weeping. Salabaetto, who had already lost most of his wits in love's flames, thought her tears genuine and her words still more so; and said:

"Madonna, I cannot provide you with a thousand gold florins, but I can lend you five hundred if you can pay me back in a fortnight. This is a piece of luck for you, since I sold my cloth yesterday; otherwise I could not have lent you a shilling."

"Oh!" said she, "have you been suffering from lack of money? Why did you not ask me? I may not have a thousand, but I have a hundred or two to give you. You take from me the courage to accept from you the service you offer me."

Salabaetto was more than captured by these words, and said:

"Madonna, I will not have you refuse on those grounds; if I had needed money as much as you do, I would have asked you."

"O Salabaetto," said she, "I see your true and perfect love for me when, without waiting to be asked for so great a sum of money, you come liberally to my aid in this necessity. Indeed I was wholly yours without this, but now I shall be much more so; and I shall ever be grateful to you for saving my brother's head. God knows I take it unwillingly, for I know you are a merchant and that merchants do all their business with money. But since necessity constrains me and I have every hope of paying you back, I will take it; and as for the remainder, if I cannot get it quickly anywhere else, I will pawn everything I have."

Saying all this with tears, she fell upon Salabaetto's neck. He comforted her and, after spending the night with her, brought her five hundred good gold florins, without awaiting any request from her, to show himself her most generous lover. She took them with laughter in her heart and tears in her eyes, Salabaetto relying on her mere promise.

As soon as she had the money, the aspect of matters began to change. Whereas Salabaetto had been perfectly free to come to the lady whenever he wanted, there now began to be obstacles, so that he could only go to her once in seven times; and when he did get in, found neither the smiles nor the caresses nor the feasts of the past. One month and then two passed after the period when he should have had his money back; and when he asked for it, he received only words in payment. Thus Salabaetto discovered the wicked woman's wiles and his own folly, and knew that he could say nothing about her except what she pleased because he had no receipt and no witness. He was ashamed to complain to anyone else, both because he had been warned beforehand and because of the jests which he rightly deserved for his stupidity. And so he wept over his folly in the deepest distress. He had received several letters from his employers telling him to exchange the money and to send it to them; so he determined to go away, so that his default would not be discovered by his failing to do this. He therefore got on a boat, and instead of going to Pisa as he ought to have done, went to Naples.

At that time there lived in Naples our fellow citizen, Pietro dello Canigiano, treasurer to the Empress of Constantinople, a man of great intellect and subtle genius, a very close friend of Salabaetto and his family. A few days later Salabaetto confided in him as a man of the greatest discretion, and dolefully related what he had done and his unlucky misfortune, asking him for advice and help in earning his living there, since he was determined never to return to Florence.

Grieved at these things, Canigiano said:

"Ill have you done; ill have you behaved; ill have you obeyed your masters. Too much money have you spent in pleasure; but for what is done some remedy must be found."

And being a man of experience he saw at once what was to be done, and told Salabaetto, who liked the advice and set out to follow it. He had a little money and Canigiano lent him some more. He made up a number of well-tied bales and bought twenty oil casks and filled them. He had them loaded and returned to Palermo. He gave a list of the bales and the value of the casks to the Customs and had them all inscribed at his valuation. He then placed them all in storage, saying that he would not touch them until other goods he was expecting had arrived.

Jancofiore at once heard about this, and learned that the goods he had brought were worth two thousand florins or more, while those he expected were worth three thousand. She felt she had got very little out of him, and thought she would pay him back the five hundred in order to get the greater part of the five thousand. So she sent for him, and Salabaetto, now fully on his guard, went to her. She pretended to know nothing about what he had brought with him, and greeted him most affectionately, saying:

"If you were angry with me because I did not repay your money when it was due . . ."

Salabaetto laughed and interrupted her:

"Madonna, I was indeed a little displeased, as a man would be when he is ready to take the heart from his body to please you! I should like you to hear how angry I am with you. I love you so much that I have sold the greater part of my possessions and have brought here goods to the value of two thousand florins, while I expect more than three thousand florinsworth from the West. I intend to set up in business and to remain here so that I can always be near you, for I feel I am happier in your love than any other lover can be in his."

"Salabaetto," said she, "since I love you better than my life I am glad of any profit of yours, and I am very happy that you have returned with the intention of remaining here, since I hope to spend many happy times with you. But I want to apologise a little because in the time just before you left, you sometimes wanted to come here and could not, and sometimes you came and were not as joyfully received as usual. Moreover, I want to apologise also for not having repaid your money at the time I promised.

"You must know that I was in great grief and trouble. Whosoever is in that state cannot be so cheerful and attend to another person as she would wish, however dear that person may be. You must know also that it is very difficult for a woman to get together a thousand gold florins. She is told lies, and does not receive what is promised; and so she has to tell lies to others. This and nothing else is the cause of my not returning your money. But I received it soon after your departure and I should certainly have forwarded it to you, if I had known where to send it. As I did not know, I have kept it for you."

She then sent for a purse which contained the money he had brought her, put it into his hand, and said:

"Count it, and see if there are five hundred."

Salabaetto was never so happy in his life, counted the money and found there were five hundred florins.

"Madonna," said he, "I know that what you say is true, but you have done enough. For this and for the sake of the love I bear you, I always place at your service any sum of money you require if I can do so. Since I shall be established here, you can test me."

Having thus renewed his love to her, in words at least, Salabaetto recommenced his intimacy with her, and she did him all honour and pleasure, and feigned the greatest love for him. But Salabaetto wanted to punish her trick with a trick of his own. One day when she had invited him to sup and spend the night with her, he arrived looking as sad and melancholy as if he wanted to die. Jancofiore embraced and kissed him, and asked why he was so sad. For a time he refused to tell her, and then said:

"I am sad because the boat carrying the goods I expected

has been captured by the pirates of Monaco. The ransom is ten thousand florins, of which my share is one thousand, and I have not a farthing to pay it. The five hundred you repaid me I sent immediately to Naples to invest in cloth which is being sent here. This is the wrong time to sell the goods I brought here with me, and I could scarcely get half the price for them. I am not yet so well known here as to be able to find someone to come to my aid. So I don't know what to say or do. If I don't send the money soon the goods will be carried into Monaco, and I shall never be able to get them again."

The lady was greatly upset by this since she felt she was losing it all. Thinking of some means of preventing their being taken to Monaco, she said:

"God knows I am sorry, out of my love for you; but what use is it to grieve so much? If I had the money, God knows I would lend it to you at once, but I haven't got it. There is a man who lent me the other five hundred florins when I needed them, but he wants a high rate of interest. He will not lend at less than thirty per cent. If you borrow from him you will have to give good security, and I myself am ready to pawn myself and all my belongings to help you. But how will you give security for the rest?"

Salabaetto saw the motive which made her offer this service and knew that she herself would be lending him the money. He first of all thanked her, and then said that under pressure of necessity he could not refuse even such heavy interest. He then said he would give as security the goods he had in the Customs, and would have them entered in the name of the person lending the money, but that he wanted to keep the key of the store-house himself, so that he could show his goods if asked and also to prevent anyone from touching or exchanging or altering them.

The lady said he spoke well, and that the security was good. Next morning, she sent for a broker in whom she had great confidence, told him the circumstances and gave him a thousand florins. These the broker lent to Salabaetto, and had the goods which Salabaetto possessed in the Customs transferred to his name. They gave each other receipts and then, parting in agreement, went about their business.

Salabaetto at once went on board ship with his fifteen hundred gold florins, and returned to Pietro dello Canigiano at Naples. He thence remitted to Florence the full amount due to the employers who had sent him out with the cloth. He paid Pietro and everyone else to whom he owed money, and rejoiced with Canigiano over the trick he had played upon the Sicilian girl. Then, determined to be a merchant no longer, he went to Ferrara.

When Jancofiore found that Salabaetto had left Palermo she was surprised and began to feel suspicious. After waiting for him two months and finding he did not return, she had the broker open the store-room. First they looked into the casks which they thought were full of oil, and found them full of sea water with a little oil on top near the bung. They then undid the bales, which contained nothing but hemp, except for two which contained cloth. In short, the value of the goods there did not exceed two hundred florins.

Jancofiore, finding herself thus tricked, long wept for the five hundred florins she had returned and still more for the thousand she had lent, often repeating: "You've got to have sharp eyes in dealing with a Florentine!" Thus, tricked and despoiled, she found that other people knew as much as she did.

When Dioneo finished his tale, the queen knew that the end of her reign had come. She praised Pietro Canigiano's advice which was proved good by its results, and also Salabaetto's sagacity which was equally displayed in carrying out the plan. She then took the laurel from her head and laid it upon Emilia's, saying in womanly fashion:

"Madonna, I know not how pleasant a queen we shall have in you, but we shall certainly have a beautiful one. Let your actions correspond to your beauties."

She then returned to her seat. Emilia felt a little shamefaced, not so much at being made queen as at being publicly praised for what women most desire; and her face became like fresh roses in the light of dawn. But she had kept her eyes lowered for a time, the blush disappeared, and she made the necessary arrangements with the steward for matters concerning the band. She then spoke thus:

"Delightful ladies, when oxen have laboured under the yoke for part of the day and are then freed and unyoked, we see them going freely at their pleasure through the woods to their pasture. We also see that gardens with many leafy trees are not less but more beautiful than woods with nothing but oaks. Therefore, since for several days we have told tales under the restraint of certain laws, I think it would be not only useful but fitting that we should wander freely like those who have laboured, and thus regain strength to return to the yoke.

"Tomorrow, when you continue your delightful tale-telling, I do not intend that you shall be bound to any particular topic in what you say. I want each one of you to speak of anything you please, being convinced that the variety of things which will be talked of will be no less charming than to speak of one topic alone. If this is done, the person who succeeds me in this kingdom will be in a stronger position to enforce the customary laws."

And having said this, she set them at liberty until supper time. Each praised the queen for what she had said in her wisdom, and then rising to their feet they went to their various pleasures. They spent the time until supper, the ladies in making garlands and amusing themselves, the young men in games and singing. They then supped merrily beside the beautiful fountain, and after supper enjoyed themselves with dancing and singing as usual. Finally the queen, in order to follow the custom of her predecessors, ordered Pamfilo to sing a song, although several of them had already sung without being asked.

Pamfilo immediately began thus:

> *O Love, so great the good, the happiness and joy I feel through you, that I am glad to burn within your fire.*
>
> *The abounding happiness of high and lofty joy within my heart, which you have caused me, cannot stay therein, but issues forth and shows my gladness in my happy face; for being in love in such a lofty and conspicuous place makes easy the dwelling in the state wherein I burn.*
>
> *I cannot tell you in my song, nor point you with my finger, Love, the good I feel; and if I must keep it hidden, for were it known, delight would change to torment; but yet I am so happy that all speech would prove but scant and weak ere I could tell a little of my joy.*
>
> *Who would have guessed my arms could ever reach so high as to have held her, or that my face would touch hers as it does when I kiss her in grace and greeting? None would believe my fortune; thus I am consumed, and hide the love which gives me happiness and joy.*

Pamfilo ended his song, in which all bore a part, and there was not one of them who devoted more attention than was necessary to noting its words and striving to guess what it was he sang that he must keep secret. And although several of them imagined several different things, none of them hit the truth.

But when the queen saw that Pamfilo's song was ended and that the young men and ladies wished to rest, she commanded everyone to go to bed.

### HERE ENDS THE EIGHTH DAY

# THE NINTH DAY

# THE NINTH DAY

*Here begins the ninth day of the* Decameron, *wherein, under the rule of Emilia, tales are told as everyone pleases on whatever subject he likes*

The light, from whose splendour the darkness fled, had already changed the dark colour of the eighth heaven to bright blue, and the little flowers in the fields were lifting their heads, when Emilia arose, and had her companions and the young men likewise called. They came, and strolled slowly along with the queen to a little wood not far from the mansion. This they entered, and watched the animals, such as deer and fawns and others, which let them come near as if fearless or tame, so free from pursuit had they been owing to the plague. They amused themselves for some time by going up close first to one and then to another, and making them run and leap. But as the sun was now high, they all wished to return home.

They went along garlanded with oak, carrying handfuls of flowers and scented plants; and any person who met them would have said: "These people will not be conquered by death, or at worst will die happy."

Singing and jesting and laughing they returned step by step to the mansion, where they found everything in good order and the servants cheerful and happy. They rested a little, and did not sit down to table until the young men and the ladies had sung six songs, each gayer than the one before. After washing their hands they were ranged at table by the steward as the queen wished; and when the food was served, all ate merrily. Rising from table, they spent some time in singing and dancing; and then, at the queen's command, retired to rest.

But at the accustomed hour each day went to the place where they gathered for tale-telling. The queen looked at Filomena, and told her that she must tell the first tale that day, and she began smilingly as follows:

# FIRST TALE

*Madonna Francesca is beloved by Rinuccio and by Alessandro, neither of whom she likes. She makes one of them lie down in a grave and sends the other to get out what he thinks to be a dead body; as they fail in the test, she gets rid of them both*

Madonna, since it is your pleasure I am delighted to be the first to run a race in the wide and open field of tale-telling which your magnificence has opened to us; if I do it well, I doubt not that those who come after me will do as well and better.

In our stories, lovely ladies, we have often showed the great powers of love. Yet I do not think it has been fully expressed or would be, even if we spoke of nothing else until the end of the year. Now since love not only leads lovers into danger of death, but even to enter the houses of the dead to take out corpses, I wish to tell you a tale, in addition to those already told, which will not only show you the power of love, but will make you see the good sense of a worthy lady, which enabled her to get rid of two men who loved her against her will.

In the city of Pistoia there lived a very beautiful widow; and two Florentines, exiled to the city, named Rinuccio Palermini and Alessandro Chiarmontesi, who were both deeply in love with her, although neither knew about the other's love. Each went prudently to work, striving to do everything he could to obtain her love.

The name of this gentlewoman was Madonna Francesca de' Lazzari. She was often urged by messages and entreaties by each of them, and rather unwisely lent an ear to them; she then wanted to get rid of them, and was unable to do so. In order to get rid of their tiresome attentions she determined to ask them to perform a service which nobody would carry out, although it would be possible to do it. Then, if they failed to perform it, she would have a good cause or pretext for refusing to receive their messages any longer.

On the day she thought of this, there died in Pistoia a man who was reputed the vilest fellow, not only in Pistoia but in the whole world, although his ancestors had been gentlemen. Moreover, he was so deformed and his face was so ugly that anyone who did not know him would have been terrified at seeing him for the first time. He had been buried in a tomb outside the church of the minor friars, a fact which she thought fell in very well with her plan. And so she said to her maid-servant:

"You know the daily annoyance and trouble I have with the messages from those two Florentines, Rinuccio and Alessandro. I have made up my mind not to satisfy them, and as they are always making great promises I want to get rid of them, by putting them to the test with something I am certain they will not do, and in this way I shall get rid of their tiresome attentions.

"My plan is this. This morning, as you know, Scannadio" (that was this bad man's name) "was buried in the churchyard of the minor friars; and the boldest men on this earth were afraid when they saw him alive, let alone dead. So you must first go to Alessandro, and say: 'Madonna Francesca sends to say that the time has now come when you may have her love which you have so long desired, and spend the night with her in the following way. For a reason which you shall know later, one of her relatives intends to bring to her house tonight the body of Scannadio, who was buried today. And she does not want it, because she is afraid of him even when dead. So she begs you to do her a great service, and to go tonight to the grave where Scannadio is buried, wrap yourself in his shroud and lie down as if you were the corpse, and wait until someone comes. Then, without moving or speaking, you must allow yourself to be taken out of the grave and brought to her house, where she will receive you and you can be with her, and depart when you like; while the rest you can leave to her.' If he says he will do it, very good; if he says he will not do it, tell him from me that he must never again appear before me and if he values his life never again send me message or messenger.

"After that, go to Rinuccio Palermini, and say: 'Madonna Francesca says she is ready to do your pleasure, if you will do her a great service. About midnight you must go to the tomb where Scannadio was buried this morning, and without saying a word at anything you see or hear, you must gently take him up and carry him to her house. There you will see why she wants this service, and you may have your pleasure of her. If you will not do this, never send message or messenger to her again.'"

The maid-servant went to them, and delivered the messages as she had been ordered. And each replied that for Francesca's pleasure, they were ready, not only to enter a tomb, but to go down to hell. The servant brought back the answer to her mistress, who waited to see whether they would be such fools as to do it.

At nightfall Alessandro Chiarmontesi left his house, stripped to his doublet, to go and lie in the tomb in Scannadio's place; as he went along terrible thoughts came into his mind, and he said to himself: "Ah! What an idiot I am! Where am I going? How do I know that her relatives have not found out that I love her and think we have been together, and have made her do this so that they can kill me in the tomb? If that happened, I should receive the harm, and nobody in the world would ever know it, and they would escape scot-free. Or how do I know that this has not been devised by some enemy of mine, with whom perhaps she is in love, and who will take advantage of it?" He then went on: "But assuming that none of these is true, yet if her relatives carry me to her house I must suppose that they will not take Scannadio's body in their arms and put it into hers. I can only suppose that they want to mutilate it because he harmed them somehow in the past. She said I was not to speak a word whatever happened. Suppose they tore out my eyes or pulled out my teeth or cut off my hands or played some similar game with me? Could I remain silent? And if I speak they will either recognise me and do me harm, or if they don't do that I shall have achieved nothing, for they will not leave me with the lady. And she will say that I broke her commands, and will never again do anything to pleasure me."

At this, he was on the point of returning home. But then his great love urged him in the opposite direction with arguments of such force that they brought him to the tomb. He opened it, got in, stripped Scannadio, wrapped himself in the shroud, closed the tomb over him, and lay down in Scannadio's place. He then began to think what Scannadio had been, and remembered what he had heard about the things which happen by night in tombs and elsewhere, so that the hair stood erect on his flesh, and he felt as if Scannadio was about to stand upright and strangle him. But with the aid of his ardent love he overcame these and other thoughts of terror, and lay there as if he were a corpse, waiting to see what would happen to him.

As midnight came near, Rinuccio left his house to do what his lady had bidden him. As he went along, he thought of many different things which might happen. He might fall into the hands of the watch, with Scannadio's body on his back, and be burned alive as a violator of graves. Or, if the matter came to light, he might acquire the hatred of Scannadio's relatives. These and many similar thoughts held him back. But then he turned again, and said to himself: "Ah! Shall I say 'No' to the very first request from this gentle lady, whom I have loved and love so much especially since I shall acquire her favours thereby? Even were I certainly to die for it, I would do what I have promised her."

Walking on, he came to the tomb, and quietly opened it. Alessandro heard him open it, and although very much afraid, remained silent. Rinuccio got in, and, thinking he held the corpse of Scannadio, took Alessandro by the feet and pulled him out. He then lifted him on to his back and started off towards the lady's house. The night was so dark that he could not see where he was going, and as he went along, he knocked Alessandro against first one and then another of the posts which were along the side of the road.

Rinuccio had nearly reached the lady's door, and she, who was waiting at the window with her servant to see if he would bring Alessandro back, was already fortifying herself to send them both away, when the watch, who were secretly posted close at hand to capture a bandit, heard the noise of Rinuccio's steps. They suddenly brought out a light to see what he was doing and where he was going, presented their spears and shields, and shouted: "Who goes there?"

When he saw them, Rinuccio had not much time to make up his mind as to what to do. He dropped Alessandro, and made off as fast as his legs would carry him. Alessandro jumped to his feet, and also made off, although hindered by the long folds of the shroud.

By the light which the watch carried the lady had clearly seen Rinuccio with Alessandro on his back and had also noticed that Alessandro was dressed in Scannadio's shroud; and she was greatly surprised at the ardour of each of them. But with all her marvelling, she laughed heartily when she saw Alessandro thrown down, and both of them run away. She was very glad at this unexpected event, and praised God for having freed her from their importunities. Returning to her bedroom, she vowed to her maid that there could be no doubt that each of them was very much in love with her, since it was obvious that they had done what she had commanded them to do.

In distress, and cursing his bad luck, Rinuccio did not

for all that go straight home. When the watch had departed, he returned to the place where he had dropped Alessandro and groped about trying to find the body, in order to complete the service required. But since he could not find it, he supposed that it had been carried off by the watch; and so returned home in grief.

As for Alessandro, he likewise returned home, not knowing what else to do, ignorant of the person by whom he had been carried, and distressed by the misfortune.

Next morning Scannadio's tomb was found open and his body was not seen, because Alessandro had put it in the bottom of the tomb. All Pistoia was filled with different views about it, and the fools thought he had been carried off by the devil.

Nevertheless, each of the two lovers informed the lady of what they had done and what had happened; and, having thus excused themselves for not having fully carried out her commands, begged her favour and her love. But she pretended not to believe them, and replied sharply that she would never do anything for them since they had not performed what she had asked; and in this way she got rid of them.

## SECOND TALE

*An abbess gets out of bed hastily in the dark to catch one of her nuns who is accused of being with a lover in bed. The abbess herself is lying with a priest and puts his breeches on her head in mistake for her veil. The accused nun sees them and points them out to the abbess; she is set free and allowed to be with her lover*

Filomena was silent, and all praised the wisdom of the lady in getting rid of the men she did not love, while they all on the contrary considered the ardent determination of the lovers to be folly rather than love. The queen then turned pleasantly to Elisa, and said: "Elisa, you must follow." And she began immediately:

Dearest ladies, as you have heard, Madonna Francesca showed wisdom in getting free from an annoyance. But a young nun by a word in season freed herself, with the aid of Fortune, from an impending danger. As you know, there are many very foolish people who set up as censors and directors of others; and, as you will see from my tale, Fortune sometimes deservedly brings them to shame. This happened to an abbess, under whose rule there lived the nun I speak of.

You must know that in Lombardy there is a convent renowned for its sanctity and religious fervour. Among the nuns was a girl of noble blood and marvellous beauty, by name Isabella. One day she came to the grating to speak with a relative, and fell in love with a young man who accompanied him. He surprised her desire in her eyes and, seeing how beautiful she was, fell in love with her; but for a long time this love remained fruitless to the great unhappiness of them both. Finally, as each wanted the other, the young man saw a way to go secretly to his nun; she agreed, and to the pleasure of each of them he visited her, not once, but many times.

But one night he was seen to leave Isabella by one of the nuns, without either of them knowing it. She told the news to some of the others. Their first idea was to denounce her to the abbess, Madonna Usimbalda, a good and holy woman in the opinion of her nuns and all who knew her. But on reflection they decided to have the abbess catch her with the young man, to prevent any possibility of denial. So they remained silent, secretly keeping watch in turns in order to catch them.

Isabella did not perceive this, and knew nothing about it; and so one night she had the young man come to her; which was immediately known to those who were on the watch. When they thought the time ripe, which was late in the night, they divided into two parties, one of which kept watch over the door to Isabella's cell, while the other ran to the abbess's door and knocked. When she replied, they said:

"Get up, madonna, get up quickly, we've found Isabella with a young man in her room!"

That night the abbess was in the company of a priest, whom she often had brought to her in a chest. She was afraid that the nuns in their zeal and haste might beat so hard at the door that it would open; so she got up quickly and dressed herself in the dark. Thinking she was picking up her nun's veil she took the priest's breeches, and, such was her haste, that without noticing it she put them on her head instead of the veil; and came out of her room. She immediately locked it behind her, and said:

"Where is this depraved woman?"

The other nuns were so fiery and eager to catch Isabella at fault that they did not notice what the abbess had on her head; and coming to Isabella's cell they helped each other to throw down the door. Rushing in, they found the two lovers in each other's arms, unable to move in their amazement at this sudden irruption.

The girl was at once seized by the other nuns and, by command of the abbess, taken to the chapter-house. The man was left alone. He dressed and waited to see what would happen, determined to injure as many of them as he could if any harm befell his young novice, and to take her away with him.

The abbess took her seat in the chapter-house in the presence of all the nuns, who had eyes only for the guilty novice. She denounced her violently as one whose wicked and depraved actions, if known, would contaminate the sanctity, chastity and good fame of the monastery. And her denunciations were followed by fierce threats.

The guilty novice in her timidity and shame did not know what to reply, save by silence to arouse the others' compassion. The abbess continued her speech, and the girl, raising her head, noticed what the abbess was wearing on her own head and the garters dangling on either side. Regaining her self-control she said:

"Madonna, God be good to you, tie up your head-dress and then say to me anything you like."

"What head-dress, you vile creature?" said the abbess, who did not see her meaning. "Have you the front to jest with me? Do you think what you have done is a subject for jests?"

"Madonna," said the girl again, "I beg you will tie up your head-dress, and then say anything you please to me."

Thereupon numbers of the nuns looked at the abbess's head, and she raised her hands to her veil; and all perceived what Isabella meant. The abbess realised her own fault and that they all saw it and that she had no excuse to offer. She changed her tone, and began to speak in very different terms, to the effect that it was impossible for anyone to defend herself from the appetites of the flesh. And she said that everyone should secretly, as they had done until then, enjoy themselves when possible.

The girl was set at liberty, the abbess went back to sleep with her priest, and Isabella with her lover. And despite those who envied her, Isabella often had him come to her again. Those nuns who had no lover secretly tried their luck to the best of their ability.

## THIRD TALE

*Master Simone, egged on by Bruno, Buffalmacco and Nello, makes Calandrino think he is pregnant. He gives them capons and money to make medicine and is cured without having a child*

When Elisa had finished her tale all the ladies gave thanks to God that the young nun had so luckily escaped the clutches of the envious community. The queen then ordered Filostrato to follow next, and, without waiting for further orders, he began thus:

Fairest ladies, yesterday's tale of the judge whose clothes were pulled off, reminded me of a tale about Calandrino which I shall tell you. Although we have said a lot about him and his friends, yet whatever is said about him can only cause merriment; and so I shall tell you the tale I had in mind yesterday.

We have already made clear who were Calandrino and the others who will be mentioned in this tale. So, without saying more about that, I must tell you that an aunt of Calandrino's died, and left him two hundred lire in small change. So Calandrino went about saying that he intended to buy a farm. He bargained with all the estate agents in Florence, as if he had possessed ten thousand florins of gold to spend; but the bargain was always broken off when it came to the point of paying.

Bruno and Buffalmacco of course knew about it, and often told him that he would do far better to enjoy the money with them than to go about buying land, as if he had to make cross-bow bolts. But, far from that, they did not even succeed in getting him to give them a single meal. In their annoyance at this, they agreed with a painter friend of theirs, named Nello, that between them they would find some way to get fed at Calandrino's expense. Without any delay they arranged together what they would do. The next morning Nello waited for Calandrino to leave his house, and before he had gone far, went up to him and said:

"Good morning, Calandrino."

Calandrino wished him a good day and a good year in

the name of God. Nello then halted and looked him in the face. Then Calandrino said to him:

"What are you looking at?"

"Didn't you feel anything wrong in the night?" asked Nello. "You don't look the same."

Calandrino immediately began to feel concerned and said:

"How? What do you think's wrong with me?"

"Oh!" said Nello, "I can't say, but you seem quite different. Perhaps it's nothing."

And so let him go. Calandrino went along, very anxious about himself, but not feeling anything amiss. Buffalmacco, who was not far off, saw him leave Nello, and then went up to him, greeted him, and asked if he felt nothing amiss.

"I don't know," said Calandrino, "but Nello told me just now that I looked quite changed. Perhaps there is something wrong with me?"

"Yes," said Buffalmacco, "and it may be more serious than just something. You look half dead."

Calandrino already began to feel rather feverish. Then along came Bruno and the first thing he said was:

"Why, Calandrino, look at your face! You look like a dead man! How do you feel?"

Hearing all of them talk in this way, Calandrino felt certain that he was ill, and said wildly:

"What shall I do?"

"I think you ought to go home," said Bruno, "and get to bed, and cover yourself up well, and send a specimen of your urine to Doctor Simone, who is so friendly with us, as you know. He'll tell you at once what you have to do, and we'll come to you, and if there's anything to be done, we'll do it."

Nello then came up, and they all went home with Calandrino, who went languidly to his bedroom, saying to his wife:

"Come and cover me up well, I feel very ill."

After he got to bed, he sent a little maid-servant with a bottle of his water to Doctor Simone, who then dwelt in the Mercato Vecchio at the sign of the Blockhead. Bruno said to his friends:

"You stay here with him, and I will go and see what the doctor says. If necessary, I'll bring him back with me."

"Ah! yes, my dear friend," said Calandrino, "go and tell me what it is, for I feel something queer inside me."

Bruno went off to Doctor Simone, arrived before the little girl with the bottle of urine, and told the doctor the joke.

Then, when the little girl arrived, the doctor had inspected the urine, and said:

"Go back and tell Calandrino to keep warm, and that I'll come to him immediately and tell him what is the matter with him and what he must do."

The little girl delivered the message, and soon after the doctor and Bruno came along. The doctor sat down beside Calandrino, felt his pulse, and then in his wife's presence, said:

"Calandrino, speaking to you as a friend, there is nothing wrong with you except that you are pregnant."

When Calandrino heard this he screamed dismally and exclaimed:

"Alas! It's your fault, Tessa. You would always lie on top. I told you how it would be."

At this, the wife, who was a modest creature, blushed red with shame, and lowering her head left the room without speaking a word. Calandrino went on complaining, and said:

"Alas, alas! What shall I do? How shall I bear this child? Where will it come out? I see that I shall die through my wife's folly; may God punish her as much as I wish to be happy! If I were well, I'd get up and beat her till I broke her bones, for it would have been well for me if I had never let her get on top. But if I escape this, then she can die of wanting it first!"

Bruno, Buffalmacco and Nello were bursting with laughter when they heard him talk, but managed to refrain. However, Doctor Monkeysimon laughed so squawkingly that you could have pulled every tooth out of his head. But finally Calandrino appealed to the doctor and begged for his advice and help.

"Calandrino," said the doctor, "don't be disturbed. Praise be God, we have found it out so soon that we can set you free in a few days with very little trouble. But you'll have to spend some money."

"Oh! Doctor! Yes, for the love of God!" said Calandrino. "I've got two hundred lire I was going to buy a farm with; if they're all needed, take them all, only keep me from having a child, for I don't know how I should bear it. I've heard women make such a noise when childbearing, although they've got a good large place to do it with, that I think if I suffered such pain I should die before I bore the child."

"Have no fear," said the doctor, "I'll make you a certain distilled drink, very good and pleasant to drink, which in three mornings will take it all away, and you'll be as fit as a fiddle. But be careful after this, and don't fall into such a folly again. For this cordial you'll have to provide three pairs of good fat capons. For the other things needed, give one of your friends five lire to buy them and have them brought to my house. Tomorrow morning, in the name of God, I'll send you this distilled drink; and begin by drinking a good large glass of it each time."

"Doctor," said Calandrino at this, "I leave it all to you."

And he gave Bruno five lire and enough money besides to buy three pairs of capons, and besought him to take the trouble to assist his friend. The doctor departed, made up some harmless medicine, and sent it to him. Bruno went and bought the capons and other things needed for a good meal, and ate them with the doctor and his other friends.

Calandrino drank the medicine on three mornings, and then the doctor came to see him with his other friends, felt his pulse, and said:

"Calandrino, you are perfectly cured. You can now go about and do anything you want, there's no need to stay in the house."

Calandrino got up very cheerfully and went about his business. He told everybody he met of the wonderful cure performed on him by Doctor Simone, who had un-pregnated him in three days without any pain at all. Bruno, Buffalmacco and Nello rejoiced at having tricked Calandrino's avarice by their device; but Monna Tessa found out what had happened, and grumbled continually about it to her husband.

## FOURTH TALE

*Cecco di Messer Fortarrigo gambles away all he has at Buonconvento and the money of Cecco di Messer Angiulieri as well. He runs after Angiulieri in his shirt, saying that he is a thief, gets the peasants to stop him, dresses in his clothes, mounts his horse and leaves him in his shirt*

The words which Calandrino spoke about his wife were received by the band with great laughter; and when Filostrato had ended, the queen ordered Neifile to speak next, and she said:

Worthy ladies, if it were not more difficult for men to show others their wisdom and virtue than their folly and vice, it would not be necessary for them to restrain their speech. This has been shown by the foolishness of Calandrino, who, in his eagerness to be cured of a sickness which his own stupidity made him think he had, quite unnecessarily mentioned in public his secret pleasures with his wife. This has brought an opposite example to my mind, viz., how the cunning of one man vanquished the wisdom of another, to the great harm and shame of the latter. And this I shall take pleasure in telling you.

Not many years ago there were two men of the same age, each called Cecco, one belonging to Messer Angiulieri and the other to Messer Fortarrigo. Although they were ill-assorted in many of their habits, they agreed so much in hating their own fathers that they became friends, and spent much time together.

Angiulieri was a handsome and educated man, and he felt it was wretched to stay in Siena with the pittance his father allowed him. He heard that a Cardinal, who was very friendly towards him, had been sent as legate to the Marches of Ancona; and made up his mind to go to this prelate, hoping to better his condition. He informed his father, and arranged to receive six months' allowance at one time, so that he could provide himself with clothes and a horse and set out in honourable wise.

He was looking about for someone to take with him as a servant. Fortarrigo heard of this and went immediately to Angiulieri, begging him in the best terms he knew to take him along, saying that he wanted to be his servant and attendant and everything, and all that with no wages but his expenses. Angiulieri replied that he did not want to take him, not because he did not know everything a servant needs to know, but because he gambled, and often got drunk as well. Fortarrigo replied that he would avoid them both, and swore it with so many oaths, to which he added so many entreaties that Angiulieri gave way and agreed.

They both set out one morning, and dined at Buonconvento. After dinner Angiulieri had a bed prepared in the inn on account of the great heat, and after undressing with Fortarrigo's help, he went to sleep, telling his servant to call him at Nones. While Angiulieri was asleep, Fortarrigo went to the tavern, and after drinking a little, began to gamble. In a very short time he lost what money he had and then the clothes from his back. Hoping to make good his losses, he went in his shirt to the room where Angiulieri was fast asleep, took all the money from his purse, and returned to his gambling, where this money soon followed the rest.

Angiulieri awoke, got up, dressed and asked for Fortarrigo. Not finding him, Angiulieri concluded that he must have got drunk and gone to sleep somewhere, as he often did. Angiulieri therefore decided to leave him, had his saddle and saddle-bags put on his horse, with the intention of getting another servant at Corsignano. When he went to pay the landlord, he found he had no money. At this the whole place was in an uproar, for Angiulieri said he had been robbed in the house, and threatened to have them all arrested and sent to Siena. Fortarrigo then appeared in his shirt, coming to take Angiulieri's clothes as he had taken his money. Seeing him about to mount, he said:

"What does this mean, Angiulieri? Are we to leave now? Wait a moment. The man who lent me thirty-eight soldi for my doublet will be here in a moment, and I'm sure he'll give it up for thirty-five in cash."

While he was speaking a man came along who informed Angiulieri that Fortarrigo must have stolen his money, by telling him the exact sum he had lost. In great anger Angiulieri abused Fortarrigo violently, and would have killed him if he had not been more afraid of the law than of God. Threatening to have him hanged in person or in effigy, he mounted his horse. As if Angiulieri had not been speaking to him but to someone else, Fortarrigo said:

"Come now, Angiulieri, enough of this; such talk gets us nowhere. Listen to this—if we pay at once, we can get it back for thirty-five soldi, but if we wait even till tomorrow he will want the thirty-eight he lent. He will do this for me, because I laid a wager in his favour. Why should we not save these three soldi?"

At this Angiulieri was in despair, especially since he saw everyone present looking hard at him and appearing to think, not that Fortarrigo had stolen his money but that Angiulieri had Fortarrigo's. So he said:

"What have I to do with your doublet? May you be hanged, for you've not only robbed me and gambled away my money, but you're now preventing my leaving, and making fun of me!"

Fortarrigo still acted as if Angiulieri was talking to someone else, and said:

"Ah! Why won't you make those three soldi for me? Do you think I can't pay you back? Ah! Do it, if you care anything about me. Why this haste? We have plenty of time to get to Torrenieri this evening. Come, pull out your purse. I might hunt all Siena and never find a doublet which suited me so well as this; and to think that I let him have it for thirty-eight soldi! It's worth forty or more, so you're harming me in two ways."

Angiulieri, in great wrath with him for having stolen his money and then keeping him in talk, made no reply but, turning his horse's head, took the road for Torrenieri. Fortarrigo, thinking of a cunning trick, trotted after him in his shirt. He had gone two miles, begging for his doublet, and Angiulieri was going fast to get this annoyance out of his ears when Fortarrigo saw some workmen in a field near the road ahead of Angiulieri. So he began to shout loudly:

"Stop him! Stop him!"

They rushed into the road in front of Angiulieri with their hoes and spades, thinking that he had robbed the man who was shouting behind in his shirt; and they seized and held Angiulieri. It was of no avail for him to tell them who he was and what had happened. And when Fortarrigo arrived, he said with an angry look:

"I don't know why I don't slay you, you treacherous thief, running off with my property!"

Then, turning to the peasants, he said:

"See, gentlemen, how he left me in the inn after having first gambled away all he had! Thanks to you and God I have recovered everything, and shall always be grateful to you."

Angiulieri said the same thing about Fortarrigo, but his words were not listened to. With the peasants' help Fortarrigo pulled him from his horse, stripped off his clothes and put them on himself, and then mounted, leaving Angiulieri in his shirt and hose. He returned to Siena and told everyone that he had won the horse and clothes from Angiulieri at dice. Angiulieri, who thought he was going in comfortable circumstances to the Cardinal in the Marches, returned poor and in his shirt to Buonconvento. Out of shame he had no desire to return to Siena at that time, but borrowed some clothes and rode to some relatives at Corsignano on the sorry nag belonging to Fortarrigo, where he stayed until his father again came to his assistance.

Thus Fortarrigo's cunning ruined Angiulieri's wise plans, although at a fitting time and place he did not go unpunished.

# FIFTH TALE

*Calandrino falls in love with a young woman. Bruno makes him a written charm and, when he touches her with it, she goes with him. He is surprised by his wife and has a painful quarrel with her in consequence*

Neifile's short tale passed without exciting much laughter or comment from the band, and the queen then turned to Fiammetta and ordered her to follow next. She merrily replied that she would do so willingly, and began thus:

Most gentle ladies, as I think you all know, there is no subject so often repeated but will please if the person who speaks of it knows how to choose the right time and place. When I consider the reason why we are here (which is for our amusement and pleasure, and nothing else), I think that this is a fitting time and place for everything which provides us with pleasure and amusement. And though such a thing were repeated a thousand times it could not give anything but pleasure each time. We have several times talked of the doings of Calandrino, but since they are all amusing (as Filostrato said recently), I want to tell you another additional tale about him. If I wanted to depart from the truth, I could easily conceal it under borrowed names; but since departure from the truth in story-telling about things which actually happened greatly diminishes the pleasure of the hearers, I shall tell it you as it actually happened, for the above-mentioned reason.

Niccolo Cornacchini, our countryman, was a rich man, and among his possessions was an estate in the Camerata. He built a large, handsome house there and made an agreement with Bruno and Buffalmacco to paint it with frescoes. Since there was a great deal of work to do, they took on Nello and Calandrino as their assistants, and then began the job. Some of the rooms had beds and other furniture and an old woman servant was there as caretaker; but, since none of the family was there, one of Niccolo's sons, a young unmarried man named Filippo, sometimes brought out a woman for his pleasure, kept her there two or three days, and then sent her away. Among those he brought out was a girl named Niccolosa, who was kept in a low house at

Camaldoli belonging to a man named Mangione, who let
her out on hire.

She was handsome and well dressed, and for a girl of her
sort well behaved and well spoken. One morning she came
out of her room in a white petticoat, with her hair loosely
knotted on her head, and went to the well in the courtyard
to wash her hands and face. At that moment Calandrino
happened to come there for water, and saluted her familiarly. She replied and looked at him, more because he was
a curious looking man than for any flirtatious reason. Calandrino began to look at her and thought her beautiful; he
then began to make advances, and did not return with the
water. But as he did not know her, he had nothing to say
to her. She had noticed his looking at her and looked at him
with a little sigh, to egg him on. This made Calandrino
immediately fall in love with her, and he did not leave the
courtyard until she was called back to Filippo's room. Calandrino returned to his work, and did nothing but heave
deep sighs. Bruno, who always watched him carefully because he took great delight in Calandrino's doings, noticed
this, and said:

"What the devil's wrong with you, friend Calandrino?
You do nothing but puff."

"Friend," said Calandrino, "if I had anyone to help me,
I should be all right."

"How's that?" asked Bruno.

"Don't tell anyone," said Calandrino, "there's a girl here
who's more beautiful than a Lamia, and she's so much in
love with me, you'd be surprised. I noticed it just now when
I went for water."

"Oh!" said Bruno, "look out that it isn't Filippo's wife."

"I think she is," said Calandrino, "because he called her,
and she went into his room. But what does that matter? I'd
steal such little bits from Christ, let alone Filippo. To tell
you the truth, friend, I like her so much I can't tell you how
much."

"Friend," said Bruno, "I'll find out who she is for you.
And if she's Filippo's wife, I'll fix up your affair in two
minutes, for I'm very friendly with her. But how shall we
manage to keep Buffalmacco from knowing? I can never
talk to her without his being there."

"I don't mind about Buffalmacco," said Calandrino, "but
we must look out for Nello; he's a relative of Tessa, and
would spoil everything."

"Well said," replied Bruno.

Bruno knew who she was, because he had seen her arrive,

and Filippo had told him about her. So, when Calandrino left his work for a time and went to look for her, Bruno told Nello and Buffalmacco about it, and they agreed together on what they would do about this love affair. When he returned, Bruno whispered:

"Did you see her?"

"Oh yes," replied Calandrino, "she's smitten me!"

"I'll go and see if she's the girl I think," said Bruno, "and if she is, leave it to me."

So Bruno went off to Filippo and the girl, and first told them the sort of man Calandrino was, and what he had said; then he arranged what each of them would do and say, for them all to get fun out of Calandrino's love-making. He then returned to Calandrino, and said:

"Yes, it's she. You'll have to go very carefully in the matter, because, if Filippo found it out, all the water in the Arno would not wash it away. But what do you want me to say to her on your behalf, if I can speak to her?"

"Ah!" said Calandrino, "tell her first that I wish her a thousand bushels of the stuff good to impregnate her, that I'm her servant, and if she wants anything. Do you understand me?"

"Yes," said Bruno, "leave it to me."

When supper came and they all left work and went down into the courtyard, Filippo and Niccolosa made friendly advances to Calandrino, who stared at Niccolosa and made the most absurd gestures at her, so that a blind man would have noticed them. Following Bruno's advice, she did everything she could think of to encourage him. She amused herself greatly with Calandrino's absurd behaviour, while Filippo pretended to be talking to Buffalmacco and the others, and not to notice what was going on. Soon afterwards they left, to Calandrino's great despair; and as they went towards Florence, Bruno said to Calandrino:

"I told you that you'd make her melt like ice in the sun. God's body, if you brought back your guitar and sang some of your love songs, you'd make her throw herself out of the window to get at you."

"Do you think so, friend?" asked Calandrino. "Shall I bring it back then?"

"Yes," replied Bruno.

"You didn't believe me today," said Calandrino, "when I told you about her. I'm quite sure, friend, that I know how to get what I want better than any man living. Who else would have been able to make such a woman fall in love with him so quickly? Do you think it could have been done by those young men who go trumpeting up and down all day, and can't collect three handfuls of nuts in a thousand years? Now I want you to see what I can do with the guitar; you'll see fine playing. Understand, I'm not such an old man as you think, as she saw at once. Anyway, I'll soon show her if I once get my hand on her. By the true body of Christ, I'll make her play so that she'll follow me like the madwoman after her child."

"Oh!" said Bruno, "you'll take her by the nose. I can see you already with your teeth like lute-keys biting her red lips and her two rosy cheeks, and then eating her all up."

These words made Calandrino feel that he had her already, and he went along singing and leaping so happily that he could have jumped out of his skin.

Next day he brought his lute, and sang several songs with her, to the immense amusement of all the others. In short, he became so excited to see her often that he scarcely did any work, and kept going to the window or the door or into the courtyard to see her. And she, cleverly behaving in accordance with Bruno's instructions, gave him every opportunity. Bruno replied to Calandrino's messages and occasionally sent one from her. When she was not there, he produced letters from her, in which she gave him great hopes, but said she was in the house of relatives and could not see him.

Bruno and Buffalmacco kept the affair in their hands, and in this way got great amusement out of Calandrino's doings. They made him buy her an ivory comb and a purse and a small knife and similar trifles, on the pretence that she had asked for them, and in exchange they brought him back one or two worthless rings, over which he went into ecstasies. Moreover, he gave them good lunches and other treats, so that they would help him on.

Things went on in this way for about two months, without advancing any further; and then Calandrino saw that the work was coming to an end and realised that if he did not bring his love to a successful end before the work was over, he would never be able to do so. He therefore kept urging and entreating Bruno, who, having first made his arrangements with her and Filippo, said to Calandrino one day when she was there:

"Friend, the girl has promised me a thousand times to do what you want, and yet she doesn't do it. I think she's leading you by the nose. Now, since she won't do what she promises, we'll make her do it, whether she wants or not, if you agree."

"Ah yes!" said Calandrino. "For the love of God let's do it soon."

"Have you the courage to touch her with a written spell I can make for you?" asked Bruno.

"Of course," said Calandrino.

"Well then," said Bruno, "bring me a little unborn paper, a live bat, three grains of incense and a blessed candle, and leave the rest to me."

Calandrino spent the whole of that evening trying to catch a bat, and at last caught one which he took to Bruno with the other things. Bruno went into a room and wrote certain absurd phrases on the card with magical characters, and then took it to Calandrino, saying:

"Calandrino, if you touch her with this writing, she will immediately follow you, and do what you want. So if Filippo goes away today, you must find her and touch her with it. Go to the small house near, which is the best place because nobody frequents it. You'll see that she'll come there. When she's there, you know what you have to do."

Calandrino was the happiest man in the world at this, took the writing, and said:

"Friend, leave it to me."

Nello, of whom Calandrino was afraid, was as much amused with all this as the others, and had a hand in the jest. So, as Bruno had arranged, he went to Calandrino's wife in Florence, and said:

"Tessa, you know how Calandrino unreasonably beat you when he brought the stones back from Mugnone. I mean that you shall have your revenge, and if you don't take it, never consider me your relative and friend again. He has fallen in love with a woman up there, and she is so light that she often shuts herself up alone with him. They have arranged to meet soon; and I want you to come along and catch him and punish him."

The wife did not see it was all a joke, but started to her feet, saying:

"Ah! You common thief, is that how you treat me? By God's Cross, it shall not go on without your paying for it!"

She put on her cloak, found a woman to accompany her, and set out at a sharp pace with Nello. When Bruno saw them coming in the distance, he said to Filippo:

"Here comes our friend."

So Filippo went up to the place where Calandrino and the others were working, and said:

"My masters, I have to go to Florence at once; work hard!"

He then went and hid in a place where he could see what Calandrino did, but not be seen himself. When Calandrino thought that Filippo had got far enough away, he came down into the courtyard. There he found Niccolosa alone and began to talk to her; while she, who knew her part well, greeted him a little more warmly than usual. Calandrino then touched her with the written spell. As soon as he had touched her, he walked towards the cottage without saying a word, and she followed him. As soon as they were inside, she closed the door, embraced Calandrino, threw him down on some straw there and straddled over him, keeping her hands on his shoulders so that he could not put his face close to hers. She looked at him, as if with great desire, saying:

"O sweet Calandrino, heart of my body, my soul, my love, my repose, how long have I wanted to have you and to hold you as I wished! Your charm enchanted me, and your guitar-playing made lattice-work of my heart. Can it be true that I have you?"

Calandrino, who was hardly able to move, said:

"Ah! sweet soul! Let me kiss you!"

"Oh, you're very hasty," said Niccolosa. "Let me first gaze my fill at you. Let me satiate my eyes with that sweet face."

Bruno and Buffalmacco had rejoined Filippo, and all three heard and saw this. Just as Calandrino was trying to kiss Niccolosa, up came Nello and Monna Tessa. And, as soon as they arrived, Nello said:

"I vow to God they're together now!"

The wife in a rage beat on the door of the cottage, broke it open and, rushing in, saw Niccolosa on Calandrino. As soon as she saw Tessa, Niccolosa sprang up and ran away to Filippo. Before Calandrino could get up, Monna Tessa ran at his face with her nails and scratched him, seized him by the hair, and dragged him to and fro, screaming:

"Cursed foul dog, so this is how you treat me! You silly old man, cursed be my love for you! Do you think you haven't enough to do in your own home that you go making love to other women? You're a nice lover! Don't you know what you are, villain? Don't you know what you are, idiot? If you were squeezed to the last drop there wouldn't come out enough juice to make a sauce. God's faith, it's not Tessa now makes you pregnant, God punish her whoever she may be, for she must be a poor creature to want such a jewel as you!"

At the sight of his wife, Calandrino felt neither alive nor

dead, and dared not make any defence. But when he had been scratched and buffeted and his hair pulled out, he found his hat and stood up, humbly begging his wife not to scream so loud if she did not want him to be cut to pieces, because the woman who had been with him was the wife of the master of the house. Said his wife:

"Let her be! God curse her!"

Bruno and Buffalmacco, who had laughed their fill over all this with Filippo and Niccolosa, came up as if they had heard the noise, and after much talk calmed Tessa down. They advised Calandrino to go to Florence and not return, so that he might not receive any harm, in case Filippo heard about it. So poor sad Calandrino, with his scratches and torn hair, returned to Florence without any desire to go back to that place again, day and night tormented and teased with his wife's scoldings. Thus ended his ardent love, after providing much mirth to his friends, and to Niccolosa and Filippo.

## SIXTH TALE

*Two young men spend the night with a man; one of them lies with the man's daughter, and his wife unwittingly lies with the other. The young man who lay with the daughter gets into the father's bed and tells him about it, thinking it is his companion. They start a quarrel. The wife guesses what has happened, gets into the daughter's bed and makes peace between them*

Calandrino had made the group laugh before, and did so again. When the ladies had ceased discussing his doings, the queen ordered Pamfilo to speak, and he said:

Fair ladies, the name of Calandrino's love, Niccolosa, makes me think of another Niccolosa, about whom I want to tell you, since her story will show you how a good woman's sudden device prevented a great scandal.

Not long ago in the Mugnone Valley there lived a good man who provided food and drink for travellers who could pay for it. Since he was poor and had only a small house, he sometimes put acquaintances up for the night, but no one else. His wife was quite a handsome woman, and by her he had two children. One was a pretty girl of about fifteen or sixteen, but not yet married; the other was a baby not a year old, whom the mother fed at the breast.

A gay, pleasant young gentleman of our city, who often passed that way, saw the girl and fell violently in love with her. She was very proud that such a young man should fall in love with her, and while she was devising means to keep him in love with her by various feignings, she fell in love with him herself. Their mutual desire would have brought this love to its fruition if Pinuccio (such was the young man's name) had not wanted to avoid any scandal to the girl and himself.

But his ardour became greater every day, and Pinuccio wanted to be with her. He determined to find some way of spending the night there, for since he knew the plan of the house he felt certain that if he could do this he would be able to go to her without anyone knowing about it. As soon as he thought of this, he put his plan into action.

With a confidential friend of his named Adriano, who knew all about this love affair, he hired two post horses and loaded them with a couple of saddle-bags stuffed with straw. They rode out of Florence and, after making a circle round, reached the Mugnone Valley after nightfall. Then, as if they were returning from Romagna, they turned and rode up to the poor man's house, and knocked at the door. As he knew them both well, he opened the door at once. Said Pinuccio:

"You'll have to put us up for the night. We thought we could reach Florence, but the best of our efforts have only brought us as far as this at this hour, as you see."

"Pinuccio," said the host, "you know how difficult it is for me to lodge gentlemen like you. But since night has caught you here and there is no time to go elsewhere, I will gladly lodge you as well as I can."

The two young men dismounted and, after attending to their horses, entered the little inn. They had brought food with them, and had supper with the host. He had only one small bedroom in which he had made up three beds to the best of his ability. Consequently there was very little space left, for two of the beds were ranged along one wall and the third opposite, so that there was only a narrow passage between them. The host had the best of these beds prepared for the two young men, and sent them to lie there. A little later, when they pretended to be asleep, although they were both awake, the host sent his daughter to bed in the second, and got into the third with his wife. The cradle containing the baby was put at the foot of the wife's bed.

Pinuccio saw all these arrangements, and a little later, when he thought everyone was asleep, he got up quietly and went to the bed where the girl he loved was lying, and lay down beside her. Although she was afraid, she received him gladly, and they enjoyed together the pleasures they desired. While Pinuccio was with the girl, a cat happened to knock something down, and woke the wife up. Thinking it was something important, she got up in the dark, and went to the place where she had heard the noise.

Adriano had paid no attention to this, but happened at that moment to get up for a natural function. As he was going out for this purpose he came upon the child's cradle, and, not being able to pass, took it from where it was and placed it beside his own bed. Then, having done what he wanted, he returned, and without troubling about the cradle, got back into bed.

The wife found that what had fallen was not important and so did not trouble to make a light to look further; she scolded at the cat and returned to the bedroom. She went straight to the bed in which her husband was sleeping, but not finding the cradle said to herself: "Oh! see what I was going to do! God's faith, I was just going to get into the guests' bed!" She searched a little further and came upon the cradle, whereupon she got into bed and lay down beside Adriano, thinking it was her husband. Adriano, who had not yet fallen asleep again, received her most gladly, and without saying a word seized her eagerly, to her great satisfaction.

Meanwhile Pinuccio had taken his pleasure of the girl as he desired. Fearing that sleep might surprise him while with her, he left her to go and sleep in his own bed. Finding the cradle there, he thought it the host's bed; so he went on, and got into bed with the host, who woke up in consequence. Pinuccio, thinking he was lying beside Adriano, said:

"I told you there was never so sweet a thing as Niccolosa. God's body, I have had the greatest pleasure a man ever had with a woman, and I went six times into the town before I left!"

The host was not best pleased to hear this news, and at first said to himself: "What the devil is he doing here?" Then with more anger than wisdom he said:

"Pinuccio, you've done a foul deed, and I don't know why you should have done it to me. But, by God's body, I'll make you pay for it."

Pinuccio was not the wisest young man in the world; he saw his mistake, but instead of trying to mend it as well as he could, he said:

"How will you pay me? What can you do to me?"

The host's wife, thinking she was with her husband, said to Adriano:

"Oh! Listen to our guests quarrelling together!"

"Let them alone," said Adriano, laughing. "God curse them! They drank too much last night."

The woman thought she heard her husband grumbling in the other bed and from Adriano's voice she realised at once where she was. Like a wise woman, she said not a word but at once arose and picked up the child's cradle. Since there was not a gleam of light in the room, she groped her way with the cradle to her daughter's bed and lay down beside her. Then, pretending that she had been awakened by her husband's clamour, she called to him and asked him why he was quarrelling with Pinuccio.

"Didn't you hear what he said he did to Niccolosa to-night?" asked the husband.

"He lies in his throat," said she. "He hasn't lain with Niccolosa, for I have been in bed with her and I should never have slept through it. You're a fool to believe it. You drink so much in the evening that you dream all night and toss up and down without knowing it, and think you are doing wonders. It's a great pity you don't break your neck. But what is Pinuccio doing there? Why isn't he in his own bed?"

Adriano saw how cleverly the woman was hiding her shame and her daughter's, and said:

"Pinuccio, I've told you a hundred times that you ought not to sleep away from home. Your habit of walking in your sleep and relating your silly dreams as truth will get you into trouble. Come back to bed, bad luck to you!"

From what Adriano and his wife said, the host began to think that Pinuccio was dreaming. So he took him by the shoulders, shook him, and said:

"Pinuccio, wake up! Go back to your own bed."

Pinuccio saw at once why they spoke in this way, and at once began to talk nonsense like a man dreaming, at which the host laughed heartily. Finally, after much shaking, he pretended to awake, and called to Adriano:

"Is it morning? Why are you calling me?"

"Yes," said Adriano, "come here."

Pretending to be very sleepy, Pinuccio at last got out of the host's bed and returned to Adriano. When day came and they got up, the host laughed and joked at him and his dreams. So with one jest and another the two young men got their horses ready, strapped on the saddle-bags, drank a stirrup-cup with the host, and rode to Florence, no less delighted with the way in which the adventure had succeeded than with the success itself.

Afterwards Pinuccio and Niccolosa found other ways of meeting; while the girl vowed to her mother that Pinuccio really had been dreaming. Thus the mother, remembering Adriano's embraces, thought that she had been the only one awake.

## SEVENTH TALE

*Talano di Molese dreams that a wolf tears his wife's throat and face and warns her to be careful. She pays no attention to the warning, and the thing happens*

When Pamfilo ended his tale, they all praised the woman's presence of mind; the queen then ordered Pampinea to speak, and she began thus:

Fair ladies, we have spoken before of the truth of dreams, which many people laugh at. But, although we have discussed this, I intend to tell you a very short tale of what happened not long ago to a woman neighbour of mine, through her not believing a dream seen by her husband.

I do not know if you are acquainted with a man of some importance, named Talano di Molese. He married a very beautiful girl named Margarita, who was very eccentric, self-willed and petulant, so much so that nobody could do anything to please her, while she would do nothing in accordance with the advice of others. This was naturally very hard for Talano to bear, but he put up with it, since there was nothing else to do.

One night Talano and Margarita were asleep in a country house they possessed; and in a dream he thought he saw her walking through a wood not far from their house. As he looked at her, he saw a large fierce wolf come out of the wood, seize her by the throat, cast her on the ground and try to drag her away as she screamed for help; she escaped from its jaws, and he saw that her throat and face were all mangled. When they got up in the morning, he said to his wife:

"Although your petulance has prevented me from ever having one happy day with you, yet I should be unhappy if ill befell you; and so, if you will take my advice, you will not go out of the house today."

She asked him why, and he then told her his dream. She tossed her head, and said:

"Those who wish ill, dream ill. You pretend to be very careful of me, but you dreamed what you would like to see happen to me. So today and always I shall be very careful not to make you happy with this or any other misfortune to me."

"I knew you would say that," said Talano, "because who scratches a scab gets that for his reward. Think what you please, I meant well; and I advise you again to stay in the house today, or at least not to go into the wood."

"Very well," said she.

But then she said to herself: "How cunningly he tried to frighten me out of not going to the wood today! He must certainly have arranged to meet one of those women there, and doesn't want me to find them. Oh, he'd not deceive a blind man, and I should be a great fool if I believed him and didn't know what he is! He certainly won't succeed. If I have to stay there all day, I must see what he is getting up to there today."

Meanwhile, the husband left the house by one entrance, and she went out by another. She hastened as secretly as she could and hid herself in the thickest part of the wood, watching and looking here and there to see if anyone were coming. While she was doing this, with no thought of the wolf, suddenly from a thick clump of trees emerged a great terrible wolf, and she had scarcely time to say: "God help me!" when the wolf was at her throat. It seized her, and began to carry her away as if she had been a small lamb.

Her throat was held so firmly that she could not scream, nor help herself in any other way. She would inevitably have been strangled as the wolf dragged her along if it had not come upon some shepherds, who shouted at it, and forced it to leave her. The shepherds recognised the unhappy woman and carried her home. After long treatment she was healed by the doctors, but all her throat and part of her face were so much scarred that, instead of being beautiful as before, she looked deformed and ugly. Thus, being ashamed to appear where she would be seen, she often miserably wept for her petulance and her refusal to believe her husband's true dream, in a way which would have cost her nothing.

## EIGHTH TALE

*Biondello plays a trick on Ciacco with a dinner; Ciacco revenges himself prudently and gets Biondello soundly beaten*

Everyone in the merry band said that what Talano had seen in his sleep was not a dream but a vision, since it had all happened exactly as he dreamed it. When everyone was silent, the queen ordered Lauretta to follow next, and she said:

Most wise ladies, those who have spoken before me today have almost all been inspired by something we have talked of formerly. I myself am now moved by Pampinea's tale of yesterday about the savage revenge of the scholar, to tell you of a vengeance which was serious enough to the person who suffered it, although not so savage as that.

I must therefore tell you that among the Florentines was a very gluttonous man, named Ciacco. His income was not sufficient to meet the expense of his gluttony, and since he was well mannered and full of witty jokes and sayings, he made himself, not a courtier, but a sarcastic buffoon. He frequented the rich and delighted to eat good food; so he dined and supped with the wealthy, although he was not always invited.

At the same time in Florence there was a man called Biondello, who had the same parasitical occupation as Ciacco. He was a pleasant little man, as neat as a fly, with his cap on his head, and a mass of yellow hair with never a single hair out of place. One morning in Lent he went to the fish market and bought two very large lampreys for Messer Vieri de' Cerchi. Ciacco saw him, and going up to him, said:

"What is the meaning of this?"

"Yesterday," replied Biondello, "three lampreys much larger than these and a sturgeon were sent to Messer Corso

Donati. They are not sufficient to entertain the gentlemen he has invited, and so he sent me to buy two more. Won't you come along?"

"Indeed I'll come," replied Ciacco.

So at the right time he went to Messer Corso's house, and found him with several of his neighbours waiting for dinner. When he was asked why he had come there, he replied:

"Messer, I have come to dine with you and your friends."

"You are welcome," replied Messer Corso, "and since it is dinner time, let us sit down to it."

So they sat down to table, and were served with peas and tunny fish, and then fried fish from the Arno, and nothing more. Ciacco then saw through Biondello's trick, and, being very angry at it, made up his mind to pay him back. Biondello made a lot of people laugh by telling them the trick; and not many days later he met Ciacco. Biondello greeted him, and laughingly asked him how he liked Messer Corso's lampreys.

"Before a week has passed," said Ciacco, "you'll be able to tell much better than I."

He then left Biondello and at once put his plan into action. He promised some money to a market-man and, handing him a glass bottle, took him to the Loggia de' Cavicciuli. There he pointed to a knight, named Messer Filippo Argenti, a tall, strong, sinewy man, haughty, irascible and hasty; and said to the market-man:

"Take this bottle to him, and speak these words: 'Messer, I am sent to you by Biondello, who begs that you will redden this bottle with your good ruby wine, because he wants to treat some of his friends.' Be careful that he doesn't get his hands on you, because he would give you a bad time and it would spoil my plan."

"Am I to say anything else?" asked the market-man.

"No," said Ciacco, "go along; when you have said this to him, come back to me with the bottle, and I'll pay you."

So the market-man went off, and delivered the message to Messer Filippo. When Messer Filippo heard it, he went red in the face, for he was very prone to wrath and thought that Biondello, whom he knew, was making a jest of him. He started to his feet, saying: "What 'reddening' and what 'friends' does he mean? God curse him and you!" And he stretched out his arm to grasp the market-man; but he was on the alert and fled away at once. He returned to Ciacco, who had watched everything from a safe distance, and told him what Messer Filippo had said. Ciacco in delight at once paid the market-man, and did not rest until he found Biondello, to whom he said:

"Were you in the Loggia de' Cavicciuli just now?"

"No," replied Biondello. "Why do you ask?"

"Because," replied Ciacco, "I know that Messer Filippo is looking for you—I don't know why."

"Good," said Biondello, "I'll go to him and make a joke."

Biondello went off, followed at a distance by Ciacco who wanted to see what would happen. Messer Filippo, who had not been able to catch the market-man, was in a great rage and chafed inwardly, for he could make nothing of the market-man's words except that Biondello, at someone's instigation, was making fun of him. And while he was chafing in this way, up came Biondello. As soon as Messer Filippo saw him, he went up and gave him a punch in the face.

"Oh! Messer!" exclaimed Biondello. "What does this mean?"

Messer Filippo took him by the hair, tore off his cap and threw his hood on the ground, still punching him hard, and saying:

"Traitor! You'll soon see what it means! What do you mean by sending me messages about 'reddening' and 'friends'? Do you think I am a boy to be hoodwinked?"

So saying, he kept smashing at his face with a fist which seemed like iron, tore out his hair, and dragging him through the mud made rags of his clothes. And he went at it so violently that Biondello had not time to say a word or to ask him why he was attacking him. He had certainly heard the "reddening" and the "friends," but did not know what they meant.

Finally, after Messer Filippo had given him a sound thrashing, a number of people gathered round and with great difficulty rescued Biondello, who was all buffeted and bruised, from his hands. They told him why Messer Filippo had done this, and reprehended him for having sent such a message, telling him that he ought to know the sort of man Messer Filippo was, and that he was not a man to be jested with. Biondello in tears tried to clear himself, and said that he had never sent to Messer Filippo for wine. And when he had collected himself a little, he went home sadly and painfully, suspecting that this was Ciacco's work. Several days later, when the marks of the bruises had left his face, he began to go about again. He happened to meet Ciacco, who said to him:

"Well, Biondello, how did you like Messer Filippo's wine?"

"I wish you had found Messer Corso's lampreys like it!" replied Biondello.

"Right!" said Ciacco. "Next time you give me such a dinner as that I'll give you another drink like the one you had!"

Biondello realised that he was more able to feel ill will towards Ciacco than he had power to hurt him, and prayed God to make his peace with him. Thereafter he was very careful not to play such tricks.

## NINTH TALE

*Two young men go to Solomon for advice. One asks what he must do to be loved, the other how to reform a shrewish wife. Solomon tells the first to love, and the other to go to the Bridge of Geese*

If Dioneo's privilege was to be respected, no one remained to tell a tale but the queen; and when the ladies had laughed their full at the unfortunate Biondello, she began merrily to speak thus:

Amiable ladies, if the nature of things is sanely examined, we may easily perceive that the whole mass of women are subjected to men by nature, by custom and by the laws, and that they are bound to submit to the discretion of men. Therefore, every woman who desires peace, rest and comfort, ought to be humble, patient and obedient to the man to whom she belongs, as well as being chaste, which is the chief and special treasure of every wise woman.

If this were not enforced by the laws, which in all things look to the common good, and by usage or custom, whose power is very great and to be revered, Nature herself would plainly display it, for she has made women delicate and fine of body, timid and fearful of mind, giving them slight bodily strength, pleasant voices and gentle movements. All of which things show that we need the control of others. It stands to reason that everyone who needs help and control should be subject, obedient and reverent to his ruler. And what rulers and helpers have we, except men? Therefore we should honour men most highly and be subject to them.

And if any woman should revolt, I consider that she would deserve sharp punishment as well as stern admonition.

I have more than once made these reflections, but I was particularly led to them by Pampinea's story of Talano's self-willed wife, to whom God sent the punishment which her husband was unable to inflict. Therefore, as I said before, in my judgment all women who are not pleasant, mild and amiable, as they are required to be by Nature, custom and the laws, are deserving of harsh and stern punishment. So I take pleasure in telling you the advice of Solomon, which is a useful medicine for curing those who are afflicted with this disease. Let no woman, who does not deserve this medicine, think that it is intended for her, although men have a proverb which says: "A good horse and a bad horse need the spur, and a good woman and a bad woman need the stick." If these words are interpreted humorously, it can easily be admitted that they are true; and even if they are to be interpreted morally, I will say they are admissible. Women are naturally pliant and yielding, and so the stick is needed to punish the iniquity of those who go too far beyond the limits assigned them; and similarly the support and terror of the stick are needed to strengthen the virtue of those who do not allow themselves to transgress.

But, let me leave sermonising, and come to what I have in mind to say. At the time when nearly the whole world had heard the great fame of the miraculous wisdom of Solomon, and how he most liberally gave proof of it to those who sought to know, many people came to him from different parts of the world for advice in their difficulties.

Among them was a noble and very rich young man, named Melisso, who set out from the city of Laiazzo, where he dwelt. As he left Antioch on the way to Jerusalem, he rode for a time beside a young man named Giosefo, who was going the same way, and, as is usual with travellers, entered into conversation with him. Melisso having learned Giosefo's rank and the place from which he came, asked him where he was going and for what reason. Giosefo said that he was going to ask Solomon's advice as to how he should deal with his wife, who was the most perverse and shrewish of women and could not be persuaded from her shrewishness by entreaties or flatteries or any other means. He then asked Melisso whence he came, where he was going and for what reason; and Melisso replied:

"I come from Laiazzo, and I have a misfortune just as you have. I am a rich young man, and I spend my money in entertaining my fellow citizens, and yet it is a strange thing to think that for all that I cannot find one person who loves me. So I am going where you are going, to find out from him what I must do to be loved."

So the two rode on together, and when they reached Jerusalem, one of Solomon's barons introduced them to his presence, and Melisso briefly stated what he needed. To which Solomon replied: "Love." When he had said this, Melisso was at once dismissed, and Giosefo then said why he was there. The only answer Solomon gave was: "Go to the Bridge of Geese." And then Giosefo was also removed from the King's presence. He found Melisso waiting for him, and told him the reply he had received. They thought over these words, and being unable to see any meaning in them or any remedy to their needs, they felt they had been scorned, and so set out on their way home.

After they had journeyed for some days, they came to a river, over which there was a fine bridge. And since a large caravan of laden mules and horses was passing over it, they had to wait until they had all crossed. And when they had nearly all passed, there was a mule which balked, as they often do, and utterly refused to cross. The mule-driver took a small stick and began to beat it, quite moderately at first, to make it go on. But the mule went first to one side and then to the other, and sometimes turned right around, and could not be made to cross over. So the mule-driver in a great rage began to beat it violently with his stick, on the head and sides and rump; but all to no avail.

Melisso and Giosefo, who were watching, kept saying to him:

"Ah! you villain! Do you want to kill it? Why don't you try to lead it gently on? It will go quicker that way than by your beating it."

Said the mule-driver:

"You know your horses and I know my mule; you leave him to me."

So saying, he recommenced beating it, and gave it so many blows on one side and the other that the mule crossed over, and the mule-driver proved he was right. And as the two young men were leaving, Giosefo asked an old man who was sitting by the bridge-head what was the name of the bridge. And he replied:

"Messer, it is the Bridge of Geese."

As soon as Giosefo heard that, he remembered Solomon's words, and said to Melisso:

"Friend, it may be that the advice Solomon gave me was

good and true, because I recognise that I haven't learned to beat my wife, and that mule-driver showed me what I ought to do."

A few days later they reached Antioch, and Giosefo invited Melisso to rest there a few days with him. Giosefo's wife received them ungraciously, and he told her to prepare such a supper as Melisso should order; and he did so in a few words, to please his friend. The lady, as she had been accustomed to do in the past, prepared a supper almost exactly the opposite to that Melisso had ordered. Seeing this, Giosefo said angrily:

"Were you not told how you should make this supper?"

"What do you mean?" she replied, turning haughtily to him. "Bah! Am I not to sup if you want to? If I was told to make it differently, I thought I'd make it the way I wanted. If it pleases you, let it please you; if not, let it alone."

Melisso was surprised at the lady's answer, and blamed her for it. And Giosefo said to her: "Woman, you are still what you were wont to be; but, trust me, I'll make you alter your ways."

He then turned to Melisso, and said:

"Friend, we shall soon see the value of Solomon's advice. But I beg you will not object to being present or that you will consider what I am about to do a mere game. Don't try to interrupt me, but remember the mule-driver's answer when we complained about his mule."

"I am in your house," replied Melisso, "and there I shall do nothing contrary to your pleasure."

Giosefo found a stick cut from a sapling oak, and went to the room where his wife had gone grumbling, after leaving the table in irritation. He seized her by the hair, threw her at his feet, and began to beat her hard with the stick. The lady first shrieked, and then threatened him. But Giosefo went on, and as she was now bruised all over she begged him for God's sake mercifully not to kill her, saying that she would never again thwart his wishes. But Giosefo still did not stop. He laid on with more fury than ever, now on her ribs, now on her buttocks, now on her shoulders, and basted her until he was weary. In short, the good lady had bruises on every bone and part of her. Having done this, he returned to Melisso and said:

"Tomorrow we shall see the result of the advice: 'Go to the Bridge of Geese.'"

After washing his hands and resting, he supped with Melisso, and then they went to bed.

The poor lady with great difficulty got up from the floor and threw herself on the bed, where she rested as well as she could. Next morning, she got up very early, and sent to ask Giosefo what he would like for dinner. Laughing over this with Melisso, he gave his orders; and then when they went home for dinner they found everything prepared exactly as he had ordered. So they highly praised the advice which at first they had not understood.

A few days later Melisso left Giosefo and returned home, where he consulted a wise man, and told him the advice he had received from Solomon. Said the wise man:

"No truer or better advice could have been given you. You know quite well that you care for nobody, and your entertainments and good services do not come from any love you bear to others, but from ostentation. Love then, as Solomon told you, and you will be loved."

Thus the shrew was chastised, and the young man by loving obtained love.

## TENTH TALE

*At the request of gaffer Pietro, Don Gianni recites spells to turn his wife into a mare; but when it comes to sticking on the tail, gaffer Pietro spoils the whole magical operation by saying he doesn't want a tail*

The tale told by the queen made the young men laugh and the ladies murmur a little; but when they were silent Dioneo began to speak thus:

Fair ladies, among many white doves a black crow adds more beauty than a snowy swan; so among many wise men one who is less wise not only adds splendour and beauty to their ripe wisdom but pleasure and amusement. You are all most discreet and moderate, and I am a witless fellow who makes your virtue more conspicuous by my defects, and so you should cherish me more than if I diminished it by greater worth in myself. Therefore I should have more freedom to show you what I am by what I say, and should more patiently be endured by you than if I were a wise man. I shall tell you a short tale whereby you may learn how carefully one should observe the instructions of those who conduct magical operations, and how small an error may ruin the whole charm.

Last year at Barletta there was a priest named Don Gianni di Barolo; and because his church was a poor one he went round the fairs of Apulia with his mare, buying and selling and hawking goods to support himself. As he went about thus he became familiar with one Pietro da Tresanti, who followed the same occupation as himself with an ass; and to show his friendship and affection he always called him gaffer Pietro. Whenever he came to Barletta, the priest always took him in and entertained him to the best of his ability. Gaffer Pietro, on his side, was a very poor man and had a little cottage at Tresanti, just big enough for himself and his pretty young wife and his ass. And whenever Don Gianni came to Tresanti, Pietro took him in and entertained him in exchange for the hospitality he had received at Barletta. But in the matter of lodging, gaffer Pietro had only one small bed, in which he slept with his pretty wife. So he could not entertain the priest as he wanted, for Don Gianni had to sleep on straw in the stable beside his mare and the ass.

The wife knew how the priest entertained her husband at Barletta, and more than once when the priest came she wanted to go and sleep with her neighbour, named Zita Carapresa di Giudice Leo, so that the priest could sleep in the bed with her husband. She often offered it to him, but he would never consent, and once said to her:

"Gammer Gemmata, trouble not about me, I am well enough. Whenever I like I can change my mare into a fair damsel and lie with her, and when I want I can change her back into a mare; and so I will never be separated from her."

The girl was amazed, but believed him, and told her husband about it, adding:

"If he's as friendly to you as you say, why don't you make him teach you these spells so that you can turn me into a mare, and go about your business with an ass and a mare, and in that way we'd both make money, and then when we got home you could turn me into a woman again!"

Gaffer Pietro, who was about as ignorant as a man can be, believed this and accepted her advice; and began to urge Don Gianni to teach him how to do it. Don Gianni did his best to wean the man from his stupidity, but not being able to, he said:

"Well, since you must have it, we'll get up tomorrow at dawn as usual, and I'll show you how it's done. The most difficult part is to stick on the tail, as you'll see."

Gaffer Pietro and Gammer Gemmata hardly slept at all that night, so eagerly did they expect it; and when it was near daylight they got up and called Don Gianni, who rose up in his shirt and went into gaffer Pietro's little room, saying:

"I don't know anyone in the world I would do this for, except for you, but since you want it, I'll do it. But you'll have to do what I tell you if you want it done."

They said they would do what he told them. So Don Gianni lighted a candle and put it into gaffer Pietro's hand, saying:

"Watch carefully what I do, and remember what I say, and if you don't want to spoil everything be careful not to utter a word whatever you may see or hear; and pray God that the tail may stick on well."

Gaffer Pietro took the candle and said he would be careful. Don Gianni then made Gammer Gemmata strip stark naked, and stand on all fours like a mare, warning her likewise not to speak a word whatever happened. He then touched her face and head, saying: "This will be a good mare's head"; then touched her hair, saying: "This will be a good mare's mane"; he touched her arms, saying: "These will be good mare's legs and hoofs"; then he touched her breasts and found them round and firm, and a part of him which wasn't called woke and stood upright, and he said: "This will make a good mare's chest"; and he did the same thing to her back and belly and buttocks and thighs and calves. Finally, nothing remained but the tail; so the priest lifted his shirt and took out the dibber used for planting men and placed it in its natural sheath, saying, "And this will make a fine mare's tail!"

Gaffer Pietro had watched everything most carefully hitherto, but he greatly disapproved of this last, and said:

"Oh! Don Gianni! I don't want a tail, I don't want a tail!"

The radical moisture by which all plants are settled had already come when Don Gianni pulled it out, saying:

"Ah! Gaffer Pietro, what have you done? Didn't I tell you not to speak, whatever you saw? The mare was nearly made but your talking has spoiled it all, and there's no way to begin it over again."

"Well enough," said gaffer Pietro, "but I didn't want that sort of tail. Why didn't you tell me to make it myself, and besides you put it on too low down."

"Because the first time you wouldn't have known how to put it on as well as I can," replied Don Gianni.

The wife stood up as they were arguing, and in all good faith said to her husband:

"Fool that you are, why did you spoil your own business and mine? When did you ever see a mare without a tail? God help me, you're a poor man, and it'll be a mercy if you're not still poorer."

Since there was no other way to make the girl into a mare, because Pietro had spoken, she dressed sadly and regretfully. Gaffer Pietro prepared to follow his old calling with his ass as usual, and went off to the fair at Bitonto with Don Gianni, whom he never again asked for such a favour.

They laughed as if they were never going to stop at this tale, which was better understood by the ladies than Dioneo had intended. But when the tale was ended and the sun began to grow cooler, the queen knew that the end of her reign had come; so she arose and took off the garland and placed it on the head of Pamfilo, the only one of them who remained to have the honour. And she said, smiling:

"Sire, since you are the last you have the great task of amending all the errors of myself and the rest who held this place before you, and so God grant you grace, as he has granted it to me, to make you a king."

Pamfilo received the honour gaily, and replied:

"Your virtues and those of my other subjects will cause me to be worthy of praise, like my predecessors."

In accordance with established custom he made suitable arrangements with the steward, and then turned to the waiting ladies, and said:

"Enamoured ladies, Emilia, our queen today, in her wisdom gave you liberty to speak on any subject you chose, in order to rest your powers. But, since you are now rested, I consider it would be well to return to our old laws. So tomorrow I want each of you to be ready to tell a tale on the subject of those who have behaved liberally or munificently in love affairs or other matters. Hearing of these things will doubtless kindle your spirits to high actions. Thus our lives, which can but be brief in these our mortal bodies, will be remembered through our fame, which all who think beyond their bellies should not only desire but seek and labour after with all their efforts."

The merry band approved the theme, and then, by permission of the new king, they got up and gave themselves to their wonted pleasures, each of them doing what he most wished to do; and thus they passed the time until supper. They went merrily to it, and were served diligently and in order; and thereafter danced as usual, and sang perhaps a thousand songs, more charming for their words than their music. The king then ordered Neifile to sing a song of her own, and she immediately and charmingly began to sing in a clear gay voice as follows:

*A girl am I and gladly do rejoice in the new season of the year, thanks be to love and to my happy thoughts.*

*Through the green meadows do I go to see the yellow flowers and white and red, the roses on their thorns and the white flowers-de-luce; and I go likening them to the face of him who loving me hath captured me, even as she that doth desire naught else save her delight.*

*When among these I find a flower that seems like him, I pluck and kiss it and speak to it, and open all my soul to it and what the heart desires, and then I plait it up with other flowers to make a garland for my fine gold hair.*

*And as by nature every flower doth give delight unto our eyes, so this one gives delight as if indeed I saw him who hath snared me with his gentle love; the greater joy its perfume gives me, speech may not express, but these my sighs true witness bear thereof.*

*Heavy and harsh they never leave my breast like other ladies' sighs; but warm and soft they come from me and speed toward my love: who, when he feels them, of himself is moved to give delight to me, and comes even at that moment when I whisper: "Come, ah! come, lest I despair!"*

Neifile's song was greatly praised by the king and all the ladies; after which, since it was already late at night, the king ordered each of them to repose until the next day.

**HERE ENDS THE NINTH DAY**

# THE TENTH DAY

## THE TENTH DAY

*Here begins the tenth and last day of the* Decameron, *wherein, under the rule of Pamfilo, tales are told of those who have acted liberally or magnificently in love affairs or in other matters*

A few small clouds in the west were still red and those in the east were already tipped with gold where the approaching rays of the sun struck them, when Pamfilo arose and had the ladies and his companions called. When they had all arrived they discussed where they should go for their amusement, and Pamfilo set out with Filomena and Fiammetta, followed by all the rest. And as they went along, they discussed their future life. After quite a long walk they found the sun was beginning to be hot, and so returned to the mansion. There they had glasses rinsed in the clear fountain, and those who wished could drink; after which they amused themselves in the pleasant shade of the garden until dinner time.

When they had eaten and slept as usual, they gathered together at the place appointed by the king, who ordered Neifile to speak first, and she began cheerfully as follows:

## FIRST TALE

*A knight in the service of the King of Spain thinks himself ill-rewarded, but the King proves that it is not his fault but the knight's misfortune, and then highly rewards him for his valour*

Honourable ladies, I ought to think it a very great favour that our king should have chosen me to speak first of such a topic as munificence, which is the light and loveliness of all virtue, even as the sun is the beauty and ornament of the whole sky. So I shall tell you a short tale, which I think quite pleasing, while to remember it cannot but be useful to you.

You must know that among the brave knights who have been produced by our city, one of the best was Messer Ruggieri de' Figiovanni. He was a rich, high-spirited man, and from his observation of the manners and the way of living of Tuscany he saw that he could show little or nothing of his bravery if he remained there. So he decided that for a time he would serve Alfonso, King of Spain, whose fame at that time had spread among all knights. So he went to Spain honourably furnished with arms, horses and followers; and was graciously received by the King.

Messer Ruggieri lived there splendidly, and performed marvellous feats of arms, and thus was soon renowned for his valour. After he had been there a considerable time and had observed the King's ways, he felt that the King bestowed his gifts of castles, towns and baronies rather recklessly, and gave them to undeserving persons. He knew his own value, and since nothing was given him, he considered it a diminution of his fame. He therefore determined to leave, and asked the King's permission, which was given him, together with one of the best and finest mules ever ridden—which was a valuable gift to Messer Ruggieri because of the distance he had to ride.

After this, the King ordered one of his trusted servants to arrange in some manner that he ride with Messer Ruggieri without appearing to have been sent by the King, that he should observe everything Messer Ruggieri said, so that he could repeat it to the King, and the next morning order Messer Ruggieri to return to the King. This servant waited for Messer Ruggieri to set out and fell into company with him, giving him to understand that he too was going to Italy.

As Messer Ruggieri rode along on the ass given him by the King, talking of one thing and another, he said about the hour of Tierce:

"I think it would be a good thing to let the animals stale."

All the animals were taken into a stable and all, except the mule, staled. They then rode on, with the King's attendant continually listening to what the knight said; and came to a stream. There they watered their beasts, and the mule staled in the water. Seeing this, Messer Ruggieri said:

"Ah! God punish you, you beast, you're made like the King who gave you to me."

The servant noted these words, and although he observed

everything the knight said all that day, he found he said nothing else which was not in the King's praise. Next morning when Messer Ruggieri went to horse, meaning to continue on his way to Tuscany, the servant delivered the King's order, and Messer Ruggieri at once turned back.

The King learned from his servant what had been said of him, and therefore sent for Messer Ruggieri, received him with a cheerful countenance, and asked him why he had likened him to the mule, or rather the mule to him. Messer Ruggieri replied with an open visage:

"Sire, I likened it to you, because you gave gifts where they ought not to have been given and did not give them where they ought to have been given; similarly the mule did not stale where it ought to have and did stale where it ought not to have done so."

"Messer Ruggieri," said the King, "my not having made gifts to you, when I have made gifts to many men who are nothing in comparison with you, did not occur because I failed to realise that you are a most valourous knight and worthy of all great gifts, but because your fortune did not allow me to make you presents, wherein your luck is at fault and not myself. I will prove to you that what I say is true."

"Sire," replied Ruggieri, "I am not angry because I have not received gifts from you, for I do not desire them in order to become richer, but because I receive no acknowledgment of my worth from you. Nevertheless, I accept your excuse as good and sincere, and am ready to look at anything you please, although I accept what you say without any proof."

The King then took him into a great hall where, as he had previously ordered, there were two large locked chests; and in the presence of many knights said to him:

"Messer Ruggieri, in one of those chests are my crown, the royal sceptre and orb, many fine girdles, clasps, rings and other valuable jewels. The other is full of earth. Choose one of them, and the one you choose shall be yours; and then you will see whether I or your Fortune were ungrateful to you."

Seeing it was the King's pleasure, Messer Ruggieri chose one of them, which the King ordered to be opened, and it was found to be full of earth. Then said the King, laughing:

"Messer Ruggieri, you can see that what I said about Fortune was the truth. But your valour deserves that I should oppose the power of Fortune. I know you do not wish to become a Spaniard, and so I shall not give you a castle or a town, but in despite of Fortune I give you the chest of which she deprived you, so that you may take it with you to your own country, and with your neighbours deservedly exult in your valour together with the testimony of my gifts."

Messer Ruggieri took it, gave the King the thanks befitting such a gift, and returned happily with it to Tuscany.

## SECOND TALE

*Ghino di Tacco captures the Abbot of Cligni, treats him for a malady of the stomach, and then sets him free. The Abbot returns to Rome, reconciles Ghino with Pope Boniface and makes him prior of the Hospitallers*

The munificence of King Alfonso to the Florentine knight was praised by them all. The king, who had taken great pleasure in it, ordered Elisa to follow next and she began immediately:

Delicate ladies, it cannot but be called praiseworthy and a great matter to be a munificent King and to have displayed munificence towards one who had served him; but what shall be said if we tell of a cleric who displayed wonderful munificence towards a person, when nobody would have blamed him if he had behaved in a hostile way? Certainly, we can only say that what was virtue in the King was a miracle in the cleric, for all clerics are more avaricious than women, and at daggers drawn with liberality. And although every man naturally desires revenge for an injury done him, the clerics, as we see, permit themselves to pursue revenge more eagerly than other men, although they preach patience and above all things commend the forgiveness of offences. The tale I shall tell you will show you how a cleric behaved with munificence.

Ghino di Tacco, a man famous for his fierceness and his robberies, was driven from Siena and declared an enemy of the Counts of Santa Fiore. He roused Radicofani against the Church of Rome and dwelt therein, causing his followers to rob everyone who passed through the neighbouring districts.

The Pope at that time was Boniface VIII, who was visited

by the Abbot of Cligni, thought to be the richest man in the world. His stomach became disordered in Rome, and the doctors advised him to go to the baths of Siena, where he would indubitably be cured. So, paying no attention to Ghino's ill-fame, he obtained the Pope's permission, and set out with great pomp of horses and servants and trappings and sumpter-mules. Hearing that the Abbot was coming, Ghino di Tacco spread his nets and, without the loss of a single boy, caught the Abbot with all his attendants and possessions in a narrow place. Having done this, he sent the ablest of his followers well attended to the Abbot, who courteously required him to dismount at Ghino's castle. The Abbot replied in fury that he would do nothing of the kind, for he had nothing whatever to do with Ghino; that he should go on, and would like to see who would stop him. To which the ambassador replied, speaking in gentle tones:

"Messer, you have come to a place where we fear nothing for ourselves except the power of God, where excommunications and interdicts are of no avail. And so be pleased to pleasure Ghino in this."

While he was speaking, the whole place was surrounded with armed robbers. The Abbot, seeing he was captured, in great annoyance set out with the messenger towards the castle, followed by all his company and possessions. He dismounted, and, at Ghino's command, was lodged alone in a small room of a rather dark, uncomfortable house; everyone else was lodged in the castle according to his rank, and the horses and all goods were placed in safety, without anything being touched. This done, Ghino went to the Abbot and said:

"Messer, Ghino, whose guest you are, sends to ask where you are going and for what reason."

The Abbot, like a wise man, had already abandoned his haughtiness, and said where he was going and why. Ghino went away, and thought he would cure him without any baths. So he had a large fire lighted in his room and a good guard kept over him, and did not visit him again until the next morning. He then carried him two slices of toast and a large glass of the Abbot's own Corniglia wine on a clean napkin, and said:

"Messer, when Ghino was younger he studied medicine, and he says that there is no medicine for a sick stomach better than that he sends you, and therefore take it and be comforted."

The Abbot, who was more hungry than eager to jest, ate the toast and drank the wine, although in annoyance; afterwards he said many haughty things, asking and advising numerous matters, and above all requesting to see Ghino. Ghino let some of these things pass as unimportant, and replied courteously to the others, saying that Ghino would visit him as soon as he could. After this, he went away and did not return until the next morning, bringing the same quantity of wine and toast. He kept him in this way for several days, until he found that the Abbot had eaten some dried beans which Ghino had brought in secretly, and intentionally had left there. So he asked him, as if on Ghino's behalf, how his stomach was; and the Abbot replied:

"I think I should be quite well if I could get out of his hands; after that I want nothing better than to eat, so well has his medicine cured me."

Ghino therefore prepared a room with his own possessions and servants, and prepared a great feast for all the Abbot's attendants and many of his own men. He then went to him the next morning, and said:

"Messer, since you feel better, it is time for you to come out of hospital."

He took the Abbot by the hand, and led him to the room prepared and there left him with his attendants, while Ghino himself went away to oversee the preparation of the banquet. The Abbot remained with his attendants and told them how he had been treated; while they on the other hand all said they had been marvellously entertained by Ghino. When dinner time arrived, the Abbot and all his attendants were served with good food and wine. Ghino still did not make himself known, but when the Abbot had passed several days in this way, Ghino collected all his baggage in a room and all his horses in a courtyard below it. He then went to the Abbot and asked him how he was, and if he felt well enough to ride. The Abbot replied that he was quite strong and that his stomach was cured, and that he should be perfectly happy when he was out of Ghino's hands. Ghino then took the Abbot to the room containing all his baggage and servants, and made him lean out a window so that he could see all his horses. He then said:

"Messer Abbot, you must know that it was not wickedness of soul which led me, who am Ghino di Tacco, to be a highway robber and the enemy of Rome, but because I was a poor gentleman driven from home, with many powerful enemies, and in that way was forced to defend my life and rank. Now I have cured you of your stomach illness, and since you seem to me to be a worthy gentleman I do not intend to treat you as I should treat others, who, when they fall into my hands as you have done, leave me so much of their possessions as I demand. But my intention is that you should leave me whatever you think fit, in consideration of the service I performed for you. All your possessions are here before you, and you can see your horses in the court-yard through that window. So take all or part, as you wish, and from this moment your staying or departing is at your disposal."

The Abbot was amazed and delighted to hear such noble words from a highway robber; his anger and annoyance at once disappeared and changed to good-will. He felt a sin-cere friendship for Ghino, and embracing him, said:

"I swear to God that to gain the friendship of a man such as I consider you to be I would suffer far greater injury than that I hitherto considered I had suffered from you! Cursed be the fate that condemned you to so damnable an occupation!"

After this the Abbot took only a very few essential things and a few horses, and returned to Rome. The Pope had heard of his captivity and had greatly regretted it; but when he saw the Abbot he asked him if the baths had done him good. The Abbot smiled, and replied:

"Holy Father, I found an excellent doctor much nearer at hand than the baths, and he cured me completely."

He then related what had happened; and the Pope laughed at it. The Abbot went on talking and, moved by the munificence of his spirit, asked a favour. The Pope, little thinking what he would ask, freely promised him what he should request. Then said the Abbot:

"Holy Father, what I have to ask of you is that you will restore your favour to Ghino di Tacco, my doctor, because he is certainly one of the finest men I ever knew. The evil he does I consider to be far more the sin of Fortune than his own. If you grant him your favour and enough to live on suitably to his rank, I have no doubt that in a short time he will appear to you such as he seems to me."

The Pope, who was a large-minded man and liked brave men, said he would gladly do so if the man was such as the Abbot said, and added that he might come to Rome in safety. Ghino therefore, at the Abbot's request, came to Court with a safe-conduct. He had not been near the Pope for long when the Pope came to think him an excellent man, was reconciled with him, and gave him a large Priory of the Hospitallers, of which order he was made knight. This he held as long as he lived, and remained a servant of Holy Church and the Abbot of Cligni.

## THIRD TALE

*Mitridanes envies the generosity of Nathan and sets out
to kill him. Nathan receives Mitridanes without making
himself known, informs him how he may be killed, meets
him in a wood as arranged, to the shame of Mitridanes,
who becomes his friend*

That a cleric should have done anything so munificent
seemed like a miracle to all who heard it; but as the ladies'
talk calmed down, the king ordered Filostrato to proceed,
and he began at once:

Noble ladies, the munificence of the King of Spain was
great, and that of the Abbot of Cligni perhaps never to be
heard of again; but perhaps it will seem to you a thing no
less marvellous to hear of one who out of sheer generosity
was prepared to give his life to another person who desired
it. And, as I shall show you by my little tale, he would
have done so, if the other man had been willing to take it.

If we may trust the words of certain Genoese and other
men who have visited those parts, it is certain that in
Cathay there was once a nobleman of inestimable wealth,
named Nathan. He lived near a road which almost of necessity was traversed by everyone going from East to West
or from West to East; and since his spirit was great and
generous and he desired to have it known by his works, he
assembled many masters and in a short space of time built
one of the finest, largest and richest palaces ever seen, and
furnished it with everything necessary to receive and to
entertain gentlemen. And since he had many servants, he
entertained magnificently everyone who passed that way.
He persevered so long in his praiseworthy custom that he
became known by fame to all the East and even to many
in the West.

When he was full of years, and still not yet weary of
generosity, his fame reached the ears of a young man named
Mitridanes, who lived in a country not far distant. Knowing
that he was just as rich as Nathan, he felt envious of the
man's fame and virtue, and determined to eclipse or to
tarnish it by greater liberality. So he built a palace like

Nathan's, and began to entertain in the most extravagant manner everybody who went to and fro in that district; so that in a short time he became quite famous.

Now one day the young man was alone in the courtyard of his palace, and a woman came to him through one of the palace doors and asked for alms. She then returned to him by a second door and again received alms, and this she did twelve times; but when she returned by the thirteenth door Mitridanes said:

"Good woman, you are somewhat importunate in your demands."

But still he gave her alms once more. But at these words, the old woman exclaimed:

"O generosity of Nathan! How wonderful you are! By thirty-two doors of his palace did I enter, even as here, and asked an alms; and never did he show that he recognised me, and each time I had what I asked. Here I only entered thirteen times, and I am recognised and reproved!"

So saying, she departed, and never came back.

Mitridanes fell into a great rage at the old woman's words, because he felt that what he had heard to Nathan's fame diminished his own, and he said to himself:

"Alas! When shall I equal the generosity of Nathan in great things, let alone surpass him as I wish, when I cannot come near him even in small things? I labour in vain, unless I can remove him from the earth. Since old age will not do it, I must do it without delay with my own hands."

Without letting anyone know his plans, he started up and went to horse with a few attendants, and in three days reached the place where Nathan lived. He ordered his attendants to pretend they were not with him and did not know him, and to look for lodging until they heard further from him.

Riding alone not far from the palace, towards evening, he came upon Nathan, also alone and plainly dressed, walking for his amusement. Not knowing who he was, Mitridanes asked if he could tell him where Nathan lived.

"My son," replied Nathan cheerfully, "nobody here can tell you better than I, and I will take you to him whenever you wish."

The young man said that this was what he desired, but that he did not wish to be seen or known by Nathan.

"This also I will do," said Nathan, "since you desire it."

Mitridanes then dismounted and walked towards the palace with Nathan, who entertained him with amusing talk. There Nathan made one of his servants take the young man's horse, and whispered into his ear to tell the whole household that nobody should tell the young man he was Nathan. As soon as they entered the palace, he placed Mitridanes in a most handsome apartment where he saw none but those deputed to his service, and where Nathan himself kept him company, doing him all imaginable honour. Now, although Mitridanes respected him as an old man, he could not refrain from asking who he was, and Nathan replied:

"I am a humble servant of Nathan's, who has grown old with him since my childhood; and I have never raised myself above what you see because, although everyone else praises him, I can praise him but little."

These words gave Mitridanes some hope that he might carry out his base intention with more skill and safety. Nathan then asked courteously who he was and what brought him there, offering his advice and aid in any way possible. Mitridanes hesitated a little before replying, but at last determined to trust in him, and after much beating about the bush asked him to pledge his secrecy, and his advice and help, and then fully revealed to him who he was and why he had come and with what intention. When Nathan heard Mitridanes's speech and cruel design, he was inwardly perturbed, but without much delay he replied with a strong mind and firm countenance:

"Mitridanes, your father was a noble man, from whom you strive not to degenerate since you have undertaken the high enterprise of being generous to all men, and I greatly praise your envy of Nathan's virtue, because if there were many such envies, the world, which is most wretched, would soon become good. The intention you have revealed to me shall certainly be kept secret, but I can rather give you useful advice than great help. About half a mile from here you can see a small wood, where Nathan goes alone every morning for a long time to take recreation. It will be easy for you to find him there and to work your will on him. If you kill him, the easiest way for you to go home is not to return by the path you came, but to take that which you will see going out of the wood to the left; it is a little wilder, but nearer your house and safer for you."

After giving this information Nathan went away, and Mitridanes secretly informed his followers (who had also entered the palace) where they were to await him the next day. Nathan did not change his mind from what he had said to Mitridanes, and next morning went to the wood to be killed. Mitridanes arose and took his bow and sword, the only weapons he had with him, mounted his horse and went to the wood. In the distance he saw Nathan walking all alone in the wood, but before killing him thought he would like to see him and hear him speak. So he ran up to him, seized him by the band he wore on his head, and exclaimed:

"Old man, you must die!"

The only reply Nathan made was:

"Then I have deserved it."

From the voice and face, Mitridanes suddenly recognised the man who had kindly received him, familiarly borne him company and loyally counselled him. His fury suddenly fell from him, and his anger was changed to shame. He threw away the sword, that he had already drawn, with which to kill him, dismounted from his horse, and threw himself weeping at Nathan's feet, saying:

"Most dear father, now plainly do I perceive your generosity, seeing how secretly you came here to give me your life, which I myself told you I wanted, though for no reason. But God, more regardful of my duty than I myself, at the moment of greatest need has opened my eyes which had been shut by miserable envy. The more ready you were to pleasure me, the more I admit I should be penitent for my error. Therefore take upon me what vengeance you think merited by my sin."

Nathan raised Mitridanes to his feet, tenderly embraced him, and said:

"My son, whether you desire to call your enterprise wicked or otherwise, there is no need to ask nor to give pardon, because I executed it not from hatred but to be more esteemed by you. Live then without fear of me, and be sure there is no man alive who loves you so much as I, considering the loftiness of your spirit which has not given itself to amassing money like a miser but to spending it. Do not be ashamed that you wished to kill me in order to become famous, and do not think that I feel amazed. High Emperors and great Kings slay many men—not one, as you wished to do—and burn countries and destroy cities to increase their dominions and consequently their fame. Thus, your desire to make yourself famous by killing me alone was not something extraordinary but very common."

Mitridanes did not excuse his base design but commended the honest excuse found by Nathan, and in talking to him said that he greatly marvelled how Nathan could have been disposed to do such a thing, and to help him to it. Said Nathan:

"Mitridanes, you must not marvel at my readiness and my advice, for since I have been of age and desirous to do the same thing that you have undertaken, nobody ever entered my house whom I did not endeavour to satisfy as far as I could in anything he asked of me. You came wanting my life. I did not want you to be the only person who ever went away from here without receiving what he asked for, so when I heard you ask for it I immediately determined to give it to you. In order that you might have it, I gave you the advice I thought likely to allow you to take my life without losing your own. Therefore I beg you to take it and satisfy yourself with it, if you desire. I do not know how I can spend it better. I have already passed eighty years in pleasures and delights, and I know that in the course of nature I can have but a short time left, like other men and all things generally. Therefore I think it much better to give my life, as I have always given and spent my treasures, than to try to keep it and to have it taken from me against my will by nature.

"A hundred years is a small gift. How much less then are the six or eight years I have left to give you! If you want it, I beg you to take it; for as long as I have been alive I have not found anyone who wanted it, and I don't know when I shall find another, if you who asked for it do not take it. And even if I should find someone else, I know that the longer I keep it the less valuable it will be; so take it, I beg, before it becomes more worthless."

In great shame Mitridanes replied:

"God forbid that by dividing it from you I should take so precious a thing as your life, or even desire it as I did just now. Not only would I not diminish the years of your life but I would gladly increase them with my own."

Nathan promptly replied:

"And if you could you would give them to me and make me do to you what I have never done to any other man, that is to take things from you when I have never taken from anyone?"

"Yes," said Mitridanes at once.

"Then," said Nathan, "do as I tell you. You, who are a young man, shall stay here in my house and be called Nathan; and I will go to yours and always have myself called Mitridanes."

"If I could act as well as you have done and do," replied Mitridanes, "I would take what you offer without overmuch hesitation; but I feel sure that my actions would diminish the fame of Nathan, and so I do not intend to spoil in another what I cannot attain to myself, and therefore will not take it."

After this and other agreeable conversations, Nathan and Mitridanes, at Nathan's request, returned to the palace, where Nathan for several days sumptuously entertained Mitridanes, and gave him every encouragement to persevere in his great and lofty enterprise. And when Mitridanes wished to return home with his companions, Nathan let him go, having showed him that he could never overcome Nathan in generosity.

## FOURTH TALE

*Messer Gentil de' Carisendi comes from Modena and takes from the grave a lady he loves, who had been buried as dead. She bears a male child, and Messer Gentil restores her and the child to her husband*

They all thought it marvellous that anyone should be liberal of his own blood, and they said that Nathan had indeed exceeded the generosity of the King of Spain and the Abbot of Cligni. But when one thing and another had been said, the king looked at Lauretta, thereby showing that he wished her to speak next so she immediately began:

Young ladies, the things related have been great and munificent. I do not think anything is left for us to say and so enjoy our tale-telling, and reach the height of the examples of munificence related, unless we turn our hand to love affairs, which always provide a most abundant supply of tales on any topic. For these reasons and also because it is suitable to our age I wish to tell you of a piece of munificence on the part of a lover, which, all things considered, will not appear less than those already related, if it is true that treasures are given, enmities forgotten, life, love and fame risked a thousand times to possess the thing beloved.

In Bologna, that most noble city of Lombardy, there lived a knight named Messer Gentil Carisendi, eminent for his worth and noble blood. This young man fell in love with a gentlewoman named Madonna Catalina, the wife of one Niccoluccio Caccianimico. And since his love was ill-requited by the lady, he went off in despair to Modena, where he had been appointed podestà.

At that time Niccoluccio was absent from Bologna, and his wife went to stay on an estate about three miles away, because she was pregnant. A sudden illness came upon her, the effect of which was to deprive her of all signs of life, and even a doctor would have said she was dead. And since her nearest relatives declared that they knew from her that she had not been pregnant long enough for the child to be perfected, without giving themselves any further trouble they buried her with much lamentation in a tomb of a neighbouring church. This event was immediately told Messer Gentil by one of his friends; and although he had received no favours from her yet he grieved much over it, and finally said to himself:

"Madonna Catalina, you are dead! While you were alive, I never received a single glance from you. But now, when you cannot defend yourself, I must take a few kisses from you, dead though you are."

It was then night; he made arrangements to keep his journey secret and went to horse with one of his servants. Without resting he rode to the place where the lady was buried, opened the tomb, entered, lay down beside her, put his face against hers and kept kissing it as he wept many tears. But man's appetite is never satisfied within any limit and always desires to go further, especially lovers'; and, making up his mind not to halt there, he said to himself:

"Ah! Now I am here why do I not touch her breasts a little? I never have touched them, and shall never touch them again."

With this desire upon him he placed his hand on her breast and held it there for a time, when he thought he felt her heart beating slightly. When he had recovered from his fear and had examined her more closely, he found that she was certainly not dead, although he thought there was only a little faint life in her. With the aid of his servant he lifted her from the tomb as gently as possible, set her before him on his horse, and secretly carried her to his house in Bologna. His mother, a wise and worthy lady, was there; and when she had heard the whole story from her son, she was moved to pity, and secretly brought Catalina back to life with hot baths and fires. When she recovered her senses, she heaved a deep sigh, and said:

"Oh! Where am I?"

"Be comforted, you are in a safe place," replied the lady.

Catalina turned and looked round her, but did not know where she was. She saw Messer Gentil before her, and in great surprise asked his mother how she had got there; and Messer Gentil then told her everything that had happened. She was grieved by this, and after having returned him thanks she besought him by the love he had borne her and also by chivalry, that she might suffer nothing in his house detrimental to her honour or her husband's, and also, since it was now day, that he would let her return to her own house.

"Madonna," replied Messer Gentil, "God has granted me the grace to bring you back from death to life through the love that I bore you; but whatever my desire may have been in the past, I do not intend either now or in the future to treat you either here or elsewhere otherwise than as a dear sister. But the benefit I conferred upon you last night deserves some reward, and so I desire you will not refuse me a favour which I shall ask of you."

The lady replied that she was willing to do so if it were virtuous and if she could do it.

"Madonna," said Messer Gentil, "all your relatives and everyone in Bologna think you are dead, and so there is no one awaiting you at your house. The favour I ask of you is that you will remain here secretly with my mother until I return from Modena, which will not be long. The reason I ask this is that I intend to make a solemn and precious gift of you to your husband in the presence of the most notable citizens of this country."

Knowing her obligations to the knight and that his request was virtuous, the lady agreed to what Messer Gentil asked and pledged him her faith, although she was very anxious to make her relatives happy by the news that she was alive. She had scarcely done speaking when she felt the pains of labour come upon her, and, being tenderly aided by Messer Gentil's mother, in a short time brought forth a fine male child; which greatly increased her happiness and Messer Gentil's. Messer Gentil ordered everything she needed and that she should be treated as if she were his own wife; after which he secretly returned to Modena.

When the period of his office expired and he was about to return to Bologna, he arranged that on the morning he returned a great banquet should be given in his house to many of the gentlemen of Bologna, including Niccoluccio Caccianimico. He returned, dismounted from his horse and met them. He found the lady healthier and more beautiful than she had ever been and the child well; so with extraordinary joy he seated his guests and had them magnificently served. He had told the lady beforehand what he intended to do and arranged with her how she should behave; and towards the end of the banquet he spoke as follows:

"Gentlemen, I remember to have heard that there is a custom in Persia, in my judgment a pleasant one, which is that when a man desires highly to honour a friend, he invites him to his house and there shows him the most precious thing he has, whether his wife, his mistress or his daughter, at the same time declaring that, if he could, he would be even more glad to show his heart in the same manner. And I mean to observe this custom in Bologna.

"You have honoured my banquet with your presence and I intend to honour you in the Persian manner, by showing you the most precious thing I have or ever shall have in the world. But before I do this I beg you will give me your opinion on something which is troubling me. A certain person had in his house a good and most faithful servant who fell seriously ill. Without awaiting the servant's end, this man had him carried out into the street and paid no more attention to him. A stranger came along and moved by pity for the sick man, took him home, and with great trouble and expense restored him to health. Now I want to know whether, if the second man retains and makes use of his services, the first master can grieve or complain should the second refuse to let him have the servant back."

After some discussion among themselves, the gentlemen agreed on their opinion, and the task of replying was alloted to Niccoluccio Caccianimico, because he was a good, ornate speaker. He first praised the Persian custom, and then said that he and the others had agreed that the first master had no further claim upon his servant, since he had not only abandoned him in such a state, but had cast him forth. As to the services taken by the second, it seemed just that the man should become his servant, because no injury, no wrong, was thereby done the first.

The knight was delighted by this opinion and that Niccoluccio had expressed it, declared that he was of the same opinion, and added:

"It is now time that I do you honour in the way promised."

He sent two of his servants to the lady, whom he had caused to be beautifully dressed and ornamented, to beg her to be pleased to come and gladden the gentlemen with her presence. She took her beautiful child in her arms and went to the hall, accompanied by two servants, and sat down beside a worthy gentleman, at the knight's request. He then said:

"Gentlemen, this is the most precious thing I have or mean to have; see if you think me right."

The gentlemen highly praised her and assured the knight that he ought to value her, and gazed closely at her. Many of them would have said who she was, if they had not thought her dead. Niccoluccio especially gazed at her, and when the knight moved a little away, he felt so anxious to know who she was that he could not refrain from asking whether she came from Bologna or was a stranger. At this question from her husband, it was difficult for the lady not to answer; but she remained silent, in obedience to the arrangement. Others asked her if that were her child, if she were Messer Gentil's wife or his relative in any other way; to all of which she made no reply. Messer Gentil then came up to them, and some of his guests said to him:

"Messer, this is a beautiful woman of yours, but she seems dumb. Is she?"

"Gentlemen," replied Messer Gentil, "that she has not yet spoken is no small argument of her virtue."

"Then do you say who she is," pursued the other.

"I will gladly do so," said the knight, "provided you will promise me that, whatever I may say, none of you will move from his seat until I have finished my story."

Everyone gave his promise, the tables were drawn, and Messer Gentil sat down beside the lady, saying:

"Gentlemen, this lady is that true and faithful servant about whom I asked you just now. She was held in small esteem by her relatives and cast out into the street as something vile and useless; I took her up, by my care and labour she was snatched from death, and God so favoured my good affection to her that He has enabled me to change her from a dreadful corpse to her present beauty. But I shall now briefly inform you how this happened to me, so that you may fully understand it all."

He then began from the point of his falling in love with her and to the great amazement of all listeners told them all that had happened until that time, adding:

"Wherefore, if you and Niccoluccio especially have not changed your opinions, this woman is rightfully mine, nor can anyone justly ask me for her."

No one replied, but all waited to hear what he would say further. Niccoluccio and the lady and the others present were weeping with compassion; and Messer Gentil then stood up, took the child in his arm and the lady by the hand, and went towards Niccoluccio, saying:

"Stand up, my relative in baptism. I do not return you your wife, whom you and your relatives cast forth; but I desire to give you this woman and her child, my godson, whom I know to have been begotten by you and whom I held at the font and named Gentil. Now, since she remained nearly three months in my house, I beg that will not make her less dear to you. I swear to you by God, Who perhaps made me fall in love with her that my love might be the occasion of her being saved as it has been, that she never lived more chastely with her father or mother or you than she has lived with my mother in my house."

So saying, he turned to the lady and said:

"Madonna, I now release you from every promise made to me and give you free to Niccoluccio."

He then placed the lady and her child in Niccoluccio's arms, and returned to his seat. Niccoluccio eagerly received his wife and child, the more happy since he was far indeed from any such hope. To the best of his ability he thanked the knight, and all the others weeping with emotion praised him greatly, and he was praised by all who heard of it. The lady was received home with great rejoicing, and gazed at for some time by all Bologna, as if she had risen from the dead. Messer Gentil always remained a friend of Niccoluccio and his relatives and the lady's relatives.

What more shall I say, gentle ladies? Do you think that a King's giving his crown and sceptre, an Abbot's having reconciled a malefactor with the Pope at no cost to himself, an old man yielding his throat to an enemy's knife, can equal the act of Messer Gentil? He was young and ardent and thought he had a just right to what others in their negligence had cast forth and he by good fortune had taken up; yet he not only chastely tempered his desire but when he possessed her, freely restored the woman whom he had desired to steal with all his might. Therefore none of the examples related seems to me similar to this.

## FIFTH TALE

*Madonna Dianora asks Messer Ansaldo for a garden in January as beautiful as one in May. Messer Ansaldo pays a large sum to a magician, and so gives it to her. Her husband declares she must keep her word and submit to Messer Ansaldo's pleasure; but when he hears of the husband's generosity he frees her from her promise, and the magician likewise refuses to take anything*

Everyone in the merry party praised Messer Gentil to the skies. The king then ordered Emilia to follow next and she began merrily, as one who desired to speak, thus:

Delicate ladies, nobody can reasonably say that Messer Gentil did not act munificently, but if anyone says that to go beyond him is impossible, it would not perhaps be hard to show the contrary. And this I mean to show you in my tale.

In Friuli, a cold but beautiful land, abounding in mountains, streams and rivers, there is a place called Udine. There dwelt a beautiful and noble lady named Madonna Dianora, the wife of a very rich and pleasant man called Gilberto. For her great worth this lady deserved that she should be loved by a great and noble baron, named Messer Ansaldo Gradense, a man of high position, known to all for his feats of arms and chivalry. In his fervent love for her he did everything he could to obtain her love and frequently sent messages to beseech her; but all in vain.

The knight's importunities were very displeasing to the lady and she saw that her refusal to do anything he asked did not prevent him from continuing to love and solicit her. She therefore thought she would get rid of him by making a strange and impossible request. So she spoke as follows to a woman who often came to her on the knight's behalf:

"Good woman, you have often assured me that Messer Ansaldo loves me above everything; you have offered me marvellous gifts from him which I have desired him to keep because I could never be brought through them to love him or to do his pleasure. But yet I should be brought to love him and to do what he wants if I could be certain he loves me as much as you say he does. Therefore if he proves it to me by what I ask him, I shall be at his command."

"Madonna," said the woman, "what do you want him to do?"

"What I desire is this," said the lady. "In the coming month of January I want near here a garden as full of green plants, flowers and leafy trees as if it were May. If he does not do this, let him never send you or anyone else to me again, for if he then went on urging me I should no longer hide this from my husband and relatives as I have done, but would complain to them and try to get rid of him."

When the knight heard the lady's request and offer, he thought it difficult and almost impossible to perform and knew that the lady had only asked it in order to deprive him of all hope; yet he determined to attempt whatever could be done. He sent out to various parts of the world to seek for someone who would give him advice and aid; and there came to him a man who offered to do it by black magic for a large sum of money, which Messer Ansaldo agreed to pay him, and cheerfully awaited the appointed time.

When this time came, the cold was intense and everything was covered with snow and ice. With his arts, the man so wrought that on the night following the calends of January, a beautiful meadow near the city appeared in the morning (according to the testimony of those who saw it) one of the fairest gardens ever seen, filled with grass and trees and all sorts of fruits. Messer Ansaldo beheld it with delight, and caused the fairest fruits and flowers to be plucked and sent secretly to his lady, with an invitation to come and see the garden she had asked for, in order that she might perceive how much he loved her and remember the promise she had made and confirmed with an oath and, like a woman of good faith, find means to carry it out.

When the lady saw the fruits and flowers, confirming what she had already heard of the marvellous garden from others, she began to repent her promise. But for all her repentance she liked to see strange things, and went with many other ladies of the city to see the garden. She praised it greatly, not without amazement, and returned home in the deepest distress, thinking of what she had bound herself to do in exchange. Her grief was such that she could not conceal it; her husband noticed the outward signs, and insisted upon knowing the reason. For a long time the lady was silent from shame, but at last under compulsion she revealed everything to him. Gilberto at first was very angry when he heard it, but then when he considered the purity of his wife's intentions, he put aside his anger, and said:

"Dianora, a chaste and wise woman never listens to any messenger on such matters and never bargains for her chastity on any consideration. The words received into the heart through the ears have more power than many people think, and almost everything becomes possible to lovers. You did ill then, first by listening and then by bargaining. But since I know the purity of your soul I will grant you what nobody else perhaps would allow, in order to free you from the bonds of the promise and also on account of the magician who may do us some harm at Messer Ansaldo's request if we disappoint him. You must go to him and do anything you can to free yourself from this promise, short of your chastity; and if that is impossible, for once you must yield him your body, but not your soul."

At this the lady wept and refused to accept such a favour from him. But, however much the lady refused, Gilberto insisted that she should do it. So at dawn next day the lady, without dressing herself very finely, went to Messer Ansaldo's house, followed by two servants and a waiting woman. When he heard that the lady had come to him, Messer Ansaldo arose in great amazement, and sent for the magician, to whom he said:

"I wish you to see the good which your art has procured me."

He then went to her and received her courteously, with no display of disorderly appetite. They all went into a fair chamber where there was a large fire, and when they were seated, he said:

"Madonna, if the long love I have borne you merits any reward, I beg you will tell me the real reason of your coming here at such an hour and with such attendants."

Shamefacedly and almost in tears, the lady replied:

"Messer, I am brought here neither by love for you nor by my plighted faith, but by my husband's command. He has sent me here, considering more the labours of your disorderly love than my honour and his own; and by his command I am prepared for once to do all your pleasure."

Messer Ansaldo was surprised at the beginning of the lady's speech, and still more by its ending. Moved by Gilberto's generosity, his passion began to change to pity, and he said:

"Madonna, since it is as you say, please God I may never harm the honour of one who pities my love. And so you shall remain here as long as you wish as if you were my sister, and whenever you want you shall freely depart, on condition that you give your husband such thanks as you think befitting such courtesy, and tell him that in future I shall always consider myself his brother and servant."

At these words the lady was very happy, and said:

"With my knowledge of your manners, nothing could have made me believe that my coming here would have any other results than those I see, for which I shall always be obliged to you."

She then took leave and returned, honourably accompanied, to Messer Gilberto, to whom she related everything which had happened, which caused him to make a close and true friendship with Messer Ansaldo.

Messer Ansaldo offered the magician the reward agreed upon, but having seen Gilberto's generosity to Messer Ansaldo, and Messer Ansaldo's generosity to the lady, he said:

"Since I have seen Gilberto so liberal of his honour and you of your love, God forbid that I should not be liberal of my reward; therefore, knowing that it is well employed by you, I intend it to remain yours."

The knight felt ashamed at this, and tried to induce him to take all or a part of it, but in vain. Three days later the magician removed the garden and departed, with Messer Ansaldo's good wishes. And the lascivious love for the lady having departed from his heart, he remained filled with sober charity towards her.

What shall we say of this, beloved ladies? Shall we place the almost dead lady and the love cooled by extinguished hope above the generosity of Messer Ansaldo, who was more warmed with love than ever and kindled with more hope, and who held in his hands the prey he had pursued so long? It seems to me foolish to think that such generosity can be compared with his.

## SIXTH TALE

*King Carlo, victorious but aged, falls in love with a young girl; ashamed of his foolish passion, he arranges honourable marriages for her and her sister*

It would take far too long to relate in full the various discussions among the ladies as to whether greater generosity were shown in the affair of Madonna Dianora by Gilberto, or by Messer Ansaldo, or by the magician. But when the king had allowed some time for discussion he looked at Fiammetta and ordered her to end the argument by telling a tale, and she immediately began thus:

Splendid ladies, I was always of the opinion that in a group like ours we should speak so fully that no opportunity for argument should be provided by overmuch narrowness in the meaning of the things said. This is much more befitting the schools than ourselves who scarcely suffice our wheels and distaffs. Therefore, since I may have some doubts in my mind and see that you are in conflict on account of what has been said, I mean to tell you a tale, not about a man of humble condition but about a valiant King and how he acted chivalrously, with never a stain upon his honour.

Every one of you must often have heard of King Carlo the elder, or the first, through whose magnificent prowess and especially by his glorious victory over King Manfred, the Ghibellines were driven from Florence and the Guelfs returned. Owing to this a knight named Messer Neri degli Uberti left the town with all his family and great wealth. He determined to live under the protection of none but King Carlo, and went to Castello da mare di Distabia to live in a solitary place and there end his life in peace. At about a bow-shot from all other dwellings he bought a piece of land among olives and hazel trees and chestnuts, which are very abundant in that country, and there he built a comfortable country house with a delightful garden about it, which according to our customs abounded in flowing water which he formed into a clear fish-pool stocked with a great many fish.

While he was giving his whole attention to beautifying his garden, it chanced in the hot weather that King Carlo went to Castellamare to rest, and while there heard so much of the beauty of Messer Neri's garden that he wished to see it. Knowing that Messer Neri belonged to the opposite party, the King wished to act in a friendly way to him, and sent to inform him that the King and four companions would sup privately with him the next evening. Messer Neri was very happy at this, made magnificent preparations, arranged with his servants everything that should be done, and received the King in his garden as handsomely as he could.

When he had looked over and praised Messer Neri's garden and house, the King washed and sat down to one of the tables set out near the fish-pool, and ordered one of his companions, Count Guido di Monforte, to sit on one side of him and Messer Neri on the other, and commanded the other three that they should wait upon him in accordance with Messer Neri's arrangements. The food was delicate, the wines excellent, the service good, with no disturbance or noise; all of which the King praised highly.

The King ate merrily and enjoyed the solitude of the place, when there came into the garden two girls about fifteen years old, with curls of hair like spun gold on which were garlands of flowers, while their faces were so delicate and beautiful they seemed more like angels than anything else. They were dressed in very thin linen garments as white as snow, tight fitting from the girdle upwards and below the girdle spreading out like a petticoat to the feet. The girl who came first carried a couple of fishing nets over her left shoulder and held a long stick in her right hand. The other had a frying-pan on her left shoulder and a bundle of wood under her left arm and tripod in her left hand, while in the other hand she carried a bottle of oil and a lighted torch. The King was greatly surprised to see them, and waited with interest to see what it meant.

The girls came forward modestly and, blushing, bowed to the King. Then the girl carrying the frying-pan laid it down near the pool with the other things she had and took the stick from the other girl; and then they both entered the water which came up as high as their breasts. One of Messer Neri's servants quickly lighted a fire, put the pan on the tripod and poured oil into it, and waited for the girls to throw out the fish to him. One of them beat the water where she knew the fish hid and the other prepared the nets, and to the great delight of the King, who watched it all carefully, they soon caught a number of fish. They threw them to the servant who put them almost alive into the pan, as they had been told to do, and then they took the finest fishes, and threw them on the table before the King and Count Guido and their father.

The fish flapped about on the table, to the great delight of the King, who took up some of them and courteously threw them back to the girls. They played in this manner until the servant had cooked the fish which had been given to him, and these were then set before the King as a side dish of rare and delightful food arranged by Messer Neri.

When enough fish had been caught and cooked, the girls came out of the water with their thin white clothes clinging to their bodies and concealing scarcely any of their beauties, and so passed blushing before the King and returned to the house.

The King, the Count and the other three gentlemen waiting upon him had watched the girls and had inwardly
praised them highly as beautiful and well formed and
charming and well behaved; but the King was especially
delighted with them. When they came from the water he had
gazed so attentively at every part of their bodies that he
would not have felt it if he had been pricked. As he thought
of them, without knowing who they were, or how, he felt in
his heart a most eager desire to please them and thereby
knew that he would fall in love if he were not careful, and
yet he did not know which of the two he liked best, so much
did they resemble each other. After thinking this over for
a time, he turned to Messer Neri and asked him who the two
girls were, and Messer Neri replied:

"Sire, they are twin daughters of mine, one of whom is
called the beautiful Ginevra and the other the gold-haired
Isotta."

The King highly praised them, and urged that they should
be married; which Messer Neri put off by saying he was unable to do so. And when the only thing left to serve at the
supper was fruit, the two girls returned dressed in fine silks
and carrying two very large silver dishes filled with various
fruits then in season, which they placed on the table before
the King. This done, they retired a short distance and sang
a song, beginning:

> None can fully tell, O Love,
> Where I have come,

so sweetly and charmingly that the King, who watched and
listened with delight, felt as if all the hierarchies of the
angels had come down to sing. After this they kneeled down
and asked the King's permission to retire, which he gave
with apparent cheerfulness, although he was sorry to have
them go.

When supper was ended the King and his companions
mounted their horses and took leave of Messer Neri, and
rode back to the King's palace, talking of one thing and another.

The King kept his love a secret, but in spite of all affairs
of state he could not forget the beautiful Ginevra's charm
and beauty, while for love of her he also loved the sister
who resembled her, and thus became so entangled in the
snares of love that he could scarcely think of anything else.
Upon various pretences he became very intimate with Messer Neri, and often visited his garden to see the fair Ginevra.

Finally, he could endure his state no longer and, not knowing what else to do, thought he would take not one but both
the girls from their father. He revealed his love and his intention to Count Guido, who, being a valiant man, replied:

"Sire, I marvel at what you tell me, and marvel more
than any other man would do since I think I know your
behaviour from childhood up better than anyone else. In
your youth, when Love might easily have pierced you with
his shafts, I knew of no such passion in you; but when I
hear of it now that you are close upon old age it seems so
strange and curious that you should fall in love like this that
it seems a miracle to me. If it fell to me to reprove you I
know what I should say to you, considering that you are still
in arms in a newly conquered kingdom, among nations unknown to you and full of deceits and treacheries, occupied
as you are with great cares and matters of state so that you
have never been able to sit down—and in the midst of all
this you give way to the flatteries of love.

"This is not the deed of a high-minded King but of a
pusillanimous youth. Moreover, and this is far worse, you
say you have determined to take his two daughters away
from the poor knight, who has done you every honour he
could in your house, and to show you the more honour displayed them almost naked before you, thereby showing
how much he trusts you and that he believes you to be a
King and not a ravening wolf.

"Has it escaped your memory that Manfred's violences to
women opened the way to this kingdom for you? What
treachery more worthy of eternal punishment was ever committed than this would be—to deprive the man who did you
honour of his hope, his consolation and his honour? Perhaps you think it would be a sufficient excuse to say: 'I did
it because he was a Ghibelline.' Is it the justice of Kings to
treat in such a way those, whoever they may be, who seek
their protection? Let me remind you, O King, that it was
very glorious to have conquered Manfred but far more
glorious to conquer oneself. Therefore do you, who have to
correct others, conquer yourself and curb this appetite, and
do not spoil what you have gloriously acquired with such a
stain."

These words sharply stabbed the King's soul and distressed him the more because he knew them to be true. So,
after several hot sighs he said:

"Count, I think that for a well-trained warrior it would be
easier to conquer any enemy rather than one's own appetite.
But though the fatigue will be great and the strength needed

inestimable, your words have so spurred me that before many days have passed I must show you by my deeds that I can dominate myself as well as conquer others."

Not many days after these words had passed, the King returned to Naples. To deprive himself of the chance of acting basely and also to reward the knight for the entertainment bestowed upon him, he determined to marry off the two girls as if they were his own daughters and not Messer Neri's, although it was hard for him to let others possess what he desired so ardently for himself. With Messer Neri's consent he bestowed magnificent dowries upon them, and gave the fair Ginevra to Messer Maffeo da Palizzi and the gold-haired Isotta to Messer Guglielmo della Magna, both of them noble knights and great barons. Having done this he set off for Apulia in an agony of grief and so quenched his fierce appetite with continual activities that he broke his amorous chains, and for the rest of his life lived free from that passion.

Some perhaps will say that it is a small thing for a King to have married off two girls; and I will admit it. But I call it a very great thing to have been done by a King in love, marrying off the girl he loved without having plucked leaf, flower or fruit of his love. Thus the King acted munificently, rewarding the noble knight highly, honouring the girls he loved in a praiseworthy way, and powerfully conquering himself.

## SEVENTH TALE

*King Pietro discovers the ardent love felt for him by Lisa who has fallen ill because of it. He comforts her, marries her to a young gentleman, and kisses her on the forehead, ever afterwards her knight*

Fiammetta reached the end of her tale and King Carlo's virile munificence was highly praised, although one of the ladies, a Ghibelline, would not praise him; then Pampinea, at the king's command, began thus:

Illustrious ladies, no wise person would contradict what you say of good King Carlo unless he bore the King ill will for some other reason; but since I have remembered an event no less commendable I wish to tell you what was done by his adversary to a girl of Florence.

At the time the French were driven from Sicily, there lived in Palermo a very rich Florentine apothecary, named Bernado Puccini, who had by his wife an only daughter, a very beautiful girl of marriageable age. And when King Pietro of Aragon became lord of the island, he and his barons held high festival at Palermo. In this festival he jousted in the Catalan style, and it chanced that Lisa, standing at a window with other ladies, saw him ride by, and as she looked at him liked him so much that she fell deeply in love with him. When the festival was over and she remained in her father's house, she could think of nothing else but her magnificent and lofty love. What most distressed her was the knowledge of her lowly birth, which gave her no hope of any happy ending; yet this did not prevent her from continuing to love the King, although she kept it secret for fear of worse things.

The King knew and cared nothing about this, which caused her a more intolerable pain than can be estimated. Her love continued to increase and one melancholy mood followed another until the girl could endure it no longer and fell ill, plainly wasting away from day to day, like snow in the sun. Her grieving father and mother did all they could to aid her with continual attentions and doctors and medicines, but all to no avail, because in despair over her love she had determined to die. Now, as her father offered to do anything she wanted, it occurred to her to try to let the King know her love and her determination before she died, if she could do so becomingly; and therefore she one day asked him to let her see Minuccio d'Arezzo.

In those days Minuccio d'Arezzo was considered a very great musician and singer and was much liked by King Pietro. Bernado thought that Lisa wanted to hear him sing and play, and as soon as Minuccio, who was a pleasant man, heard of it, he went to her. After trying to cheer her up with kindly words, he played to her on his viol and then sang her some songs, which were so much smoke and flame to the love of the girl whom he thought he was consoling. The girl then said that she wished to say a few words to him in private, and when everyone had left the room, she said:

"Minuccio, I have chosen you as the most trustworthy keeper of my secret, hoping first that you will never reveal it to anyone but the person I desire to know it, and then that you will help me to the extent of your power. And this I beg of you.

"You must know then, Minuccio, that on the day when our lord, King Pietro, made the great feast for his triumph, I saw him jousting and love of him lit such a fire in my soul that it has brought me to what you see. Knowing how ill my love befits a King and being unable either to drive it away or to lessen it, I have determined to die as the lesser suffering, since to bear it is too much for me.

"True it is that I shall depart disconsolate if he does not first know of it. I know of nobody who can more fittingly make him know my condition than you, and so I want to entrust it to you and beg you will not refuse to do it, so that, dying consoled, I may escape these woes."

This she spoke weeping, and then was silent.

Minuccio was amazed at her greatness of spirit and her fierce determination. He suddenly saw how he could virtuously assist her, and said:

"Lisa, I pledge you my faith, and you may live certain that I shall never deceive you; I praise you for your lofty enterprise in having raised your spirit to so great a King; and I offer you my aid whereby I hope, if you wish for comfort, that before the third day has passed I shall so act that I think I shall bring you news which will be most dear to you. Not to waste time, let me go and start at once."

Lisa once again besought him eagerly and promised him to be comforted, and then said good-bye. Minuccio departed and went to one Mico da Siena, in those days quite a good rhymester, and by his entreaties forced him to write the following song:

> *Go forth, O Love, to my Lord and tell him the pain I endure, tell him I am near to death, hiding my desire from fear.*

> *With folded hands, O Love, I beg you to go to my Lord. Tell him my heart so sweetly is in love that I desire and love him often; and that I fear to die from the great fire which burns in me and do not know how I may escape the heavy pain I bear, desiring him in fear and shame. Ah! Let him know my woe, for love of God!*

> *Since I have been in love with him, O Love, you never gave me courage greater than my fear to show my desire even once to him who keeps me in such pain. And to die thus is bitter to me. Perhaps it would not dis-*

*please him if he knew what pain I feel, if you had given
me strength to make known to him my state.*

*Since it was not your pleasure, Love, to grant me so
much grace as to make known my heart unto my
Lord, alas, by sign or semblance, I beg of you, sweet
my lord, to go to him and to remind him of the day I
saw him with shield and lance bearing his arms like
other knights, and gazed at him, and fell in love with
him, so that my heart is dying.*

These words Minuccio immediately set to soft and piteous
music as the matter required, and the third day went to
Court when King Pietro had already sat down to eat and
sent him orders to sing something to his viol. He then played
and sang the song so sweetly that everyone in the hall
seemed like shadow men, so silent and earnest were they to
listen, the King more than anyone else. And when Minuccio
had finished his song, the King asked him whence it came,
for he believed he had never heard it before.

"Sire," replied Minuccio, "the words and music were
composed not three days ago."

The King then asked for whom, and he replied:

"I dare not reveal it save to you only."

Desirous to hear this, the King arose from the table and
took him into another room, where Minuccio related to him
everything he had heard. The King was delighted, praised
the girl, and said that he would have compassion upon so
worthy a girl. He then told Minuccio to go to her and comfort her on his behalf, and to say that the King would come
to visit her about Vespers that day without fail.

Minuccio was most happy to bear such good news to the
girl, and at once went to her with his viol, and told her
everything in private; after which he sang her the song to his
viol. The girl was so pleased and happy that evident signs of
returning health appeared in her at once. Without knowing
or trying to guess what might happen, she eagerly awaited
Vespers when she would see her lord.

The King was a generous and kindly lord, and, having
several times thought over what Minuccio had told him,
while he knew the girl and her beauty very well, felt more
pity than ever. About the time of Vespers he mounted his
horse, as if riding out for recreation, and came to the
apothecary's house. There he asked to see a very beautiful
garden which belonged to the apothecary, and after some

time enquired of Bernado how his daughter was and if he had yet arranged a marriage for her.

"Sire," replied Bernado, "she is not yet married and has been and is very ill. It is true that she has improved marvellously since Nones today."

The King immediately saw what this improvement meant, and said to Bernado:

"Faith, it would be a pity that so beautiful a creature should be taken from the world; we desire to visit her."

So a little afterwards he went to her bedroom, accompanied only by Bernado and two attendants; he went to the bedside where the girl was eagerly awaiting him propped up a little, took her by the hand, and said:

"Madonna, what is the meaning of this? You are young and should be a comfort to others, yet you allow yourself to be ill. We pray you, for love of us, to be pleased to take comfort in such a way that you may be soon well."

Feeling herself touched by the hand of him whom she loved above all things the girl indeed felt a little modest shame but also as much pleasure in her soul as if she had been in Paradise. And she replied to the best of her ability:

"My lord, the cause of my sickness was my attempt to bear very heavy burdens with my small strength; but thanks to you, you will soon see me free from it."

The King alone understood the girl's hidden meaning and thought more and more highly of her, and often cursed Fortune for making her the daughter of such a man. And after staying with her for some time and comforting her, he departed.

This kindness on the King's part was highly commended and considered a great honour to the apothecary and his daughter, who remained as glad as any woman could be with her lover. Aided by hope she grew well in a few days and became more beautiful than ever. The King had discussed with the Queen what reward should be given her for so great a love, and when the girl was well he mounted his horse and, accompanied by many of his barons, went to the garden and sent for the apothecary and his daughter. The Queen and many of her ladies also came there and received the girl with the greatest kindness. Then the King, standing beside the Queen, said to Lisa:

"The great love you bear, brave girl, deserves great honour from us, and for love of us we will that you should be contented. The honour is this—that since you should be married we will that you should accept the husband we shall bestow upon you, ourselves none the less ever intending to be called your knight, while we ask no more of your love than a single kiss."

The girl blushed deep red with shame and, obedient to the King's pleasure, answered in a low voice:

"My lord, I am very sure that if it were known that I am in love with you, most people would consider me mad, thinking perhaps that I am out of my mind and ignorant of my own rank and yours. But God, who alone sees the hearts of mortals, knows that at the hour I first loved you I knew you to be a King and myself to be the daughter of Bernado the apothecary, and that it ill became me to set the love of my spirit so high. But, as you know better than I, none of us loves by deliberate choice but from appetite and pleasure. I have often opposed all my strength to these laws but in vain, and so I loved, love and always shall love you.

"True it is that when I felt myself taken with love of you I determined that your will should always be mine. Therefore, if you told me to stand in a fire and I thought it would please you, it would be a delight to me; how gladly then will I take a husband and cherish him whom you are pleased to give me, since this will be an honour and estate to me. You know how honourable it is for me to have you, a King, as my knight; and therefore I say no more of this. As for the kiss which is all you ask of my love, it shall only be yielded you with the Queen's permission. Nevertheless, for the kindness of the Queen and you to me, God through me renders you thanks and reward!"

She was then silent. The Queen was greatly pleased by the girl's reply, and thought her as wise as the King had said. The King sent for the girl's father and mother, and having found they agreed to what he intended to do, he sent for a young but poor gentleman, named Perdicone, to whom he handed a ring and there, with his consent, betrothed him to Lisa. In addition to many valuable jewels which the King and Queen gave the girl, the King also gave them Ceffalu and Calatabellotta, two excellent and very fruitful estates, saying:

"We give you these as your lady's dowry; what we intend to do for you, you shall see when the time comes."

He then turned to the girl, and said:

"We now desire to take the fruit of your love which is ours."

And he took her head in both his hands and kissed her on the forehead.

Perdicone and Lisa's father and mother and Lisa herself were delighted, and made a great and merry marriage feast.

And, as many affirm, the King most faithfully observed his pact with the girl. As long as he lived he always called himself her knight, and whenever he rode out on any feat of arms bore no token or badge save that which she sent him.

Acting thus he captured the souls of his subjects; he set an example to others and acquired eternal fame. But today there are few who stretch the bow of the intellect to such matters, for most lords have become cruel and tyrannical.

### EIGHTH TALE

*Sofronia thinks she is the wife of Gisippus, but in fact is married to Titus Quintus Fulvius with whom she goes to Rome. There Gisippus arrives in poverty and thinks he has been treated contemptuously by Titus, and therefore says he has killed a man in order to die himself. Titus recognises him and, to save him, says he killed the man; whereupon the real murderer then confesses. Octavius sets them all at liberty; Titus gives Gisippus his sister in marriage and shares his property with him*

When Pampinea had ceased speaking and all, especially the Ghibelline, had praised King Pietro, Filomena began thus at the king's command:

Magnificent ladies, who does not know that Kings can do very great things when they want, and that therefore they are specially called upon to be generous to others? The man who has power and does what is befitting him, does well; but we should not marvel so much at him or praise him so highly as we ought to do with another who accomplished the same thing when less is expected of him. Therefore, if you think the works of Kings so excellent and praise them so much, I have no doubt you will admire and praise those of our equals when their deeds resemble or exceed those of Kings. And so I propose to tell you of the praiseworthy and generous deeds of two citizens, friends.

At the time when Octavius Cæsar had not been saluted Augustus, but reigned over Rome as one of the Triumvirate, there lived in Rome a gentleman called Publius Quintus Fulvius. He had a son named Titus Quintus Fulvius, who, on account of his high intelligence, was sent to learn philosophy

at Athens and was warmly recommended by his father to a
very old friend, a nobleman named Chremes. Titus was
lodged by him in his own house along with his son Gisippus,
and both were sent to learn philosophy under the discipline
of the philosopher Aristippus.

The manners of the two young men were so similar that
from familiarity they developed so great a friendship and
fraternity that nothing but death could separate them.
Neither was happy except when with the other. They began
their studies together, and since each was endowed with the
the highest intelligence they rose to the glorious heights of
philosophy side by side and with great commendation. In
this way they spent three years to the great delight of
Chremes, who looked upon them both as his own children.
At the end of this time Chremes, who was old, departed this
life, like all things else. They felt an equal grief as at the loss
of a common father, nor could the friends and relatives of
Chremes discover which of the two was the more in need of
consolation.

Some months later the relatives and friends of Gisippus,
including Titus, urged him to marry; and found him a girl
of noble birth and the greatest beauty, a freewoman of
Athens, aged about fifteen, by name Sofronia. When the
wedding was close at hand, Gisippus one day asked Titus,
who had not yet seen her, to come with him to visit her. As
she sat between them in her house, Titus, who was naturally
interested in the beauty of his friend's wife, looked closely
at her, found every portion of her most pleasing to him,
and, as he praised her, fell as deeply in love with her as
ever a lover could, although he showed no signs of it.

After spending some time with her, they departed and returned home. Titus went alone to his room, and there began
to think of the charming girl; and the more he thought of her
the more he fell in love with her. After heaving many deep
sighs he said to himself:

"Ah! Titus, wretched is your life! Where and in whom
have you set your soul and love and hope? Do you not
know that you should look upon this girl as your sister, both
on account of the favours you have received from Chremes
and his family, and on account of the close friendship between you and Gisippus, whose betrothed she is? Whom
then do you love? Wither do you let yourself be carried by
deceitful love? Whither by flattering hope? Open the eyes
of your mind, and know yourself, wretch! Make way for
reason, curb your lascivious appetite, temper your unhealthy
desires, and direct your thoughts elsewhere. Oppose your

lust in its beginnings, and conquer yourself while there is yet time. What you wish to do is not befitting, is not comely. You should flee from what you desire to pursue even if you are sure of winning it (which you are not), if you have any regard for what is required by true friendship and what you owe it. What then will you do, Titus? Leave this unbecoming love if you would do what is befitting."

But then he thought of Sofronia and all his thoughts turned in the opposite direction; he condemned everything he had said, and went on:

"The laws of love are stronger than any others; they break divine laws as well as those of friendship. How often has the father loved his daughter? The brother his sister? The stepmother her step-son? Things more monstrous than for a man to love his friend's wife have already occurred a thousand times. Moreover I am young, and youth is entirely subject to the laws of love. What pleases love must therefore please me. Virtuous deeds belong to my elders; I can only will what love wills. Her beauty deserves all men's love; if I, a young man, love her, who can rightly reprove me for it? I do not love her because she is Gisippus's, but should love her whosoever's she were. It is Fortune's error for yielding her to my friend Gisippus rather than to another. And if she must be loved (as she deservedly must for her beauty), then, if Gisippus hears of it, he should be more happy to have me love her than another."

Thus, making a mock of himself, he continued in this argument, going first to one side and then to the other, and spent not only that day and night but many others, until for lack of food and sleep he was compelled to take to his bed. Gisippus for several days had noticed that he was thoughtful and now saw he was ill, felt grieved, and used every art and device to cheer him up, never left his side, and often and insistently asked him the cause of his pensiveness and illness. Titus several times invented false tales which Gisippus found out; but finally, when Titus found himself constrained, he answered in this manner with many sighs and laments:

"Gisippus, if it had pleased the gods I would rather have died than continue to live, when I think how Fortune has led me to a point where my virtue has been tested and where, to my great shame, I have been beaten. But indeed I expect soon that reward which befits me, I mean death, which will be more precious to me than to live with the remembrance of my baseness, which I shall reveal to you, though not without blushing, for I neither can nor ought to conceal anything from you."

He then began from the beginning and revealed to his friend the reason for his thoughts, and the contest among them, and to which side the final victory inclined, and how he was dying for love of Sofronia, affirming that since he knew how unbecoming this was in him he had made up his mind to die as a penance, which he thought would soon come to pass. When Gisippus heard this and saw his weeping, he was silent for a time, for he too was absorbed, though more temperately, by his delight in the beautiful girl. But then without hesitation he decided that his friend's life should be dearer to him than Sofronia. So, with his own tears claiming the other's tears, he replied, weeping:

"Titus, if you were not so much in need of comfort as you now are, I should complain of you to yourself as a man who has violated our friendship by keeping your great passion so long concealed from me. And although you thought it unvirtuous, yet unvirtuous things are no more to be concealed from a friend than virtuous ones, because since a friend delights in virtuous things with his friend, so he strives to uproot the unvirtuous things from his friend's mind. But let us leave that for the present, and come to that which I know to be of greater importance. I do not wonder that you love Sofronia who is my betrothed, but I should wonder if it were otherwise, knowing as I do her beauty and the nobility of your spirit which is the more apt to feel passion in proportion to the excellence of the thing which delights you. And the more reasonable your love of Sofronia, the more unjust your complaint of Fortune (although you do not express it) for yielding her to me, since you think your love would be right if she were anyone's but mine. But, if you are wise as you are wont to be, to whom could Fortune have yielded her more favourably for you than to me? Whoever else had her—however justified your love might then be—would have loved her more for himself than for you, which you had no need to fear from me if you know me to be the friend I am. The reason is this—that so long as we have been friends I do not remember ever to have had anything which was not yours as much as mine.

"Therefore, if matters had gone so far forward that it could not be otherwise, even then this should be as with other things; but it has not gone so far that I cannot make her yours only, and this I will do. For I do not know how my friendship could be dear to you if I did not make my will yours in something which may virtuously be done. True, Sofronia is betrothed to me, and I love her greatly, and was awaiting the marriage with great eagerness. But since you, who have more understanding than I, more eagerly desire a thing so precious as she, be sure that in this my room you shall see, not my—but your—wife. Therefore, put off your pensiveness, drive away melancholy, call back your lost health and content and happiness, and from this hour onward await cheerfully the reward of your love which is so much more worthy than mine."

At these words of Gisippus's, Titus felt the pleasures of flattering hope but at the same time equally felt ashamed, for his reason showed him that the greater was Gisippus's generosity the more unseemly was it for him to make use of it. Therefore, without ceasing to weep, he answered as follows with great difficulty:

"Gisippus, your true and generous friendship clearly shows me what I ought to do. God forbid that I should ever take from you as mine the woman God has given to you as the more worthy. If He had seen that she was more suitable for me, neither you nor anyone else ought to think that she would have been granted to you. Therefore, cheerfully enjoy your choice and wise council and His gift, and leave me to waste away in tears, which He has prepared for me as one unworthy of such good as she, which tears I shall either conquer and shall thus be dear to you, or they will conquer me and I shall be out of my pain."

"Titus," said Gisippus, "if our friendship permits me to force you to follow my wishes and can induce you to follow them, this is a case when I mean to take full advantage of it. If you do not yield amicably to my entreaties, I shall make use of such compulsion as befits a friend in order to make Sofronia yours. I know the strength of love's powers and I know that they have led lovers to an unhappy death, not once but many times. I see you so near it that you can neither turn back nor conquer your tears, and if you proceed you will be overcome, and I without any doubt should soon follow you.

"Therefore, even if I loved you for no other reason, your life is precious to me for the sake of my own. Sofronia then shall be yours, and you will not easily find another so pleasing to you. I shall transfer my love to someone else, and shall thus have contented us both. Perhaps I should not be so generous if it were as hard and difficult to find wives as it is to find friends. Since I can very easily find another wife but not another friend I prefer—I will not say to lose her, for I shall not lose her by giving her to you, but to transfer her from good to better, to another me—to transfer her, I say, than to lose you. So, if my entreaties have any power over you, I beg you to cast off this sorrow and at one and the same time to comfort yourself and me, and with good hope to make ready to enjoy that happiness which your hot love desires of the person you love."

Titus was ashamed to consent to allow Sofronia to be his wife and so remained silent, pulled in the other direction by his love and Gisippus's entreaties.

"Gisippus," said he, "I do not know if I can say that I am pleasing myself more, or you, by doing what you tell me will please you so much. But since your generosity is such that it vanquishes my natural shame, I will do it. But I tell you this—I do it as a man who knows that he is receiving from you both the woman he loves and his life. May the gods grant that I may yet prove to you with honour and benefits to yourself how much gratitude I feel for what you are doing for me in greater pity for me than I feel for myself."

After these words Gisippus said:

"Titus, if we are to succeed in this matter I think we must act as follows: as you know, Sofronia has been betrothed to me after long discussion between my parents and hers, and so if I now went and said I do not want her as my wife, great scandal would arise and would anger her relatives and mine. I should care nothing about that if I thought that thereby she would become your wife. But if I did that I fear that her relatives would speedily give her to another, who perhaps would not be you, and so you would have lost the woman I should not have gained. Therefore, if you agree, I think I should continue as I have begun, bring her home to the house as mine and make a wedding feast, and then we can arrange that you secretly lie with her as if she were your wife. Then at a fitting time and place we will let them know what we have done. If they like it, all well and good; if they do not, yet the thing will be done and nothing can then undo it, so they will be forced to accept it."

Titus liked the plan. Therefore, when Titus was well and happy again, Gisippus received her into his house as his wife. A great feast was made, and when night came the women left the bride in her husband's bed and went away. Titus's room was next to Gisippus's and they communicated; so, when Gisippus went to his room after all lights had been extinguished he passed softly into Titus's and told him to go and lie with his lady. At this Titus was overcome with shame and wanted to change his mind and refuse to go; but since Gisippus was as determined in spirit as in his words, he sent him there after a long argument.

When he reached the bed, he took the girl as if to embrace her, and softly asked her if she would be his wife. Thinking he was Gisippus, she said "yes," and he slipped a beautiful and valuable ring on her finger, saying:

"And I will be your husband."

He then consummated the marriage, and took long amorous pleasure of her, and neither she nor anyone else perceived that it was not Gisippus who lay with her.

The marriage of Titus and Sofronia was in this position, when his father Publius died, and a letter was sent him that he must return to Rome at once to attend to his affairs. He therefore arranged with Gisippus to go and take Sofronia with him, but this could not be done secretly without telling her how things were. So one day they took her to a room and told her everything that had happened, and Titus proved it to her from many incidents between them. After gazing somewhat scornfully at one and then the other, she began to weep exceedingly and complained of Gisippus's deception. Before a word of all this was mentioned in Gisippus's house, she went to her father's house and told him and her mother of the deceit Gisippus had practised upon her and then, adding that she was the wife of Titus, and not of Gisippus as they believed.

Sofronia's father was bitterly angered by this, and raised a great quarrel between his relatives and those of Gisippus. The talk and disturbance was loud and long. Gisippus became hated by his relatives and by Sofronia's, and they all said that he deserved severe punishment as well as reprehension. But he maintained that he had done a good action, and that Sofronia's relatives should thank him for having married her to a better man than himself.

Meanwhile, Titus heard all this with the greatest distress. He knew that the character of the Greeks made them the more noisy and threatening, the less they met with opposition; while otherwise they would become humble and even abject. So he made up his mind not to endure their insults further without reply. He had a Roman soul and Athenian wit, and therefore managed to collect the relatives of Gisippus and Sofronia in a temple. He then came in, accompanied only by Gisippus, and spoke thus to them as they sat waiting:

"Many philosophers believe that whatever is done by mortal man comes to pass through the will and foresight

of the immortal gods, and therefore some assert that all
which is done or will be done happens of necessity, although
others say that this necessity applies only to what has been
done. If these opinions are examined with care, it will
plainly appear that to reprehend something which cannot
be hindered is doing nothing less than attempting to show
oneself wiser than the immortal gods, of whom we are
compelled to believe that they govern and dispose of us and
our affairs with eternal wisdom and without error.

"You may easily see what mad presumption and folly it
is to question their deeds and how those who most eagerly
do this are the most deserving of chains. In my opinion,
you are all like this, if it be true what I have heard you
say and go on saying because Sofronia has become my wife,
when it was intended that she should be Gisippus's; for
you have not considered that from all eternity it had been
decreed that she should not be Gisippus's wife but mine, as
is now plain from the event.

"But, since many persons think it a heavy matter, hard of
understanding, to speak of the secret providence and intention of the gods, I will descend to the counsels of men, pre-
supposing even that the gods had nothing to do with what
has happened. In speaking thus, I shall be compelled to do
two things very contrary to my habits; one is to praise myself, the second to blame and condemn others. But I shall
do it because the present matters require it, while I do not
intend to depart from the truth in either.

"Your complaints, which arise more from anger than
reason, your continual murmurings and outcries, insult, vil-
ify and condemn Gisippus because from his own desire he
gave me for my wife the woman you meant to give him,
wherein I consider that he is highly to be praised. My reasons are these: first, he did what a friend ought to do; second, he acted more wisely than you would have done.

"It is not my intention here to discuss what the sacred
laws of friendship demand that one friend should do for
another; it is sufficient only to recall that the bonds of
friendship are closer than those of blood and parenthood,
for our friends are our own choice while our parents are the
result of Fortune. Therefore, you should not marvel if Gisippus prefers my life to your affection, since I am his
friend.

"Coming now to the second reason, which I must demonstrate to you with more insistence (which is that he was
wiser than you are), it appears to me that you have understood nothing of the gods' providence, while you are still

less aware of the effects of friendship. I say then that your foresight, your counsel and your reflection decided to give Sofronia to Gisippus, a young man and a philosopher. Gisippus's gave her to a young man and a philosopher. Your counsel gave her to an Athenian, and Gisippus's to a Roman. Yours to a young nobleman, his to one more noble. Yours to a rich young man, his to one much richer. Yours to a young man who not only did not love her, but scarcely knew her; his to a young man who loved her beyond his own happiness and more than his own life.

"Examine now whether what I have said is not true and more to be praised than what you did. That I am a young man and a philosopher like Gisippus, my face and studies declare, without need for further demonstration. He and I are of the same age, and we have advanced step by step together in our studies. True it is that he is Athenian, and I a Roman. If we are to dispute about the fame of our cities, I shall say that I belong to a free country and he to one subject; I shall say that my city is queen of the world and his city obedient to mine; I shall say that my city is pre-eminent in war, power and the arts, whereas his can only be praised for the arts.

"Moreover, however humble I might seem to you here as a scholar, I was not born from the dregs of the Roman people. My own houses and the public buildings of Rome are filled with the ancient statues of my ancestors, and the Roman annals are filled with the triumphs conducted by the family of Quintus to the Capitol of Rome. Nor has it declined with age, for the glory of our name is today more flourishing than ever.

"From very shame I am silent as to my wealth, for I consider that decent poverty is the ancient and best patrimony of the noble citizens of Rome. If this opinion be condemned by the vulgar, and riches be praised, then I must tell you I am abundantly wealthy, not because I am avaricious but because I am Fortune's friend. I know it is true that you were and would be happy to have Gisippus as a relative; but I should be no less dear to you in Rome, since in me you will have an excellent guest, a useful, solicitous and powerful patron both for private needs and public occasions.

"Now leaving the will free and looking at the matter reasonably, who would commend your counsel more than my Gisippus's? Assuredly, no one. Sofronia then is well married to Titus Quintus Fulvius, a rich and noble and antique citizen of Rome, the friend of Gisippus. If anyone laments or complains about that, he is not doing what he ought to do, and does not know what he is doing. Perhaps some will say that they do not complain that Sofronia is the wife of Titus, but do complain of the manner in which she became so—stealthily, furtively, without the knowledge of her friends and relatives. Nor is this a miracle or any new thing.

"I set aside those women who have taken husbands against the wishes of their fathers, those who have fled with their lovers and thus have been mistresses before they were wives, those who have pleaded for marriage more by pregnancy and children than with their tongues, and whom necessity has advanced. None of these happened to Sofronia, who was discreetly, soberly and orderly given in marriage by Gisippus. Some will say that he married her to a man she ought not to have married. These are foolish and womanly laments, proceeding from a lack of thought. This is not the first time Fortune has made use of devious ways and new methods to attain her pre-determined ends. What do I care whether a cobbler or a philosopher attends to some affair of mine, and whether it be in secret or openly, if the rseult is good? If the cobbler is indiscreet I ought to be careful to see that he has nothing more to do with it, and thank him for what he has done. If Gisippus has married Sofronia well, it is a superfluous folly to regret the manner and to complain of him. If you have no confidence in his wisdom, take care that he marries no one else, and thank him for this.

"Nevertheless you must know I did not seek, either by trickery or fraud, to lay any stain on the honour and nobility of your blood in the person of Sofronia. Although I took her secretly to wife, I did not come like a ravisher to take her virginity nor did I wish like an enemy to possess her otherwise than honourably; but I was ardently aflame for her delicate beauty and virtue, and I knew that you loved her so much that if I had sought her in the manner you perhaps think I ought to have adopted, I should not have had her, owing to your fear that I should take her to Rome.

"Therefore I made use of the secret means which now are revealed to you, and I made Gisippus consent in my name to what he was unwilling to do. Although I loved her eagerly, I sought her embraces not as a lover but as a husband, and, as she herself can bear true witness, I did not approach her until I had wedded her with the customary words and a ring, asking her whether she would be my wife, to which she said 'Yes.' If you think her deceived, you should blame her and not me, because she did not ask who I was. The great wrong, the great sin, the great crime wrought by Gisippus, my friend whom I love, is that he secretly married Sofronia to Titus Quintus. For this you slander, menace and plot against him. What more could you do if he had given her to a peasant, a ruffian or a slave? What chains, prison, crucifying will suffice?

"But let us leave this. The time has come, before I expected it, when my father has died, and I must return to Rome. Since I wish to take Sofronia with me, I have told you what I should perhaps otherwise have kept secret. If you are wise, you will cheerfully accept it, for if I had wished to insult or outrage you I could have left her here scorned; but God forbid that such baseness should ever dwell in a Roman soul!

"Sofronia then is mine, by the consent of the gods and the force of human laws, by the praiseworthy wisdom of my friend Gisippus and by my own lover's wit; and you, peradventure thinking yourselves wiser than the gods and other men, show me that you stupidly condemn this in two ways which to me are very annoying. First, you retain Sofronia, which you have no right to do except so far as it please me; second, you treat Gisippus as an enemy, when you are under great obligations to him. I do not at present mean to show you how foolishly you are acting in these matters, but I advise you as my friends to put aside your anger and get rid of your fury. Restore Sofronia to me, and let me depart and live cheerfully as your relative. Be certain of this, whether what is done pleases or displeases you, I shall take Gisippus from you, and as soon as I return to Rome I shall undoubtedly regain her who is rightfully mine, however much you object. And by perpetual enmity I shall make you learn from experience what the anger of the Romans can achieve."

Having said this, Titus rose to his feet with an angry countenance, took Gisippus by the hand, and left the temple, shaking his head at them in a threatening way to show how little he cared for them. Those who remained, partly persuaded to friendship and family alliance with Titus by his reasonings, and partly terrified by his final words, agreed together that it would be better to have Titus as their relative (since Gisippus had not wanted it) than to lose Gisippus as a relative and to have Titus as an enemy into the bargain. They therefore went after Titus and told him they were willing Sofronia should be his, and that they wanted to have him as their relative and Gisippus as a good friend. After a friendly and family meeting, they departed, and sent Sofronia back to him. Like a wise woman, she made a

virtue of necessity, and devoted to Titus the love she had
felt for Gisippus. She set out with Titus for Rome, and
there was received with great honour.

Gisippus remained in Athens, held in low esteem by
nearly everybody; and not long afterwards through the in-
trigues of the citizens, he was driven out of Athens, poor
and helpless, and condemned to perpetual exile. Gisippus,
having thus become not only poor but a beggar, made his
way as best he could to Rome, to find if Titus remembered
him. He learned that Titus was alive and respected by all
the Romans, and, having found his house, waited about
until Titus came. In his miserable condition he was unwilling to speak, but strove to be seen, so that Titus might
recognise him and call him. Titus passed by, and Gisippus
thought he had seen and scorned him; and remembering
what he had done for him in the past, Gisippus departed in
anger and despair.

It was already night; he was hungry and penniless, knew
not where to go, and desired death above all things. He
came to a deserted part of the city and saw a large cave,
where he spent the night on the bare ground in an evil plight,
falling asleep when he was worn out with weeping.

Towards morning, two men who had been thieving during the night came to the cave with their spoils. A quarrel
started, and the stronger killed the other man, and went
away. Gisippus heard and saw what happened, and felt he
had found the means of obtaining the death he so much desired, without killing himself. So he remained there until
the police officers, who had heard of the deed, came there
and haled Gisippus savagely away. When he was examined,
he said he had killed the man and had never been able to
leave the cave. Therefore the Prætor, by name Marcus
Varro, ordered that he should be crucified, as was then the
custom.

At that moment Titus happened to come to the Prætor's
court, and, looking at the wretch's face as he was told what
had happened, suddenly recognised Gisippus, and marvelled
at his miserable fate and how he had got there. He desired
ardently to help him, and, seeing no other way to help him
except to set free his friend by denouncing himself, immediately thrust forward and said:

"Marcus Varro, I claim the poor man whom you have
condemned, because he is innocent. I have offended the
gods enough with one crime, by slaying the man whom your
officers found dead this morning; and I will not further offend them by the death of another innocent man."

Varro was amazed, and regretted that the whole Court had heard what he said. But, since he could not honourably do anything but what the laws commanded, he had Gisippus brought back, and in the presence of Titus said to him:

"How could you be so mad as to confess without any torture that you did something you had not done, when it was a matter of your life? You said you killed the man last night, and now this man comes and says that he and not you killed him."

Gisippus saw the man was Titus, and realised at once this had been done to save him, out of gratitude for the services received from him. So, weeping piteously, he said:

"Varro, in truth I killed him; and Titus's pity is now too late to save me."

But Titus said:

"Varro, as you see, this man is a foreigner, and he was found unarmed beside the murdered man. You can see that his miserable condition makes him want to die; set him free then, and punish me who have deserved it."

Varro marvelled at their insistence, and guessed that neither of them was guilty. He was thinking how to set them free when there came in a young man, named Publius Ambustus, an abandoned sinner, known as a thief to all the Romans, and the man who had really committed the murder. He knew that neither of the two men was guilty, and such a softening of heart came over him for their innocence that he was moved by compassion, and said to Varro:

"Prætor, my deeds bring me to solve this debate between these two, and I know not what god within me urges me to make plain my crime. You must know that neither is guilty. I killed the man towards morning last night, and I saw that other poor man asleep while I was dividing the spoil with the man I killed. There is no need for me to clear Titus. His fame is known to all that he is not a man of that sort. Set them free then, and punish me as the laws require."

The news of this came to Octavius, who sent for all three of them, and desired to know the reason why each of them wanted to be condemned; and they told him. Octavius set free the first two because they were innocent, and the third for love of them. Titus first reproved Gisippus for his mistrust, and then rejoiced greatly with him, and took him home, where Sofronia with tears of pity received him as a brother. After he had rested, Titus dressed him in the clothes suited to his rank and virtue and, after sharing equally with him all his money and possessions, gave him his young sister Fulvia as his wife. He then said:

"Gisippus, it is now for you to decide whether you will remain here with me, or whether you will return to Achaia with all I have given you."

Constrained on the one side by the decree of exile from his own city and on the other by the love he owed to Titus's friendship, Gisippus determined to become a Roman. There, he with his Fulvia and Titus with his Sofronia lived long and happily in a large house, and each day became closer friends—if that were possible.

Friendship, then, is a most sacred thing, worthy not only of singular reverence but of being commended with perpetual praise, as the most discreet mother of liberality and honour, the sister of gratitude and charity, the enemy of hatred and avarice, ever ready, without waiting to be asked, to do virtuously to another what it would wish done to itself. Its sacred results are today most rarely to be seen in two persons, for to the shame and sin of men's miserable cupidity which makes them look only to their own interest, friendship has been driven to the ends of the earth and left in perpetual exile.

What love, what wealth, what family tie could have made Gisippus feel so deeply in his heart the fervour and tears and sighs of Titus, so that he gave his friend his own beautiful and loved wife—save only friendship! What laws, what threats, what fear would have made the young arms of Gisippus abstain from embracing the girl (who perhaps invited it) in dark and solitary places or in his own bed—save only friendship! What rank, what merit, what advantages would have made Gisippus careless of losing his own relatives and Sofronia's, careless of the insulting gibes of the multitude, careless of scorns and jests to content his friend—save only friendship!

Moreover, what could have urged Titus (when he could blamelessly have feigned not to see him) unhesitatingly to procure his own death to save Gisippus from the cross, which he himself had provoked, save only friendship! What could have made Titus most liberal in sharing his great patrimony with Gisippus, whom Fortune had deprived of all he had, save only friendship! What could have made Titus most unsuspiciously eager to give his sister to Gisippus, although he saw him in extreme poverty and misery, save only friendship!

We see men desire a multitude of relatives, crowds of brothers, a great quantity of sons, and to increase the number of their servants with their wealth. And they do not perceive that any one of them dreads more the slightest danger to himself than he is solicitous to avert great dangers from his father, brother or master; whereas we see exactly the contrary in a friend.

## NINTH TALE

*Saladin, disguised as a merchant, is entertained by Messer Torello, who afterwards goes on a Crusade and sets a time to his wife, after which if he does not return she may re-marry. Messer Torello is captured, and his skill in dressing hawks brings him to the notice of the Sultan, by whom he is recognised and highly honoured. Messer Torello falls ill; then by magic arts he is carried back to Pavia at the very moment when his wife is about to re-marry. She recognises him, and they return home together*

Filomena ended her tale and Titus's munificent gratitude was praised by all, when the king, reserving to Dioneo his right to speak last, began thus:

Fair ladies, Filomena is undoubtedly right in what she says about friendship, and she has every reason to complain, as she did at the end, that friendship is now so little accepted by mankind. If we were here to correct or reprove the world's faults, I could follow up her words with a long speech. But our object is different, and it occurs to me to relate to you in a long but pleasant tale one of Saladin's liberalities. From the things you will hear in my tale you will see that, although our vices prevent us from obtaining anyone's complete friendship, we may at least take delight in rendering service, in the hope that some day it will be rewarded.

I say then that, as some relate, in the time of the Emperor Frederick the First, a general Crusade was undertaken by all Christians for the recovery of the Holy Land. Saladin, the Sultan of Babylon and a most valiant Prince, hearing something of this, determined to go personally and observe the preparations of the Christian Princes, so that he could better resist them. He made all his arrangements in Egypt, pretended he was going on a pilgrimage, and set out with two of his wisest and most important councillors, and only three servants, in the guise of merchants. They passed through many Christian provinces, and as they rode through Lombardy towards the Alps, it happened that one evening on the way from Milan to Pavia they met a gentleman, by name Messer Torello d' Istria da Pavia, who was going with his attendants, hounds and hawks, to stay at a handsome estate he had in the Ticino. When Messer Torello noticed them, he saw they were gentlemen and foreigners, and wished to honour them.

Saladin asked one of the attendants how far it was to Pavia and if they could get there in time to enter the city; but Torello, not giving the attendant time to speak, replied himself:

"Gentlemen, you cannot reach Pavia in time to enter the city today."

"Then," said Saladin, "since we are foreigners, will you be kind enough to tell us the best inn where we can lodge?"

"Gladly," replied Messer Torello. "I was just about to send one of my servants to Pavia on an errand; I will send him with you and he will guide you where you will find the best inn."

He then gave orders to the most intelligent of his servants as to what to do, and sent him off with them. He himself rode straight to his house, and arranged the best supper he could, with tables set out in the garden. That done, he waited for them at the door. The attendant rode along talking of different things with the gentlemen, and led them by side roads to his master's house, without their noticing it. And when Messer Torello saw them, he went to meet them on foot, saying with a laugh:

"Gentlemen, you are very welcome."

Saladin, who was very quick-witted, guessed that the gentlemen had doubted whether they would have accepted his invitation, if he had invited them when he met them, and so, artfully, had them brought to his own house, so that they could not refuse to spend the evening with him. He returned his salutation, and said:

"Messer, if a man might ever complain of courteous men, we might do so of you, for you have taken us out of our way, and you force us to accept your hospitality without our having deserved such kindness except by a single greeting."

"Gentlemen," said the knight, who was a wise and well spoken man, "if I may guess from your appearance, what you will receive from me will be but poor entertainment compared with what is befitting you. But indeed there is nowhere outside Pavia where you could be well lodged, and therefore do not regret having gone a little out of your way to be lodged not quite so ill."

When he had said this, the servants surrounded the gentlemen as they dismounted, and led away their horses. Messer Torello conducted the three gentlemen into the rooms prepared for them, had their riding boots taken off and refreshed them with cool wines, and retained them in conversation until supper time.

Saladin and his companions and servants all knew Latin, so they could all make themselves perfectly well understood. Each of them thought that the knight was the most pleasant, courteous man and the best talker they had ever met. Messer Torello, on the other hand, thought they were far more important and magnificent personages than he had at first supposed, and therefore regretted that he could not entertain them that evening with company and with a more ceremonious banquet. He determined to atone for it next day, and, having told one of his servants what he wanted done, sent him to his wife, a most excellent and high-minded woman, who was at Pavia—which was close at hand, and where none of the gates was ever locked. After this he took the gentlemen into the garden, and courteously asked who they were. Saladin replied:

"We are merchants of Cyprus on our way from Cyprus to Paris about our affairs."

"Would to God," replied Messer Torello, "that our country produced such gentlemen as I see the merchants of Cyprus are!"

After spending a short time in conversation about other things, supper was served. He had them sit at his own table, to do them greater honour, and they were well served, as far as an impromptu supper could provide.

Soon after the tables were removed, Messer Torello saw they were tired, and so took them to excellent beds to sleep; soon after which he went to bed himself.

The servant carried the message to Messer Torello's wife in Pavia. She, whose spirit was rather regal than feminine, immediately called together Messer Torello's friends and servants, prepared everything befitting a great banquet, sent out invitations by torch-light to many of the noblest citizens, hung out carpets and arras and hangings, and arranged everything in accordance with her husband's message.

Next day the gentlemen arose, and Messer Torello went

to horse with them and ordered out his hawks. He took them to a neighbouring marsh, and showed them how the birds flew. Saladin asked for someone to lead them to the best inn of Pavia, and Messer Torello said:

"I will take you, for I have to go there."

They believed him, and were glad, and together they set out. About Tierce they came to the city, and, thinking they were going to the best inn, went with Messer Torello to his house, where quite fifty of the noblest inhabitants had gathered to receive the gentlemen, whose bridles and stirrups were immediately held for them. As soon as Saladin and his companions saw this, they saw what had happened, and said:

"Messer Torello, this is not what we asked of you. Last night you did sufficient and more than we required; therefore you might well let us go on our way."

"Gentlemen," said Messer Torello, "I owe more to Fortune than to you for what happened yesterday, since I met you on the road at the time when you had to come to my little house. But today I shall be indebted to you, as will all these gentlemen; and if you think it courteous to refuse to dine with them, you can do so if you wish."

Vanquished by this, Saladin and his companions dismounted and were gaily conducted by the gentlemen to the rooms which had been richly decorated for them. When they had put off their travelling clothes and rested a little, they came to the great hall which was splendidly arrayed. Water was poured on their hands and they were ceremoniously marshalled to their places and magnificently served with all kinds of dishes, so much so that the Emperor himself could not have been better entertained. Although Saladin and his companions were great Princes and accustomed to see the finest things, yet they greatly marvelled at this, and the more so when they considered the knight's rank, for they knew he was a citizen and not a Prince.

After they had eaten and the tables had been removed and they had talked for a time, the gentlemen of Pavia, at Messer Torello's desire went off to rest, since it was very hot. He remained with his three guests, whom he took to a room, and there sent for his wife so that they might see everything that he held dear. She was tall and handsome and dressed in rich clothes, and came into the room with her two children, who looked like two angels, and saluted the guests. They stood up when they saw her and greeted her respectfully. They had her sit down with them, and made much of the two children. After they had been conversing pleasantly for a short time, Messer Torello went away, and she asked them who they were and where they were going. And they made her the same answer as to Messer Torello. Then the lady said gaily:

"Then I see my woman's idea will be useful, and so I beg you as a special grace that you will not refuse or despise a little gift I shall have brought to you. Remember that women give small gifts, in accordance with their small hearts, and so take them, looking more to the good will of the giver than to the value of the gift."

She then had brought to each of them two pairs of robes, one of cloth and the other of silk, fit for Princes rather than for citizens or merchants, and three taffeta coats and linen garments, saying:

"Take these; I have dressed you in clothes like my husband. Although the other things are not worth much, still, they may be useful to you, since you are far from your wives, and have a long way to go and return, and since merchants are neat and fastidious men."

The gentlemen were amazed and saw that Messer Torello was determined to omit no courtesy to them. From the richness of the clothes, far above the status of a merchant, they began to suspect that Messer Torello had recognised them. But one of them answered the lady:

"These are very great gifts, madonna, and could not be lightly accepted, were it not that we are constrained by your request, which cannot be refused."

Messer Torello then returned and the lady, after commending them to God, departed and made like gifts to the servants, suitable to their rank. Messer Torello besought them to spend the rest of the day with him; so, after their siesta, they put on their new clothes and rode through the city with him. And when supper time came, they supped magnificently with a large and honourable company. At a fitting time they went to bed, and when they got up next morning, in place of their tired hacks they found three good fat palfreys, and likewise new strong horses for their servants. Seeing this, Saladin turned to his companions, and said:

"I swear to God that there was never a more complete or courteous or shrewd man than this. If the Christian Kings are such Kings as he is a knight, the Sultan of Babylon would not be able to resist one of them, let alone all those we have seen preparing to invade him."

Knowing it would be useless to refuse them, they thanked him courteously, and mounted. Messer Torello, with a large company, went with them a great distance on their way. Although the Sultan was reluctant to part from Messer Torello (so much had he already taken a liking to him), yet, since he was in a hurry to push on, he begged them to return. And, though Messer Torello regretted leaving them, he said:

"Gentlemen, I shall do so since you wish it. But this I must say. I do not know who you are, and do not ask to know more than you wish to tell; but whoever you may be, you will never make me believe that you are merchants. And so I commend you to God."

After taking leave of the rest of the company, the Sultan replied to him: "Messer, perhaps we shall be able one day to show you our merchandise and so convince you. God be with you."

Saladin then departed with his companions, determined if his life lasted and he were not worsted in the coming war that he would honour Messer Torello no less than he had been honoured by him. He spoke much of him and his wife and all his deeds and actions and possessions, praising them all to his companions. And when at the expense of much fatigue he had gone through the whole of the West, he and his companions took ship to return to Alexandria, where with full information they prepared for defence.

Messer Torello returned to Pavia and for a long time wondered who the three could have been, but never came anywhere near the truth.

The time for the Crusade arrived, and there were great preparations on all sides. In spite of his wife's tears and entreaties, Messer Torello determined to go. When everything was ready, and he was about to start, he said to his wife, whom he loved profoundly:

"Lady, as you see, I am going on this Crusade, both for the honour of my body and the salvation of my soul. I leave our goods and our honour in your keeping. Now it is certain that I am going, but a thousand things may happen which make my return uncertain. And so I wish you to grant me a favour. Whatever happens to me, if you have no certain news of my life, wait a year and a month before you remarry, beginning from this day of my departure."

The lady wept bitterly, and replied:

"Messer Torello, I do not know how I shall bear the grief in which you leave me by going. But if my life proves stronger than grief and it should happen otherwise to you, live and die secure in the knowledge that I shall live and die the wife of Messer Torello."

"Lady," said Messer Torello, "I am most certain that as far as concerns you, what you have promised would be carried out. But you are a young and beautiful woman of noble family, and your great virtue is known to everyone. So I have no doubt that if nothing is heard of me, there will be many gentlemen who will ask for you as wife from your brothers and relatives. And however much you wish, you will not be able to defend yourself from their exhortations, and you will be forced to agree to their wishes. That is why I ask this limit, and not a greater one."

"I will do what I can to carry out what I have said," replied the lady, "and I will certainly obey what you enjoin upon me, although I might want to do otherwise. I pray God that neither you nor I may be brought to such an end within that time."

The lady then embraced Messer Torello with tears, and taking a ring from her finger, gave it to him, saying: "If I should happen to die before you return, remember me when you see this."

He then mounted his horse, said farewell to everyone, and went on his way. Coming to Genoa with his company, he went on board a galley and in a short time came to Acre, where he joined the remainder of the Christian host, wherein almost immediately there began a great plague and mortality. While this sickness still lasted, Saladin, either by good fortune or design, captured almost all the surviving Christians and imprisoned them in many different towns. Among them was Messer Torello, who was taken to Alexandria. He was known to nobody there and was afraid to reveal his identity, and so was forced by necessity to train hawks—in which he was extremely skilled—and in this way came to the notice of Saladin, who had him brought out of captivity and made him his falconer.

Messer Torello was called Saladin's Christian, and neither recognised the Sultan nor was recognised by him. All his thoughts were turned towards Pavia, and several times he tried without success to make his escape. Certain Genoese came as ambassadors to Saladin to ransom their fellow citizens, and when they were leaving, Messer Torello wrote to his wife that he was alive and would come to her as soon as he could and she should wait for him; and he earnestly asked one of the ambassadors, whom he knew, to convey the letter to his uncle, the abbot of San Pietro in Ciel d'Oro.

About this time Messer Torello was one day talking with Saladin about the hawks, when Messer Torello happened to smile, and made a movement with his mouth which

Saladin had noticed in his house at Pavia. This movement made Saladin remember Messer Torello, and so he looked at him more carefully and thought he recognized him. Changing the conversation, he said:

"Tell me, Christian, which is your country in the West?"

"Sire," replied Messer Torello, "I am a Lombard from a city called Pavia, a poor man of humble birth."

When Saladin heard this he felt his suspicions almost certainties, and said to himself:

"God has granted me the opportunity to show this man how much I thought of his courtesy."

Without saying another word, Saladin had all his clothes brought into a room to which he took Messer Torello, and said:

"Look, Christian, and tell me if you ever saw any of these clothes before."

Messer Torello looked about and saw the clothes his wife had given to Saladin. It seemed impossible that they should be there, but still he said:

"Sire, I recognise none of them. But it is true that these two are like the clothes in which I clad three merchants who stayed at my house."

Then Saladin, able to restrain himself no longer, tenderly embraced him, saying:

"You are Messer Torello d' Istria, and I am one of the three merchants to whom your wife gave those clothes, and now the time has come for me to show you my merchandise, as I said might happen when I left you."

Hearing this Messer Torello was both happy and ashamed—happy that he had had such a guest, ashamed because he felt he had entertained him but poorly. Then said Saladin:

"Messer Torello, since God has sent you here, you must feel that not I but you are the master."

They rejoiced greatly together, and Saladin had him clothed in royal garments, and led him forth in the sight of all his great barons, speaking much praise of him and commanding that all who valued his favour should honour Messer Torello as if he were the Sultan himself. And this each of them immediately did, but especially the two lords who had been with Saladin in his house. The height of this sudden glory in which Messer Torello found himself to some extent withdrew his thoughts from Lombardy, especially since he had every hope that his letters had reached his uncle.

In the camp or army of the Christians on the day when

Saladin captured them, there died and was buried a knight of Provence, of small importance, named Messer Torello of Dignes. Now, since Messer Torello d' Istria was known to the whole army through his nobility, everyone who heard the news "Messer Torello is dead" thought this meant Torello d' Istria and not Torello of Dignes. And the subsequent event of their being captured prevented them from learning the truth. Thus many Italians returned with this piece of news, and some of them were so reckless as to say that they had seen him dead and had been present at his burial. When his wife and relatives heard it, the news gave them inexpressible grief, as it also did to all who had known him.

It would be a long task to relate the lady's grief and sadness and woe; but when after some months of continual mourning her grief had begun to subside, she was courted by the most eminent men in Lombardy, while her brothers and other relatives urged her to marry again. At first she refused many times and with great lamentations, but being constrained she finally agreed to do what her relatives asked, on condition that she should be allowed to remain unmarried for the period she had promised Messer Torello.

While the lady's affairs in Pavia were in this state and only about a week remained before she was to marry again, Messer Torello in Alexandria happened to meet a man whom he had seen go on board the galley which was to take the Genoese ambassadors to Genoa. He therefore called to him, and asked what sort of a voyage they had had, and when they had reached Genoa.

"My lord," said the man, "the galley had an ill voyage, as we heard in Crete, where I remained on shore. When it was near Sicily a dangerous gale arose and drove it on the shores of Barbary, and not one man escaped; two of my own brothers perished in it."

Messer Torello believed what he said (and indeed it was perfectly true), and, remembering that the period of time he had asked his wife to give him would expire in a few days, that no news of him could have come to Pavia, he felt certain that his wife would be on the point of remarrying. Consequently he fell into such distress that he lost his appetite and took to his bed, determined to die.

The news of this came to Saladin, who had the greatest affection for him, and went to see him, and thus after many entreaties and questionings discovered the reason of his grief and sickness. Saladin reproached him for not having spoken of it sooner, and then told him to cheer up, saying that he would manage things in such a way that Messer Torello would be in Pavia on the appointed day, and told him how. Messer Torello believed Saladin, and, since he had often heard that this was possible and had been done, he was comforted and begged Saladin to carry it out.

Saladin ordered one of his magicians, whose skill he often proved, to discover some means whereby Messer Torello could be carried to Pavia in his bed in a single night. The magician replied that it could be done, but that for his own good Messer Torello should be conveyed in his sleep.

Having arranged this, Saladin returned to Messer Torello. Seeing that he was determined either to be in Pavia on the given day if he could or to die if he could not, Saladin said:

"Messer Torello, God knows that you are in no wise to be reproved for loving your wife affectionately and for suspecting that she may be married to another, for among all the ladies I ever saw I think her behaviour, her manners, her garb, apart from her beauty which is but a perishable flower, are most to be commended. Since Fortune has brought you here, it would have greatly delighted me for us to live together as equal princes in the government of my kingdom for as long as we lived together. God has not granted me this, for it has come into your mind either to die or to return to Pavia at the appointed date; but I should greatly have liked to know it in time so that I could have sped you to your home with the honour, grandeur and the company your virtues deserve. This too has not been granted me. You desire to be there at once, and so I shall send you there, as I can, in the way I have told you."

"Sire," replied Messer Torello, "your words show me the effects of your kindness, which I never deserved to this supreme degree; but even if you had not spoken I should have lived and died most certain of it. But since I have made this determination, I beg that what you tell me may be done quickly, because tomorrow is the last day she will still await me."

Saladin said that it should be accomplished without fail. Next day, with the intention of sending him that night, Saladin ordered that in a great hall there should be prepared a rich and handsome bed of cushions, all of which were made of velvet and cloth of gold, in accordance with their customs. Over the bed was a coverlet worked in designs of very large pearls and most precious stones, and two pillows befitting such a bed. This done, he ordered that

Messer Torello (who was already recovered) should be
clothed in Saracen clothes of the richest and most beautiful
kind ever seen, while about his head was wound one of his
longest turbans

It was now late, and Saladin with many of his barons
went to Messer Torello's room, sat down beside him, and
said, almost in tears:

"Messer Torello, the hour which must separate us draws
near; and since I cannot go with you or send anyone along
with you because the manner of your travelling forbids it,
I must take leave of you in this room, and have therefore
come here Before I commend you to God, I beg you by the
love and friendship between us that you will remember me.
Then, if possible, before our lives end, I beg that when you
have arranged your affairs in Lombardy you will come at
least once to see me, to make up for the loss of pleasure in
seeing you which your haste to be gone imposes on me. To
make this easier, do not shrink from visiting me with letters
and from asking what you please of me, for I will certainly
do it more gladly for you than for any other man living."

Messer Torello could not restrain his tears, and being
hindered by them replied in a few words that it was impossible Saladin's benefits and virtue should ever leave his
memory, and that he would indeed do what the Sultan
commanded, if life were granted him. Saladin then tenderly
embraced and kissed him with many tears, and said:

"Go, in God's care."

He then left the room. After this, all the barons took
their leave, and went with Saladin to the room where the
bed had been prepared. Since it was now late and the magician was waiting and in haste to despatch him, there came a
doctor with a certain drink, telling him that it would
strengthen him This Messer Torello drank, and in a short
time fell asleep. By Saladin's command he was carried in his
sleep to the handsome bed, and beside him was laid a large
beautiful crown of great value, which was marked in a
way to show plainly that it was sent by Saladin to Messer
Torello's wife.

After this he placed on Messer Torello's finger a ring, set
with a carbuncle of such brilliance that it seemed like a
torch, while its value could scarcely be estimated. He was
girt with a sword, whose ornaments could not easily be
valued. On his chest was fastened a clasp, set with pearls
whose like was never seen, and other precious stones. Then,
on either side of him was set a large gold bowl filled with
double ducats, and many strings of pearls and rings and

girdles and other things, which would take long to describe. This done, he kissed Messer Torello once again, and told the magician to hurry; and immediately in Saladin's presence the bed and Messer Torello disappeared, and Saladin remained talking of him with his barons.

Messer Torello, with all the above-mentioned gems and ornaments, had reached the church of San Pietro in Ciel d'Oro, as he had asked, and was still asleep when the sacristan, having rung the angelus, entered the church with a light in his hand. Suddenly he saw the rich bed, and was not only surprised but terrified, so that he fled. When the Abbot and the monks saw him fly, they were amazed and asked him the reason; and the monk told them.

"Oh," said the Abbot, "you're not such a child now or so new to this church that you should be frightened so easily. Let us go and see what has scared you so much."

They lit more torches, and the Abbot with all his monks entered the church, where they saw the marvellous rich bed, and the knight sleeping on it. While they were doubtfully and timidly looking at the noble gems, without going too near the bed, the effect of the potion came to an end and Messer Torello awoke and heaved a deep sigh. The Abbot and monks saw this and fled in terror, shrieking "Lord help us!"

Messer Torello opened his eyes and looked about him, and saw he was in the place where he had asked Saladin to send him, which gave him great joy. He sat up and looked at some of the things about him; although he already knew Saladin's munificence, he now thought it greater than ever and knew it better. Nevertheless, when he heard the monks run away and knew the reason, he did not move but called to the Abbot by name, and begged him to have no fear, since it was Torello his nephew. At this the Abbot was still more frightened, since for several months he had believed Torello was dead. But in a little time, feeling reassured by good reasons and finding himself still called, he made the sign of the holy cross, and went up to Messer Torello, who said:

"Why are you suspicious, father? I am alive, thank God, and returned here from beyond the seas."

Although Torello had a long beard and was dressed in Arab clothes, the Abbot soon recognised him, and being completely reassured took him by the hand, saying:

"My son, you are welcome." And then proceeded: "You must not be surprised at our fear, because there is not a man in this place but thinks you are dead; so much so that I must tell you Madonna Adalieta, your wife, overcome by the entreaties and threats of her relatives, has agreed to marry again, and this morning is to go to her new husband —the marriage feast and everything connected with it are all prepared."

Messer Torello arose from the rich bed and greeted the Abbot and the monks with marvellous cheer. He begged every one of them to say nothing about his return, until he had done what he had to do. After this, he had the rich gems placed in safe keeping, and told the Abbot all that had happened to him until that moment. The Abbot, delighted at his good fortune, returned thanks with him to God. Messer Torello then asked the Abbot who was his wife's new husband; and the Abbot told him.

"Before my return is known," said Messer Torello, "I want to see how my wife behaves at this wedding feast. I know it is not customary for churchmen to go to such banquets, but out of love for me I should like you to arrange for us to go there together."

The Abbot replied that he would gladly do so. It was now full day, and he sent to the bridegroom to say that he would like to come to the wedding feast with a friend. And the gentleman replied that he would be happy for them to come.

At the appointed hour, Messer Torello, still in the same clothes, went to the bridegroom's house with the Abbot, gazed at by everyone he met but recognised by no one. And the Abbot told everyone he was a Saracen, sent as ambassador by the Sultan to the King of France.

Messer Torello was placed at a table opposite the lady, whom he beheld with the greatest joy, while he thought from her face that she looked discontented with her new marriage. She also looked several times at him, but she did not recognise him on account of his long beard and foreign clothes, and her firm belief that he was dead.

When Messer Torello thought the time had come to find out whether she remembered him, he took from his finger the ring she had given him when he set out, and called to a boy who was serving at his table, saying:

"Say to the bride from me that in my country the custom is when a stranger, as I am here, eats at a bride's feast, that to show her pleasure at his coming to eat with her she sends him her own wine-cup filled with wine, and when the stranger has drunk, the cup is covered, and the bride drinks the wine that is left."

The boy took the message to the lady. She thought the stranger was a great personage, and, being a well-bred woman, wished to show that she was pleased at his coming; so she ordered them to wash a large gold cup which stood before her, to fill it with wine and take it to the gentleman.

Messer Torello put the ring in his mouth, and while drinking managed to let it fall in the cup without anyone noticing. Leaving only a little wine, he covered up the cup, and sent it back to his wife. To carry out the custom, she took the cup, uncovered it, carried it to her mouth, saw the ring, and gazed at it without saying anything. She saw that it was the ring she had given Messer Torello at his departure, took it in her hand and looked closely at the man she had thought a foreigner. She recognised her husband, and overthrew the table in front of her, as if she had gone mad, screaming:

"There is my husband! It is Messer Torello!"

She ran to the table where he was sitting, and without caring for her clothes or what was on the table, threw herself across it and closely embraced him; and nobody there could get her to loose him, until Messer Torello told her to restrain herself a little since there would soon be plenty of time for them to embrace. Whereupon she stood up. The banquet was in confusion, but in part happier at the return of such a knight. At his request every man was silent, and then Messer Torello related all that had happened to him from the day of his departure until that moment, ending up by saying his being there alive must not displease the gentleman who, thinking him dead, had married his wife.

Although the gentleman was a little irate, he replied freely and like a friend that Messer Torello should dispose of what was his as he wished. The lady took off the new husband's ring and crown, and put on the ring she had taken from the cup and the crown sent her by the Sultan. They then left the house and with all the wedding pomp returned to Messer Torello's house, where he rejoiced with his relatives and friends and all the citizens, who looked upon him almost as a miracle.

Messer Torello gave some of the gems to the man who had paid for the wedding banquet, and some to the Abbot and many others. He sent several letters to the Sultan to announce his happy return, declaring himself Saladin's friend and servant; and then lived many years with his virtuous wife, with more chivalrous courtesy than ever.

Thus ended the trials of Messer Torello and his beloved wife, and such was the reward of their ready and cheerful courtesy. Many attempt to do the same, but do it with so ill a grace that they make their guests pay more for it before-hand than it is worth; and thus if no reward follows, neither they nor anyone else should be surprised.

### TENTH TALE

*The Marquess of Saluzzo is urged by his subjects to take a wife and, to choose in his own way, takes the daughter of a peasant. He has two children by her and pretends to her that he has killed them. He then pretends that he is tired of her and that he has taken another wife and so brings their own daughter to the house as if she were his new wife, after driving her away in her shift. She endures it all patiently. He brings her back home, more beloved by him than ever, shows her their grown children, honours her and makes others honour her as marchioness*

When the king had ended his long tale, which, to judge by their looks, had greatly pleased everyone, Dioneo said, laughing:

"The good man who was waiting to bring down the ghost's stiff tail that night would not have given two cents for all the praise you give Messer Torello!"

Then, knowing that he was the only one left to tell a tale, he began:

Gracious ladies, as far as I can see, today has been given up to Kings, Sultans and such like persons; so, not to wander away too far from you, I shall tell you about a Marquess, but not of his munificence. It will be about his silly brutality, although good came of it in the end. I do not advise anyone to imitate him, for it was a great pity that good did come to him.

A long time ago the eldest son of the Marquess of Saluzzo was a young man named Gualtieri. He was wifeless and childless, spent his time hunting and hawking, and never thought about marrying or having children, wherein he was probably very wise. This displeased his subjects, who several times begged him to take a wife, so that he might not die without an heir and leave them without a ruler, offering to find him a wife born of such a father and mother as

would give him good hopes of her and content him. To
which Gualtieri replied:

"My friends, you urge me to do something I was determined never to do, seeing how hard it is to find a woman
of suitable character, and how many of the opposite sort
there are, and how wretched is the life of a man who takes
a wife unsuitable to him. It is foolishness of you to think
you can judge a girl by the characters of her father and
mother (from which you argue that you can find me one
to please me), for I do not see how you can really know the
fathers' or the mothers' secrets. And even if you did know
them, daughters are often quite different from their fathers
and mothers.

"But you want me to take these chains, and I am content
to do so. If it turns out badly I want to have no one to complain of but myself, and so I shall choose for myself. And
I tell you that if you do not honour the wife I choose as
your lady you will find out to your cost how serious a thing
it is to have compelled me by your entreaties to take a wife
against my will."

They replied that they were content, if only he would take
a wife.

For some time Gualtieri had been pleased by the character of a poor girl in a hamlet near his house. He thought
her beautiful, and that he might live comfortably enough
with her. So he decided that he would marry her without
seeking any further, and, having sent for her father, who
was a very poor man, he arranged to marry her. Having
done this, Gualtieri called together all his friends from the
surrounding country, and said:

"My friends, it has pleased you to desire that I should
marry, and I am ready to do so, more to please you than
from any desire I have of taking a wife. You know you
promised me that you would honour anyone I chose as your
lady. The time has now come for me to keep my promise
to you and you to keep yours to me. I have found a girl
after my heart quite near here; I intend to marry her and
to bring her home in a few days. So take thought to make a
handsome marriage feast and how you can honourably receive her, so that I may consider myself content with your
promise as you may be with mine."

The good men cheerfully replied that they were glad of it,
and that they would consider her their lady and honour her
as their lady in all things. After which, they all set about
preparing a great and handsome wedding feast, and so did
Gualtieri. He prepared a great and fine banquet, and invited

many friends and relatives and noblemen and others. Moreover, he had rich and beautiful dresses cut out and fitted on a girl, who seemed to him about the same build as the girl he proposed to marry. And he also purchased girdles and rings and a rich and beautiful crown, and everything necessary to a bride.

When the day appointed for the wedding arrived, Gualtieri about the middle of Tierce mounted his horse, and so did those who had come to honour him. Everything being arranged, he said:

"Gentlemen, it is time to go for the bride."

Setting out with all his company he came to the hamlet and the house of the girl's father, where he found her drawing water in great haste, so that she could go with the other women to see Gualtieri's bride. And when Gualtieri saw her, he called her by her name, Griselda, and asked where her father was. She blushed and said:

"He is in the house, my lord."

Gualtieri dismounted, told everyone to wait for him, entered the poor little house where he found the girl's father (who was named Giannucole), and said to him:

"I have come to marry Griselda, but first I want to ask her a few things in your presence."

He then asked her whether, if he married her, she would try to please him, and never be angry at anything he said or did, and if she would be obedient, and several other things, to all of which she said "Yes." Gualtieri then took her by the hand and led her forth. In the presence of all his company he had her stripped naked, and then the clothes he had prepared were brought, and she was immediately dressed and shod, and he had a crown put on her hair, all unkempt as it was. Everyone marvelled at this, and he said:

"Gentlemen, I intend to take this girl as my wife, if she will take me as her husband."

He then turned to her, as she stood blushing and irresolute, and said:

"Griselda, will you take me as your husband?"

"Yes, my lord," she replied.

"And I will take you as my wife," said he.

Then in the presence of them all he pledged his faith to her; and they set her on a palfrey and honourably conducted her to his house. The wedding feast was great and handsome, and the rejoicing no less than if he had married the daughter of the King of France.

The girl seemed to have changed her soul and manners with her clothes. As I said, she was beautiful of face and body, and she became so agreeable, so pleasant, so well-behaved that she seemed like the daughter of a nobleman, and not Giannucole's child and a cattle herder; which surprised everyone who had known her before. Moreover, she was so obedient and so ready to serve her husband that he felt himself to be the happiest and best matched man in the world. And she was so gracious and kindly to her husband's subjects that there was not one of them but loved her and gladly honoured her, while all prayed for her good and prosperity and advancement. Whereas they had said that Gualtieri had showed little wisdom in marrying her, they now said that he was the wisest and shrewdest man in the world, because no one else would have known the lofty virtue hidden under her poor clothes and village garb.

In short, before long she acted so well that not only in the marquisate but everywhere people were talking of her virtues and good actions; and whatever had been said against her husband for having married her was now turned to the opposite. She had not long been with Gualtieri when she became pregnant, and in due time gave birth to a daughter, at which Gualtieri rejoiced greatly.

Soon after this the idea came to him to test her patience with a long trial and intolerable things. He said unkind things to her, seemed to be angry, and said that his subjects were most discontented with her on account of her low birth, and especially when they saw that she bore children. He said they were very angry at the birth of a daughter and did nothing but murmur. When the lady heard these words, she did not change countenance or cheerfulness, but said to him:

"My lord, you may do with me what you think most to your honour and satisfaction. I shall be content, for I know that I am less than they and unworthy of the honour to which you have raised me by your courtesy."

Gualtieri liked this reply and saw that no pride had risen up in her from the honour done her by him and others.

Soon after, he informed his wife in general terms that his subjects could not endure the daughter she had borne. He then gave orders to one of his servants whom he sent to her. The man, with a dolourous visage, said:

"Madonna, if I am to avoid death I must do what my lord bids me. He tells me I am to take your daughter and . . ."

He said no more, but the lady, hearing these words and seeing the servant's face, and remembering what had been said to her, guessed that he had been ordered to kill the

child. She went straight to the cradle, kissed and blessed
the child, and although she felt great anguish in her heart,
put the child in the servant's arms without changing her
countenance, and said:

"Do what my lord and yours has ordered you to do. But
do not leave her for the birds and animals to devour her
body, unless you were ordered to do so."

The servant took the child and told Gualtieri what the
lady had said. He marvelled at her constancy, and sent the
servant with the child to a relative at Bologna, begging her
to bring her up and educate her carefully, but without ever
saying whose daughter she was.

After this the lady again became pregnant, and in due
time brought forth a male child, which delighted Gualtieri.
But what he had already done was not enough for him. He
pierced the lady with a worse wound, and one day said to
her in pretended anger:

"Since you have borne this male child, I cannot live at
peace with my subjects, who complain bitterly that a grandson of Giannucole must be their lord after me. If I am not to
be driven out, I fear I must do now as I did before, and in
the end abandon you and take another wife."

The lady listened to him patiently, and her only reply
was:

"My lord, content yourself and do what is pleasing to you.
Do not think about me, for nothing pleases me except as
it pleases you."

Not many days afterwards Gualtieri sent for his son in
the same way that he had sent for his daughter, and while
pretending in the same way to kill the child, sent it to be
brought up in Bologna, as he had sent the girl. And his wife
said no more and looked no worse than she had done about
the daughter. Gualtieri marvelled at this and said to himself
that no other woman could have done what she did; and if
he had not seen that she loved her children while she had
them, he would have thought she did it to get rid of them
whereas he saw it was from obedience to him.

His subjects thought he had killed his children, blamed
him severely and thought him a cruel man, while they felt
great pity for his wife. And when the women condoled
with her on the death of her children, she never said anything except that it was not her wish but the wish of him
who begot them.

Several years after his daughter's birth, Gualtieri thought
the time had come for the last test of his wife's patience.
He kept saying that he could no longer endure to have

Griselda as his wife, that he knew he had acted childishly
and wrongly when he married her, that he therefore meant
to solicit the Pope for a dispensation to marry another
woman and abandon Griselda; for all of which he was reproved by many good men. But his only reply was that it
was fitting this should be done.

Hearing of these things, the lady felt she must expect to
return to her father's house and perhaps watch cattle as she
had done in the past, and see another woman take the man
she loved; at which she grieved deeply. But she prepared
herself to endure this with a firm countenance, as she had
endured the other wrongs of Fortune.

Not long afterwards Gualtieri received forged letters
from Rome, which he showed to his subjects, pretending
that the Pope by these letters gave him a dispensation to
take another wife and leave Griselda. So, calling her before
him, he said to her in the presence of many of his subjects:

"Wife, the Pope has granted me a dispensation to leave
you and to take another wife. Now, since my ancestors were
great gentlemen and lords of this country while yours were
always labourers, I intend that you shall no longer be my
wife, but return to Giannucole's house with the dowry you
brought me, while I shall bring home another wife I have
found more suitable for me."

At these words the lady could only restrain her tears by
a great effort, beyond that of women's nature, and replied:

"My lord, I always knew that my lowly rank was in no
wise suitable to your nobility; and the rank I have had with
you I always recognised as coming from God and you, and
never looked upon it as given to me, but only lent. You are
pleased to take it back, and it must and does please me to
return it to you. Here is the ring with which you wedded
me; take it. You tell me to take the dowry I brought you;
to do this there is no need for you to pay anything nor
shall I need a purse or a sumpter horse, for I have not forgotten that I came to you naked. If you think it right that
the body which has borne your children should be seen by
everyone, I will go away naked. But in exchange for my
virginity, which I brought here and cannot carry away, I
beg you will at least be pleased to let me take away one shift
over and above my dowry."

Gualtieri, who was nearer to tears than anyone else present, managed to keep his countenance stern, and said:

"You shall have a shift."

Those who were present urged him to give her a dress, so
that she who had been his wife for thirteen years should not

be seen to leave his house so poorly and insultingly as it would be for her to leave it in a shift. But their entreaties were vain. So the lady, clad only in her shift, unshod and with nothing on her head, commended him to God, left his house, and returned to her father accompanied by the tears and lamentation of all who saw her.

Giannucole (who had never believed it was true that Gualtieri would keep his daughter as a wife and had always expected this event) had kept the clothes she had taken off on the morning when Gualtieri married her. So she took them and put them on, and devoted herself to drudgery in her father's house, enduring the assaults of hostile Fortune with a brave spirit.

After Gualtieri had done this, he told his subjects that he was to marry the daughter of one of the Counts of Panago. He therefore made great preparations for the wedding, and sent for Griselda to come to him; and when she came, he said:

"I am bringing home the lady I have just married, and I intend to do her honour at her arrival. You know there is not a woman in the house who can prepare the rooms and do many other things needed for such a feast. You know everything connected with the house better than anyone, so you must arrange everything that is to be done, and invite all the women you think fit and receive them as if you were mistress of the house. Then, when the marriage feast is over, you can return home."

These words were a dagger in Griselda's heart, for she had not been able to dispense with the love she felt for him as she had her good fortune, but she said:

"My lord, I am ready."

So, in her coarse peasant dress, she entered the house she had left a little before in her shift, and had the rooms cleaned and arranged, put out hangings and carpets in the halls, looked to the kitchen, and set her hand to everything as if she had been a scullery wench of the house. And she never paused until everything was ready and properly arranged.

After this she invited all the ladies of the surrounding country in Gualtieri's name, and then awaited the feast. On the wedding day, dressed in her poor clothes, she received all the ladies with a cheerful visage and a womanly manner.

Gualtieri had had his children carefully brought up in Bologna by his relative, who was married into the family of the Counts of Panago. The daughter was now twelve years old, the most beautiful thing ever seen, and the boy was seven. He sent to her and asked her to come to Saluzzo with his son and daughter, to bring an honourable company with her, and to tell everyone that she was bringing the girl as his wife, and never to let anyone know that the girl was anything else. Her husband did what the Marquess asked, and set out. In a few days he reached Saluzzo about dinner time, with the girl and boy and his noble company; and all the peasants of the country were there to see Gualtieri's new wife.

The girl was received by the ladies and taken to the hall where the tables were spread, and Griselda went cheerfully to meet her, saying:

"Lady, you are welcome."

The ladies had begged Gualtieri, but in vain, to allow Griselda to stay in her room or to lend her one of her own dresses, so that she might not have to meet strangers in such a guise. They all sat down to table and began the meal. Every man looked at the girl and said that Gualtieri had made a good exchange, and Griselda above all praised her and her little brother.

Gualtieri now felt that he had tested his wife's patience as far as he desired. He saw that the strangeness of all this did not alter her and he was certain it was not the result of stupidity, for he knew her to be an intelligent woman. He thought it now time to take her from the bitterness which he felt she must be hiding behind a smiling face. So he called her to him, and in everyone's presence said to her smilingly:

"What do you think of my new wife?"

"My lord," replied Griselda, "I see nothing but good in her. If she is as virtuous as she is beautiful, as I well believe, I have no doubt that you will live with her the happiest lord in the world. But I beg you as earnestly as I can not to give her the wounds you gave the other woman who was your wife. I think she could hardly endure them, because she is younger and because she has been brought up delicately, whereas the other laboured continually from her childhood."

Gualtieri saw that she really believed he was to marry the other, and yet spoke nothing but good of her. He made her sit down beside him, and said:

"Griselda, it is now time that you should reap the reward of your long patience, and that those who have thought me cruel and wicked and brutal should know that what I have done was directed towards a pre-determined end, which was to teach you to be a wife, then how to choose and keep a wife, and to procure me perpetual peace so long as I live with you. When I came and took you to wife, I greatly feared that this would not happen to me; and so, to test you, I have given you the trials and sufferings you know. I have never perceived that you thwarted my wishes by word or deed, and I think that in you I have the comfort I desire. I mean to give you back now what I deprived you of for a long time, and to heal the wounds I gave you with the greatest delight. Therefore, with a glad spirit, take her whom you think to be my wife and her brother as your children and mine. They are the children whom you and many others have long thought that I had cruelly murdered. And I am your husband, who loves you above all things, believing I can boast that no man exists who can so rejoice in his wife as I in you."

He then embraced and kissed her. She was weeping with happiness. They both arose and went to where their daughter was sitting, quite stupefied by what she had heard, and tenderly embraced her and her brother, thus undeceiving them and many of those present.

The ladies arose merrily from table and went with Griselda to her room. With better hopes they took off her old clothes and dressed her in one of her noble robes, and brought her back to the hall a lady, which she had looked even in her rags.

They rejoiced over their children, and everyone was glad at what had happened. The feasting and merrymaking were prolonged for several days, and Gualtieri was held to be a wise man, although they thought the testing of his wife harsh and intolerable. But above all they esteemed the virtue of Griselda.

The Count of Panago soon afterwards returned to Bologna. Gualtieri took Giannucole away from his labour and installed him as his father-in-law, so that he ended his days honourably and in great content. He afterwards married off his daughter to a nobleman of great wealth and distinction, and lived long and happily with Griselda, always honouring her as much as he could.

What more is to be said, save that divine souls are sometimes rained down from Heaven into poor houses, while in royal palaces are born those who are better fitted to herd swine than to rule over men? Who but Griselda could have endured with a face not only tearless but cheerful, the stern and unheard-of tests imposed on her by Gualtieri? It would perhaps not have been such a bad thing if he had chosen one of those women who, if she had been driven out of her home in a shift, would have let another man so shake her fur that a new dress would have come from it.

Dioneo's tale was over, and the ladies talked about it, taking first one part and then another, blaming some things and praising others. The king looked up at the sky and saw that the sun was already sinking towards the hour of Vespers, and so, without rising, he spoke thus:

"Beautiful ladies, as I think you know, human wisdom does not wholly consist in remembering past things and knowing the present; but grave men esteem it the highest wisdom to be able to foresee the future from a knowledge of both.

"As you know, it will be a fortnight tomorrow since we left Florence to find some amusement to support our health and vitality, and to escape the melancholy, agony and woes which have continued in our city since the beginning of the plague. In my opinion we have virtuously performed this. We have told merry tales, which perhaps might incline to concupiscence; we have eaten and drunk well, played and sung music, all of which things incite weak minds to things less than virtuous; but so far as I have seen there has not been one word or one act on your part or on ours which could be blamed. I have noticed only continual virtue, concord and fraternal familiarity; which is certainly most pleasing to me in your honour and in mine. Now, through too long a habit something might arise which would turn to annoyance, and if we stay away too long an opportunity for scandal might occur; and moreover each of us has now for one day exercised the honour which now dwells in me. I therefore think, if you agree, that it would be well for us to return to the place from which we set out. And, if you consider the matter, our being together is already known round about, and so our company might be increased in such a way as to destroy our pleasure. If you approve my advice, I shall retain the crown until we leave, which I think should be tomorrow. If you decide otherwise, I am quite ready to crown someone for tomorrow."

The discussion between the ladies and young men was long, but at last the king's advice was adopted as wise and virtuous, and they determined to do as he had said. So, having called the steward, he discussed with him what should be done next morning, and then, standing up, gave the company their freedom until supper time.

The ladies and the rest arose, and as usual amused themselves in different ways. They came to supper merrily, and after that began to sing and dance and play music. After Lauretta had danced, the king ordered Fiammetta to sing a song, and she began pleasantly as follows:

> If Love came to us without jealousy, no woman living—whoever she might be—would be so glad as I!
>
> And if a woman should be pleased to find in her lover gay youth, the very pinnacle of virtue, eagerness and prowess, wisdom, manners, eloquent speech and perfect grace—I should be pleased, who love them all and see them in my hope.
>
> But since I see that other ladies are as wise as I, I tremble with my fears and dread the worst—which is that others may desire the man I love; and so my wondrous fortune turns to woe and sighing, and all life seems ill.
>
> If my lover were but as faithful as he is valiant, I should feel no jealousy. But now so many ladies seek for lovers that I think all men are faithless. This stabs my heart and makes me wish to die; I dread each woman who looks at him, and fear I may be robbed of him.
>
> Therefore in God's name I beg all ladies not to work this wrong on me; for should any seek to do me harm by word or sign or flattery, either I shall turn fool at learning it or she shall weep her bitter foolishness!

When Fiammetta had ended her song, Dioneo, who was sitting beside her said laughingly:

"Madonna, you would be very courteous to let all women know this, so that no one in ignorance may deprive you of a possession, whose loss would make you so angry!"

After this, they sang several other songs, and when it was nearly midnight, the king commanded that they should all go to bed.

Next morning they arose after the steward had already sent off all their baggage, and returned to Florence under the guidance of their prudent king. The three young men left the seven ladies in Santa Maria Novella, where they had met; and after taking leave of them went about their business. And the ladies returned home.

**END OF THE TENTH AND LAST DAY**

# CONCLUSION

Most noble ladies, for whose delight I have given myself
over to this long task, I believe that with the aid of divine
grace it is more through your pious prayers than any merit
of mine that I have carried out what I promised to do at
the beginning of this work. So now, after giving thanks,
first to God and then to you, I shall rest my pen and weary
hand. I know that these tales can expect no more immunity
than any others, as I think I showed in the beginning of the
Fourth Day; and so before I rest, I mean to reply to certain
objections which might be made by you or others.

Some of you may say that in writing these tales I have
taken too much license, by making ladies sometimes say
and often listen to matters which are not proper to be said
or heard by virtuous ladies. This I deny, for there is nothing so unchaste but may be said chastely if modest words
are used; and this I think I have done.

But suppose it to be true—and I shall not strive with you,
for you are certain to win—I reply that I have many arguments ready. First, if there is any license in some of them,
the nature of the stories demanded it; and if any understanding person looks at them with a reasonable eye he will see
that they could not be related otherwise, unless I had altered them entirely. And if there are a few words rather
freer than suits the prudes, who weigh words more than
deeds and take more pains to appear than to be good, I say
that I should no more be reproved for having written them
than other men and women are reproved for daily saying
"hole," "peg," "mortar," "pestle," "sausage," "Bologna
sausage," and the like things. My pen should be allowed no
less power than is permitted the painter's brush; the painters are not censured for allowing Saint Michele to slay the
serpent with a sword or lance and Saint Giorgio to kill the
dragon as he pleases. They make Christ male and Eve female, and they fasten sometimes with one nail, sometimes
with two, the feet of Him who died for the human race on
the Cross.

In addition, anyone can see that these things were not
told in church, where everything should be treated with

reverent words and minds (although you will find plenty of license in the stories of the church); nor were they told in a school of philosophers, where virtue is as much required as anywhere else; nor among churchmen or other philosophers in any place; but they were told in gardens, in pleasure places, by young people who were old enough not to be led astray by stories, and at a time when everyone threw his cap over the mill and the most virtuous were not reproved for it.

But, such as they are, they may be amusing or harmful, like everything else, according to the persons who listen to them. Who does not know that wine is a most excellent thing, if we may believe Cinciglione and Scolaio, while it is harmful to a man with a fever? Are we to say wine is wicked because it is bad for those who are feverish? Who does not know that fire is most useful and even necessary to mankind? And because it sometimes destroys houses, villages and towns, shall we say it is bad? Weapons defend the safety of those who wish to live in peace, but they also kill men, not through any wrong in them but through the wickedness of those who use them ill.

No corrupt mind ever understands words healthily. And just as such people do not enjoy virtuous words, so the well-disposed cannot be harmed by words which are somewhat less than virtuous, any more than mud can sully sunlight or earthy filth the beauty of the skies.

What books, what words, what letters are more holy, more worthy, more to be revered than those of the divine Scripture? Yet many people by perversely interpreting them have sent themselves and others to perdition. Everything in itself is good for something, and if wrongly used may be harmful in many ways; and I say the same of my tales. Whoever wants to turn them to bad counsel or bad ends will not be forbidden by the tales themselves, if by any chance they contain such things and are twisted and turned to produce them. Those who want utility and good fruits from them, will not find them denied; nor will the tales ever be thought anything but useful and virtuous if they are read at the times and to the persons for which they are intended.

Those who have to say paternosters and play the hypocrite to their confessor can leave them alone; my tales will run after nobody asking to be read. And yet bigots say and even do such little trifles from time to time!

There will also be people to say that if some of the tales here were absent it would be all the better. Granted. But I